I0824159

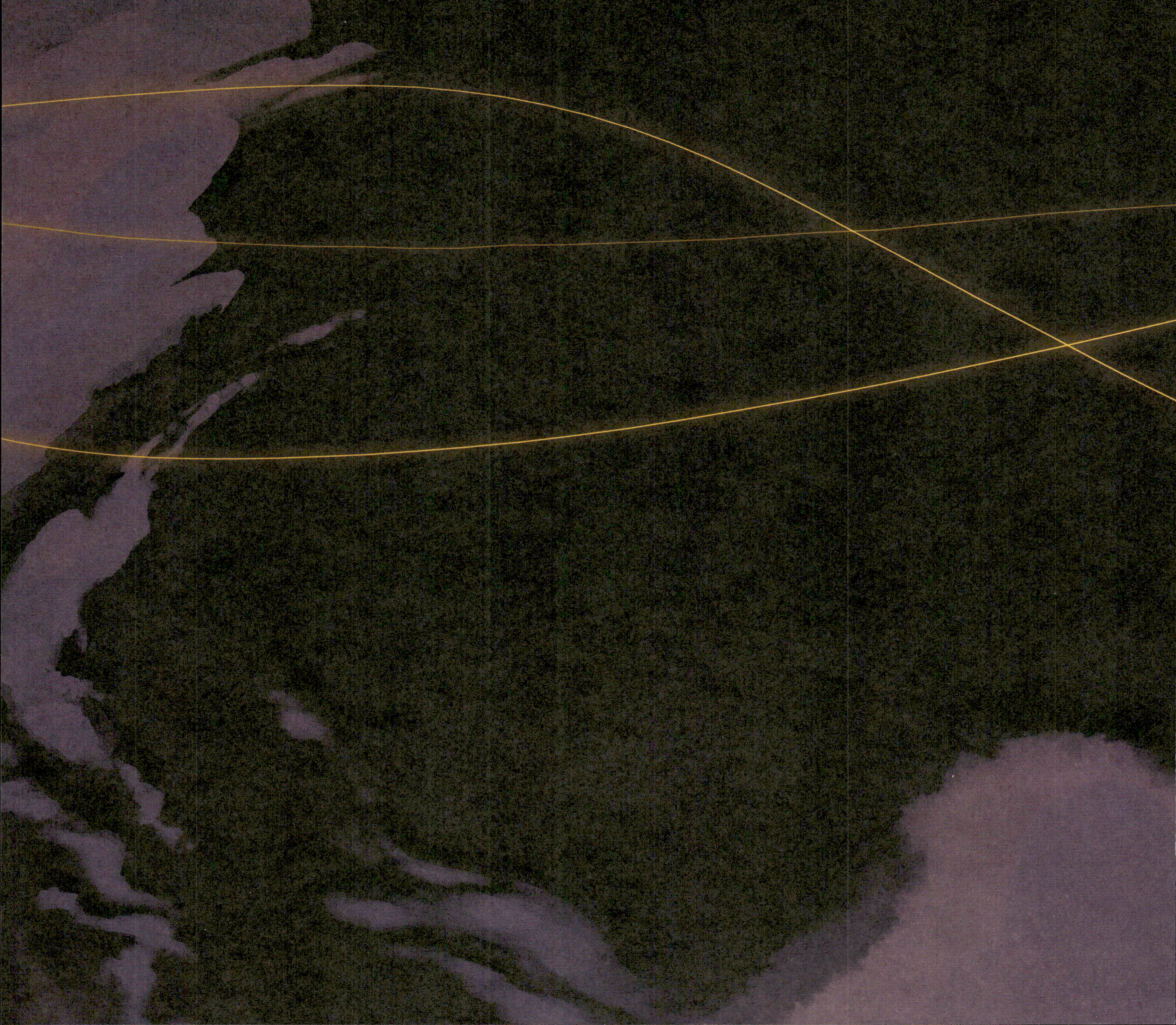

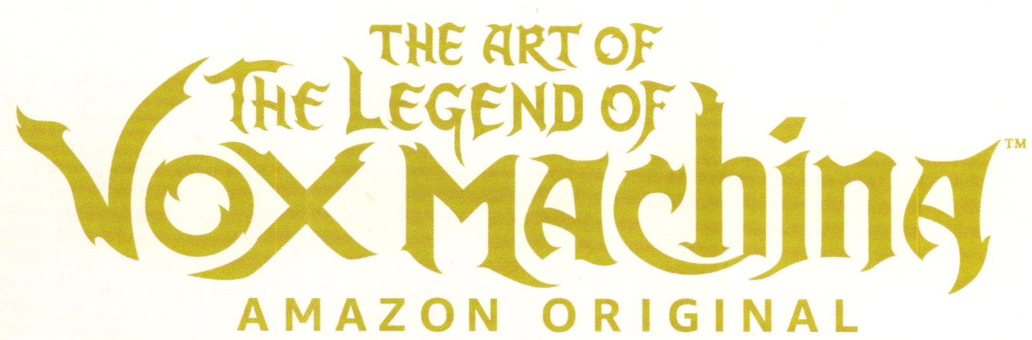
THE ART OF
THE LEGEND OF
VOX MACHINA™
AMAZON ORIGINAL

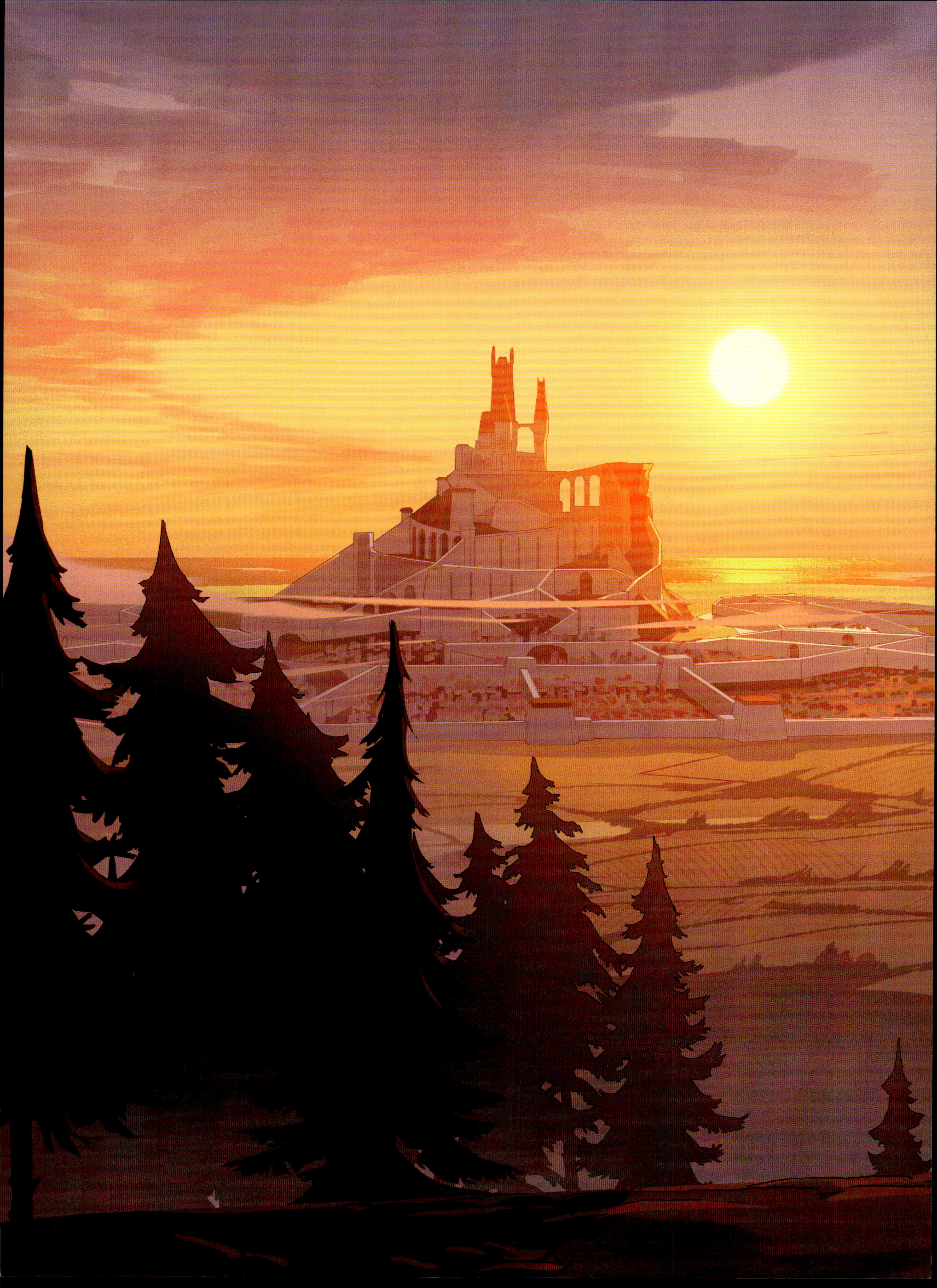

THE ART OF THE LEGEND OF VOX MACHINA™

Written by
MEREDITH KECSKEMETY

Introductions by
ARTHUR LOFTIS

PHIL BOURASSA

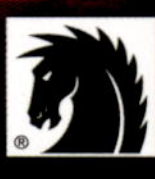

DARK HORSE BOOKS

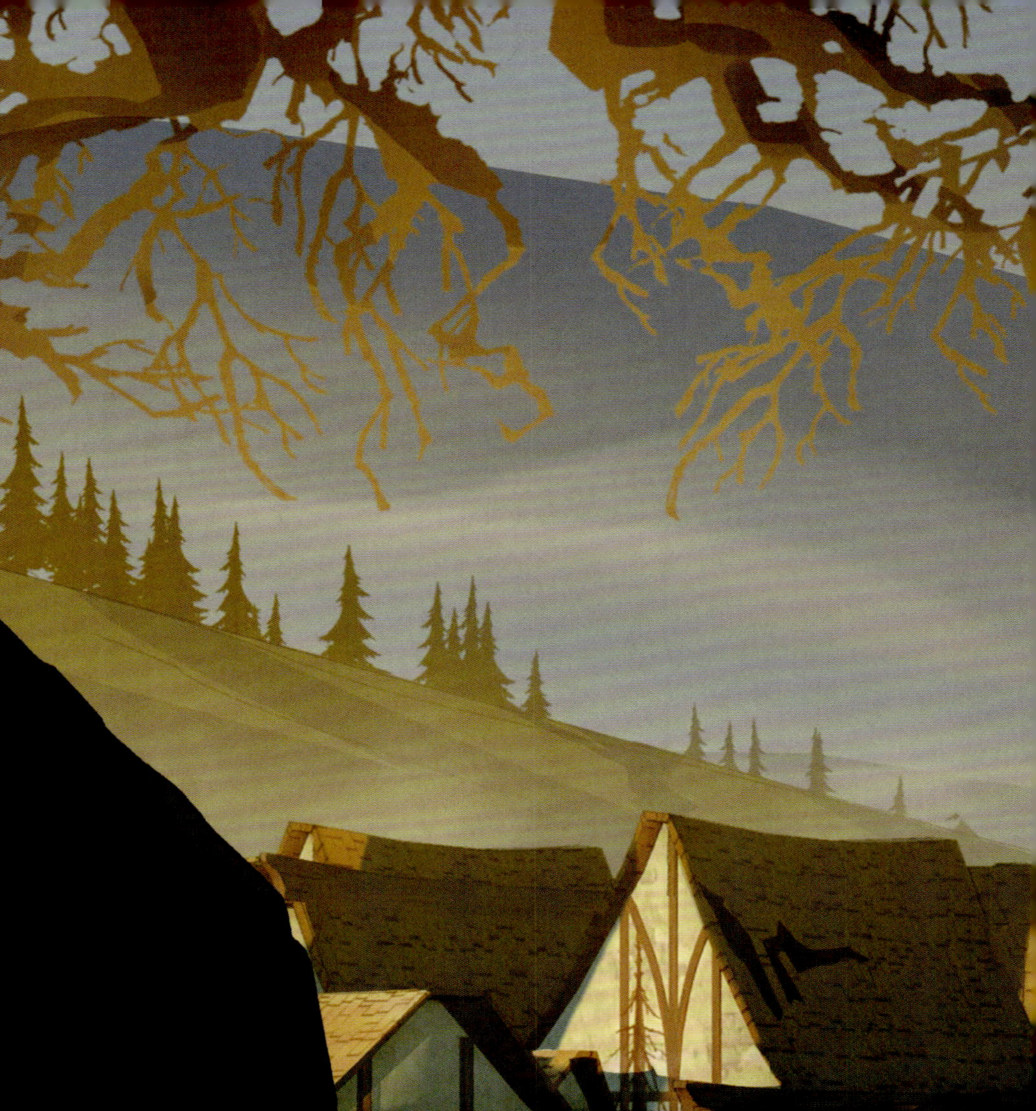

President and Publisher
MIKE RICHARDSON

Editor
RACHEL ROBERTS

Assistant Editor
ANASTACIA FERRY

Concept Designer and Deluxe Edition Designer
ANITA MAGANA

Designers
ANITA MAGANA
CINDY CACEREZ-SPRAGUE
LIN HUANG

Digital Art Technician
AJ NEWELL

Special thanks to Matthew Mercer, Laura Bailey, Taliesin Jaffe, Ashley Johnson, Liam O'Brien, Marisha Ray, Sam Riegel, Travis Willingham, Dani Carr, Niki Chi, and Shaunette DeTie at Critical Role, Josh Topal and Jamie Kampel at Amazon, Kay Tinder at Titmouse, and to Kari Yadro at Dark Horse Comics.

Published by Dark Horse Books. A division of Dark Horse Comics LLC
10956 SE Main Street, Milwaukie, OR 97222

DarkHorse.com

First Edition: December 2024
Standard Edition ISBN: 978-1-50674-759-0
Deluxe Edition ISBN: 978-1-50674-760-6
Digital ISBN: 978-1-50674-808-5

10 9 8 7 6 5 4 3 2 1
Printed in China

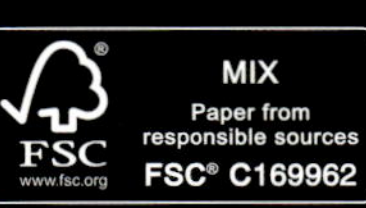

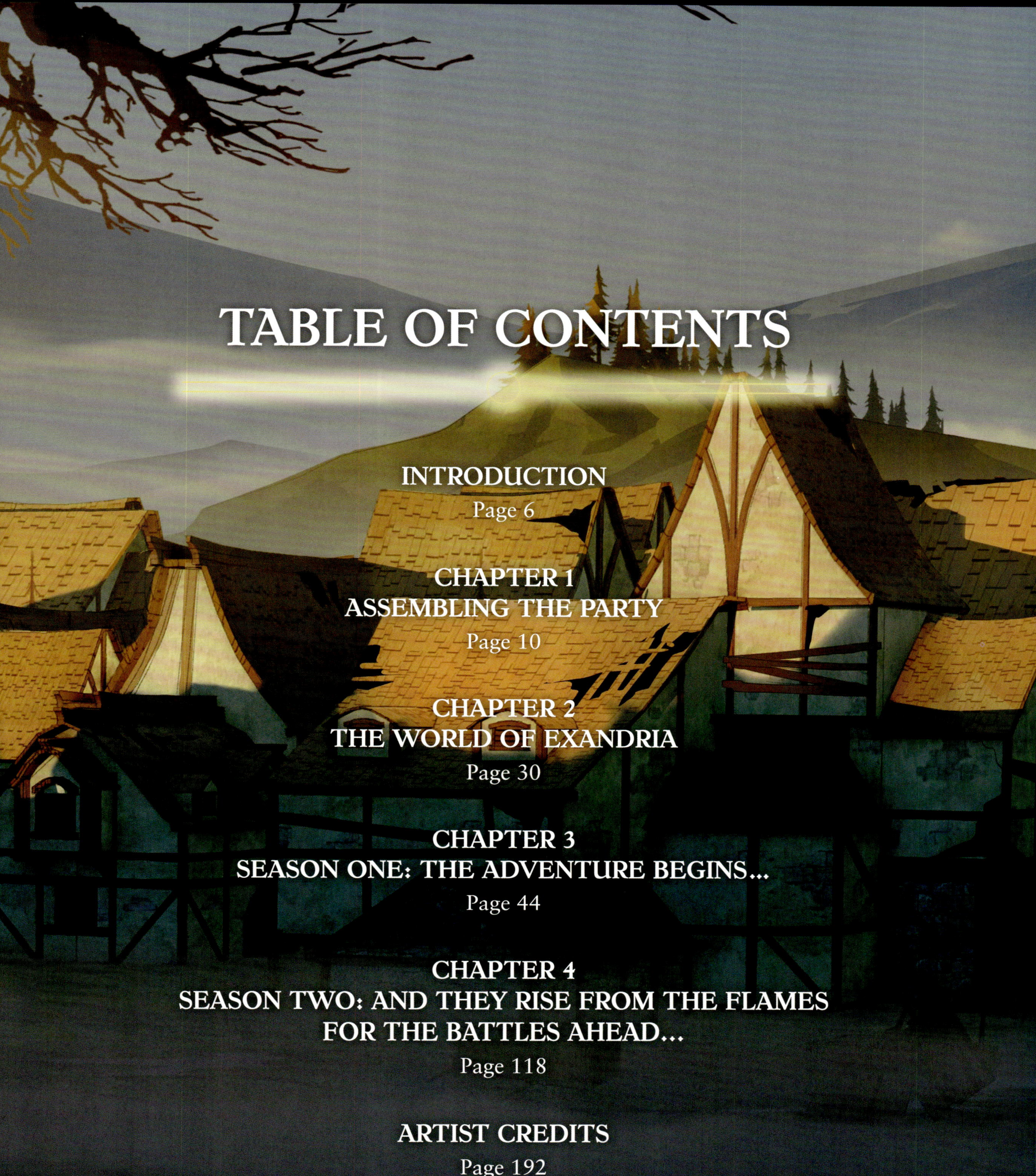

TABLE OF CONTENTS

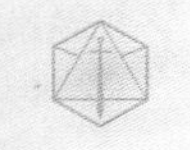

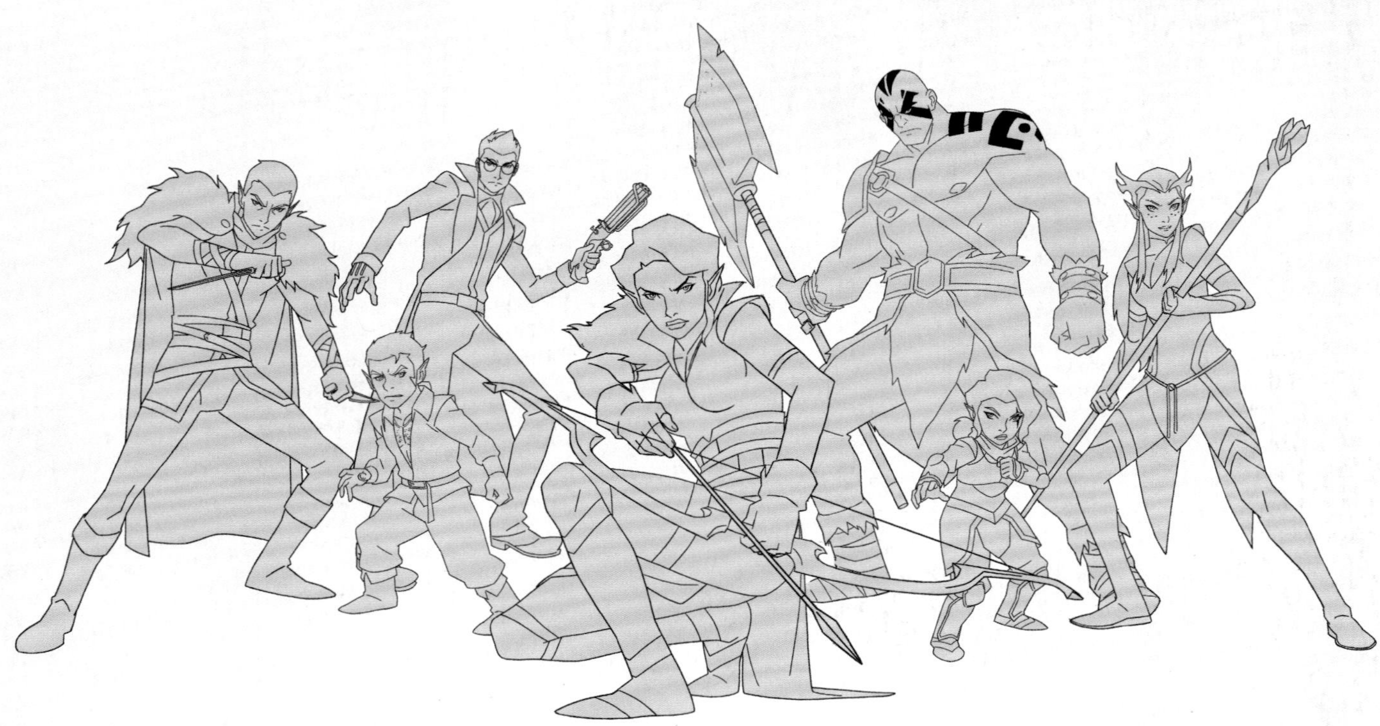

INTRODUCTION

I landed on this project by pure chance and serendipity. Looking back, it's one of those twists of fate that seem so against the odds that it's hard to reconcile the likelihood of it having happened at all. I'll explain.

One early morning in fall 2018, I quite randomly found myself sitting across the aisle from Travis Willingham and Laura Bailey on a flight bound for New York Comic Con. We were headed to the annual convention to promote our various projects and, amused by the sheer coincidence of the encounter, spent most of the flight talking about their efforts to adapt and pitch their already wildly successful streaming tabletop RPG as an animated series.

I had originally become acquainted with the voice acting power couple a few years prior when we attended back-to-back press premieres for a project that Travis and I had worked on. In the years between, Critical Role had become a full-blown geek culture phenomenon, and I was more than a little curious what they were planning to do with their distinctly unique IP. Before parting ways in New York, we discussed the possibility that I might take a stab at the character designs for their nascent show, which, as a big ol' fantasy geek myself, and a fan of the talent involved, filled me with excitement and imagination.

It wasn't until many months after that fortuitous flight, after Critical Role's historically successful fan-funded Kickstarter and subsequent partnership with Titmouse Animation, that I was officially invited to team up with Supervising Director Sung Jin Ahn, Art Director Arthur Loftis, and a small but dedicated collection of industry pros to create the look of the characters and the world for *The Legend of Vox Machina* animated series.

It was a happy roll of the cosmic dice, and a serendipitous beginning to what would come to define itself as one of the great joys of my animation career. A sentiment I'm sure is shared widely amongst the many collaborators whose work is collected in this volume.

Much in the same way as the amazing characters and world of Critical Role sprang organically from the tabletop misadventures of a group of brilliant friends and would go on to light up the imaginations of legions of fans, the art team responsible for the work in this book was brought together by circumstance, opportunity, and passion in order to translate the magic of Critical Role into a new medium. The artwork collected here reflects the combined efforts of a talented and diverse team of artists, whose life paths, creative inclinations, and professional relationships collided at the right moment to lend their various abilities, and channel their own inspirations, into bringing this special show to life. It is our great pleasure to share some of that inspiration with fans, both old and new, who made this whole wonderful journey possible.

It's been almost six years since that 6am flight out of LAX, and not a day has passed that I don't thank my lucky stars for the good fortune and uncanny timing of it all. ◆

PHIL BOURASSA, LEAD CHARACTER DESIGNER

Here at Titmouse, *The Legend of Vox Machina* is a show that holds a special place in our nerdy hearts. As a studio, tabletop gaming runs deep in our veins. During my earliest days with the company, I found out that the conference rooms were available

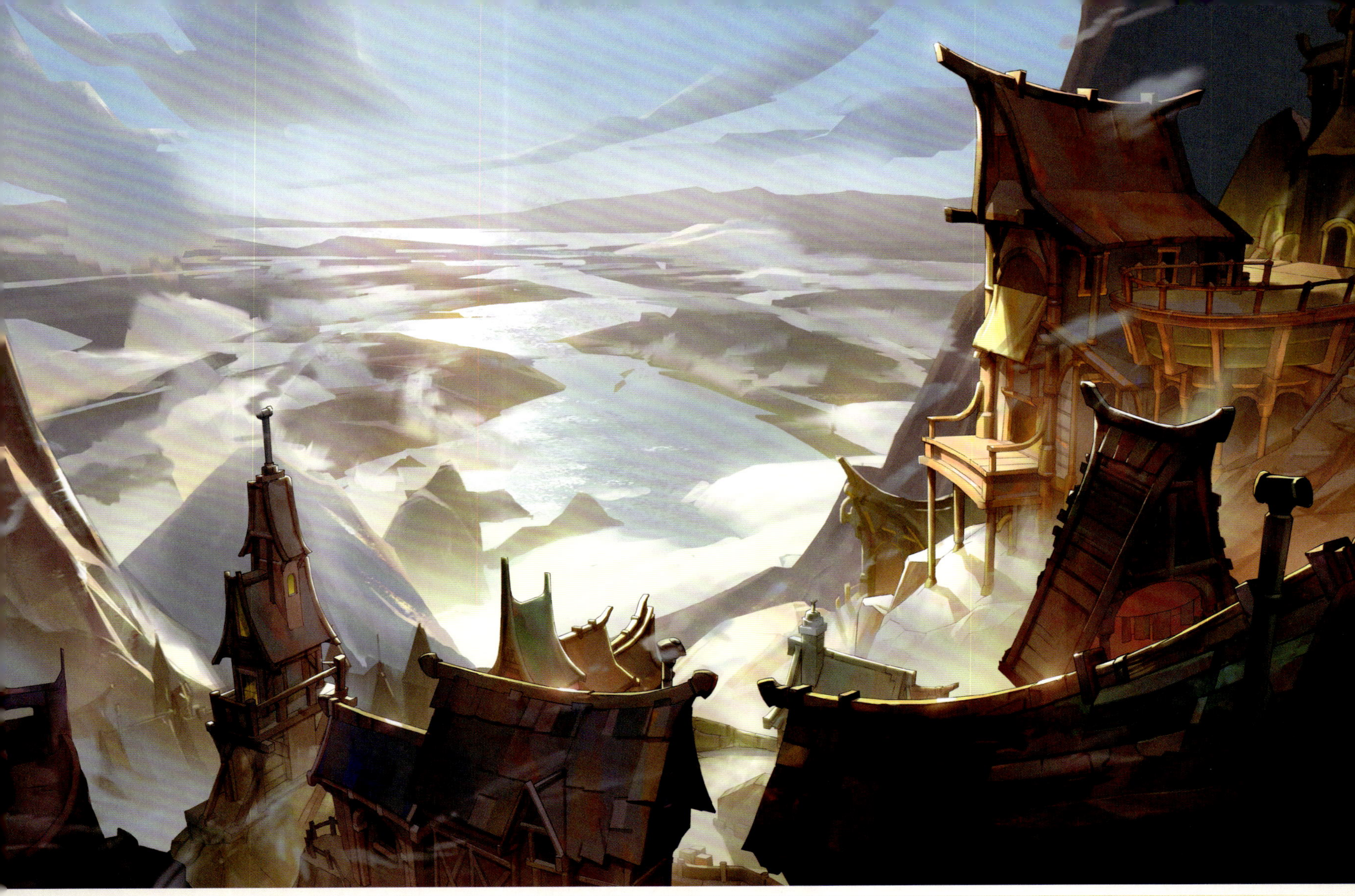

after-hours for people to run RPG campaigns or play various miniature wargames. It was in those first few years working in animation that I made lifelong friends who I still roll dice with on a regular basis. In a world dominated by video games played on your computer or console, tabletop gaming felt like an amazing way to hang out with friends in person again–to make jokes, create stories, and feel like part of a larger community. That feeling was part of what made Critical Role so fun to watch. These were friends improvising character moments, singing, laughing, and yet telling an enthralling story with highs and lows beyond what I thought was possible in a gaming session. I was absolutely hooked from the start, and completely stunned when I was asked years later to join the project.

Since then, we've made two seasons of the animated adaptation and are well on our way to finishing a third. In that time, nothing has diminished how awestruck I've been by the generosity of the Critters–the Critical Role fans. They funded the first season of the show, making this entire animated series possible. In my mind, we have all been making this show together, and this art book is a testament to the power of compassion to bring something positive to the world. Collectively, they saw promise in the stories of a group of nerdy voice actors and lent their support to making something new out of thin air. If you've been with us from the start, then I hope as you flip through these pages you feel a sense of pride in what you've enabled our talented team to do. If you're new to the world of Critical Role, welcome! I hope you find the same sense of community in these stories that we all did. ◆

ARTHUR LOFTIS, ART DIRECTOR

A TTRPG Adventuring Party is a very personal experience. Regardless of streams, social media followings, and yes, even animated series adaptations, the questing experience can never fully be shared with anyone but your party. Upon learning that I would be working alongside the creators of Critical Role and be privy to their collaboration with other artistic visionaries in their own right to bring *The Legend of Vox Machina* to life, my immediate feelings were those of reverence. Grog, Keyleth, Percy, Pike, Scanlan, Vax and Vex were not only characters they had created, but they were reflections of themselves. And they were brave enough to share those reflections with an audience.

My goal in writing this book is for every level of fan to understand the absolute devotion that went into making *The Legend of Vox Machina*. At every level, the attention to detail may have been obsessive, but it was born from a passion to give Ashley, Laura, Liam, Marisha, Matthew, Sam, Taliesin, and Travis a vision worthy of their party's tale.

I dedicate this book to every party I've ever had the honor of rolling dice with, and the stories we've told along the way... ◆

MEREDITH KECSKEMETY

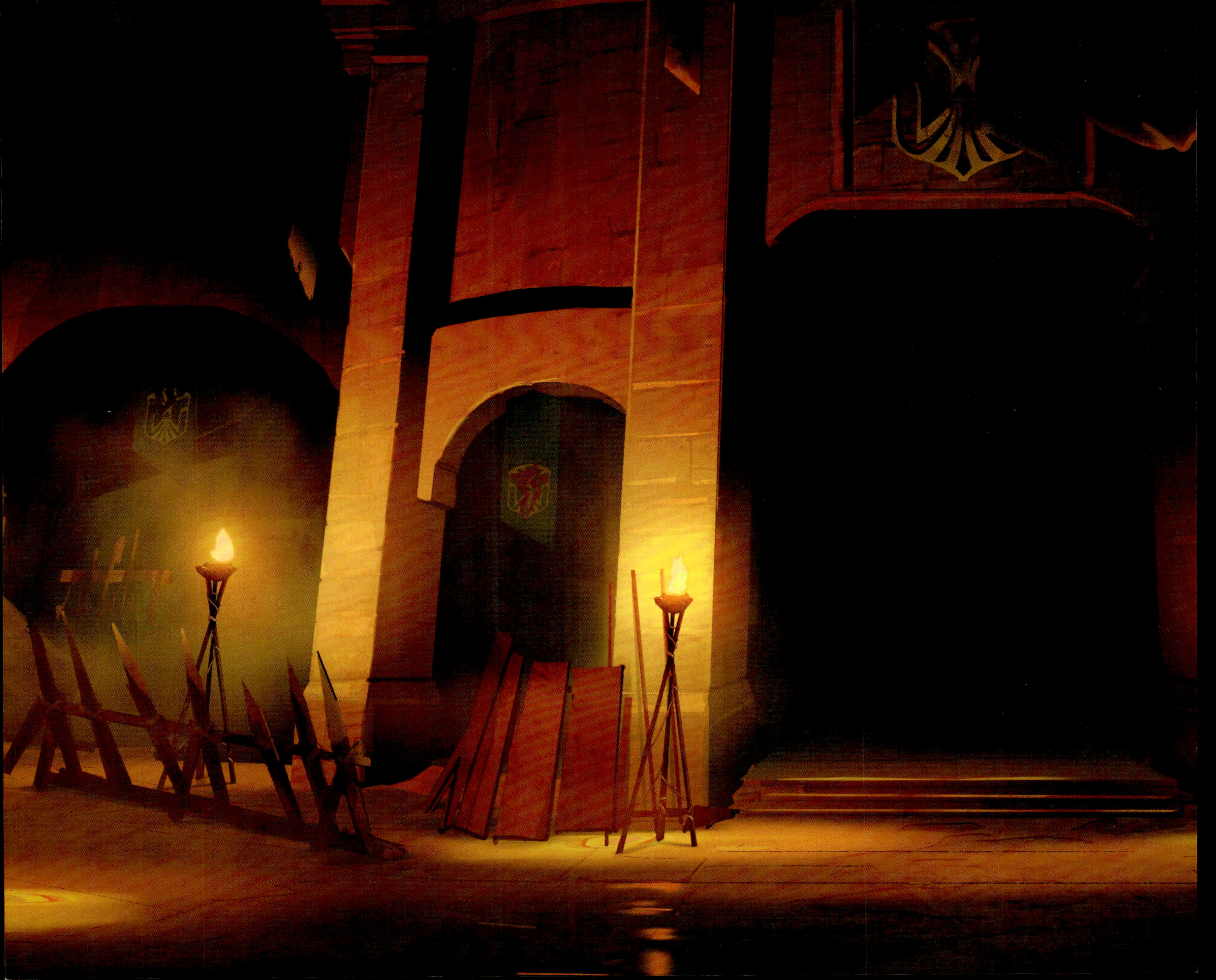

CHAPTER ONE

DESIGNING VOX MACHINA

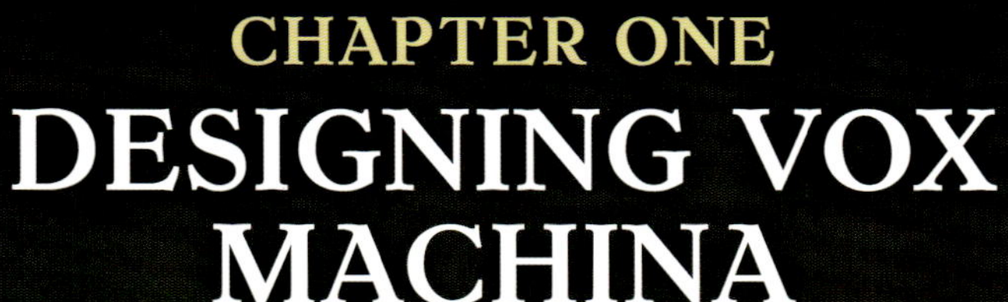

"Vox Machina, what a fucking joke." – AGAR, S1E1 "THE TERROR OF TAL'DOREI: PART 1"

When designing each member of Vox Machina, it was important for the design team to capture the essence of each character in the silhouette. If a fan is seeing just the outline of each character, they should be able to identify which one they are looking at easily. Having a dynamic range of silhouettes was also important so they can look interesting as a group. Grog has to fill out the background and be this imposing figure, while Pike and Scanlan's statures allow for a lot of play with height levels in the foreground.

"Early in design, each character's RPG archetype was also considered. Percy and Vax are dexterity builds, so they're never going to look super buff. They need to be agile and strike dynamic poses. Staging was another big consideration for group shots. Dealing with such large characters next to very small ones required some cheating to get everyone in a shot together." – PHIL BOURASSA (CHARACTER DESIGNER)

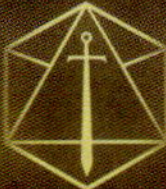

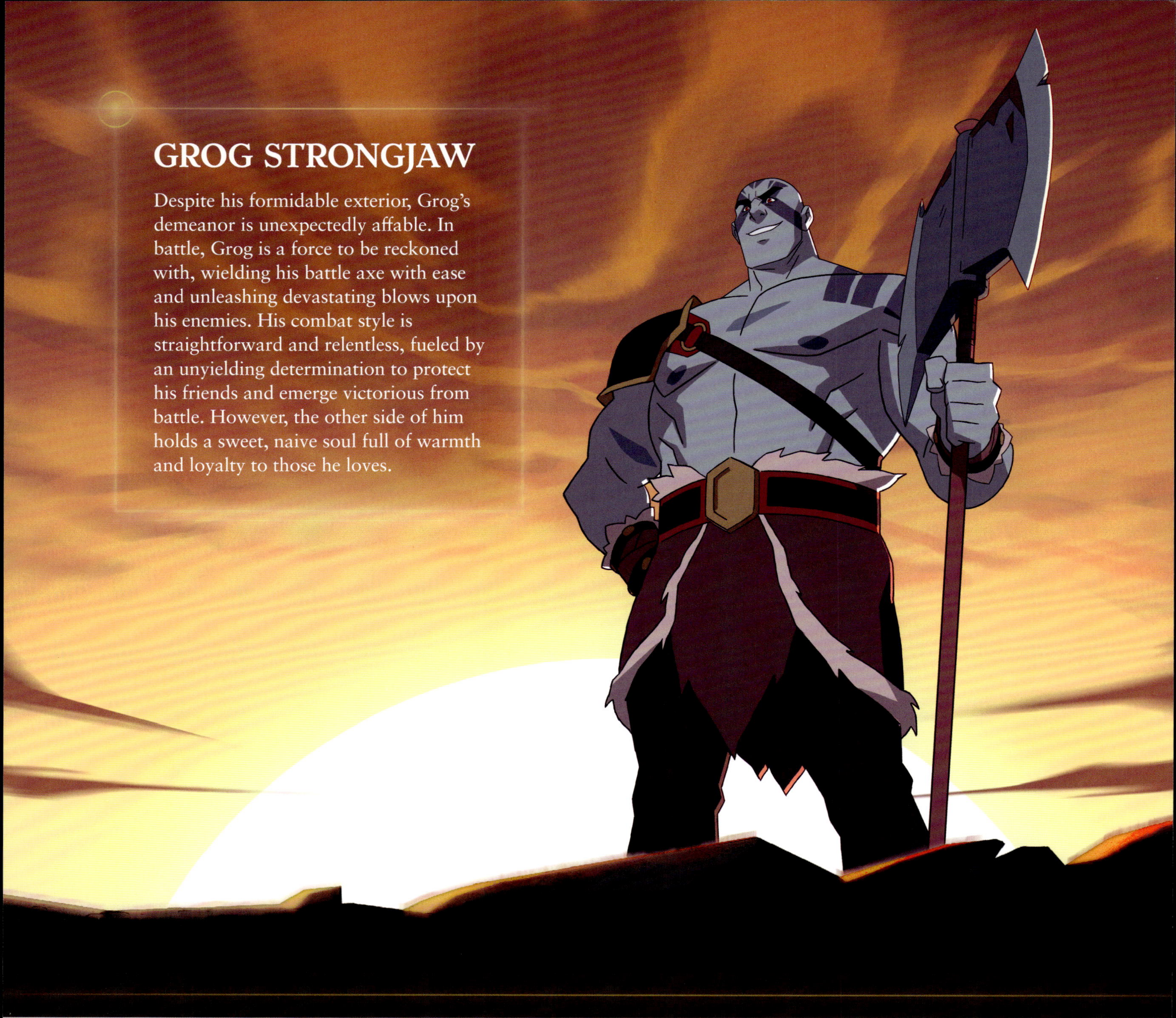

GROG STRONGJAW

Despite his formidable exterior, Grog's demeanor is unexpectedly affable. In battle, Grog is a force to be reckoned with, wielding his battle axe with ease and unleashing devastating blows upon his enemies. His combat style is straightforward and relentless, fueled by an unyielding determination to protect his friends and emerge victorious from battle. However, the other side of him holds a sweet, naive soul full of warmth and loyalty to those he loves.

Early Concepts

"He's not just a tough guy; he's also a little kid. You want to convey his childlike softness as well. Some of my early concept designs were too fierce and badass. As we worked on them, it was clear that "fierce-ness" is only part of him."

– PHIL BOURASSA (CHARACTER DESIGNER)

Author's note: I'd be wary of calling Grog a "child" in writing, but fortunately for us, he can't read.

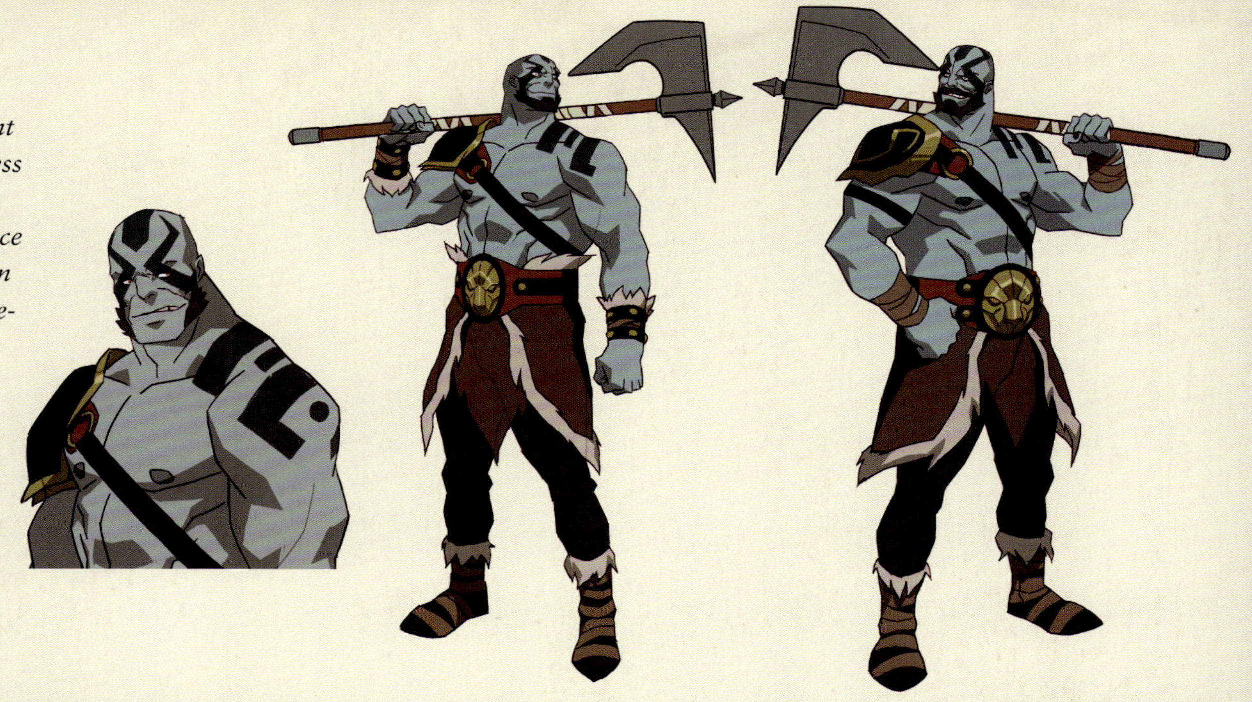

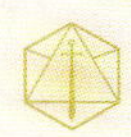

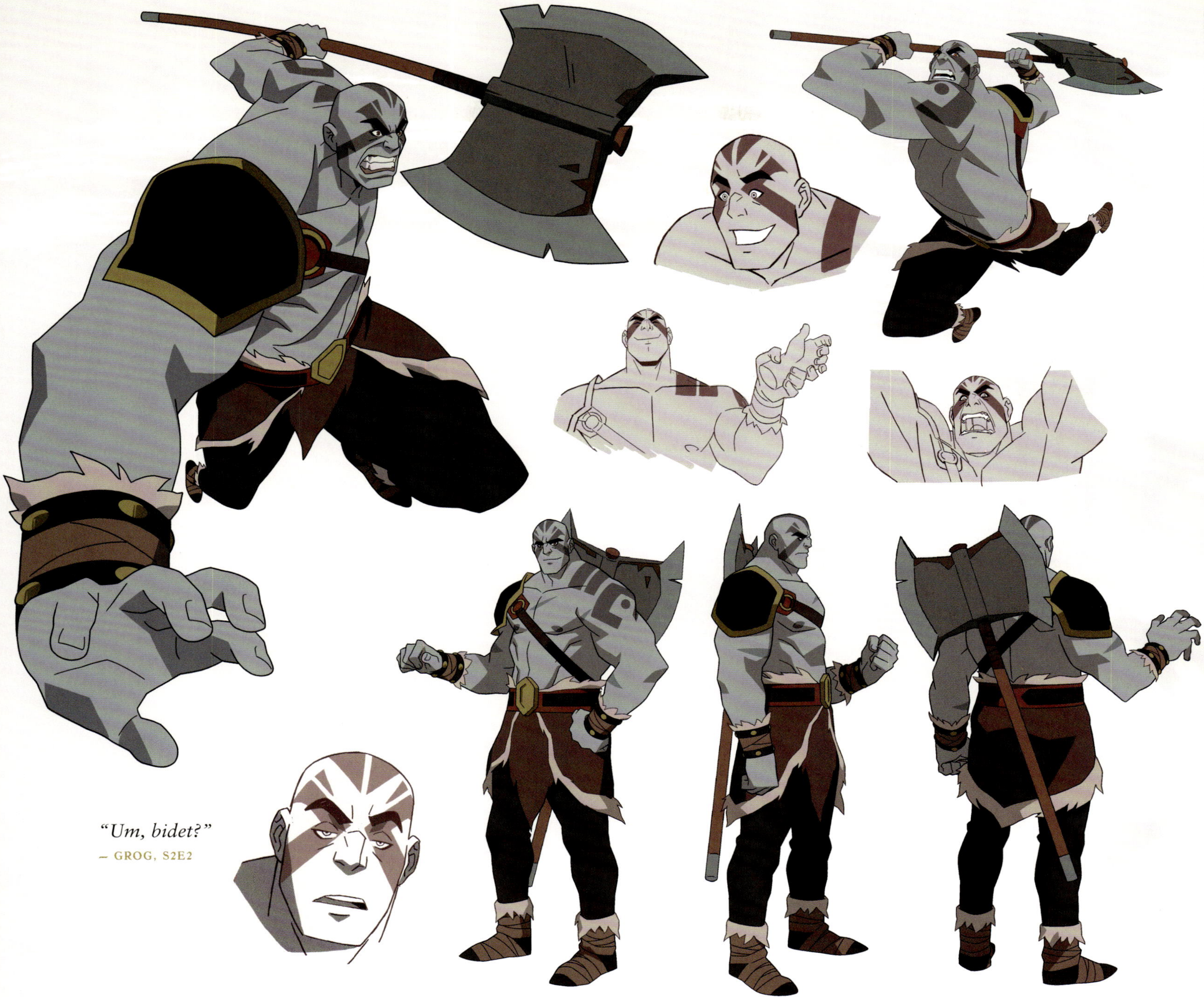

"Um, bidet?"
— GROG, S2E2

Grog's Axe and Dwarven Belt

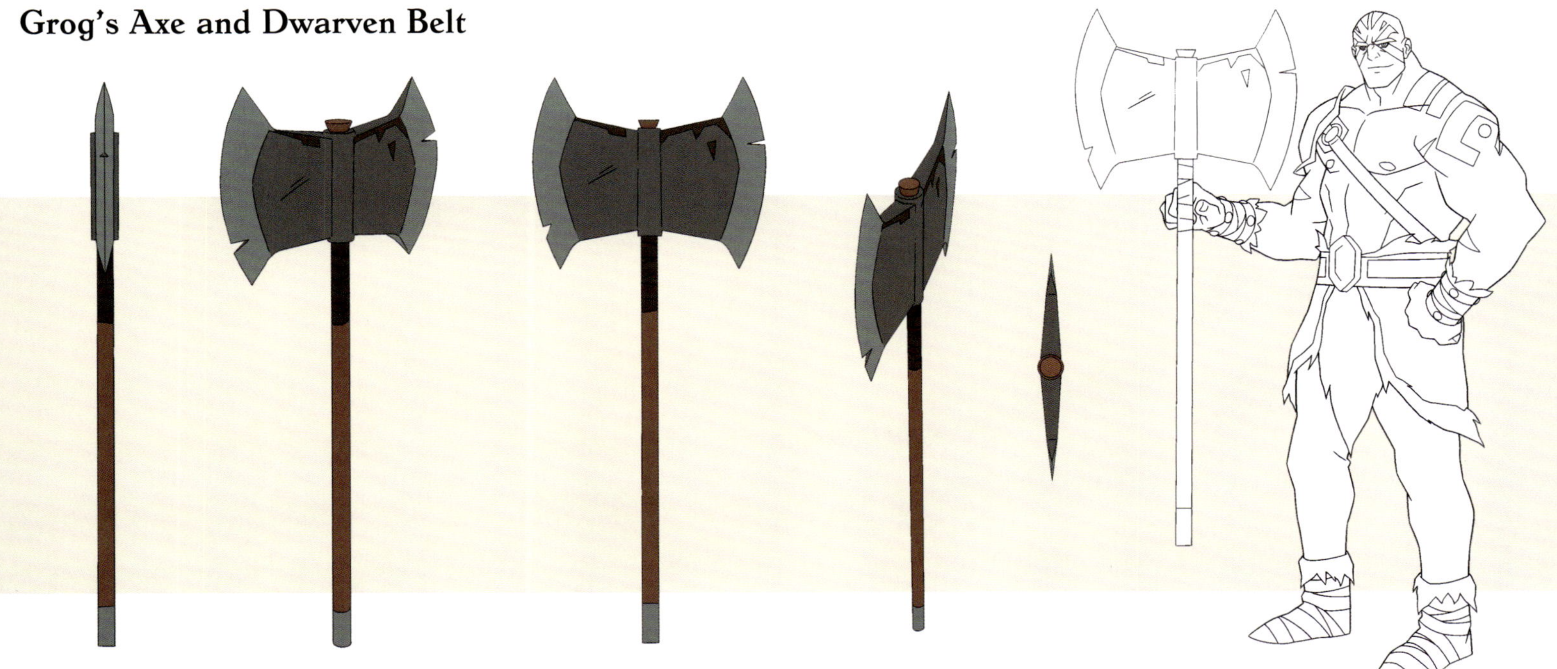

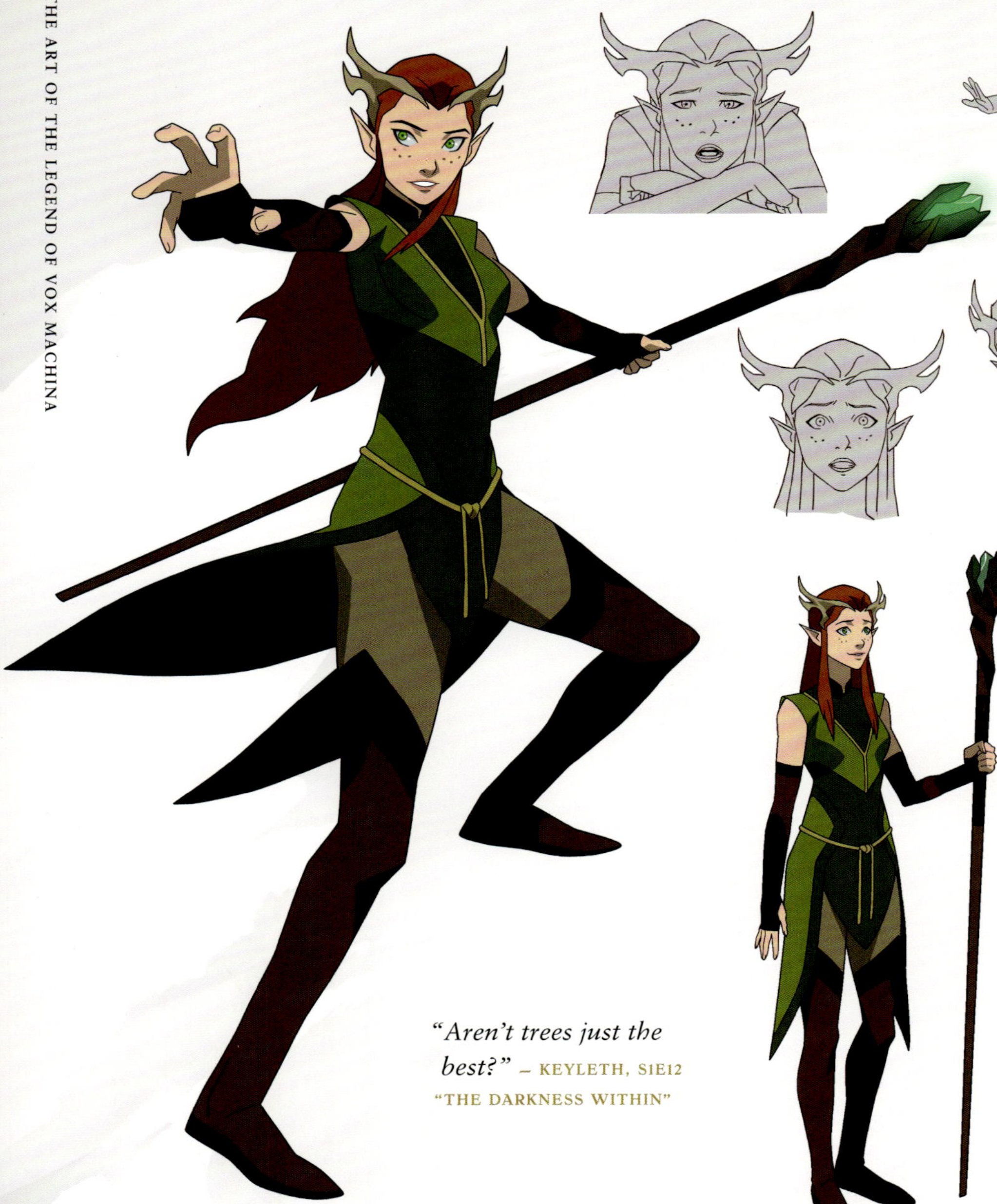

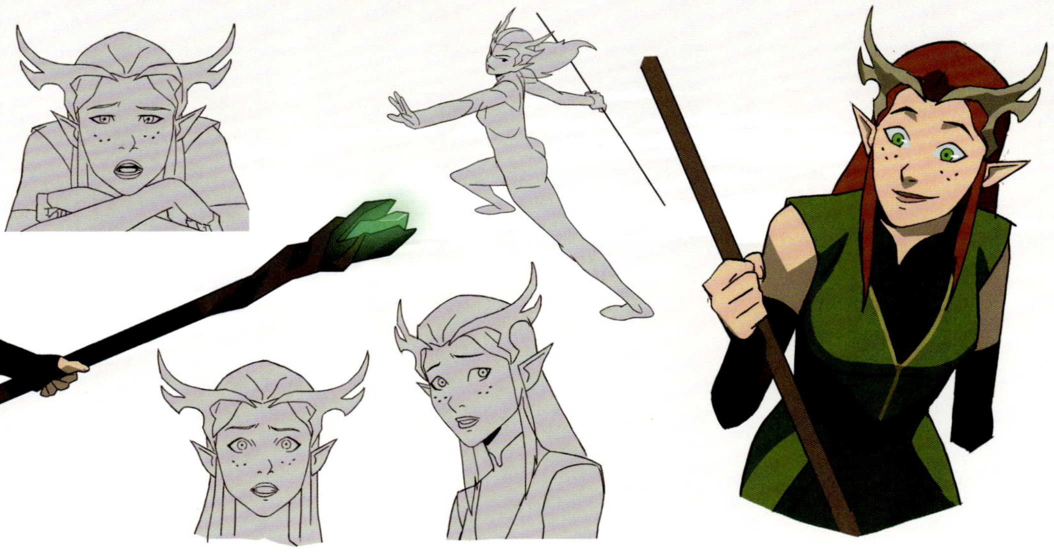

"Aren't trees just the best?" – KEYLETH, S1E12 "THE DARKNESS WITHIN"

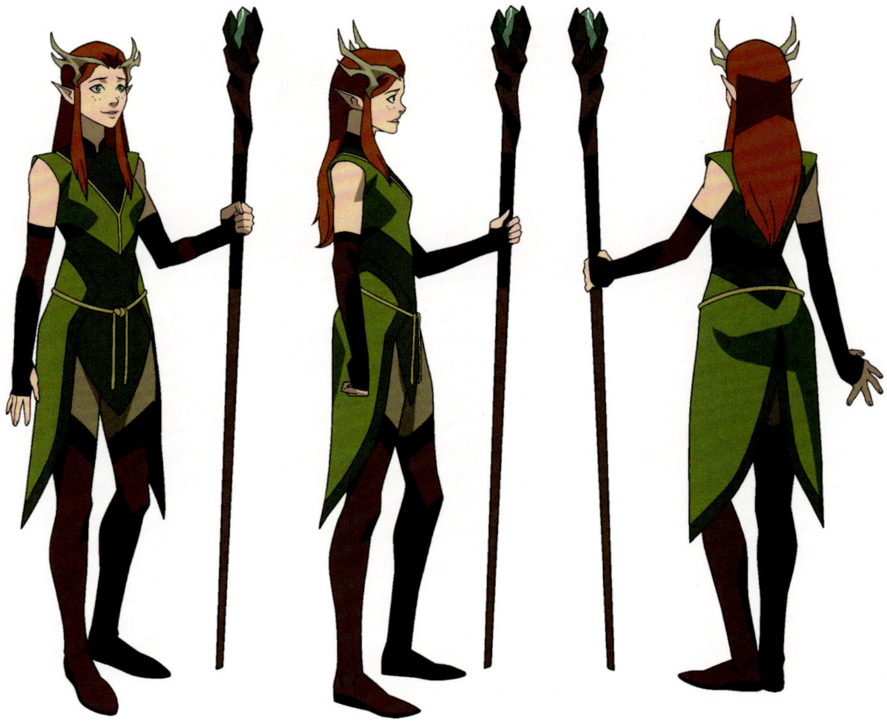

Keyleth's Staff and Minxie Transformation

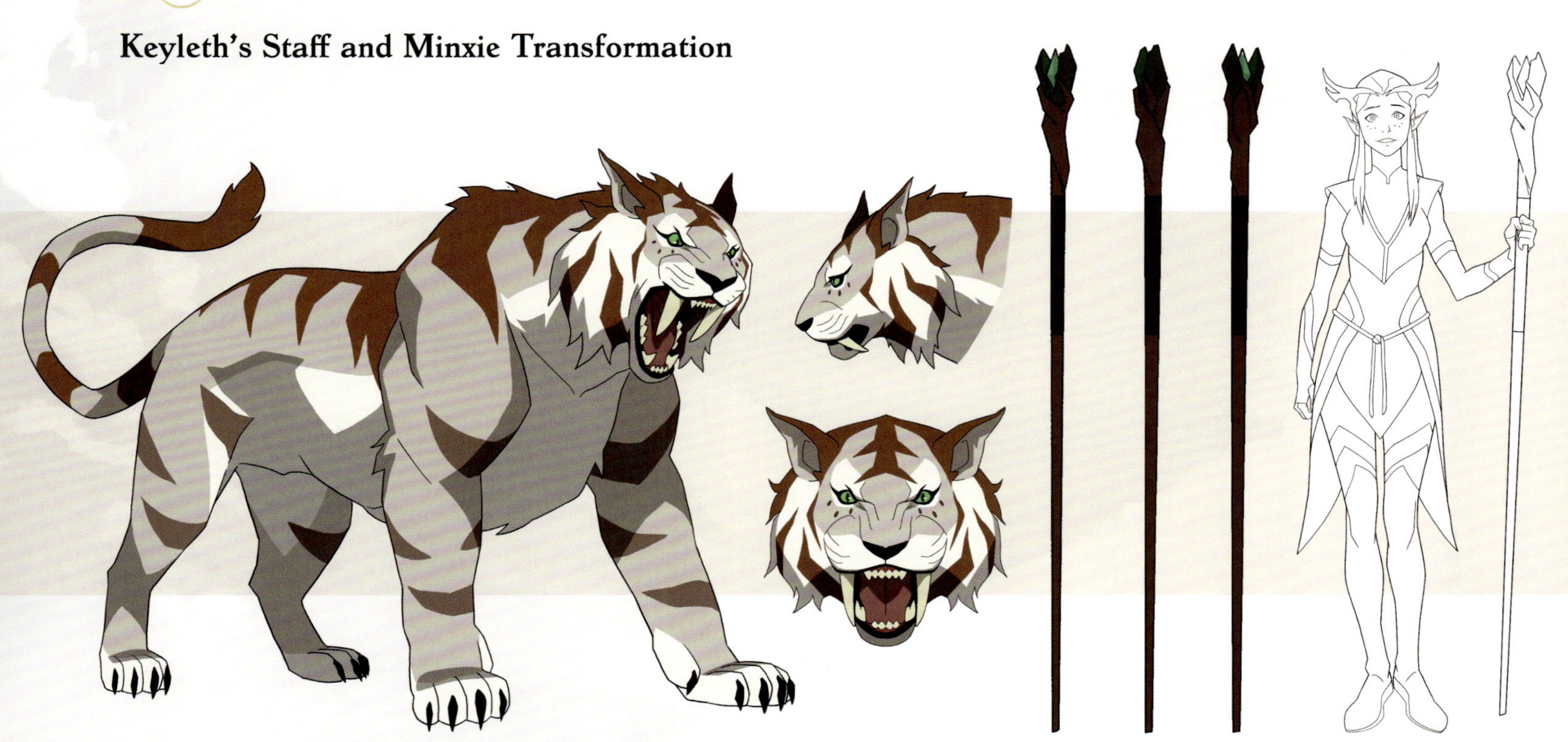

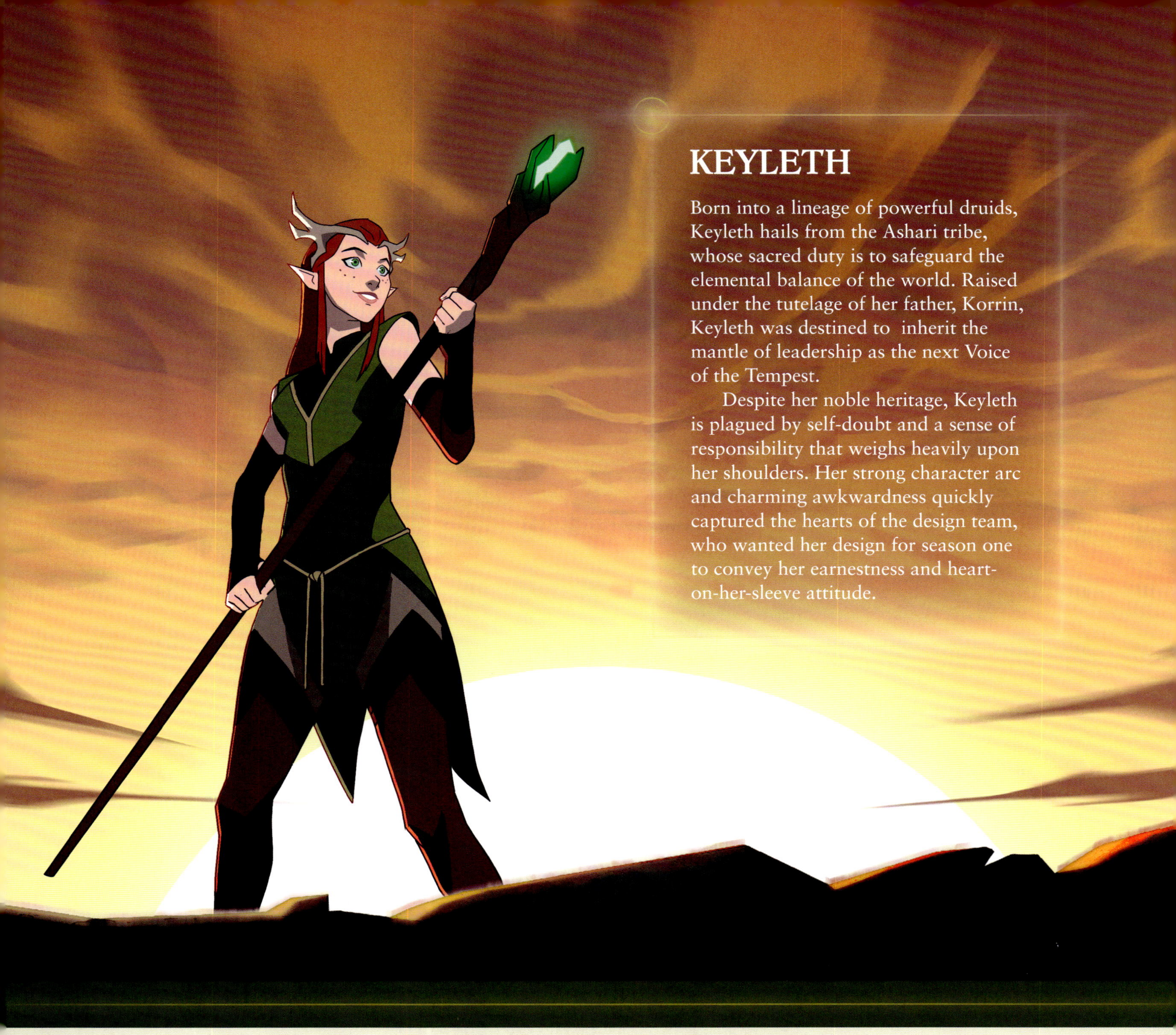

KEYLETH

Born into a lineage of powerful druids, Keyleth hails from the Ashari tribe, whose sacred duty is to safeguard the elemental balance of the world. Raised under the tutelage of her father, Korrin, Keyleth was destined to inherit the mantle of leadership as the next Voice of the Tempest.

Despite her noble heritage, Keyleth is plagued by self-doubt and a sense of responsibility that weighs heavily upon her shoulders. Her strong character arc and charming awkwardness quickly captured the hearts of the design team, who wanted her design for season one to convey her earnestness and heart-on-her-sleeve attitude.

Early Concepts

Her powers encompass a wide range of abilities, from controlling the weather to communicating with animals and plants, making her a formidable force. Finding the right design to capture the natural foundation of her powers was an important consideration when developing the look of Keyleth's magic.

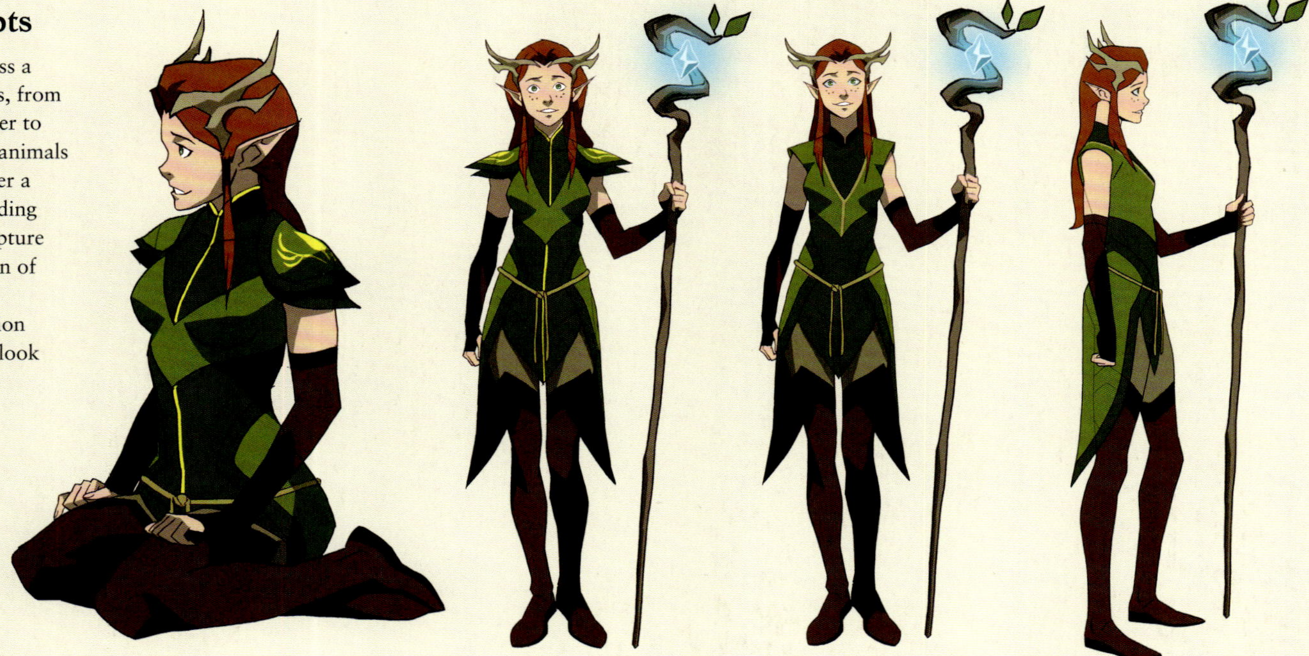

PERCIVAL DE ROLO

Percival Fredrickstein Von Musel Klossowski de Rolo III, commonly known as Percy, is a complex and enigmatic character. Born into the prestigious de Rolo family, his life was irrevocably altered when his family was brutally murdered before his eyes by the treacherous Briarwoods. Bent on revenge and fueled by a thirst for justice, Percy embarked on a quest to avenge his family's death and liberate Whitestone from the grip of tyranny.

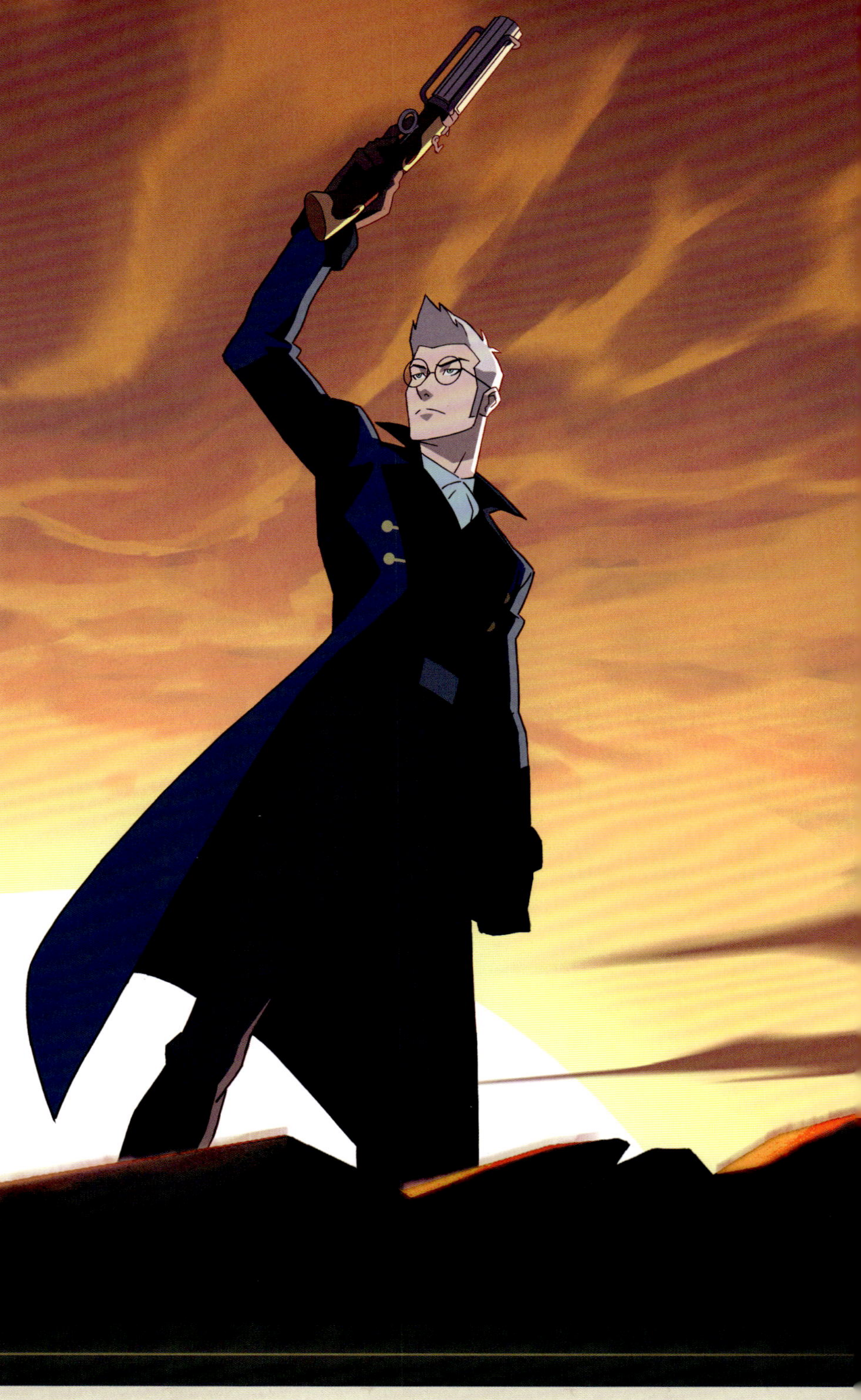

Early Concepts

Armed with his intellect and a talent for invention, Percy became known as the "gunslinger" of Vox Machina. Yet, beneath Percy's stoic exterior lies a tortured soul haunted by guilt and remorse. Despite his best efforts to bury his past and focus on the task at hand, the specter of his family's murder looms large, driving him to desperate measures in his quest for vengeance. As the series unfolds, Percy's character undergoes a profound transformation, evolving into a reluctant hero and a steadfast friend.

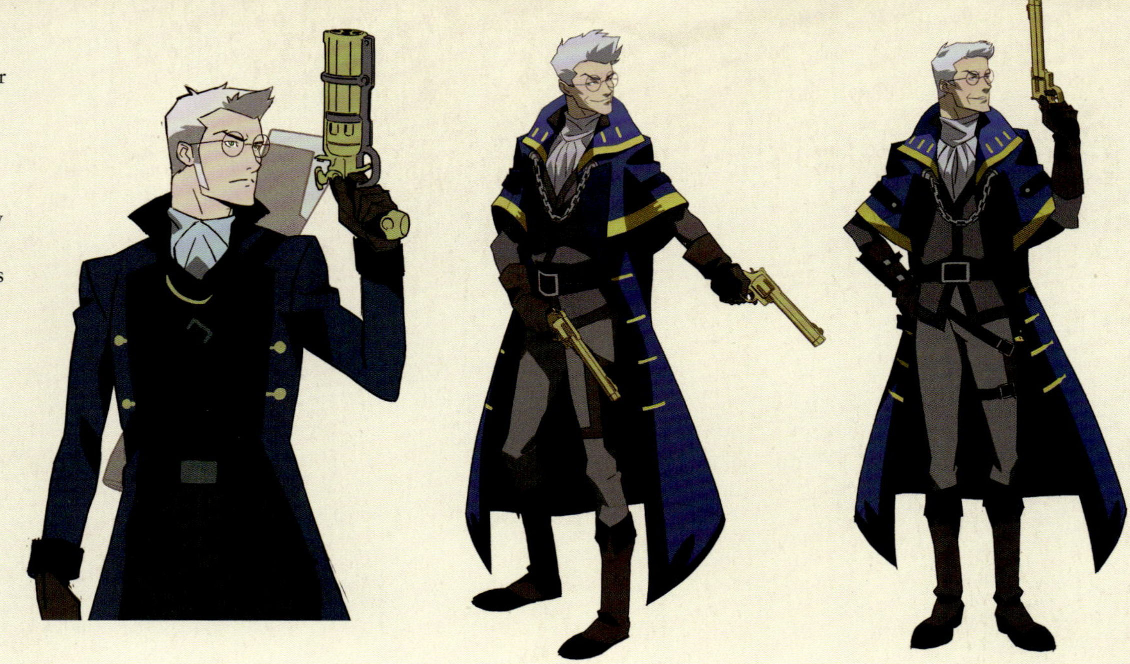

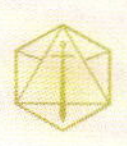

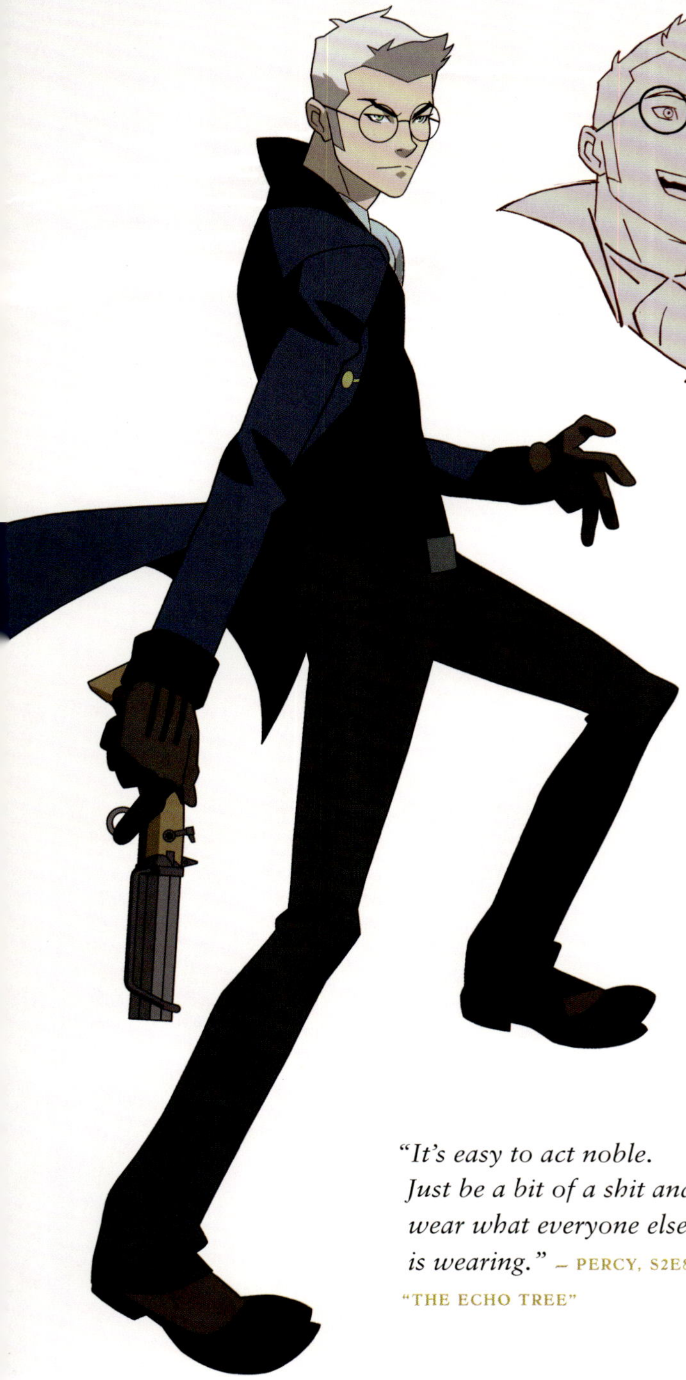

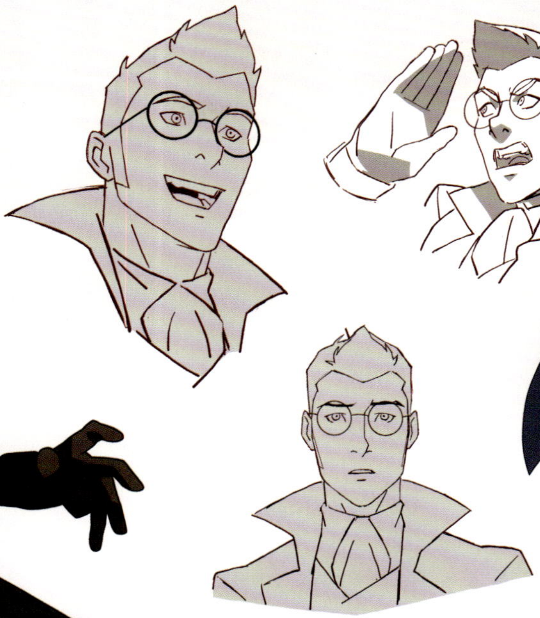

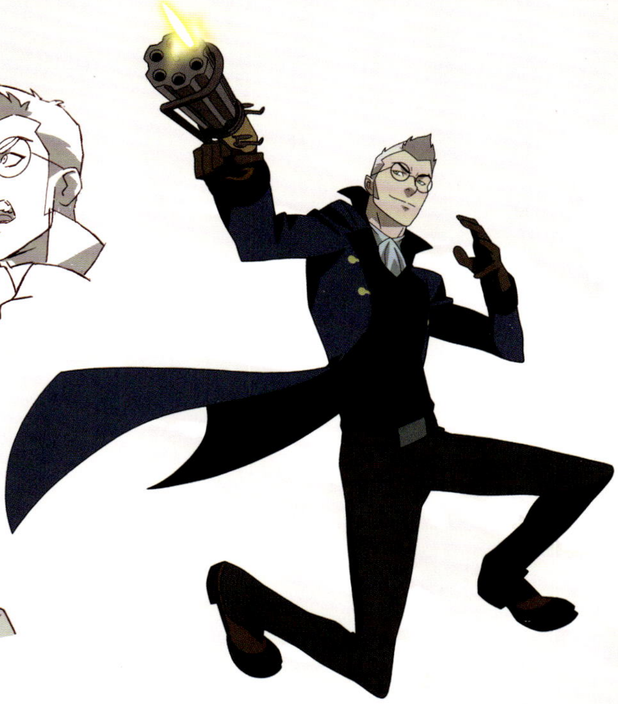

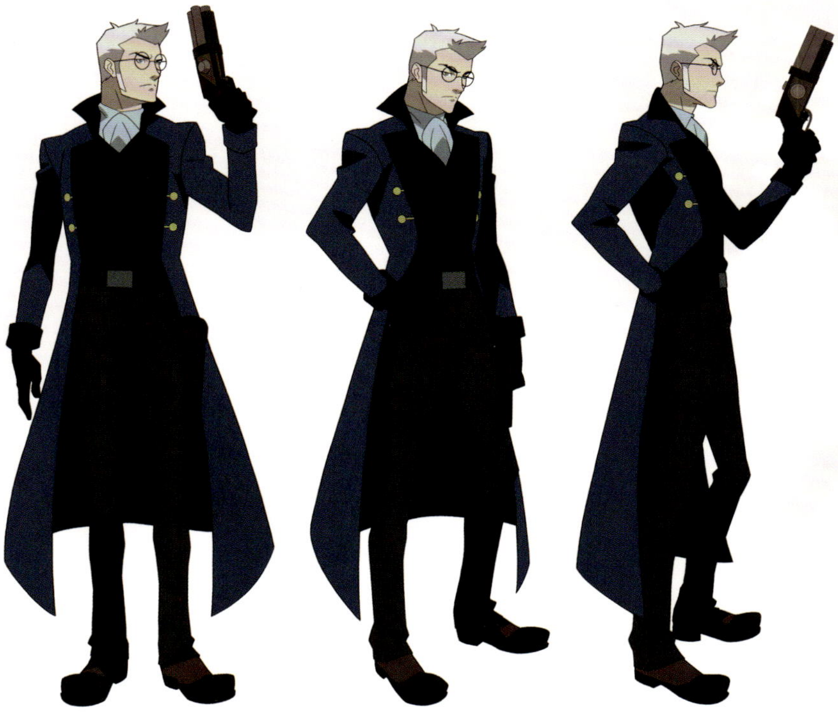

"It's easy to act noble. Just be a bit of a shit and wear what everyone else is wearing." — PERCY, S2E8 "THE ECHO TREE"

Percy's Pepperbox and Mask

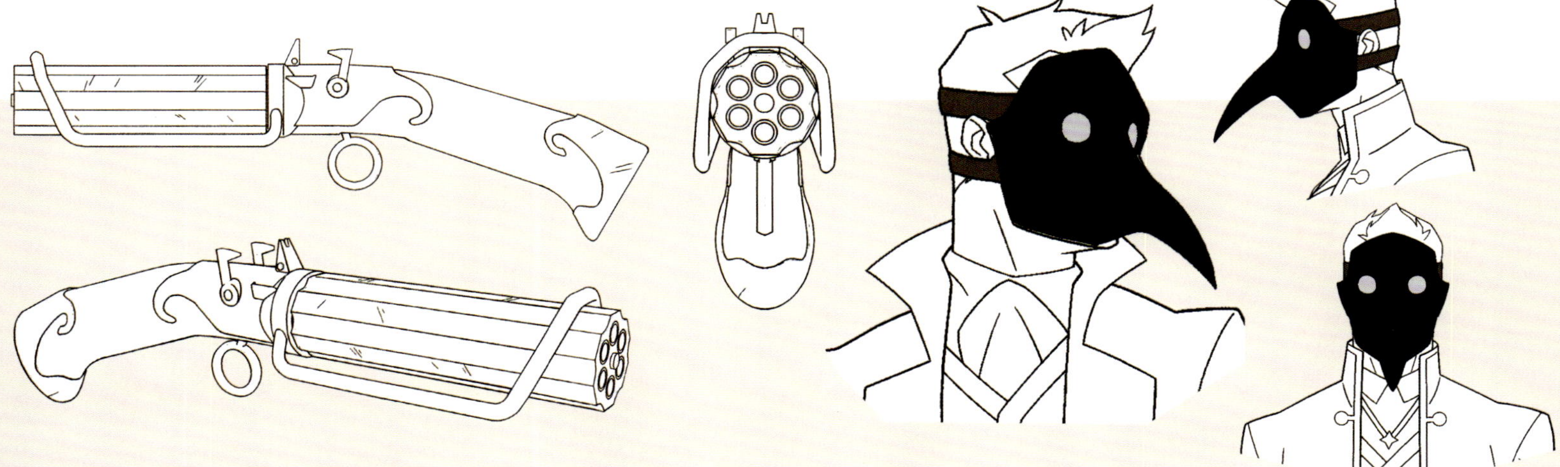

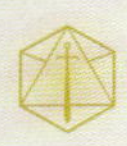

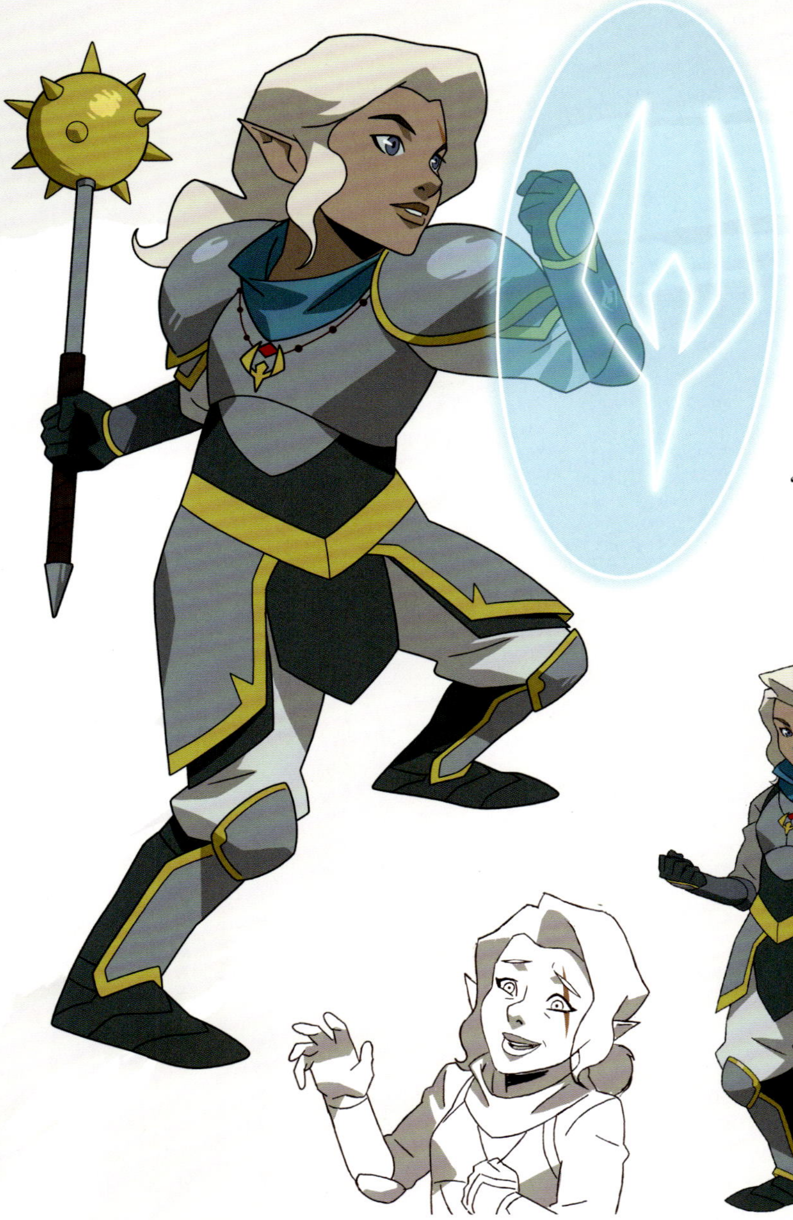

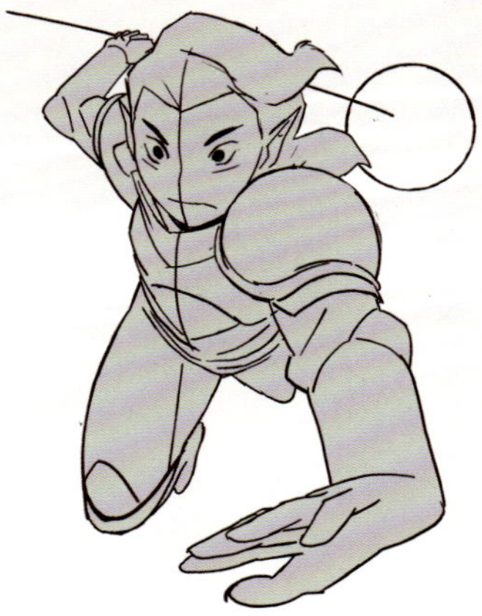

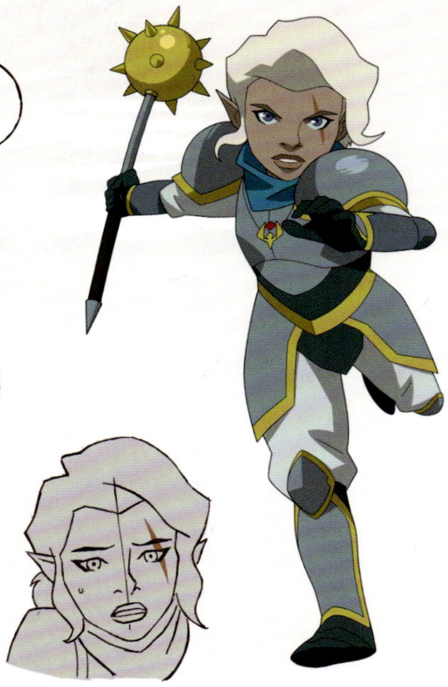

"Maybe we could try doing some good this time?"

— PIKE, S1E1 "THE TERROR OF TAL'DOREI: PART 1"

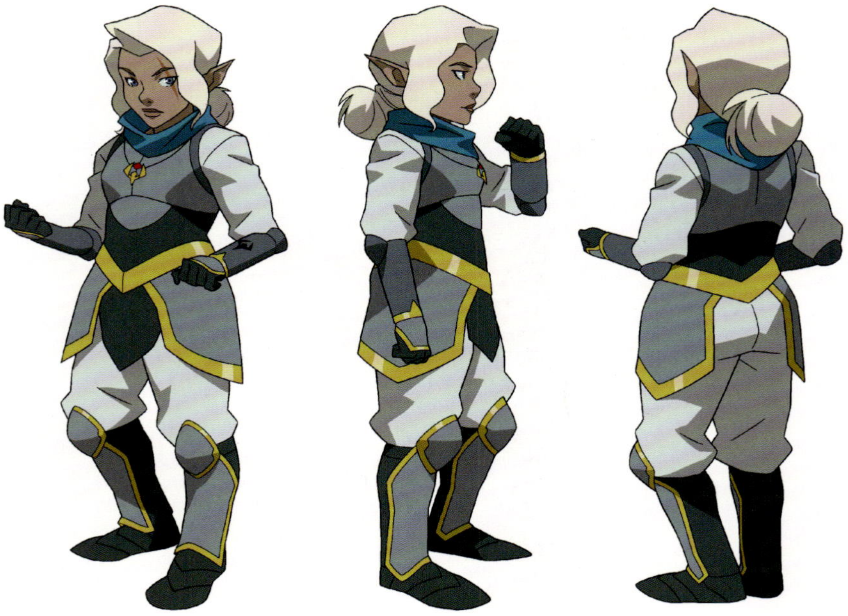

The Everlight

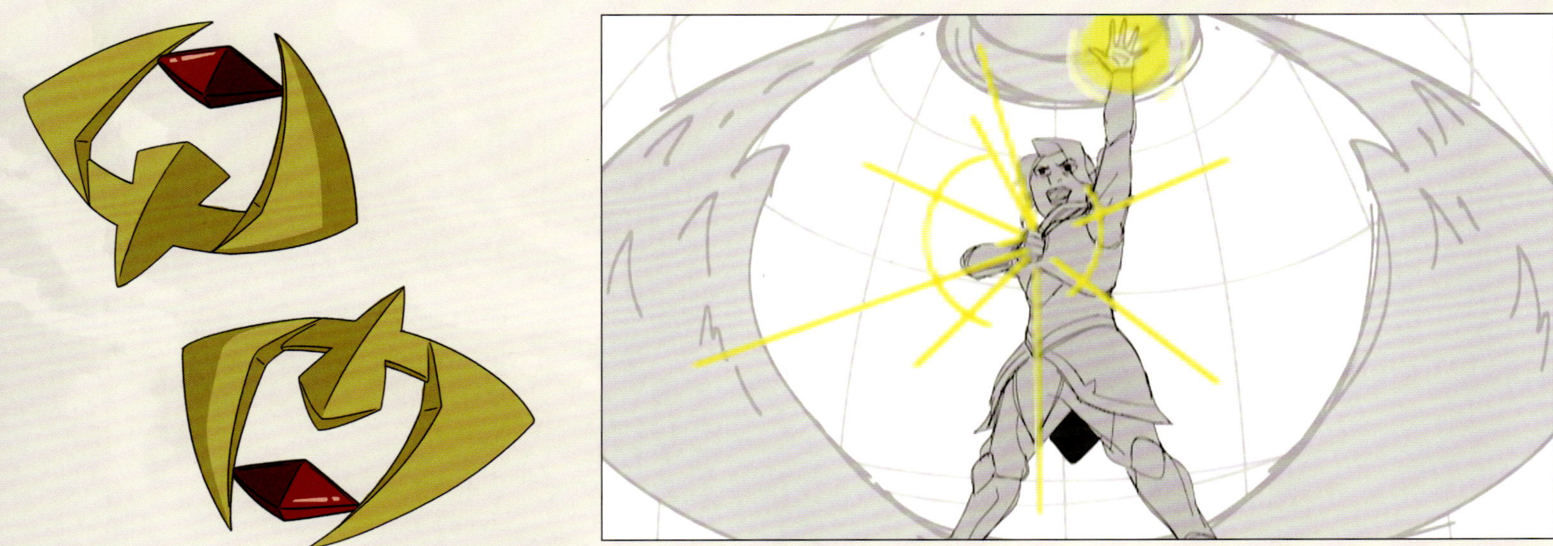

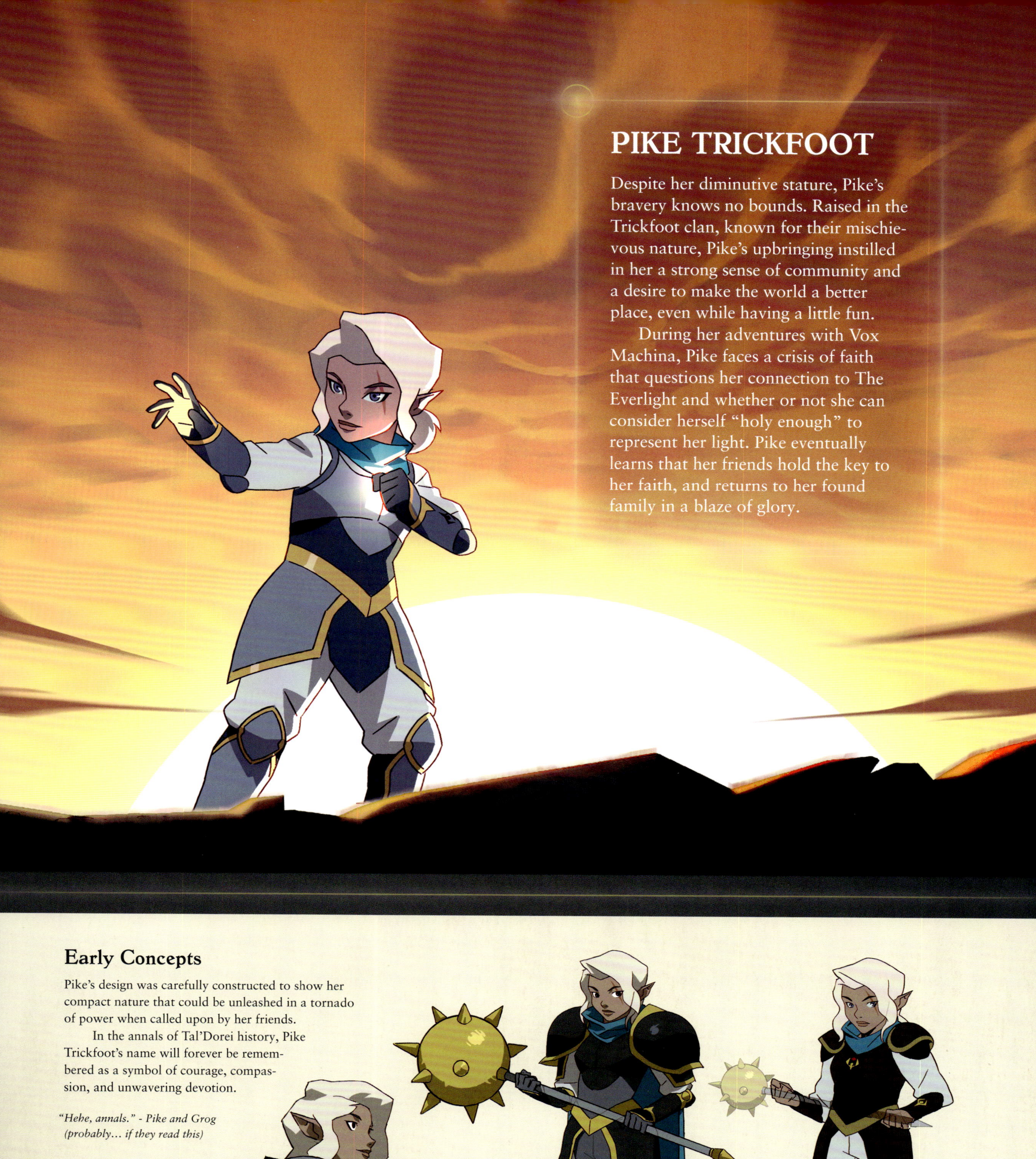

PIKE TRICKFOOT

Despite her diminutive stature, Pike's bravery knows no bounds. Raised in the Trickfoot clan, known for their mischievous nature, Pike's upbringing instilled in her a strong sense of community and a desire to make the world a better place, even while having a little fun.

During her adventures with Vox Machina, Pike faces a crisis of faith that questions her connection to The Everlight and whether or not she can consider herself "holy enough" to represent her light. Pike eventually learns that her friends hold the key to her faith, and returns to her found family in a blaze of glory.

Early Concepts

Pike's design was carefully constructed to show her compact nature that could be unleashed in a tornado of power when called upon by her friends.

In the annals of Tal'Dorei history, Pike Trickfoot's name will forever be remembered as a symbol of courage, compassion, and unwavering devotion.

"Hehe, annals." - Pike and Grog (probably... if they read this)

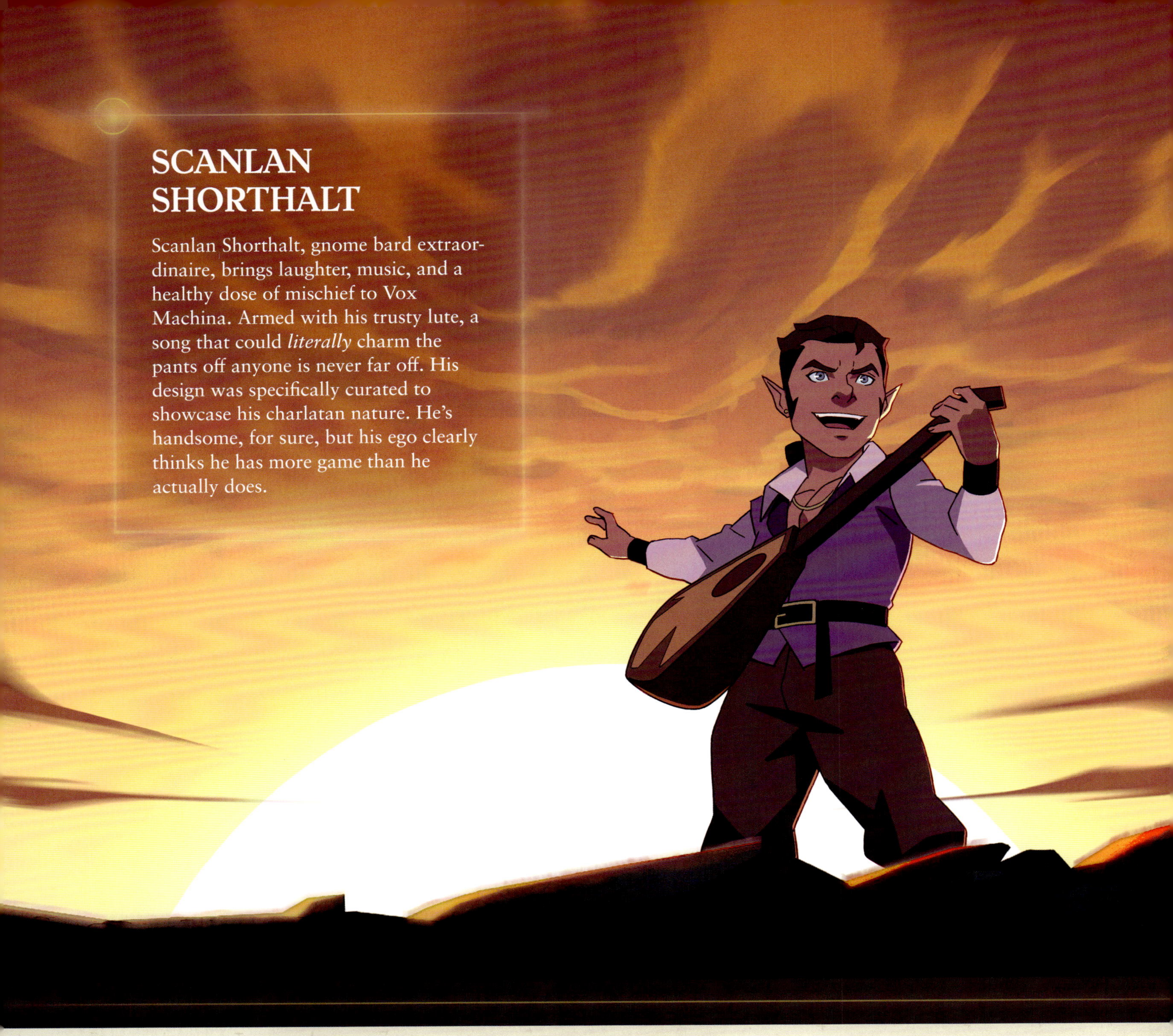

SCANLAN SHORTHALT

Scanlan Shorthalt, gnome bard extraordinaire, brings laughter, music, and a healthy dose of mischief to Vox Machina. Armed with his trusty lute, a song that could *literally* charm the pants off anyone is never far off. His design was specifically curated to showcase his charlatan nature. He's handsome, for sure, but his ego clearly thinks he has more game than he actually does.

Early Concepts

Beneath his flamboyant exterior, however, lies a complex soul grappling with insecurities and a deep-seated need for validation and belonging. Despite his tendency to mask his vulnerabilities with humor and bravado, Scanlan's desire for his friends' approval is something not even a sold-out crowd could fulfill.

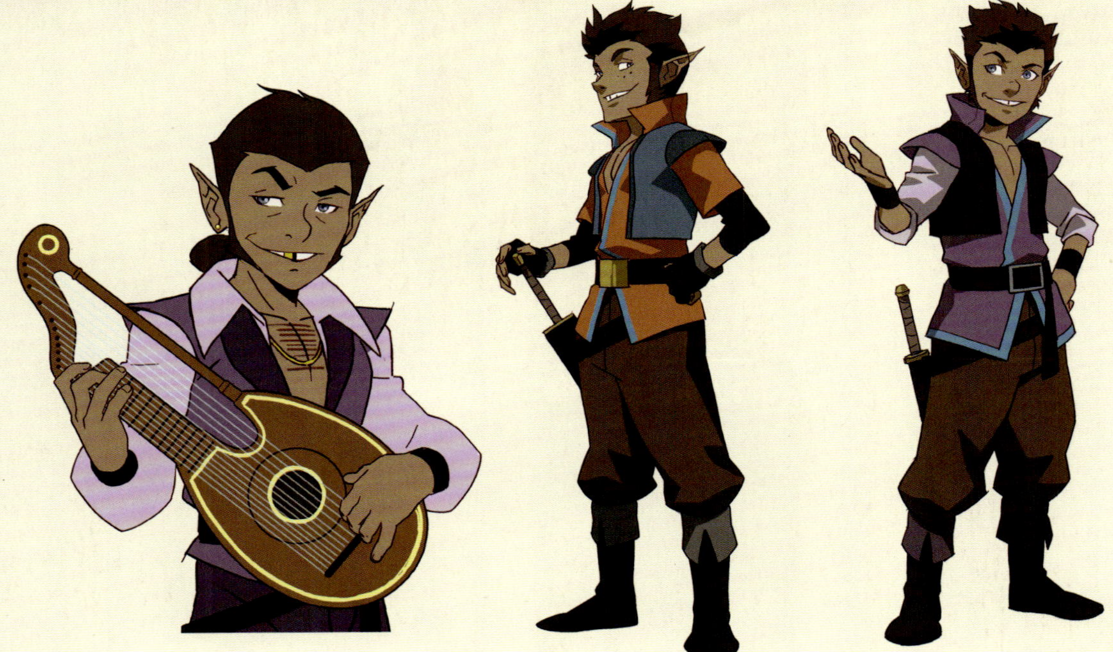

"I'm sort of an adventurer, rebel leader, musician. Some would say philosopher."

– SCANLAN, S2E10 "THE KILLBOX"

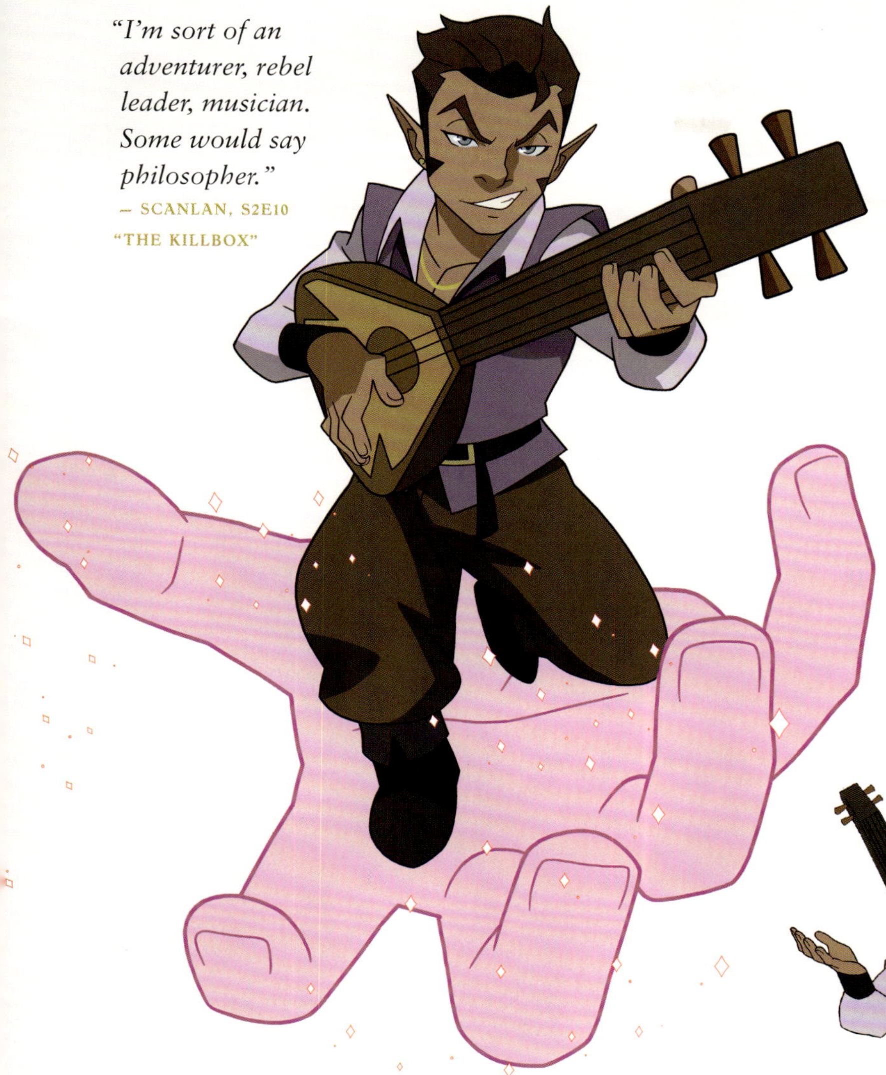

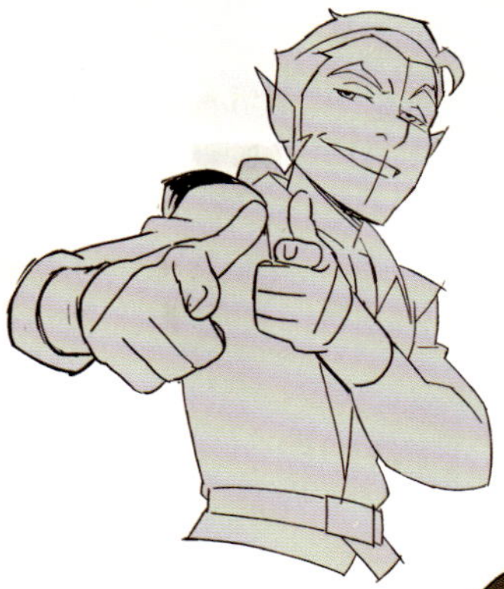

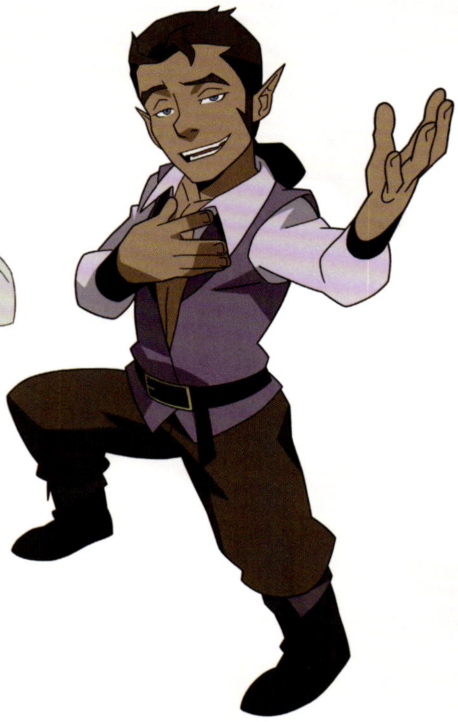

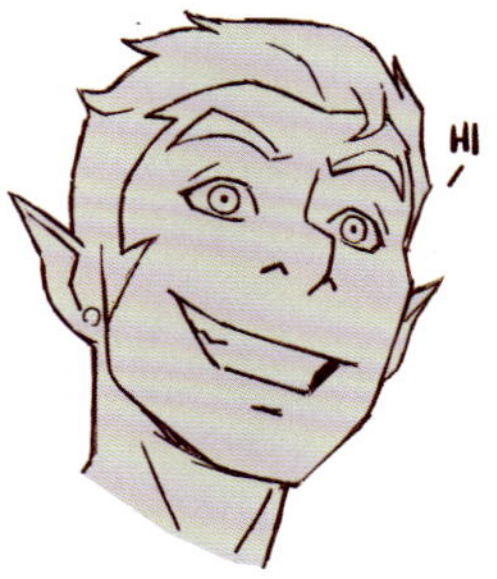

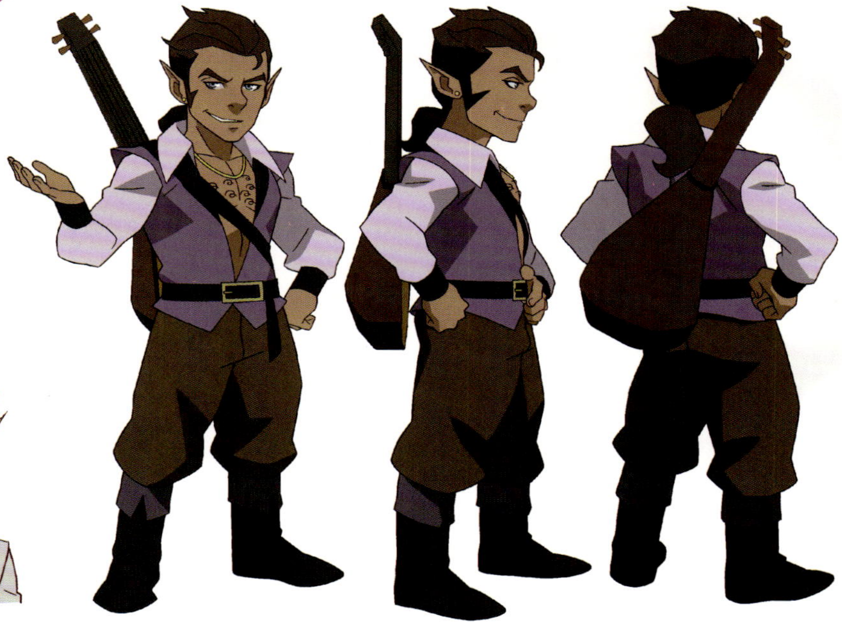

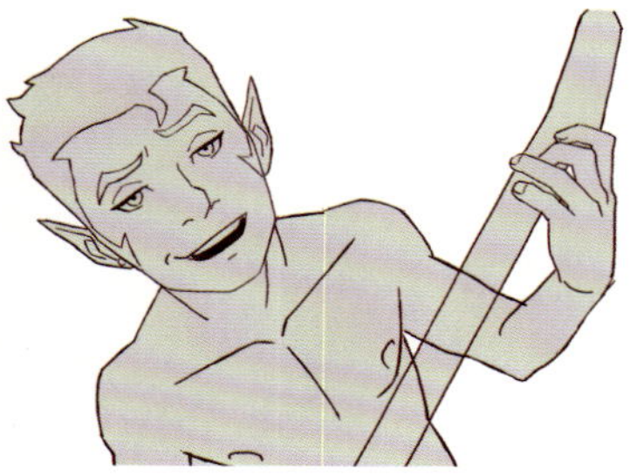

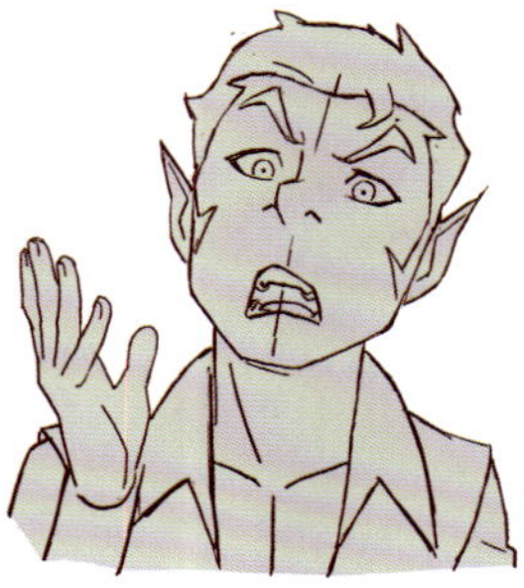

Scanlan's Lute and Magic

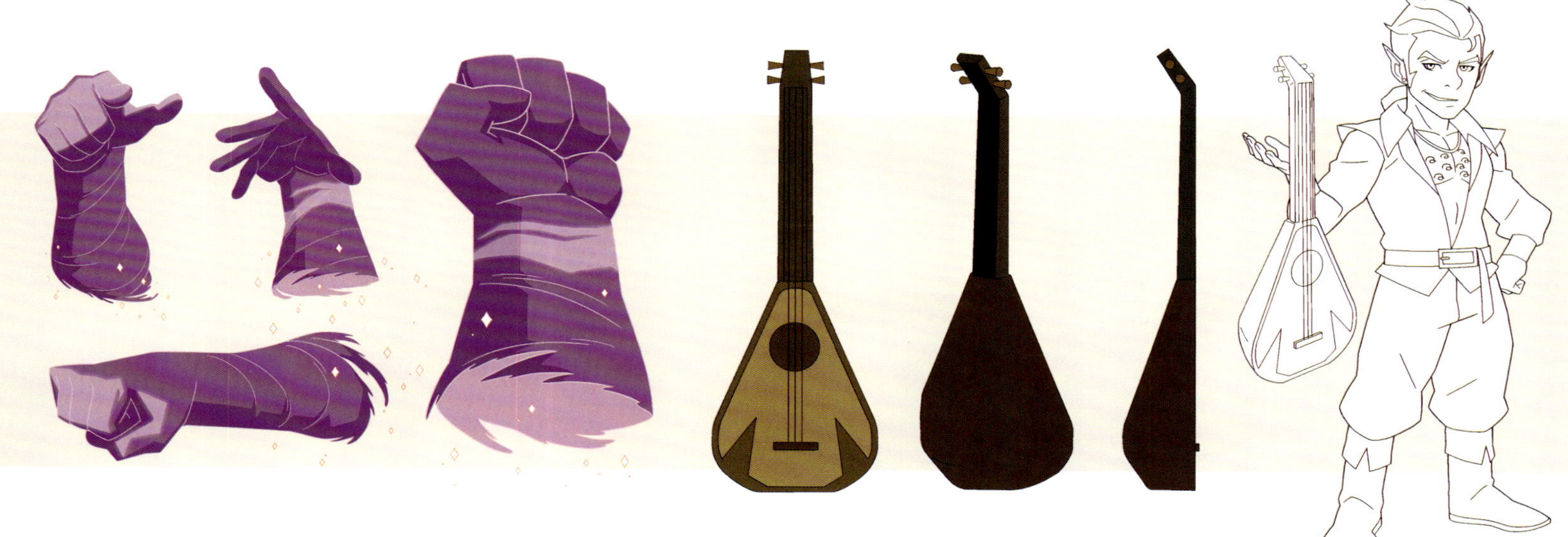

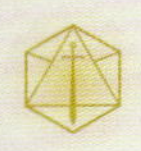

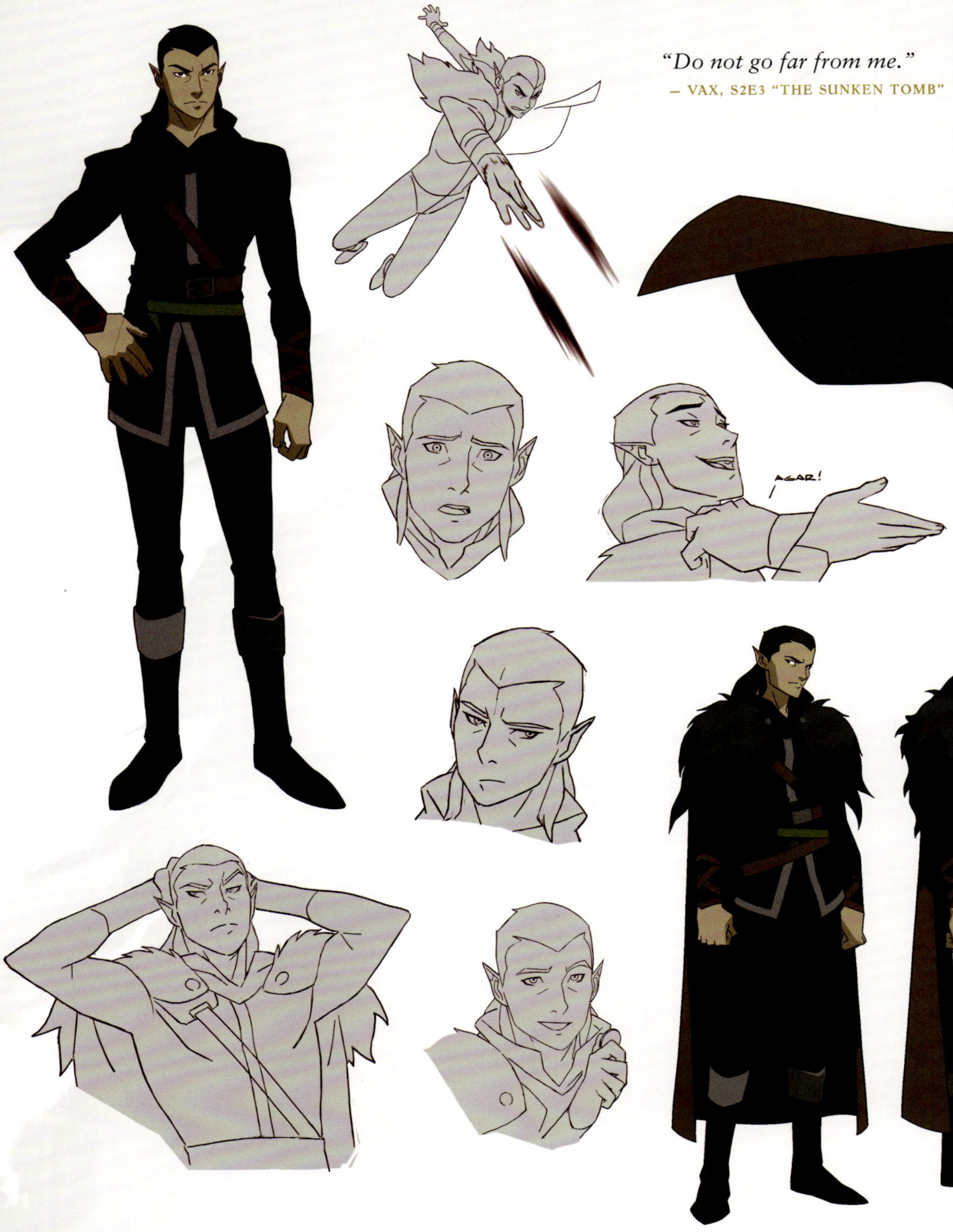

"Do not go far from me."
– VAX, S2E3 "THE SUNKEN TOMB"

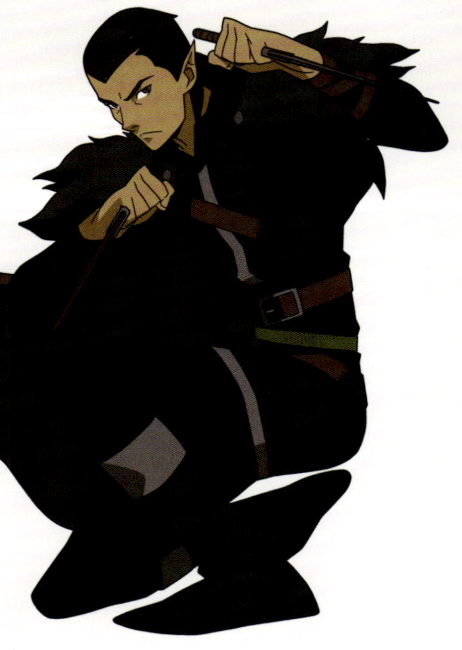

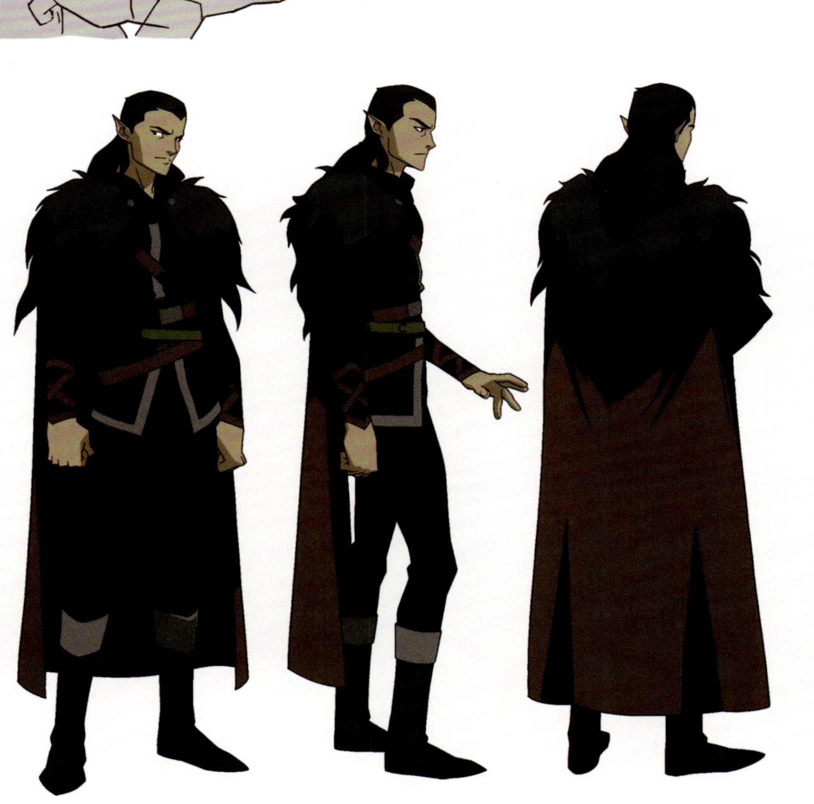

Vax's Daggers

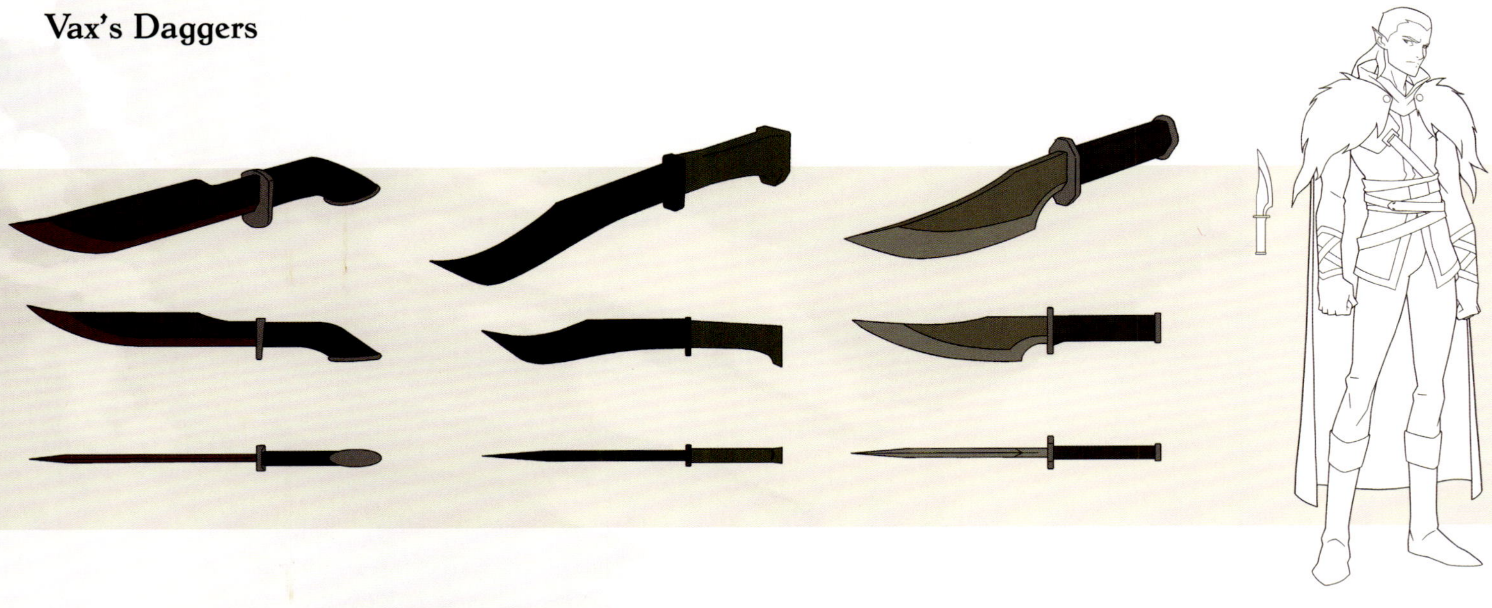

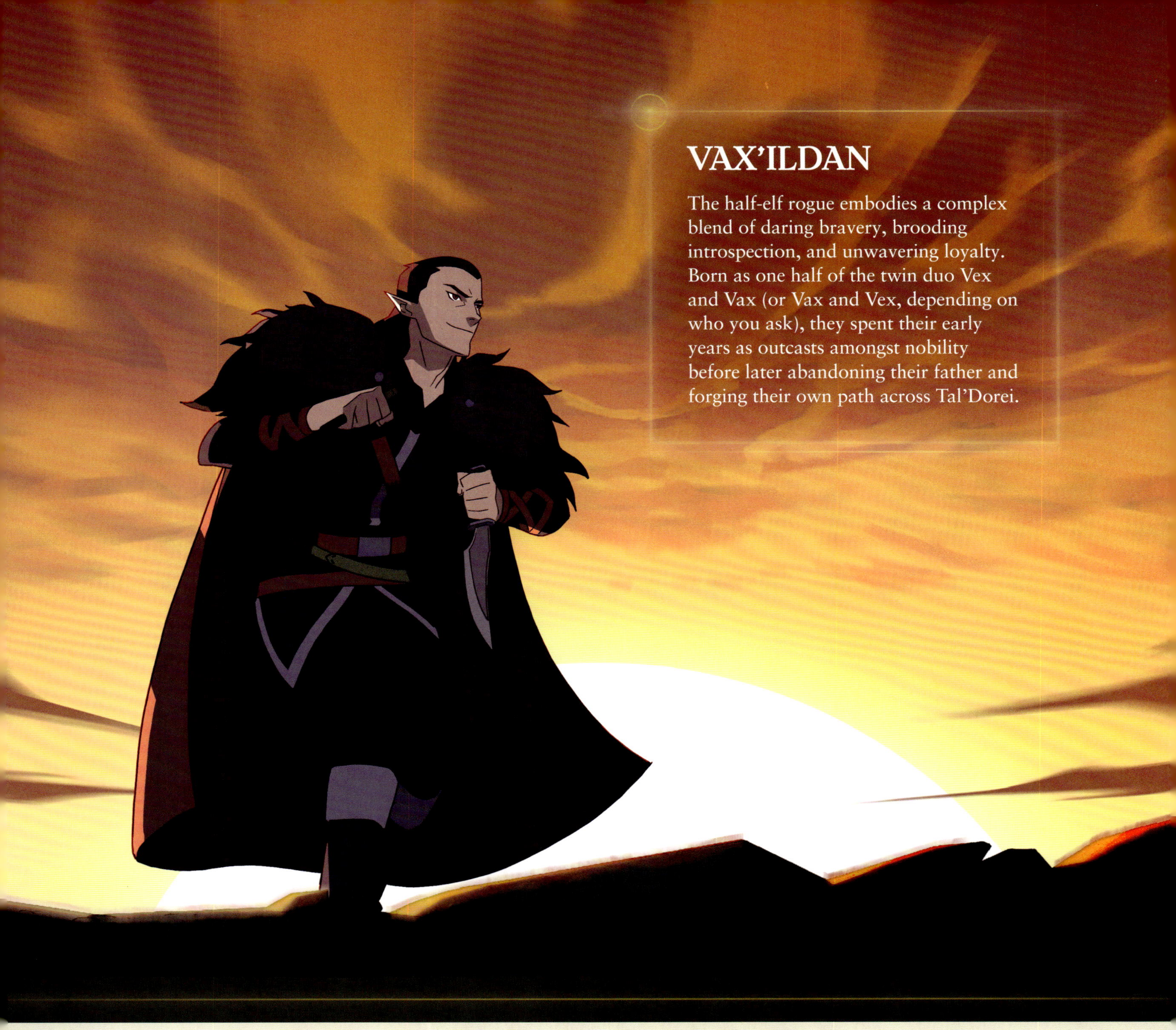

VAX'ILDAN

The half-elf rogue embodies a complex blend of daring bravery, brooding introspection, and unwavering loyalty. Born as one half of the twin duo Vex and Vax (or Vax and Vex, depending on who you ask), they spent their early years as outcasts amongst nobility before later abandoning their father and forging their own path across Tal'Dorei.

Early Concepts

Vax has always straddled two worlds, and the threads of fate seem to hold a bit more tightly to this shadowy figure. His design was influenced by his ability to navigate the world with the grace of a dancer and the cunning of a fox, slipping through the shadows and striking swiftly when the moment is right.

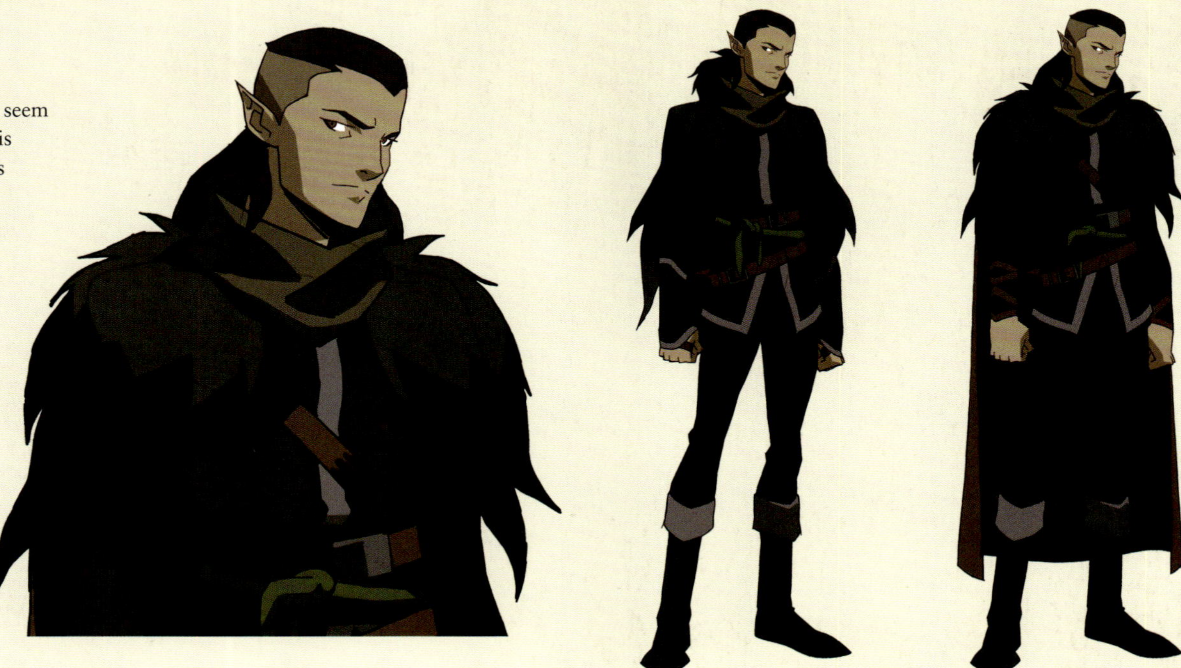

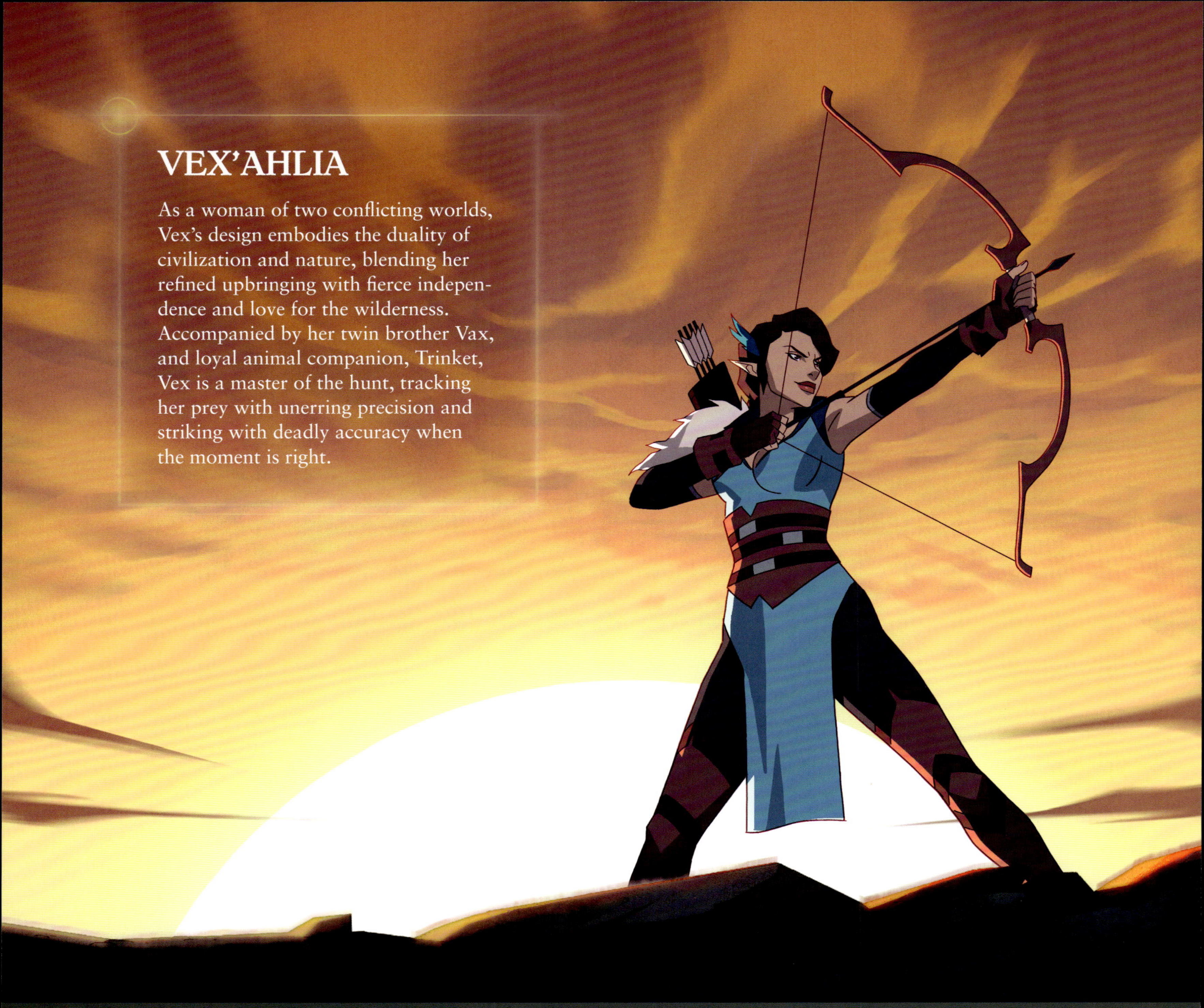

VEX'AHLIA

As a woman of two conflicting worlds, Vex's design embodies the duality of civilization and nature, blending her refined upbringing with fierce independence and love for the wilderness. Accompanied by her twin brother Vax, and loyal animal companion, Trinket, Vex is a master of the hunt, tracking her prey with unerring precision and striking with deadly accuracy when the moment is right.

Early Concepts

It was important for Vex's look to convey not only her keen fighting prowess but also her feminine wiles and sharp-witted savvy, which are key when navigating tense diplomatic situations. She often serves as the voice of reason within Vox Machina, offering sage counsel and blunt observations while facing down their foes. Beneath her tough and sometimes aloof exterior, however, lies a heart of gold that allows her to be fiercely loyal to her friends and protective of those she holds dear.

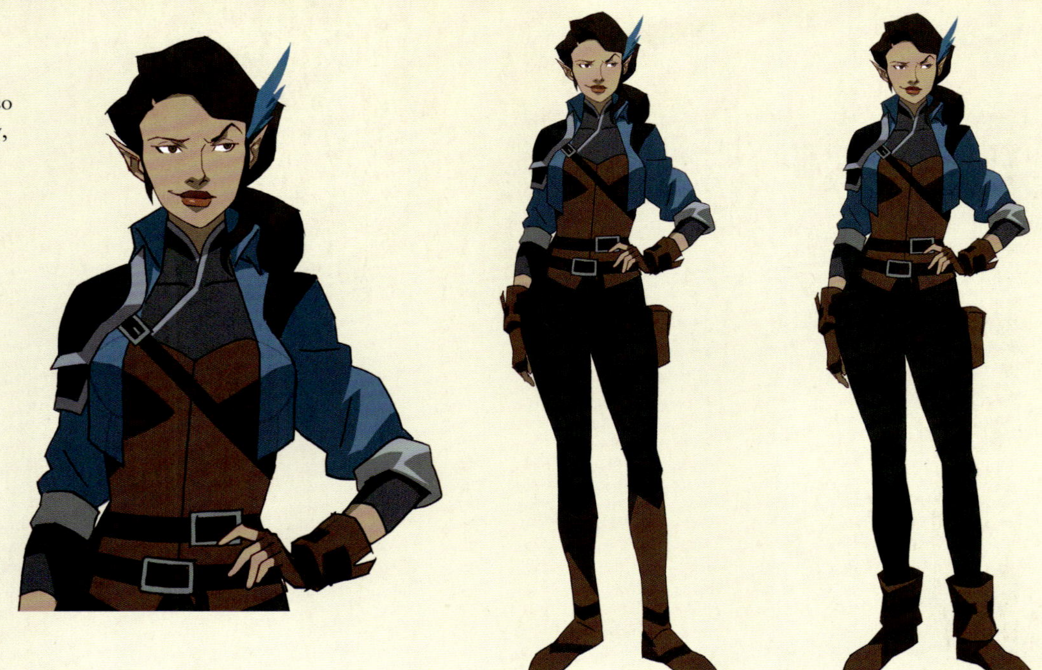

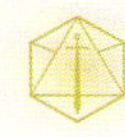

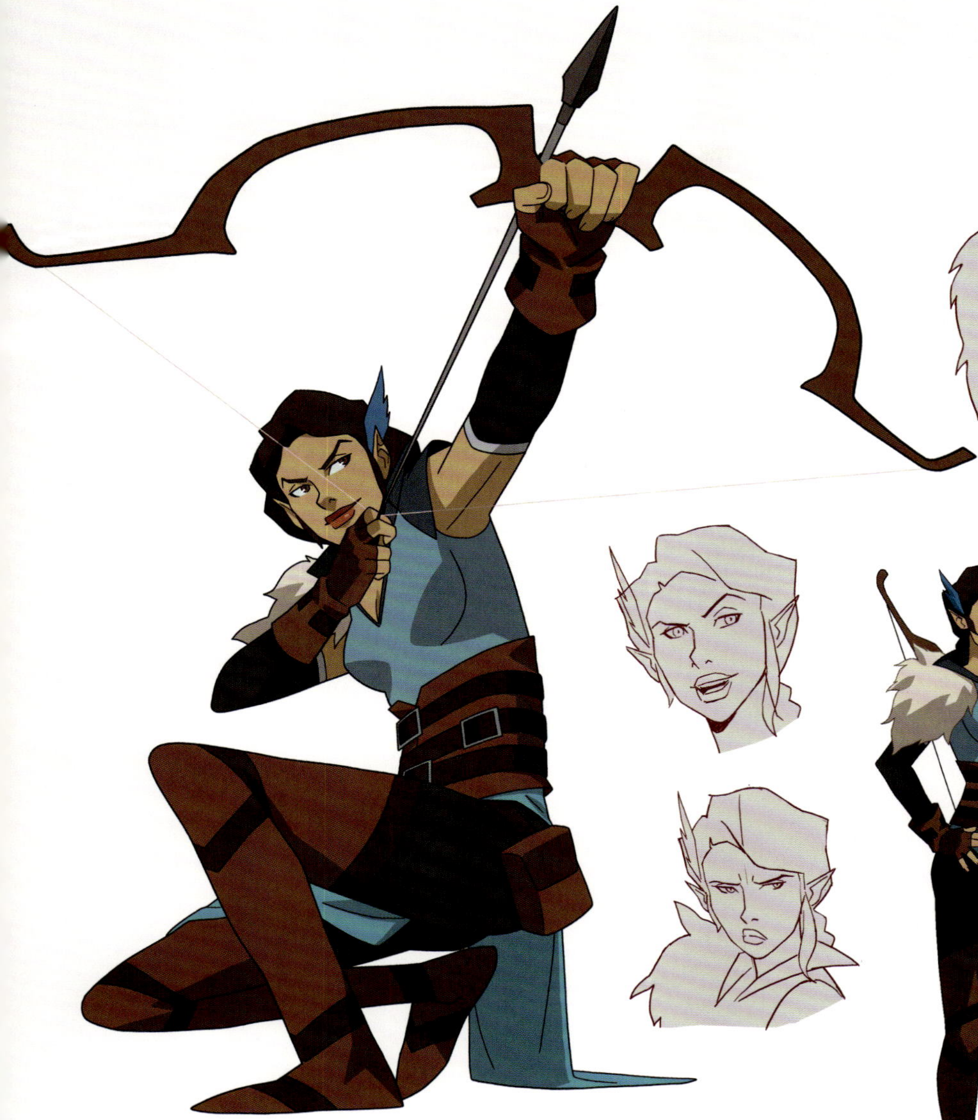

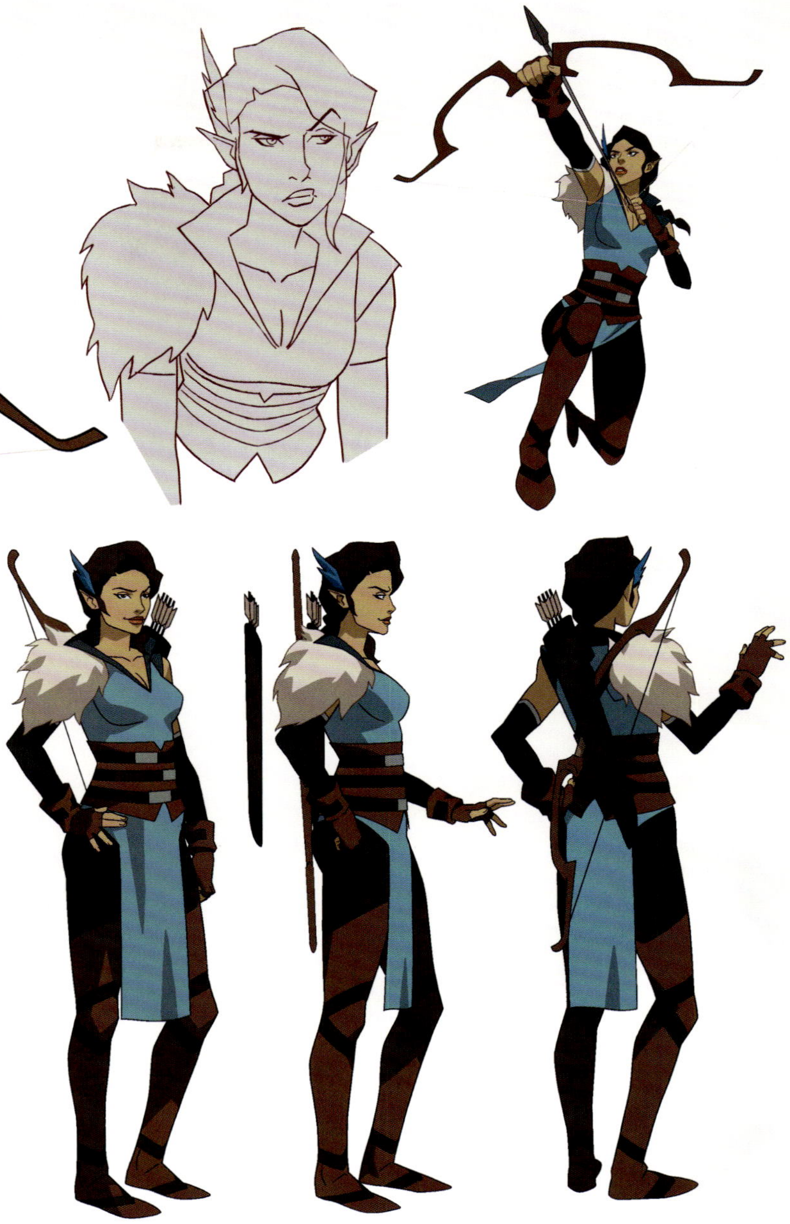

"The deadlier the traps, the richer the reward."
– VEX, S2E3 "THE SUNKEN TOMB"

Vex's Bow

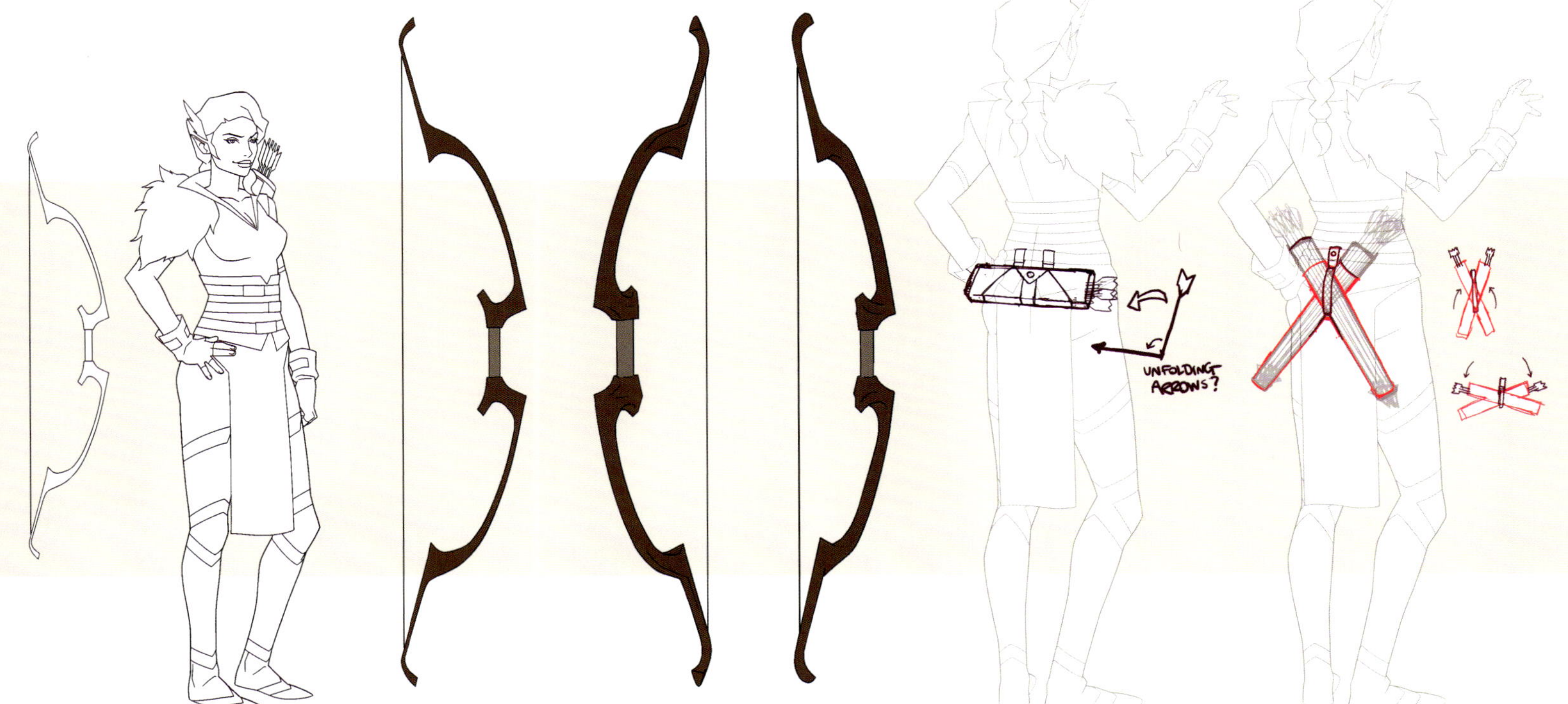

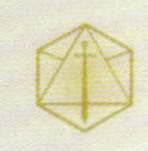

Trinket

Trinket is not just a bear; he's a steadfast companion, a loyal protector, and an indispensable member of Vox Machina. A wild animal captured as a cub, Trinket's fate intertwined with that of Vex's. As Vox Machina's guardian bear, Trinket has faced countless dangers alongside his companions. From battling fearsome monsters to navigating treacherous dungeons, he fearlessly charges into the fray, always ready to defend his friends with tooth and claw.

"They do have a bear. It looked quite ferocious." – SOVEREIGN URIEL TAL'DOREI III, S1E1 "THE TERROR OF TAL'DOREI" PART 1"

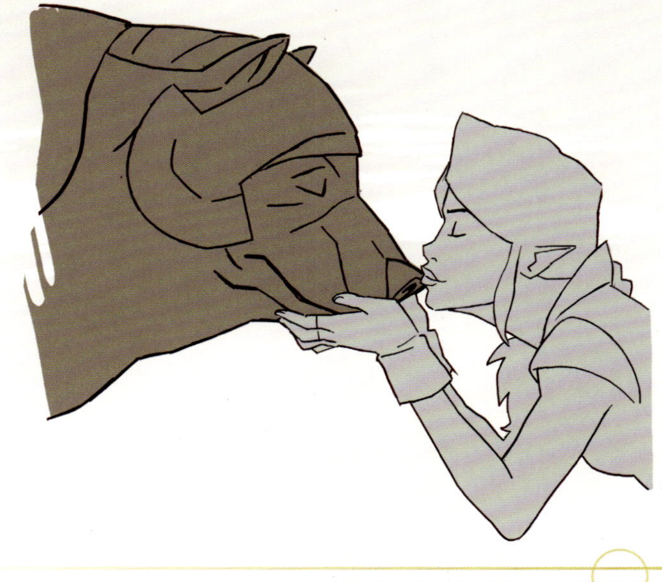

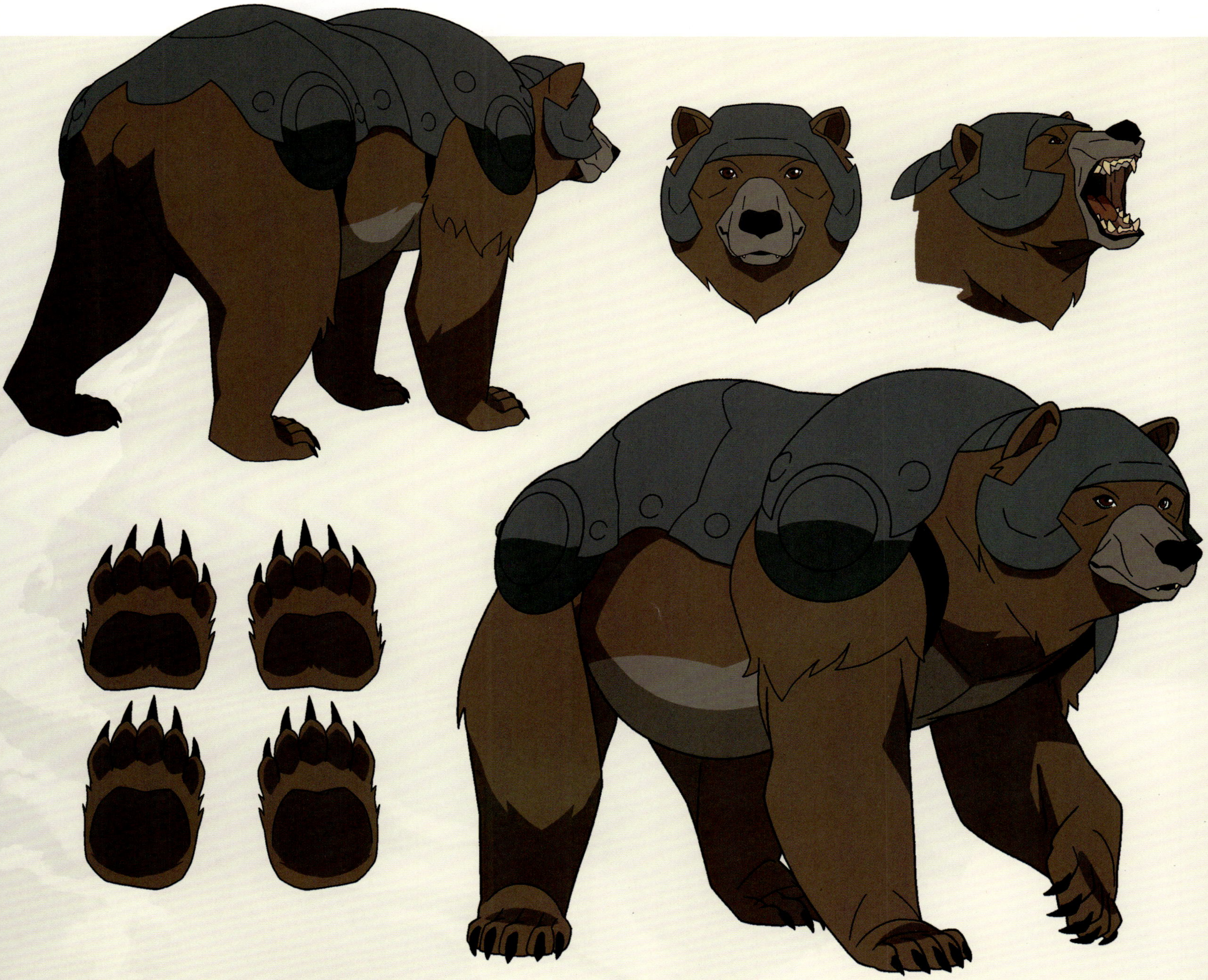

Figuring out how to design armor for a bear was also a fun challenge for the design team as they worked with the animation team to finesse how Trinket could move on screen. Any character with four legs is an added challenge when coordinating their movement, so Trinket's design was particularly important to keep streamlined (but also cute!)

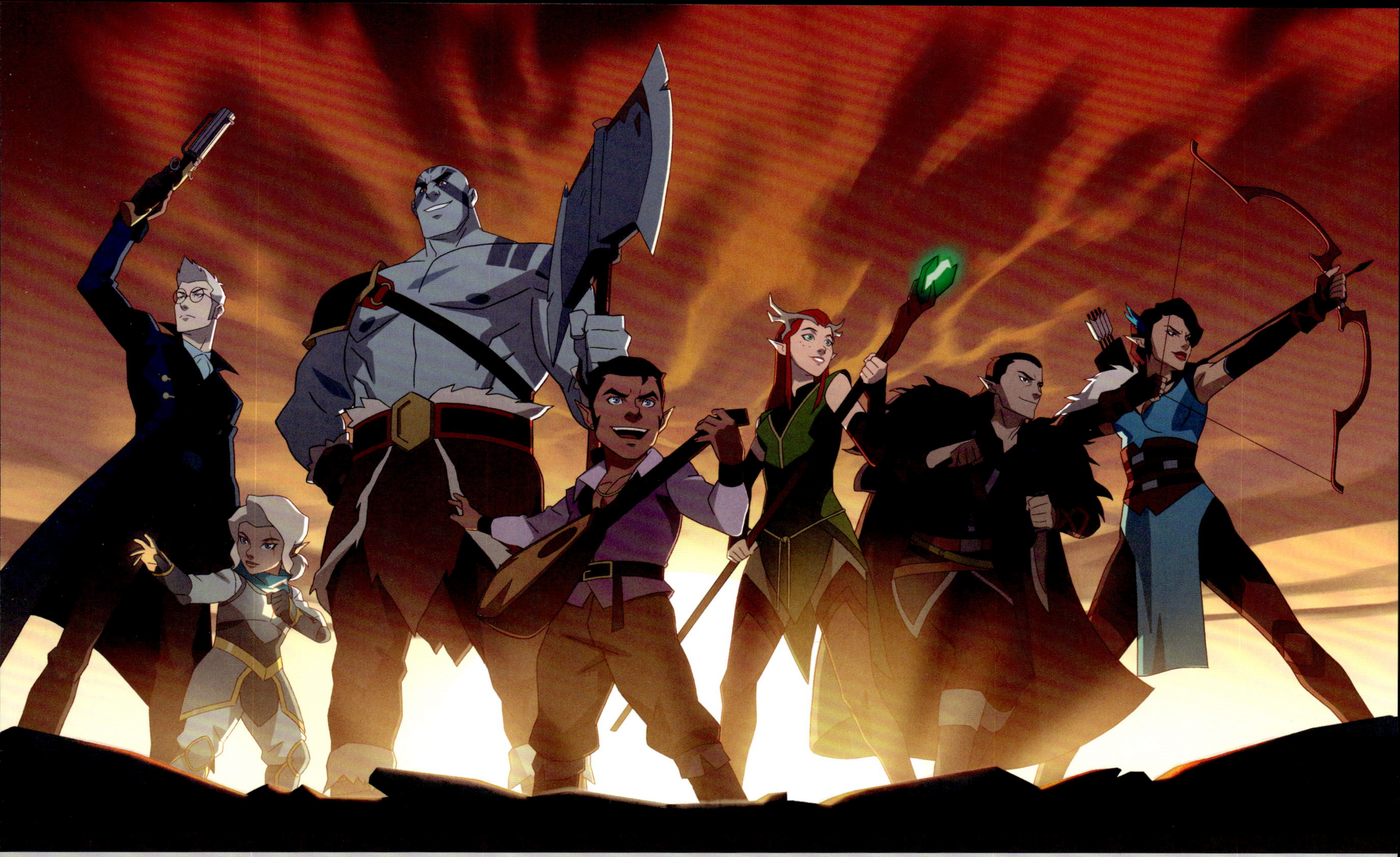

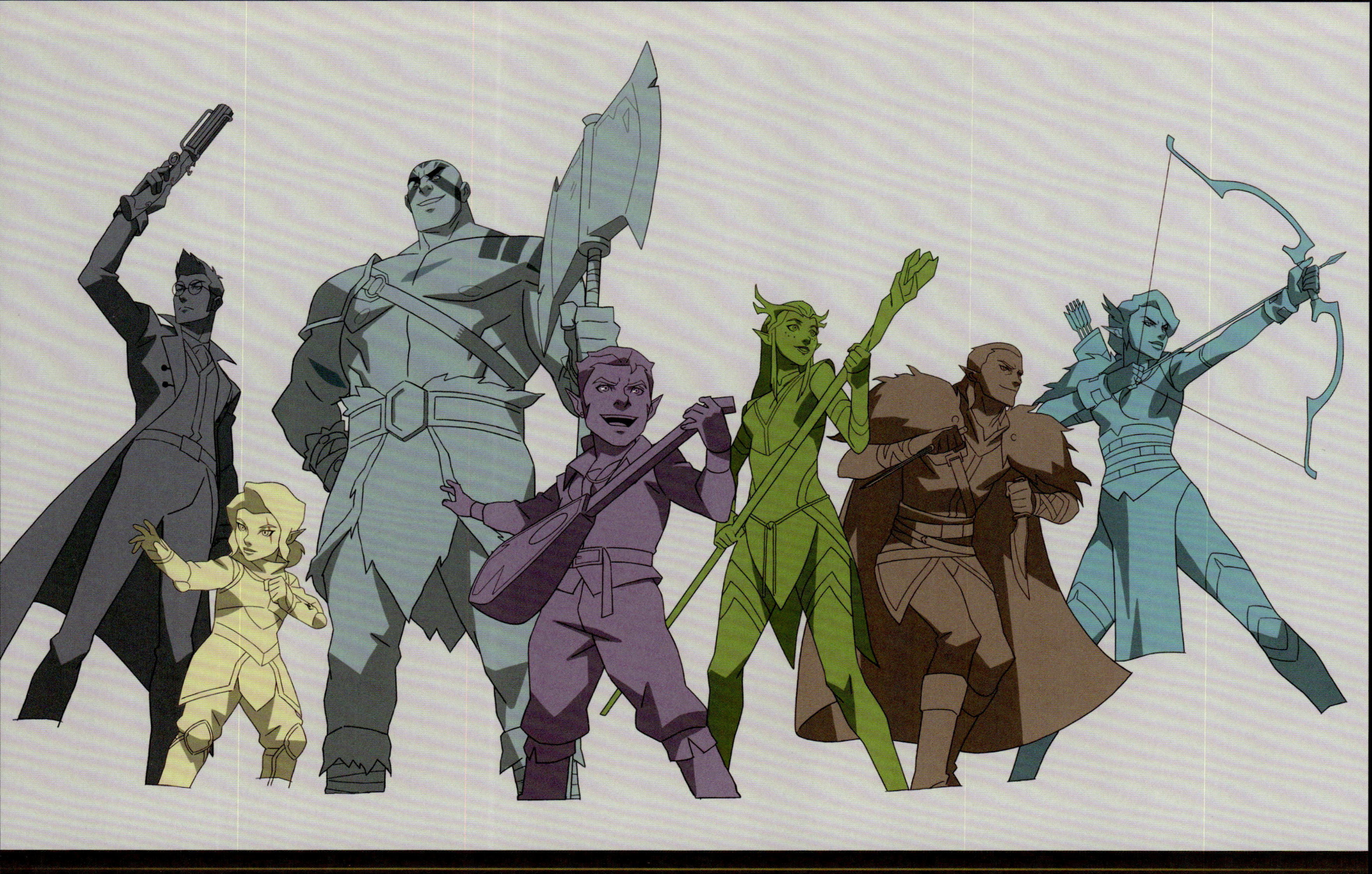

Vox Machina Heroic Pose

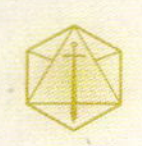

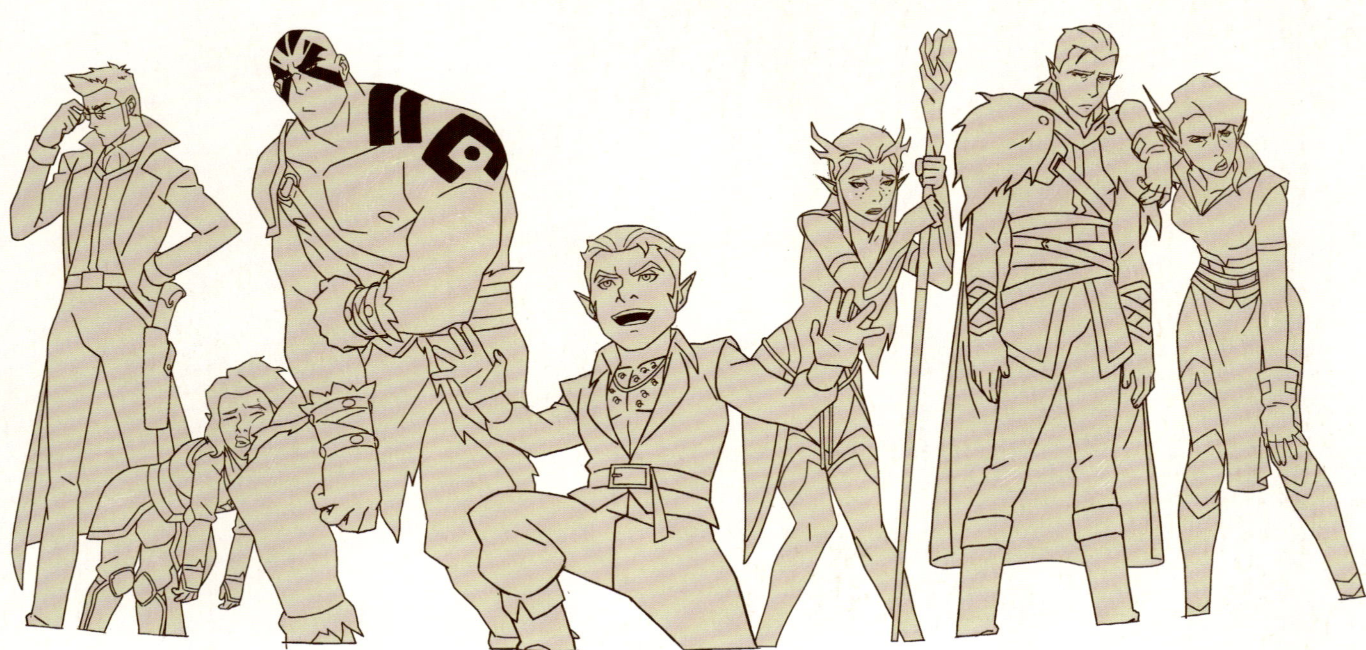

INTERVIEW Q&A WITH PHIL BOURASSA

Character Designer Phil Bourassa already had an impressive resume full of critically acclaimed legacy characters upon joining the crew for The Legend of Vox Machina. Having such a distinct and sought-after style, his character sensibilities fell naturally into place alongside Arthur Loftis's art direction.

What was your first reaction to finding out you were going to be designing characters for the series?

I was excited to have the chance to contribute to something so special and unique. The origin story of how the series came to be is so special. I had worked with Travis (Willingham) before I even knew about Critical Role, and I was really excited to contribute to this show. The stream had achieved massive popularity in this short time span and we're in at the ground floor for its animated adaptation.

I've worked on a lot of legacy IP, and I love drawing Superman and Batman, but this is completely original material. When you're working on old legacy properties, you don't get to interact with the OG creators. There's something really fricken cool about sitting in the room with the Critical Role cast and setting that template. It was such a humbling honor to play in this sandbox.

When does a character designer enter the process in animation, and what did you have to work off of?

Oftentimes character development is done before there is even a script. It is not uncommon to work from an outline or pitch bible with simple character descriptions and nothing else. In terms of Vox, I wasn't the first designer to take a crack at the characters. They had a pitch deck with character concept art, so I had a lot to work with. Going into it, I was unfamiliar with the characters, so I watched a few episodes of the stream, but you can't just watch nine hours and get the whole overview, so I had to pick up a lot in my conversations with the Critical Role cast and Arthur Loftis (series Art Director).

It's great working with characters with well-established visual identities regardless of the medium. These characters hadn't been done in animation, but there's tons of official campaign art and fan art to get the direction. They came to me saying we wanted to see this in Phil's style. I have to admit that early on, I was nervous to begin working with Arthur and Sun Jin (series Supervising Director), because they were new people, and I wasn't sure if they would respond to my style. But we immediately found a rhythm, and it was such a joy to discover that this was really going to work.

Who is your favorite character to see fan art for?

I've seen a lot of great fan art, but I feel like people have a lot of fun with Scanlan. He's so over the top and absurd because Sam is such a riot. However, Pike is probably my current favorite to draw. I don't see a lot of fan art of her, but it's always nice to see. She's like a little tornado, and I love drawing her compact nature. You can do a lot of fun things visually when posing her out.

How closely did you work with the individual cast members on the look of their character?

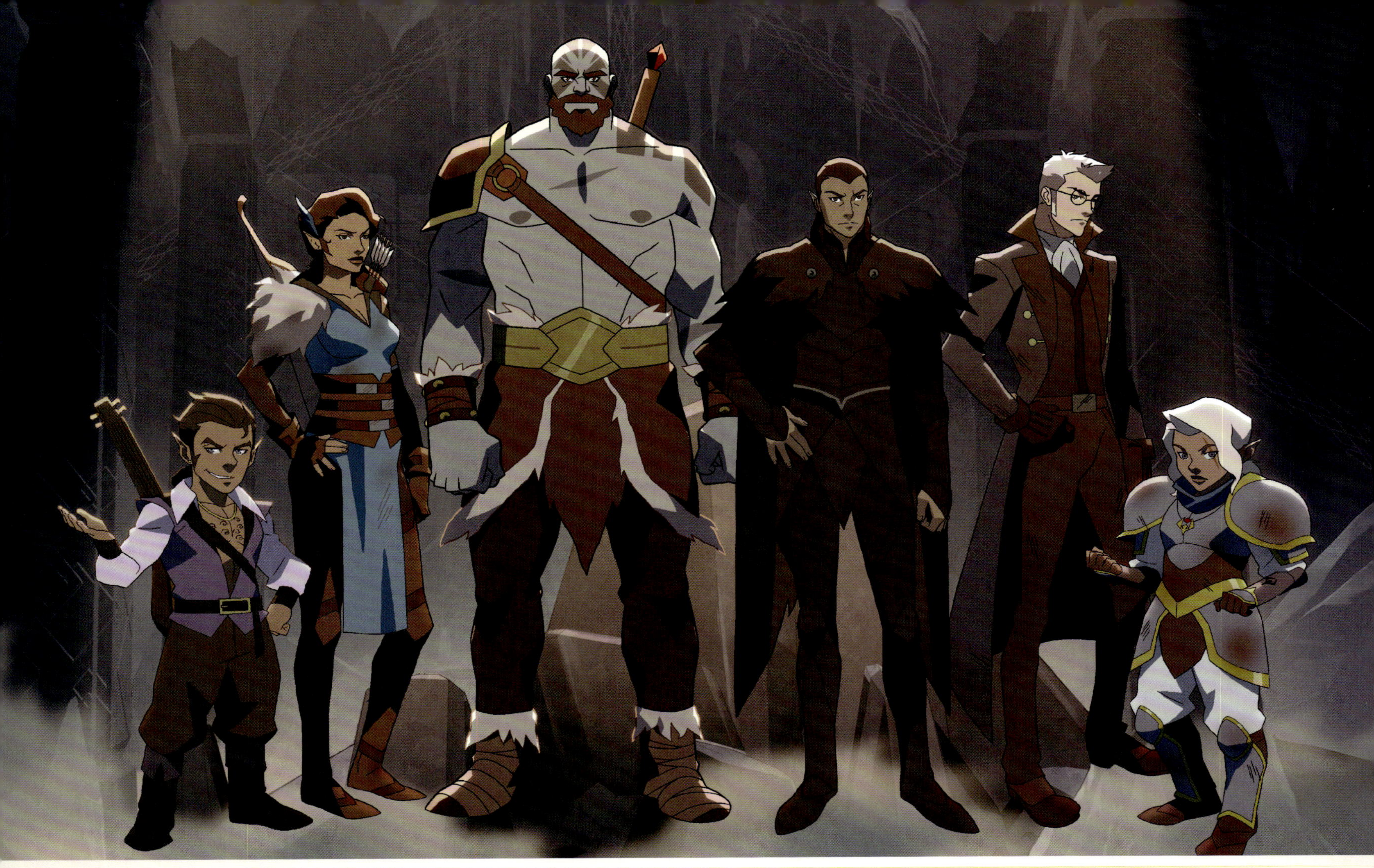

Everyone had a say, especially in the beginning, when it came to their character. Travis, Sam, and Matt are kind of the point guys that I see regularly, but they have all been friends for years so they know how each member would react to each design before even asking.

It was important to me to get every cast member involved because, at the end of the day, you want Ashley to LOVE the Pike design and you want Marisha to LOVE Keyleth's look because they're the experts. These characters are avatars of these artists. They were also their first characters too–so they are their alter egos in a way, and it feels a little more personal.

What is your favorite part of the character design process?

That depends entirely on the week. I really enjoy the concept stage, when the possibilities are endless. However, it can be creatively exhausting when you're constantly coming up with fresh takes and know only a few of them will end up on screen. You really have to convince everyone that it's the best idea when you're doing concepts, and you might not even think it's the best idea. It's the most fulfilling but most challenging stage.

I also really like doing the turnarounds and expression sheets once you've figured out a character. Turns are super mechanical, so you're using a different part of your brain where it's easier to get in the zone and flesh out the details.

What is your least favorite part of the character design process?

Drawing mouth charts. I once had to draw thirty mouth charts in two weeks, and it was not fun. They're technical but not in a fun way. You have to create a code for each mouth position and a lot of artists tend to draw mouths too exaggerated so it can look like the characters are screaming all the time.

What is one skill you think is essential to character design that is often overlooked by newbies?

For designers of any experience level, it's easy to fall back on idiosyncratic tropes, forgetting that we are storytellers first. The needs of the story and the character have to take priority over pure style choices. It's fine to draw something because it looks cool, but you have to have a story justification ready for your design choices. Every word that a writer or director conveys to me to describe a character, I try to use that in my design. That's why I want people to be specific because I'm going to latch onto that description. I might bring something back that might not match what's in everyone's mind, but it will conform to the essence of the description and vibe.

Which character would you want to be trapped on a deserted island with and why?

I'm going with my girl Keyleth. She has the charming awkwardness and is easy to relate to. And who better to be stranded in the wilderness than someone who has mastery over the elements and nature magic? I do have to point out that there's probably no one less useful in a protracted real-life crisis than someone whose only skill is drawing cartoons, so hopefully, she likes my jokes. The rest of the characters would probably eventually kill me because I'd be doing nothing. ◆

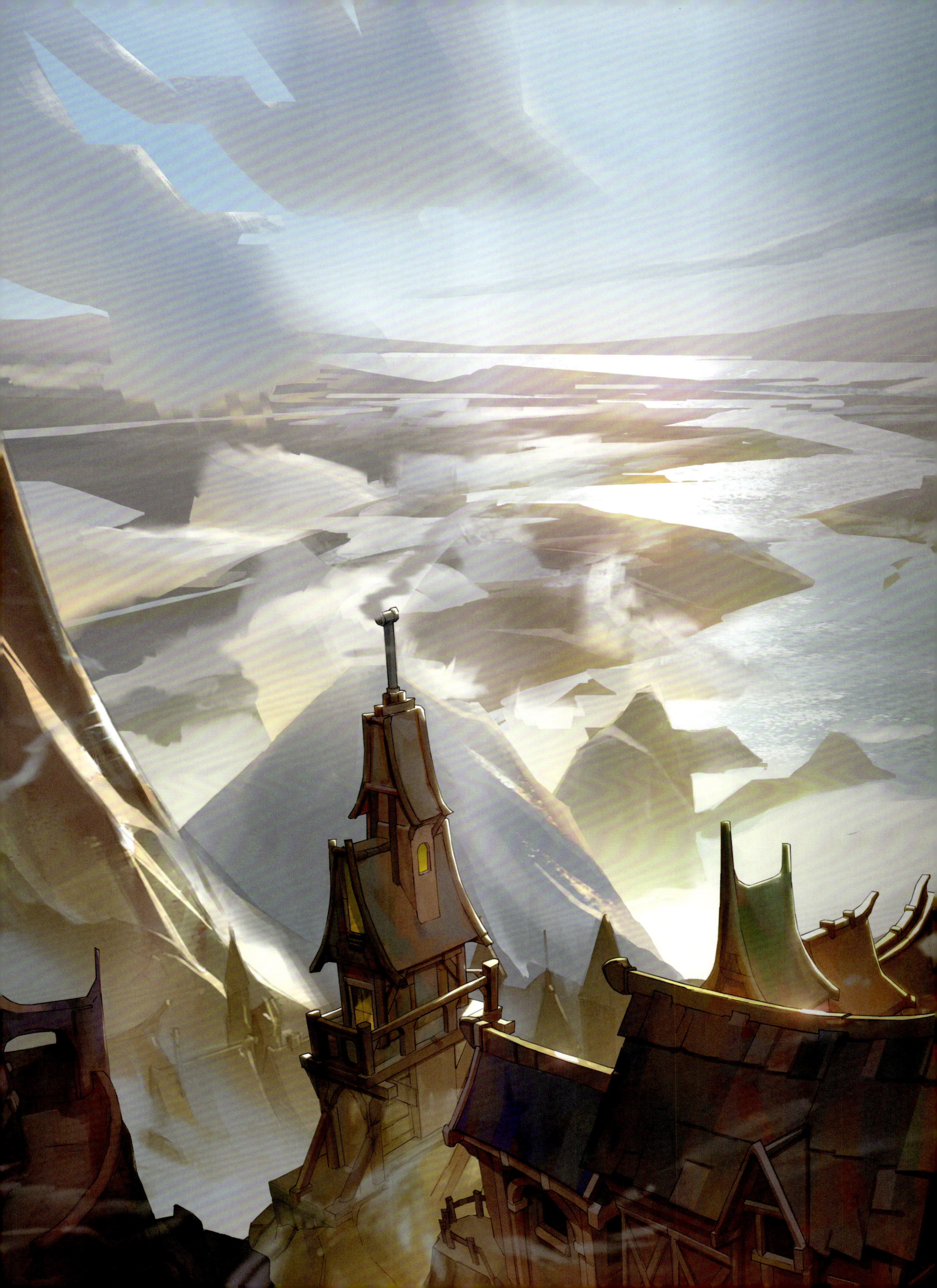

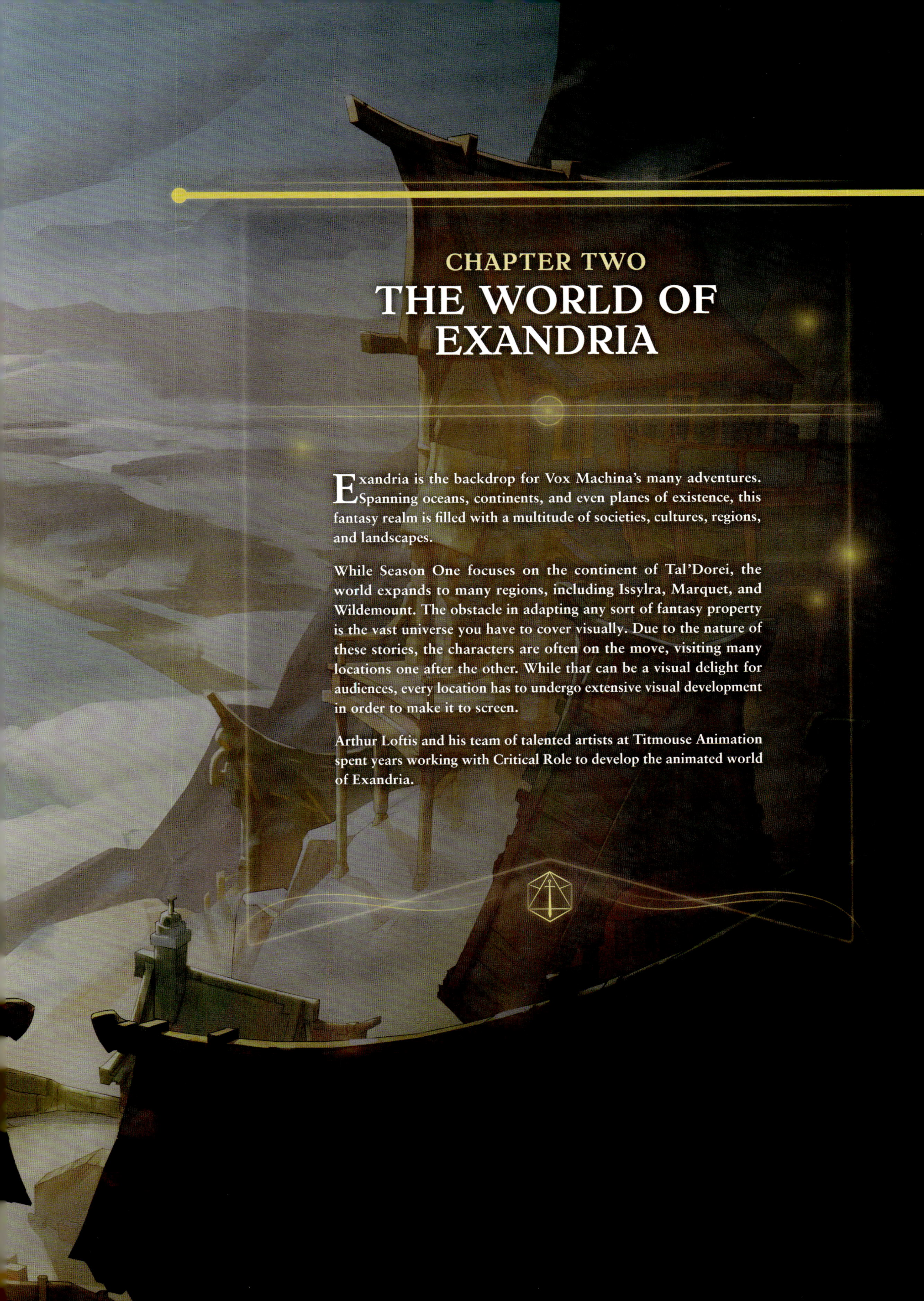

CHAPTER TWO
THE WORLD OF EXANDRIA

Exandria is the backdrop for Vox Machina's many adventures. Spanning oceans, continents, and even planes of existence, this fantasy realm is filled with a multitude of societies, cultures, regions, and landscapes.

While Season One focuses on the continent of Tal'Dorei, the world expands to many regions, including Issylra, Marquet, and Wildemount. The obstacle in adapting any sort of fantasy property is the vast universe you have to cover visually. Due to the nature of these stories, the characters are often on the move, visiting many locations one after the other. While that can be a visual delight for audiences, every location has to undergo extensive visual development in order to make it to screen.

Arthur Loftis and his team of talented artists at Titmouse Animation spent years working with Critical Role to develop the animated world of Exandria.

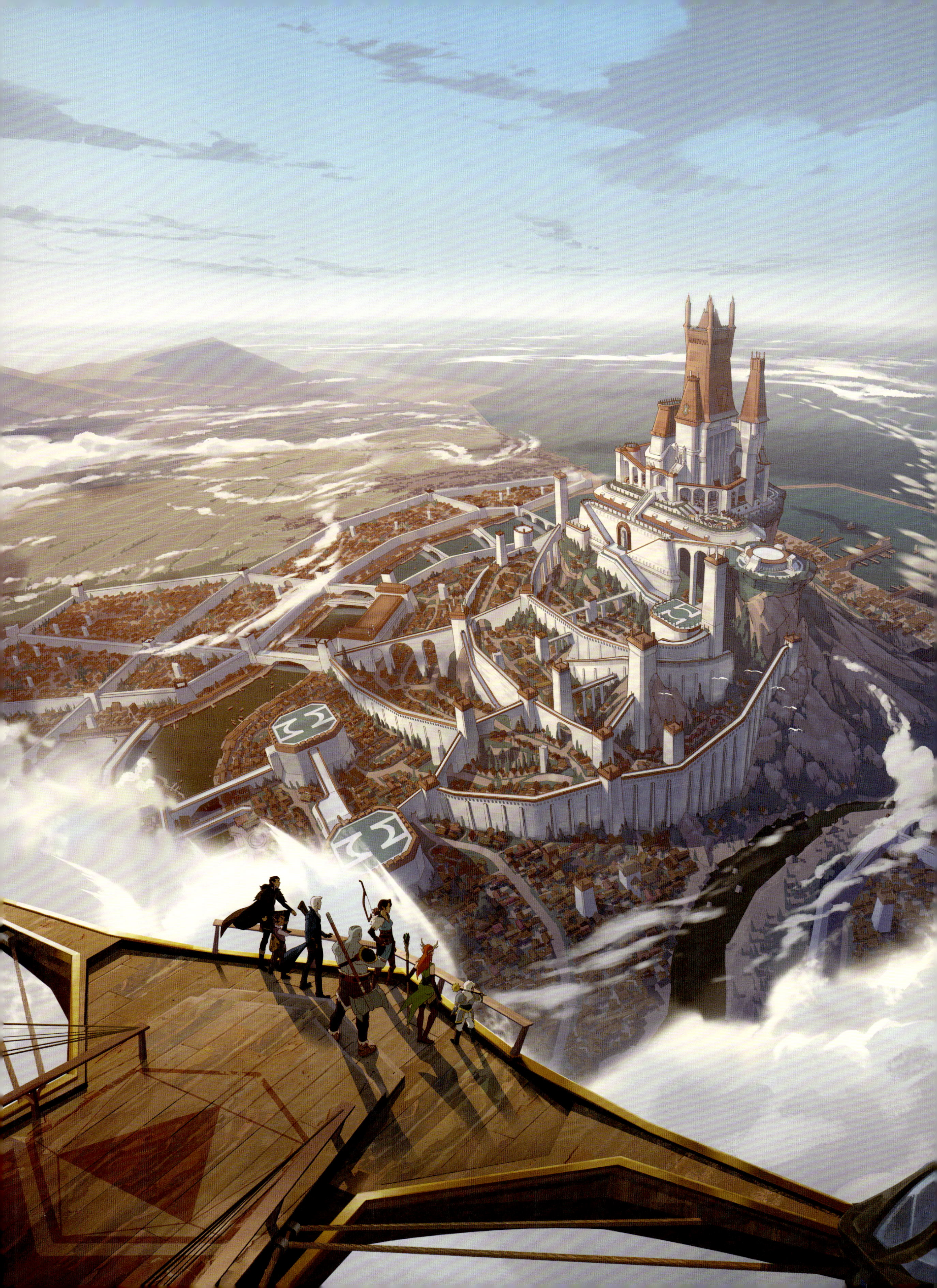

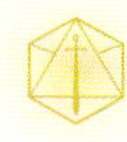

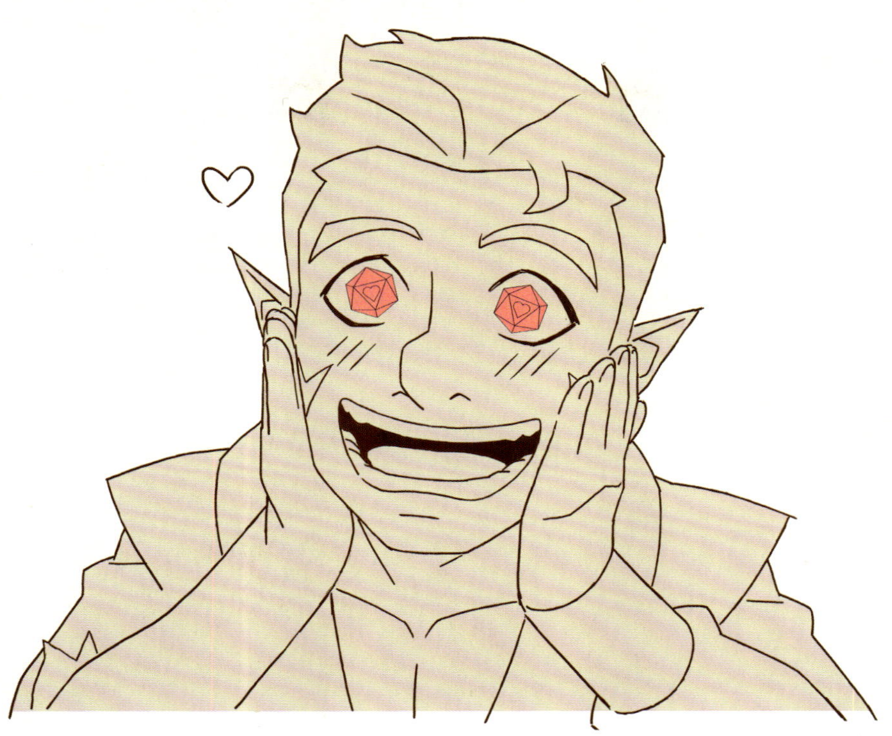

INTERVIEW Q&A WITH ARTHUR LOFTIS

Arthur Loftis, art director extraordinaire, joined the crew of Vox Machina *fairly early in the process. Originally a background designer for the Kickstarter promotional video, his love of Critical Role and passion for the material shown through his work made him a natural choice when the team was looking for an art director on the series.*

What is the job of an Art Director on a show?

An Art Director is like the North Star for the design team. It is their job to establish the look of the show, from backgrounds and character designs to paintings and special effects. They have to communicate between the different teams and act as an intermediary between artists and executives. As an individual designer, your job is to get lost in the specific technical details of an individual design. An Art Director is meant to look at the bigger picture and think about the series and character arcs as a whole. The ideal art director is a compass, pointing the other designers in the right direction.

What was your first reaction to finding out you were going to be Art Directing the series?

Disbelief and excitement.

What were your first steps in finding inspiration for the design and overall look of the show?

When I first started, I didn't know Phil would be coming onto it. Once I found out we were getting Phil, I realized there were a lot of ideas and similar shape language behind our work. My own design sensibilities really lined up well with Phil's character designs, and knowing that gave me a direction to continue pushing. Our work, while totally different on its face (he's a character guy, I'm a background guy), shares slightly exaggerated proportions, and we both have backgrounds in traditional media. I wanted to keep that in the show, so we found ways to keep the idea of gouache-like facets of color in the backgrounds, and a lightly textured outline that gives you the sense of drawing with graphite.

Was it hard to pivot from being a fan to being a main creative force behind this beloved IP?

Yes, but it was also my strongest asset. It's nice having someone in the room who knows the context of everything. Sung Jin Ahn (Supervising Director) and I work very well together because he came into it from outside the fandom, so he's able to take a step back from it and focus on whether the story is working or not. He is able to separate himself from the worry of fan service or Easter eggs, and call out something if it's clearly not working. That is the exact kind of person you want in that Supervising Director seat. But then, when it comes down to the design of the world and having all those fun extras baked into the set dressing and character design, that is where having a superfan as Art Director comes in handy. I can tell Phil Bourassa

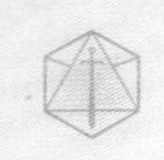

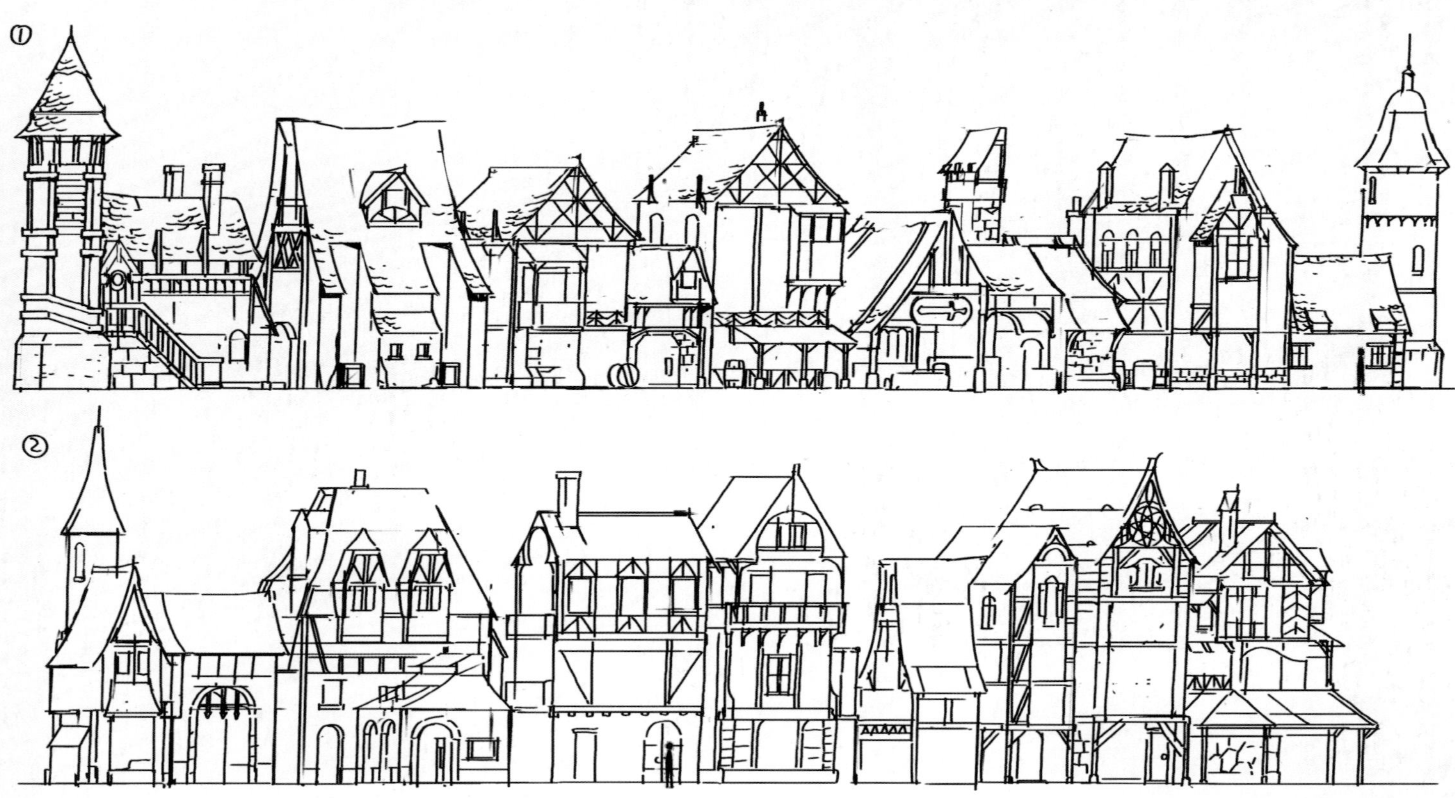

THE RESOURCES THE KICKSTARTER GAVE US ALLOWED US TO MAKE THIS LOVE LETTER TO THE AUDIENCE AND FANS.

(Character Designer) important details to include that could be fun for fans to spot, but they're not words coming out of a character's mouth, so it won't mess with the story.

How did you go about distinguishing the series art from the massive amount of fan art already out there?

There's a lot of amazing fan art out there, but a lot of it is very illustrative. It's not designed to move, which you need for animation! So going into the series, we knew we'd seen a lot of beautiful painted art, but we hadn't seen a ton of animation being made with these characters yet. I knew from our team's collective experience we could really wow them by taking it to a level that no one thought was possible before the Kickstarter.

Knowing that this show was picked up for two seasons off the bat, did that have any impact on your process?

We took it one season at a time in order to not get overwhelmed, but I knew the whole story of where we were going and where we were coming back to. We sunk a lot of time into designing Emon and Whitestone because I knew these were forever locations and that time wouldn't be wasted if we really went in on those. With that being said, knowing that we would have to blow up Emon in the end, I was really excited to do that. It's like making your own disaster movie. I was sure it was going to be the hardest thing we had to do in the show, but everyone pulled out all the stops.

If you could go back and tell day 1 Arthur one piece of advice for tackling this show, what would that be?

You don't need to know everything. There's an expectation you put on yourself to have all the answers and it's more important to remind yourself to ask questions. You're coming in with knowledge and it's important you share that knowledge, but if you don't know something, learn it from the team and disseminate that to everyone else.

What do you hope fans think of when they look back on the art from this show and its impact in animation?

I hope that they know that the resources the Kickstarter gave us allowed us to make this love letter to the audience and fans. The origin story of the show is not just the characters, it's the meta-story of fans making this project possible. They have a great amount of control over what gets put on screen, and that is wonderful.

Which setting would you want to build a summer home in?

Definitely Vasselheim. It's not "summery" at all, but if I could live anywhere in the Critical Role universe, it would be there. First off, it's the most defensible city. And I'm just really happy with how the designs came out. There are so many cool locations that would be thrilling to see at eye level. ◆

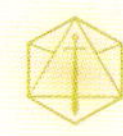

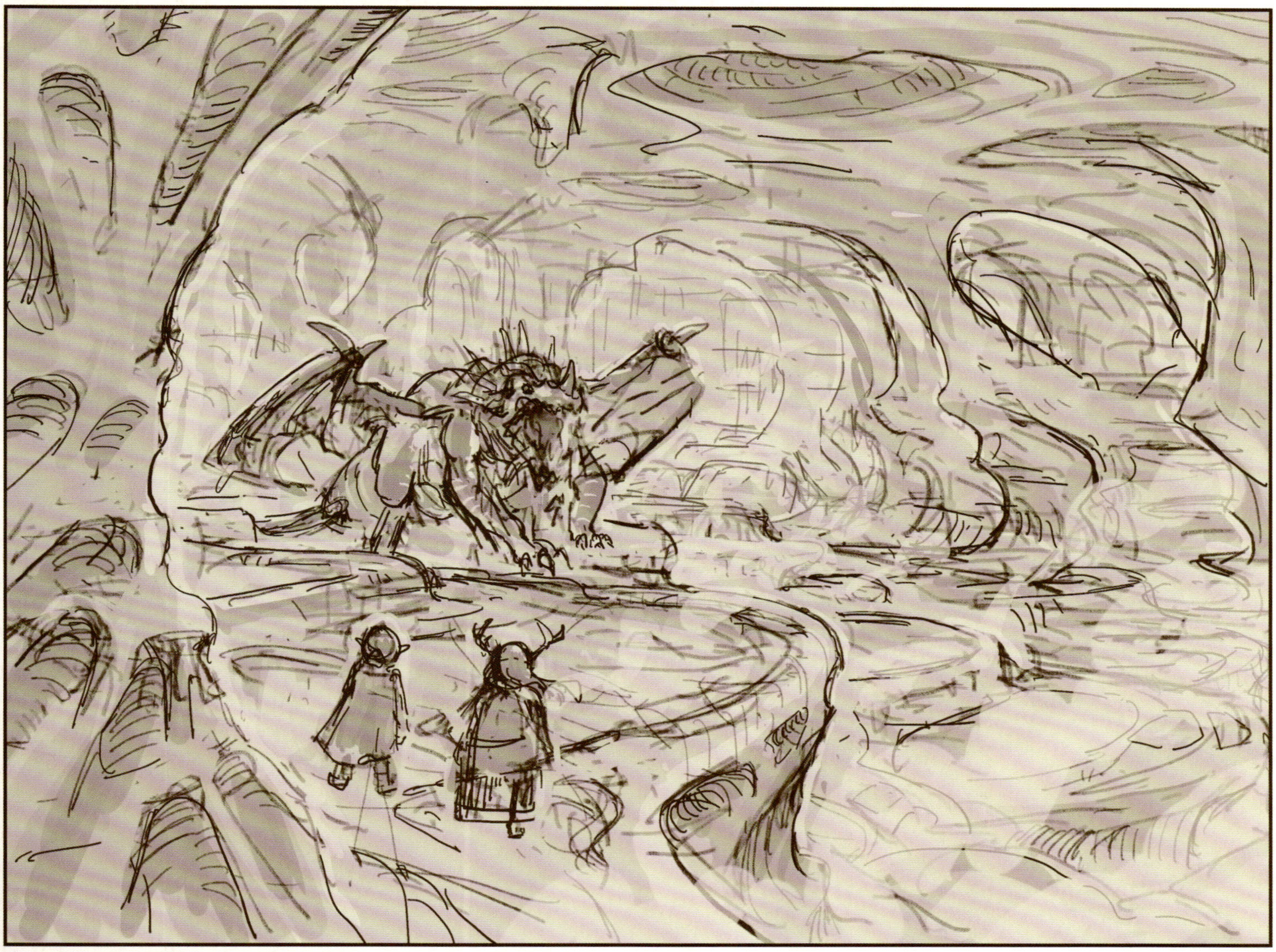

Early concepts design.

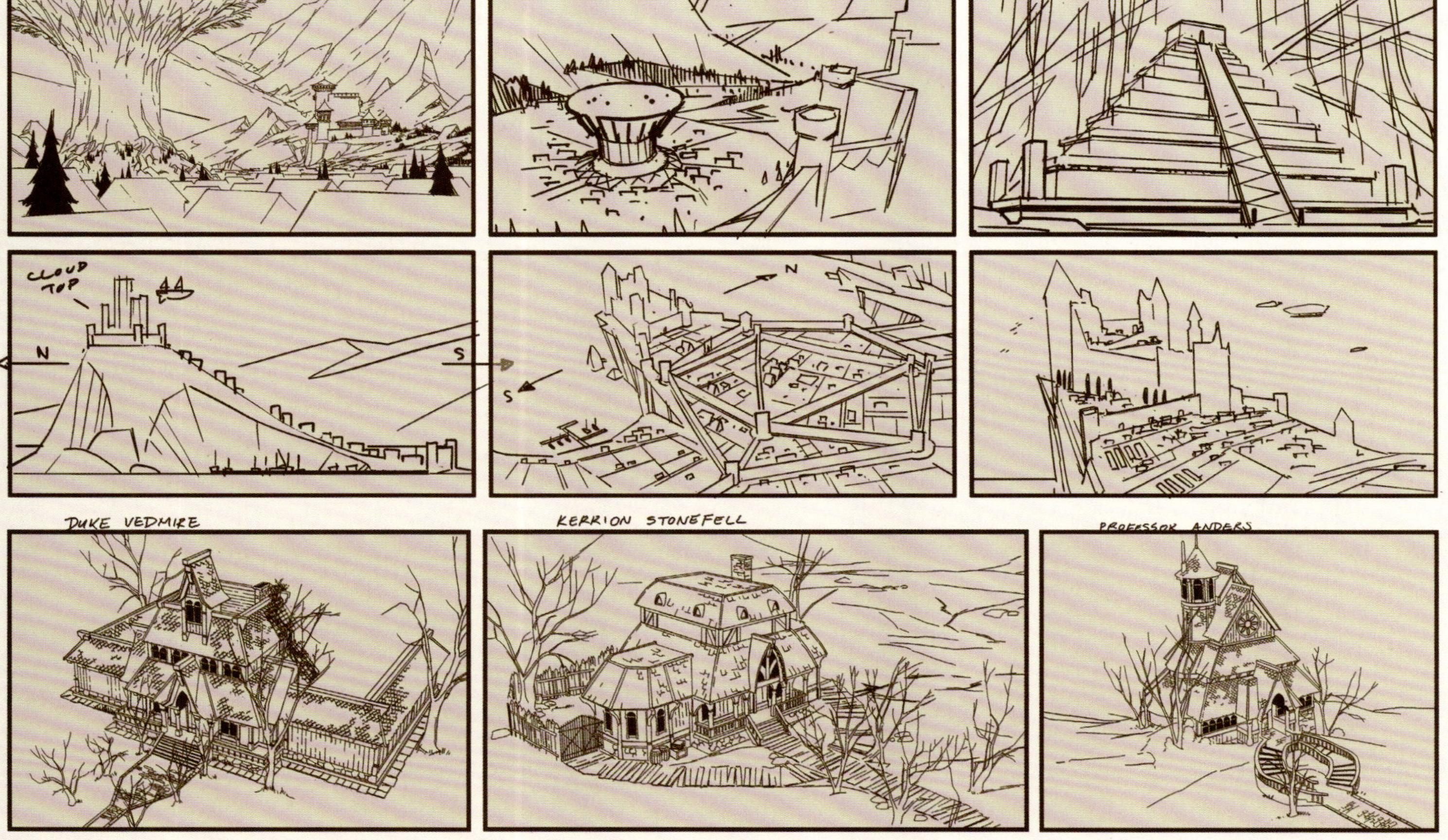

Early concepts design of Whitestone Mansions.

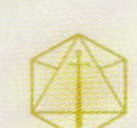

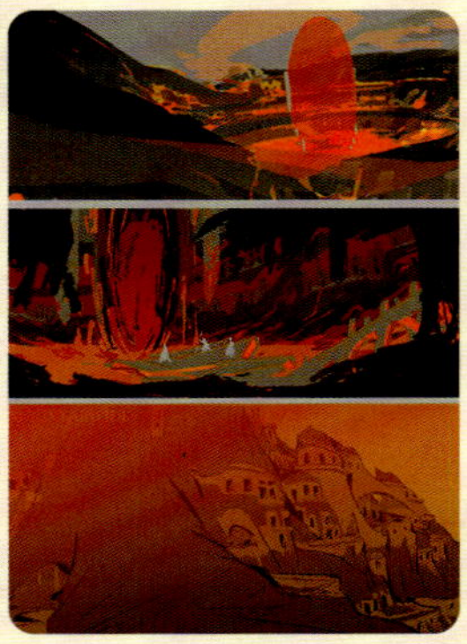

PYRAH

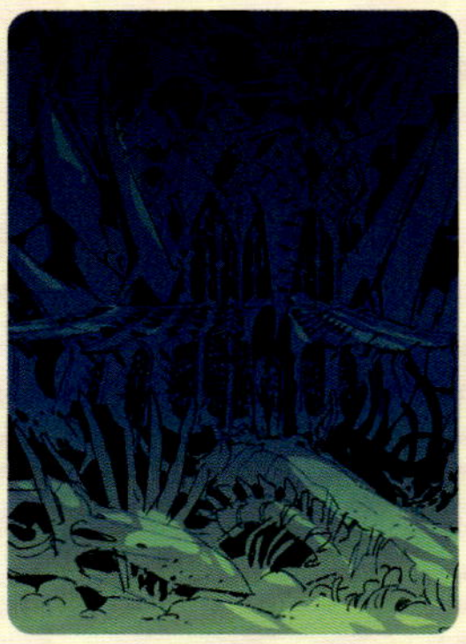

SUNKEN TOMB

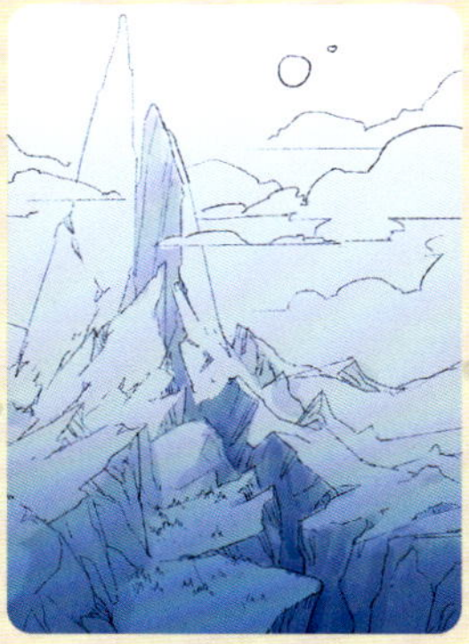

RIMECLEFT

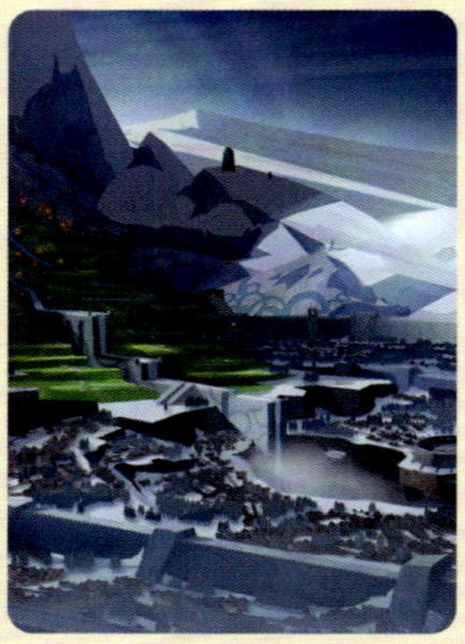

VASSELHEIM

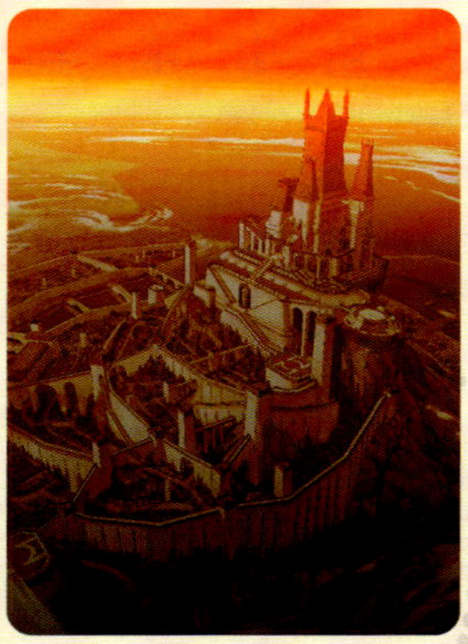

WEST

EMON

N
W
E
S

THE OZMIT SEA

TERRAH

FORT DAXIO

KRAGHAMMER

SEASHALE MOUNTAINS

TORIAN FOREST

EMON

EMERALD OUTPOST

DAGGERBAY

DAGGERBAY MOUNTAINS

THE SHIFTING KEEP

VISA ISLE

THE MIRESCAR

FESHUN NARROWS

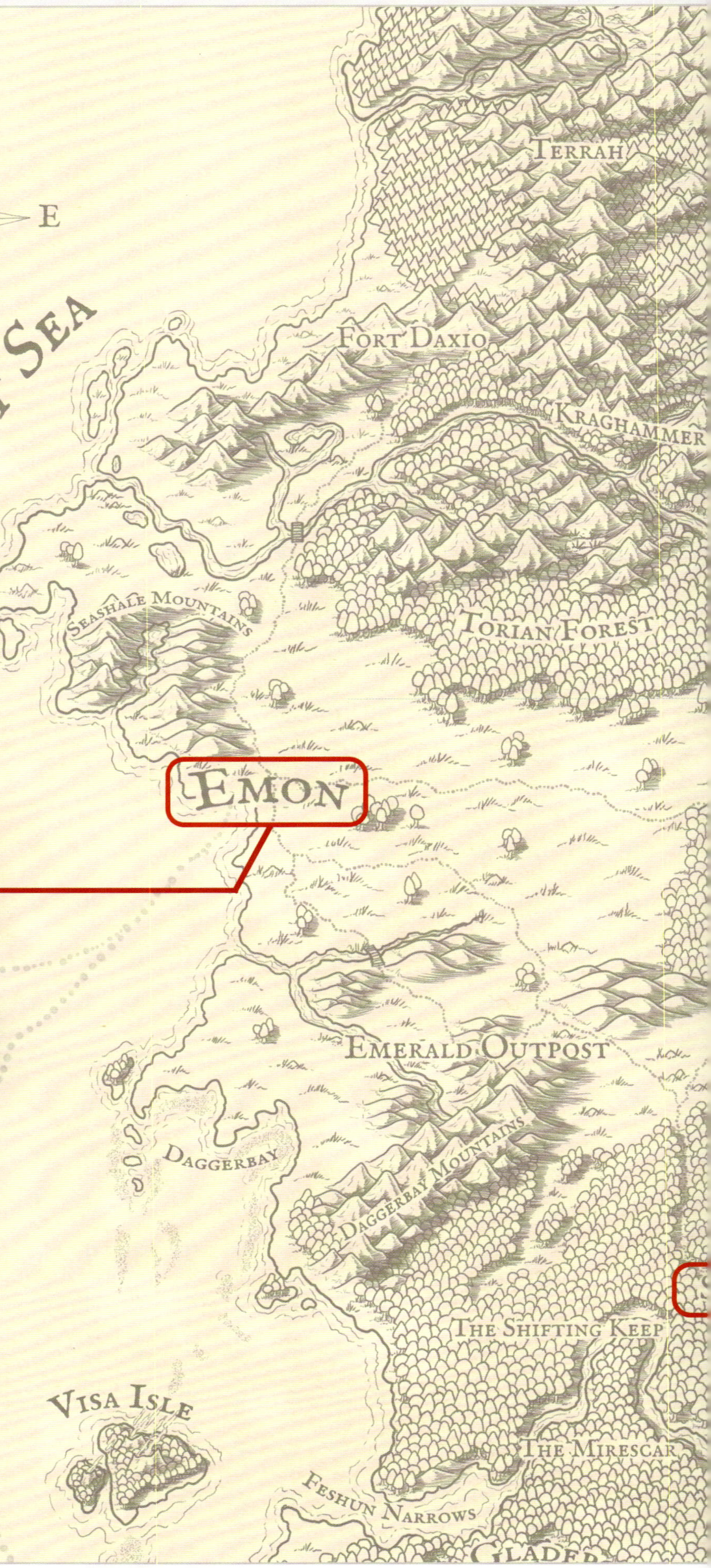

Designing Exandria

The story of Critical Role is one that constantly defies expectations, and bringing the world of Exandria to life in animation was no different. When beginning his exploration of the world, Arthur Loftis researched various topographies across the globe and found specific regions within Exandria that could be home to those natural elements. The art team thought out everything from vegetation to land elevation to architectural history during the series' visual development.

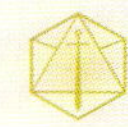

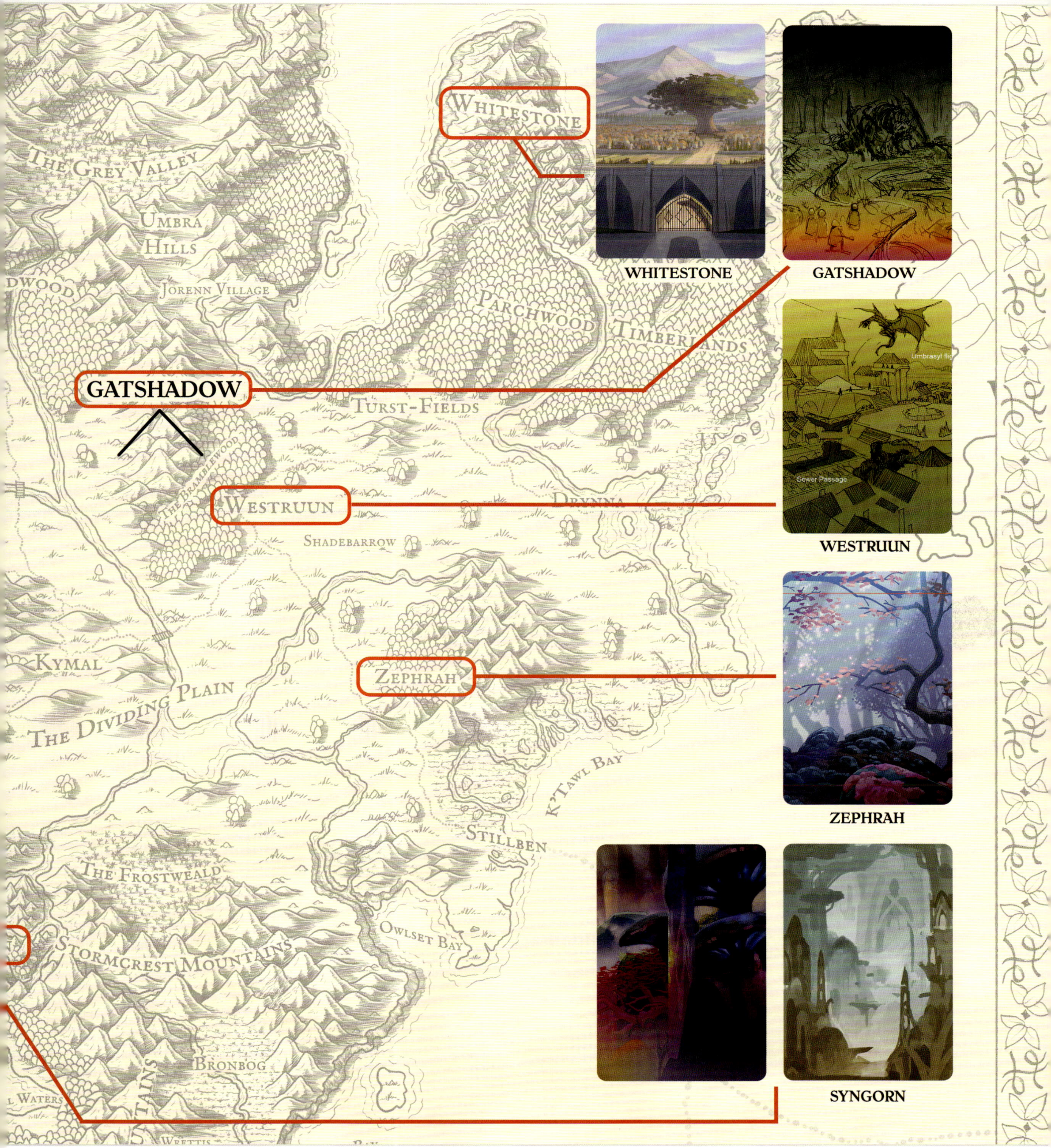

WHITESTONE

GATSHADOW

WESTRUUN

ZEPHRAH

SYNGORN

While we only visit a handful of locations in season one, the art team knew that more would need to be built out for season two, so they began to pull in ideas early to help flesh out each setting.

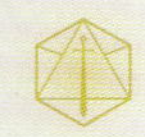

Translating a TTRPG Setting for Animation

One cannot begin adapting a Tabletop RPG for animation without considering the visual language of magic. Magic permeates every aspect of life in Exandria, from the powerful spells wielded by wizards to the mystical creatures that roam its wilds. Each character has to have their own signature look with their magic so the audience can differentiate spells on screen. The art department on *The Legend of Vox Machina* quickly outlined color and shape templates for each character's magical abilities.

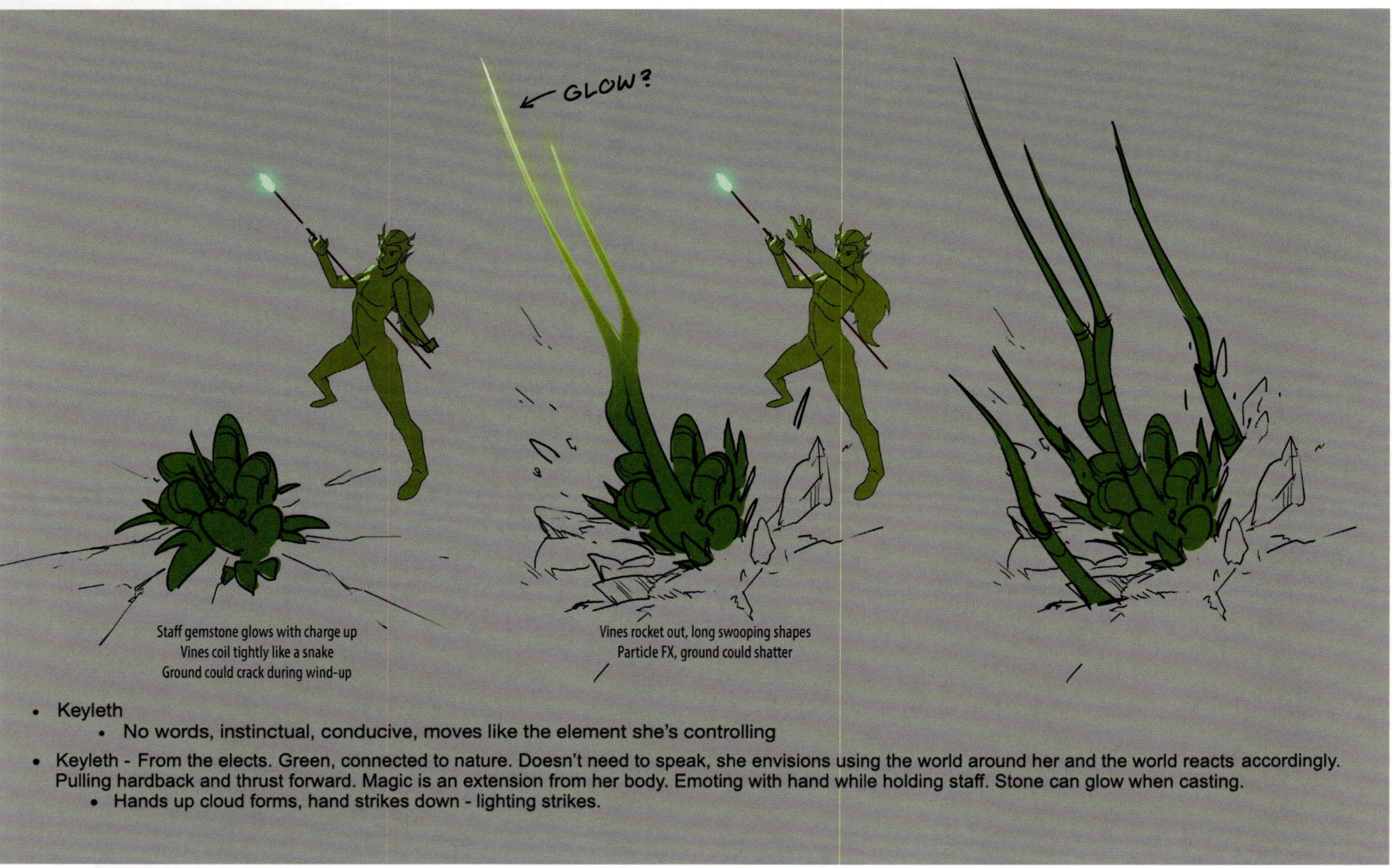

"I warned you those vines have thorns." – VEX, S1E10 "DEPTHS OF DECEIT"

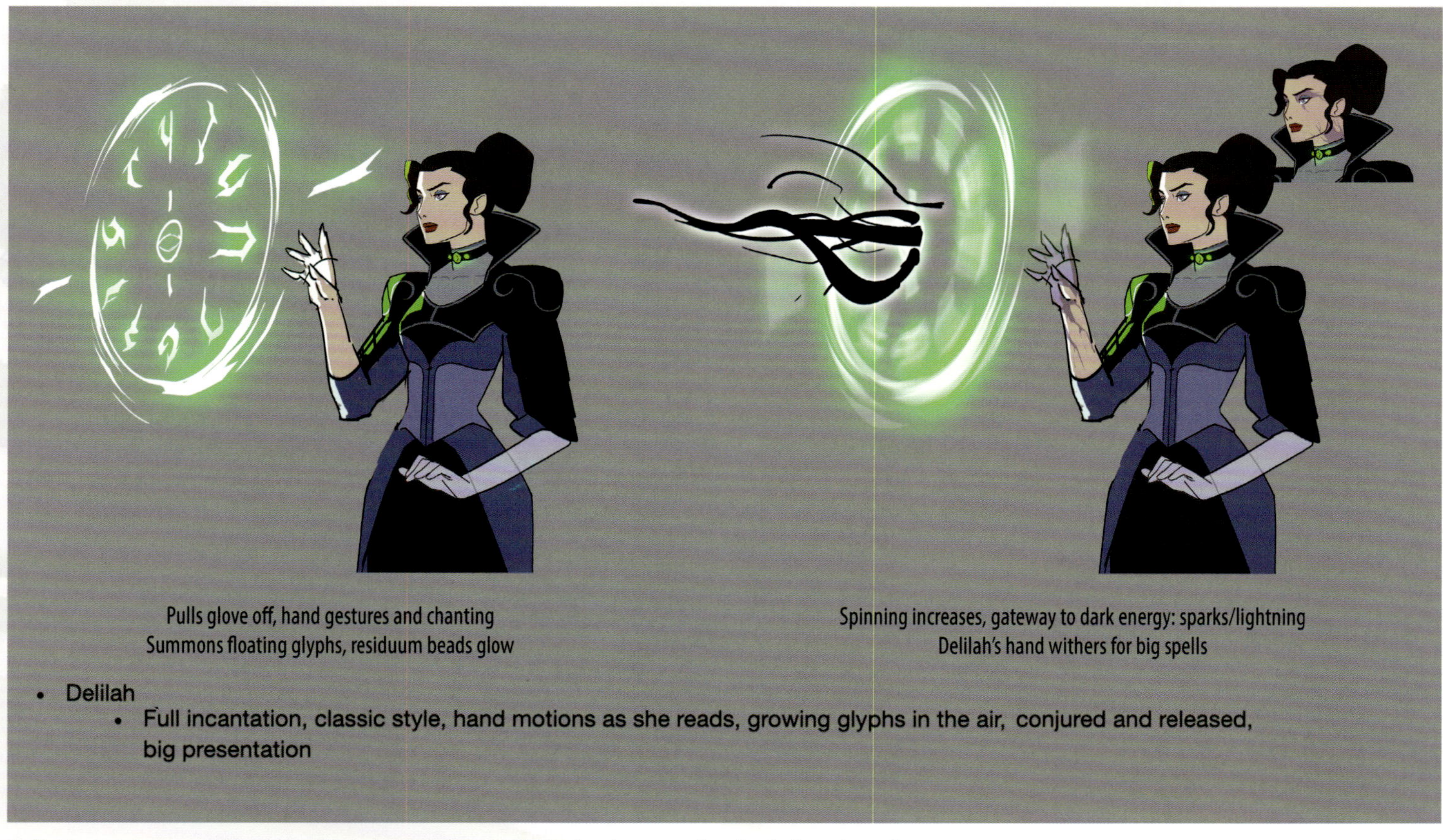

Delilah's magic is necrotic in nature and is designed to appear as if it is drawing energy from her body as the spell continues.

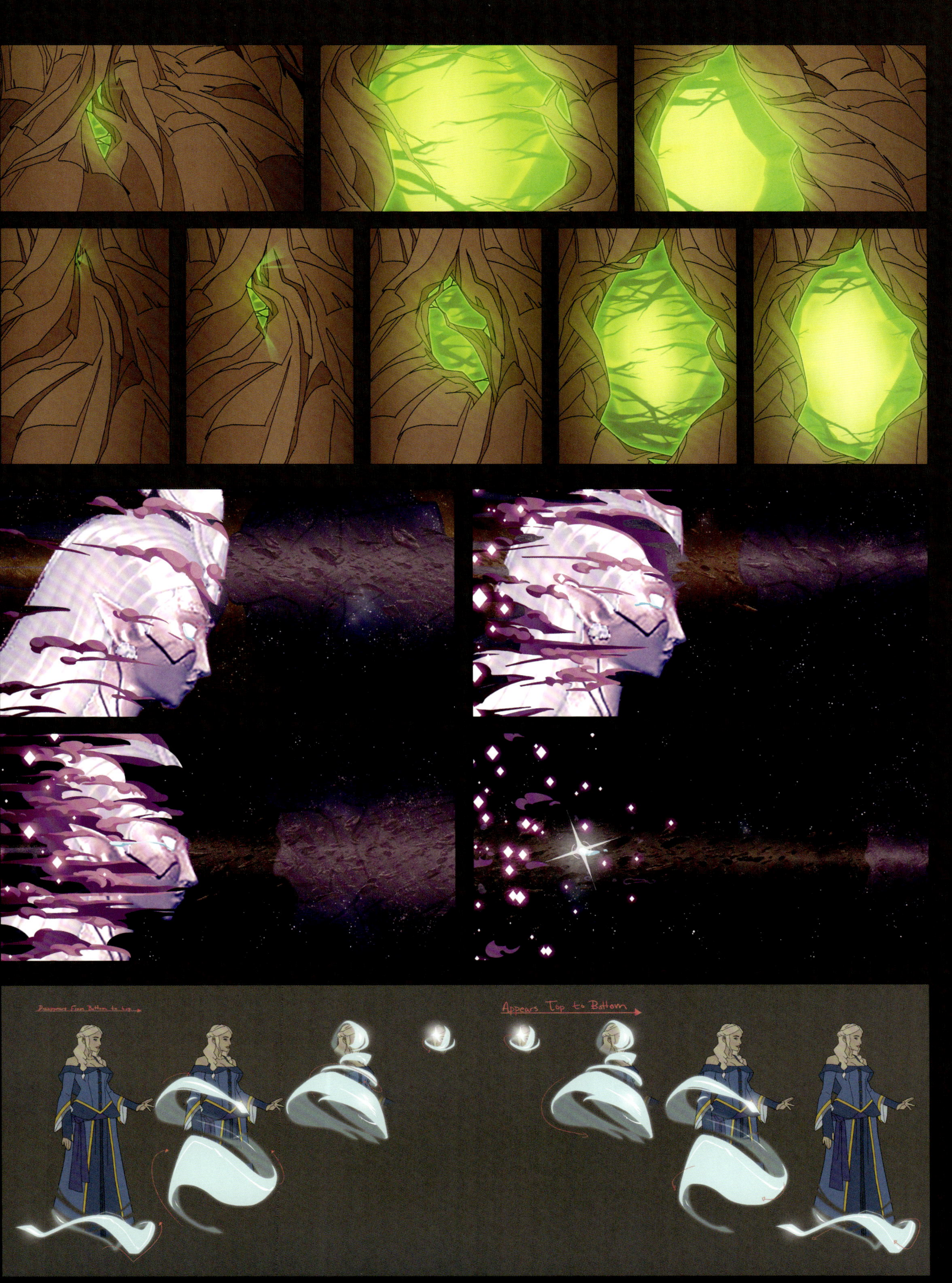

Many of the magical effects are refined in post-production by composite artists. They will follow keys that guide them on how every effect should be layered to give each spell its unique appearance.

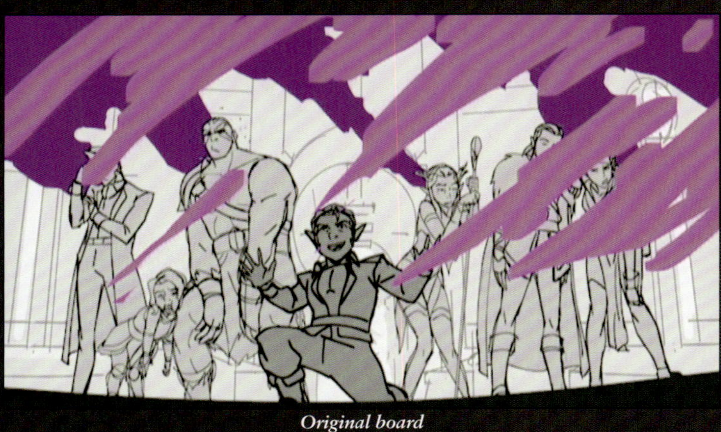
Original board

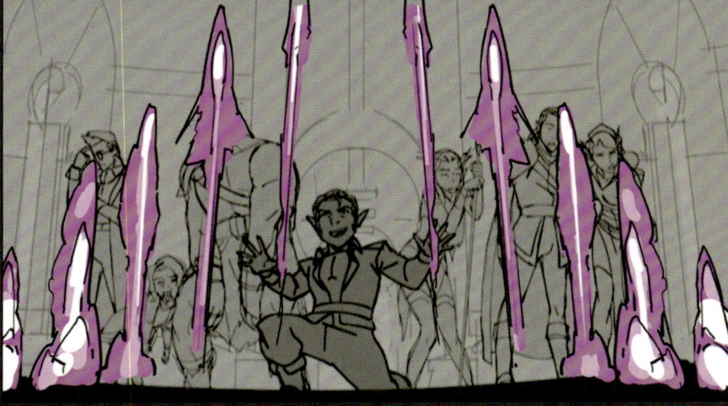
Over the top fireworks/flames/waterworks

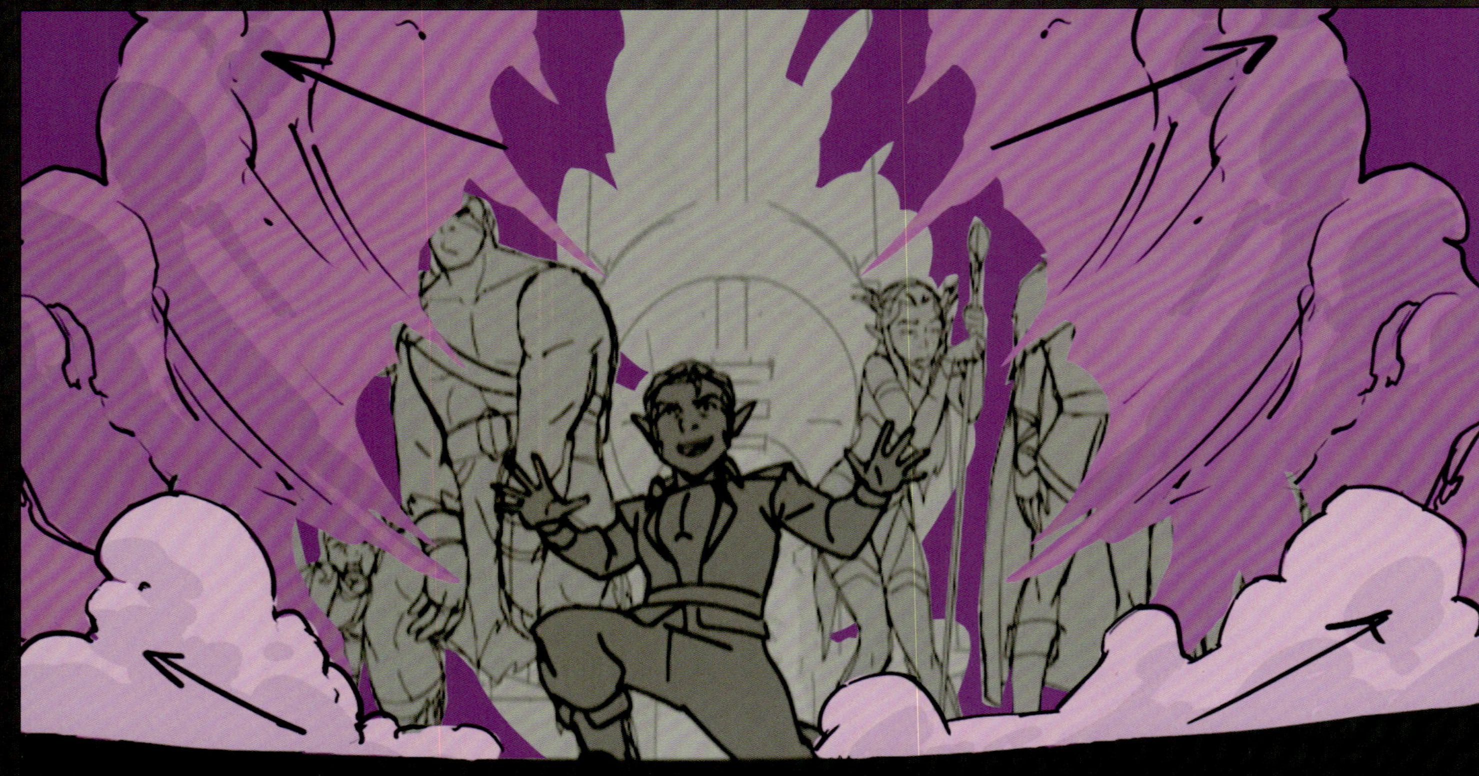
Illusory "curtains" of smoke ripple out

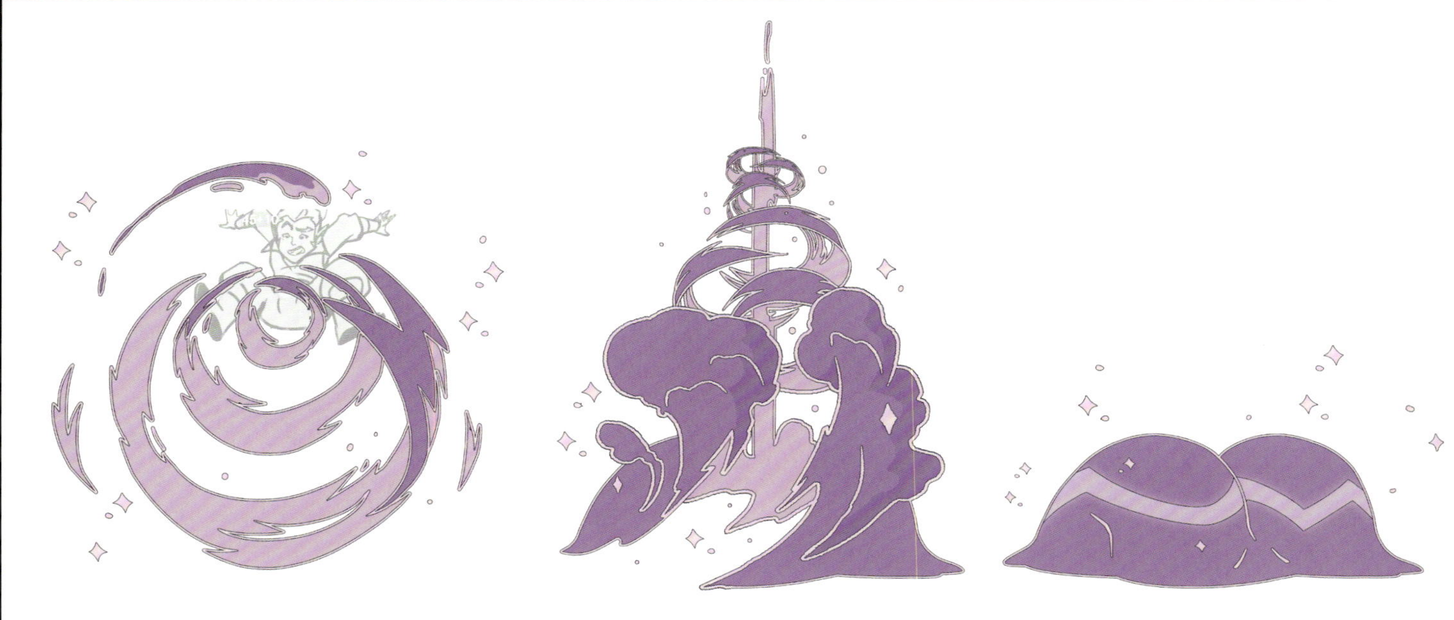

Scanlan's magic was always his signature purple with a lot of smoky flare. Perfect for that showstopping number when you need a bit of extra drama.

"I'll save our asses with some butt stuff." – SCANLAN, S2E2 "THE TRIALS OF VASSELHEIM"

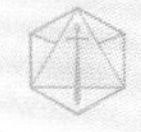

Font Design

Throughout the series, there are various magical texts written in different arcane languages. The design team developed their own font to include whenever these instances came up in the script where an unreadable text appeared on screen.

For example, the font can be seen in The Book of the Whispered One and on the Obelisk.

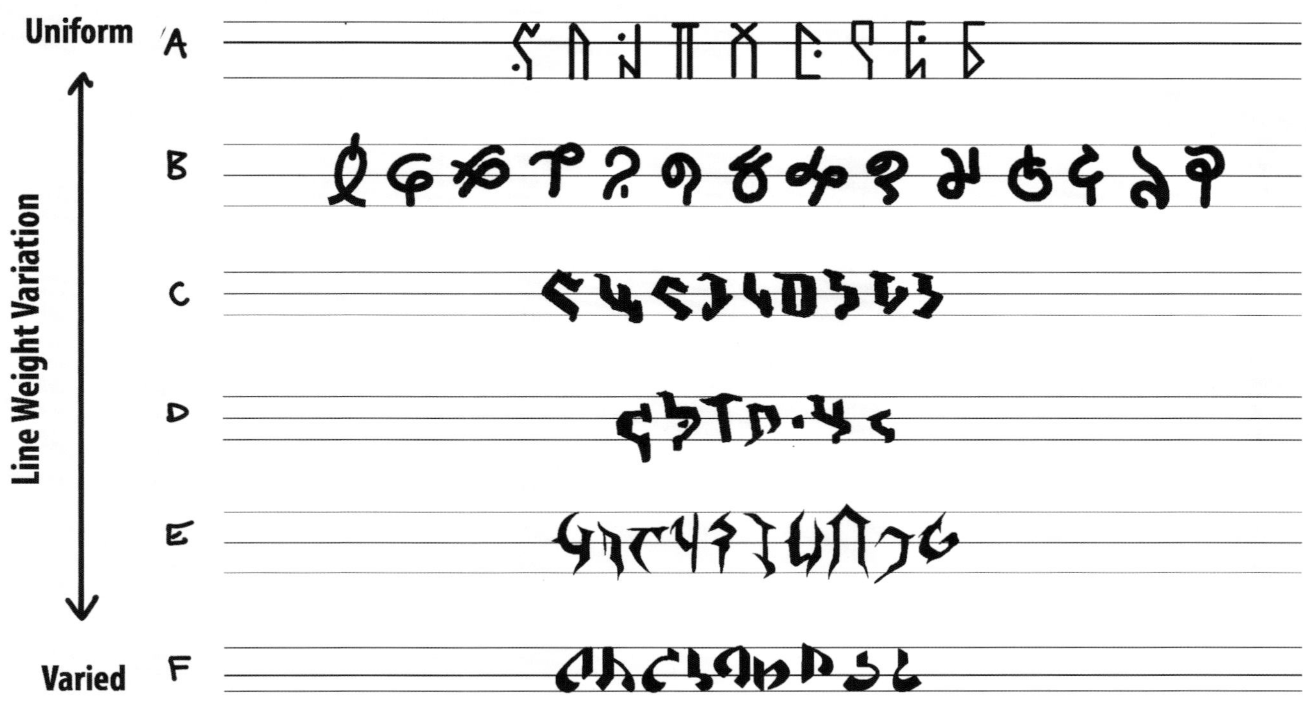

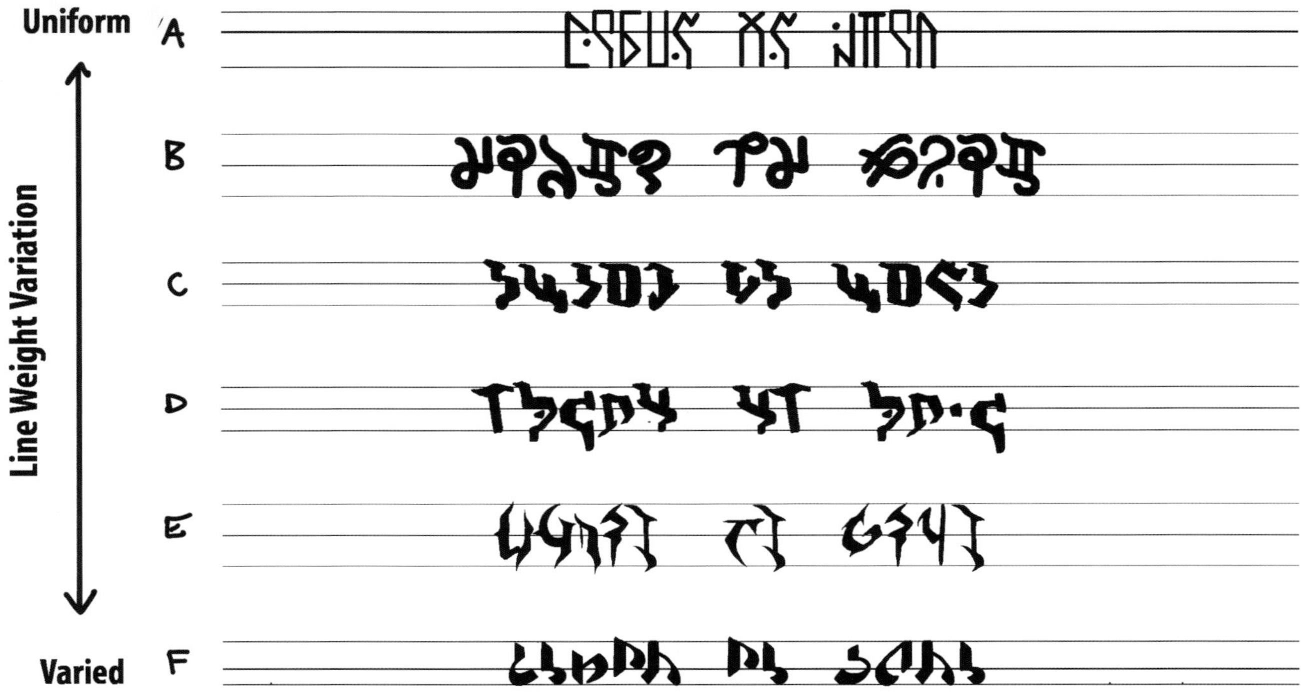

Different font variations that were pitched for the series.

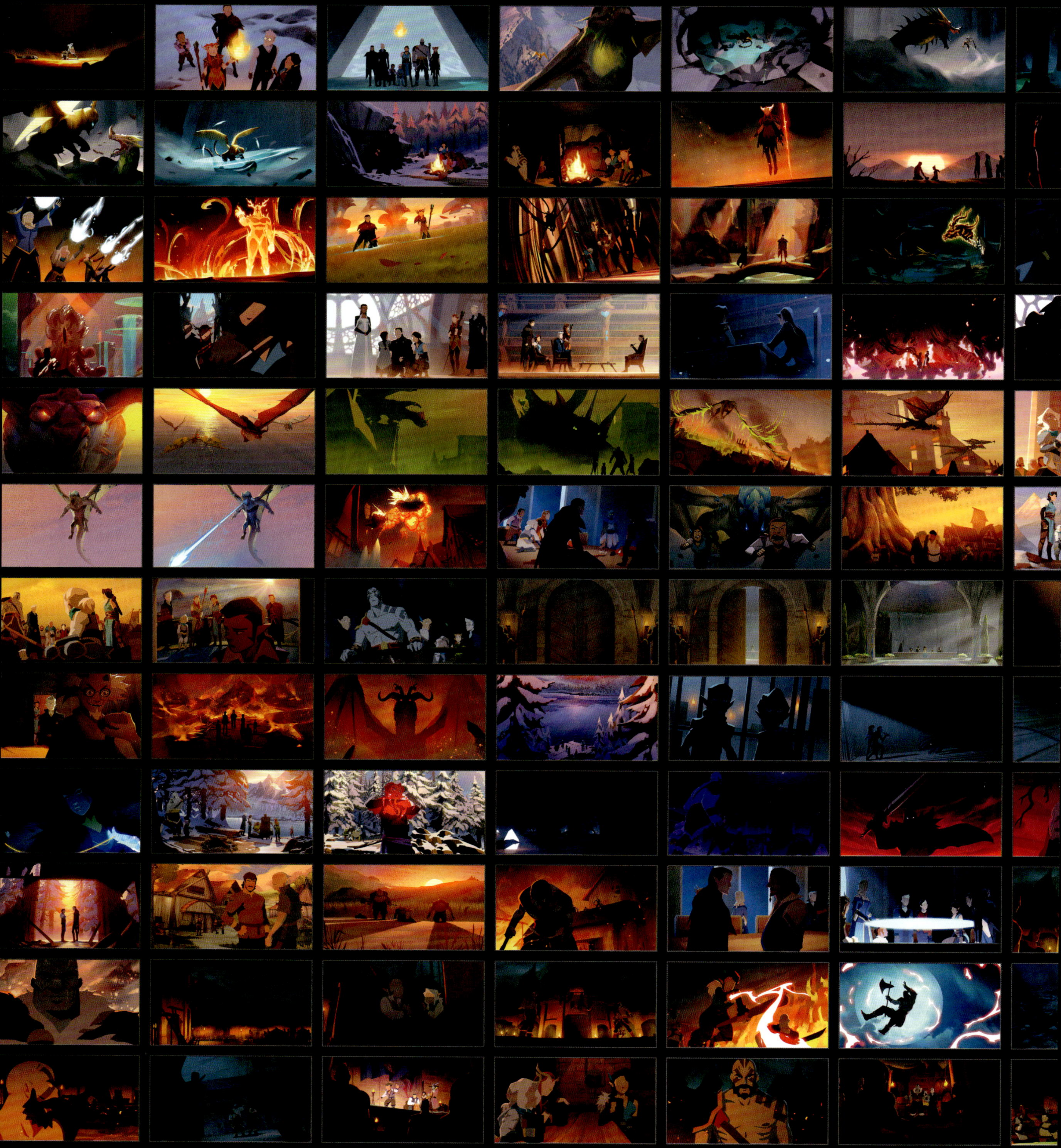

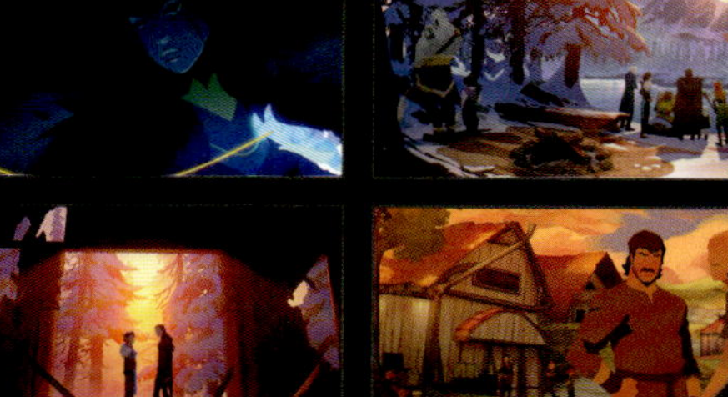
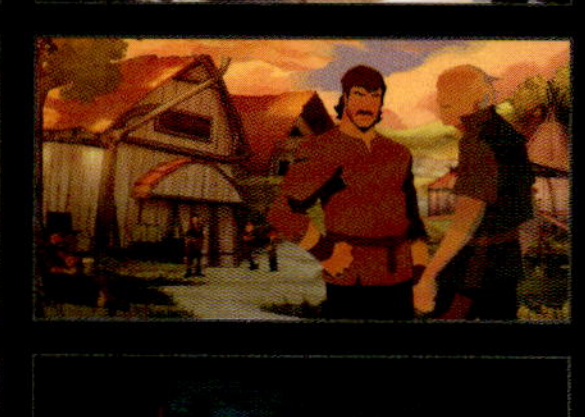
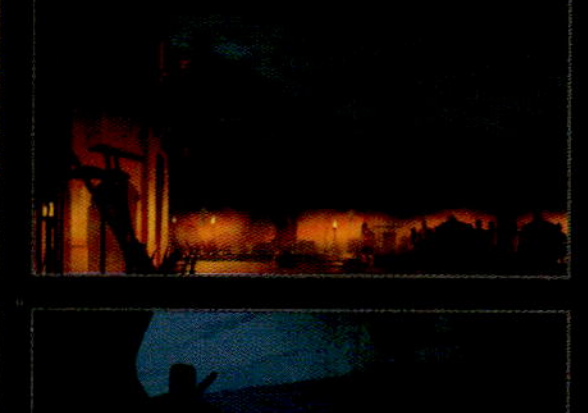
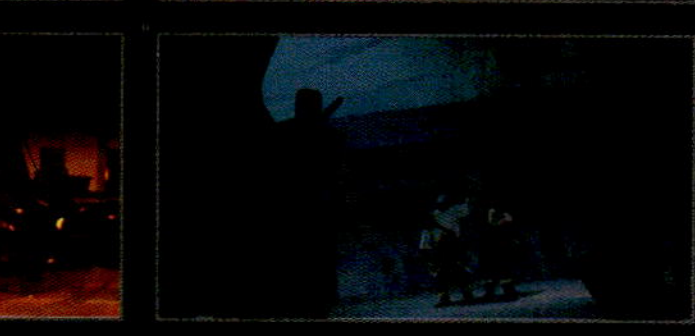
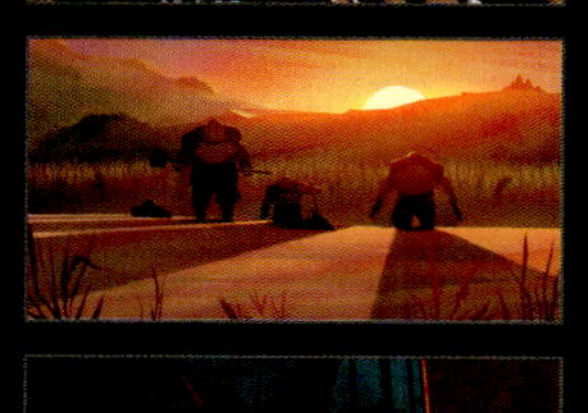
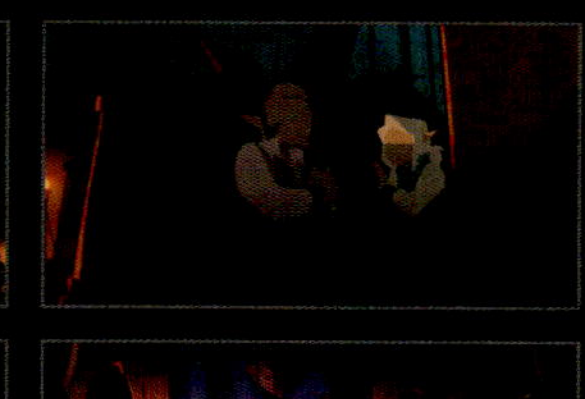
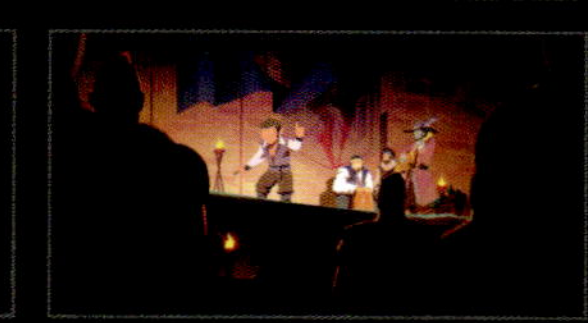
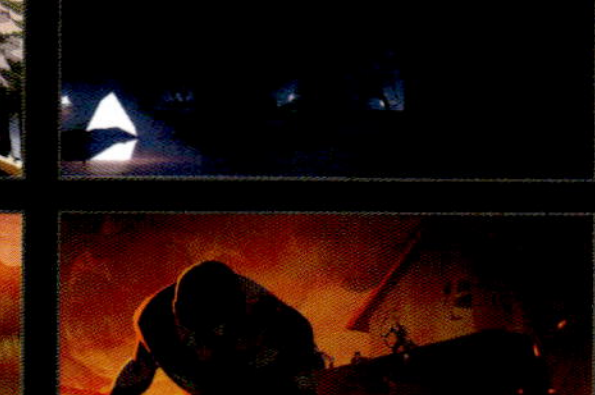

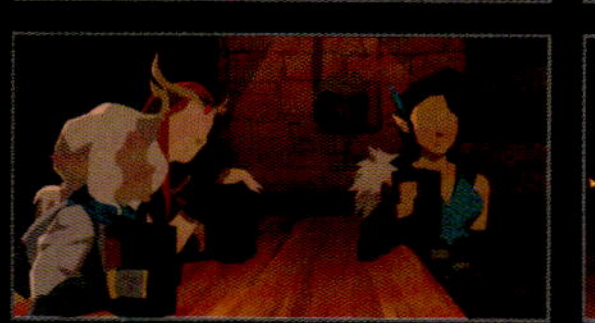
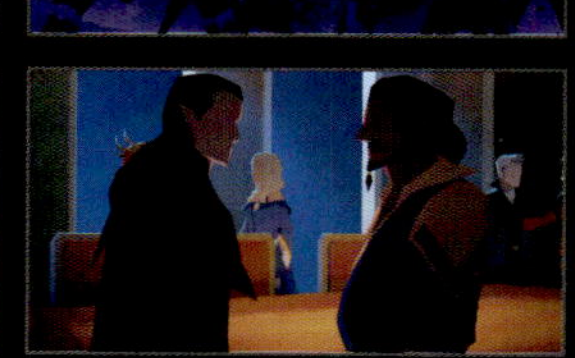
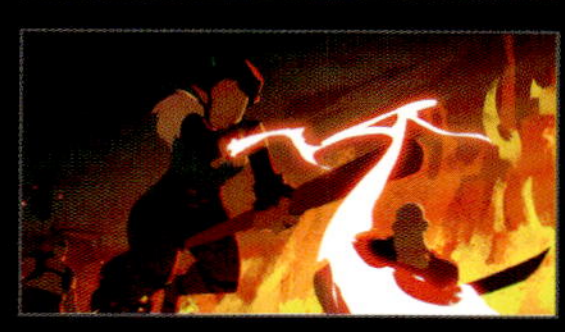
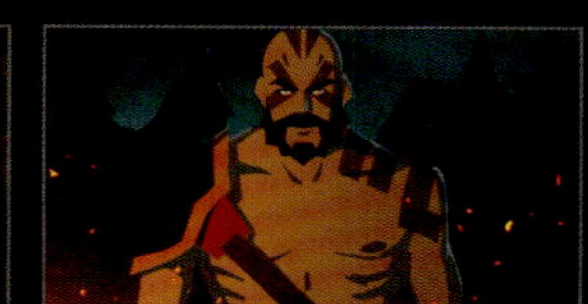
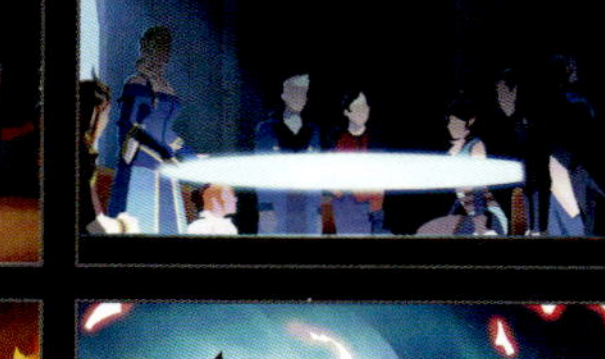
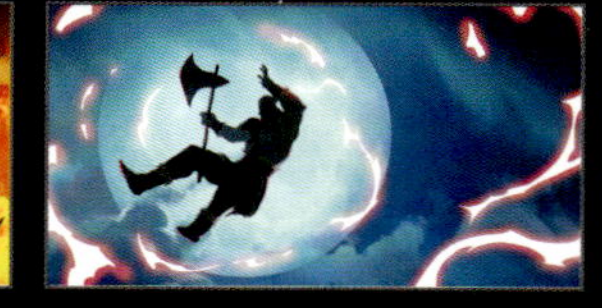
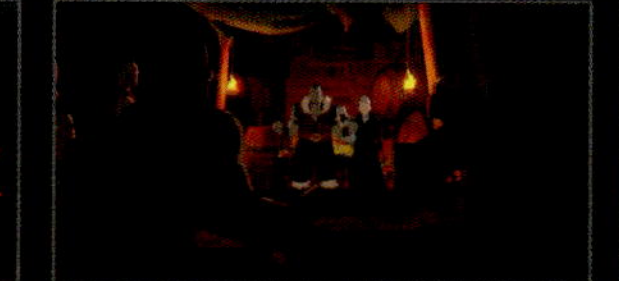

Color Scripts

Color scripts are an important step in the design process for *The Legend of Vox Machina*. In animation, you can't move a light around to change the time of day or up the drama like you would on a live-action set. Someone has to draw those various rim lights, and if they don't connect from scene to scene, it is virtually impossible to fix after the fact.

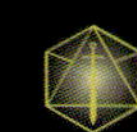

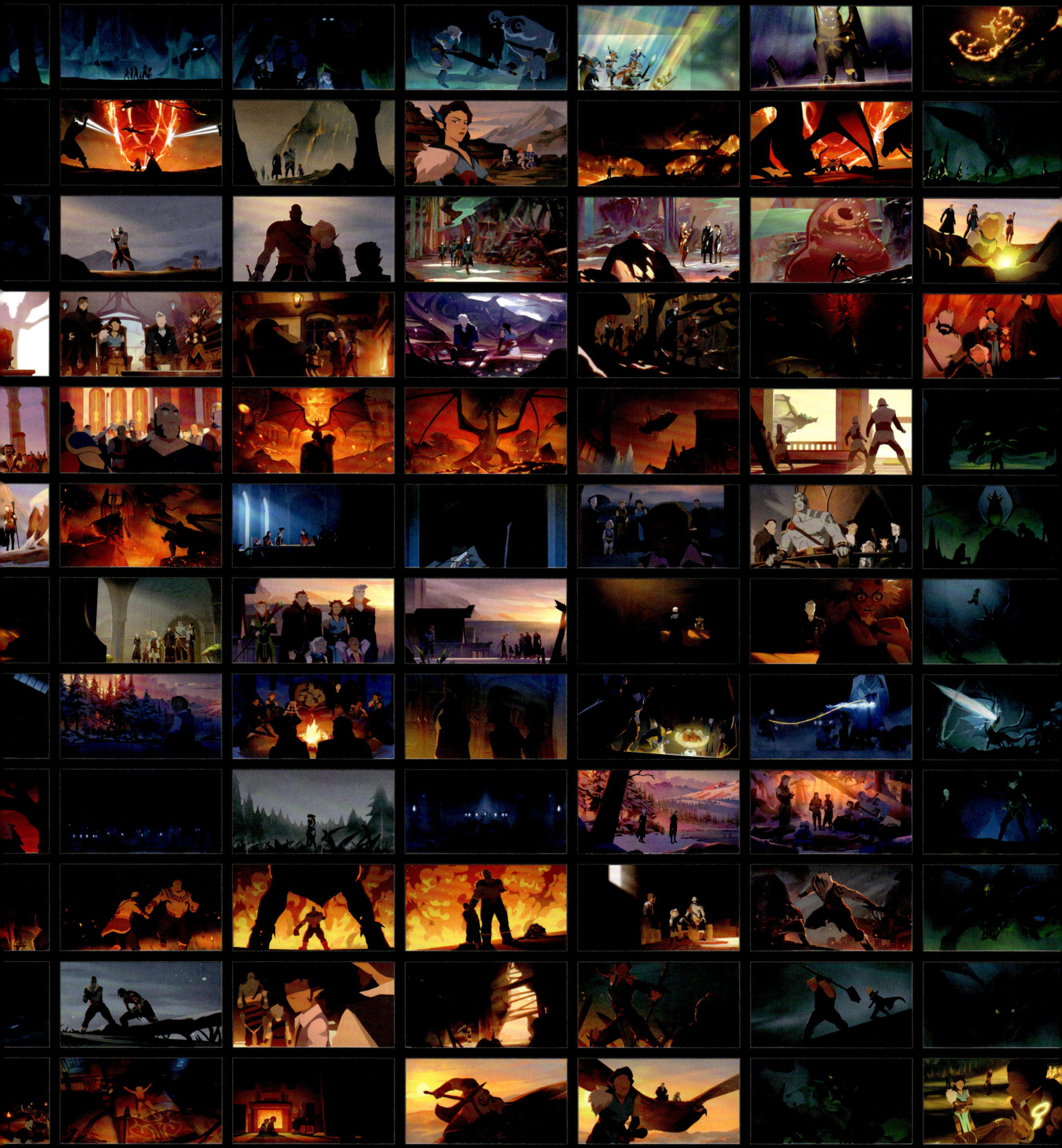

Color Scripts painted by Howard Chen

These color scripts serve as a guide to knowing how characters and props will look when the light is coming from one direction versus the reverse shot or how the color of a scene will change depending on the time of day in the script. The lighting on *Vox Machina*, in particular, is very cinematic, so giving the animators that information upfront is crucial. Background painters will also utilize color scripts to start their background paintings, as will the compositors, who add additional lighting and visual effects once the animation is complete.

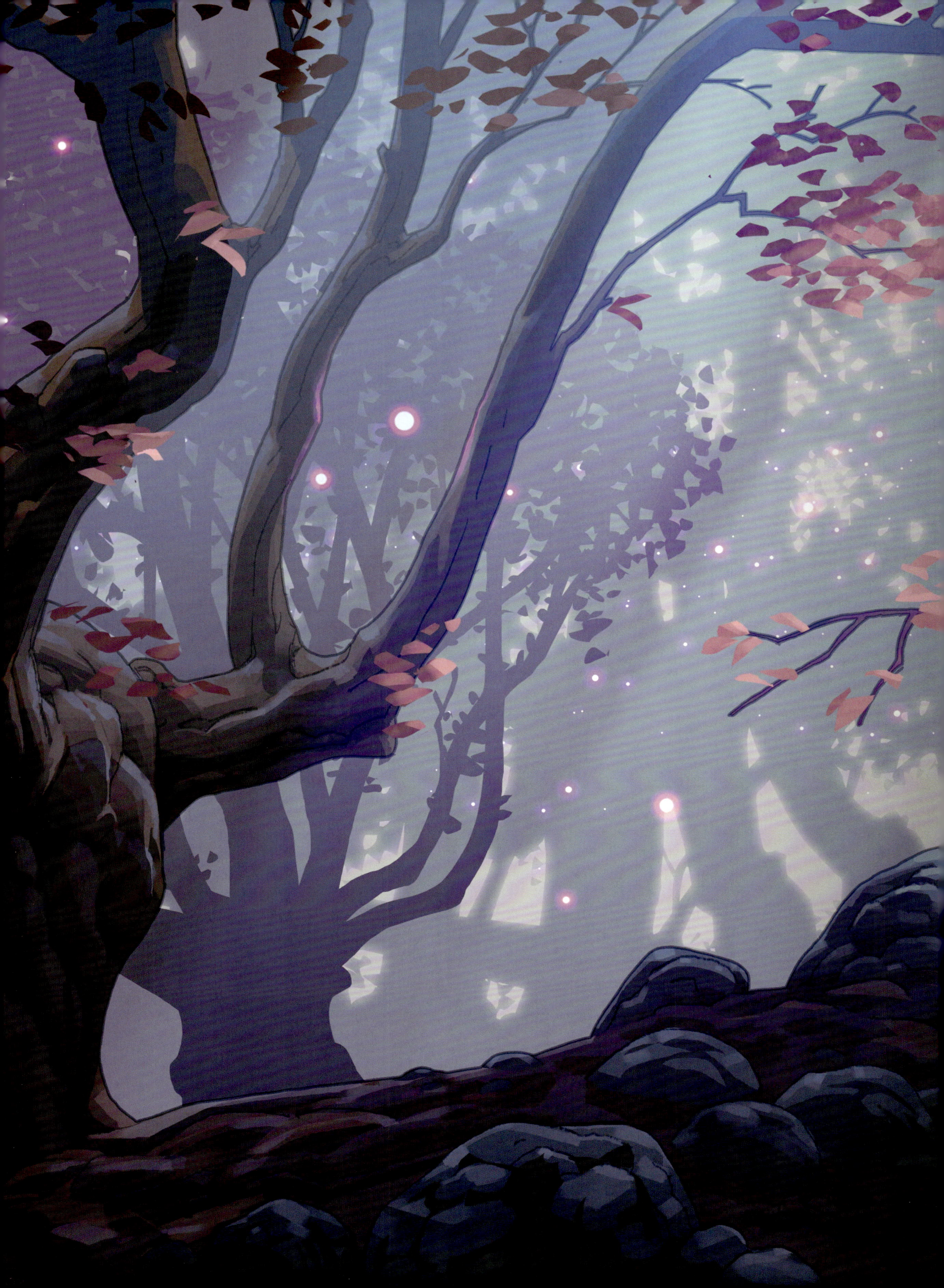

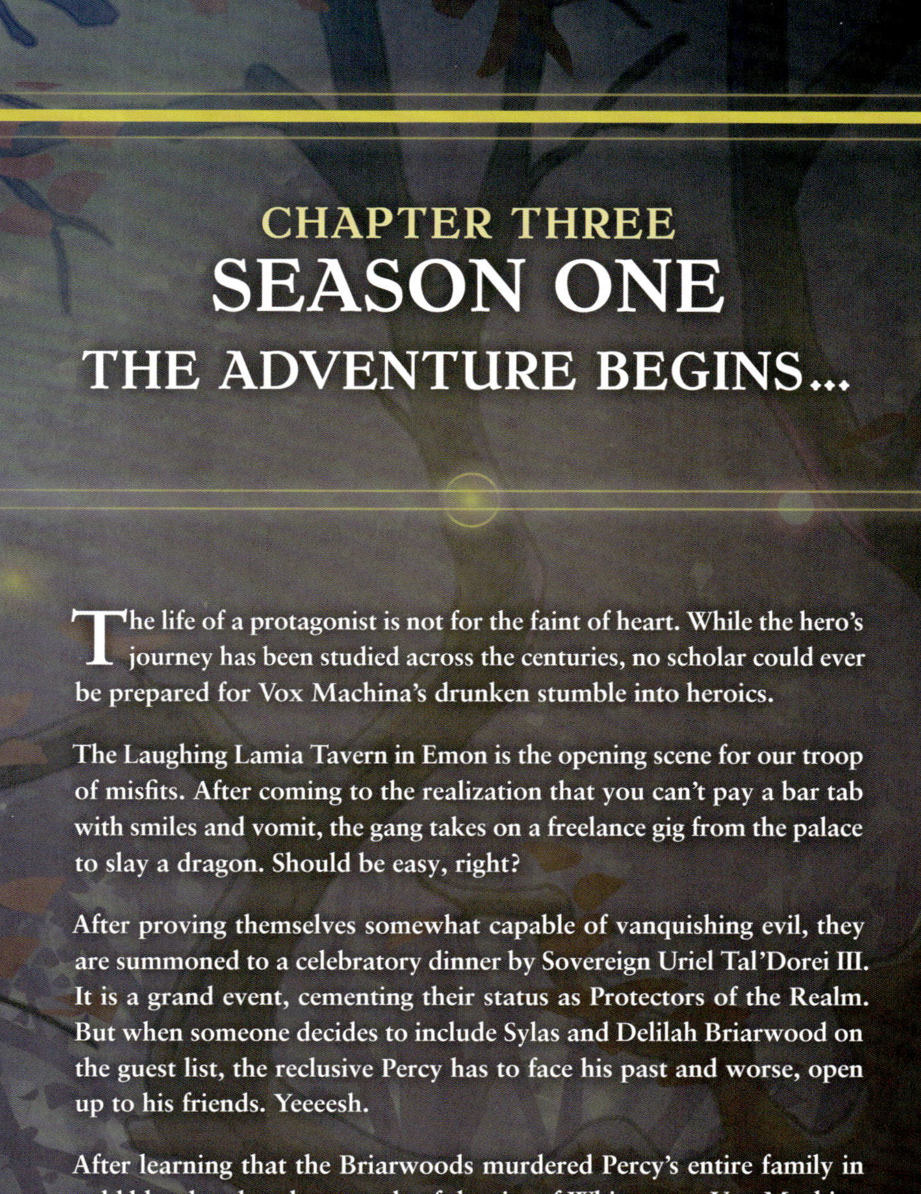

CHAPTER THREE

SEASON ONE

THE ADVENTURE BEGINS...

The life of a protagonist is not for the faint of heart. While the hero's journey has been studied across the centuries, no scholar could ever be prepared for Vox Machina's drunken stumble into heroics.

The Laughing Lamia Tavern in Emon is the opening scene for our troop of misfits. After coming to the realization that you can't pay a bar tab with smiles and vomit, the gang takes on a freelance gig from the palace to slay a dragon. Should be easy, right?

After proving themselves somewhat capable of vanquishing evil, they are summoned to a celebratory dinner by Sovereign Uriel Tal'Dorei III. It is a grand event, cementing their status as Protectors of the Realm. But when someone decides to include Sylas and Delilah Briarwood on the guest list, the reclusive Percy has to face his past and worse, open up to his friends. Yeeeesh.

After learning that the Briarwoods murdered Percy's entire family in cold blood and took over rule of the city of Whitestone, Vox Machina march bravely into battle.

Vox Machina march into battle.

Vox Machina walk slowly into battle after almost bailing several times and getting run off the road by a vicious pack of undead wolves. Regardless of how, they end up making it to Whitestone, all body parts intact, ready to lead the citizens in a revolution worthy of song!

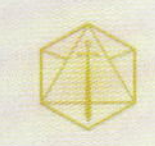

EPISODE 1 & 2

THE TERROR OF TAL'DOREI PARTS 1 AND 2

"After a truly dazzling musical intro followed by a twenty-minute standing ovation from the Council of Tal'Dorei, the gang and I embark on a quest to save Emon from this dick of a dragon named Brimscythe. We obviously crushed it, and everything went down without incident." – A RECOUNTING OF "THE TERROR OF TAL'DOREI PARTS 1 AND 2" BY SCANLAN SHORTHALT

The Tavernkeeper

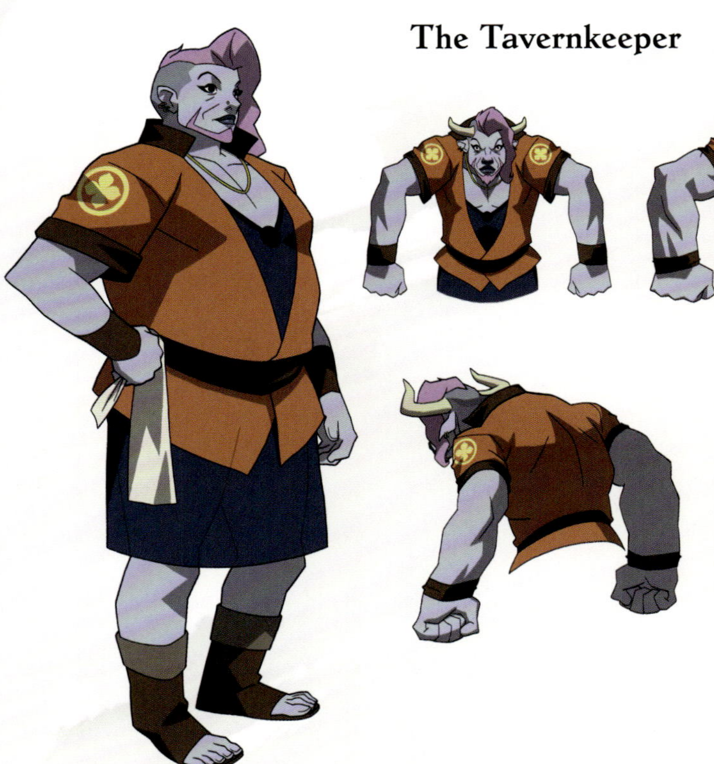

In the early days of the series' development, fans voted on a character they wanted to see as the tavern-keeper in Vox Machina's local drinking haunt. The result? A nonbinary changeling bard who is probably in the wrong line of business if they're already over all the bar fights.

Matt Mercer

One of the many Matt Mercer cameos throughout the series. Just don't pee on his leg, and tell him it's Scanlan.

Sovereign Uriel Tal'Dorei III

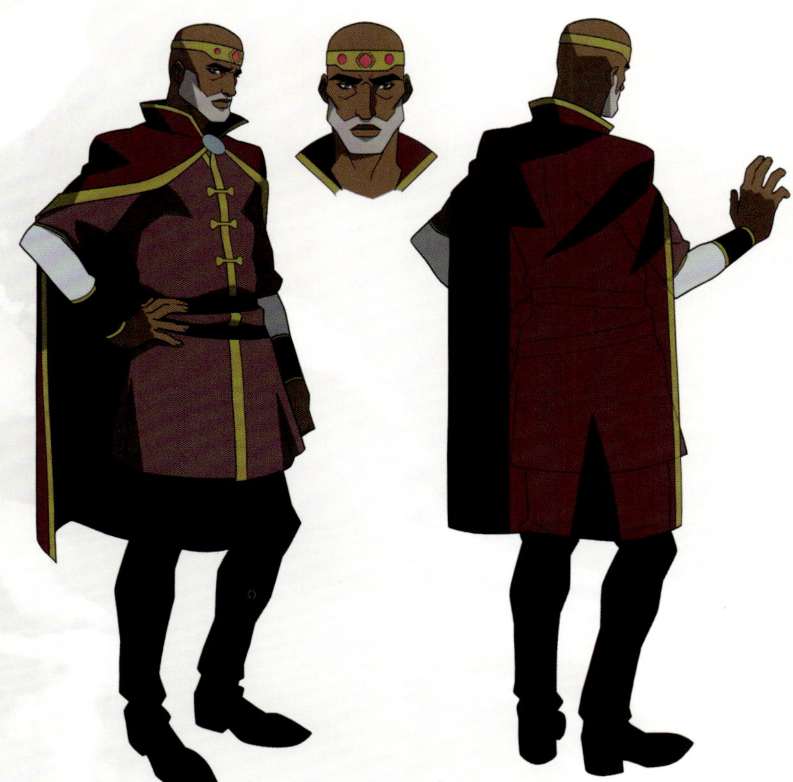

The ruler of Tal'Dorei who calls upon Vox Machina for help when danger arises. His design needed to evoke sophistication while still having a vulnerability that could be exploited by Sylas Briarwood.

Sir Gregory Fince

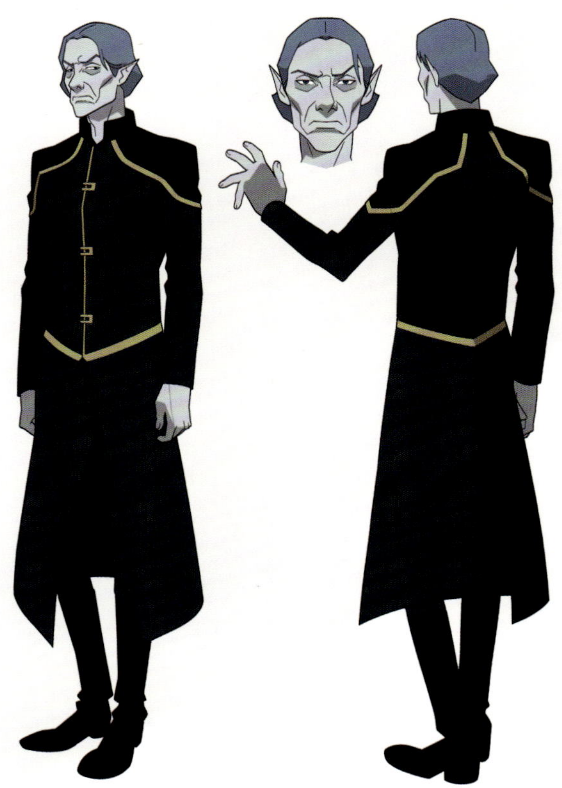

As Master of Defense on the Tal'Dorei council, he advises the Sovereign on all matters regarding the protection of the realm. His sly, greasy appearance and blunt military strategy triggers Vox Machina's suspicions about his true identity. Turns out he's just an asshole.

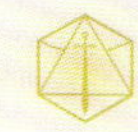

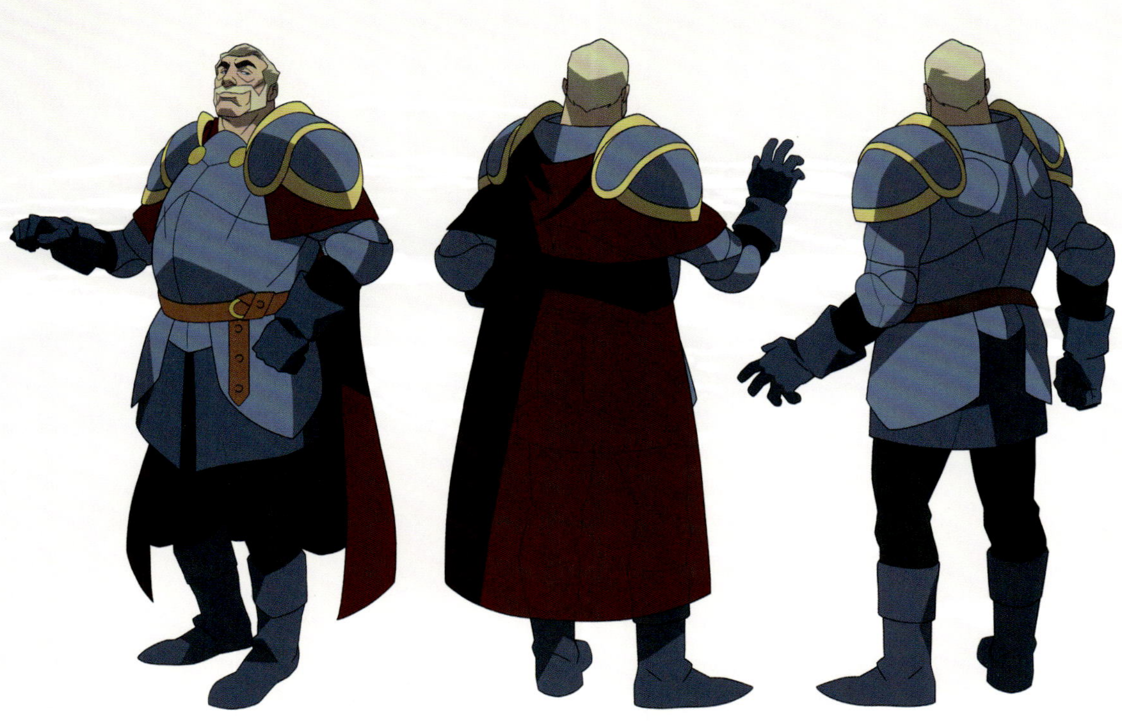

General Krieg / Brimscythe

Didn't your mother ever tell you not to judge a book by its cover? As General of the Sovereign's armies, Krieg embeds himself within Emon society to weaken it from the inside, only to reveal himself to be the formidable dragon Brimscythe.

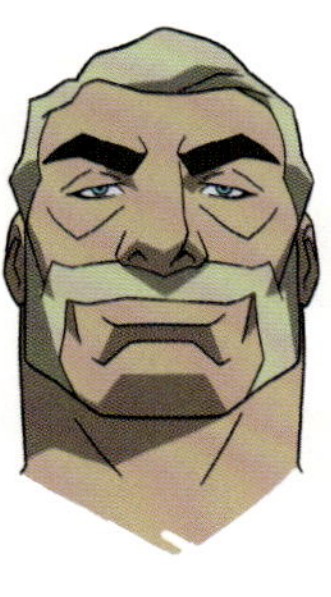

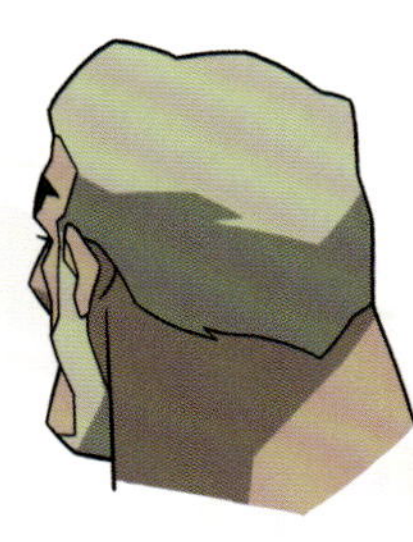

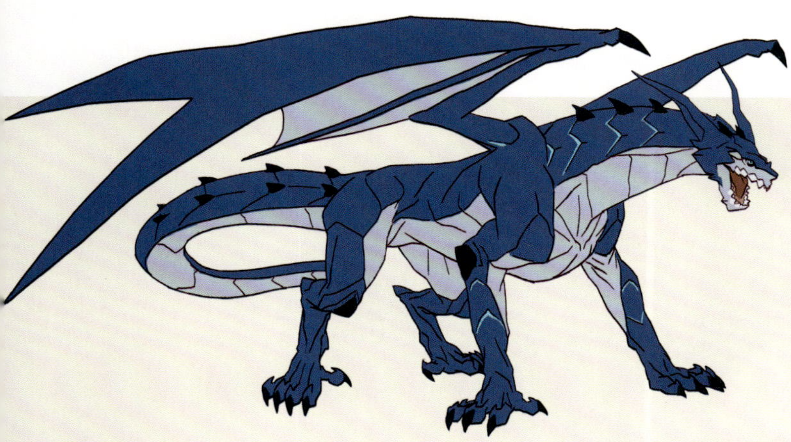

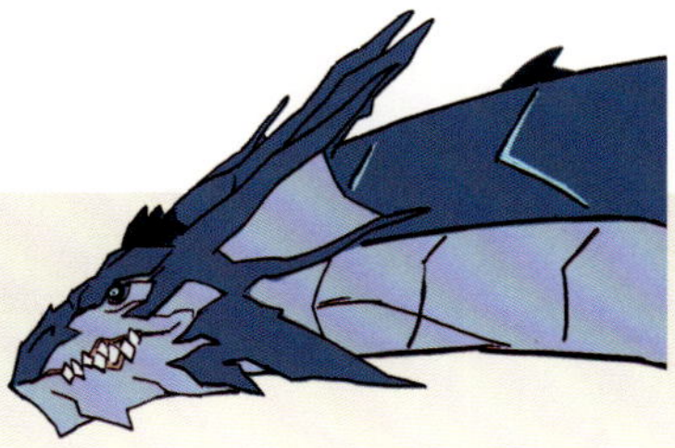

Brimscythe Transformation

For complicated animation sequences, character designers often draw "special poses" to aid the animators in modeling.

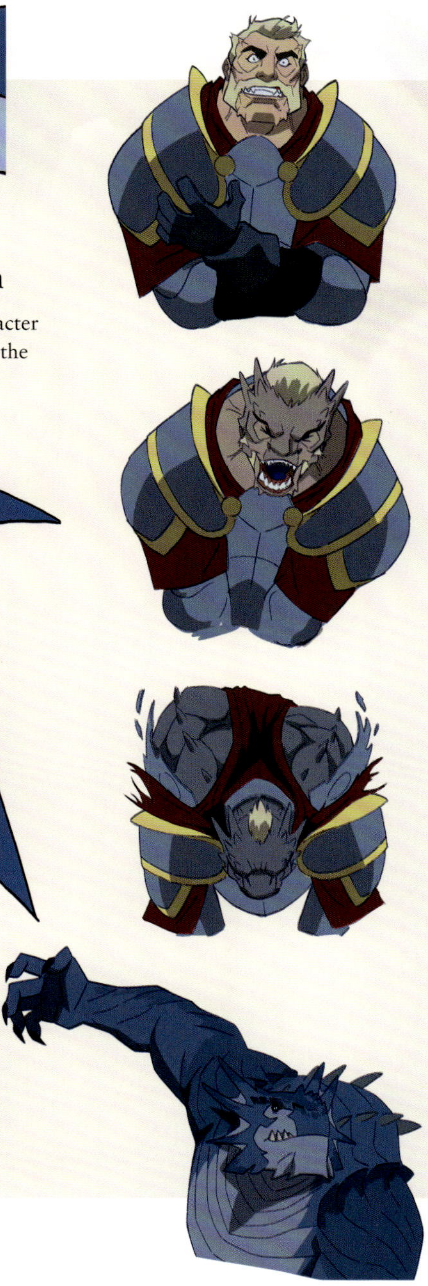

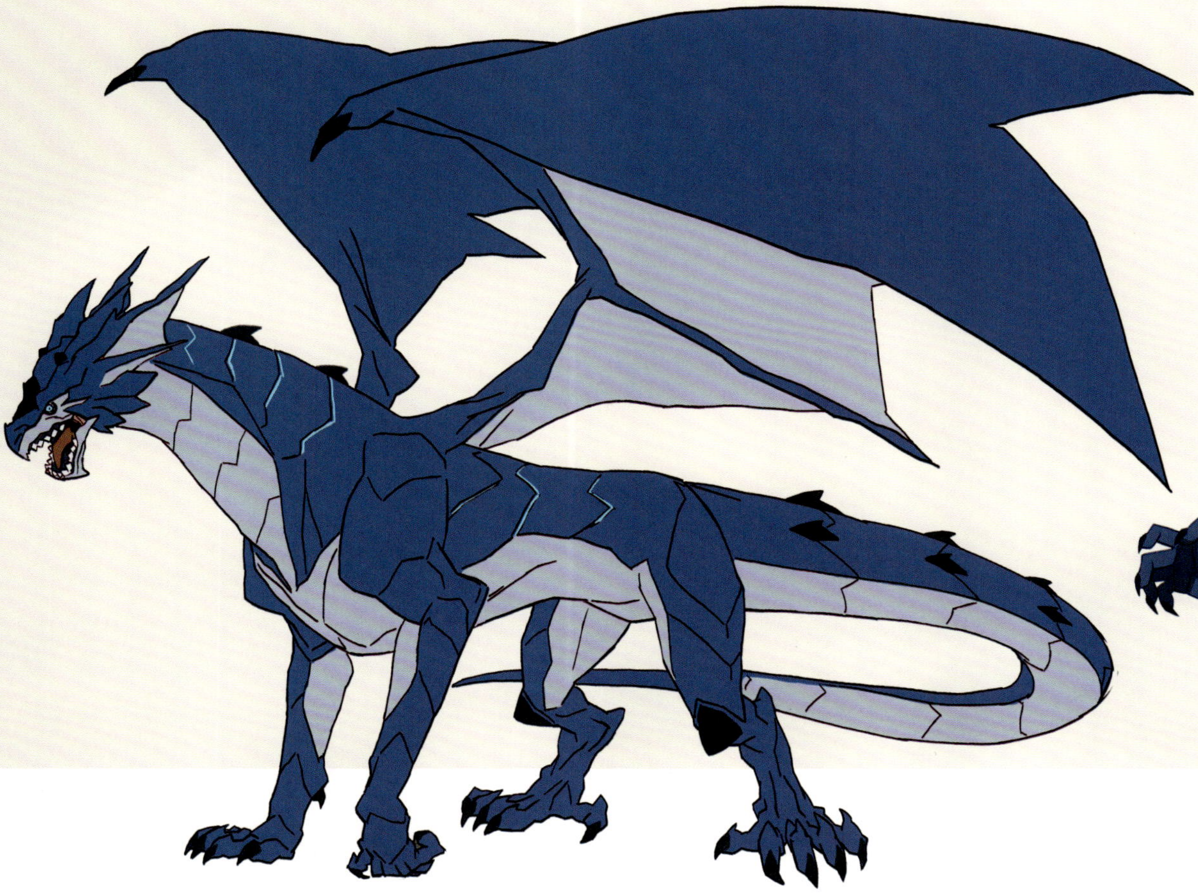

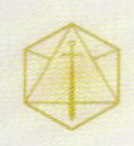

Shaun Gilmore

A true fan favorite, Gilmore could charm the pants off just about anybody (and he has the closet full of discarded clothing to prove it). If you couldn't tell, purple is his favorite color.

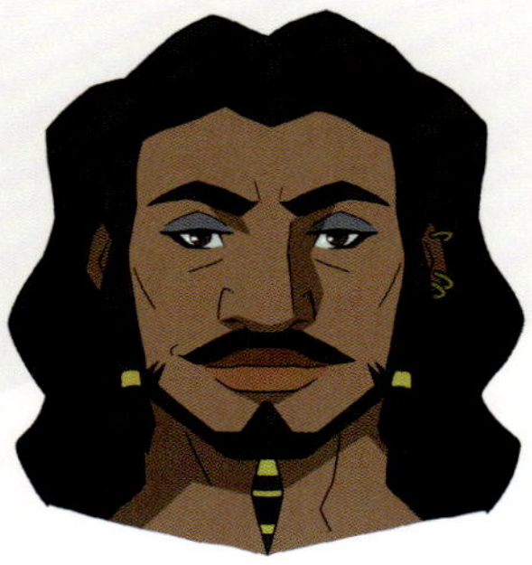

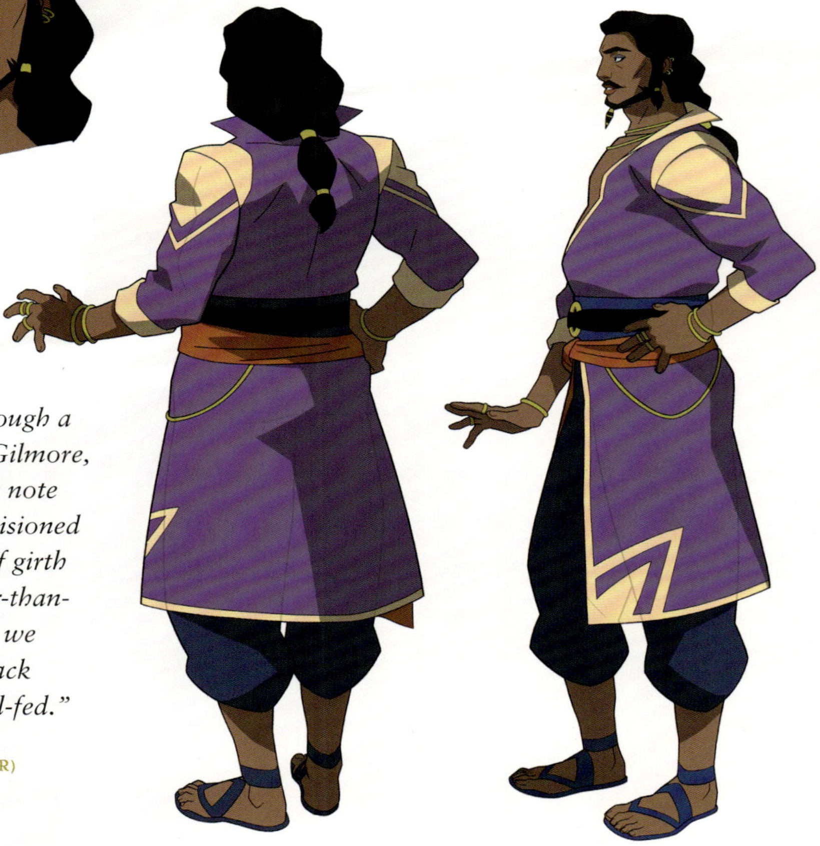

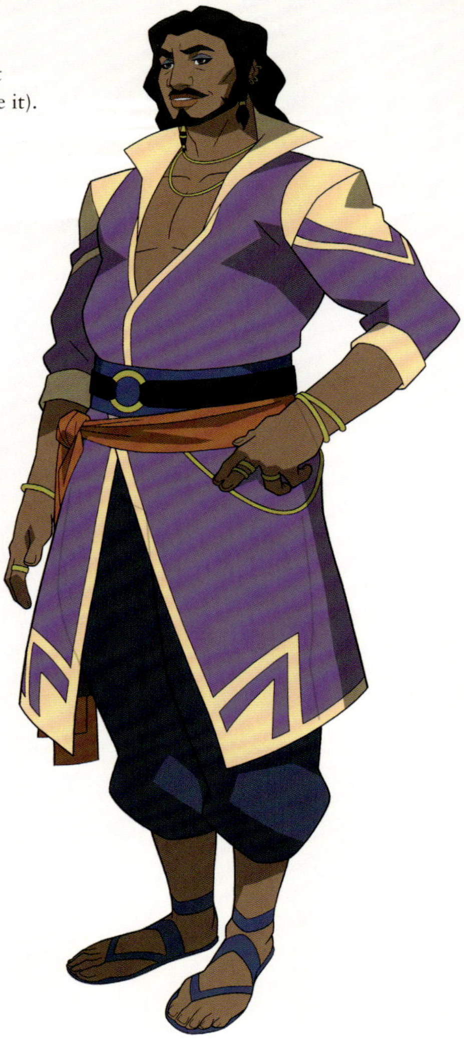

"After working through a few variations of Gilmore, Mercer gave us the note that he always envisioned him having a bit of girth to match his larger-than-life personality, so we made sure to go back and make him well-fed."

– PHIL BOURASSA (CHARACTER DESIGNER)

Lady Allura Vysoren

Lady Kima of Vord

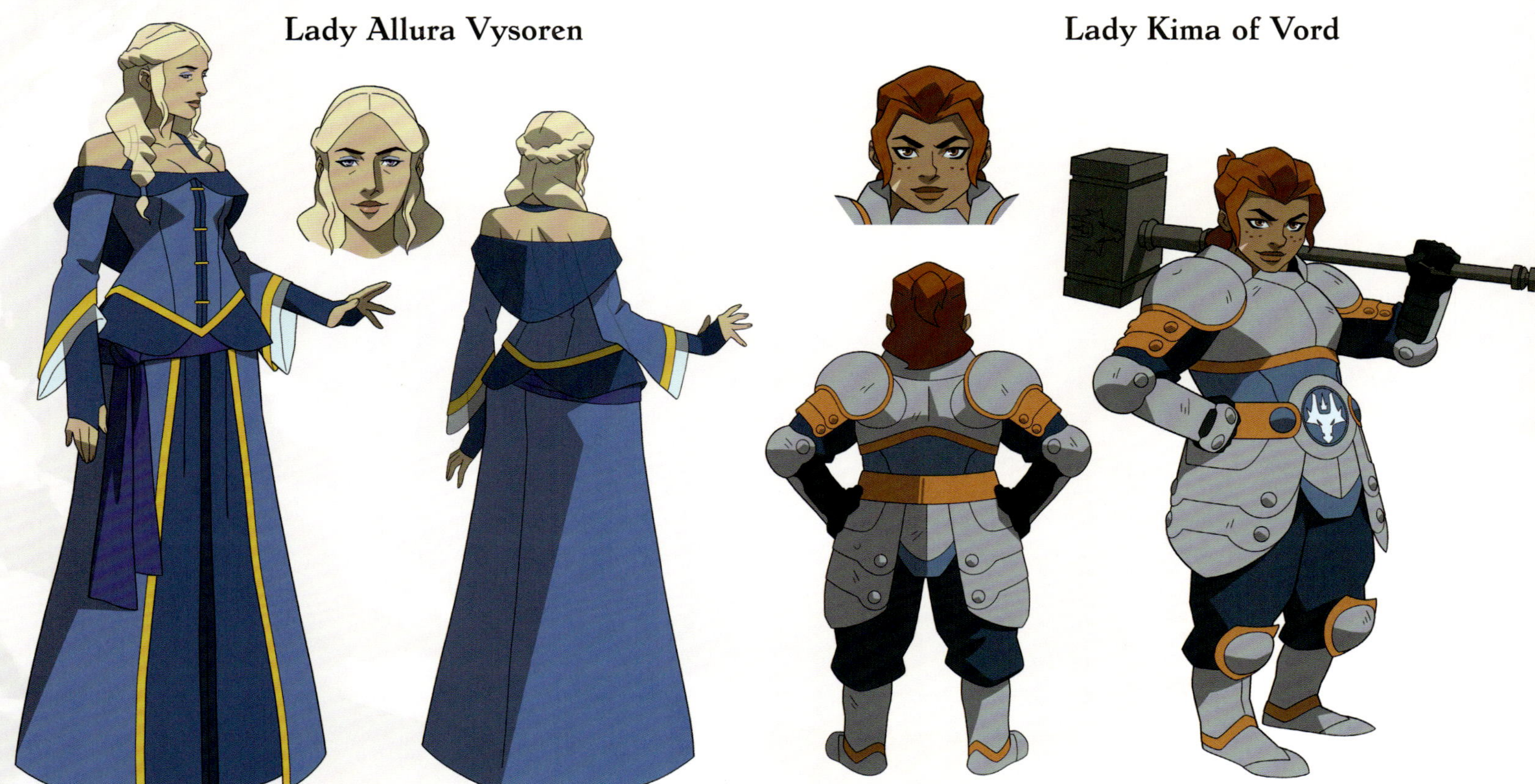

As Master of Arcana on the Council of Tal'Dorei, Lady Allura often aids Vox Machina on their quests to protect the realm.

Her design was inspired by Galadriel from *The Lord of the Rings* with more of a relatable spin to keep her grounded and down to earth. The subtle age lines added to her face convey her years of experience as an adventurer before meeting Vox Machina.

Like Pike, Kima is a powerhouse in a small package. Her contrasting proportions make her the perfect character to design in animation. Her silhouette is sturdy and strong with a giant weapon to further exaggerate her size. She may come off as a tad abrasive, but this doesn't sway Allura in her love of her.

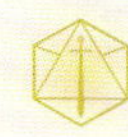

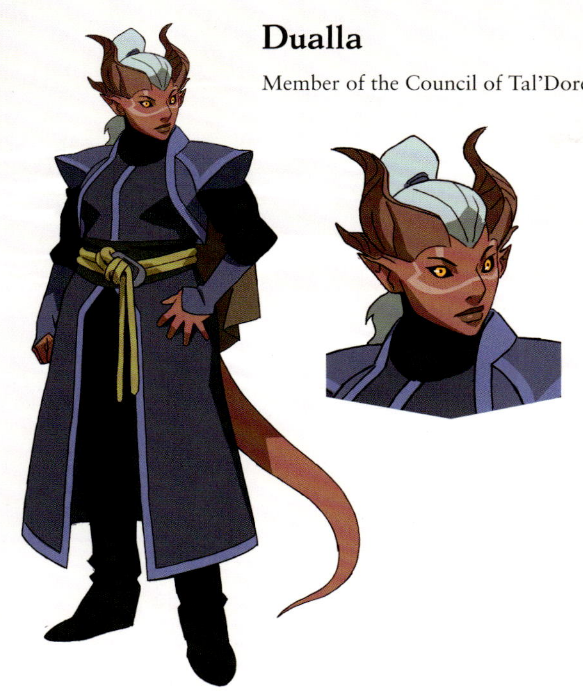

Dualla

Member of the Council of Tal'Dorei.

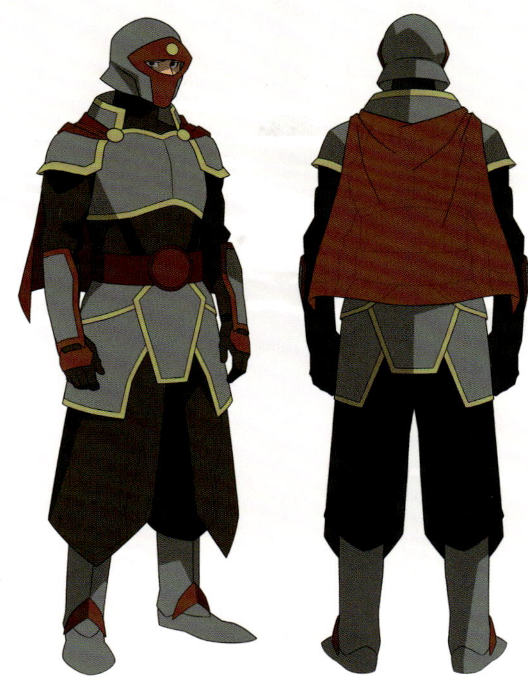

Emon Guard

Turnaround of a standard guard in Emon. Every character designed for the series is given a "turnaround" for storyboard artists and animators to reference.

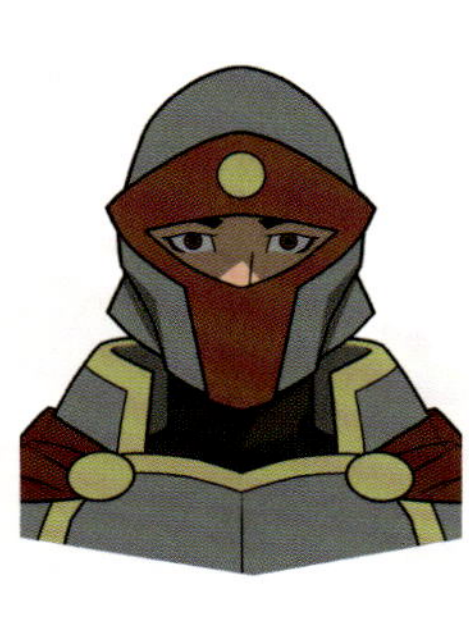

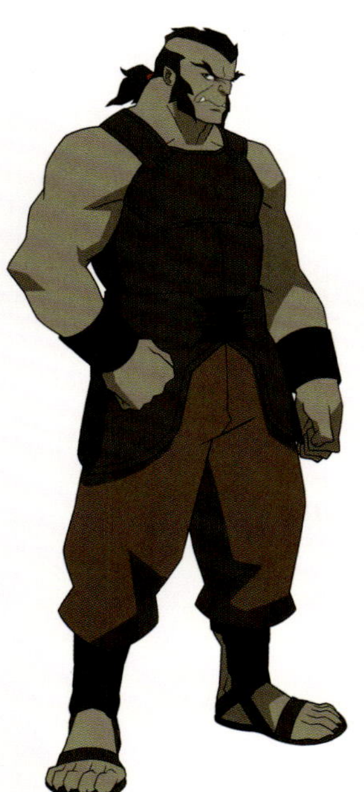

Agar

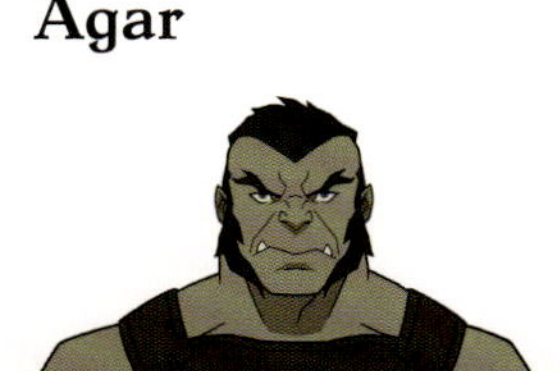

is the show's first half-orc design to go through the design pipeline and thus serves as a species template for all other half-orcs in the series. A keen eye can spot his Agar's Assassins tattoo on his hand, which is eventually chopped off during their brawl.

Agar's Assassins

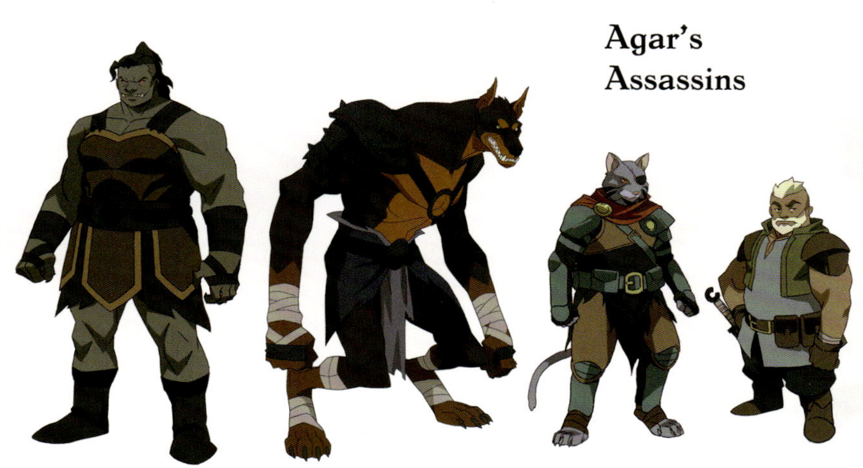

It wouldn't be Vox Machina without a sloppy bar fight. The gruff rival gang known as Agar's Assassins found themselves on the wrong side of that fight… and down a right hand in the process.

Adventuring Party

A completely original license free adventuring party. (Author's note: Scanlan has taken it upon himself to serve as legal counsel for this book).

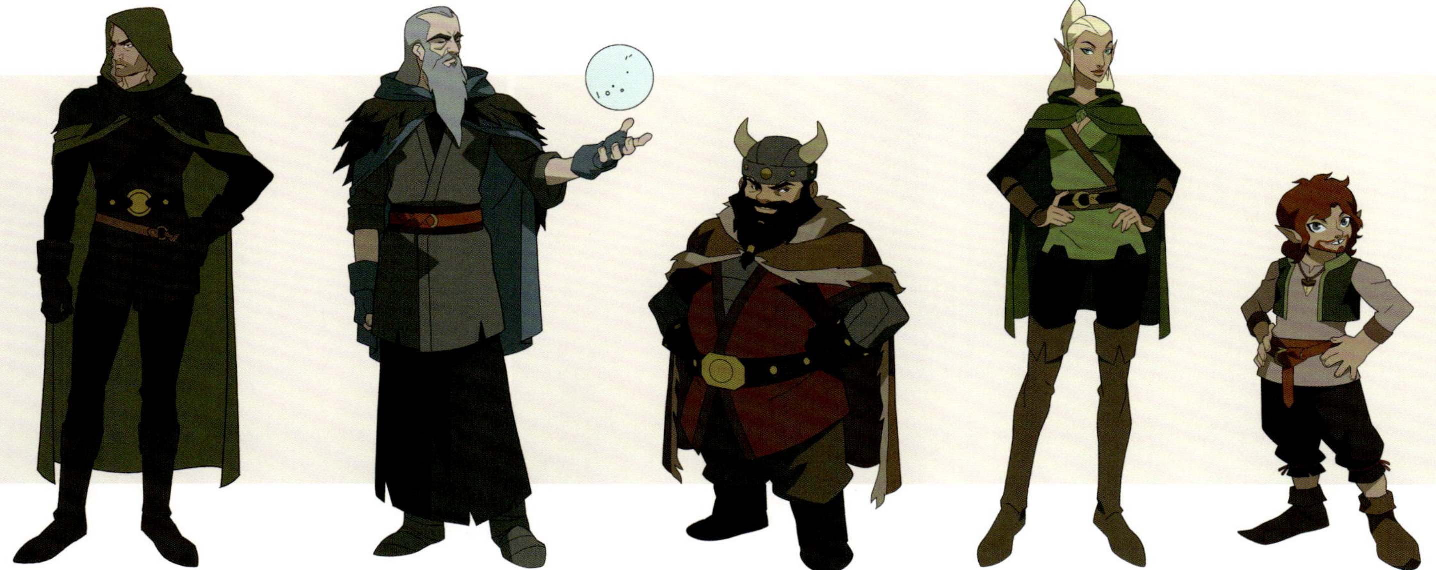

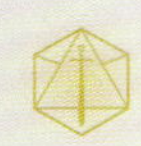

Emon

As the central city of Tal'Dorei, hitting the vast scale of this home base location for Vox Machina was key for the design team. When designing Emon's layout, Arthur Loftis (Art Director) researched Matt Mercer's 2D renderings for the original campaign while also taking into account where certain areas of the city would be located in a real-world situation to ensure security and functionality.

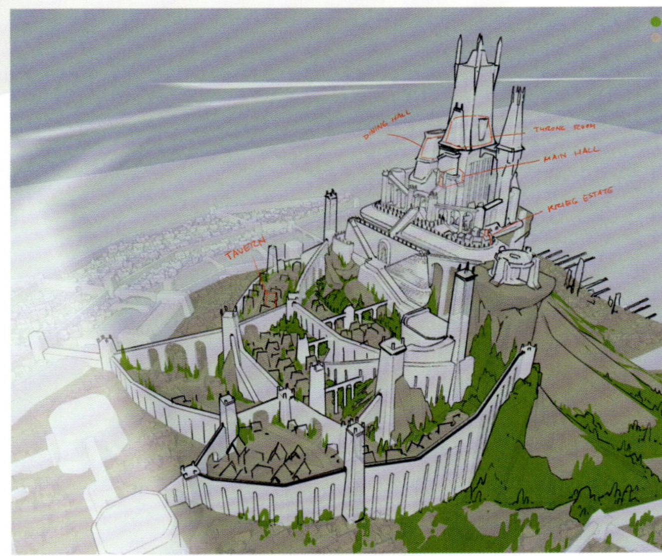

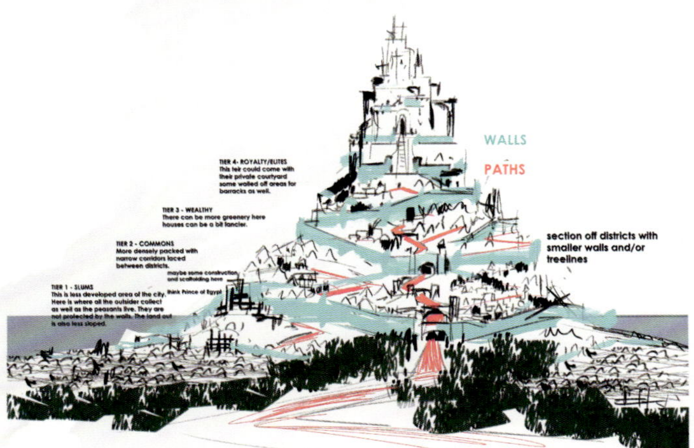

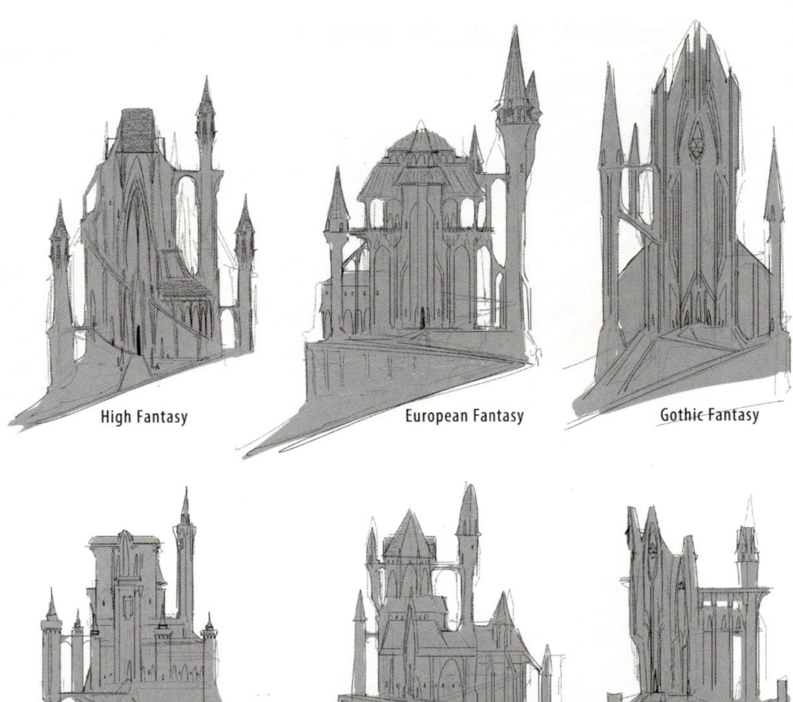

Design took inspiration from Art Deco for the shape language throughout Emon, using it to give the audience something modern they wouldn't see anywhere else in the world.

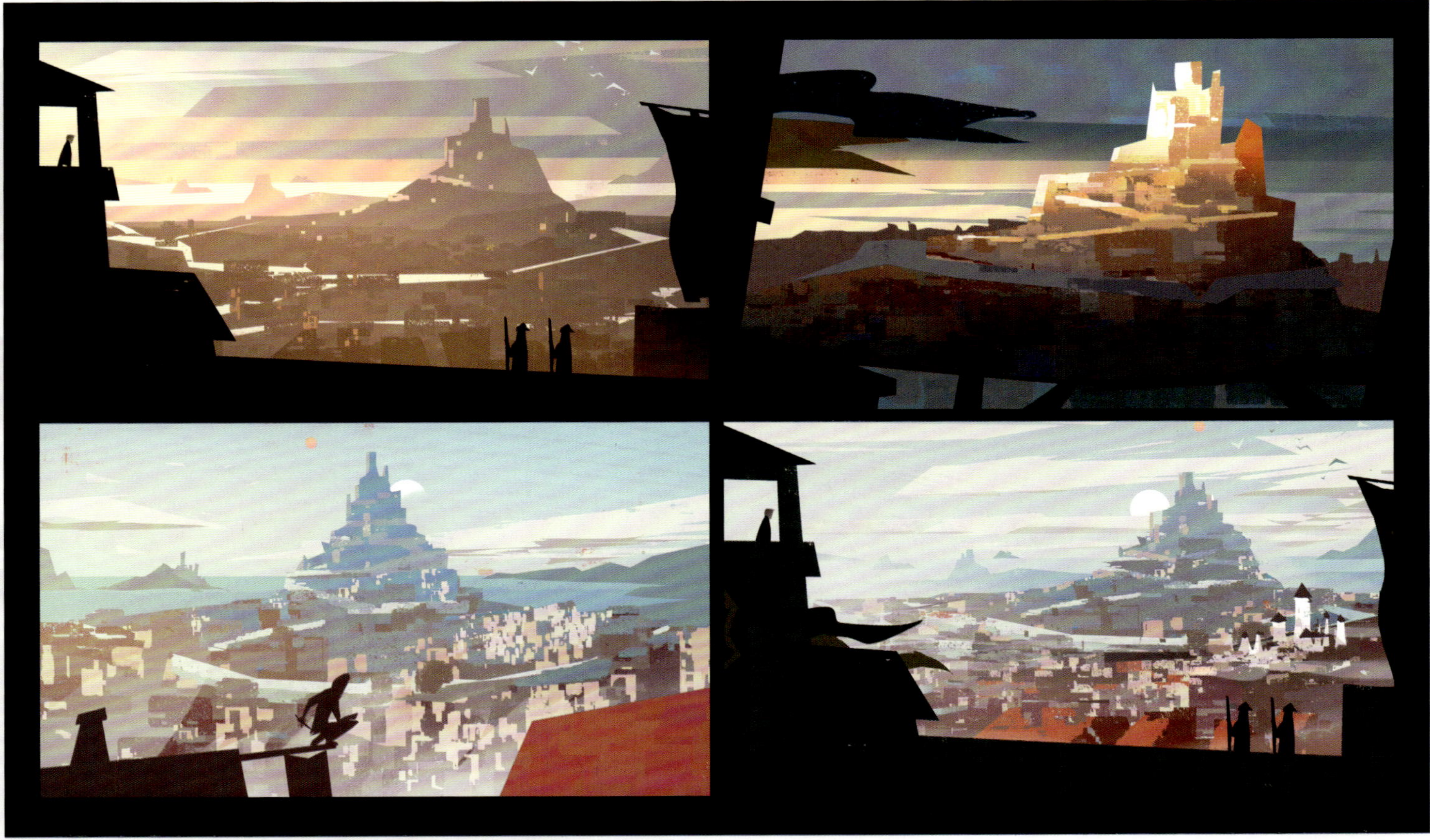

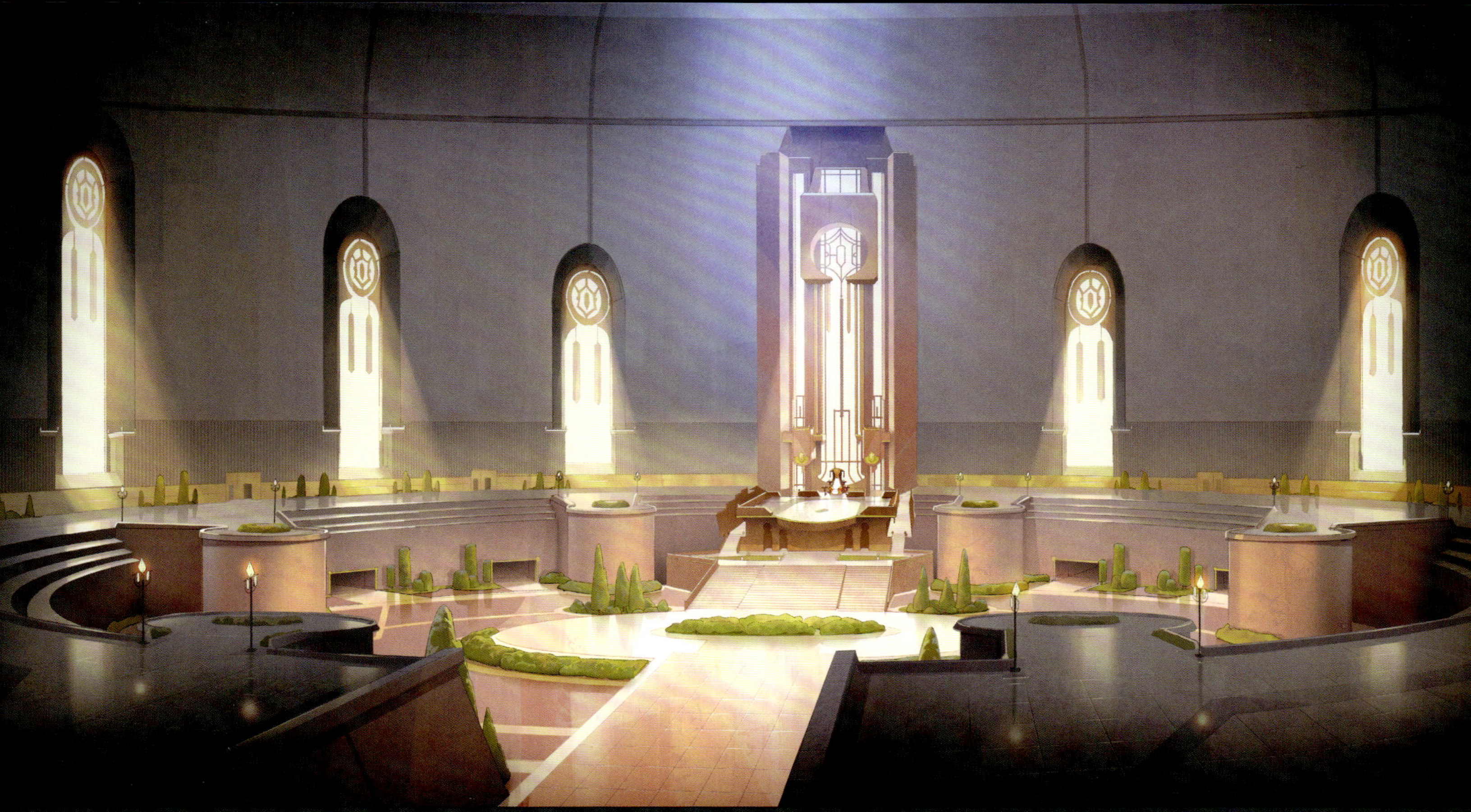

Throne Room

Wanting to instill shock with size, Loftis originally designed the council chamber to be even grander than this (if you can believe it). After reining in the scale, the design settled into this regal hall worthy of the ruler of Tal'Dorei.

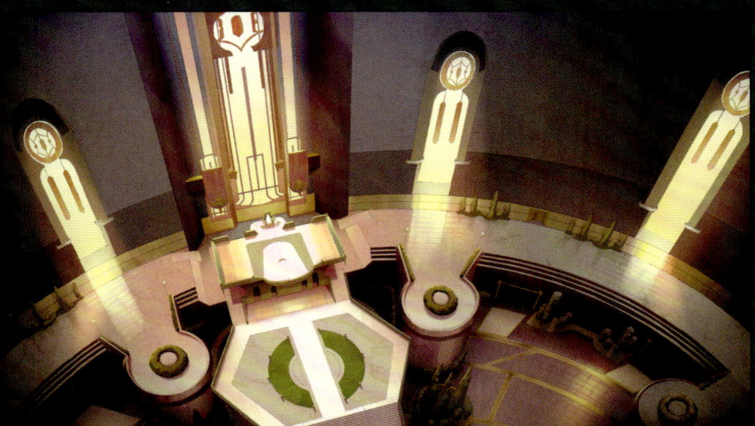

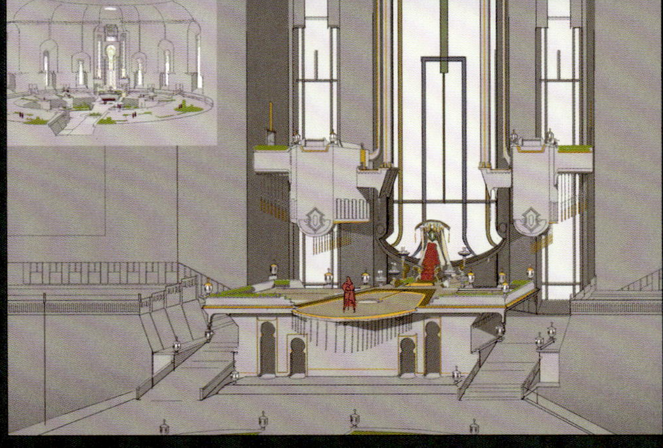

Color and Concept art of the throne room.

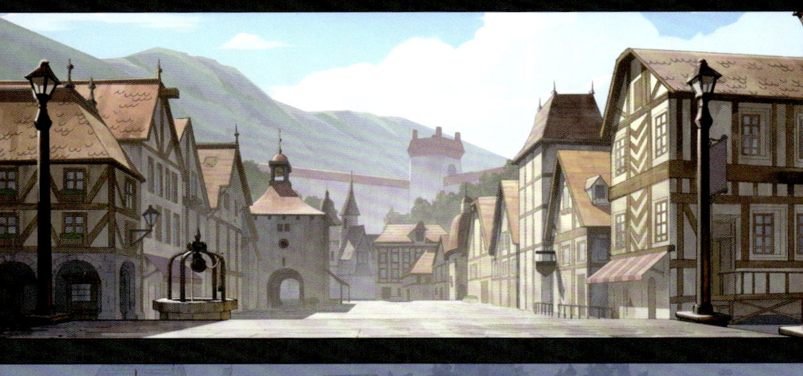

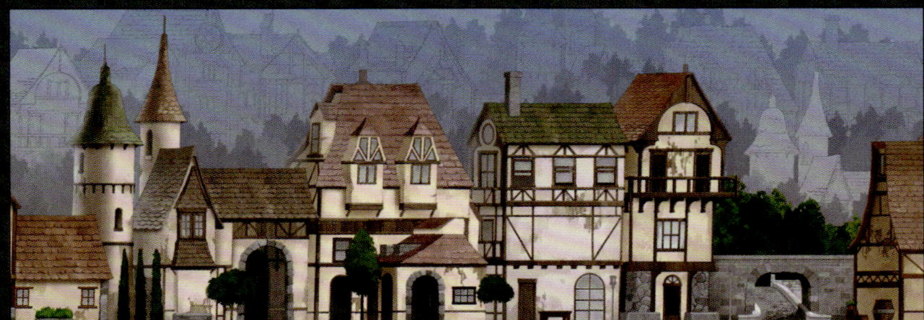

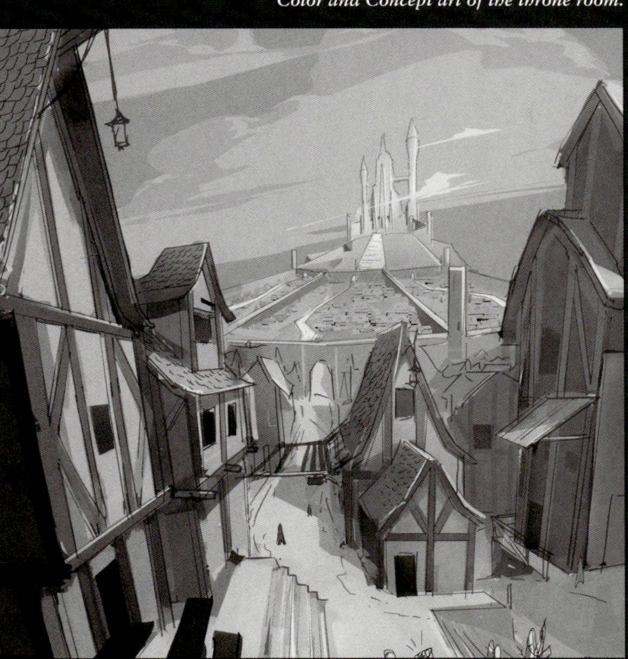

Concept art for building out the city of Emon.

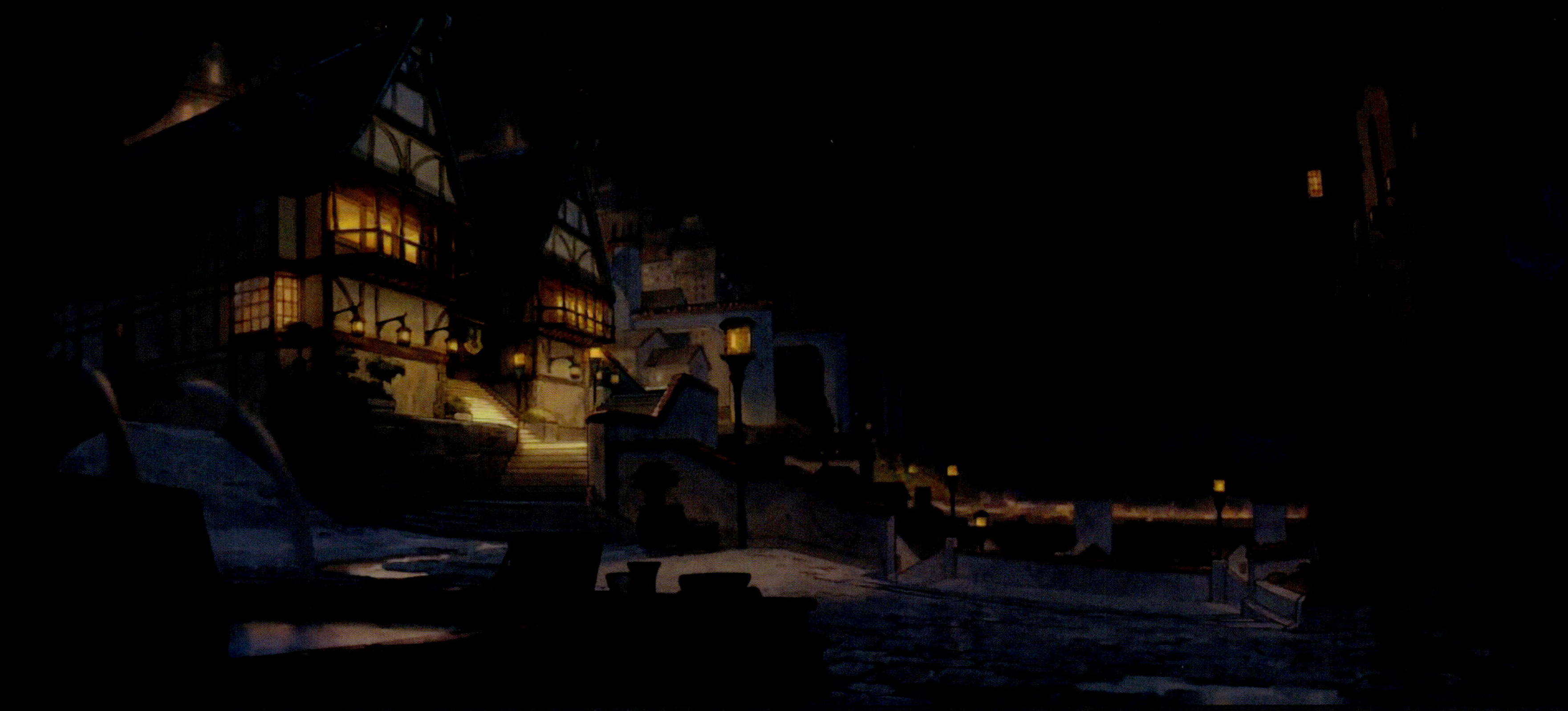

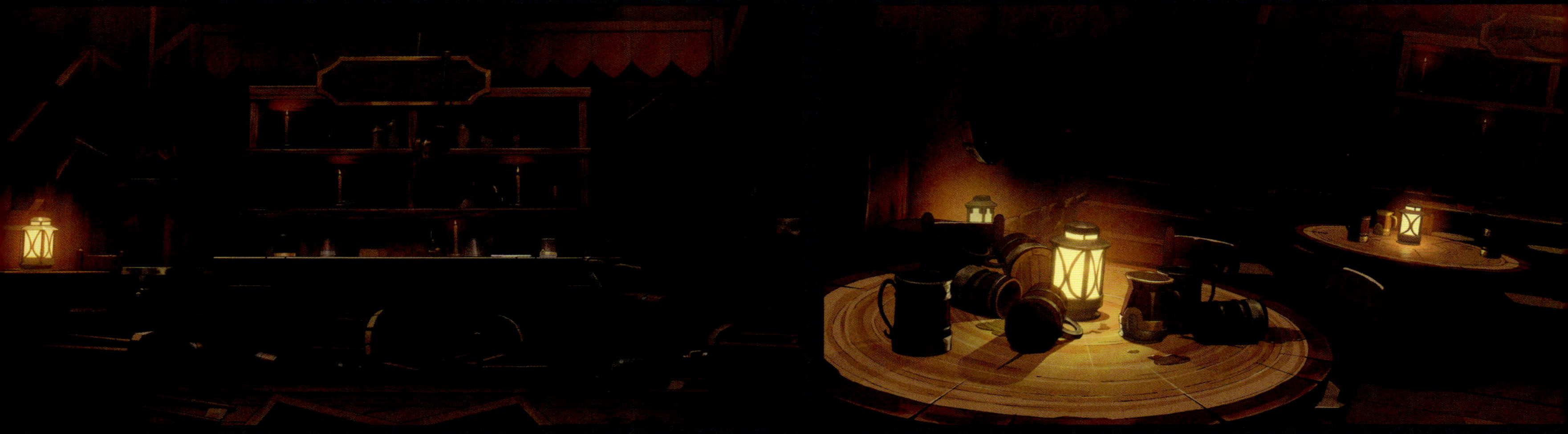

Laughing Lamia Tavern

Site of the first bar room brawl to kick off Episode One, The Laughing Lamia Tavern is home to many unique patrons, from the rowdy regulars to those just passing through Emon.

Designer Jessica Woulfe originally gave the tavern a serpent motif, and after the fan vote chose the tavernkeeper to be a bard, they decided to pepper the interior with various instruments.

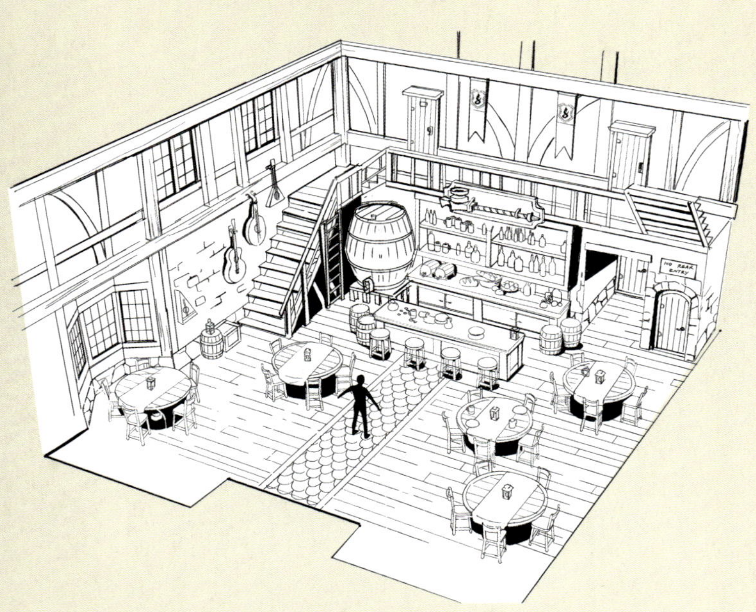

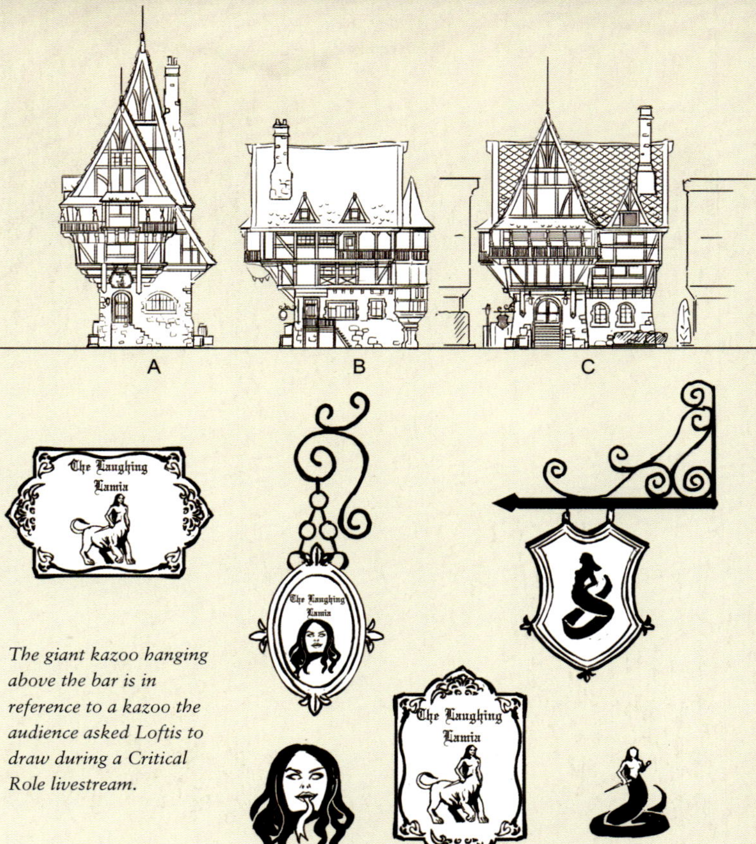

The giant kazoo hanging above the bar is in reference to a kazoo the audience asked Loftis to draw during a Critical Role livestream.

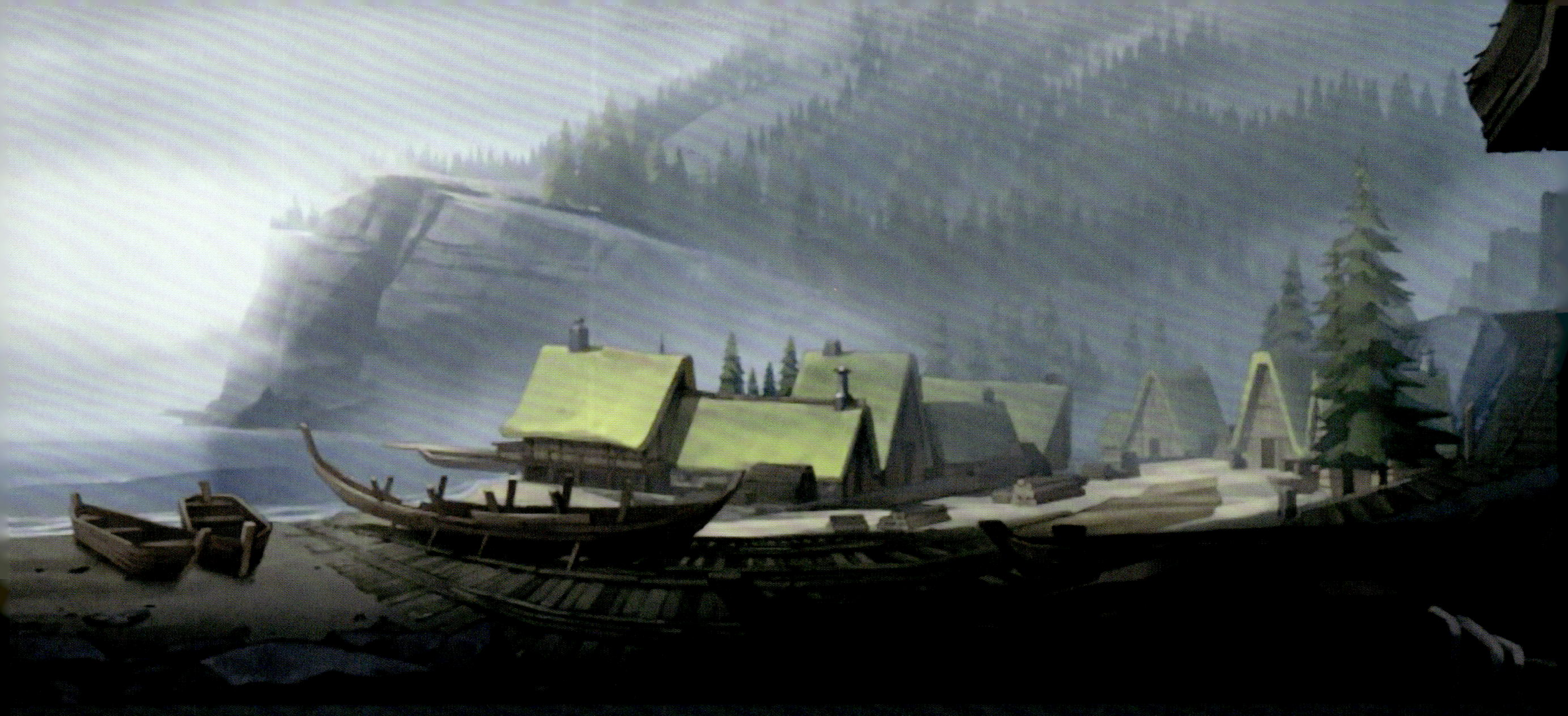

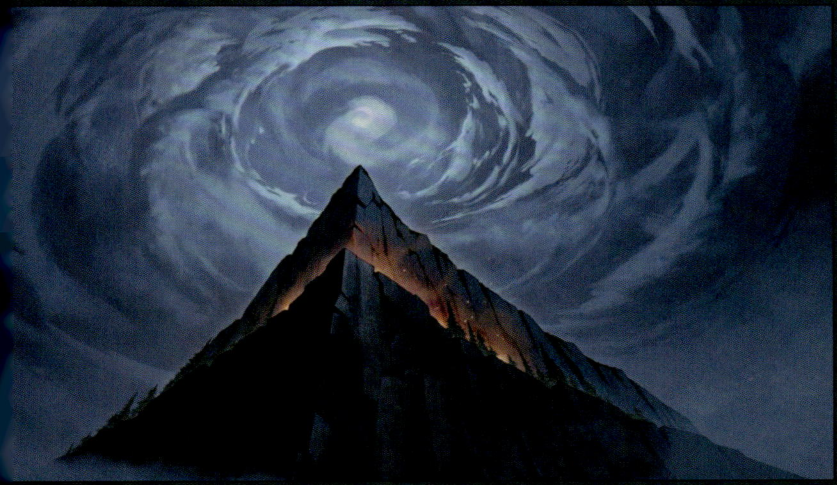

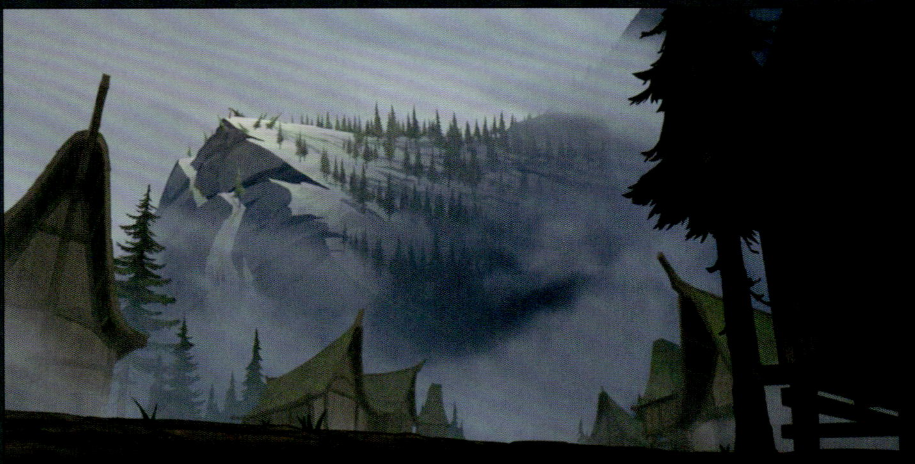

Shale Steps

Located in a coastal area of Emon, the cliffs themselves are meant to appear like frozen waves crashing on shore. Vox Machina's first encounter with the dragon Brimscythe is on said cliffside.

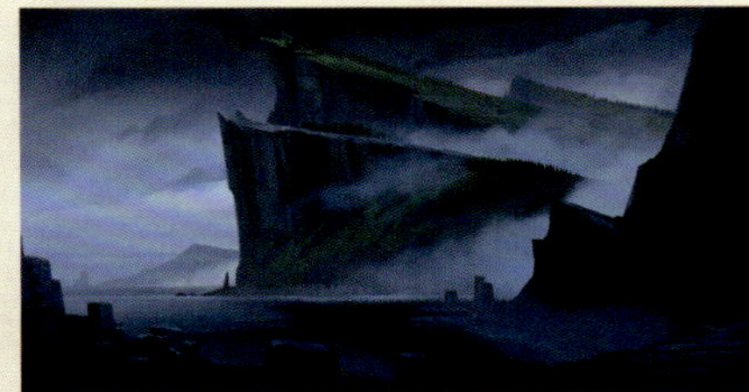

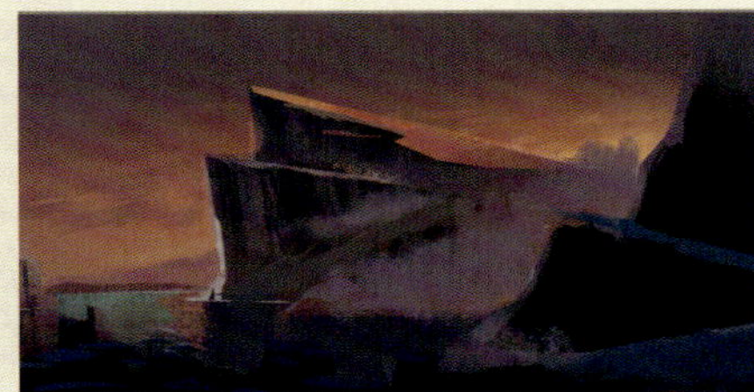

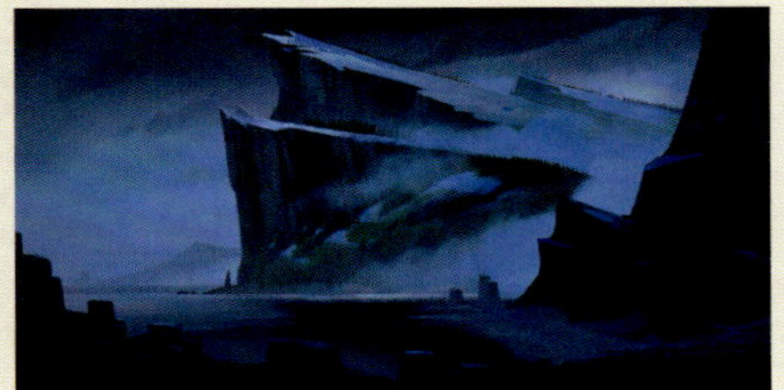

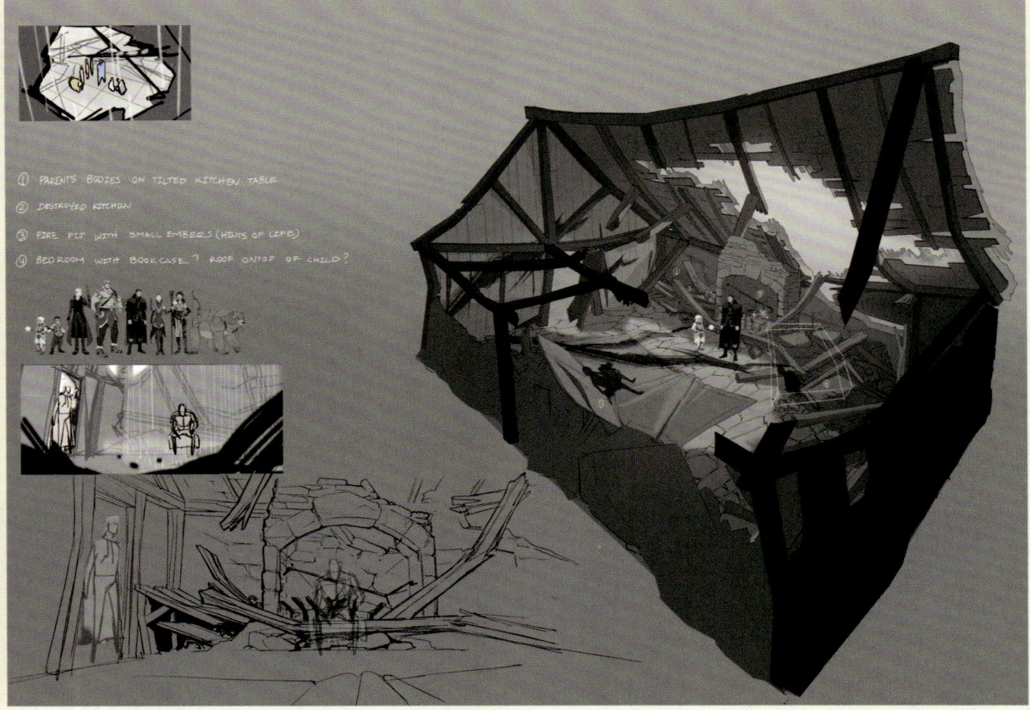

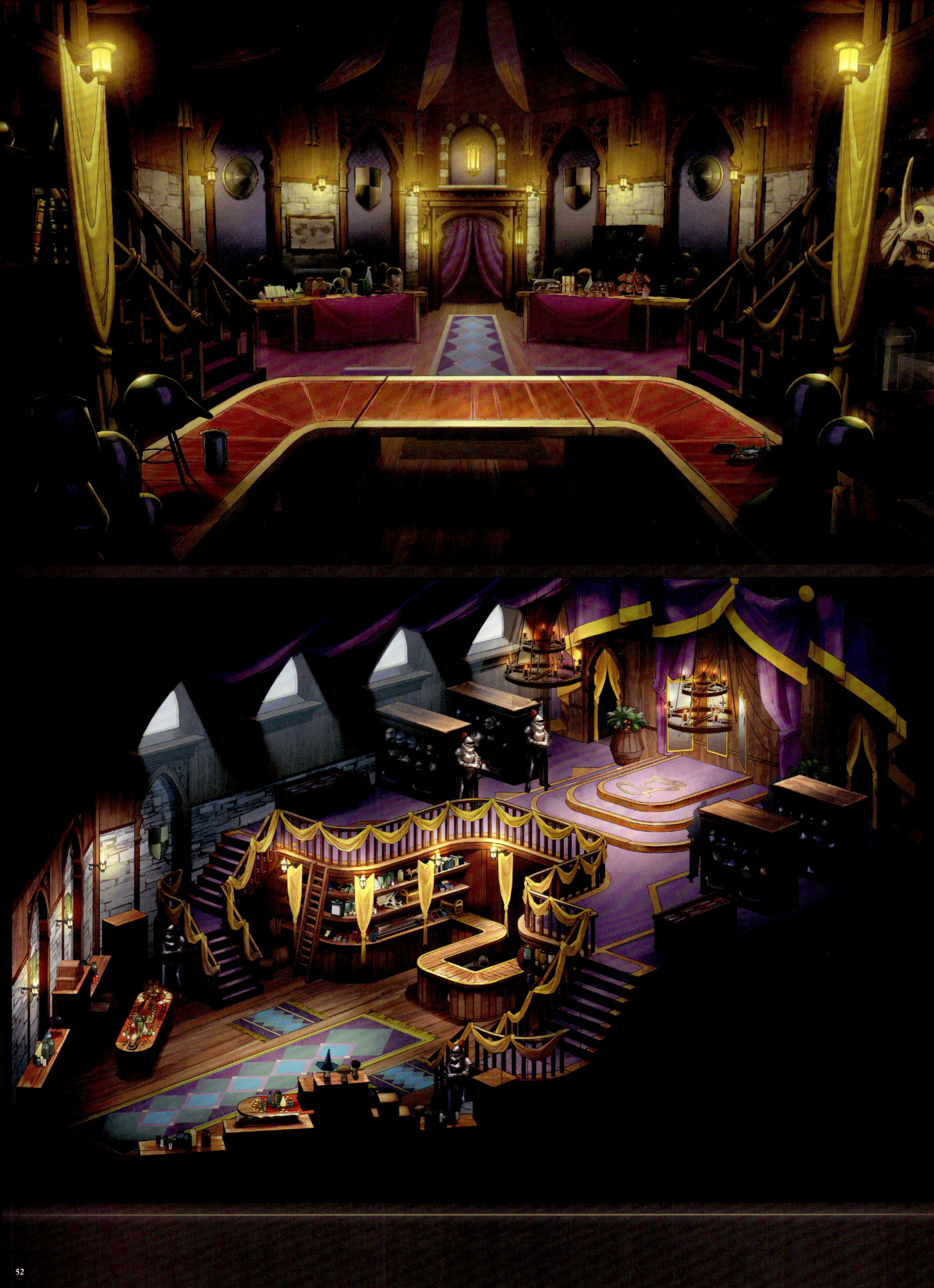

Gilmore's Glorious Goods

Resident Critter Arthur Loftis (Art Director) wanted to ensure the fans would have an exciting hunt for Easter Eggs within Gilmore's shop. Scattered throughout, you can see references to the original campaign stream as well as future campaigns from Critical Role.

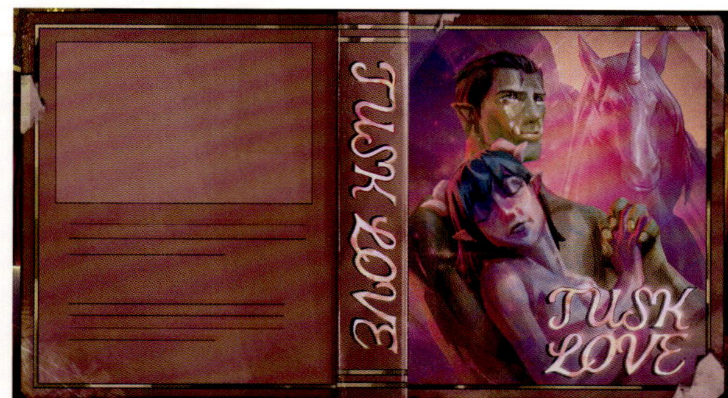

Tusk Love Book—A reference to Critical Role's later campaign The Mighty Nein.

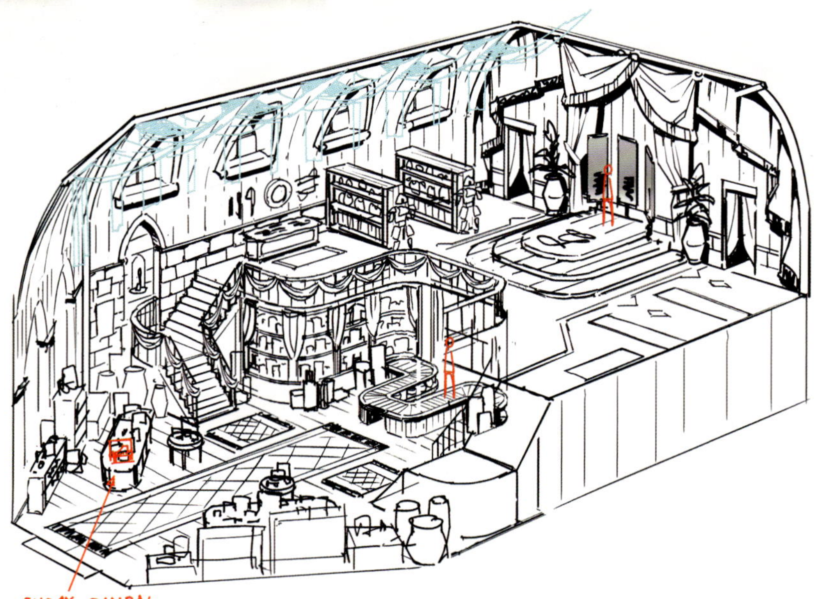

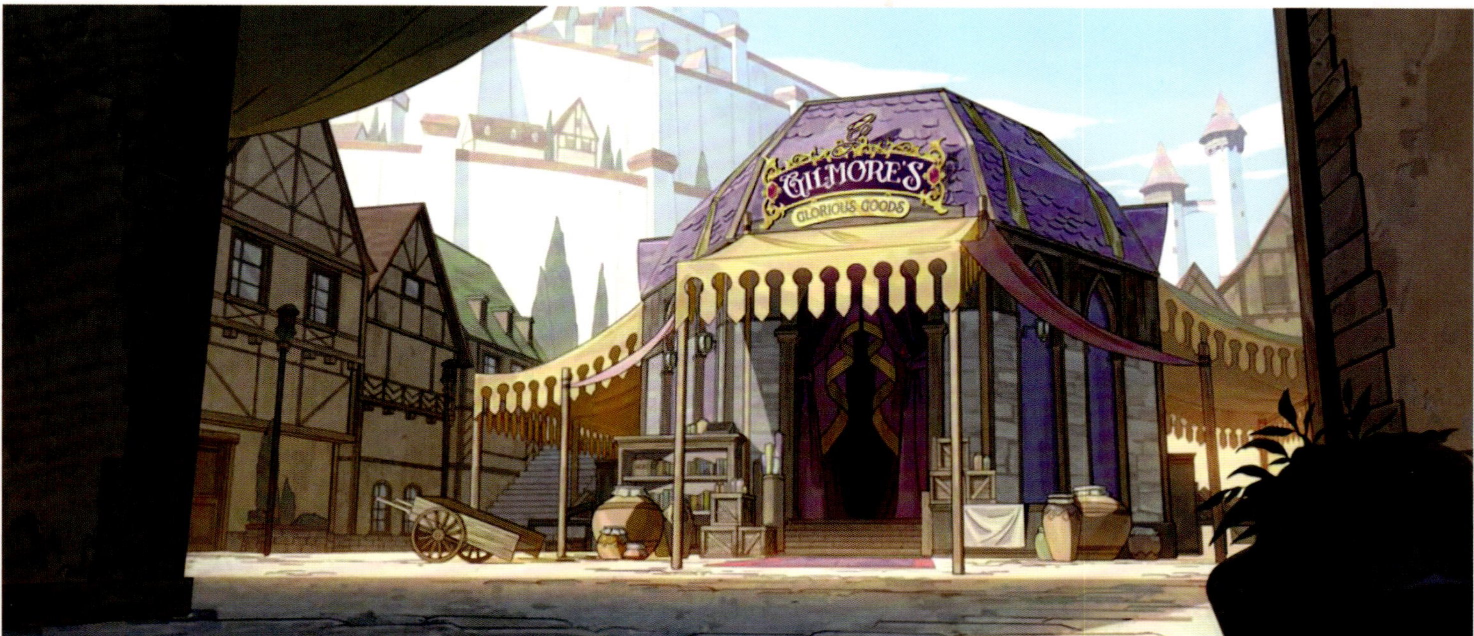

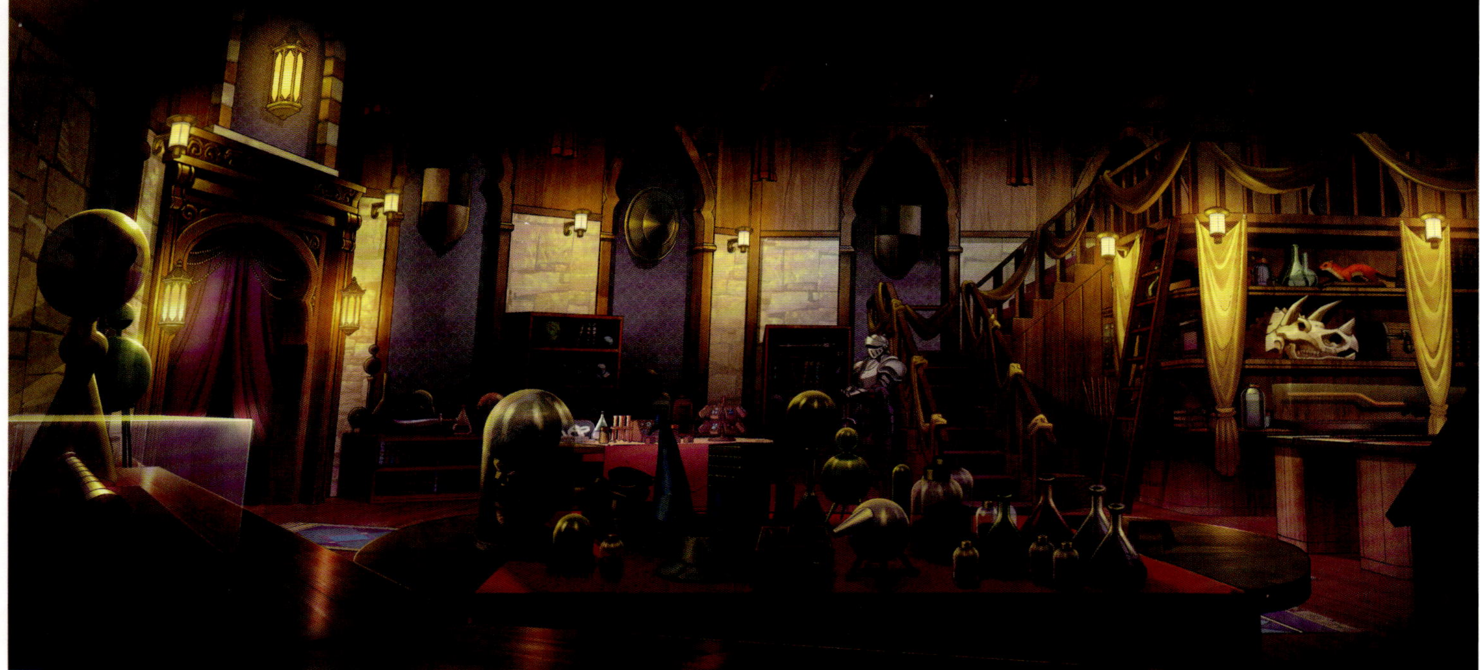

Gygax Sandal—A legend in itself, Gary Gygax cobbled the sandal himself, and it is auctioned off annually for charity at Gary Con. The winner becomes its "steward" for the year. After Chris Prynoski (Titmouse President and Executive Producer) became its steward during production, the art team was inspired to include it in the shop.

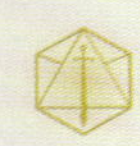

Krieg Manor

Home to General Krieg–designers wanted it to look overly glossy and polished, alluding to Krieg's vanity.

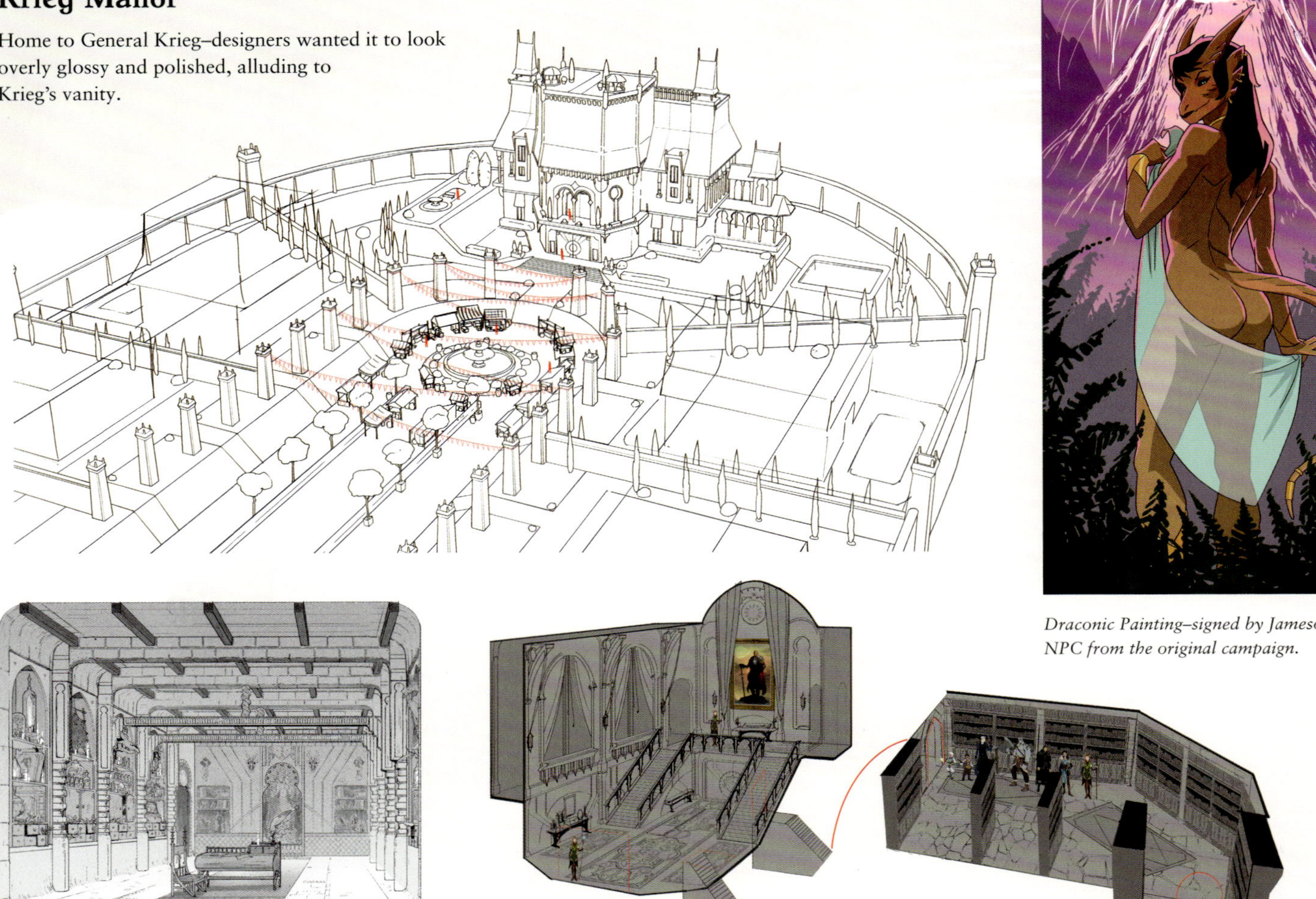

Draconic Painting–signed by Jameson, an NPC from the original campaign.

Brimscythe's Lair

A tribute to the classic "dungeon crawl," Brimscythe's lair hides behind a portal within General Krieg's manor fit for a dragon's hoard. Just be sure to watch out for that lair action.

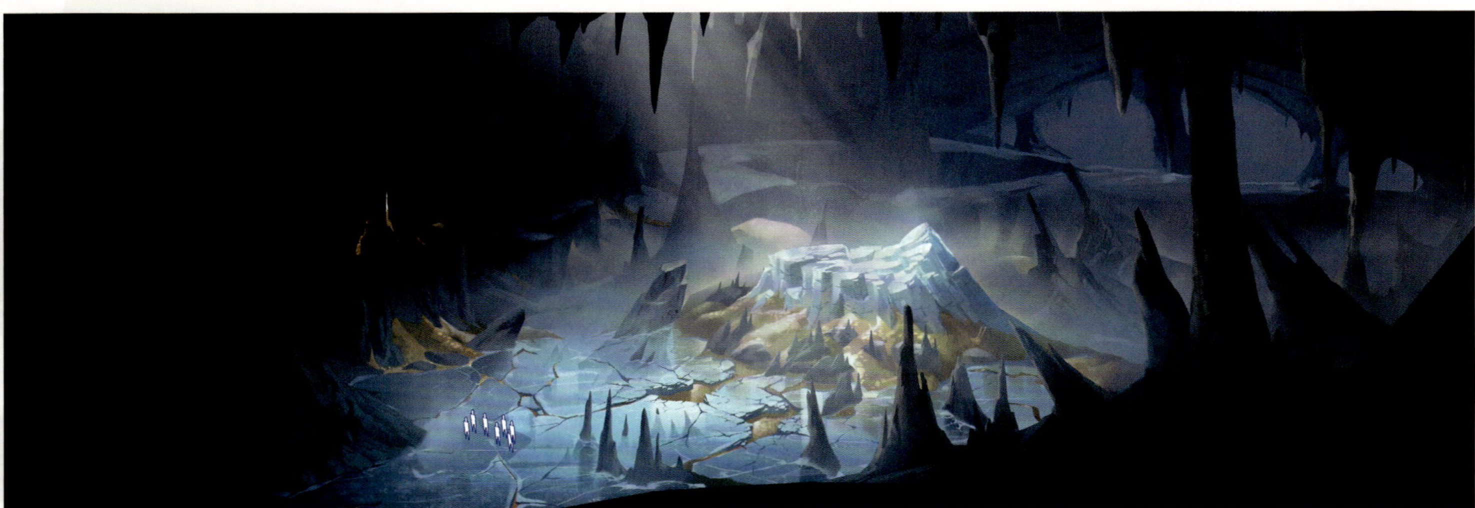

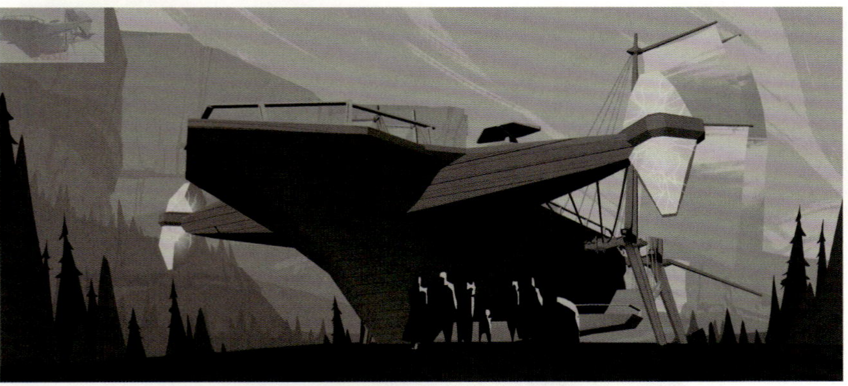

Airship

The airship was one of the first CG pieces the design team had to tackle in the series. Arthur Loftis originally drew the airship as in the background of an early Emon concept design, and the writing team ran with it, working it more into the story to showcase it.

> *"Isn't this ship amazing, there's TWO bathrooms downstairs."*
>
> – SCANLAN, S1E1 "THE TERROR OF TAL'DOREI PART 1"

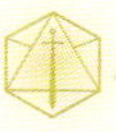

FROM SCRIPT TO SCREEN

MEETING GILMORE

EXT. GILMORE'S GLORIOUS GOODS - DAY

An exotic and extravagantly painted MAGICAL SHOP, draped with purple cloths and tassels.

INT. GILMORE'S GLORIOUS GOODS - CONTINUOUS

Enter a lavish store filled with everything anyone could want, *for a price*. Magical weapons and items, potions, armor - Gilmore has it all!

Vax and Pike enter through a door draped with purple cloth. The place is empty.

57 GILMORE (O.S.)
Enter. I see you've come seeking assistance of the arcane.

From a balcony, REVEAL-

SHAUN GILMORE, the most fabulous store owner in all of Tal'Dorei!

Middle Eastern in appearance and clad in gold-trimmed purple garb, fingers studded with jeweled rings.

57 GILMORE (CONT'D)
Welcome to Gilmore's Glorious Goods! Enchanted Curios and magical artifacts at discounted prices. I take gold, silver, platinum-
(Sees Vax and GASPS)
Why if it isn't the mysterious Vax'ildan! I was hoping you would swing back through again.

He strolls over and gives Vax an EPIC hug. As they flirt with each other:

58 VAX
(delighted to see him)
Glad to see you've lost none of your charm... Gilmore.

Gilmore is all smiles.

59 GILMORE
Oh, listen to you. Don't. Stop. I can't take it.
(then)
I've missed your visits.

ON Pike, uncomfortable, she waves awkwardly.

59A PIKE
Hi.

GILMORE
So, are you here on business, or pleasure?

Pike wanders around checking out various magical items. In the foreground she finds a book titled "Tusk Love".

Vax goes on as Pike flips through pages, tilting her head in curiosity.

60 VAX
Business, I'm afraid. We need information on blue dragons. Particularly... how to kill them.

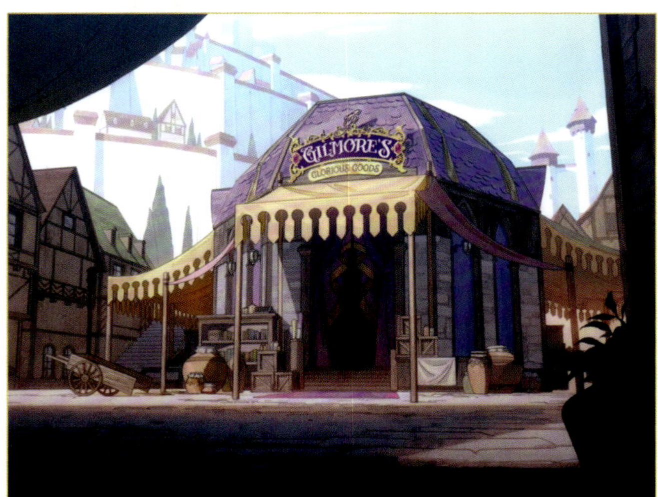

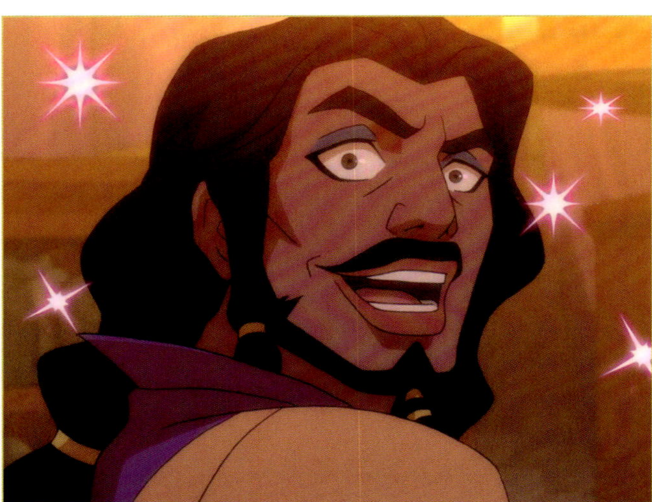

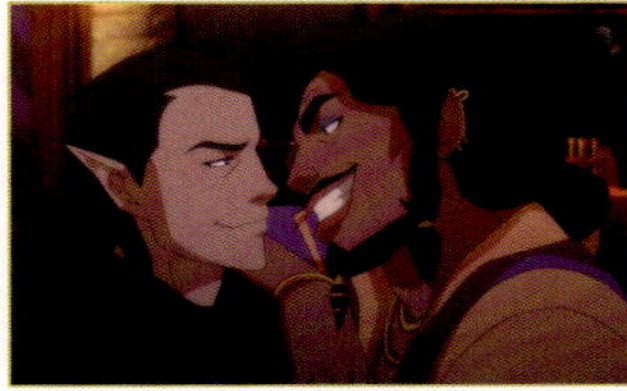

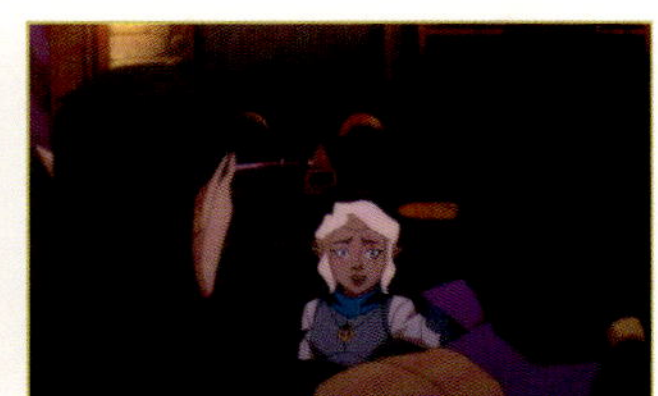

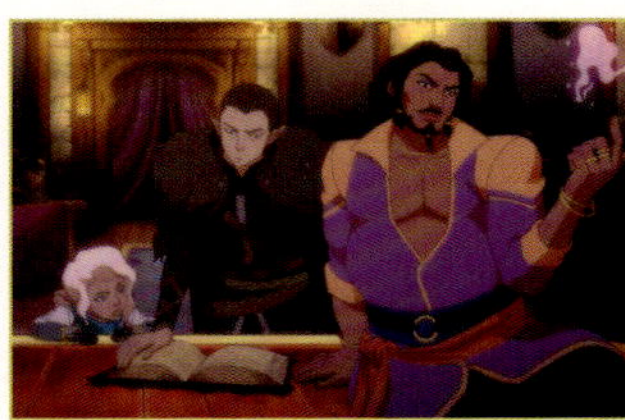

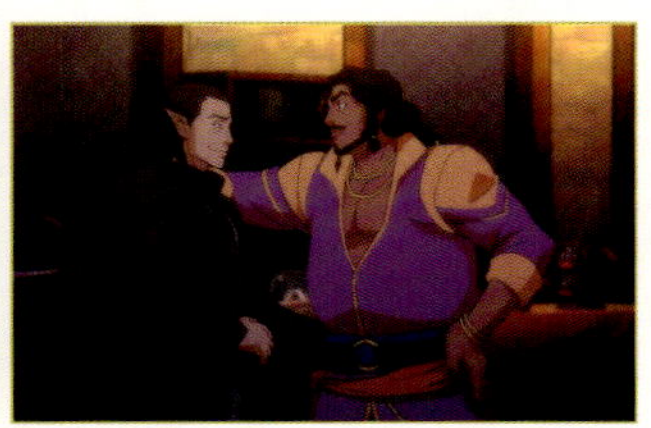

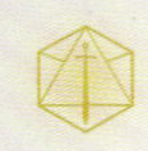

EPISODE 3

THE FEAST OF REALMS

"I love a dinner party as much as the next guy, but this one was kind of a snooze. Not sure why The Briarwoods chose to party crash. I could've given them several other ideas for a proper night out on the town in Emon. Instead, they trigger an aggro side of Percy that none of us have ever seen. Come on, 'your soul is forfeit'? What kind of gothic emo boy fantasy are we living in here?" – A RECOUNTING OF "THE FEAST OF REALMS" BY SCANLAN SHORTHALT

Sylas Briarwood

Having returned from the dead after his wife's bargain with The Whispered One, he walks among the living as a creature stuck between life and death. Though his vampiric nature leaves him bloodthirsty and ready for a fight, he harbors a passionate love for his wife and would follow her to the ends of the earth.

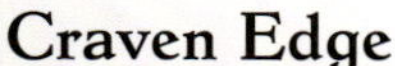

Craven Edge

Sylas's sinister sword that, like Sylas, drinks the blood from its victim. The more blood it drinks, the larger it grows.

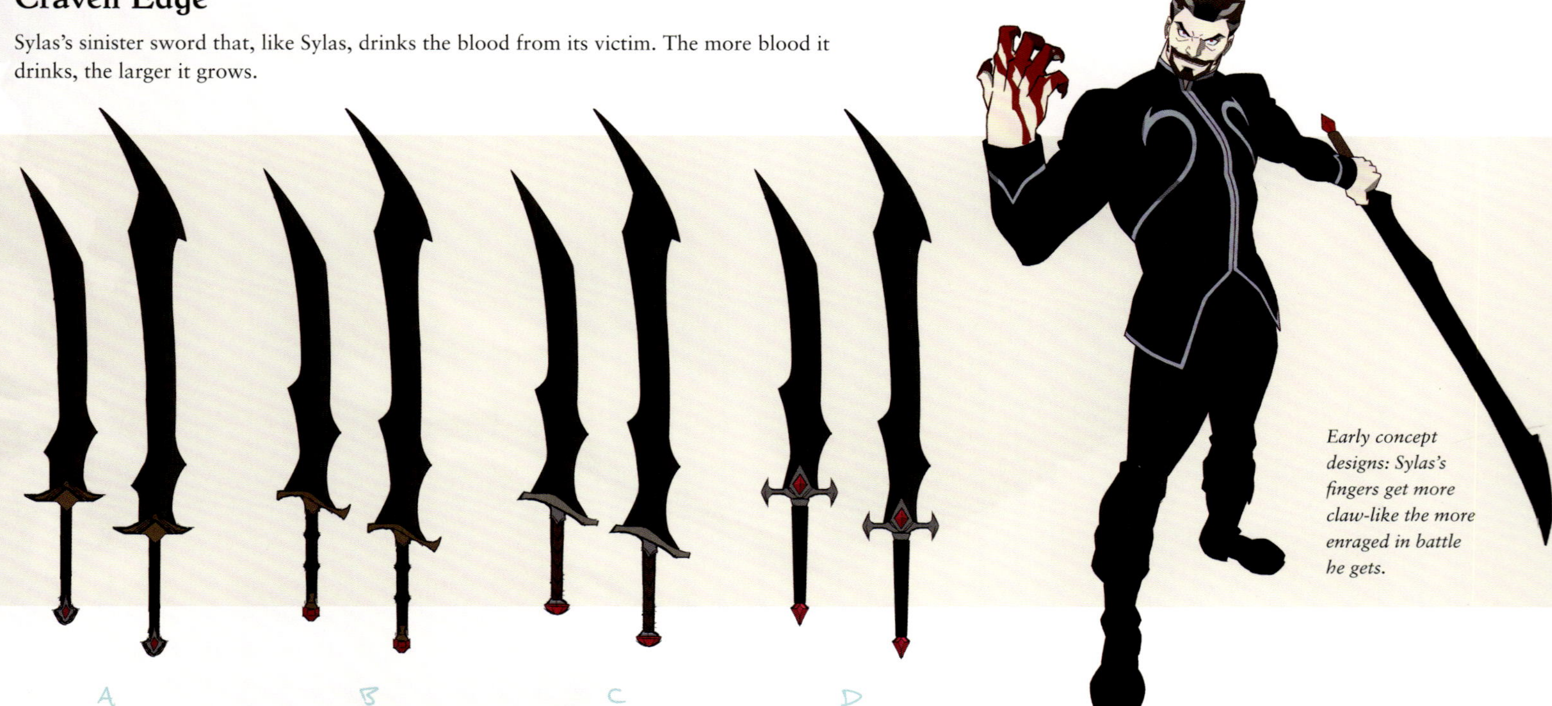

Early concept designs: Sylas's fingers get more claw-like the more enraged in battle he gets.

Delilah Briarwood

Scarred by the untimely death of her beloved Sylas, Delilah strikes a deal with The Whispered One for him to return as a vampire. Her design highlights her refined and elegant nature while alluding to the necrotic power she wields. In other words, she's a real bad bitch.

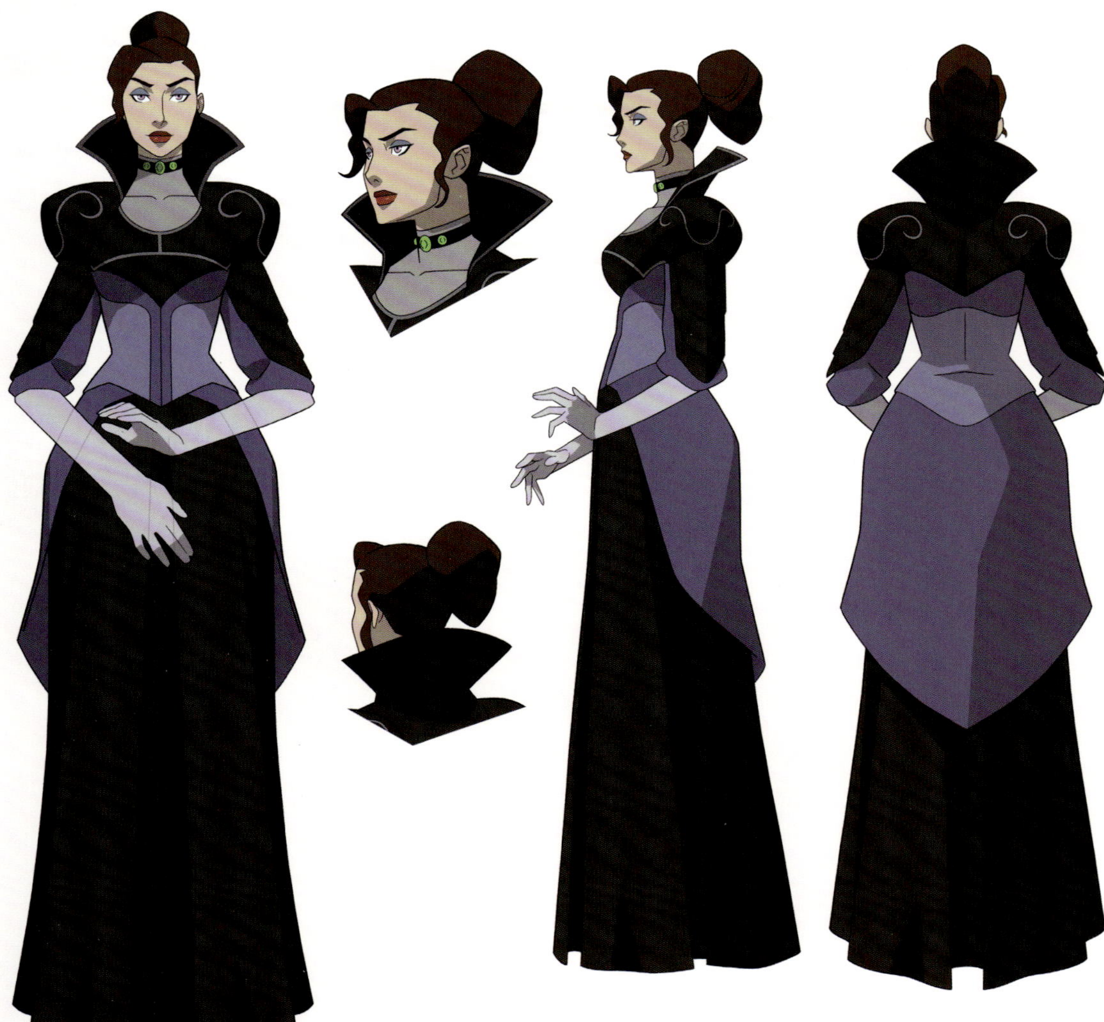

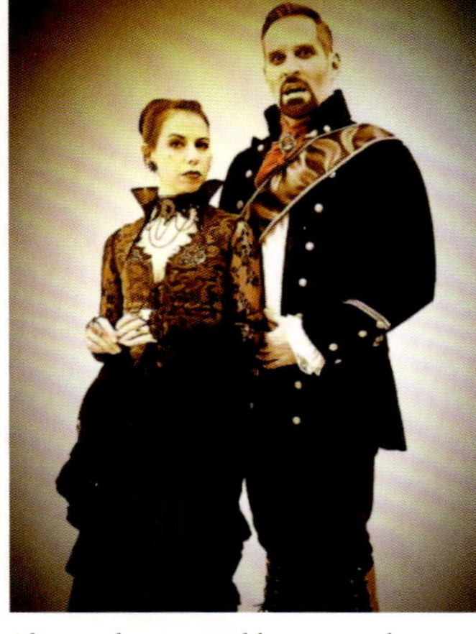

Photo reference used by artists of Laura Bailey and Travis Willingham dressed as Delilah and Sylas for Halloween in 2016.

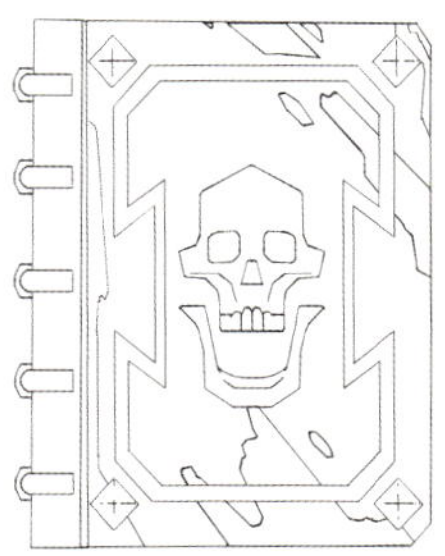

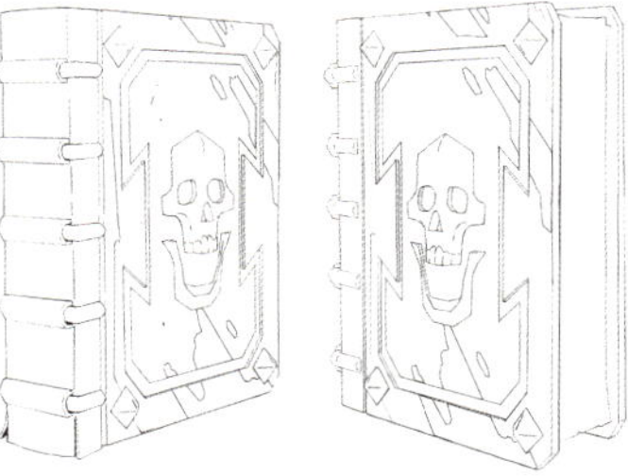

Delilah's Necklace

Given to her by The Whispered One, the writers initially gave her this necklace because when she originally takes out Pike during their first battle, they were worried about the attack being too OP. An idea was floated that she had three "charges" of this powerful spell to keep her abilities in check, but it became unnecessary to track after fleshing out the rest of the season.

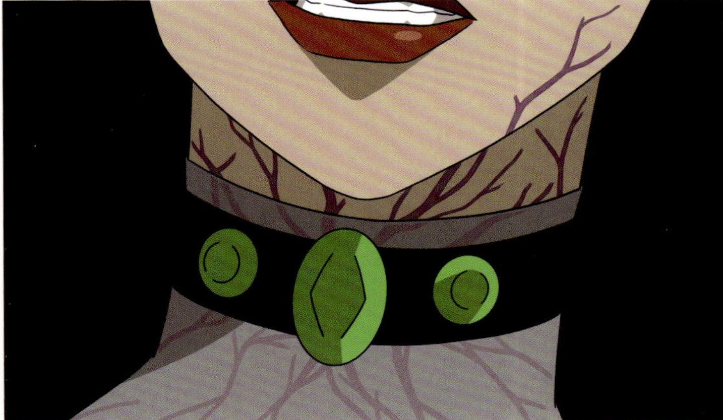

"When they arrived in Whitestone, The Briarwoods came as allies. But they brought dark ambitions and allowed no one to stand in their way. Not even children. They slaughtered us in cold blood, seizing my ancestral home." – PERCY, S1E4 "SHADOWS AT THE GATES"

Weapons Check Guard

Matt Mercer as... the weapons check guy! Be sure to leave a tip; he's had a rough night.

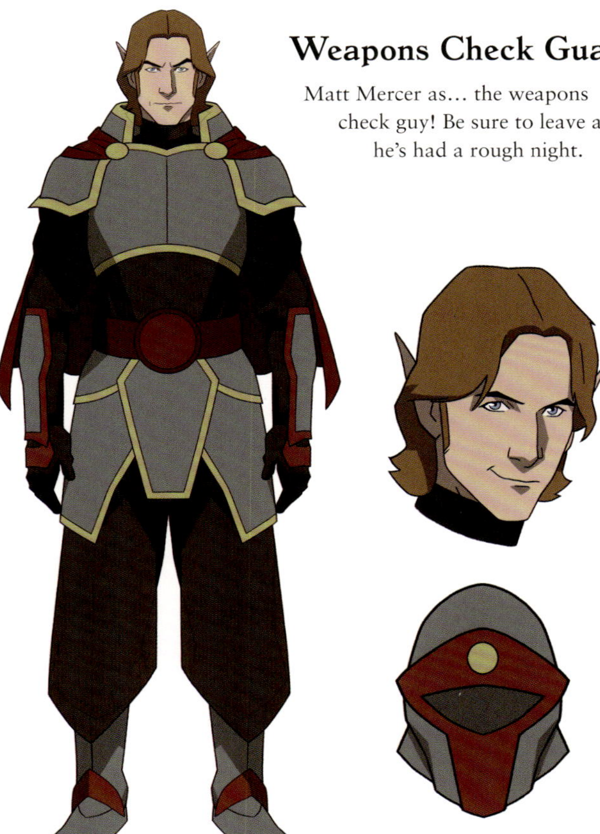

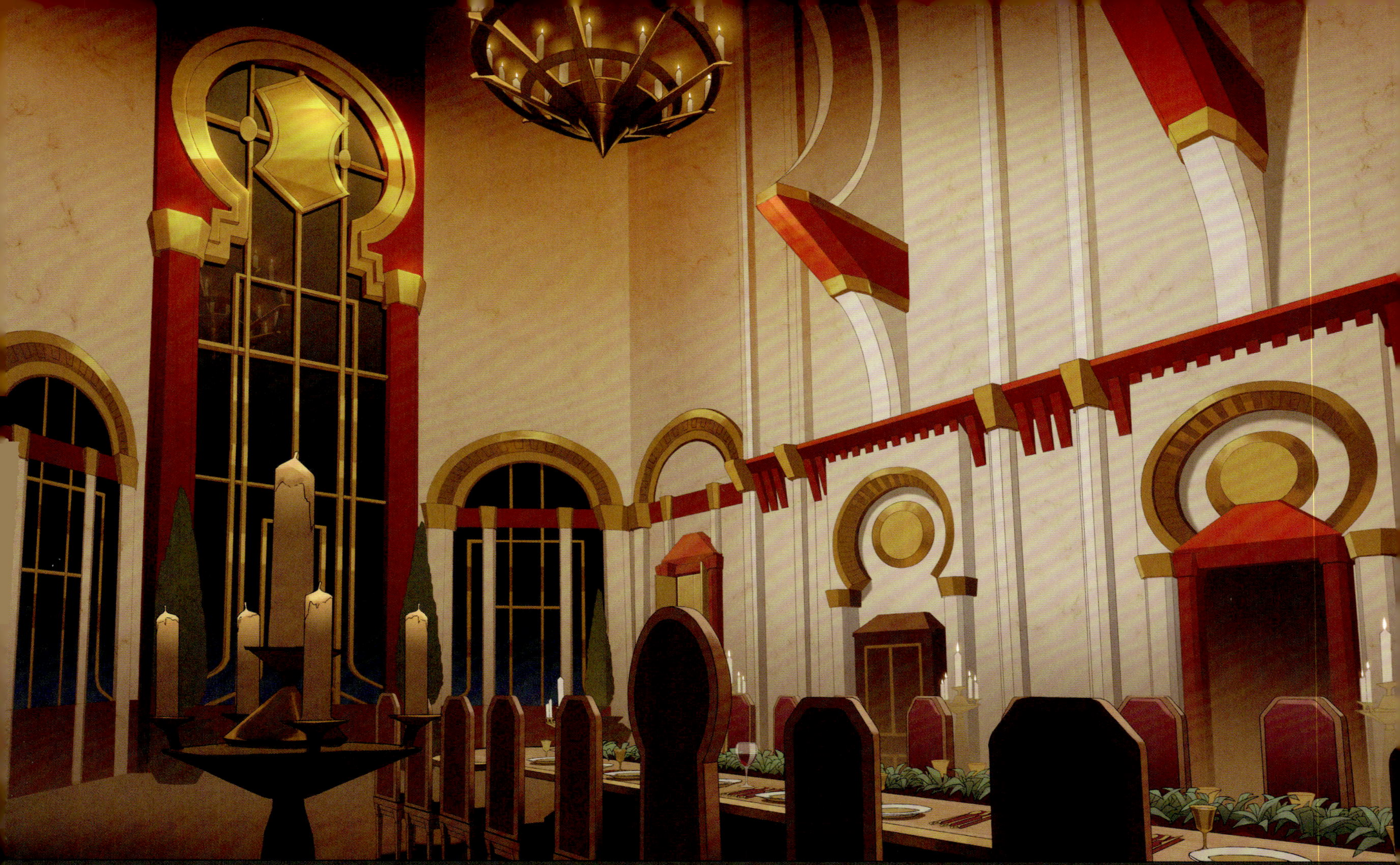

Emon Palace Ballroom

A grand room for all of Sovereign Uriel Tal'Dorei's receptions and banquets. Also a great stage for Scanlan to debut his hit single, *"Pull My Beads of Love."*

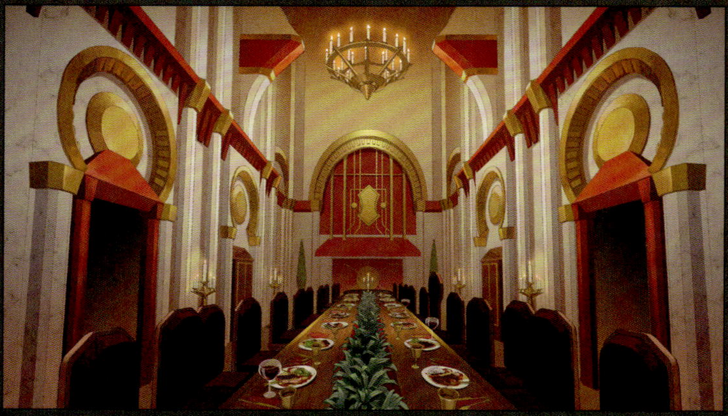

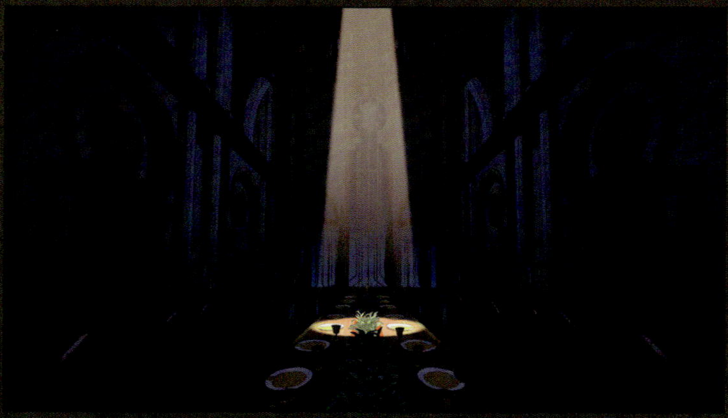

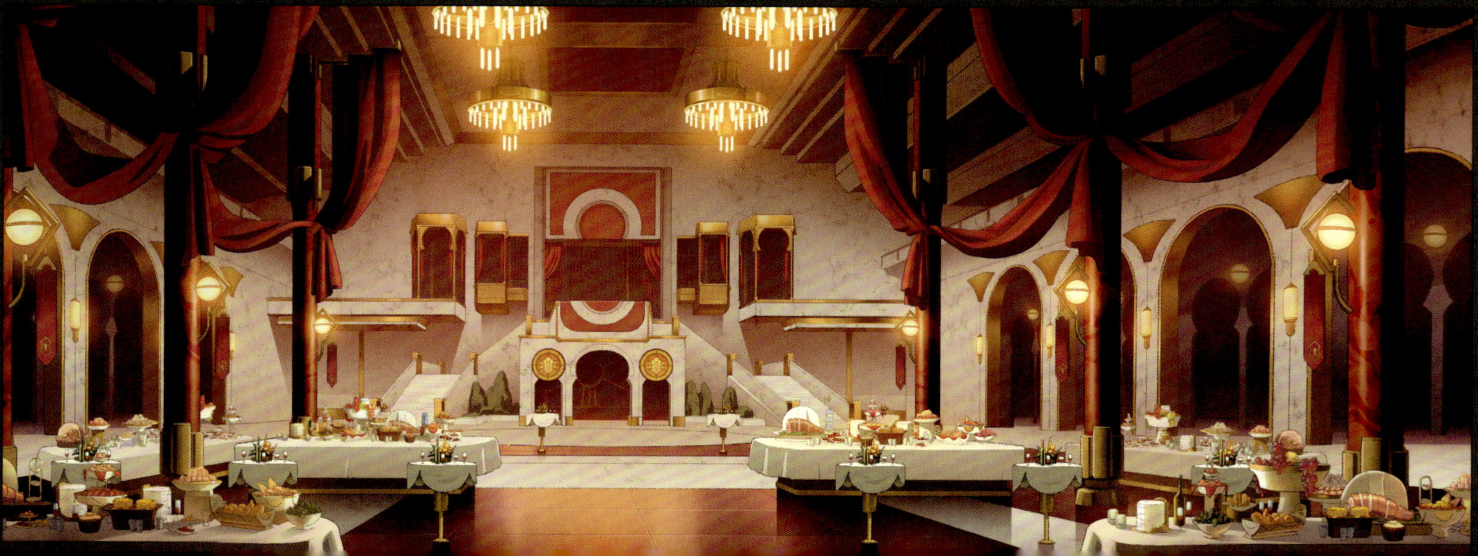

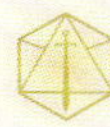

Briarwood Carriage

Vax's Belt a.k.a. Simon (The Snake)

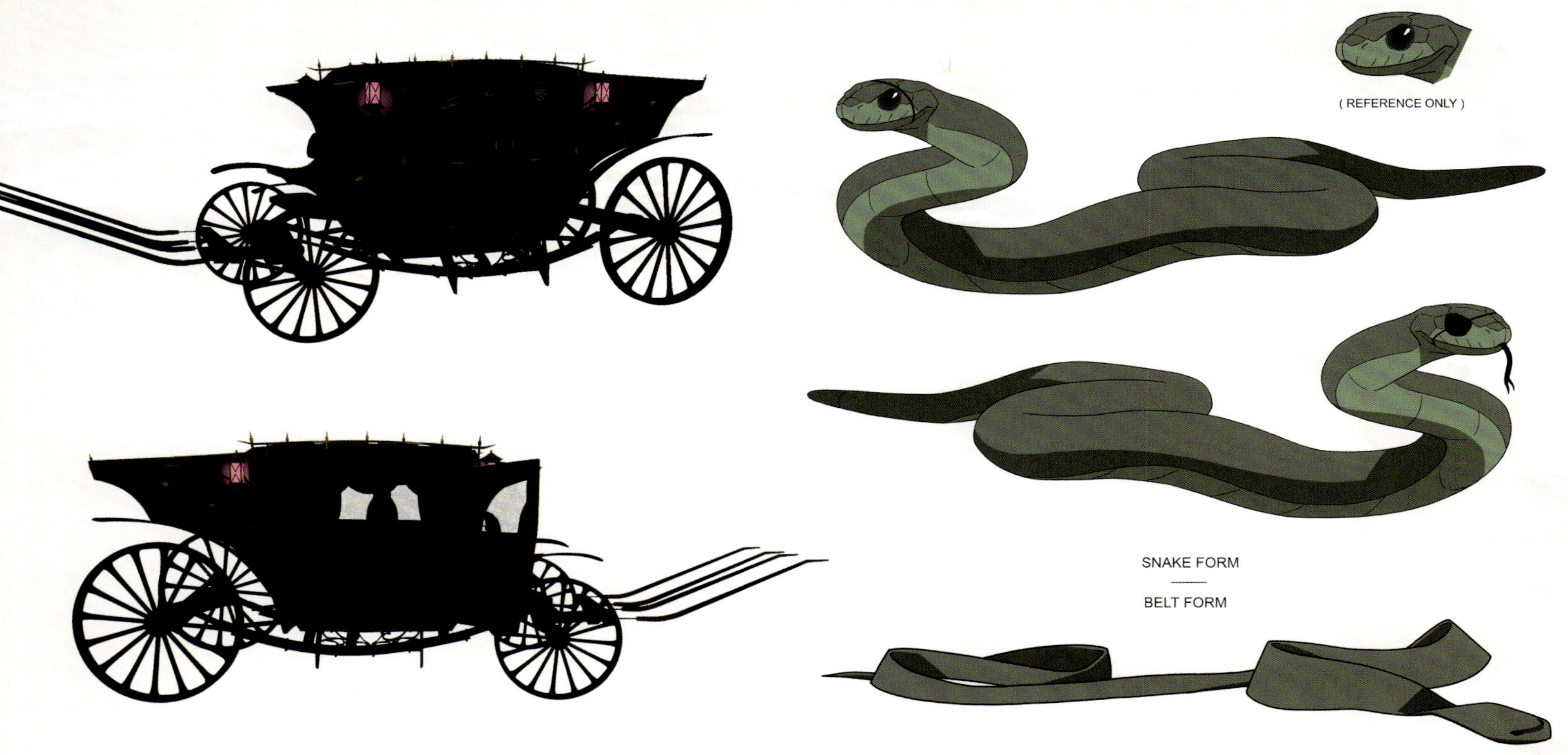

CG renderings of the Briarwood Carriage.

Formalwear Designs for Vox Machina

Even Grog needs a fancy loincloth from time to time.

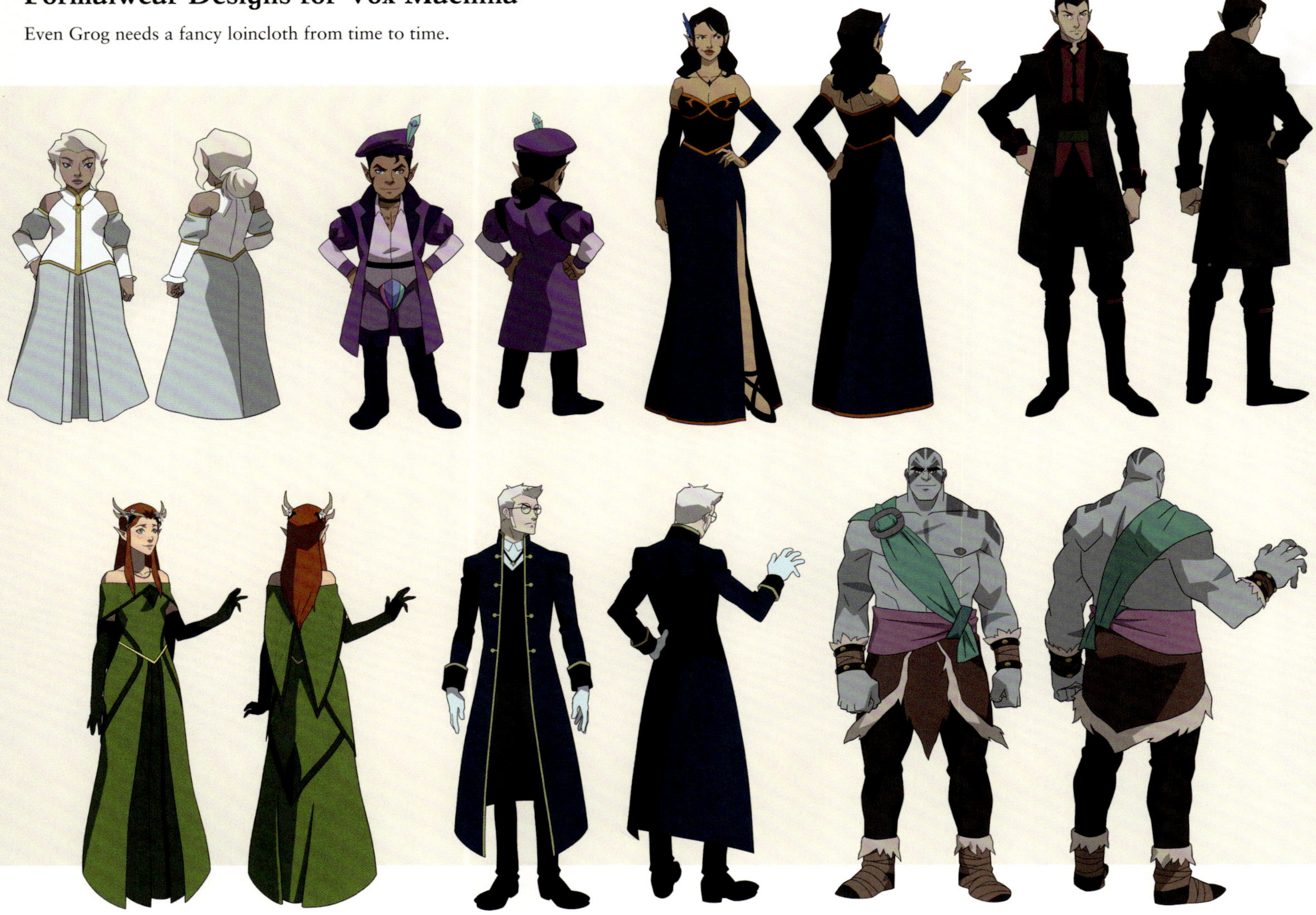

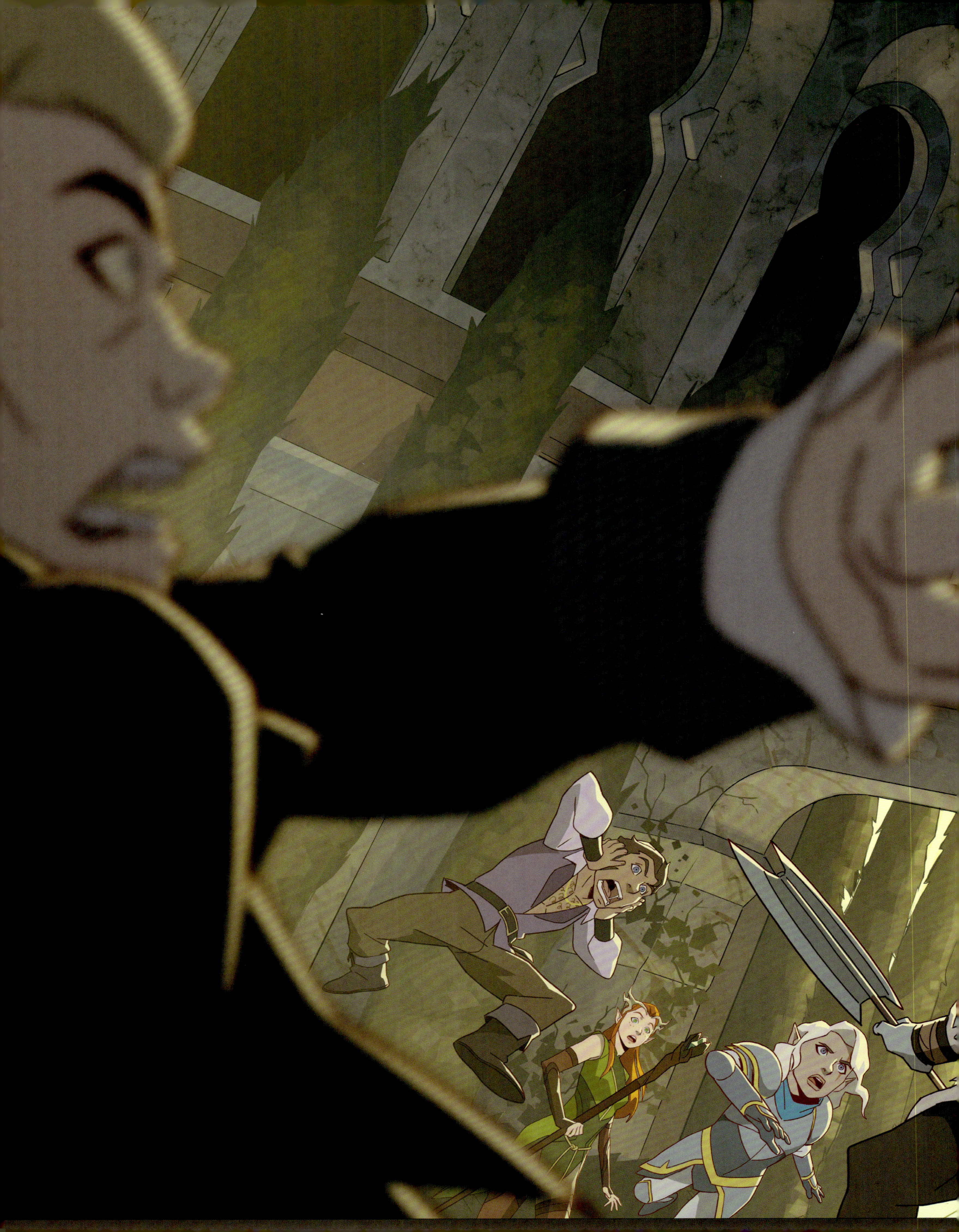

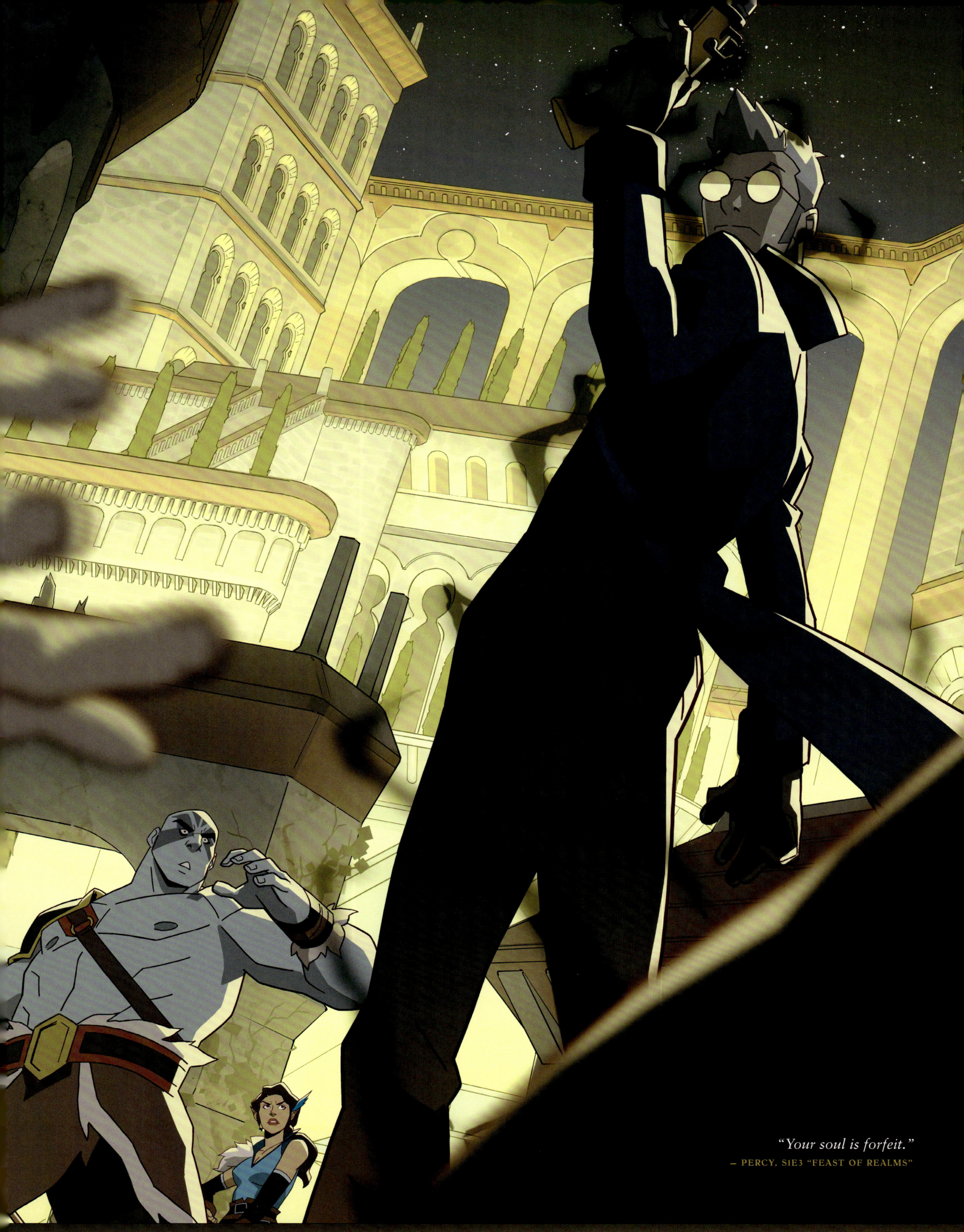

"Your soul is forfeit."
– PERCY, S1E3 "FEAST OF REALMS"

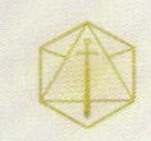

EPISODE 4

SHADOWS AT THE GATES

"After the Sovereign's dinner party is ruined, Vox Machina take the fall. Just shows how much saving the city from a dragon gets you. If you ask me, the whole thing could've easily been blamed on food poisoning. Have you seen the state of the palace kitchens lately? Anyway, your classic horror movie ensues when wraiths attack the keep, and while we really would have loved to see the justice system do its job, it was time to get the fuck out." – A RECOUNTING OF "SHADOWS AT THE GATES" BY SCANLAN SHORTHALT

Jarett Howarth

Loyal to the kingdom above all else, Jarett takes his duty of keeping Vox Machina under house arrest very seriously.

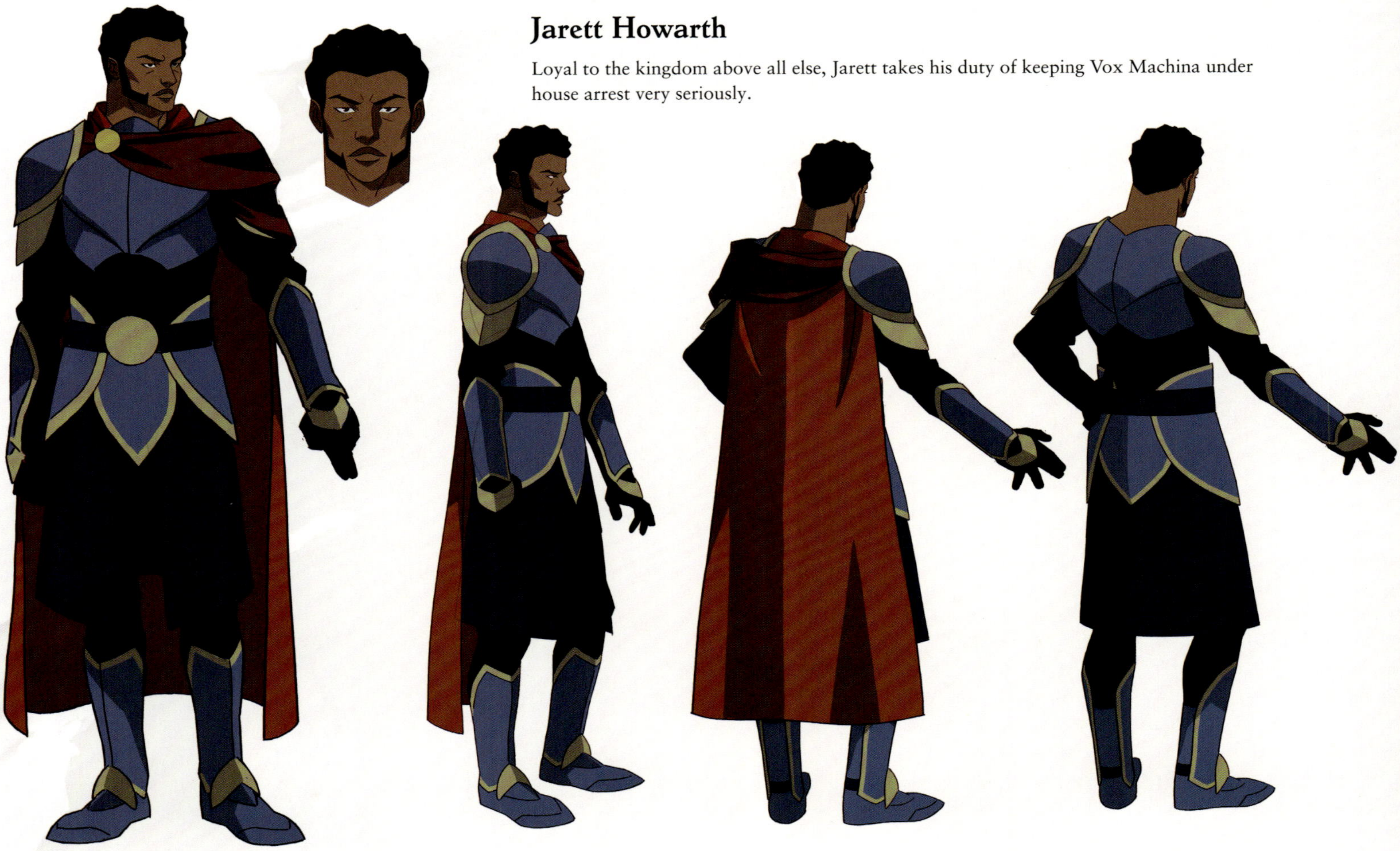

Wraiths

Sent by Delilah Briarwood, these creatures of the dead give us a ghastly look at the terror the Briarwoods can unleash. Their design was notably complicated to animate, but the art team was determined to push the visceral horror feel throughout.

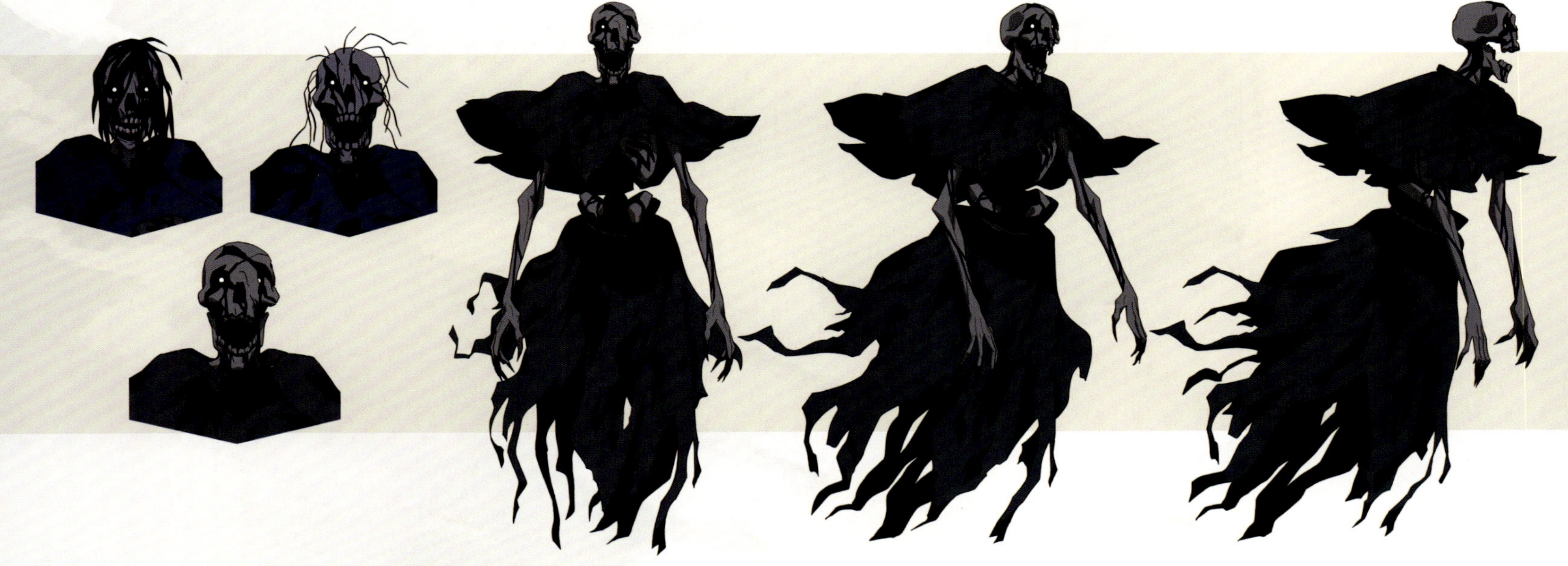

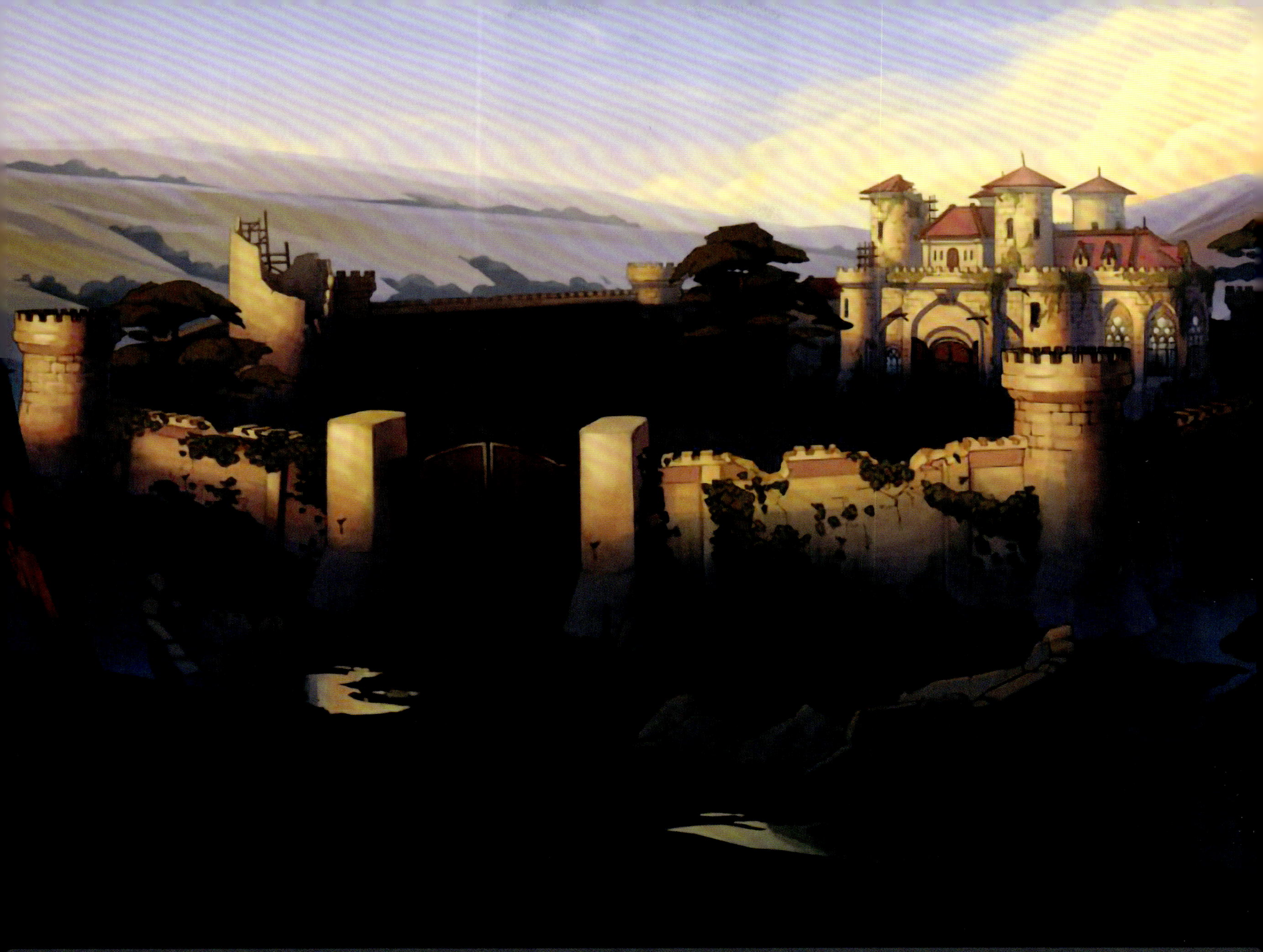

The Keep

A recurring trope in many a TTRPG game, as a reward for their bravery in fighting off the dragon Brimscythe, Vox Machina are offered a key to a keep instead of gold. Finally, a place to call home. Until they're all arrested and forced into house arrest–then it just becomes another prison they have to break out of.

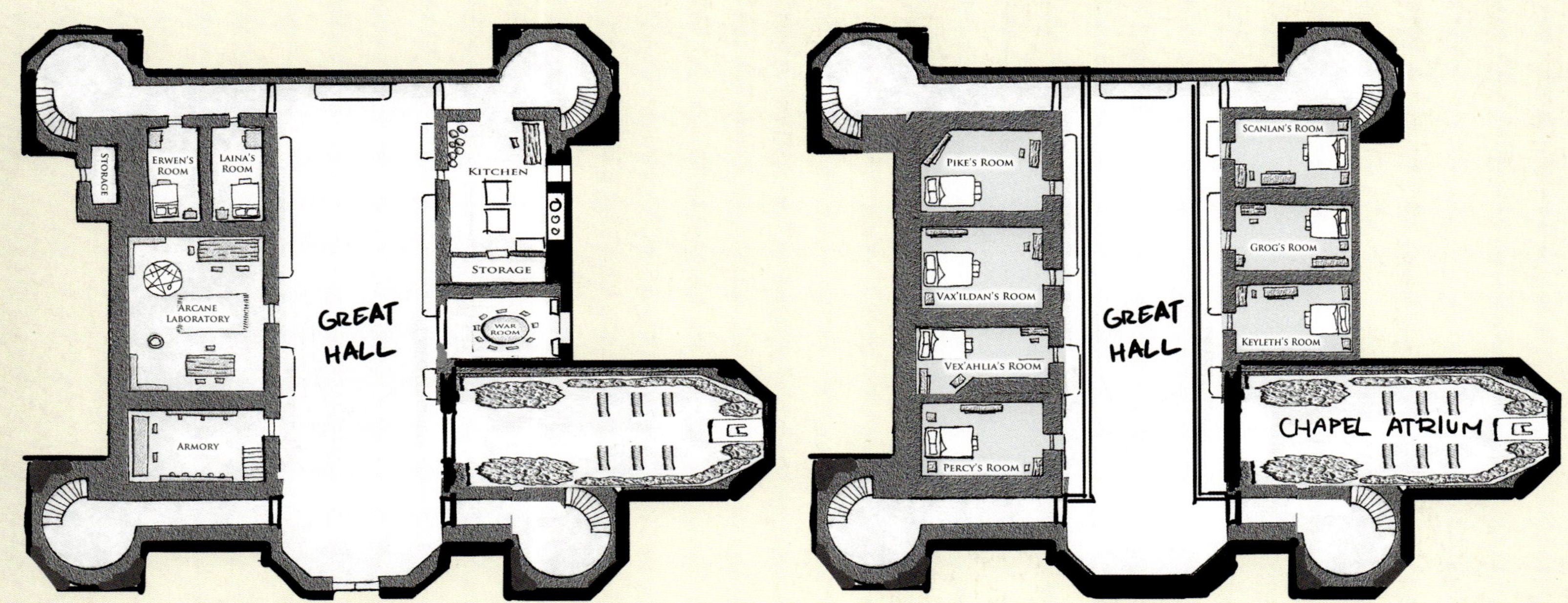

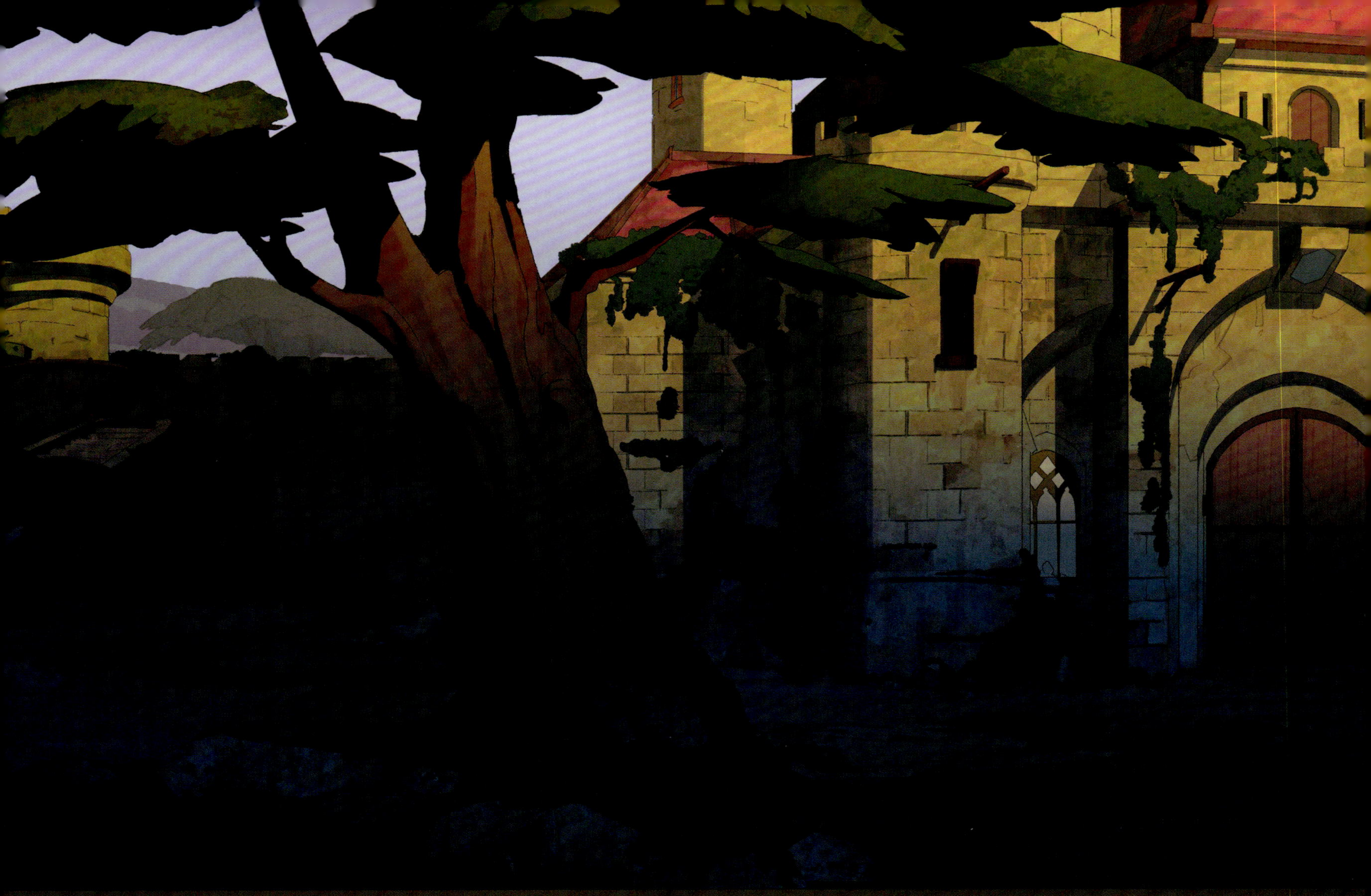

The Keep Exterior and Chapel

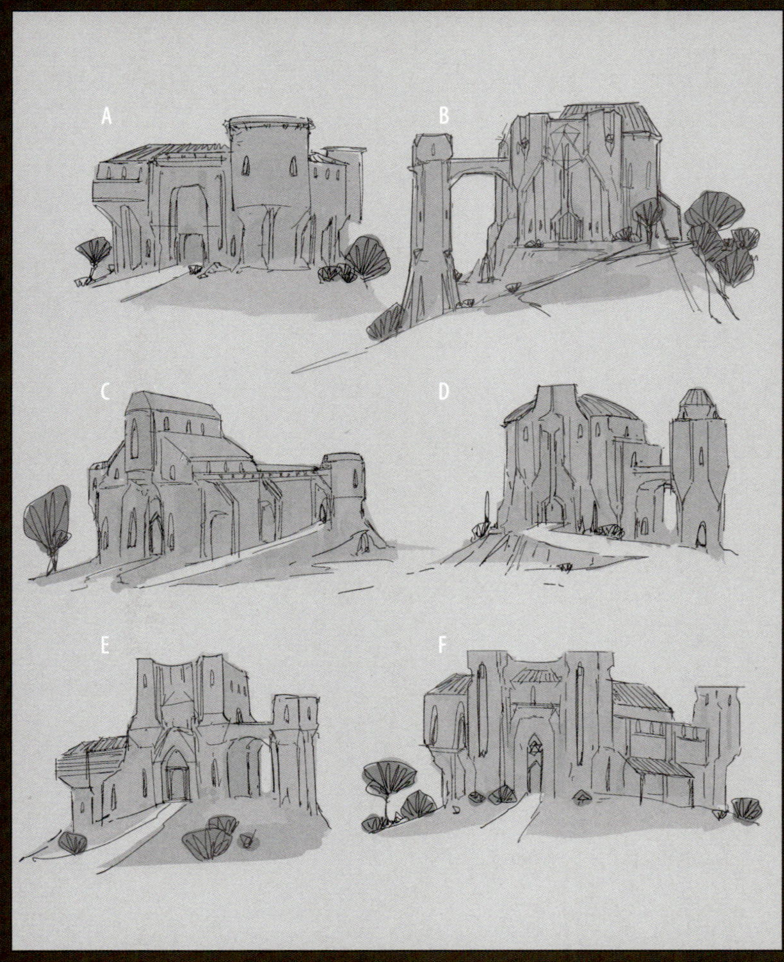

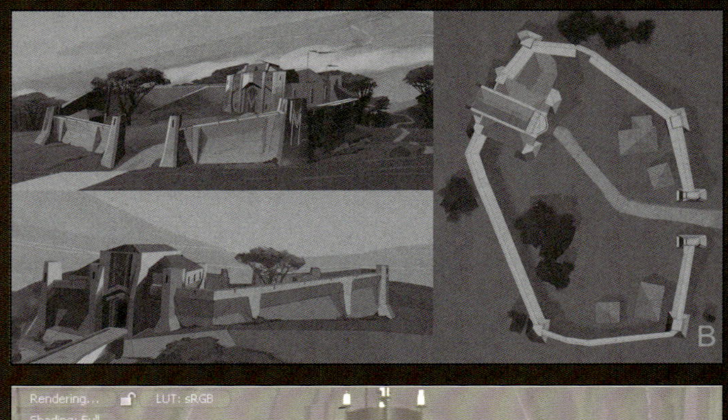

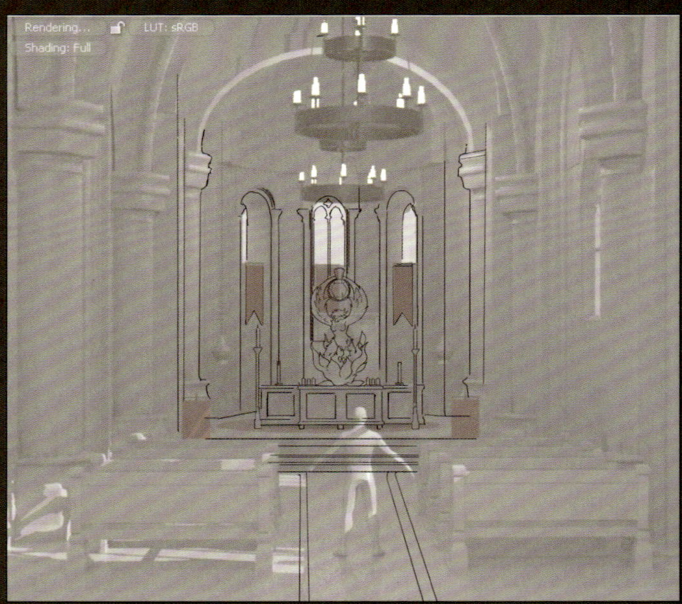

Sketches and renderings of the Keep's exterior by Arthur Loftis (Art Director). Interior sketch of Pike's chapel to The Everlight.

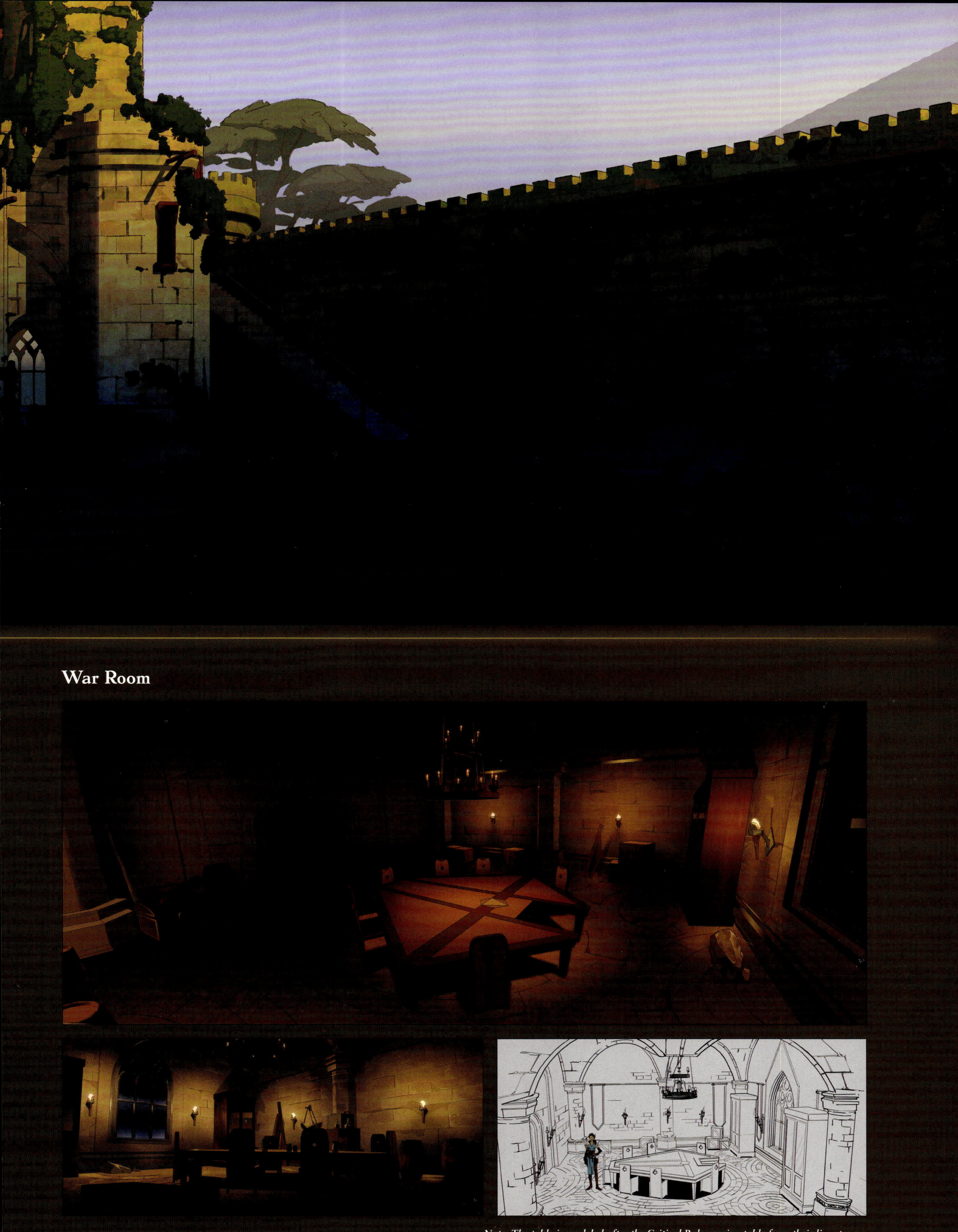

War Room

Note: The table is modeled after the Critical Role gaming table from their live stream.

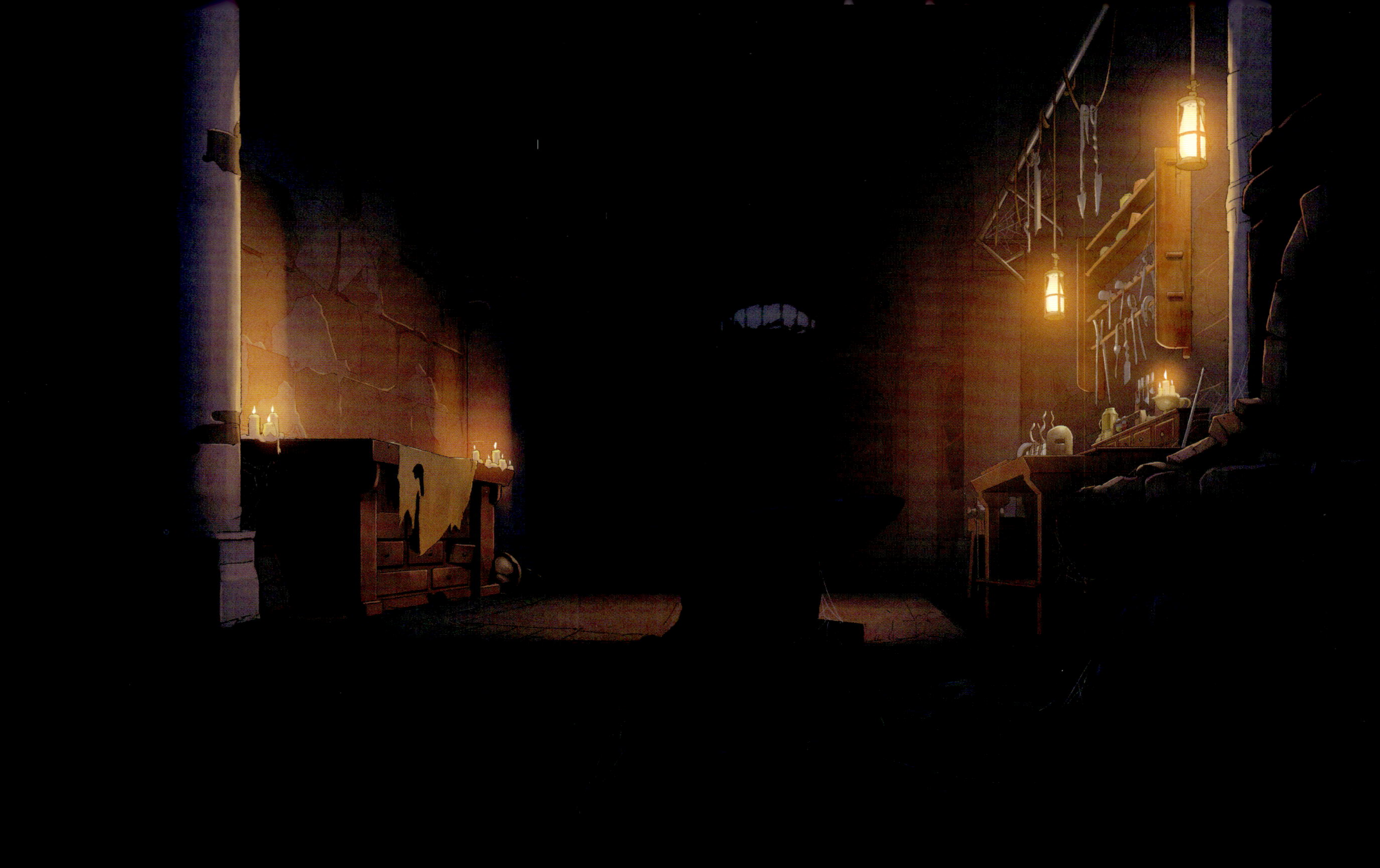

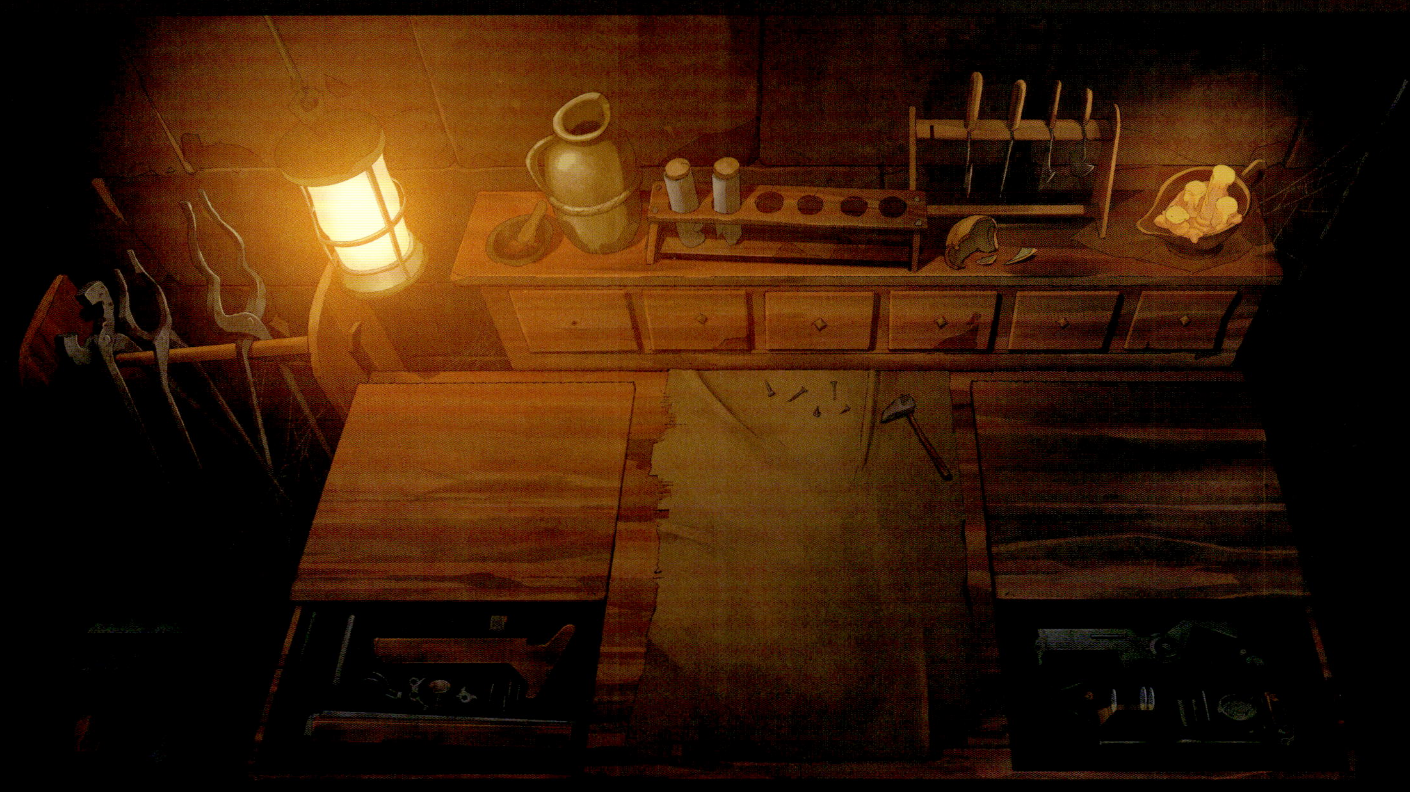

Percy's Workshop

Designs of Percy's workshop within Greyskull Keep. Mostly used for brooding.

Kitchen

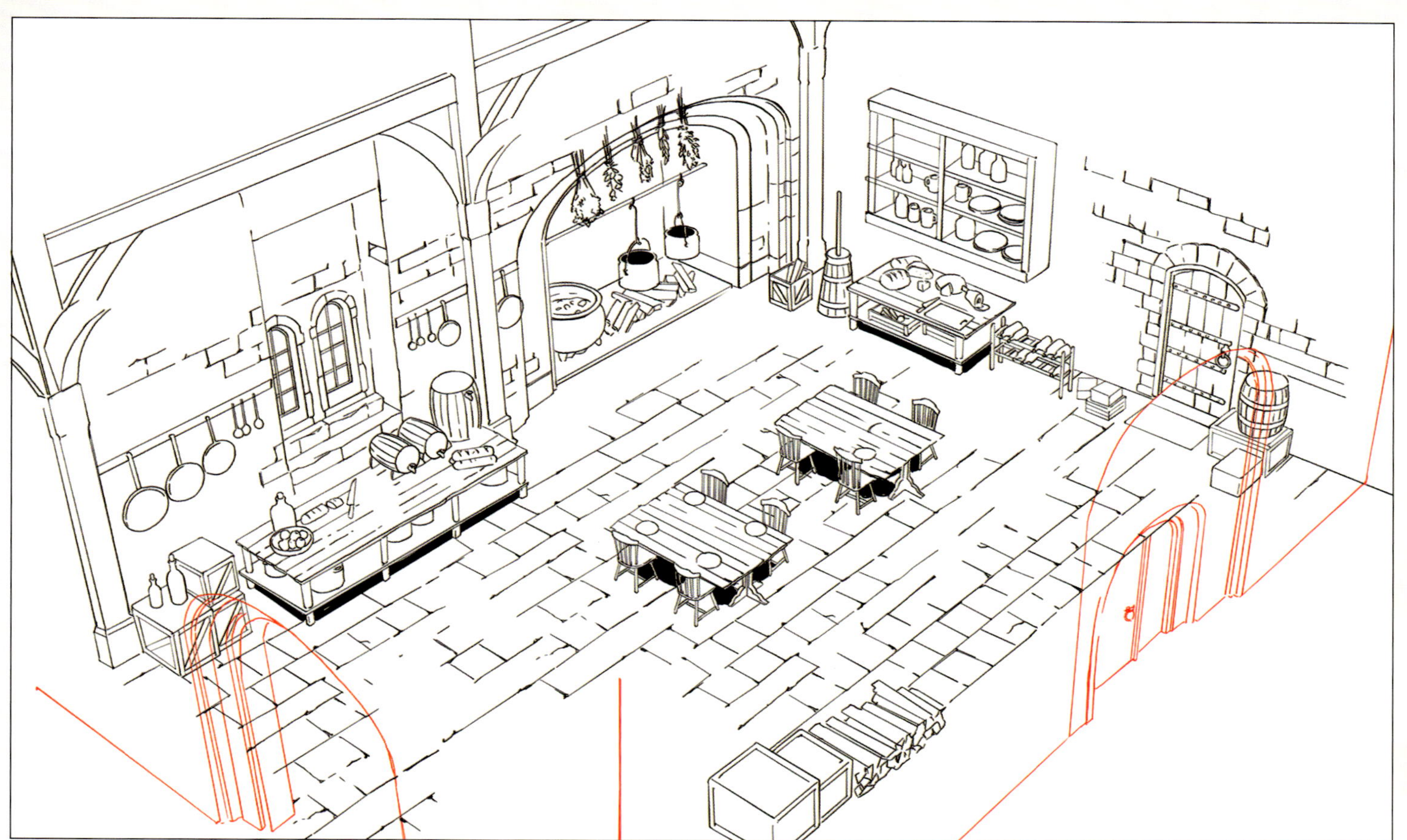

Layout of the kitchen in Greyskull Keep, complete with sandwich-making ingredients.

The Book of the Whispered One

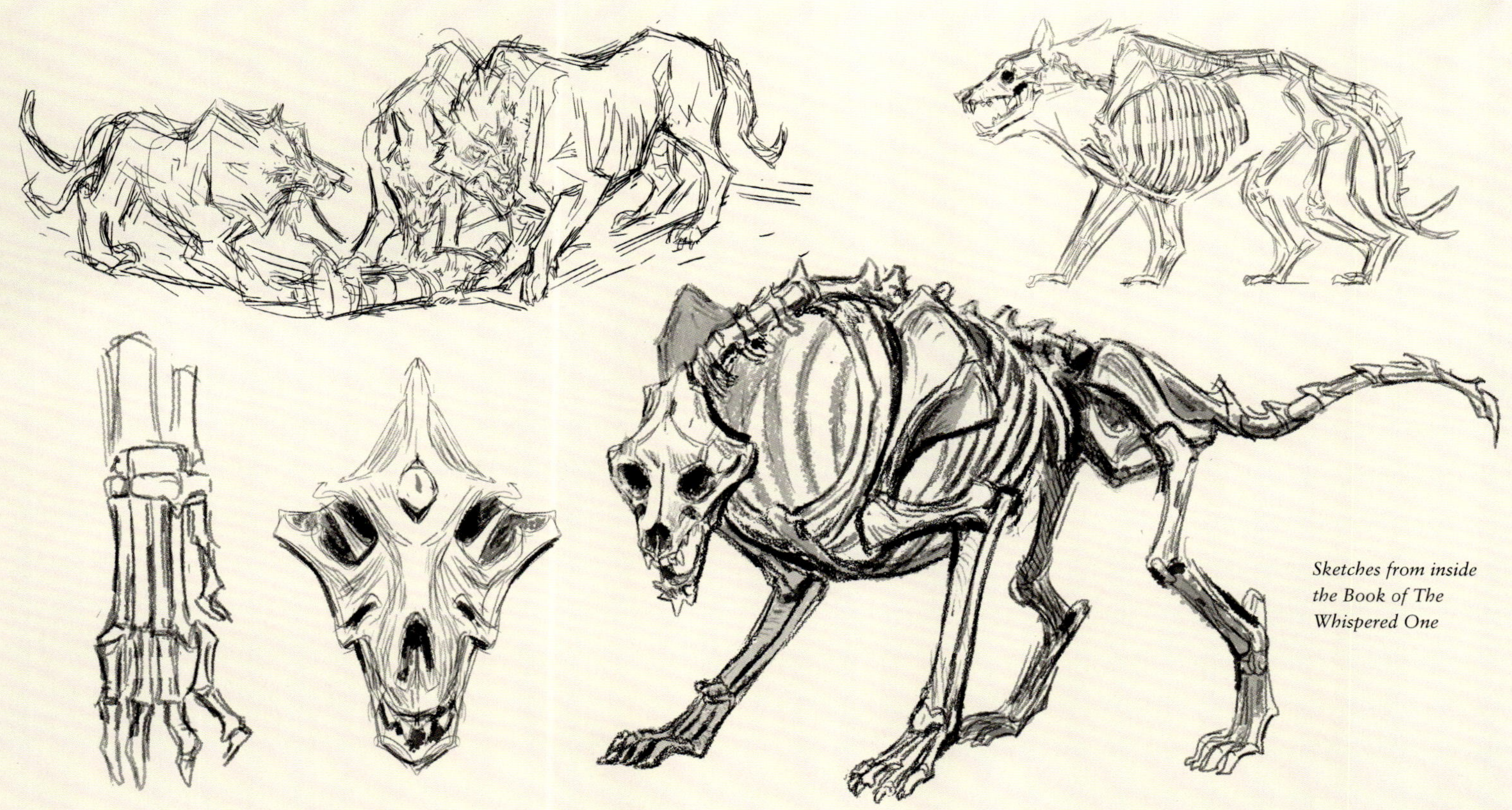

Sketches from inside the Book of The Whispered One

Vax: So, what does it say?
Scanlan: Oh, it says pyramid, spirits of the dead, and right here in tiny letters it says, "Fuck you, Vax." – S1E1 "SHADOWS AT THE GATES"

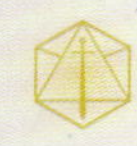

EPISODE 5

FATE'S JOURNEY

"We're off to Whitestone to kick some vampire ass! Vax catches the feels for 'Kiki,' Percy broods some more, and we all put our animal-handling checks to the test against some undead wolves. Yeeeesh. Glad I was able to easily translate Delilah's ancient book and completely prepare us for what's ahead." – A RECOUNTING OF "FATE'S JOURNEY" BY SCANLAN SHORTHALT

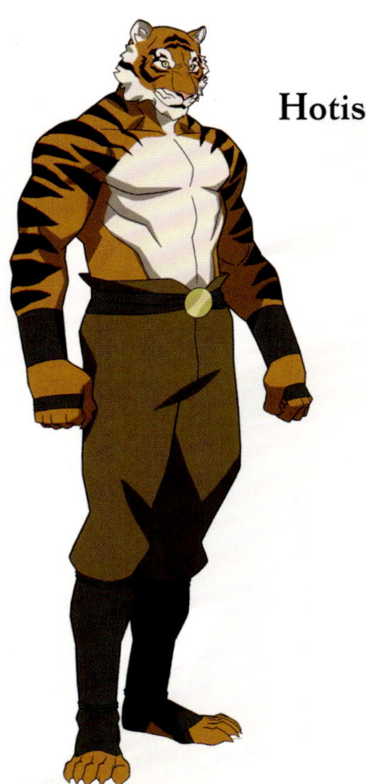

Hotis

A character from the live-streamed campaign, Hotis makes a cameo in this episode during a flashback scene in which Vox Machina recounts the strangest creature they ever killed.

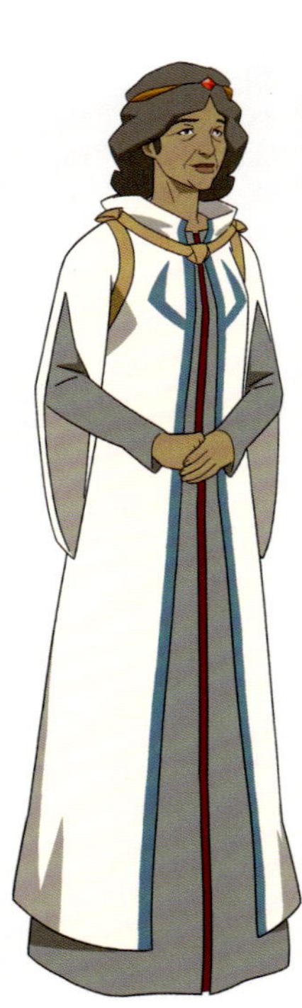

Head Cleric

A Cleric of the Everlight Pike seeks counsel from during her faith crisis.

"Whatever has happened to you, child, The Everlight accepts you as you are." – S1E5 "FATE'S JOURNEY"

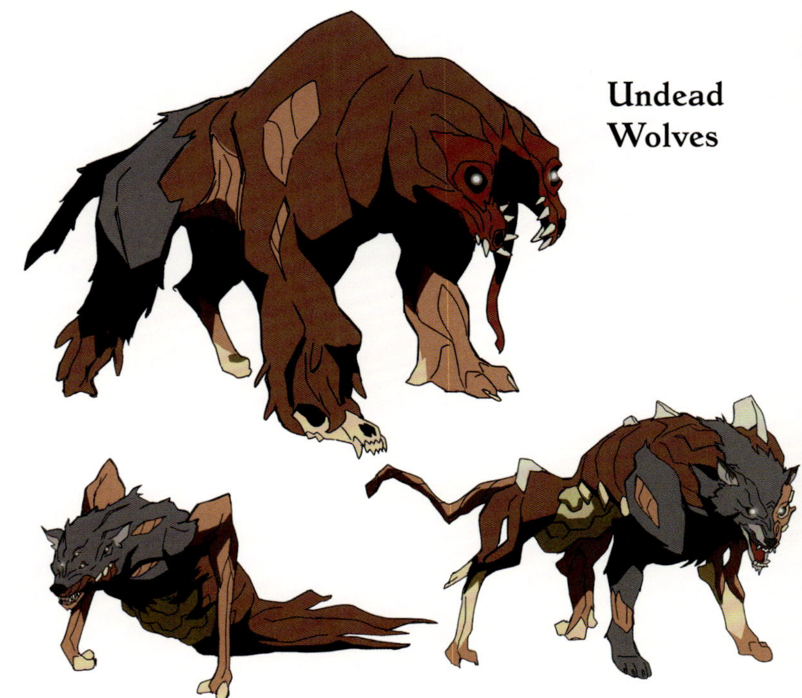

Undead Wolves

Early designs of the undead wolves that chase Vox Machina on their journey to Whitestone. These are meant to evoke the idea that Delilah mixed different creatures together during her necrotic experimentation. The designs were later simplified to aid with movement in animation.

Whitestone

Nestled in the valley of the Alabaster Sierras mountain range sits the gothic countryside town of Whitestone. While the design team pulled from the campaign when exploring the town's overall look, they also built upon the lore, exploring the histories of where its people came from and how they found themselves in Whitestone.

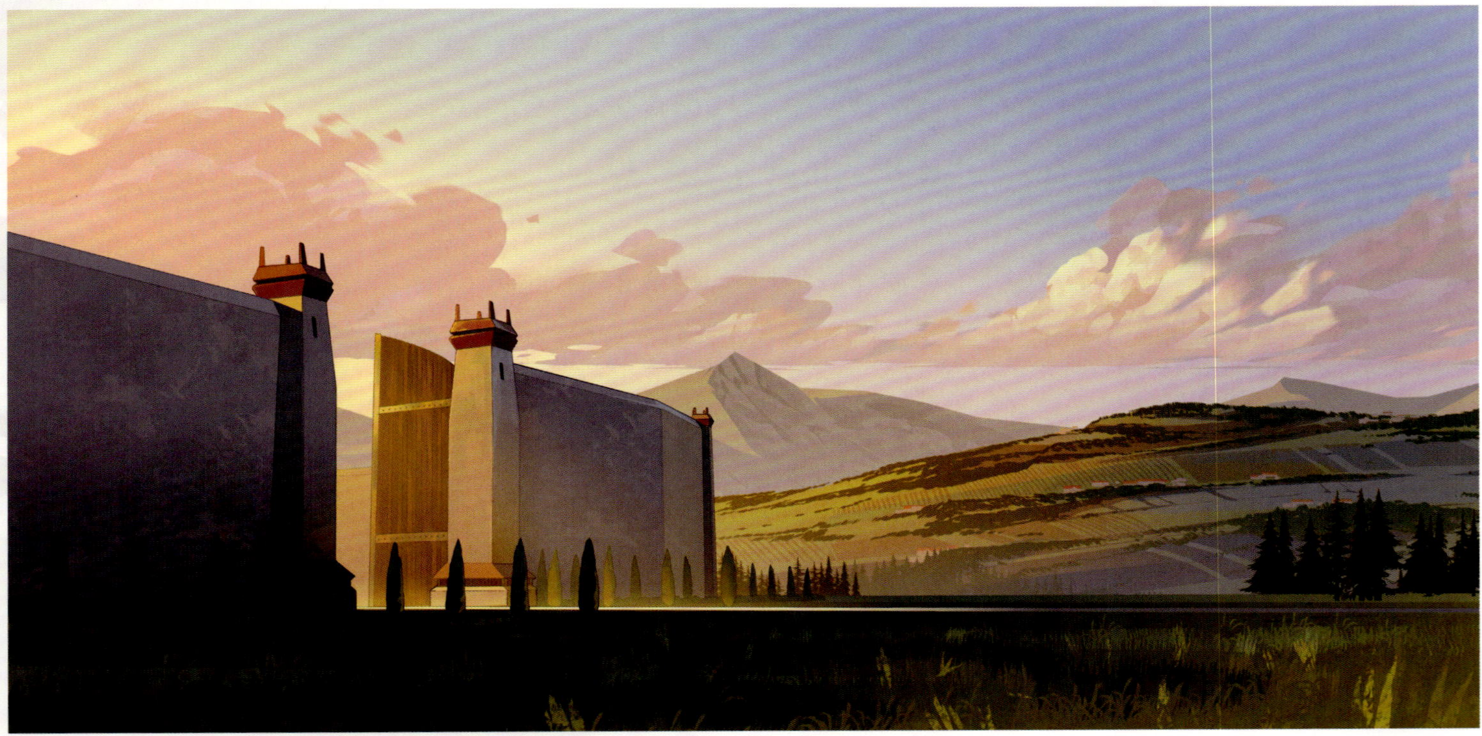

Storyboards from the Undead Wolves Chase

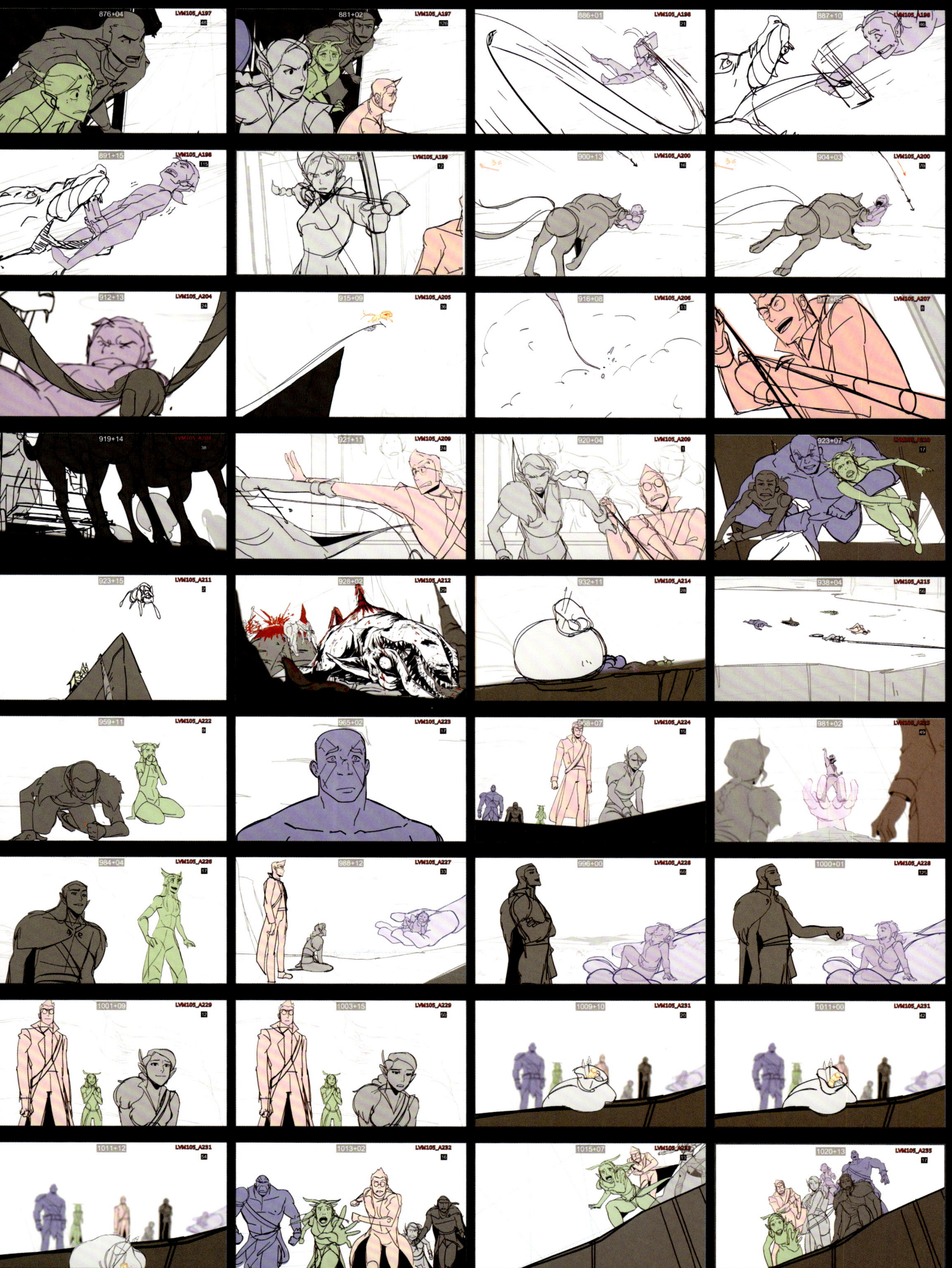

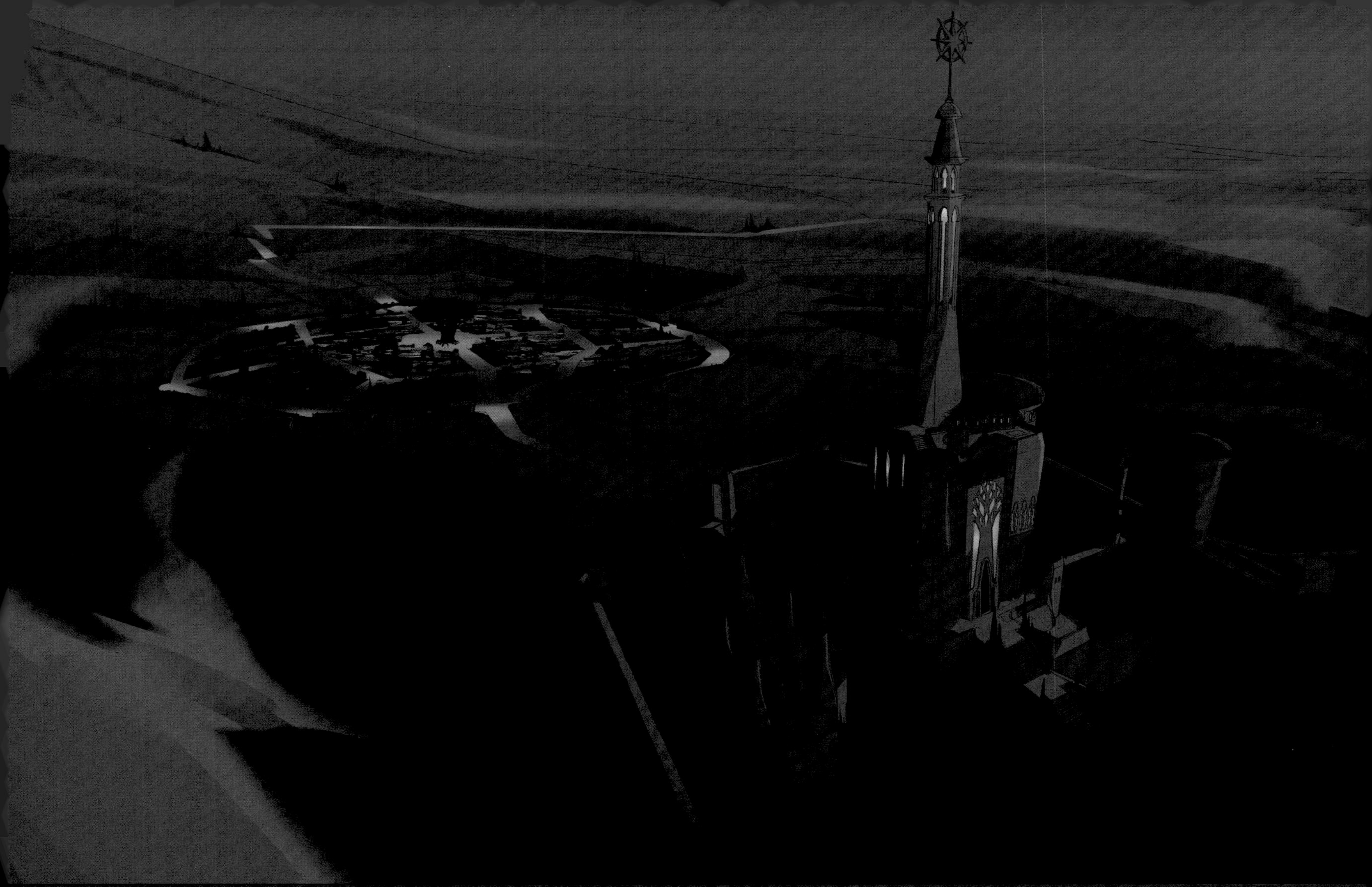

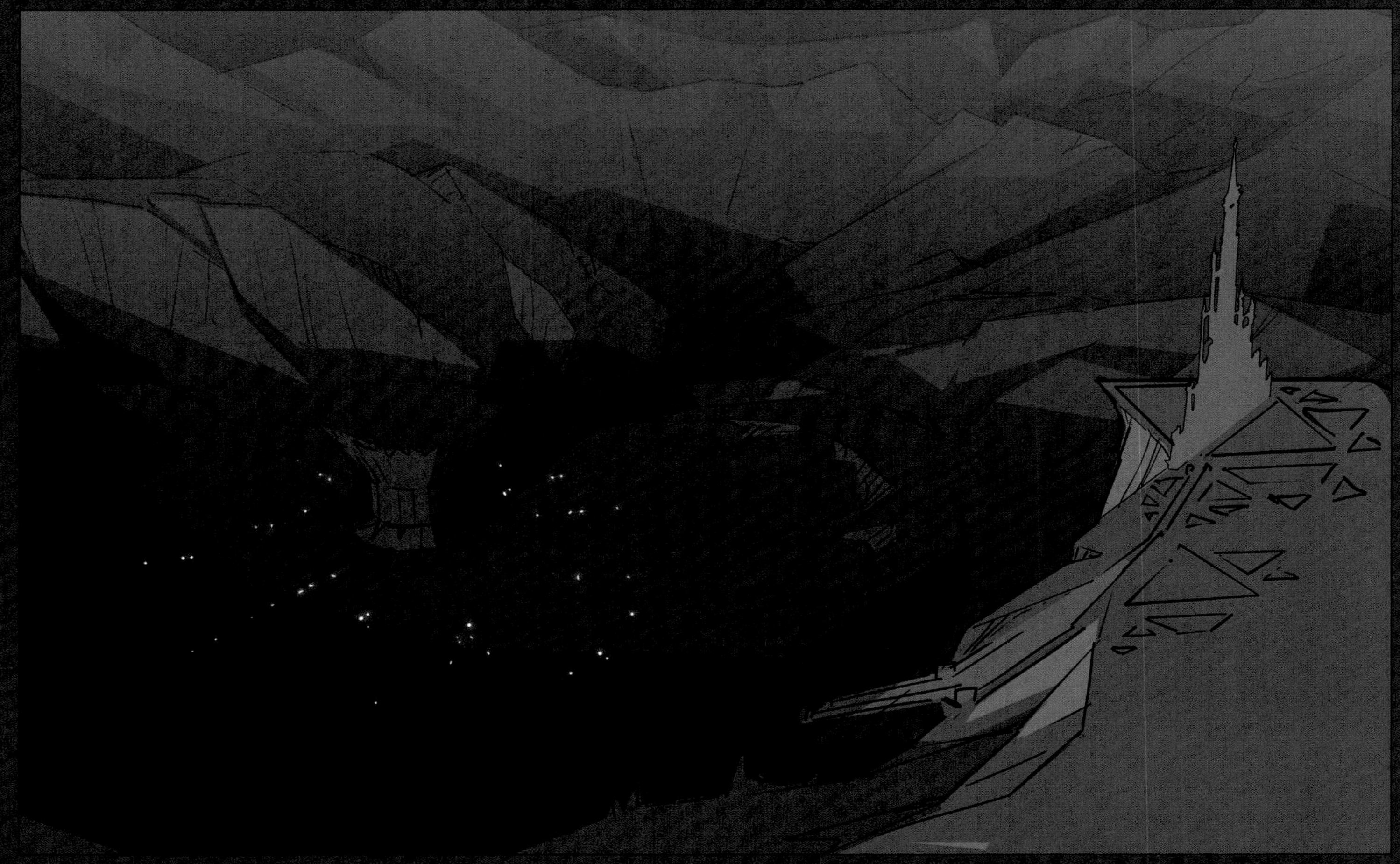

"When its people originally came over from Wildemount on boats, I imagined the craftspeople who made those boats were the same people to build the homes. They naturally used those skills and incorporated that seafaring design into the architecture of the town. You will see the roofs shaped like boat hulls as a nod to that history." — ARTHUR LOFTIS

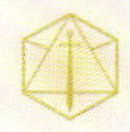

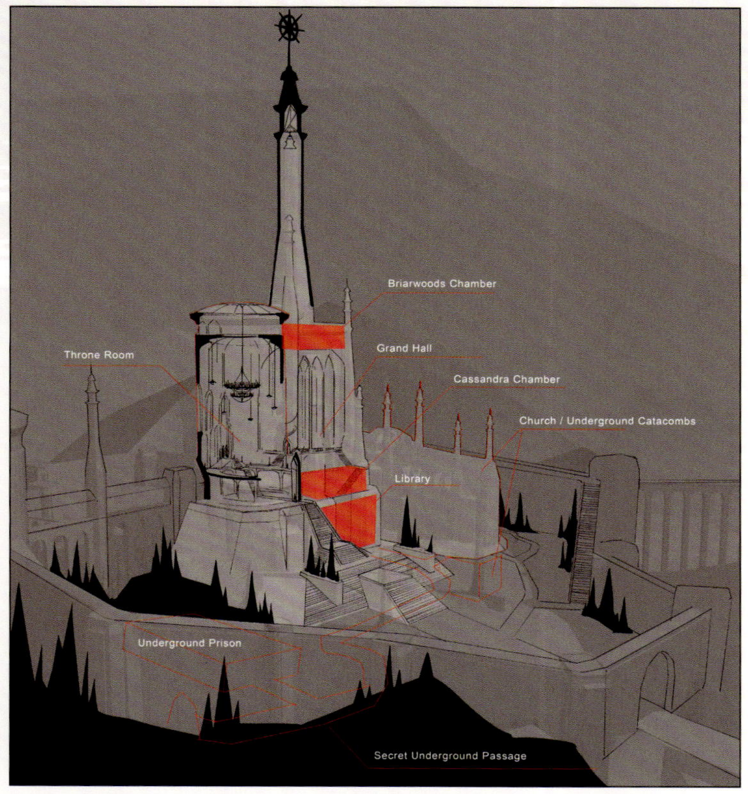

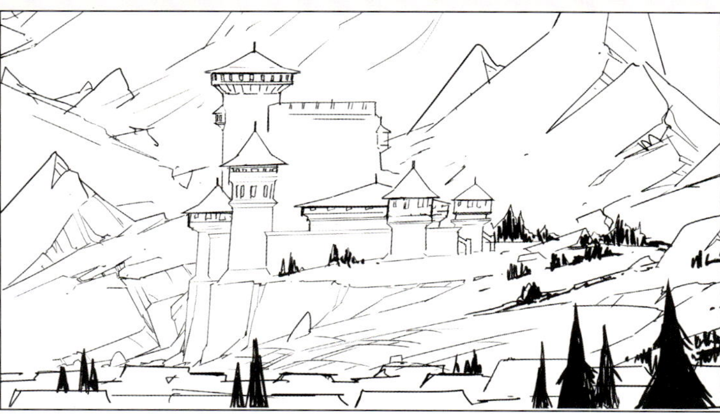

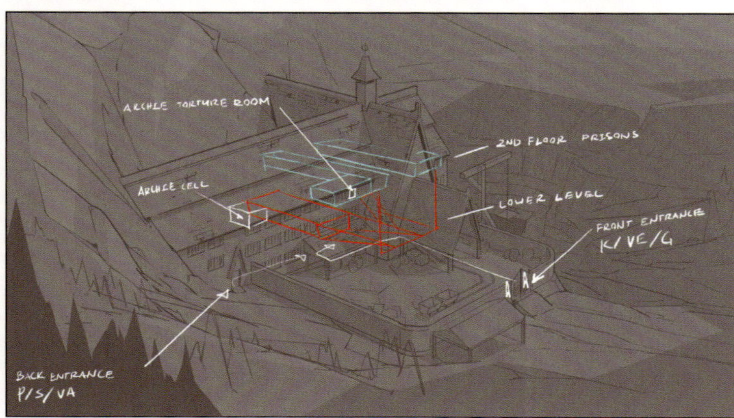

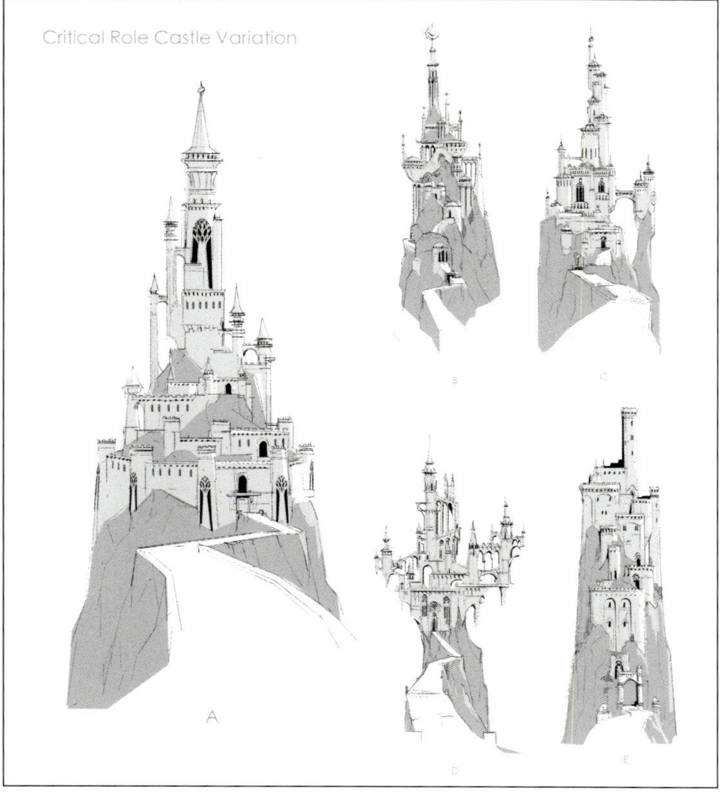

Carriage

Tracking characters within a moving carriage is challenging during wide shots, so the design team devised the solution of putting a torn canopy over the top to strategically hide characters during those moments.

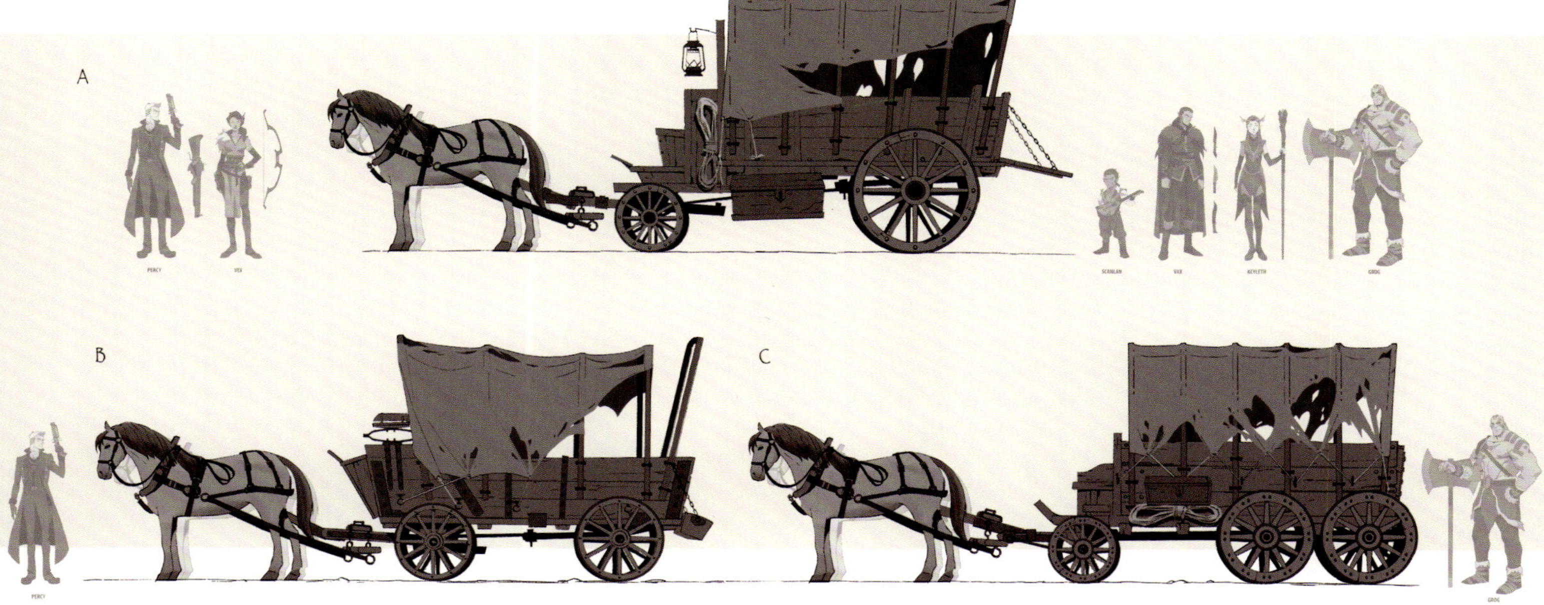

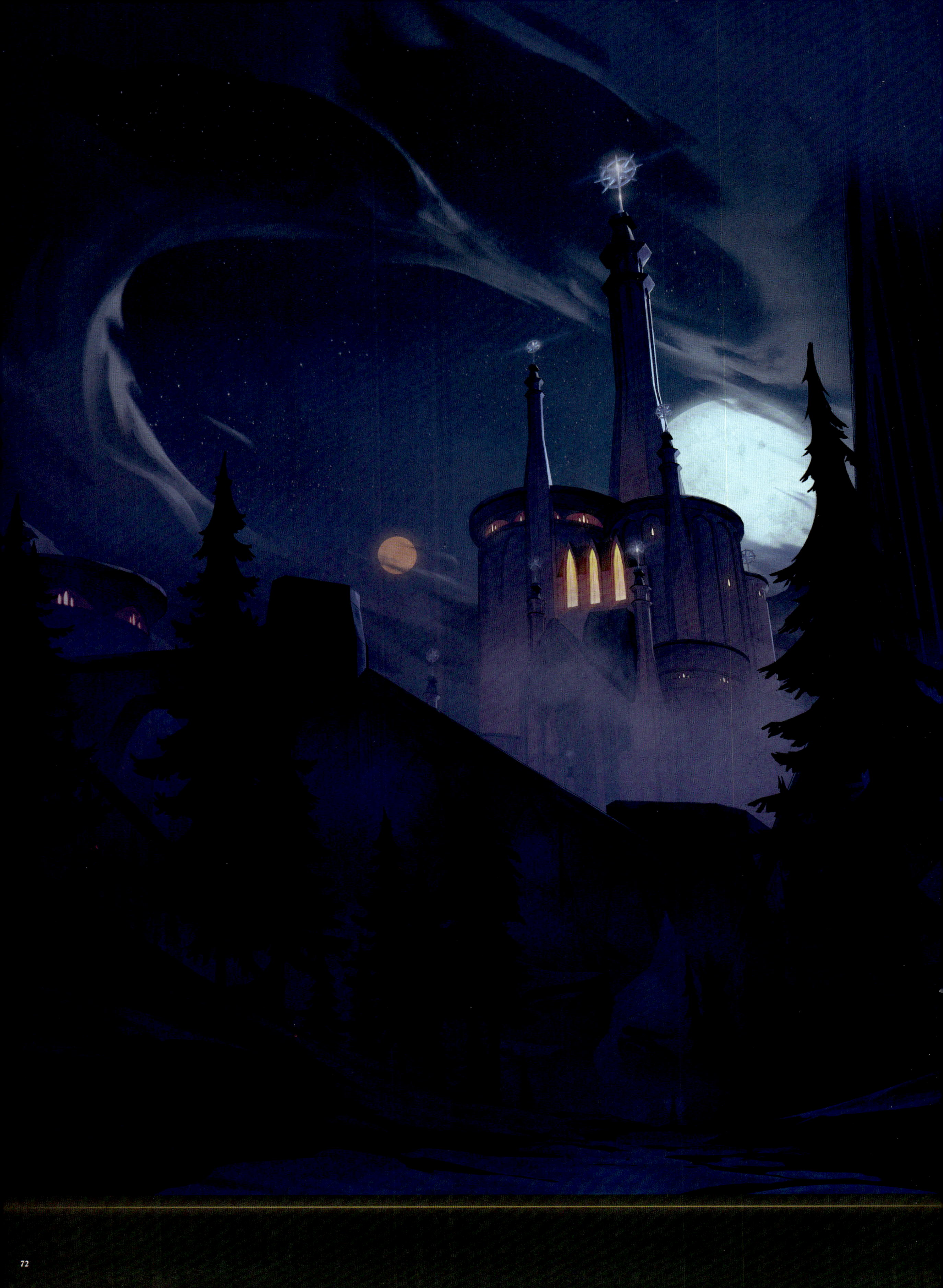

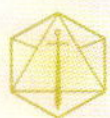

The Sun Tree

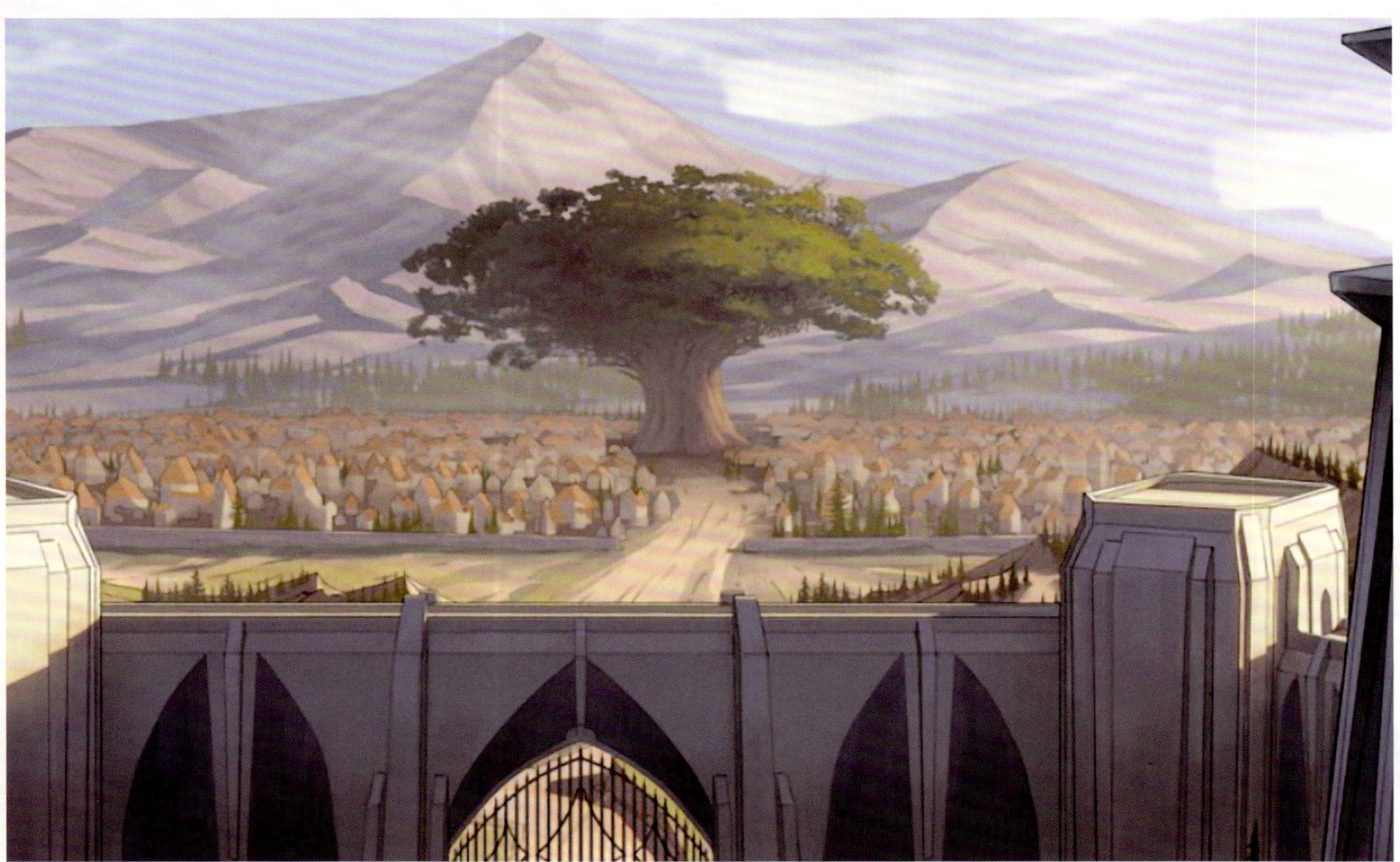

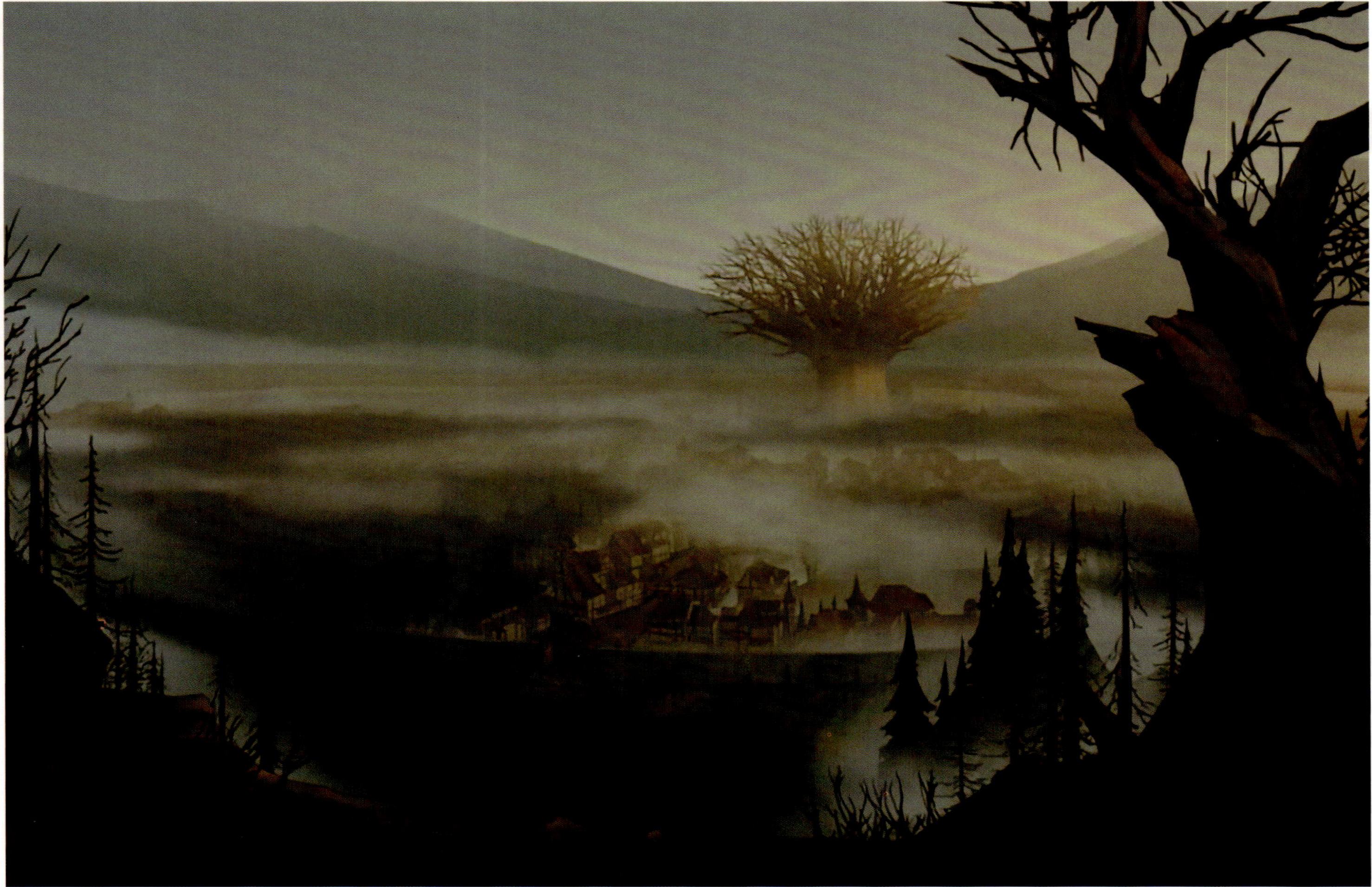

"Canonically, there was an epic battle among gods called The Calamity. We made the location of the Sun Tree where that battle ended all those years ago. I always pictured two gods fighting; one lands the finishing blow, and it creates a crater in the middle of that mountain range. That's the valley the city sits inside of. It's fertile because of the divine energy radiating from the Sun Tree." – ARTHUR LOFTIS

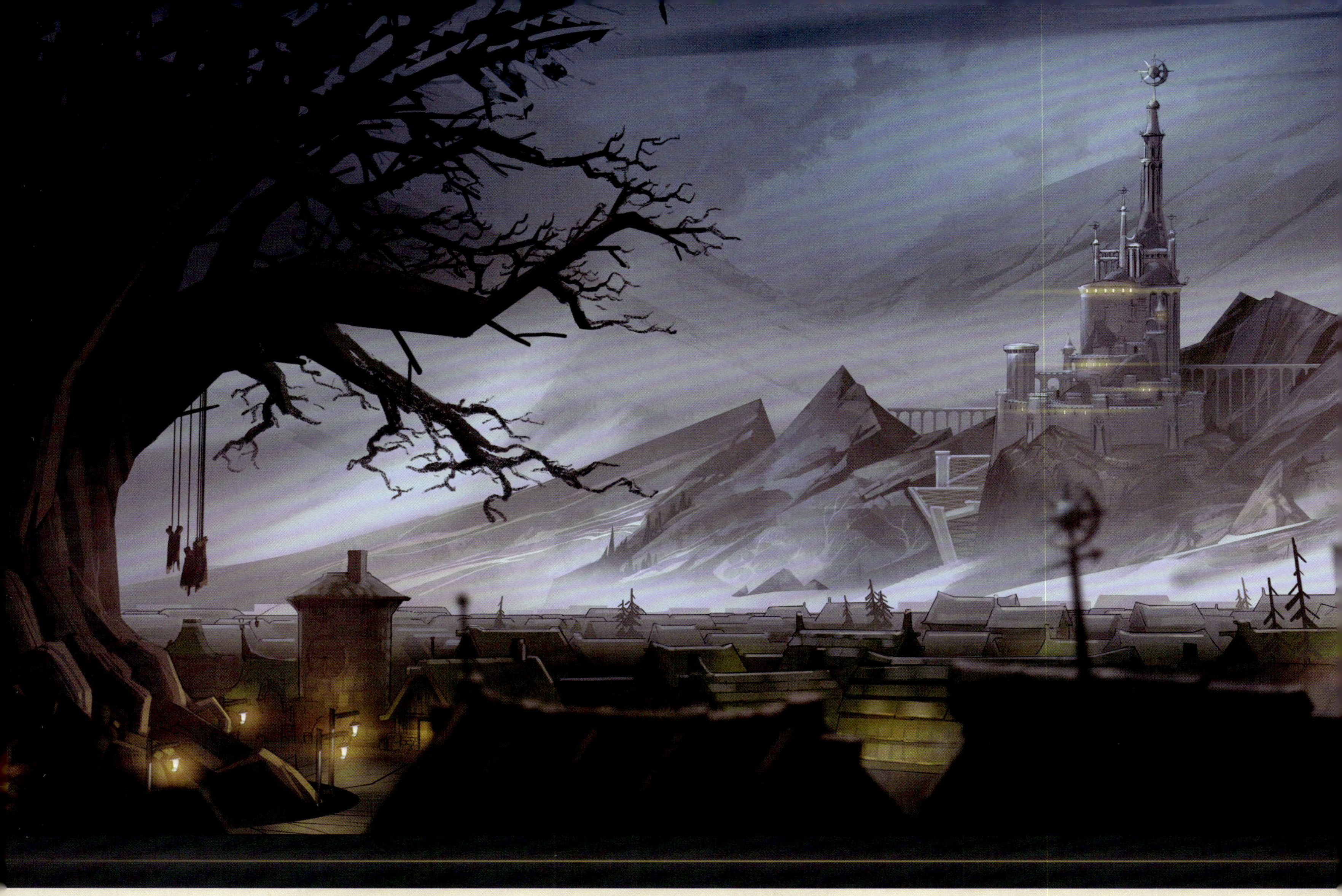

"Vox Machina" Hanging from the Sun Tree

In the final moments of the episode, Vox Machina arrives at The Sun Tree only to discover bodies dressed up to look like them, strung up in this macabre scene. The team wanted to capture the emotion felt by the cast during the original campaign when Mercer described the scene, and they slowly realized that those villagers were supposed to be Vox Machina.

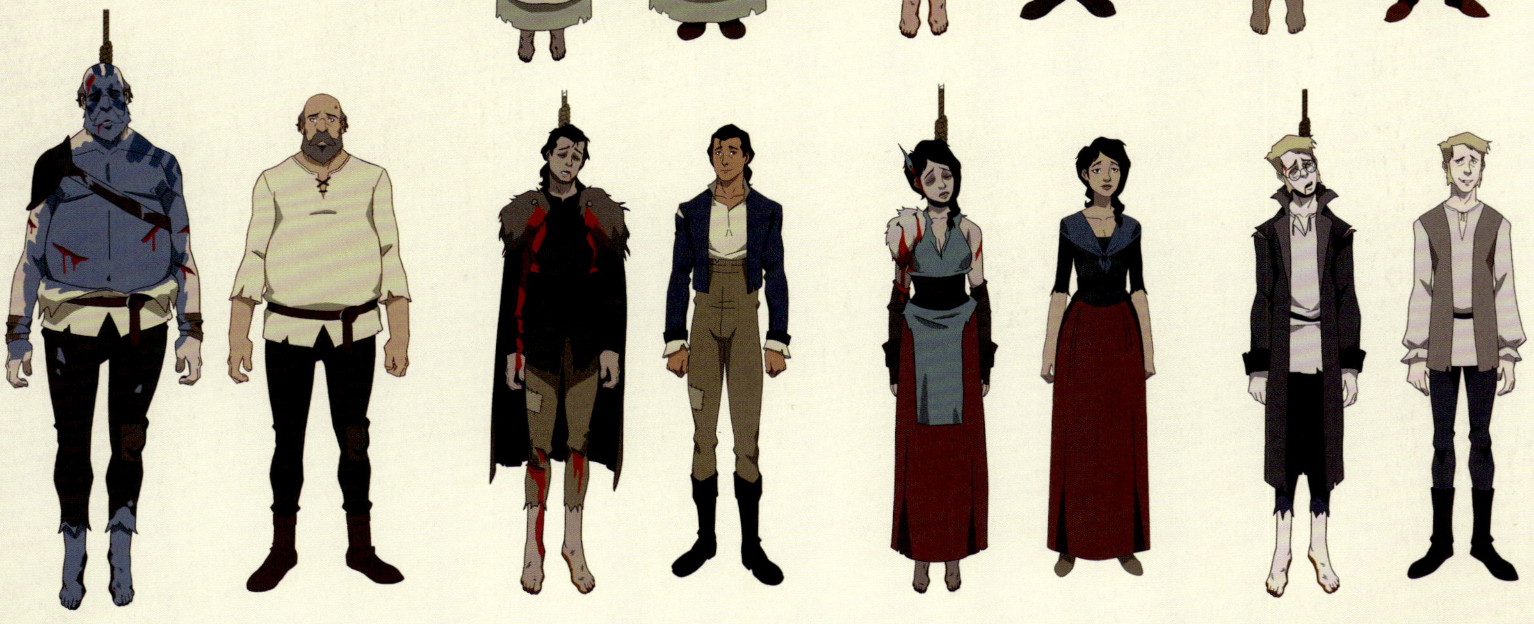

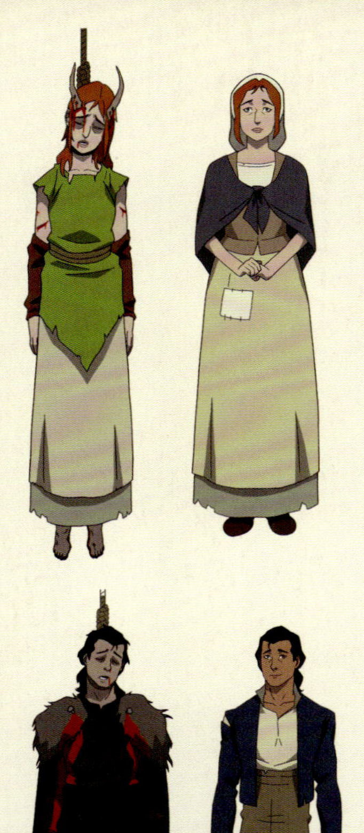

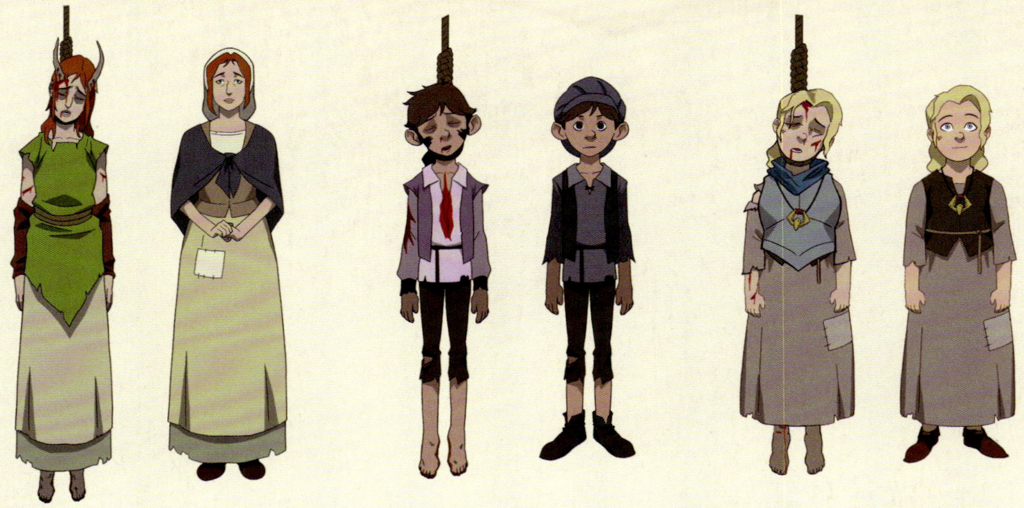

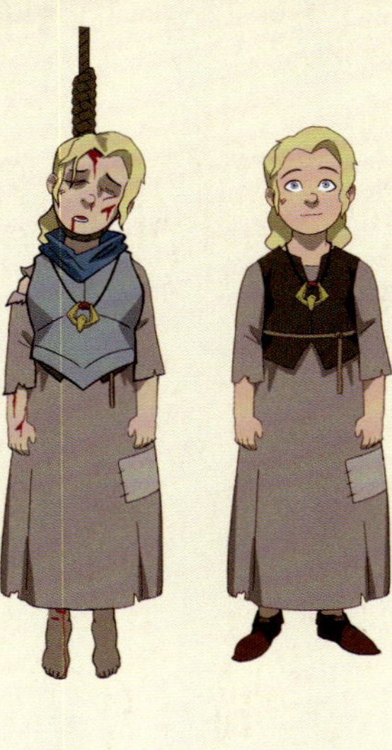

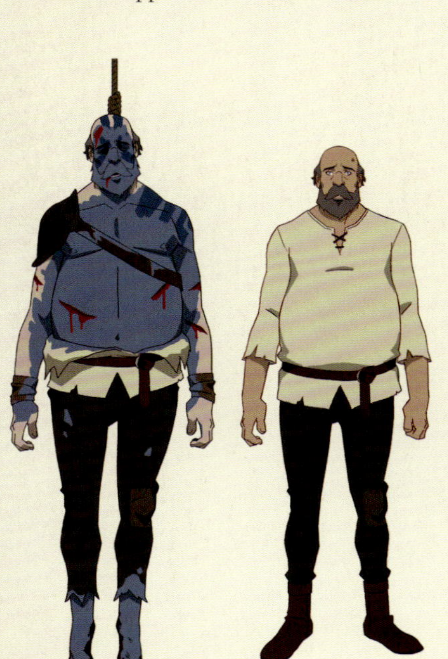

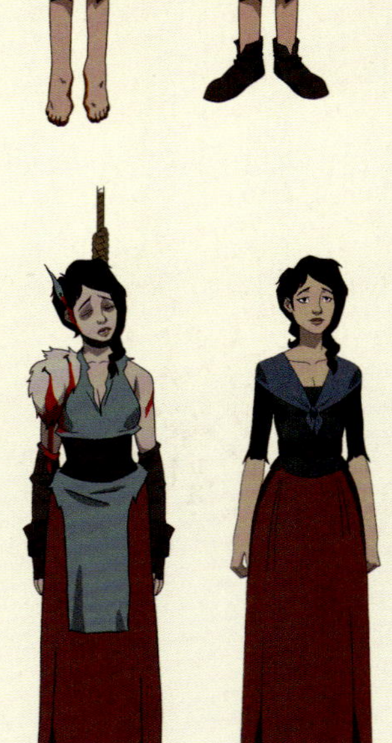

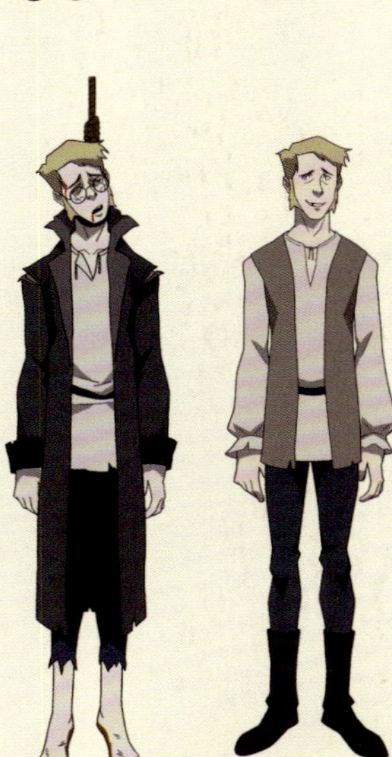

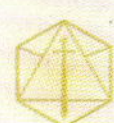

Everlight Temple

The Everlight Temple design is inspired by solar farms and is meant to work with the sun. The artists constructed the temple so that mirrors would reflect the sun's holy light into this clockwork mechanism, harnessing its light into a pointed laser. Within the tower, gears are placed to look like an orrery, a mechanical model of the planets.

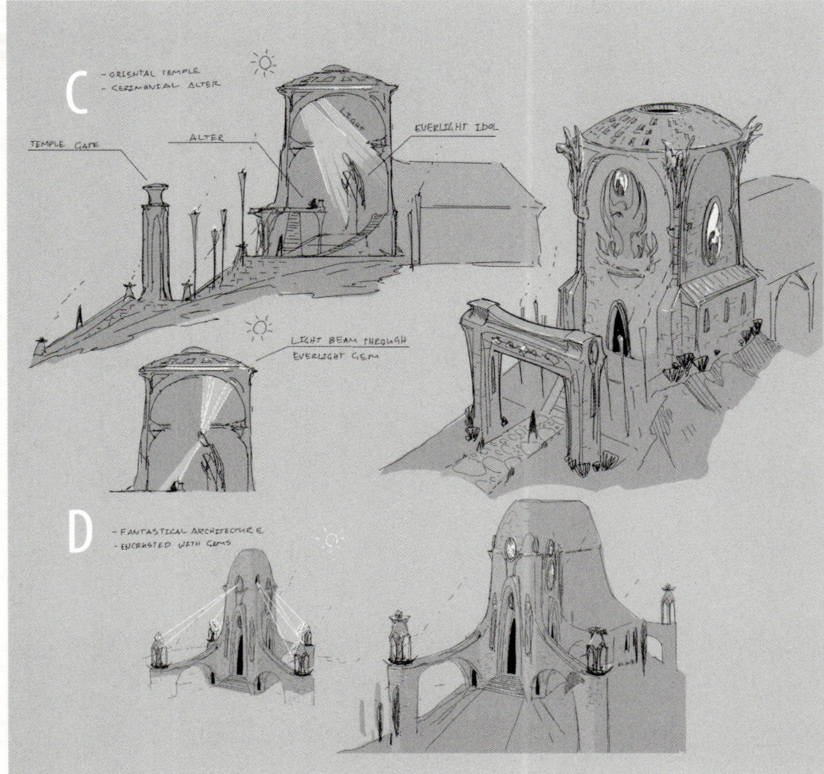

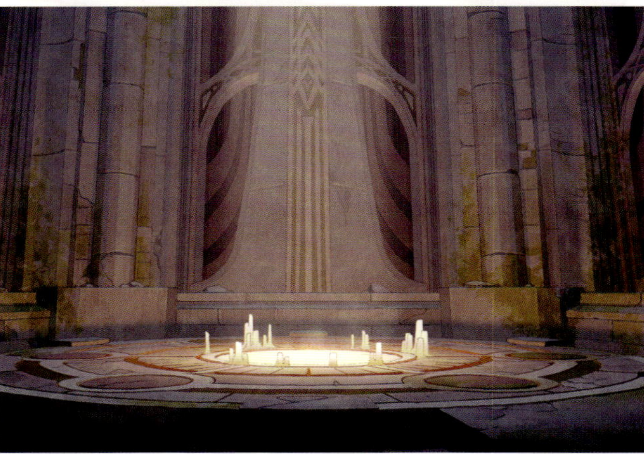

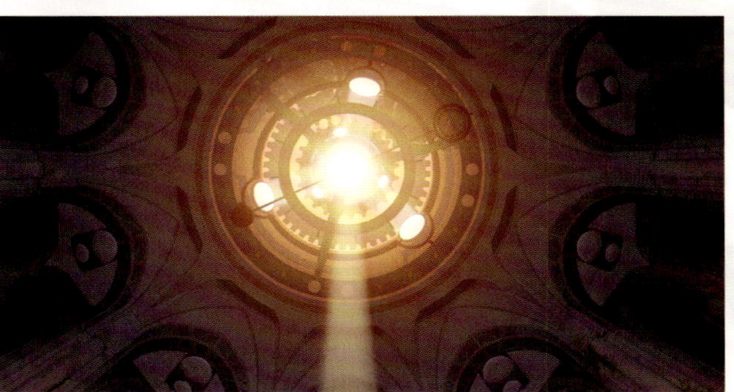

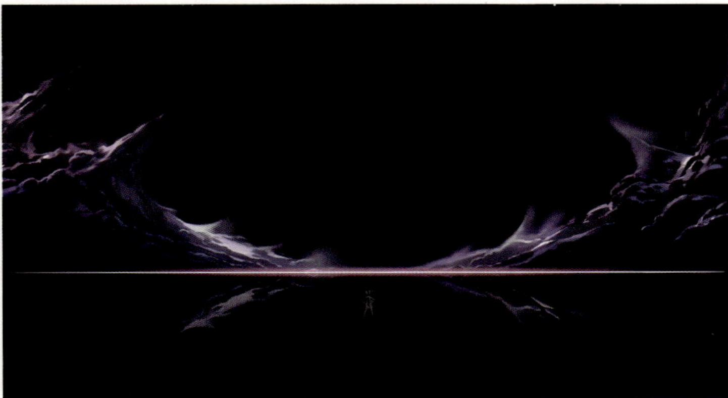

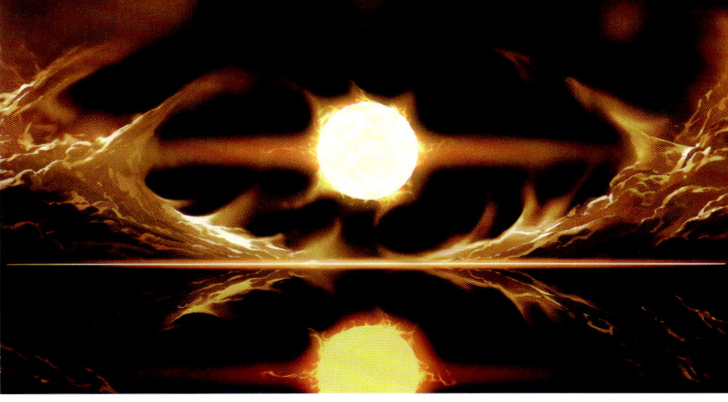

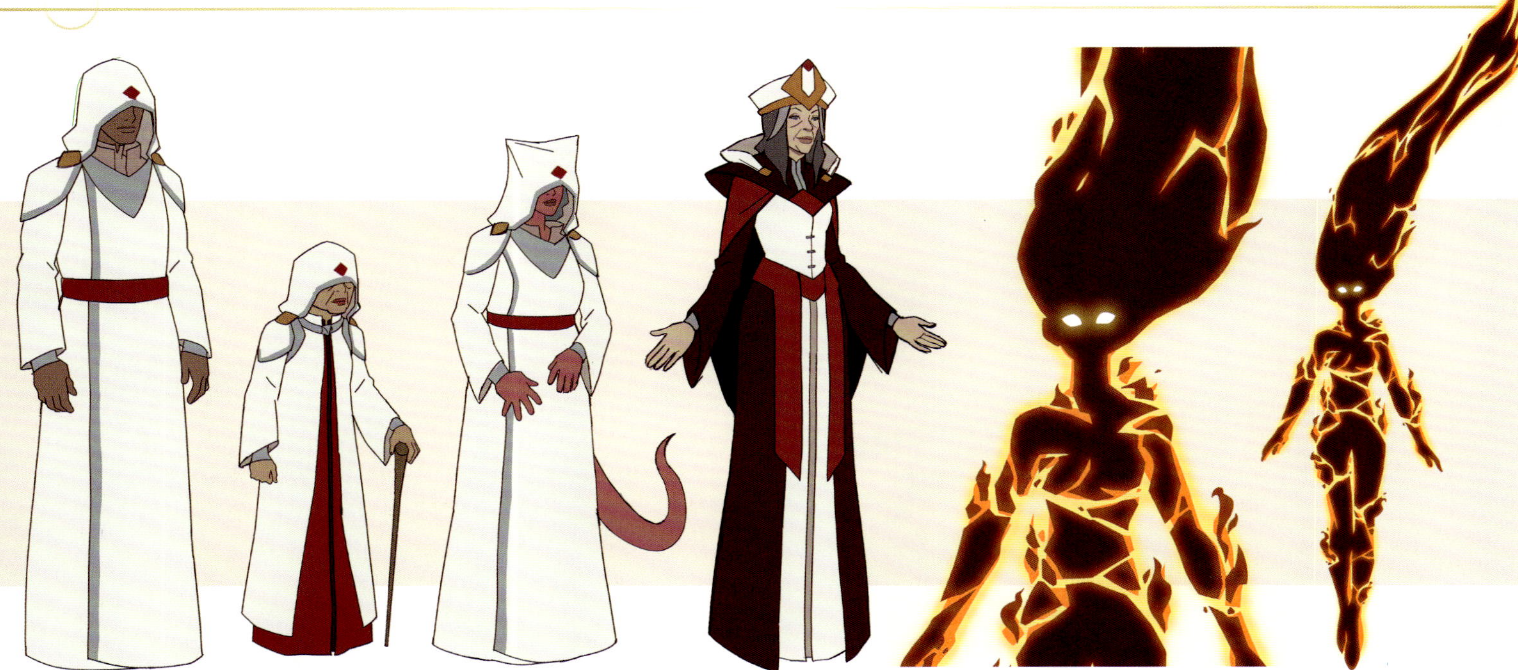

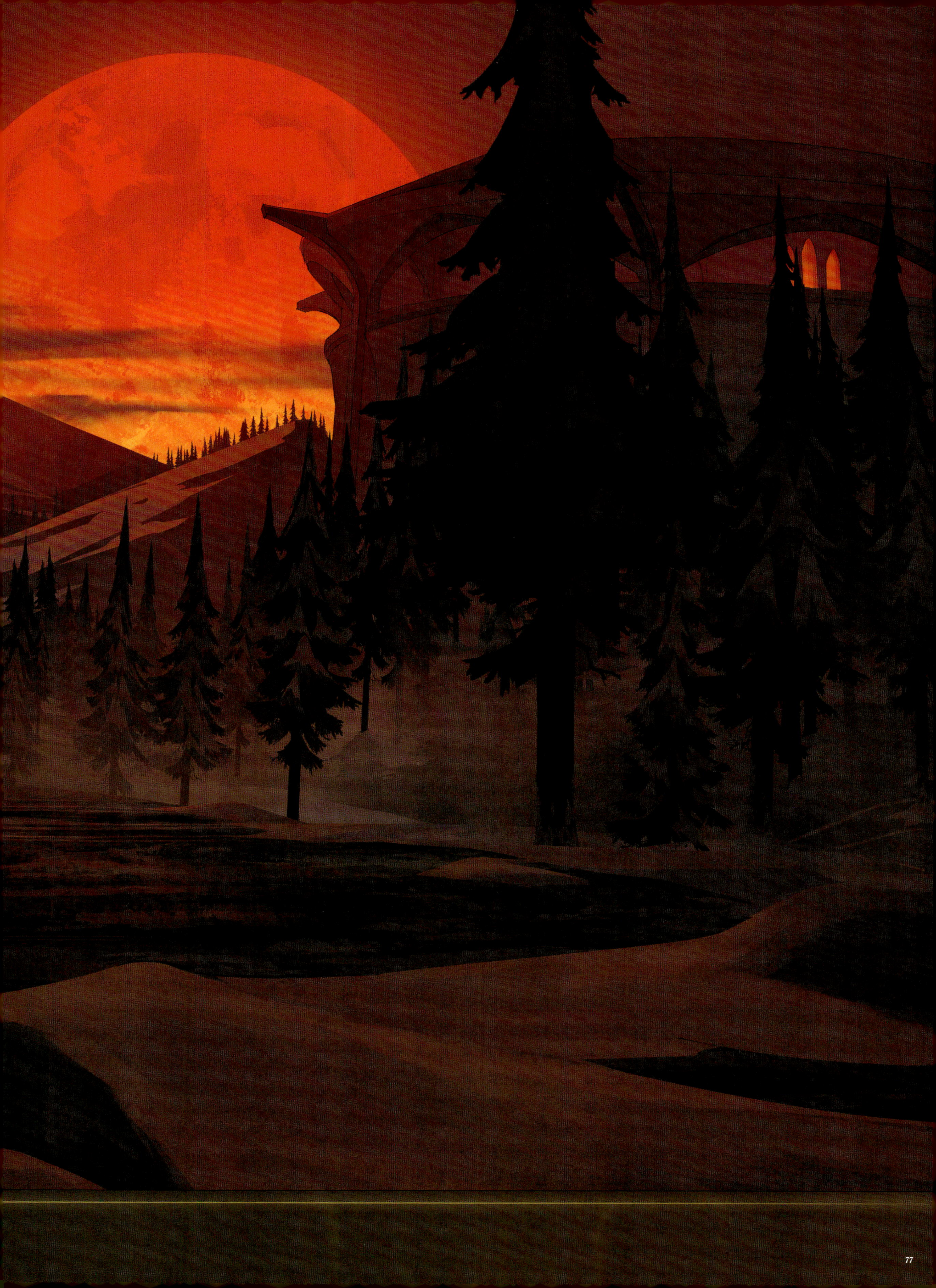

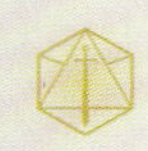

EPISODE 6

SPARK OF REBELLION

"Everybody loves a good prison break episode! I, once again, save literally everybody with my quick thinking and devilish charm. Percy takes down Stonefell and gets a little smoky in the process, but we're not concerned... yet. Oh, and Percy's long-lost sister is alive! What a trip, huh?" – A RECOUNTING OF "SPARK OF REBELLION" BY SCANLAN SHORTHALT

Kerrion Stonefell

The sadistic torturer, Kerrion's outsides are just as ugly as his insides. His clothing consists of an ill-fitted uniform that appears to be a few ranks above his station. Character designers decided to give him the backstory that he stole the coat from a person of greater rank to make himself look more important—an aspirational uniform, if you will.

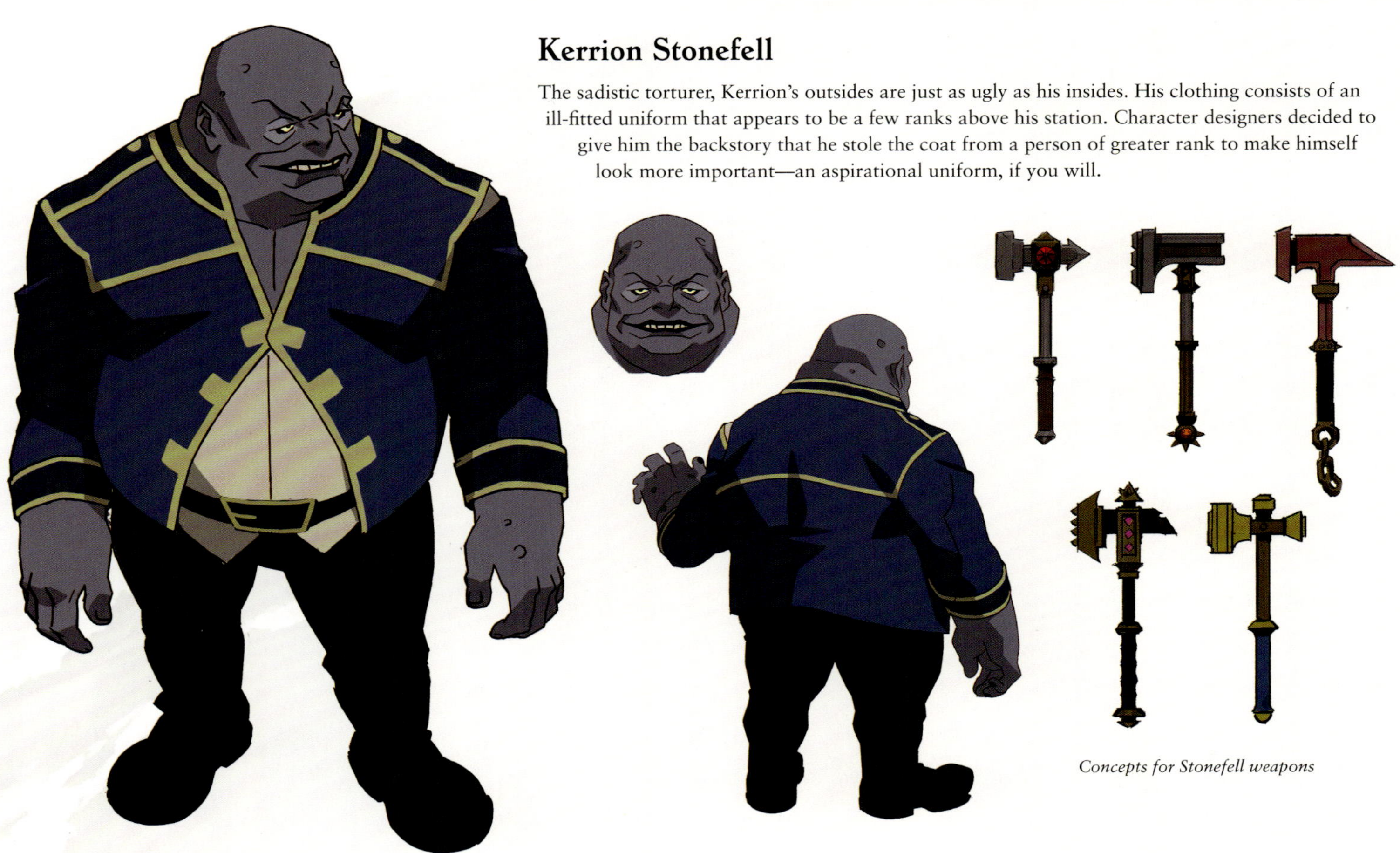

Concepts for Stonefell weapons

Matt Mercer Cameo

Matt Mercer (minus an eye) makes an appearance as a Whitestone rebel.

Keeper Yennen

While Archie is the "heart" of the rebellion, Keeper Yennen is the "soul." She stands tall as the unyielding rock for the people of Whitestone and those resisting the Briarwoods.

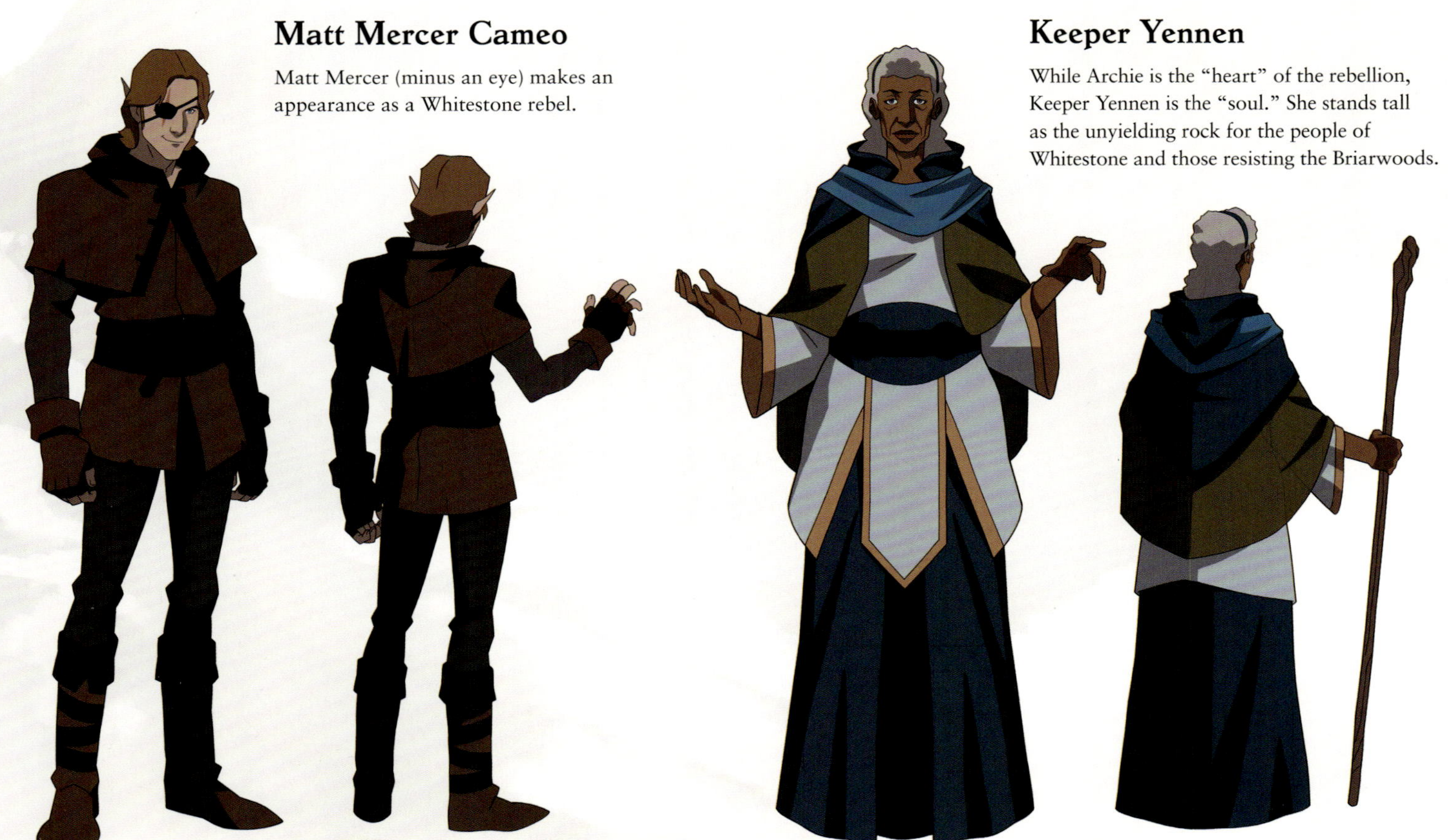

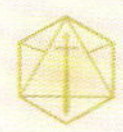

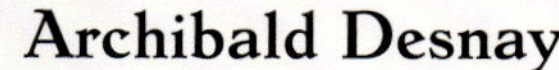

Archibald Desnay

A departure from the campaign character, Archie is considered the "heart" of the Whitestone rebellion. As Percy's childhood friend, he co-opted the de Rolo family crest to be the symbol of their cause.

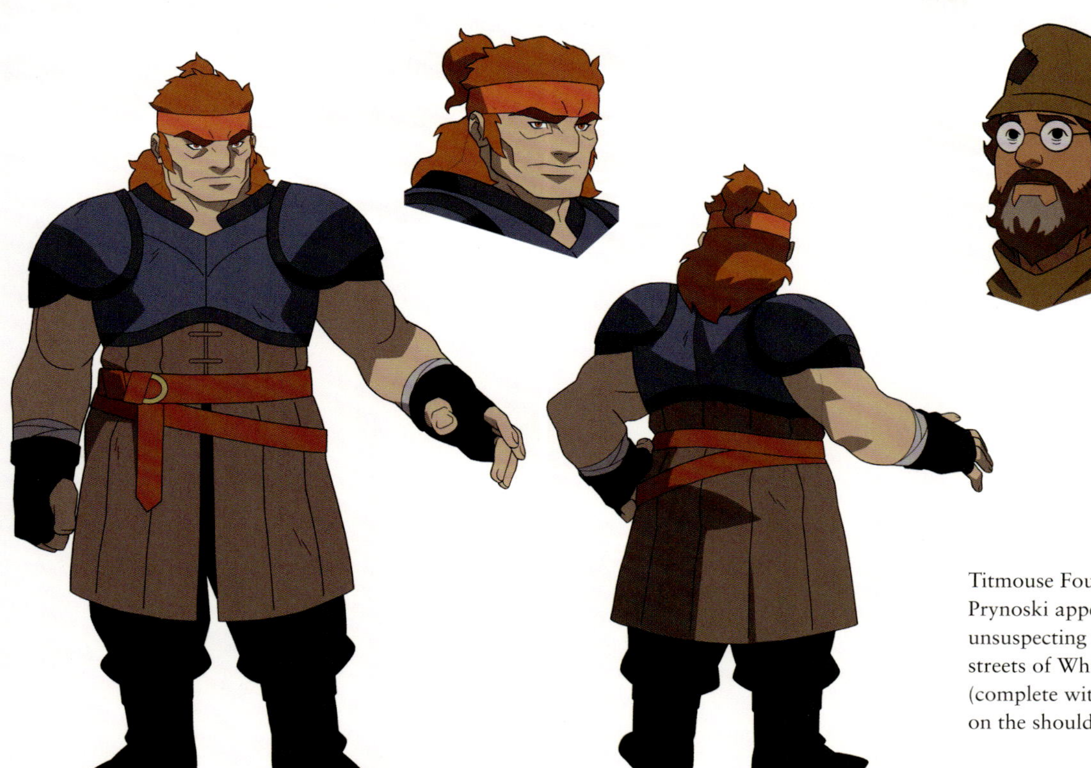

Beggar Man–Chris Prynoski

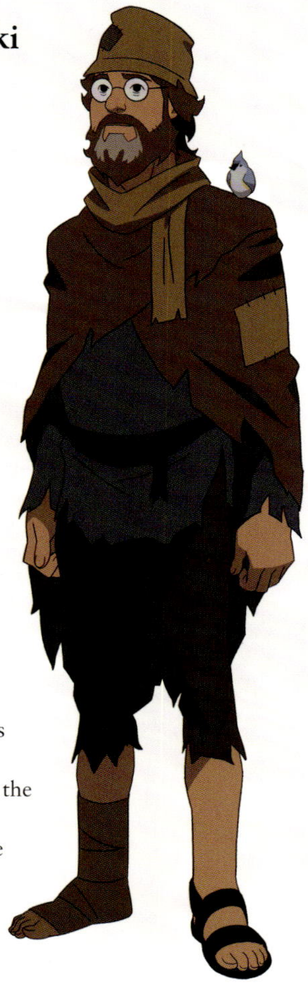

Titmouse Founder Chris Prynoski appears as an unsuspecting beggar on the streets of Whitestone (complete with titmouse on the shoulder!)

Undead Giants

Designs of the Undead Giants resurrected by Delilah Briarwood to patrol Whitestone and keep the rebels at bay.

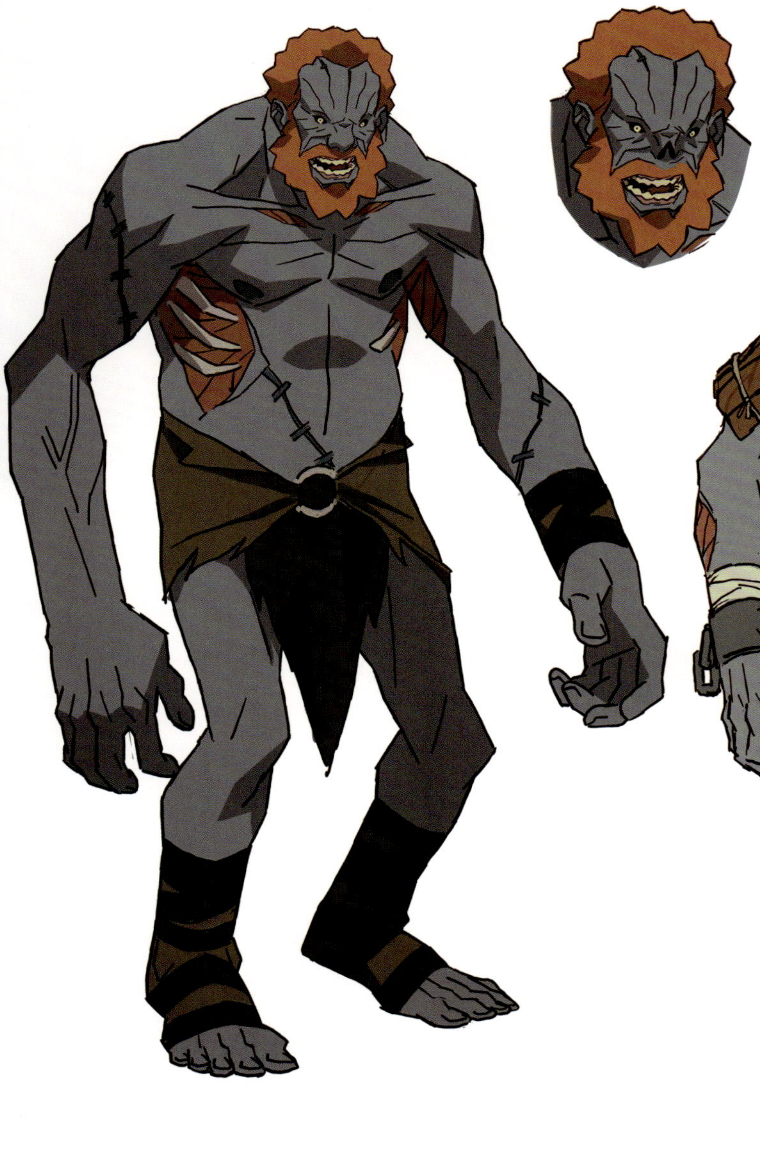

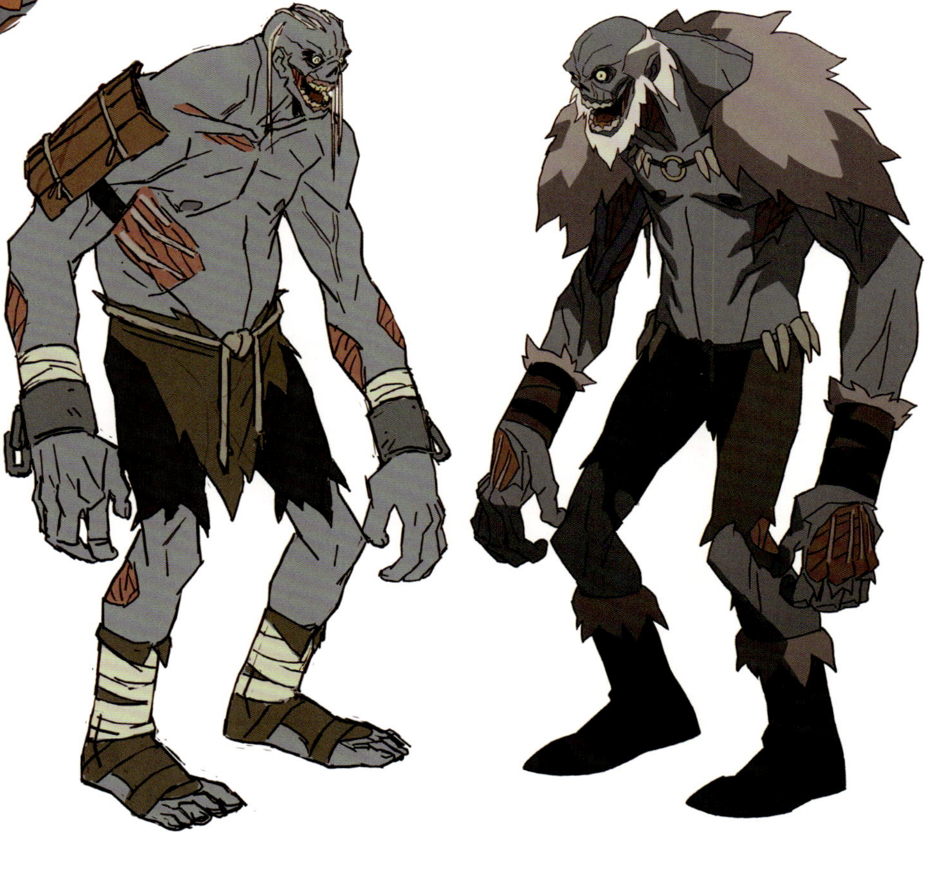

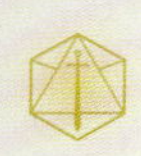

Bryn

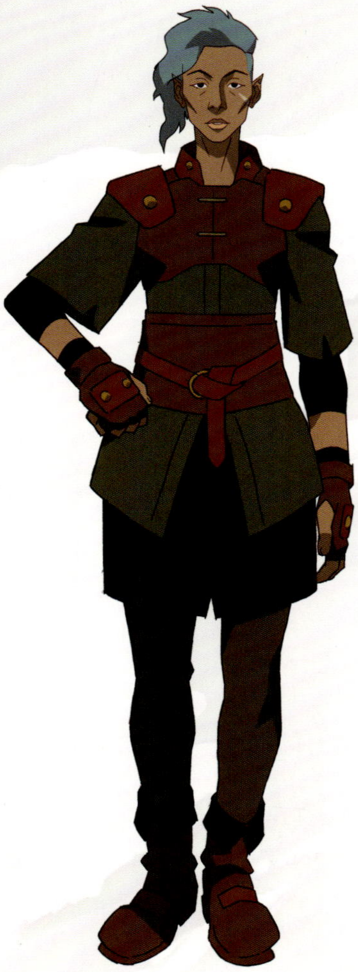

Rahlia

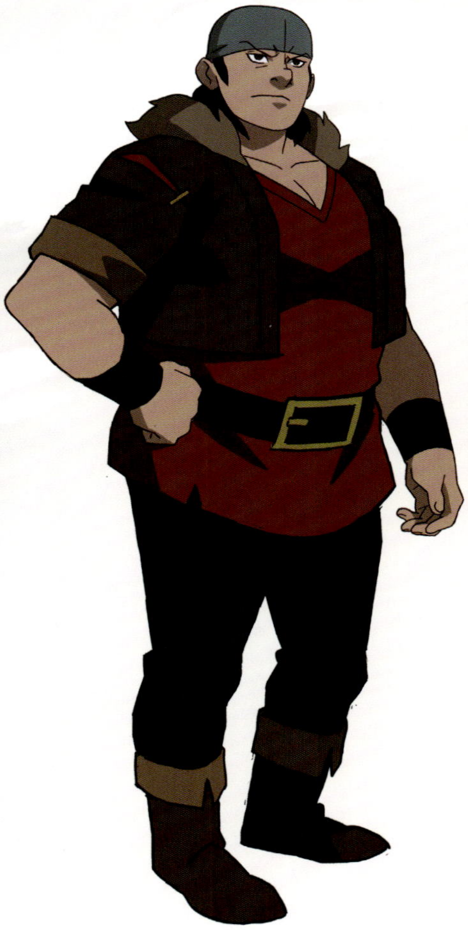

Pale Guard

A turnaround of a Pale Guard–a guard of Whitestone.

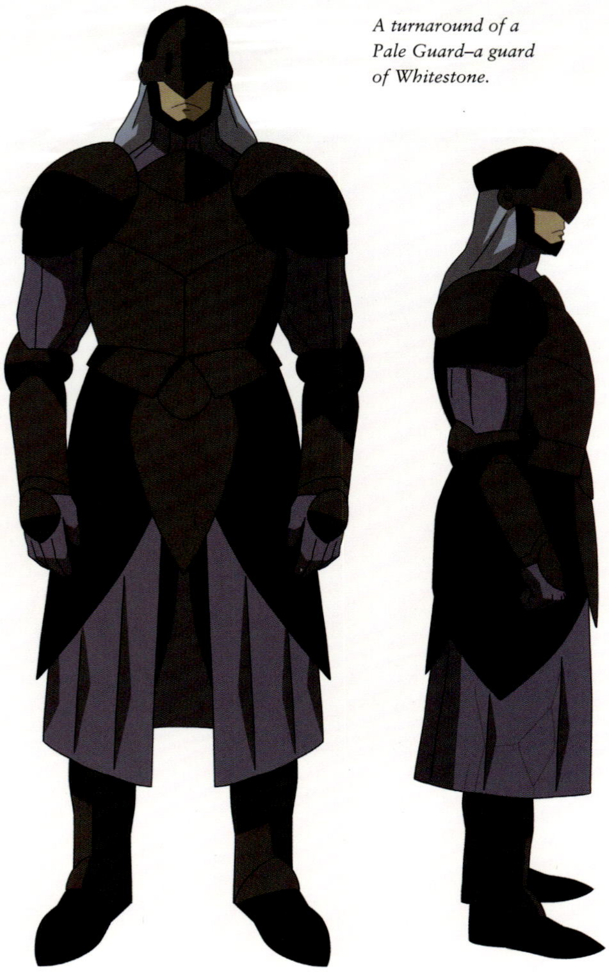

Whitestone Rebels

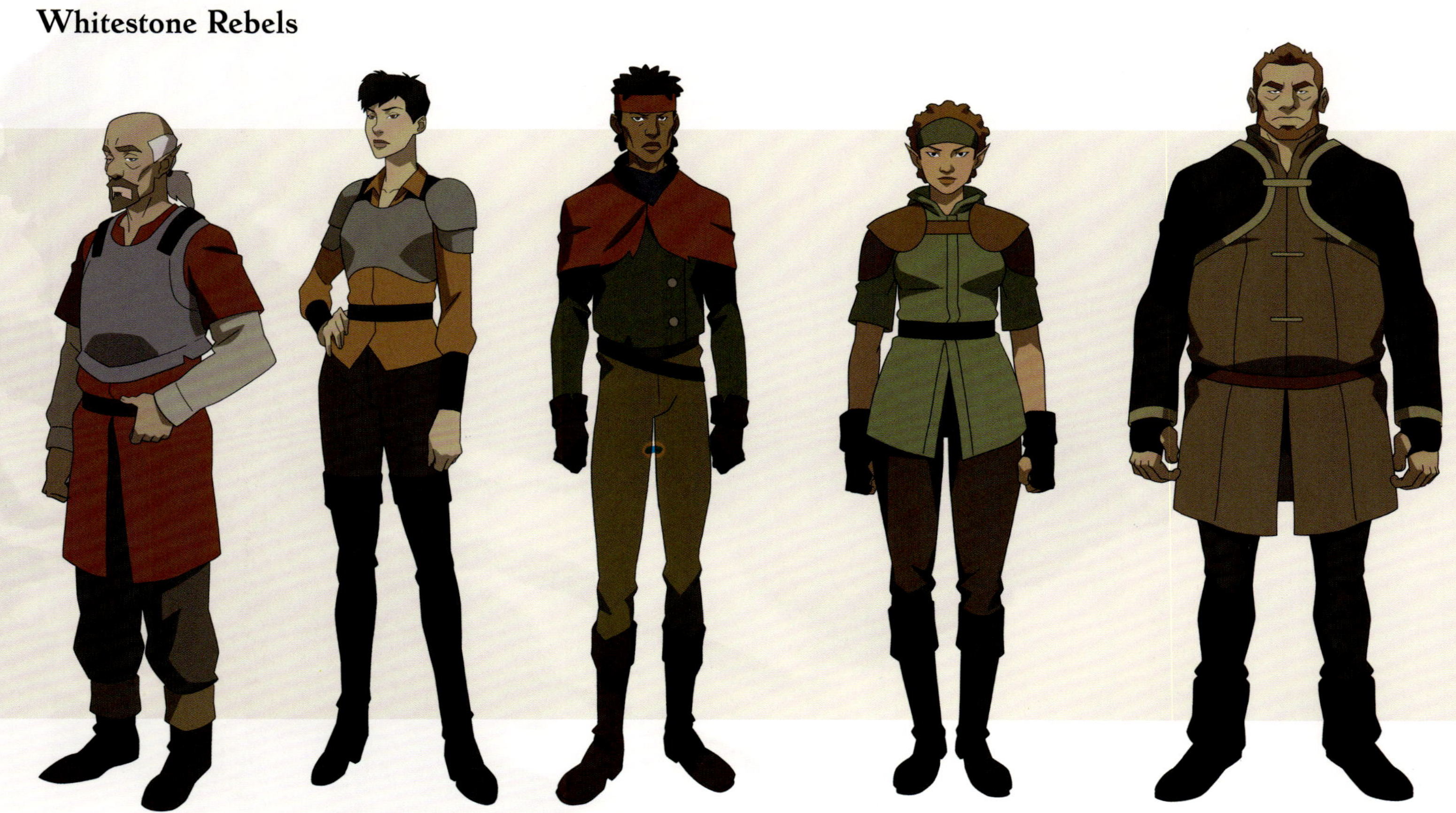

Rebel Hideout

The audience's first look at Whitestone is this ramshackle rebel hideout, designed to show their struggle in the fight against the Briarwood and allude to the fact that they are barely getting by.

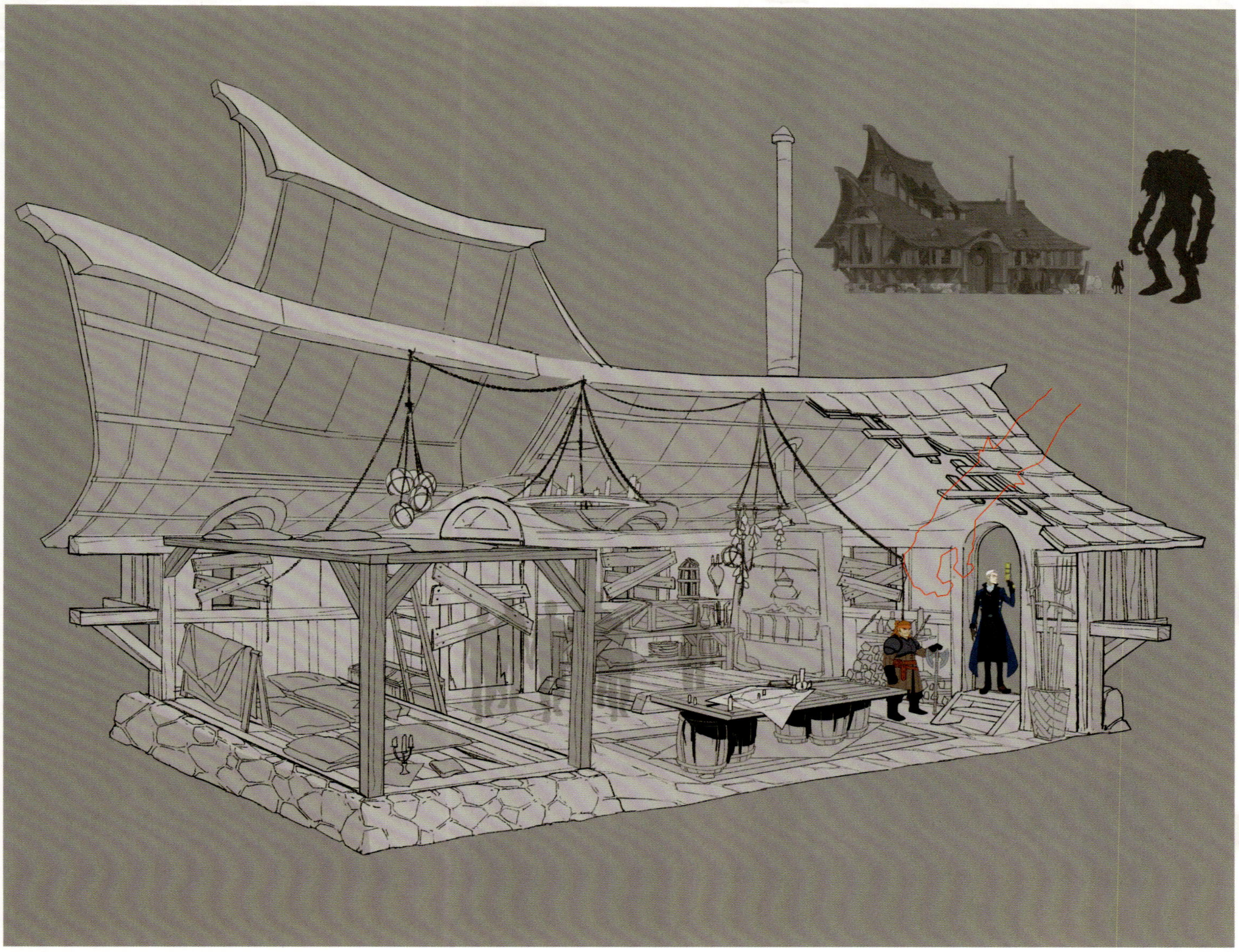

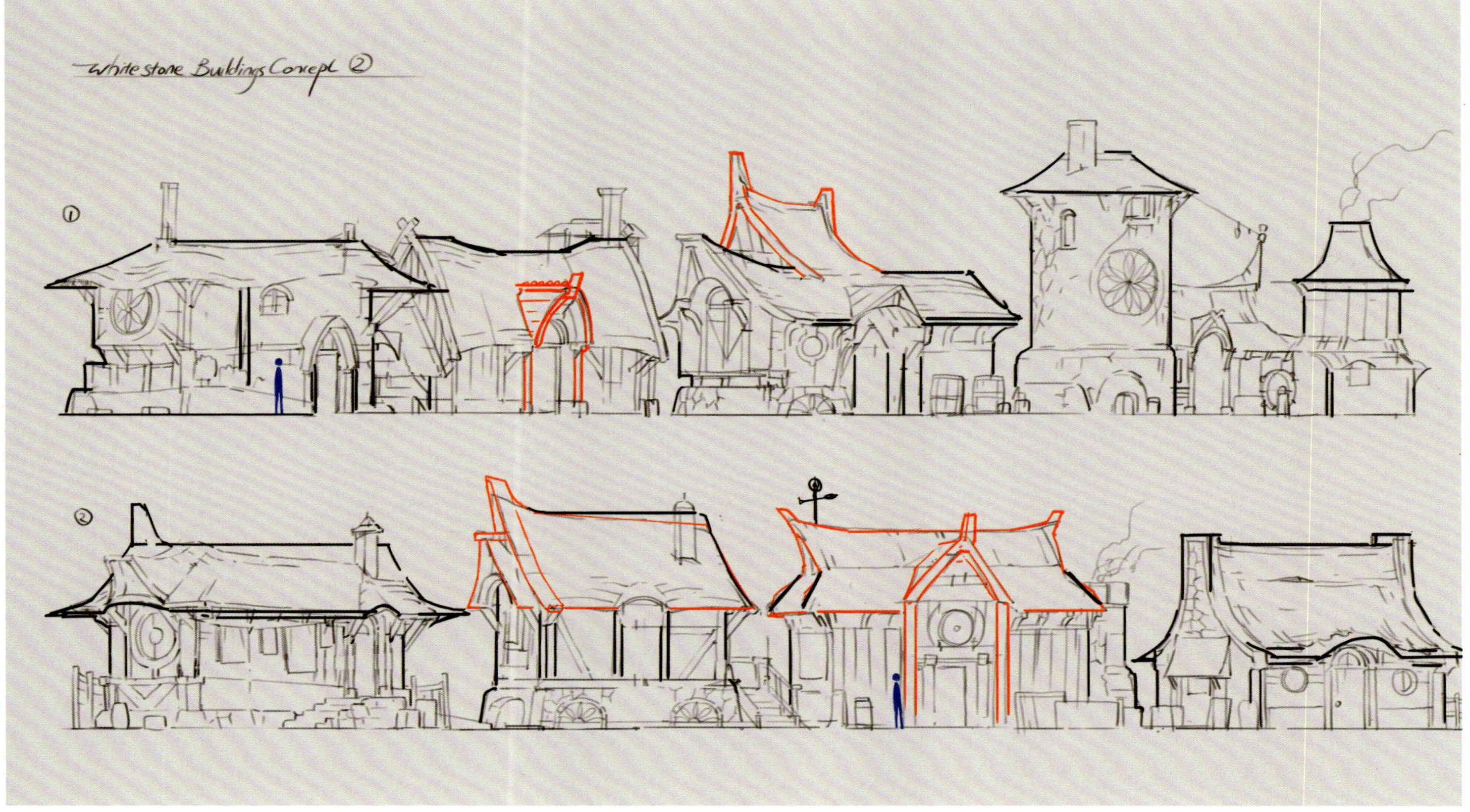

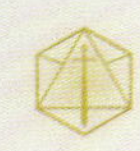

Whitestone Prison

"Whitestone is a mining town, named for the stone that is refined to create residuum, a powerful magical component. We wanted to show that Whitestone never had need for a prison before Sylas and Delilah took over, so we designed this building as a repurposed mining structure with carts and a storage yard. The cells might have been storerooms a few years ago, but they've been refitted with metal bars to hold people who would fight against the new regime." – ARTHUR LOFTIS

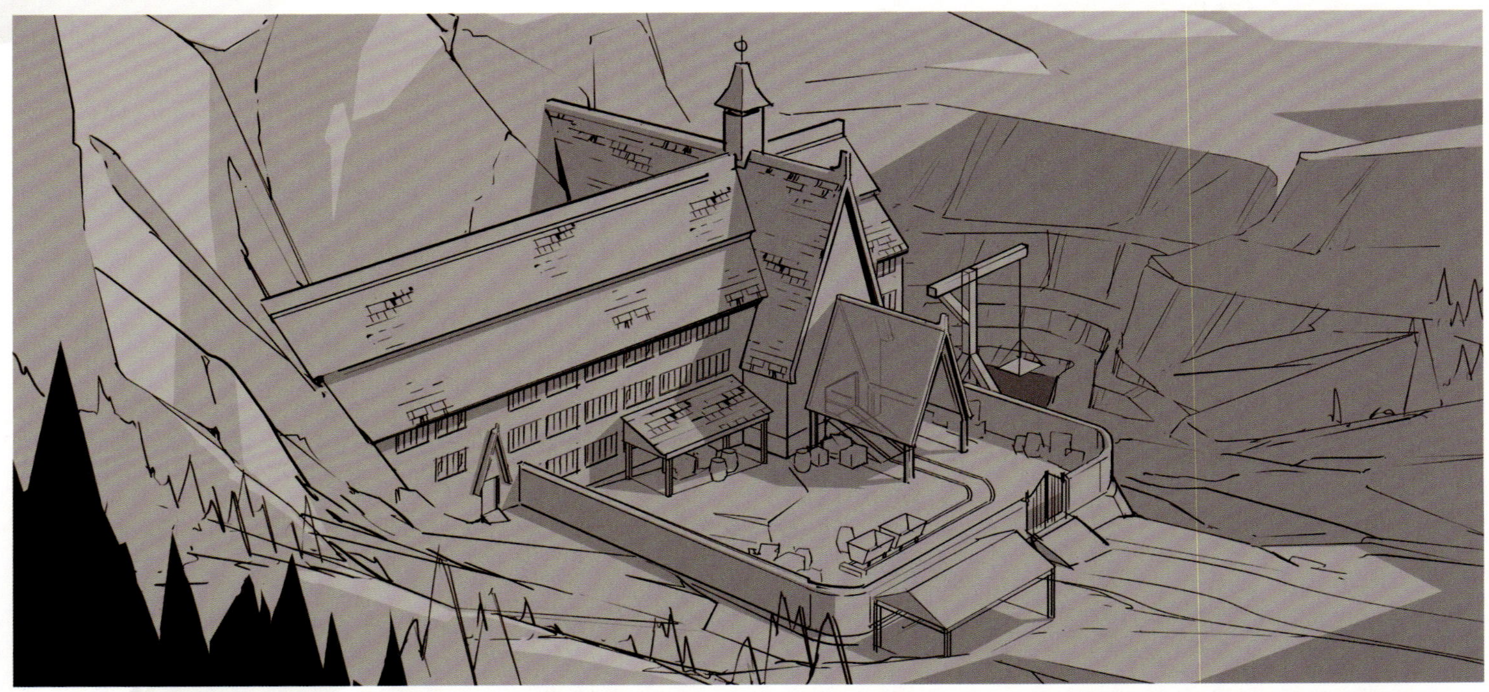

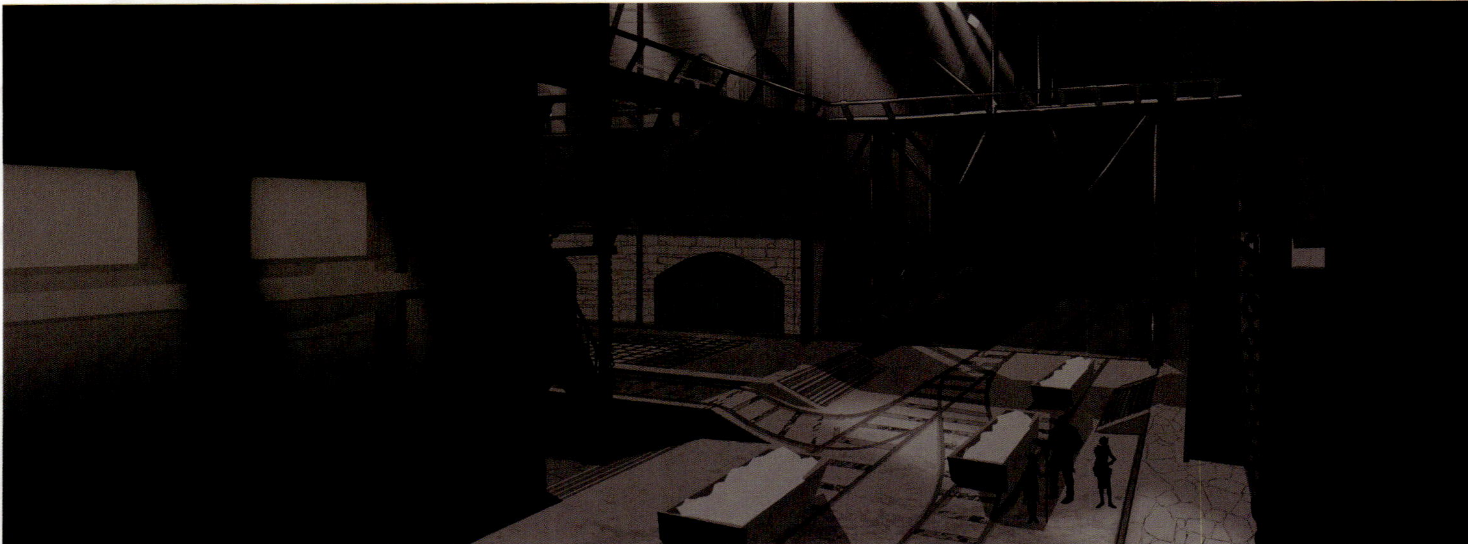

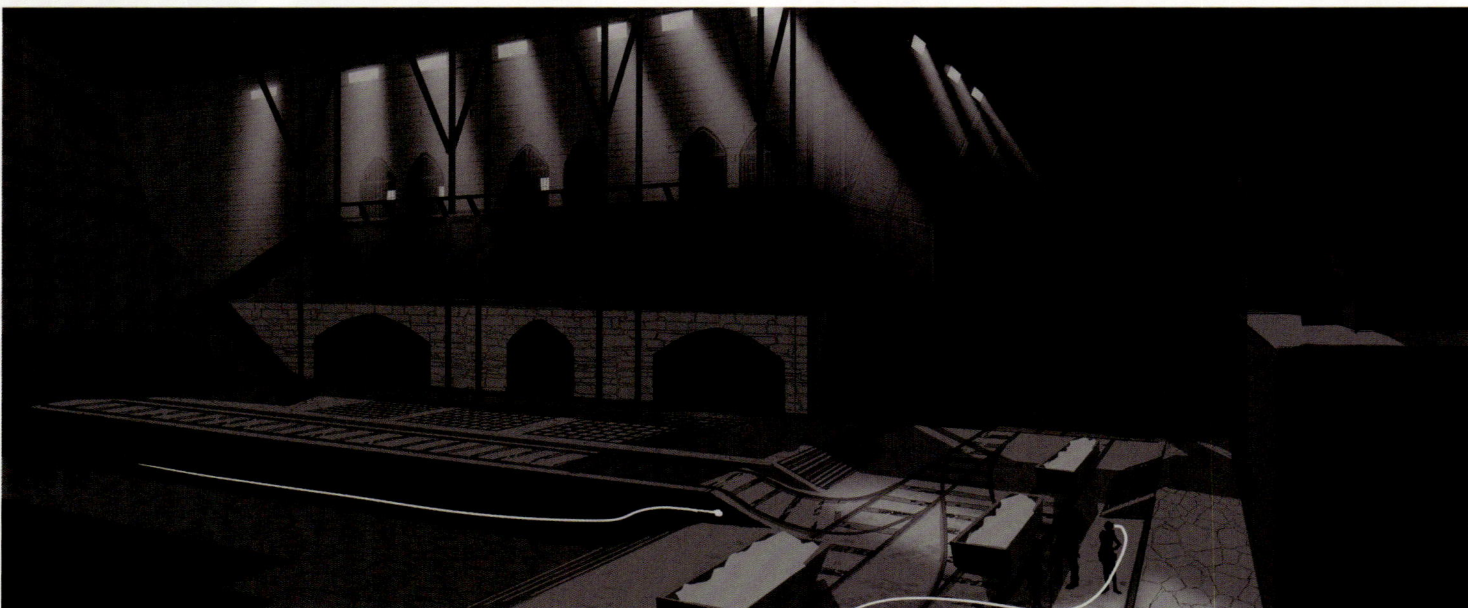

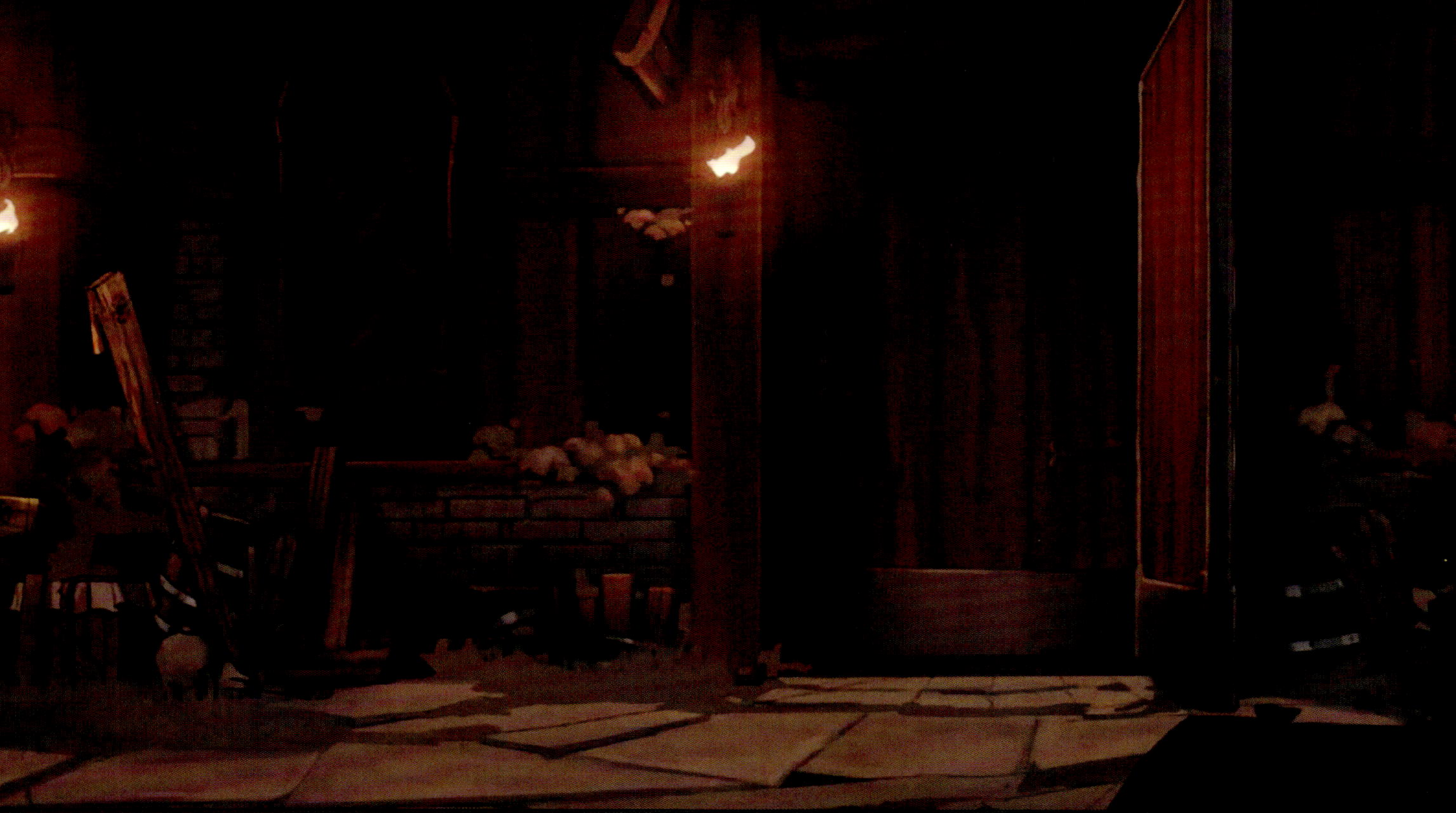

Whitestone Tavern

Serving as another secret rebel hideout, the signage in front pays homage to the Sun Tree. The cellar is where the rebels have stored supplies to fight the Briarwoods.

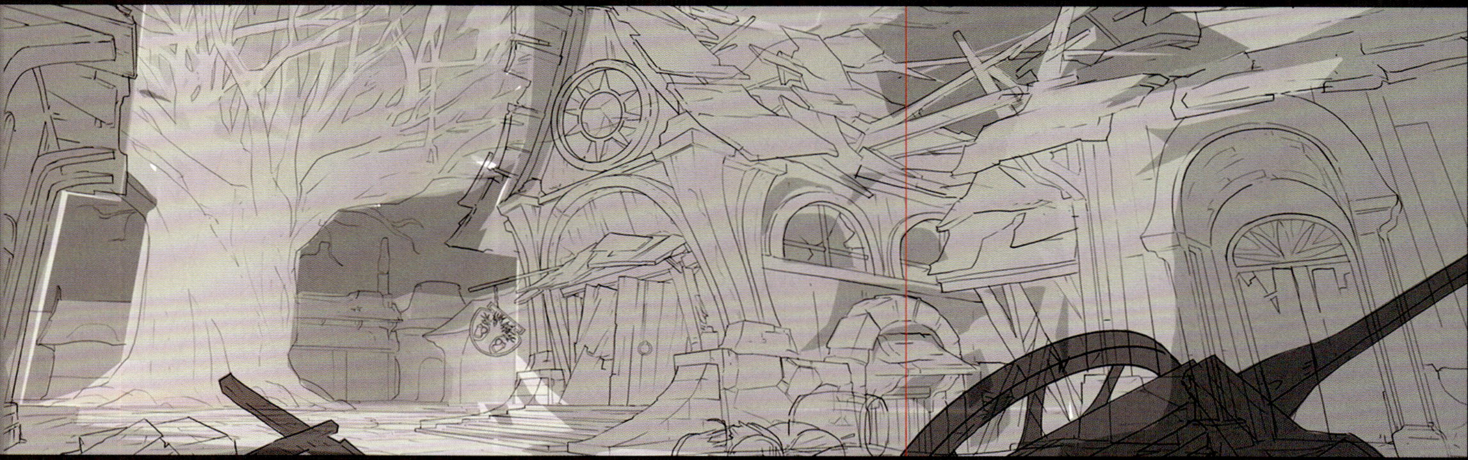

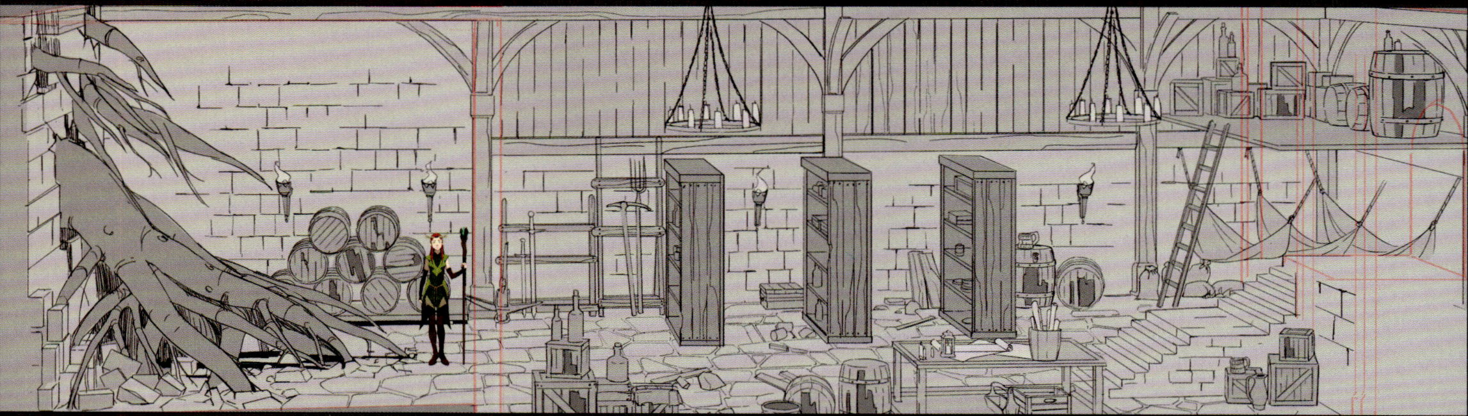

Keeper Yennen: Thanks to the Briarwoods, all our resources are dwindling. Including ale.
Grog: I will fucking murder everyone! – S1E6 "SPARK OF REBELLION"

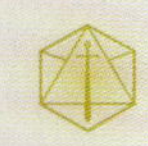

EPISODE 7

SCANBO

"Just a little ol' episode I like to call, 'the time Scanlan burned down Vedmire's motherfucking house!' You want to see me vomit fire? Turn into a dinosaur? Shoot lightning out of my crotch? I swear to gods that last one is true. Definitely a night I will not shut up about for the rest of my extremely long life." – A RECOUNTING OF "SCANBO" BY SCANLAN SHORTHALT

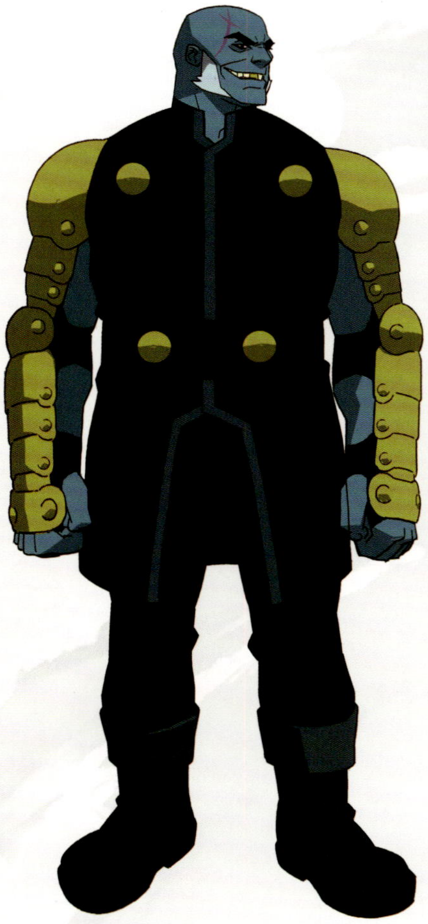

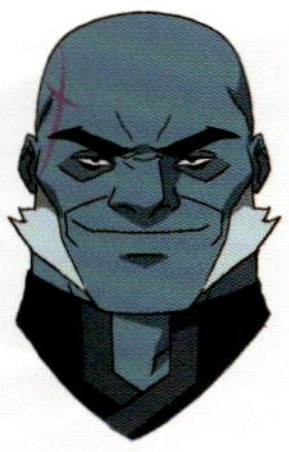

Duke Vedmire

Vedmire's look is that of a beast in a suit. The Briarwoods hired him to aid in their takeover of Whitestone, and paid him with a house and fancy clothes. Having discovered a taste for the finer things in life, he loves dressing up and being "fancy." To amp up the drama of his showdown with Scanlan, the character team pushed his size to have him tower over any foe.

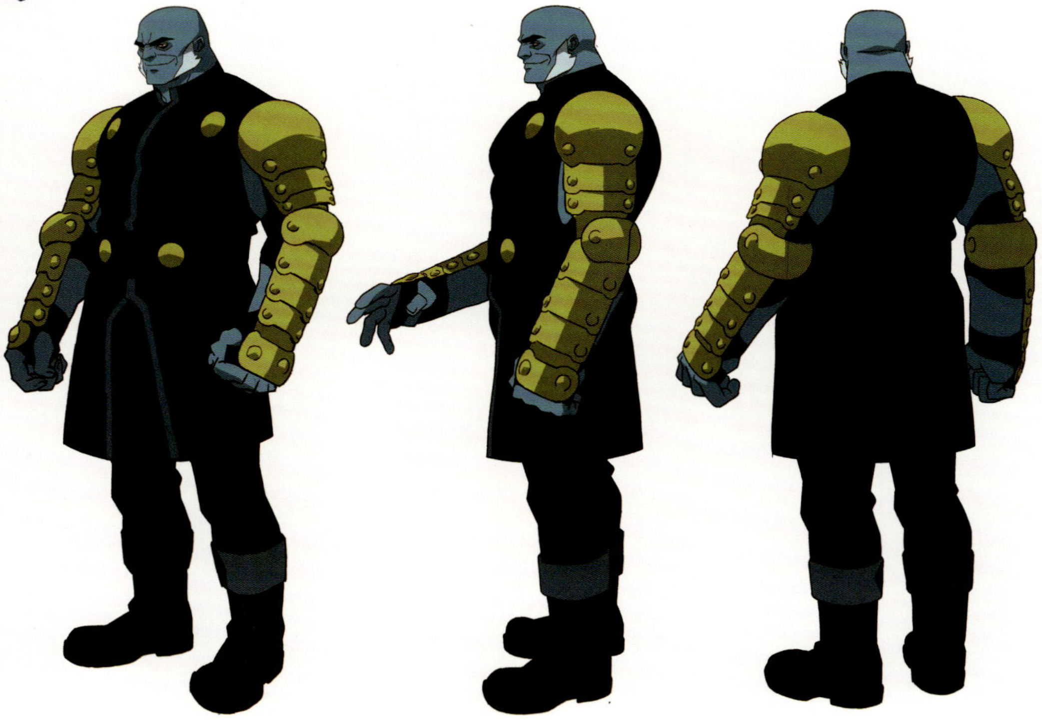

Early designs of Duke Vedmire (bottom left)
Weapon designs for Duke Vedmire (bottom right)

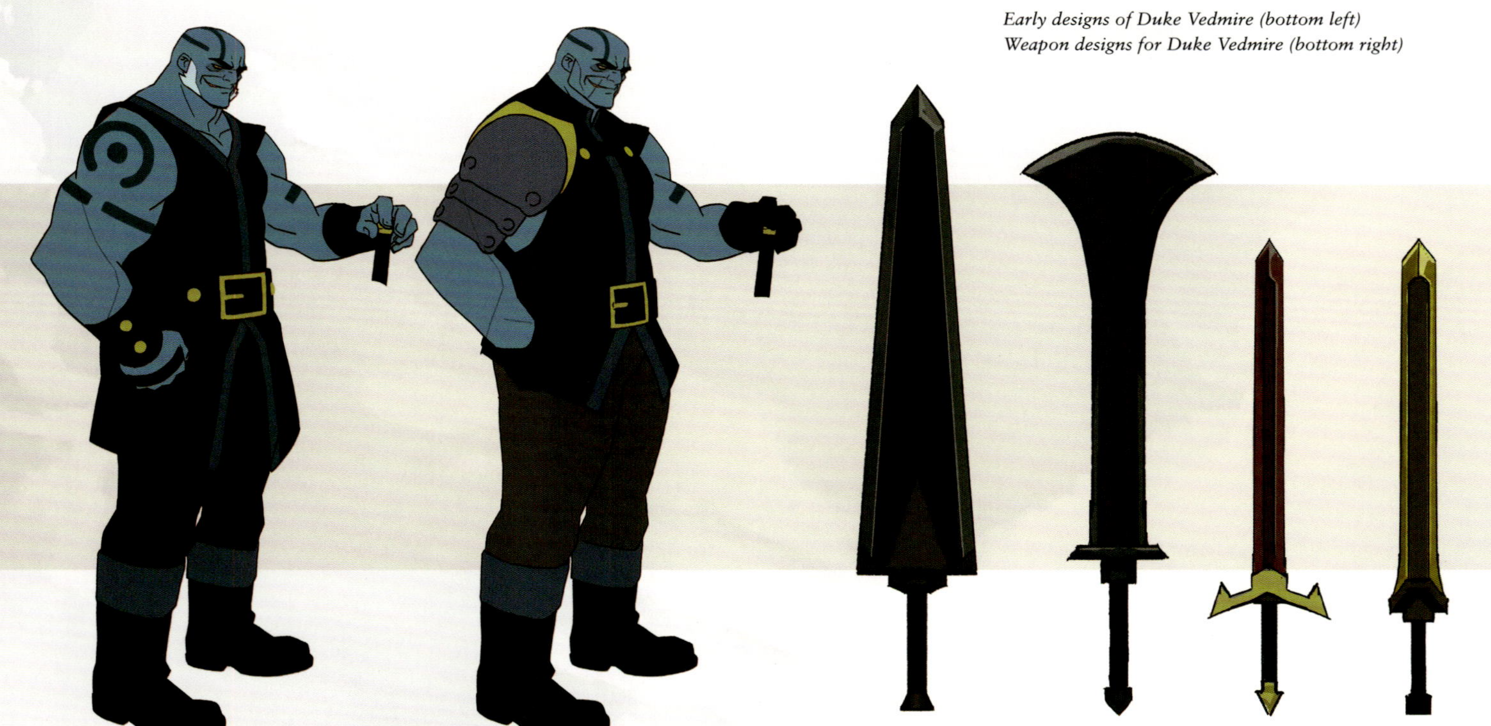

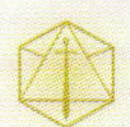

Young Percy

I think we can all agree Percy dresses better now.

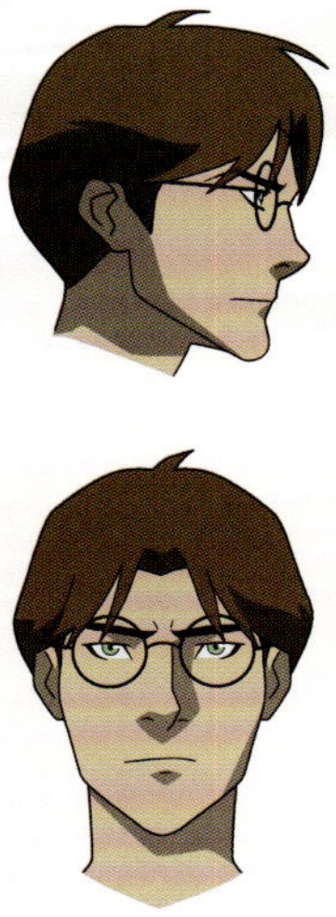

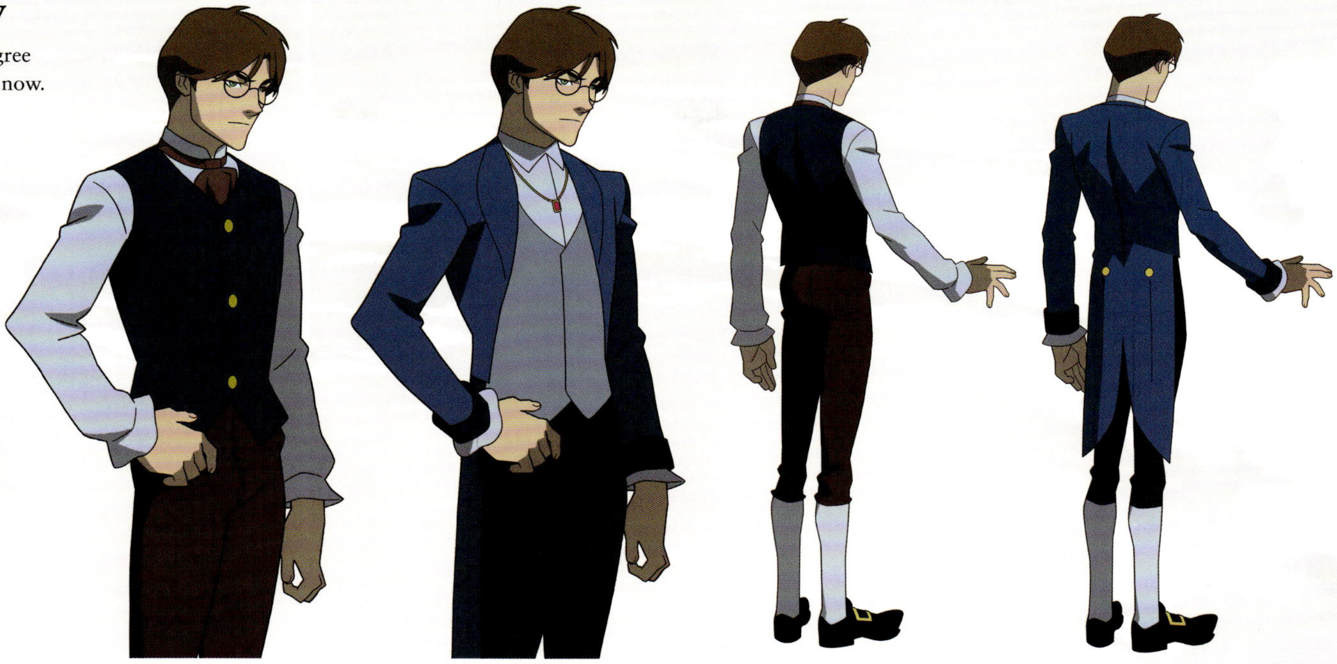

Percy's Family

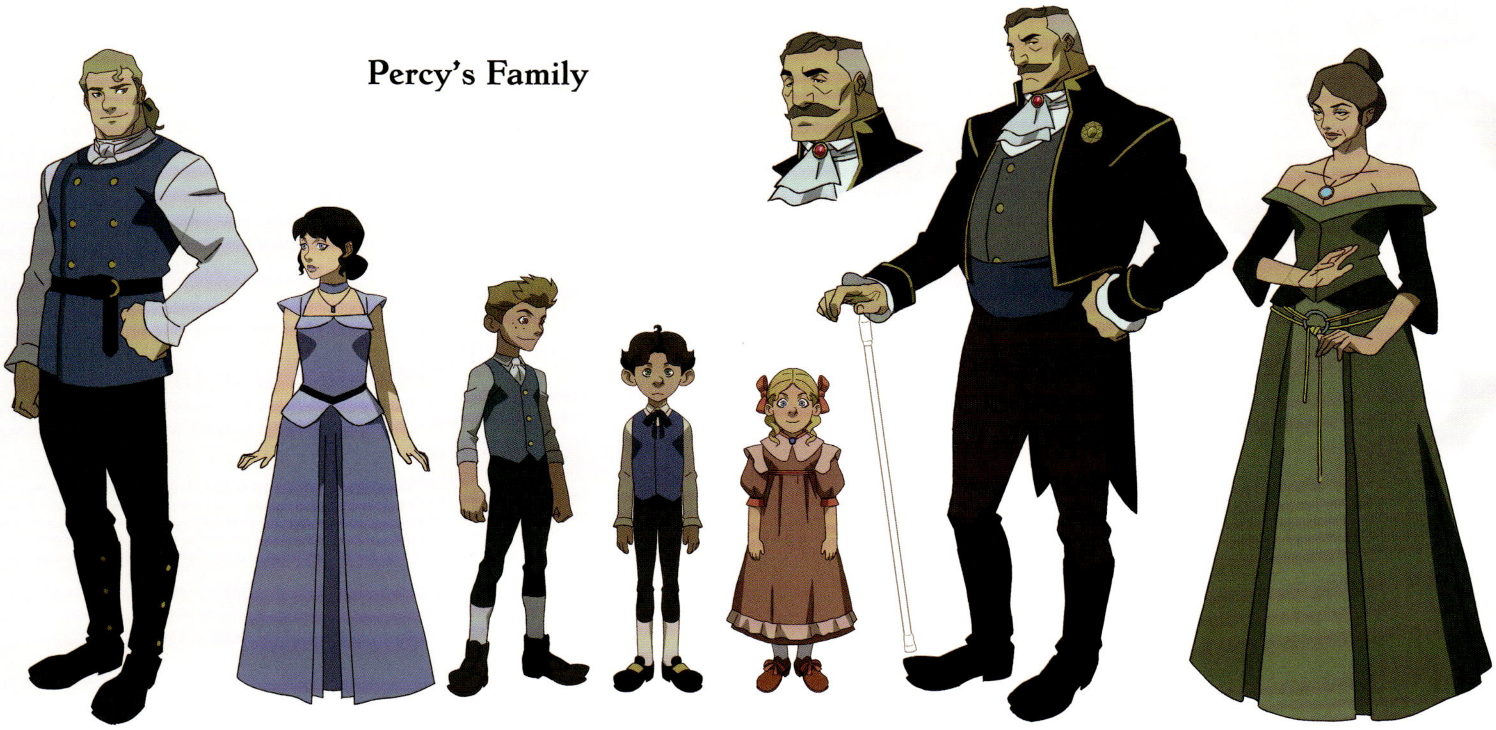

The de Rolos

In *Scanbo*, we get a look at Percy's childhood and family prior to the Briarwoods' reign of terror.

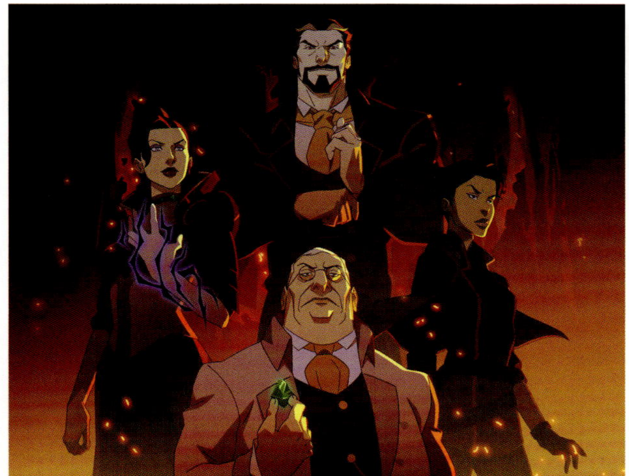

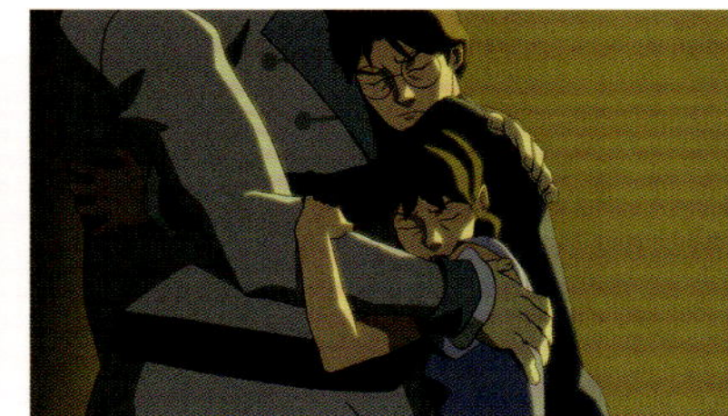

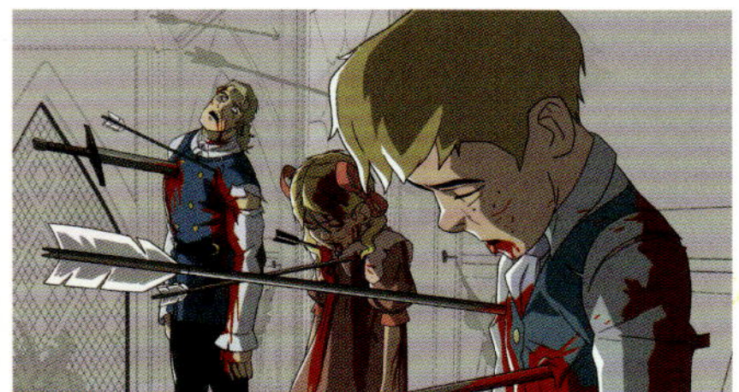

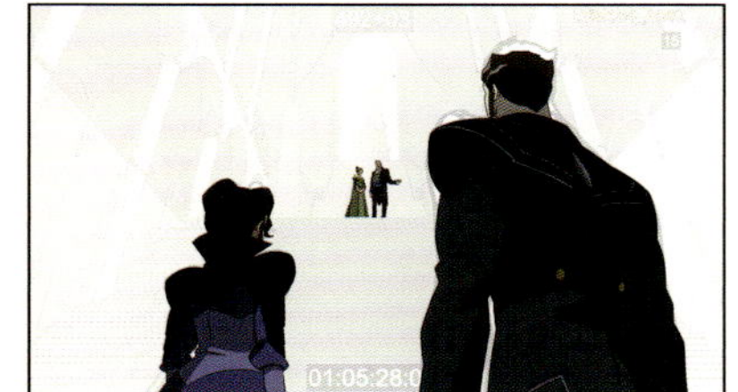

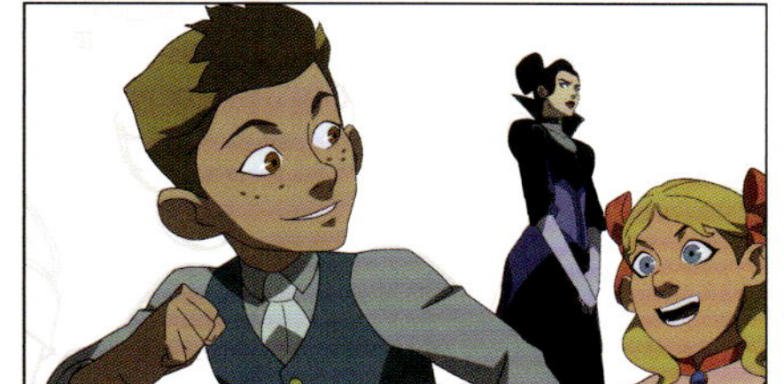

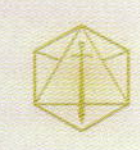

Vedmire's Mansion

Adorned with many of Vedmire's hunting trophies, the design team took inspiration from the hunting lodge aesthetic to emphasize Vedmire's enjoyment of killing for sport. Considering that this home once belonged to Whitestone nobility prior to the Briarwoods' rule, the architecture has Sun Tree symbolism hidden throughout as a nod to its history.

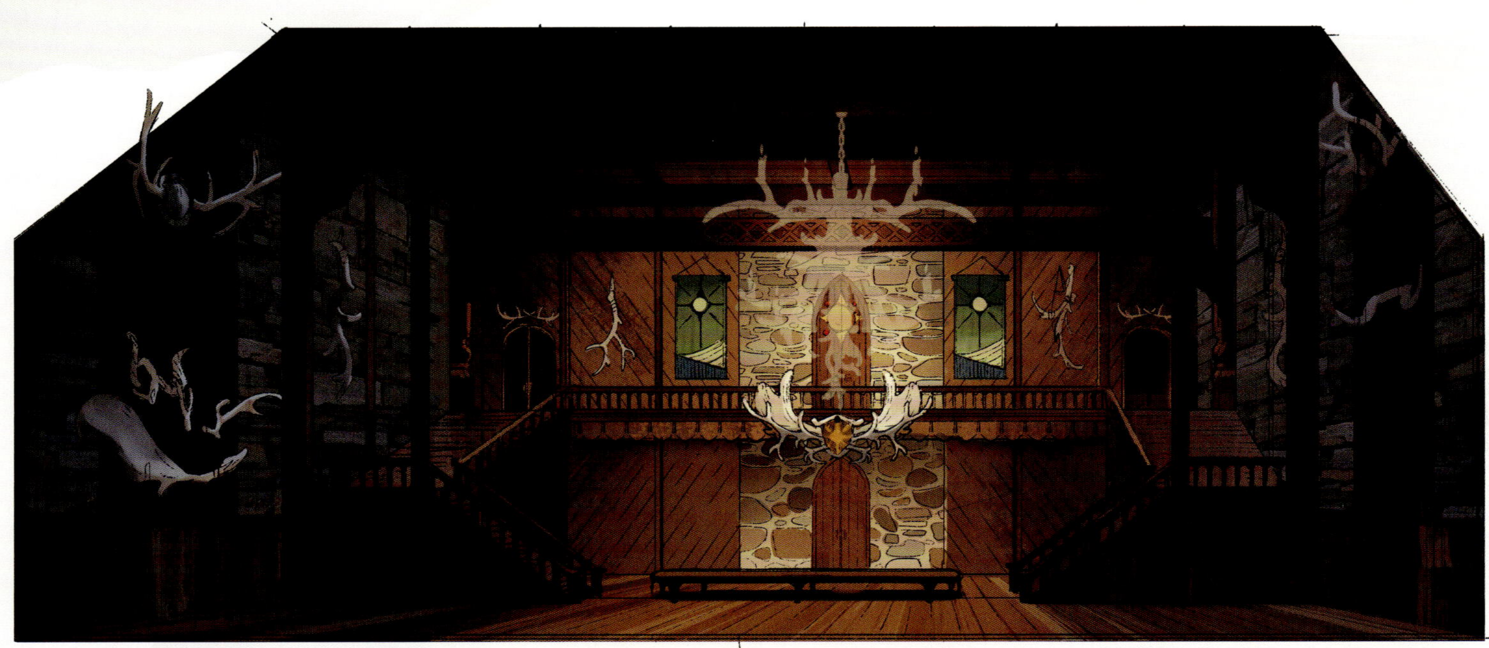

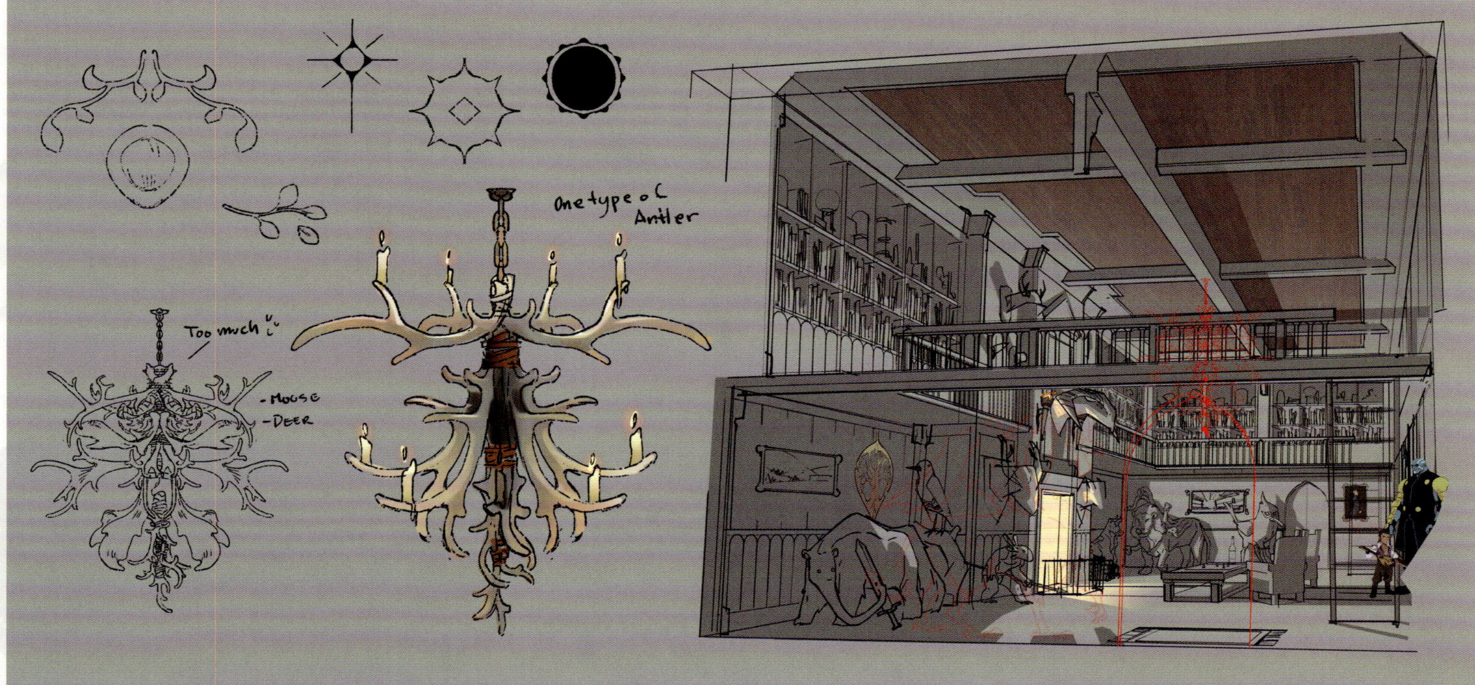

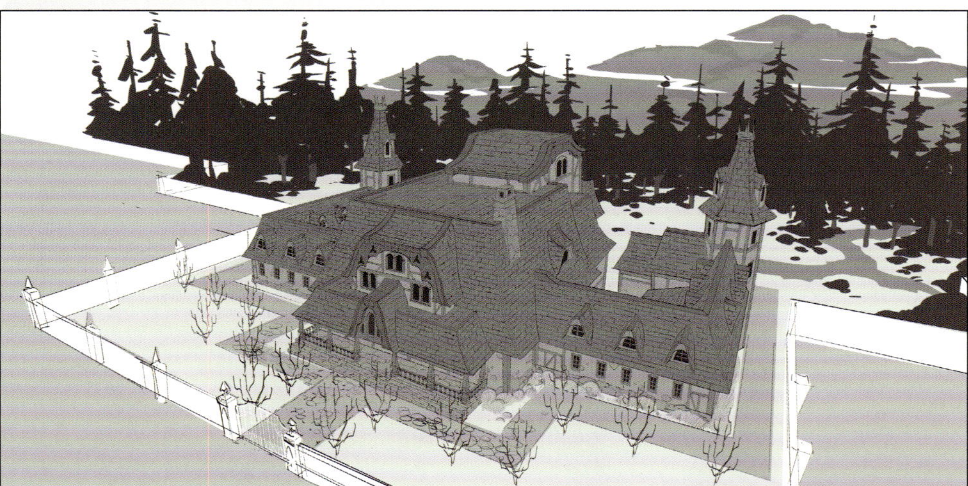

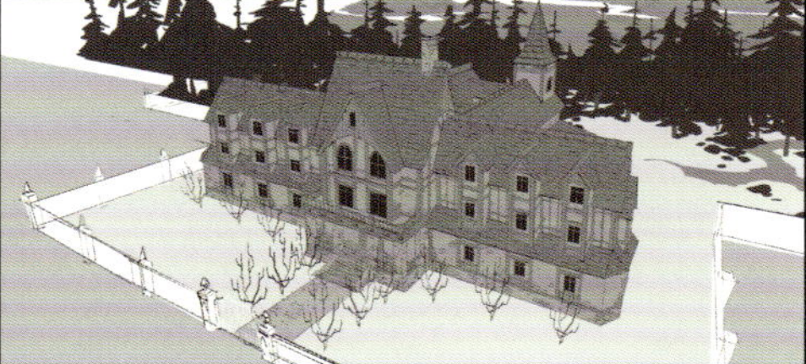

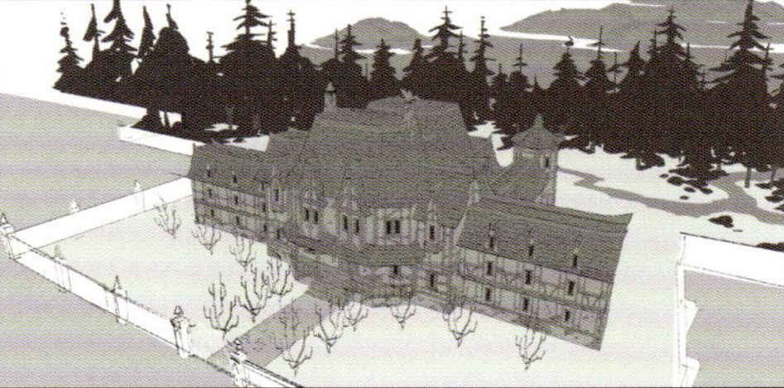

"Funny story actually, I thought this was 74 Whitestone Drive, but it must've been 74 Whitestone Avenue." – SCANLAN, S1E7 "SCANBO"

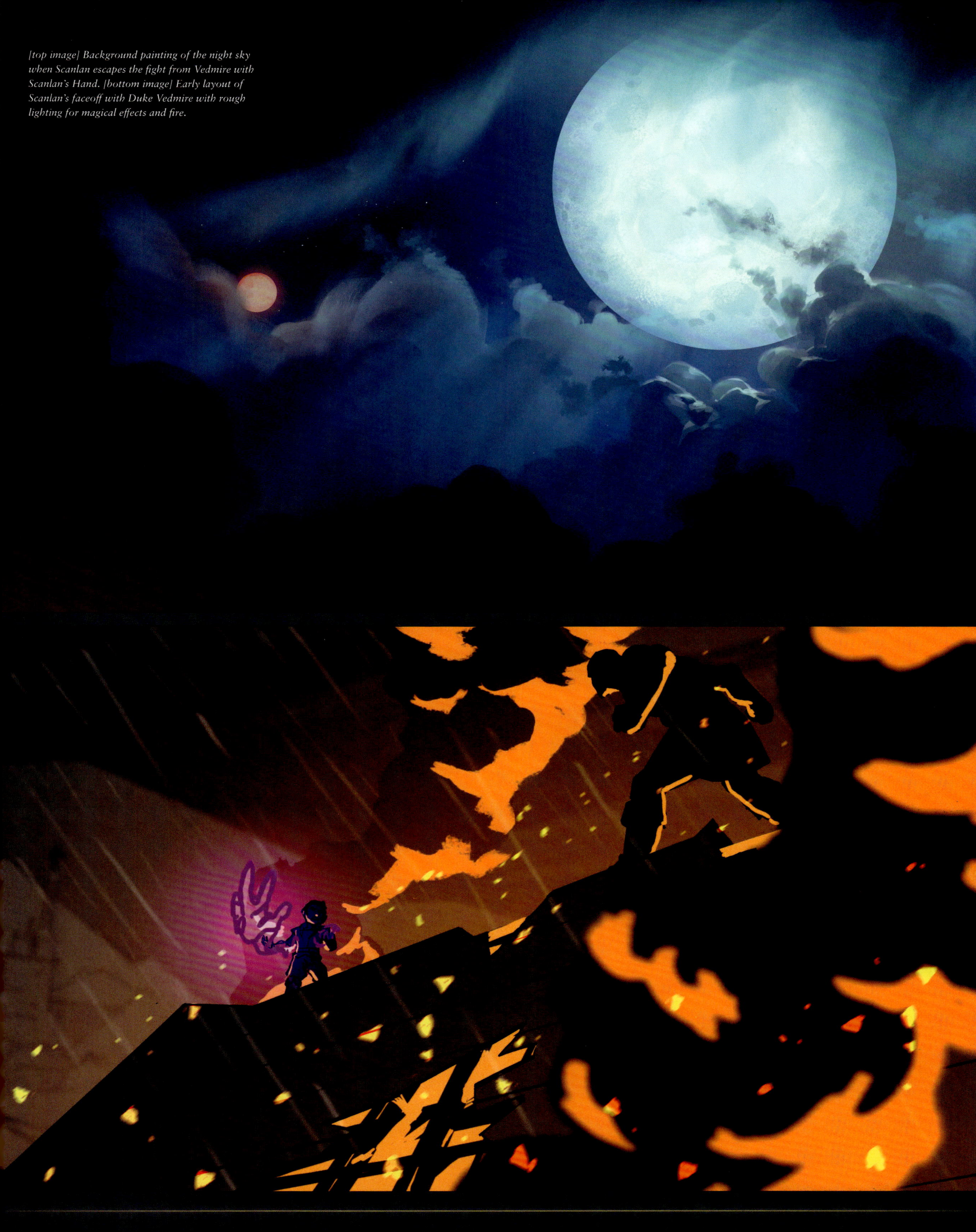

[top image] Background painting of the night sky when Scanlan escapes the fight from Vedmire with Scanlan's Hand. [bottom image] Early layout of Scanlan's faceoff with Duke Vedmire with rough lighting for magical effects and fire.

"I'm afraid this performance is over. You're weak. You're small. And in this world, that means you lose." DUKE VEDMIRE, S1E7 "SCANBO"

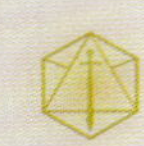

Creating "The List"

With Percy's family murdered, he found himself alone and powerless. Abandoning the family name, he wandered the streets until his thirst for revenge took him to a place so dark he was overtaken by the demon Orthax. Together, they developed a "Pepperbox." This spawn of science fires like a gun, with six chambers. On those six chambers, the names of his intended targets appear on the barrels, ready to meet their mark.

NAMES ON THE LIST

- Kerrion Stonefell
- Professor Anders
- Delilah Briarwood
- Sylas Briarwood
- Anna Ripley
- Cassandra De Rolo (appears later)

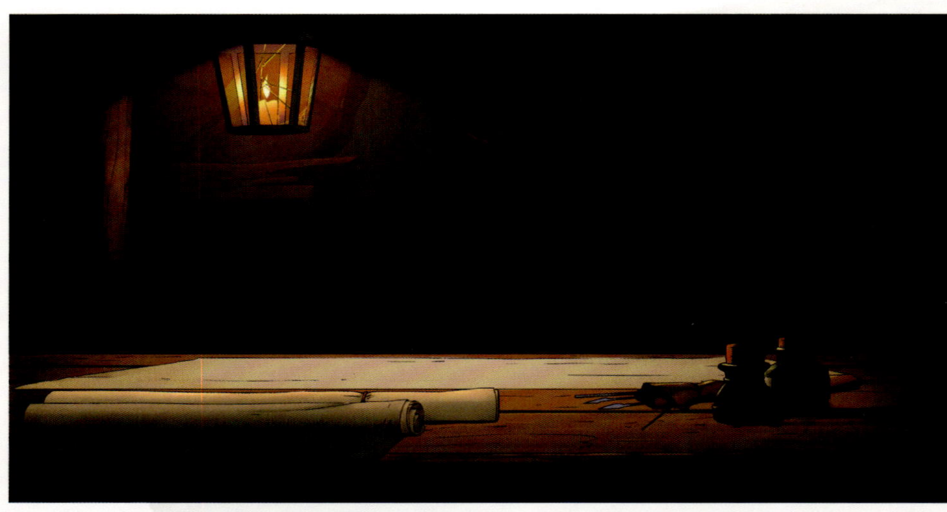

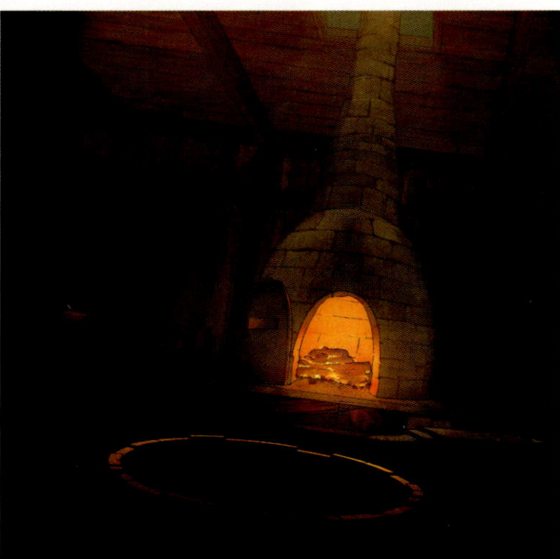

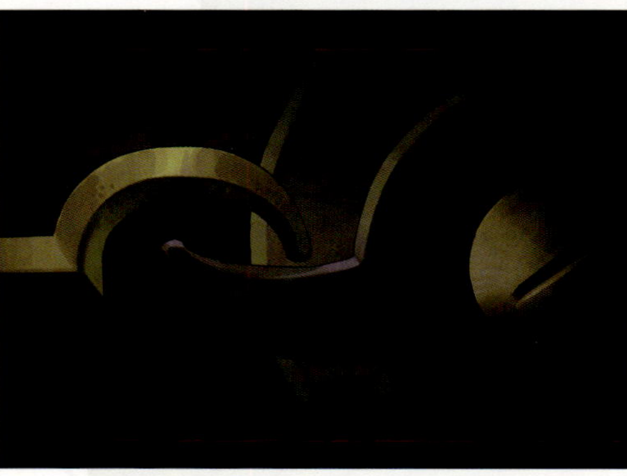

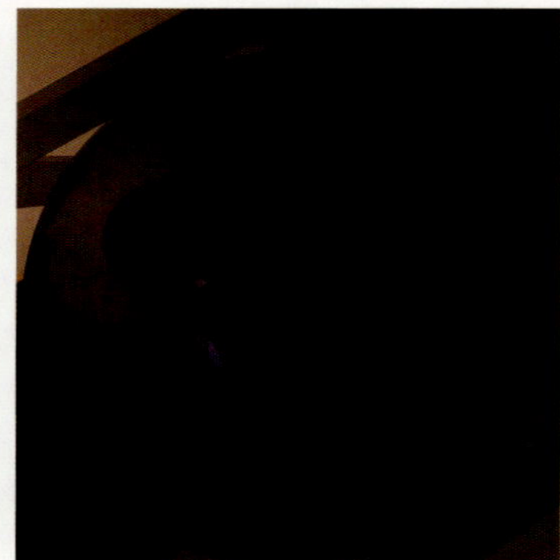

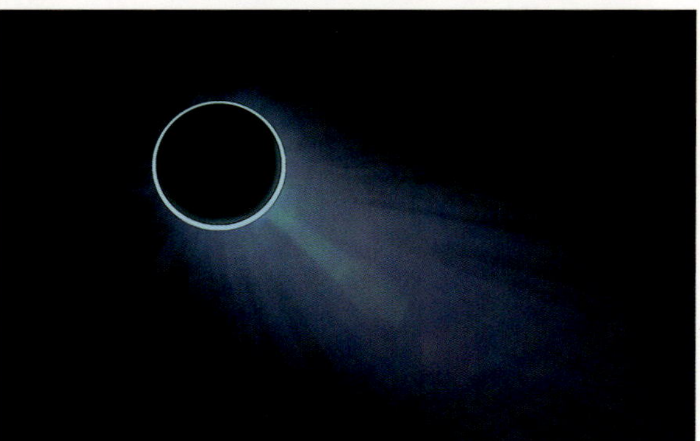

"I dreamt of a machine that would tip the scales of fortune in my favor." – PERCY, S1E7 "SCANBO"

Shape-Change Scroll

In another fan-favorite moment from the campaign, Scanlan uses this shape-change scroll discovered in Brimscythe's lair to transform into a triceratops. Who said dinosaurs were extinct?

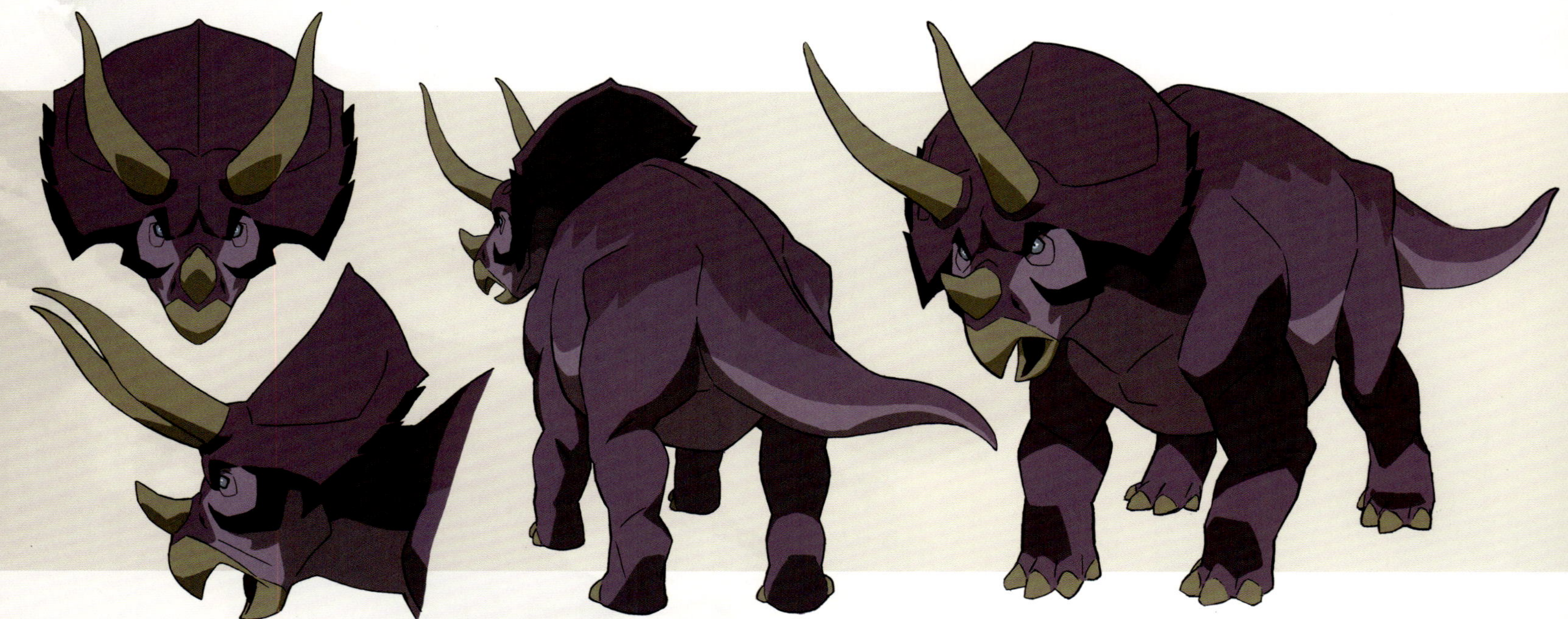

Storyboards from Scanlan and Vedmire's Showdown

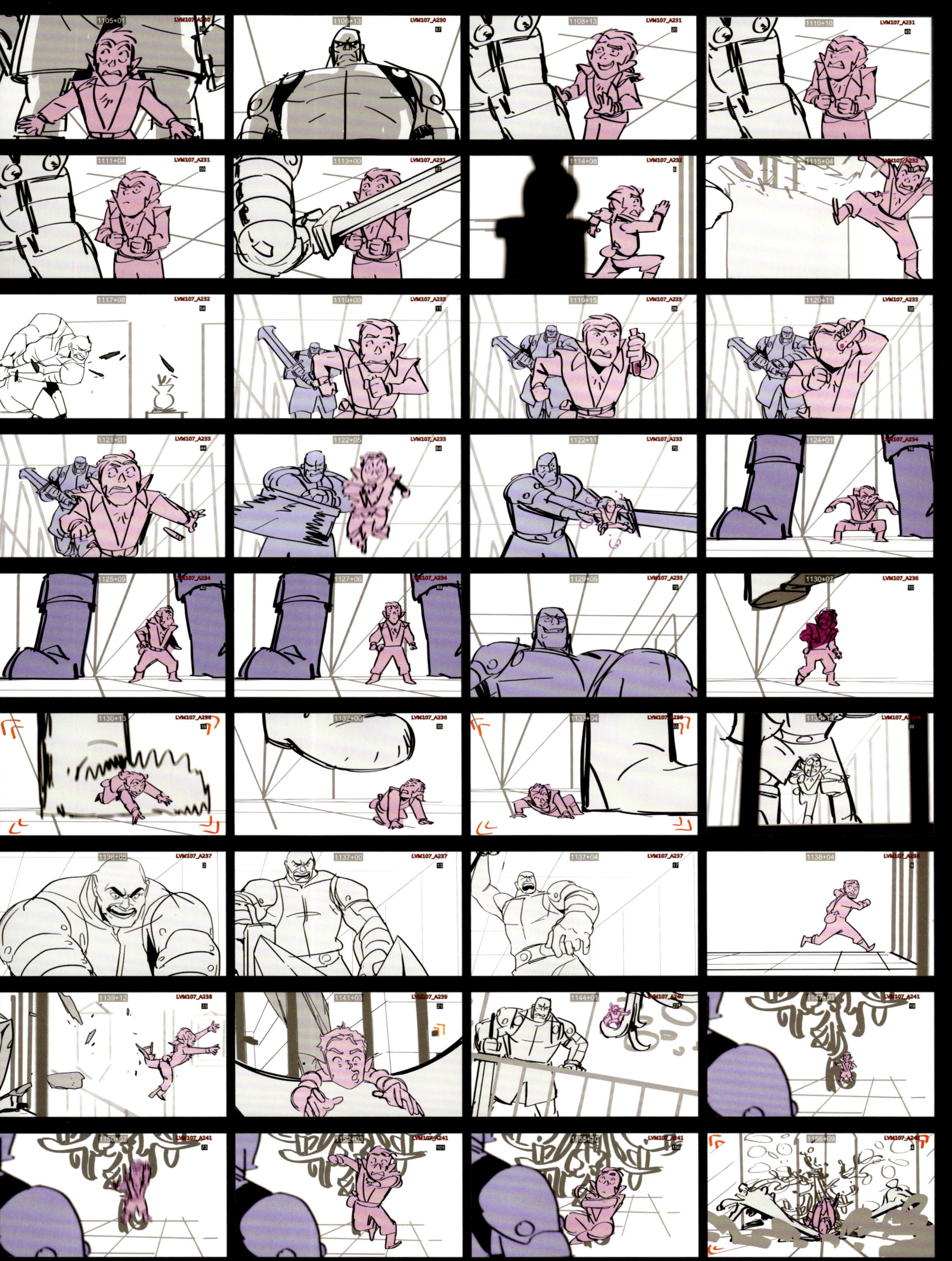

"Not bad–I should remember that spell." –SCANLAN, S1E7 "SCANBO"

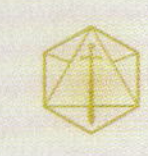

EPISODE 8

A SILVER TONGUE

"We find Cassandra. Cassandra almost dies. Keyleth saves her. Grog becomes evil for a minute thanks to Anders's silver tongue. But then we rip it out of his skull, so Grog's okay! Unfortunately, Pikey's not doing so well on her faith journey, and when Delilah decides to raise a zombie horde against us… we could really use a Priest right about now." – A RECOUNTING OF "A SILVER TONGUE" BY SCANLAN SHORTHALT

Professor Anders

Cassandra de Rolo

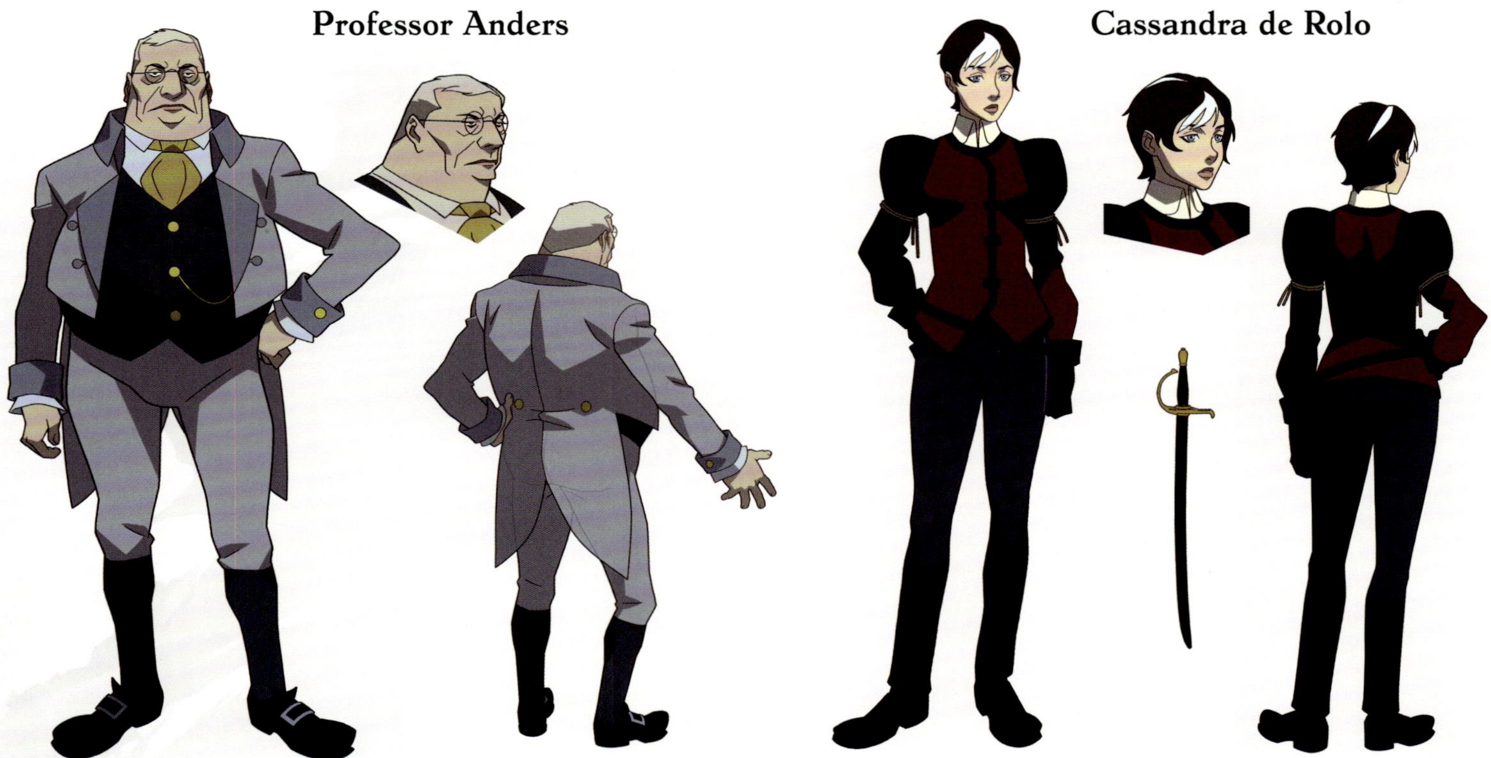

Percy's former tutor, Anders aided the Briarwoods in their coup of Whitestone by using his knowledge of the castle to help them sneak inside the gates. His magic allows him to control people and objects with his voice, harnessed by a silver tongue.

While initially coming off as haughty, cold, and direct, when you get to know her, Cassandra is actually haughty, cold, and direct. She is a skilled fighter with a rapier and has the royal grooming fit for a leader, even if we are slow to trust her after the Briarwood reign.

Minxie

Images blocking out Keyleth's transformation to Minxie for the animation team.

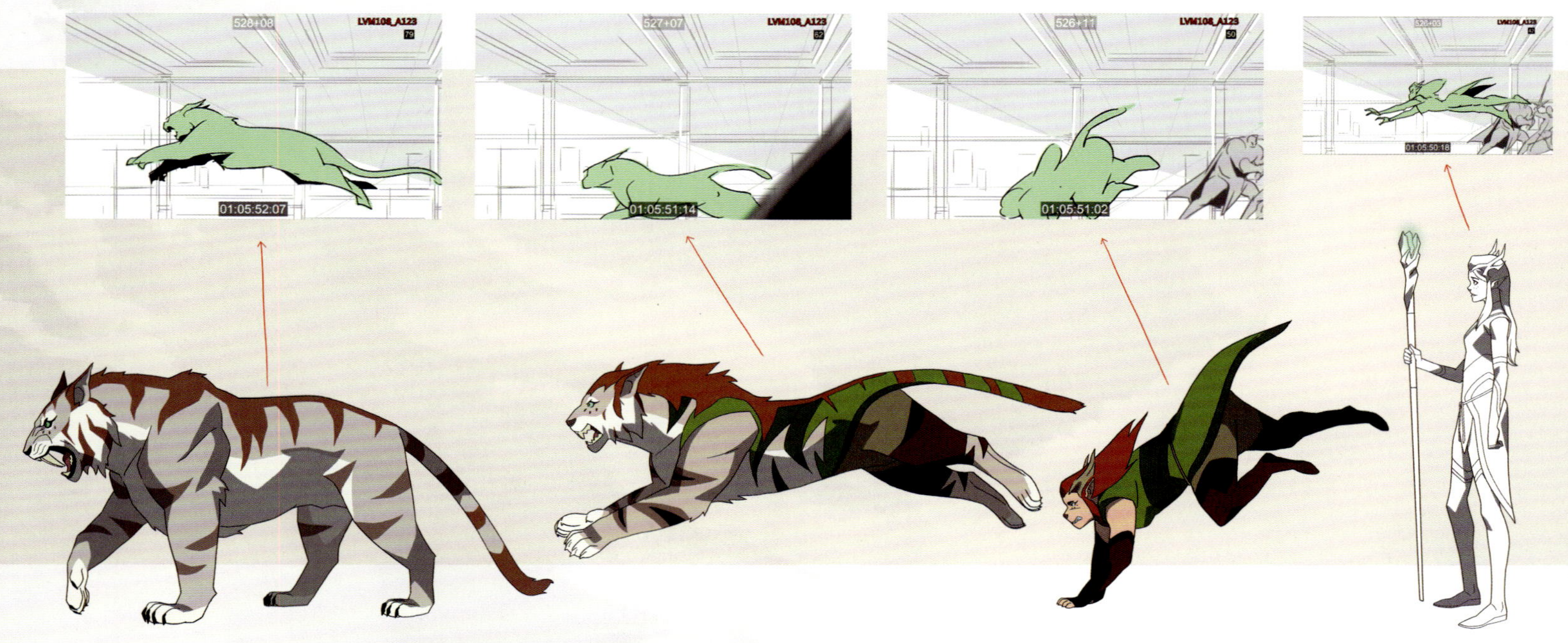

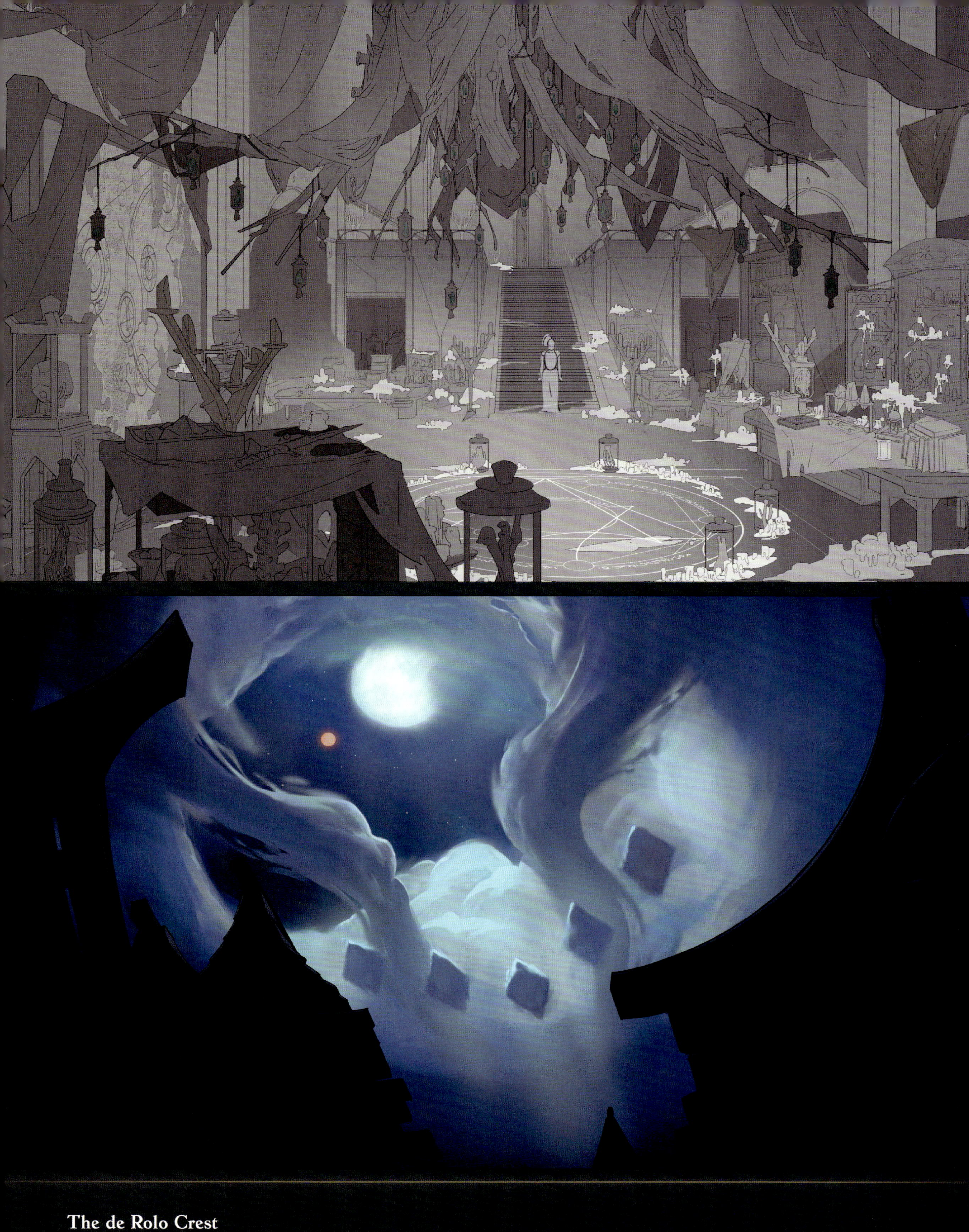

The de Rolo Crest

Formed in the sky via Keyleth's skywriting ability, it serves as a call to arms for those in Whitestone who are ready to overthrow the Briarwood.

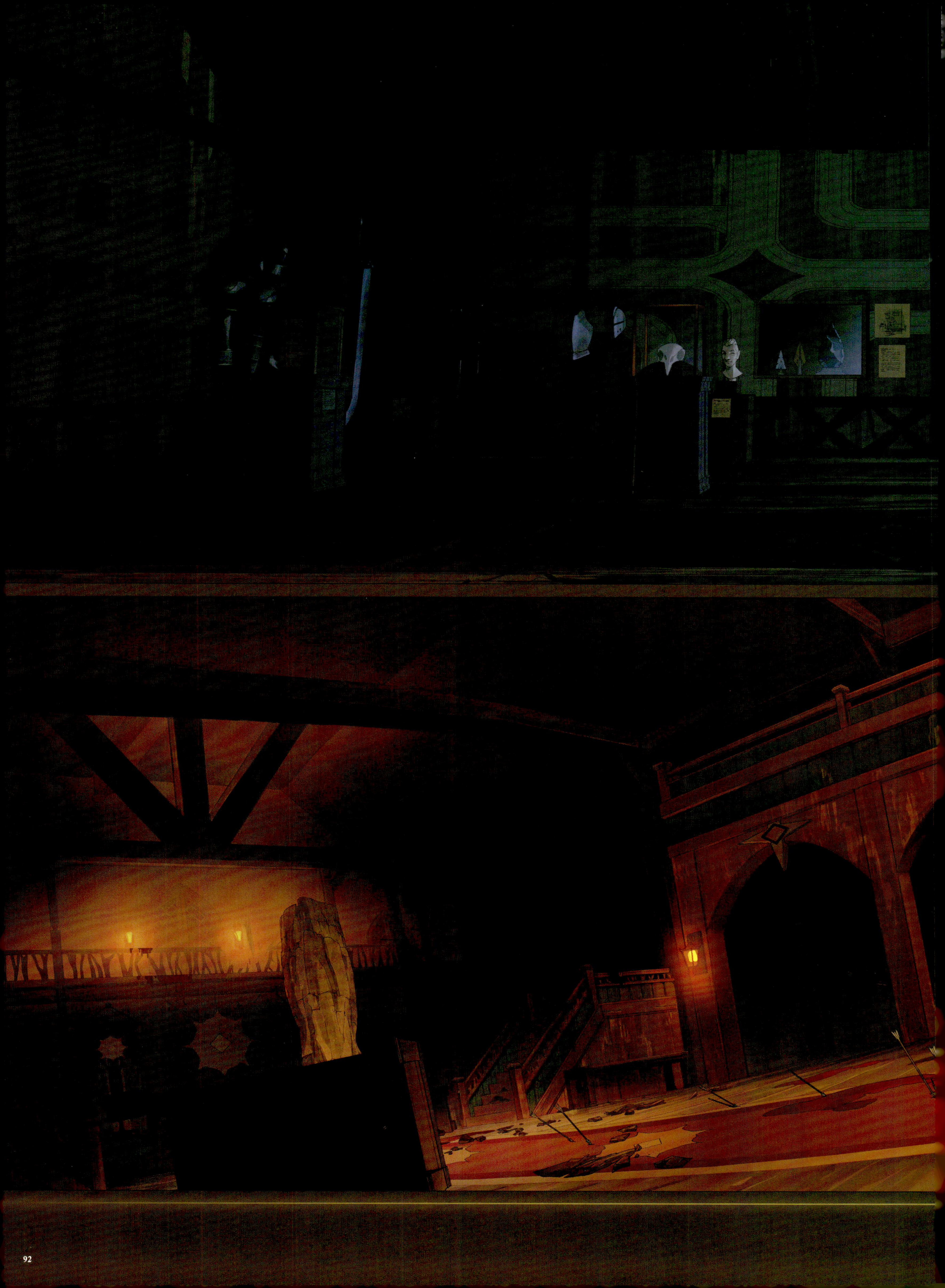

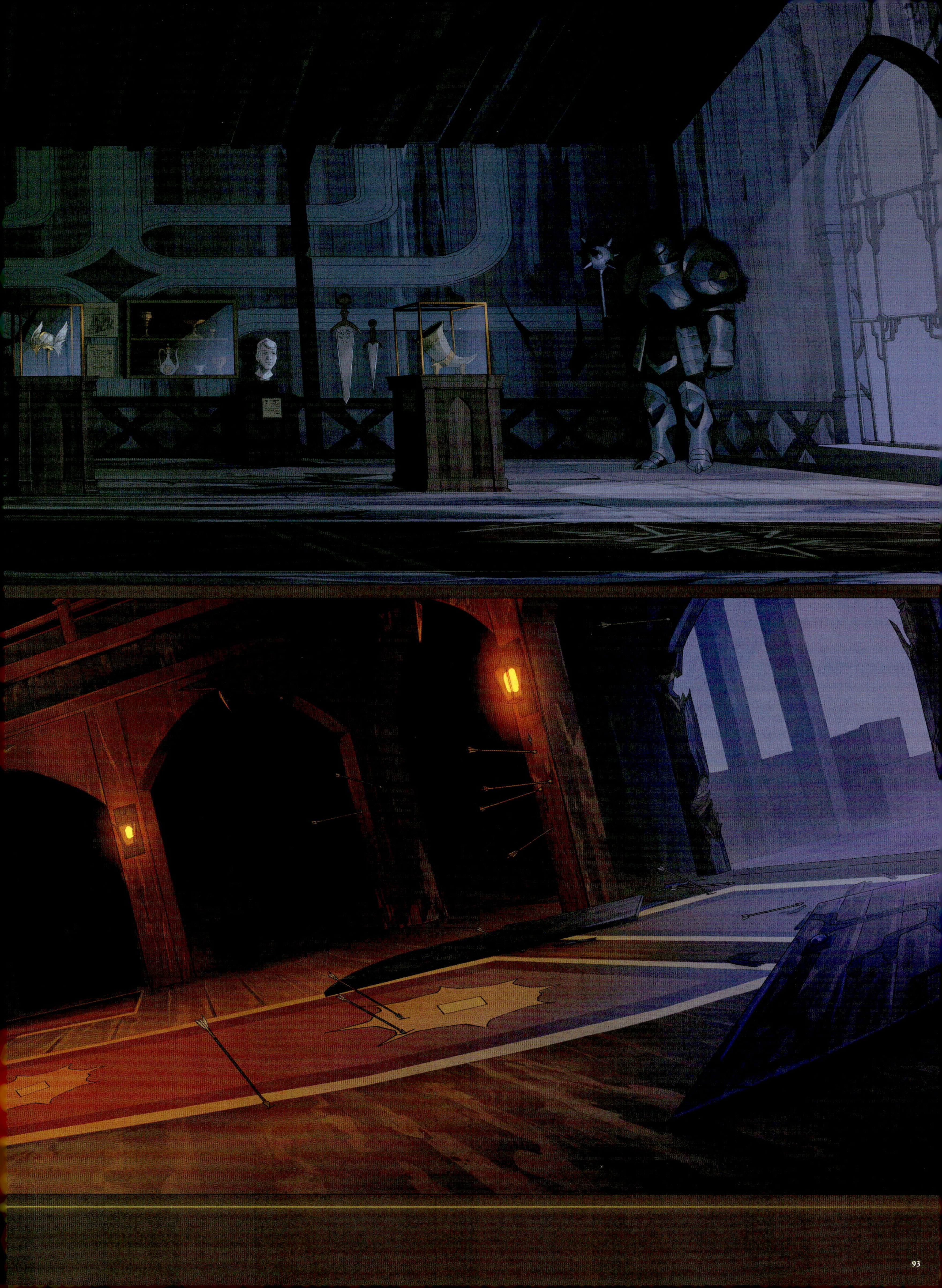

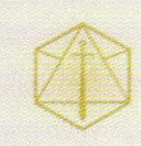

Professor Anders's House

"Anders was described to us by Mercer as a pseudo-intellectual who wears all the trappings of a learned man but is actually just an egotistical collector. We staged the showdown between him and Percy in Anders' trophy room, designed as a miniature museum of relics he has amassed from different corners of Tal'Dorei. This was a great spot to include a few easter eggs, like portraits of various Critical Role crew on the walls–Rachel Romero, Ed Lopez, Ben Van Der Fluit, and our own supervising director Sung Jin Ahn." – ARTHUR LOFTIS (ART DIRECTOR)

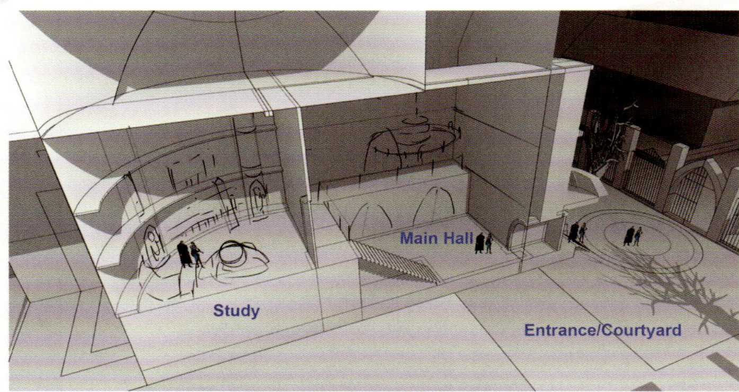

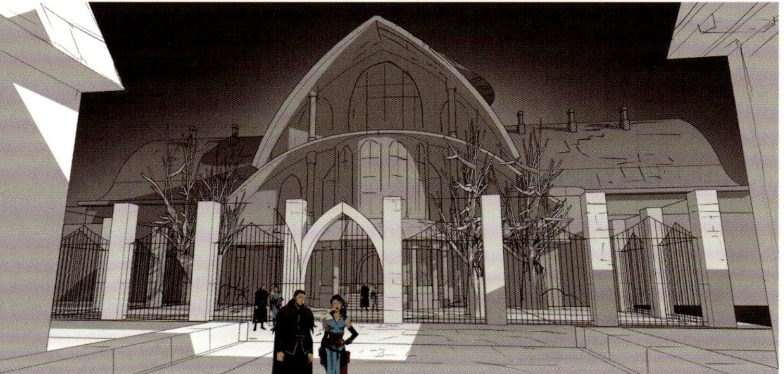

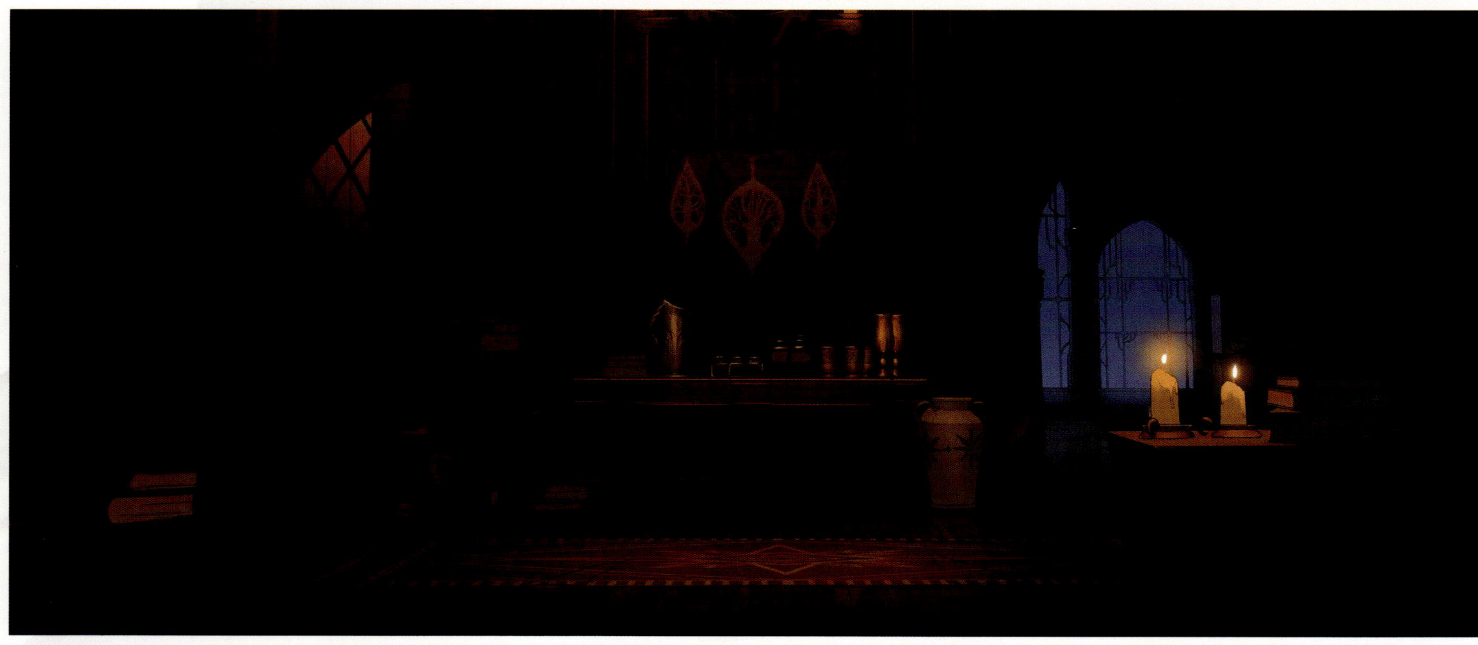

Suits of Armor

Lining the walls of Anders's study, these suits of armor come alive when commanded by Anders to attack Vox Machina.

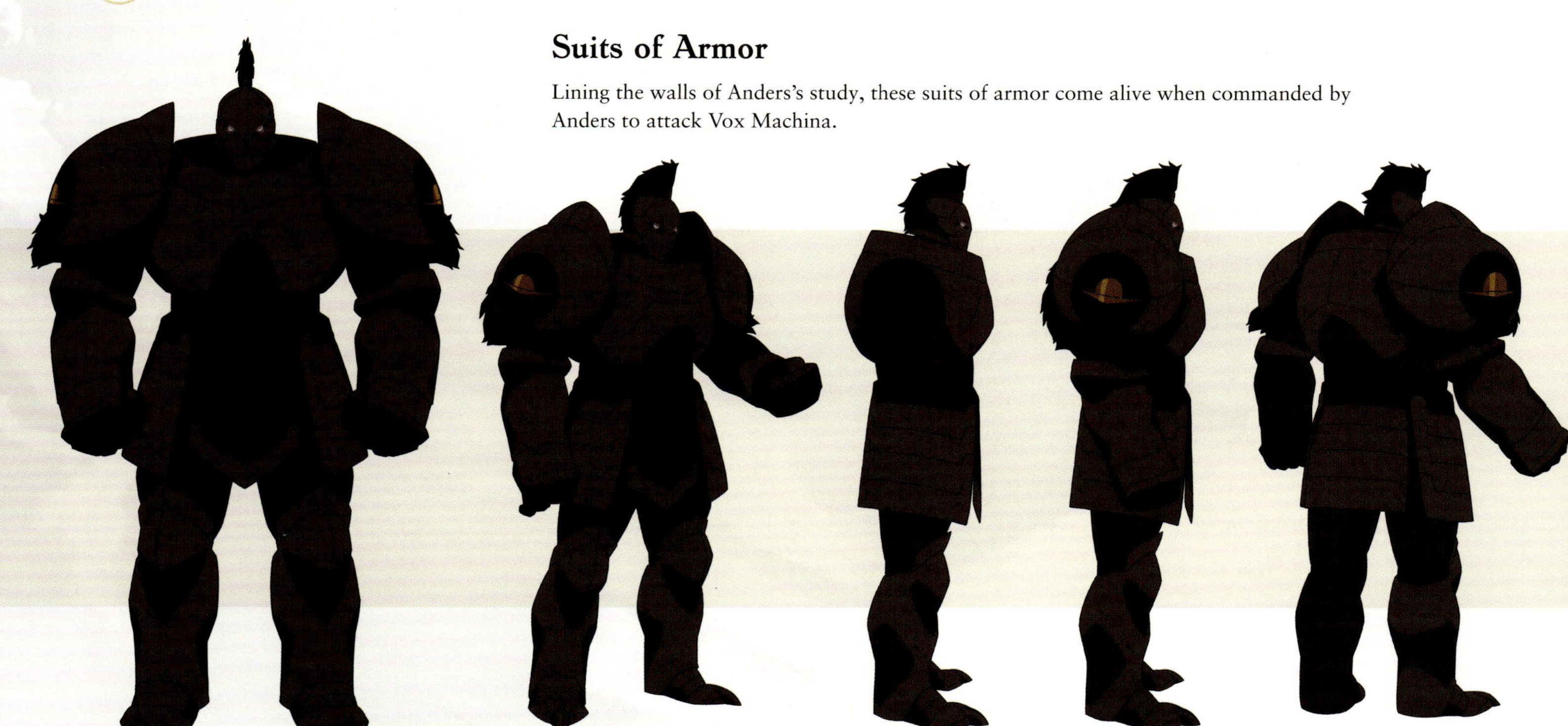

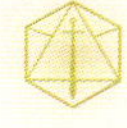

FROM SCRIPT TO SCREEN

PIKE'S COMMUNE WITH THE EVERLIGHT

There's a figure in darkness in the distance.

A LOUD SOUND AND FLASH OF DARKNESS SEEM TO ATTACK HER. She rears back, then slowly backs away in fear.

Suddenly, the darkness envelops her as several black tentacle arms rise and begin tugging at her. They drag her through the darkness, keeping her aloft above the ground. HANDS FROM EVERYWHERE surround her, SQUEEZING the life from her...

INT. TEMPLE OF THE EVERLIGHT - NIGHT

Pike floats above the floor with her eyes closed, IMMENSE PAIN evident on her face, blood streaming from her nose. She <groans> in pain. The flames around her are lit with fury.

The door BURSTS open and the clerics RUSH back in -- and right to her side.

67 HEAD CLERIC
Pike! Can you hear us?

She doesn't answer, but her body continues to thrash. The clerics look worried -

68 CLERIC
We're losing her.

INT. INKY VOID (PIKE'S VISION)

In the blackness, Pike fights back, <screaming>, as the darkness ties her down, grabbing her by the throat. The darkness starts to climb up her body.

IT climbs up her chest and shoulders, almost reaching her face.

70 PIKE
I can't go. I won't go. Not without an answer.

Pike begins to sink into the darkness, like quicksand.

71 PIKE
No please! Everlight!!!!!

With her last breath, she screams for the Everlight as she sinks under the inky blackness...

INT. PRISTINE PLANE (PIKE'S VISION) - CONTINUOUS

Suddenly, a bright burning light appears. Pike's unconscious body is lifted out of the liquid substance, which instead of the inky blackness, is a shining bright. Pike floats above the surface, surrounded by BLINDING WHITE. Pike rises, gaining consciousness, to greet the bright burning sun in front of her.

72 PIKE
You heard me? Thank you. I-I was trying so hard to find you.

In the center of the pale expanse, the flaming sun glows brighter. She covers her eyes from the brightness.

73 PIKE
Everlight...? Is that really you?

...the flame grows even bigger, revealing a FIGURE IN THE LIGHT.

A female voice, deep and lush, answers.

74 EVERLIGHT
Speak, child. Who are you?

75 PIKE
I'm... lost. I tried to live up to your standards; to be a steward of your faith. But I failed. I need to find my way back to your Light.

76 EVERLIGHT
Lies will not lead you back.

The flame FLARES UP, angry and bright.

77 PIKE
I'm- I'm not lying! <PAINED CRY>

The flames grow even more intense, pressing towards Pike.

Pike braces herself from the flames, scared and taken aback. She covers her face to protect herself, recoiling in pain with seemingly no way out...

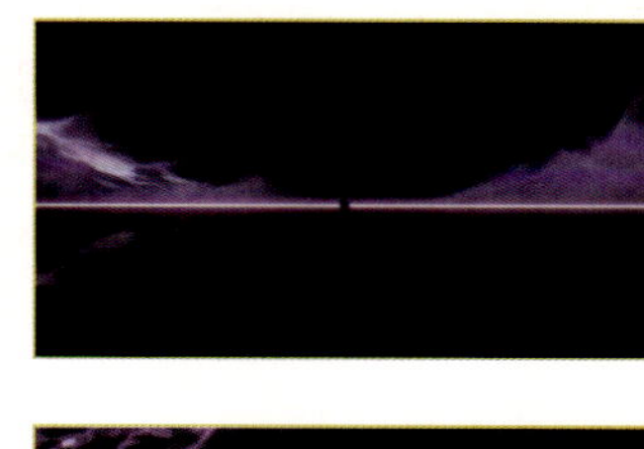
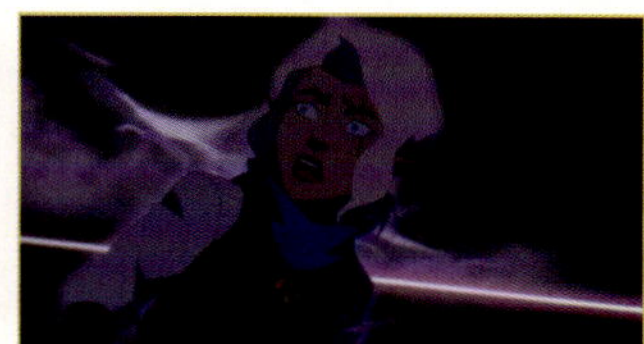
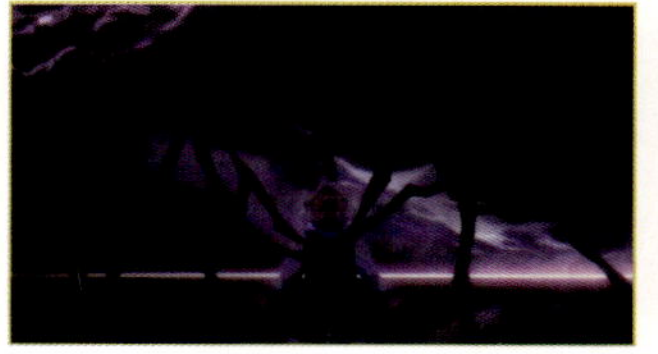
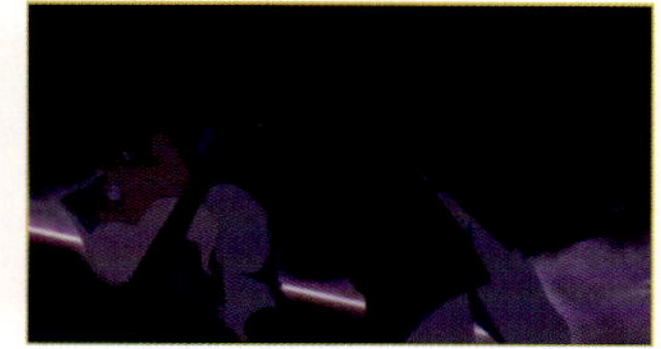
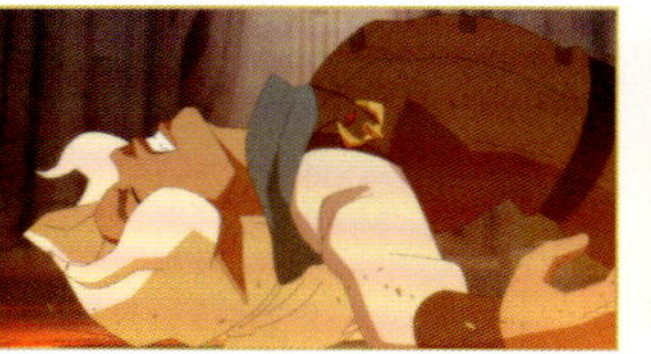
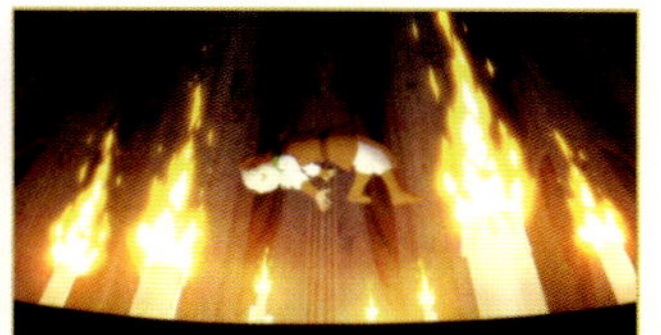
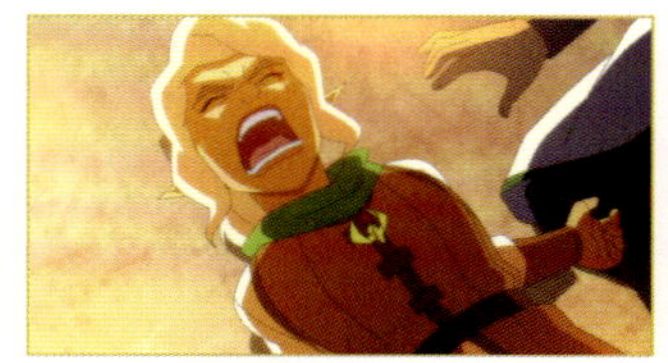
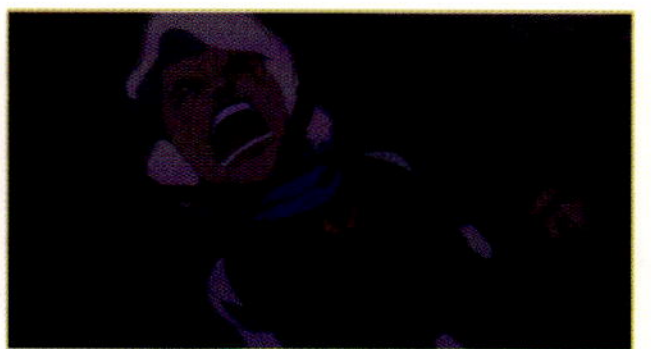
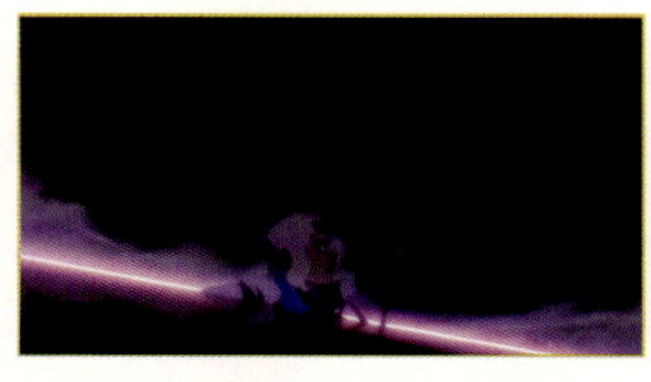
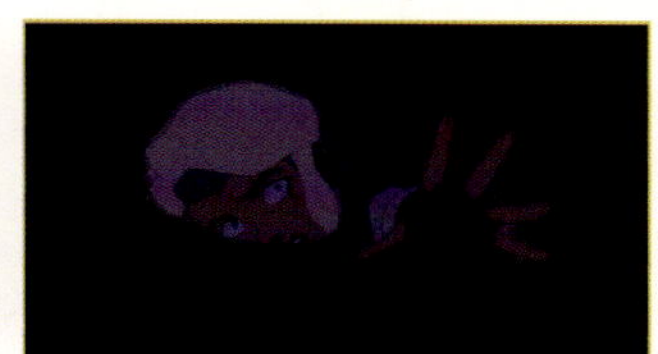
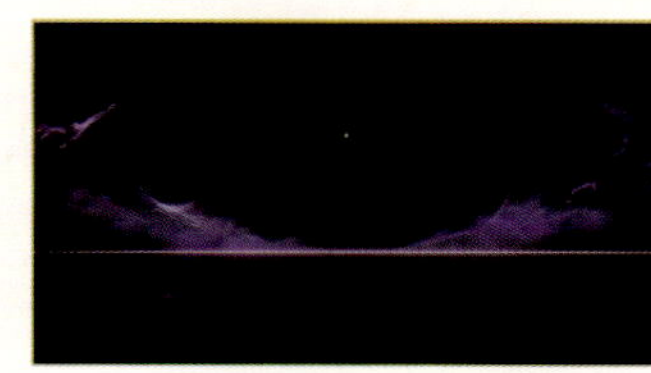
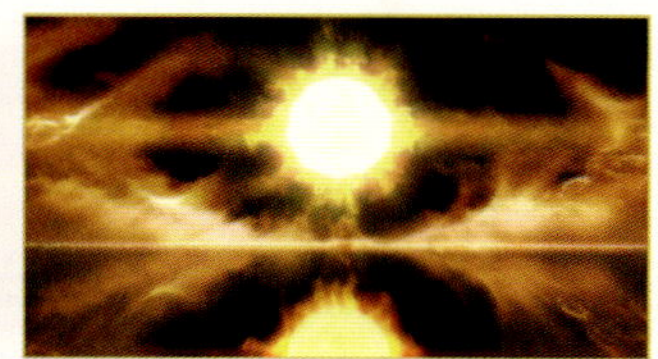
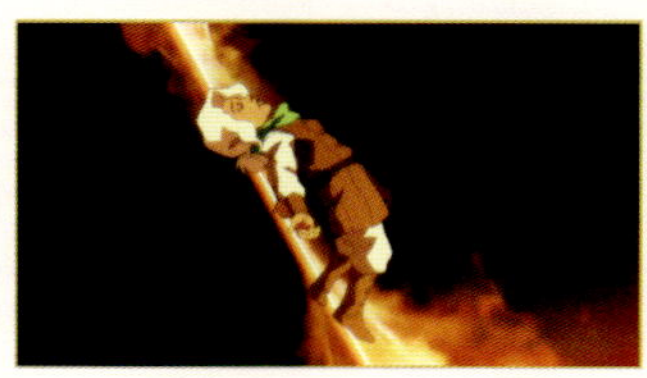
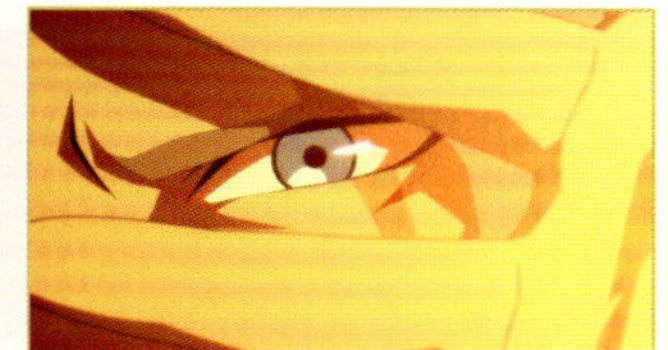
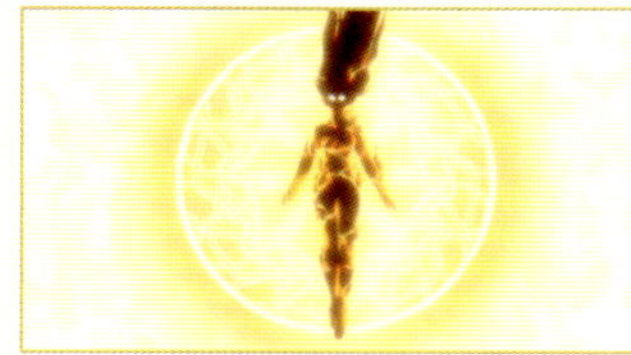
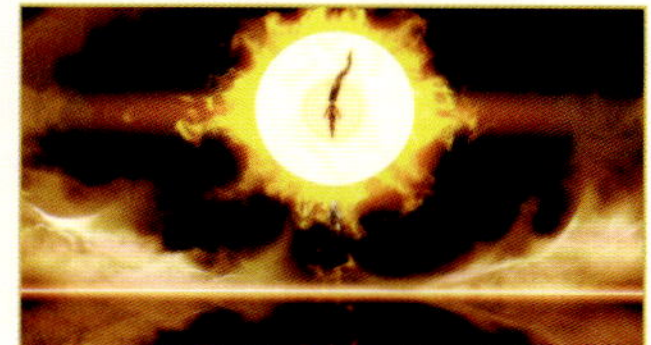

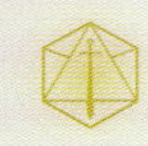

EPISODE 9

THE TIDE OF BONE

"The heroes known as Vox Machina take on a zombie horde in an epic fight that takes sweet Archie to an early grave. Cassandra does her sister thing and gets Percy to finally step up and be a leader, prompting him to give an okay speech that spurs us into battle. Pike FINALLY decides to show up and help out a bit, but most importantly, I almost have a threesome with a zombie!" – A RECOUNTING OF "THE TIDE OF BONE" BY SCANLAN SHORTHALT

Undead Horde

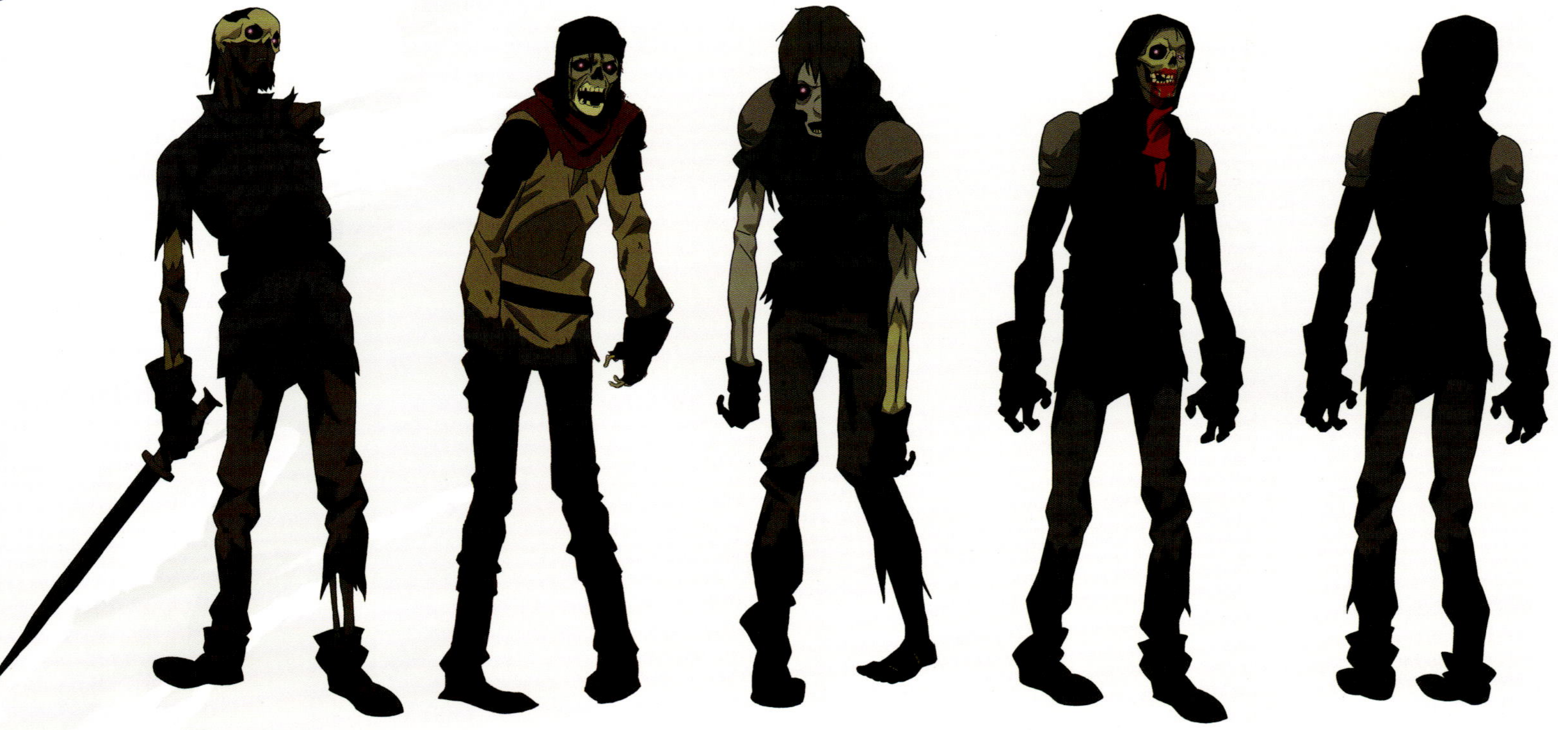

Creating an undead army took a literal alive army of artists to complete. Many shows will limit the number of designs in large group shots and just repeat models, but the team on Vox Machina wanted every zombie to have a unique design and movement cycle to really give the fight a realistic feel.

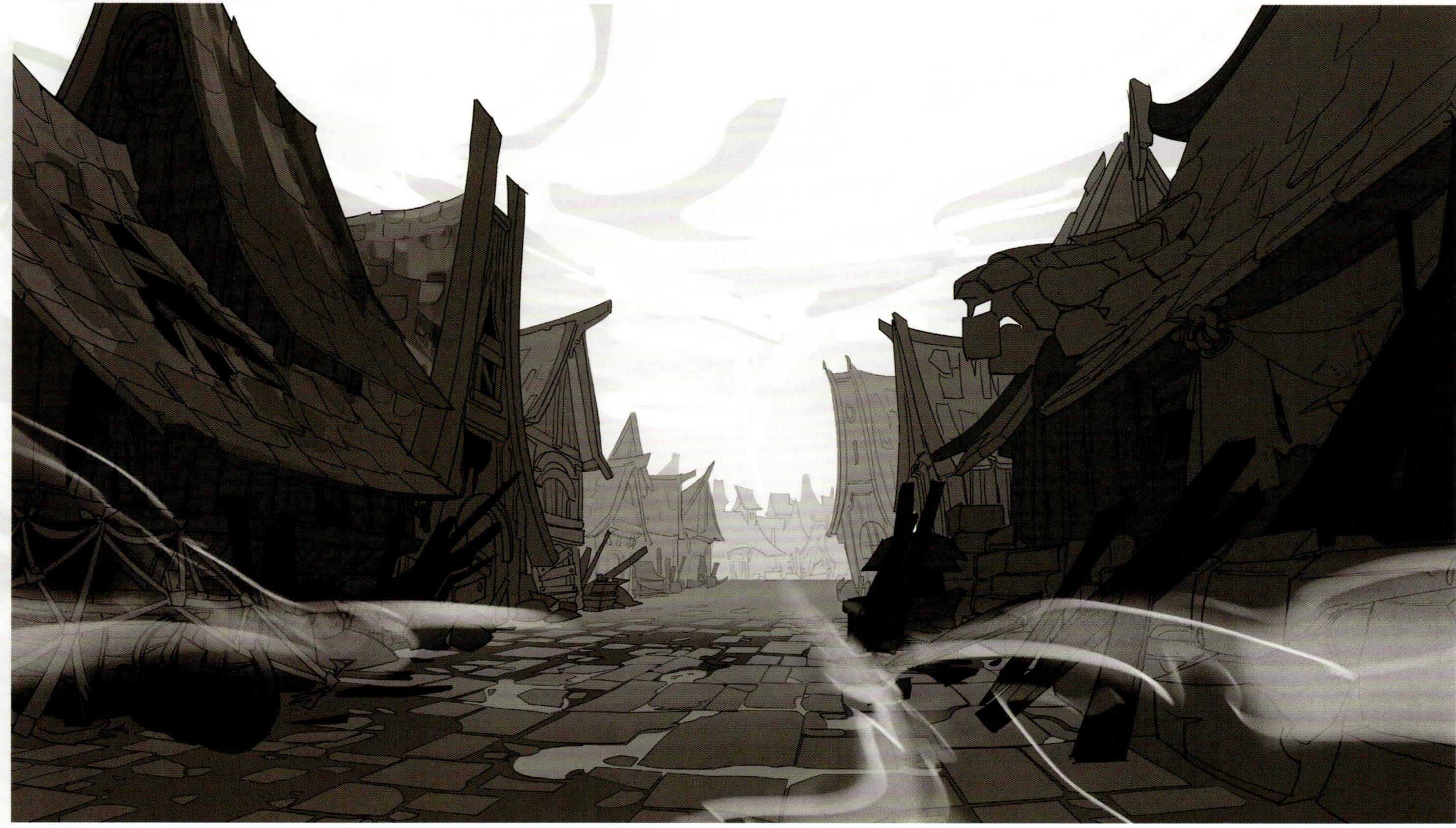

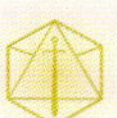

Astral Projection of Pike

When you can't get the real thing, astral projection Pike is a pretty close second. Radiating with the holy energy of The Everlight, Pike returns to help Vox Machina live to fight another day.

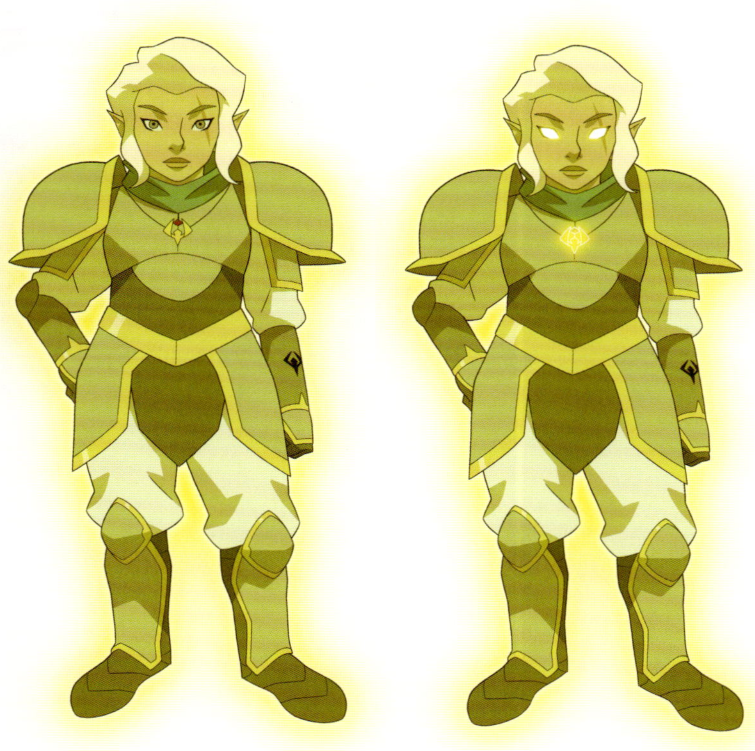

Bad News

The only weapon powerful enough to take down an undead giant in one shot. Good thing its only single use or this thing would be seriously OP.

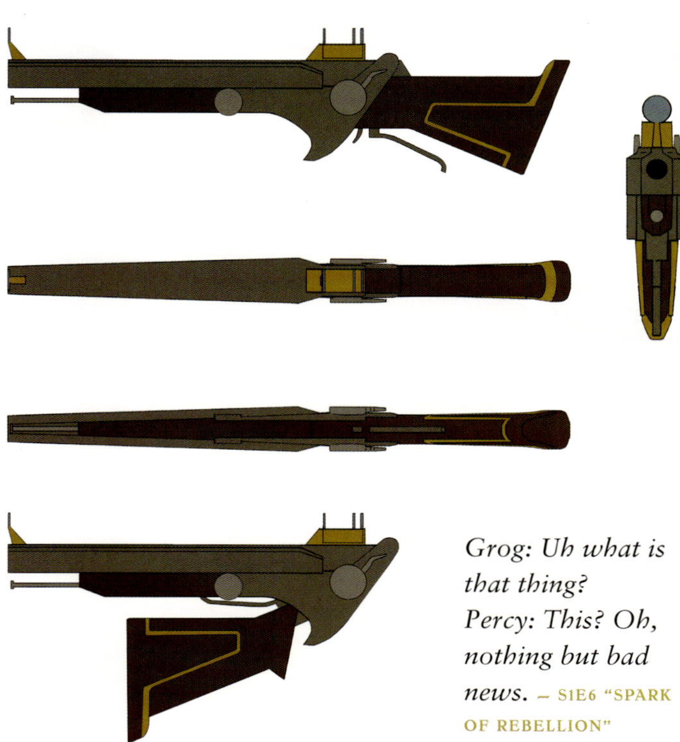

Grog: Uh what is that thing?
Percy: This? Oh, nothing but bad news. — S1E6 "SPARK OF REBELLION"

Whitestone Dungeon

A secret passage into Whitestone Castle and the perfect place for someone from Percy's past to make an untimely return.

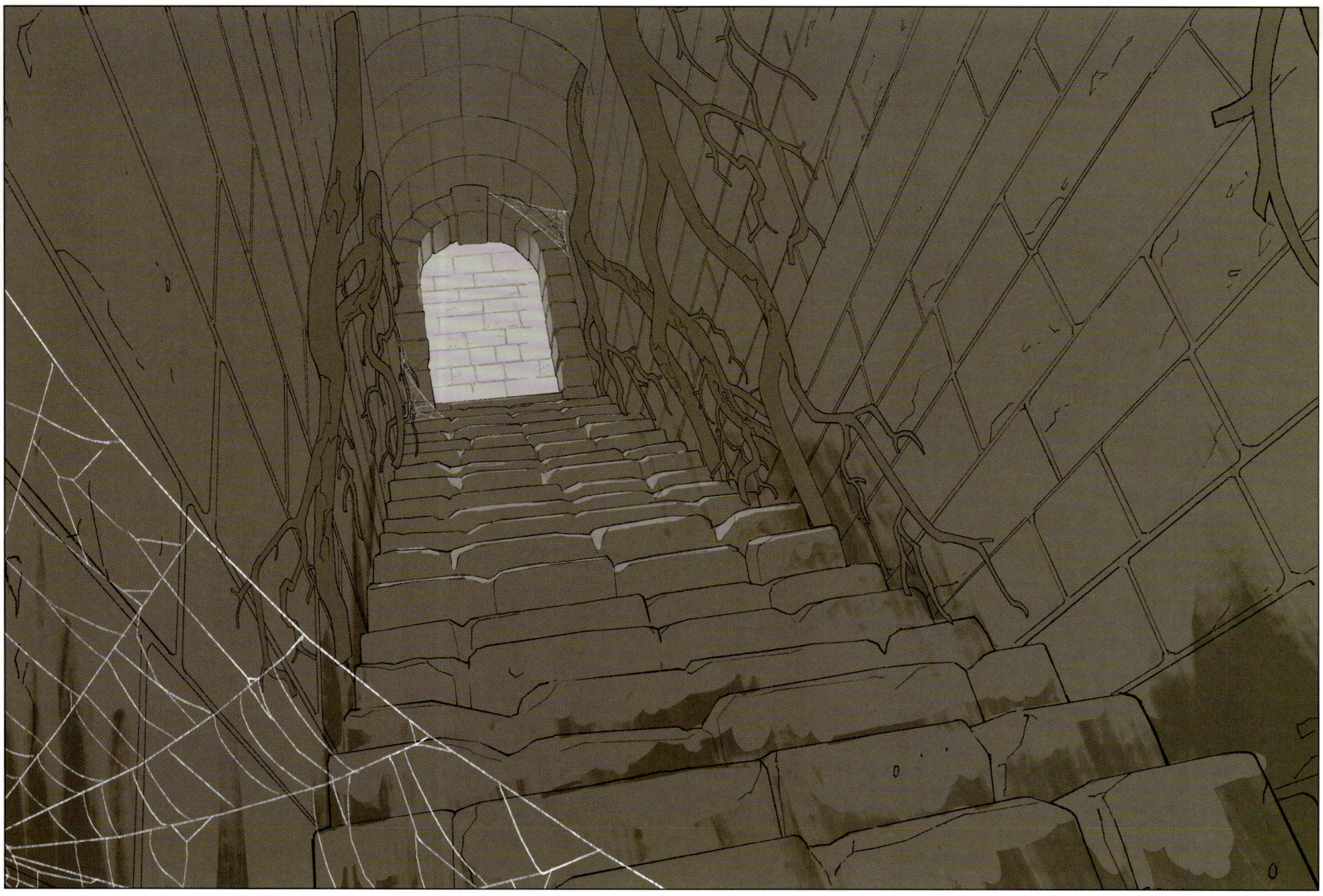

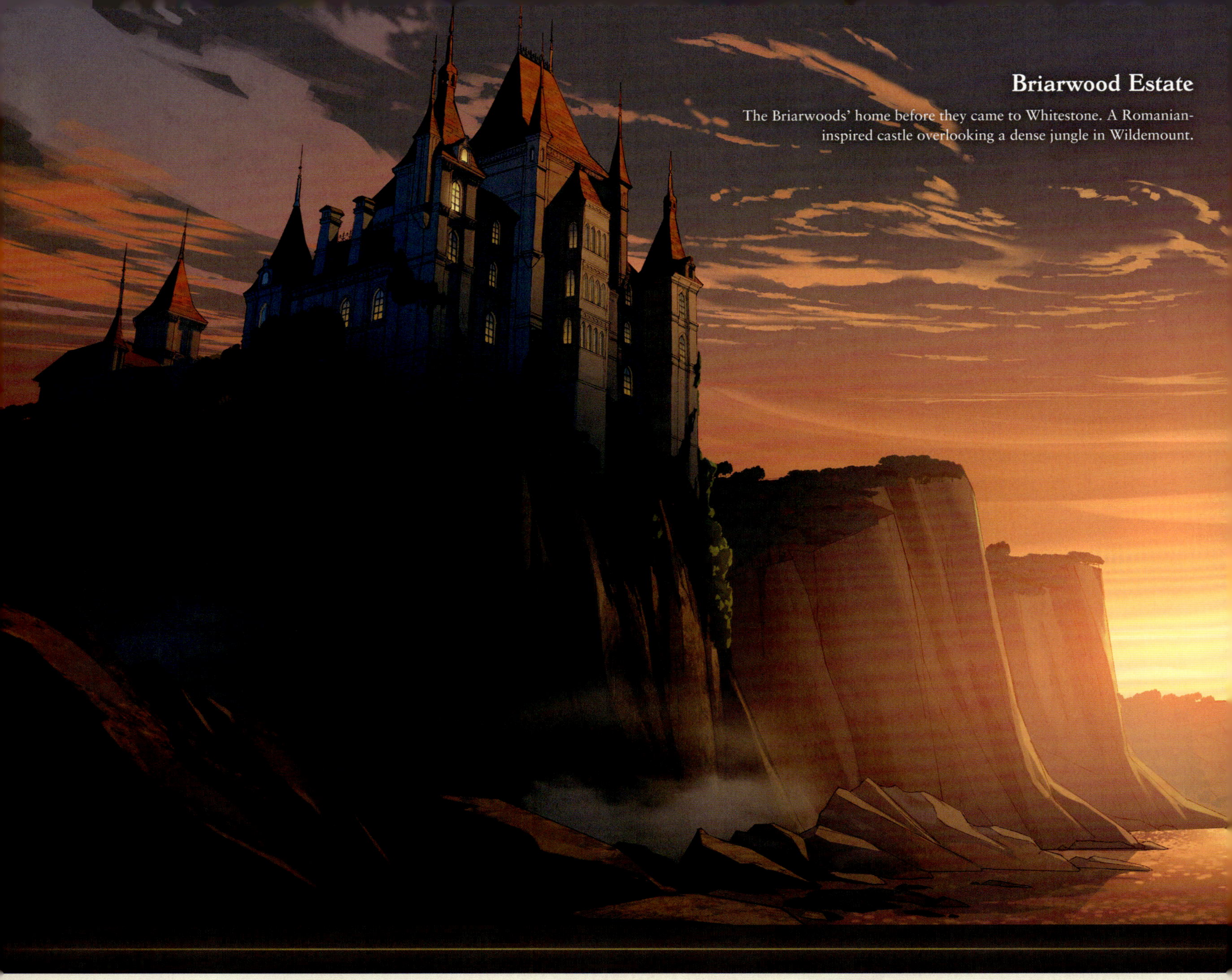

Briarwood Estate

The Briarwoods' home before they came to Whitestone. A Romanian-inspired castle overlooking a dense jungle in Wildemount.

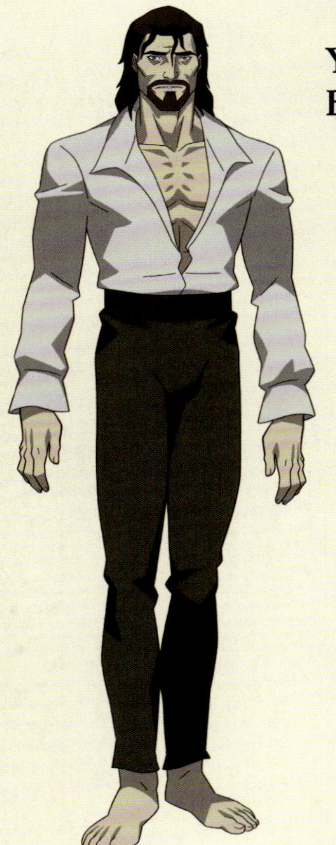

Young Sylas Briarwood

He might not be a vampire yet, but he's still got it.

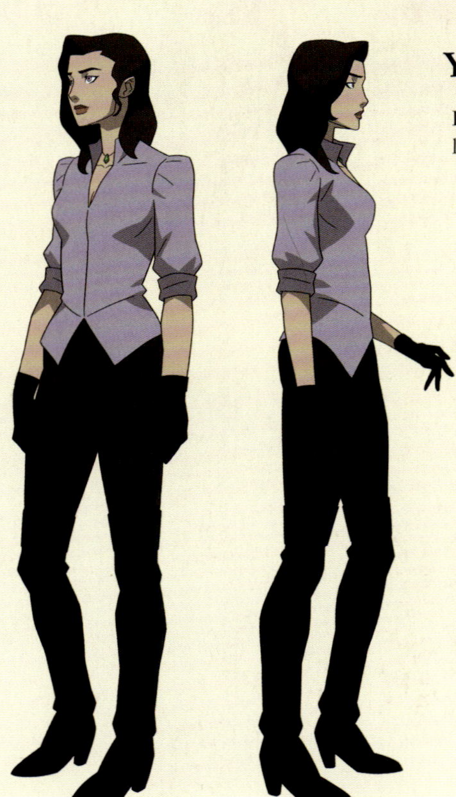

Young Delilah Briarwood

Prior to Whitestone, Delilah was young, in love, and desperate to keep Sylas alive.

"I am Lord Percival Fredrickstein von Musel Klossowski de Rolo III. On the day the Briarwoods took Whitestone, I watched my family die. Despite my desire for vengeance, I fled and fear kept me from my home. We have all lost. But Archie never feared, never wavered. He willingly gave his life for all of us. For Whitestone. His sacrifice, your sacrifice, and that of my family shall not be in vain. Today is for Archie, for the DeRolos, for Whitestone!"

– PERCY, S1E8 "THE TIDE OF BONE"

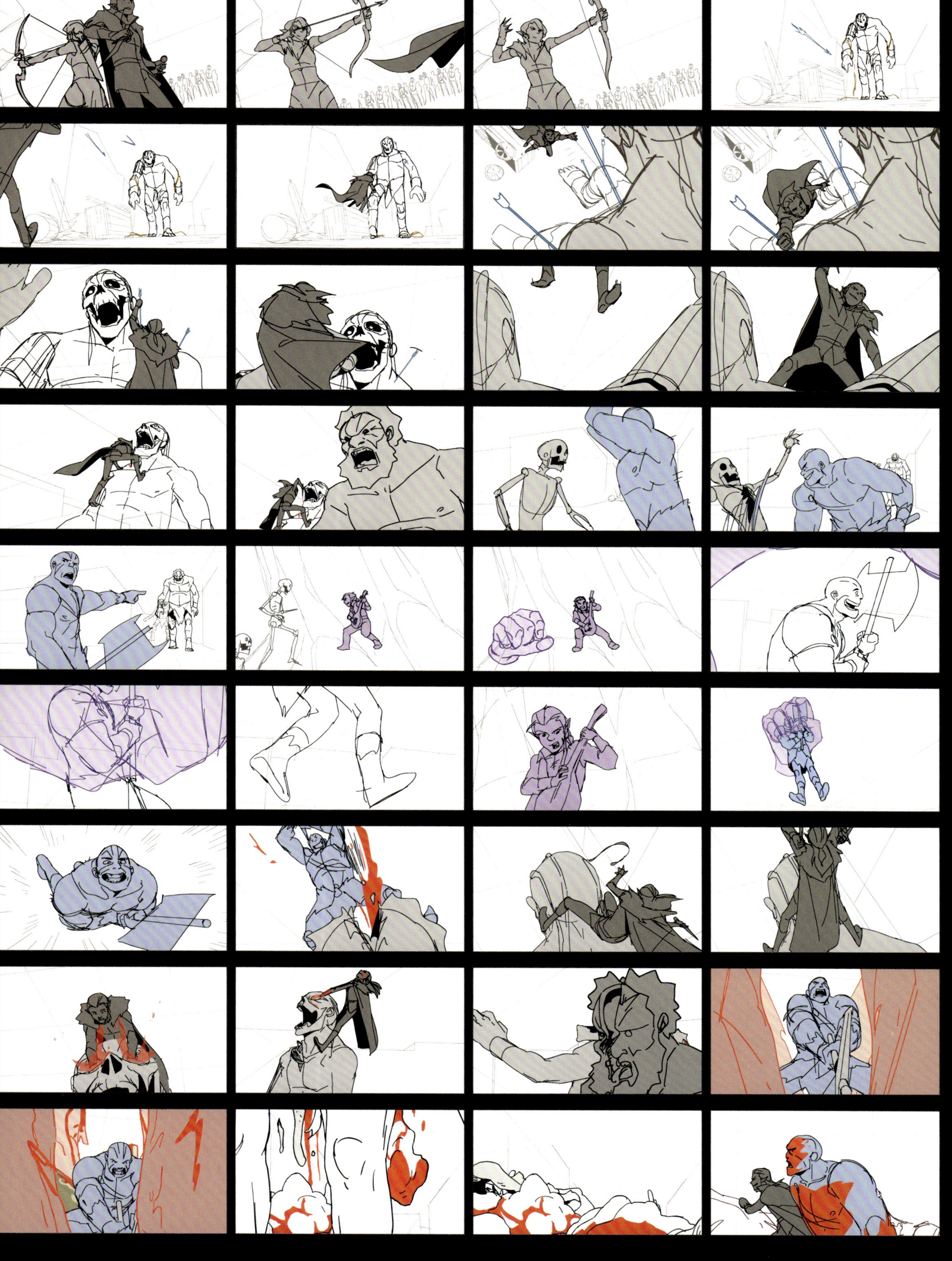

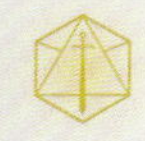

EPISODE 10

DEPTHS OF DECEIT

"Deception! Betrayal! Vox Machina is taken by surprise when Cassandra reveals she's been working with the Briarwoods the entire time (although I want it on record that I knew the entire time.) After killing Percy's ancestors… again, we all get a great centerfold shot of naked Grog swimming through acid that will be burned into my retinas for decades to come." – A RECOUNTING OF "DEPTHS OF DECEIT" BY SCANLAN SHORTHALT

Dr. Anna Ripley

An engineer and alchemist dedicated to science above all else, she cares little about the moral implications of her work. While working for the Briarwoods, she tortured Percy and Cassandra for information on the process of refining Whitestone residuum for use in a ritual that would bring back The Whispered One.

She's designed another pepperbox similar to Percy's, but an explosion during its creation is what led her to lose her hand.

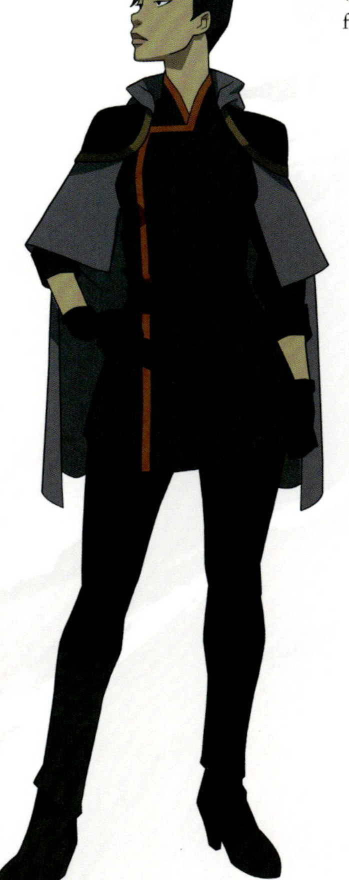

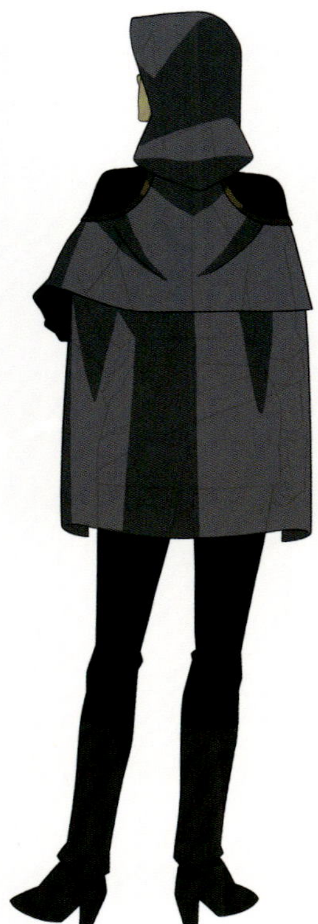

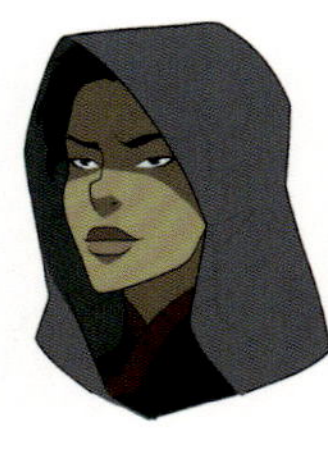

"At the moment, you're the luckiest person in Whitestone. Because you're at the bottom of my list." – PERCY, S1E10 "DEPTHS OF DECEIT"

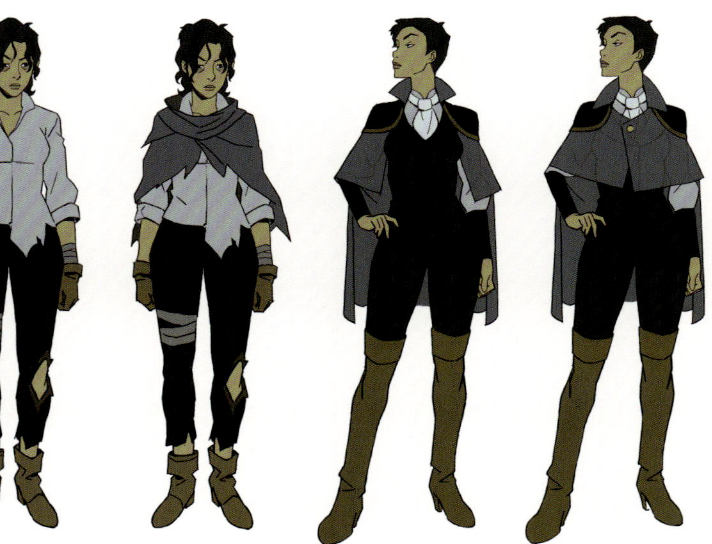

Ripley designs during her imprisonment in Whitestone and from Percy's flashback visions.

De Rolo Mausoleum

Lined by reliefs of long-passed De Rolo ancestors, one could call the battle that ensues here the epitome of overkill.

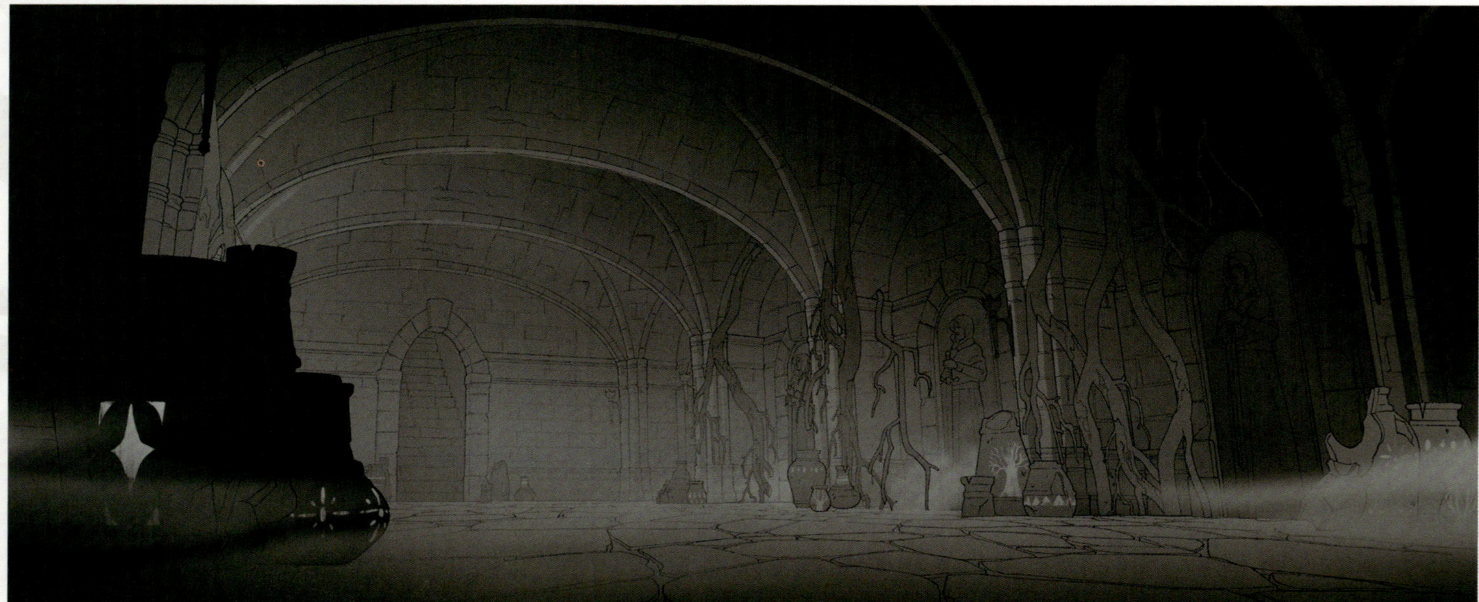

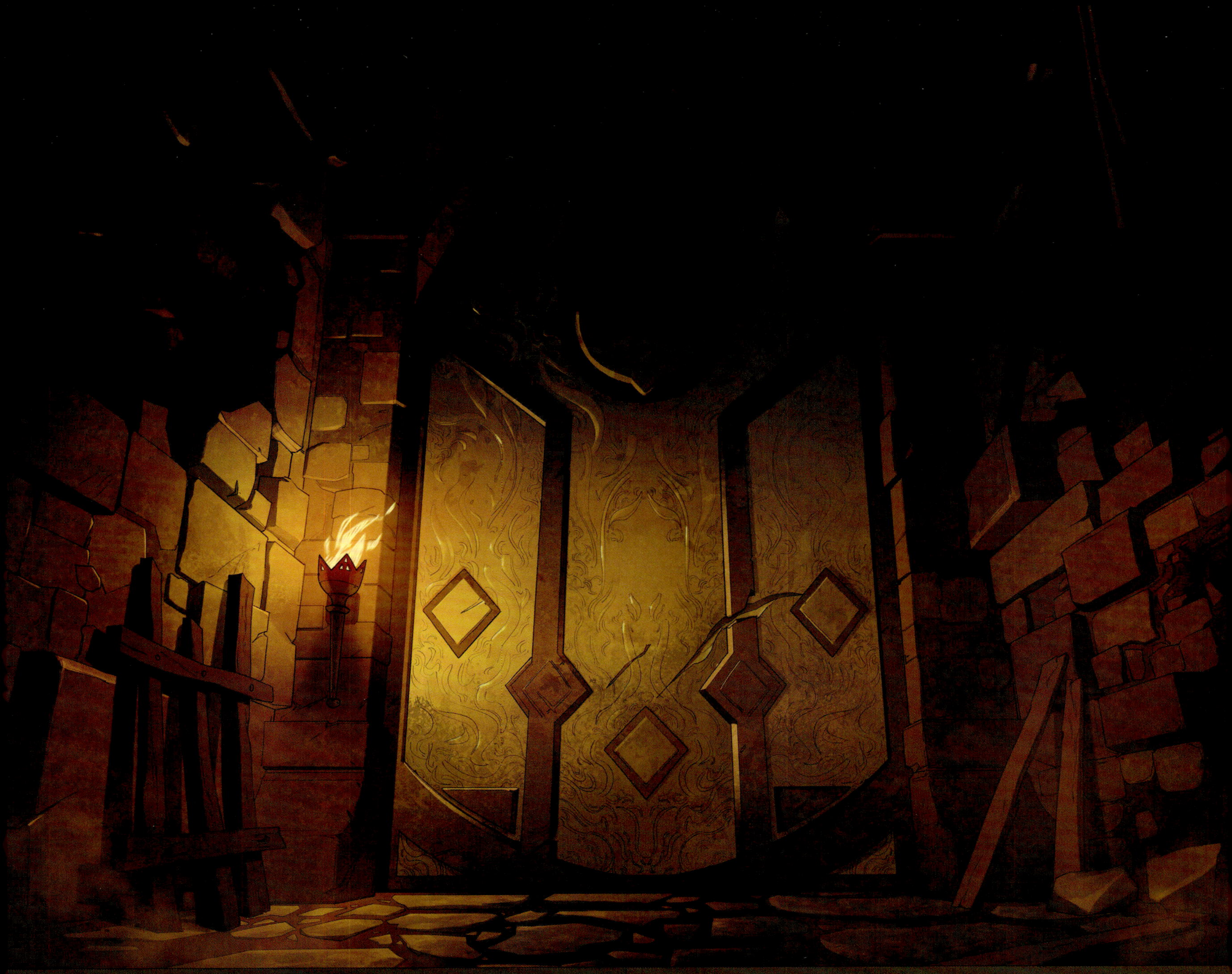

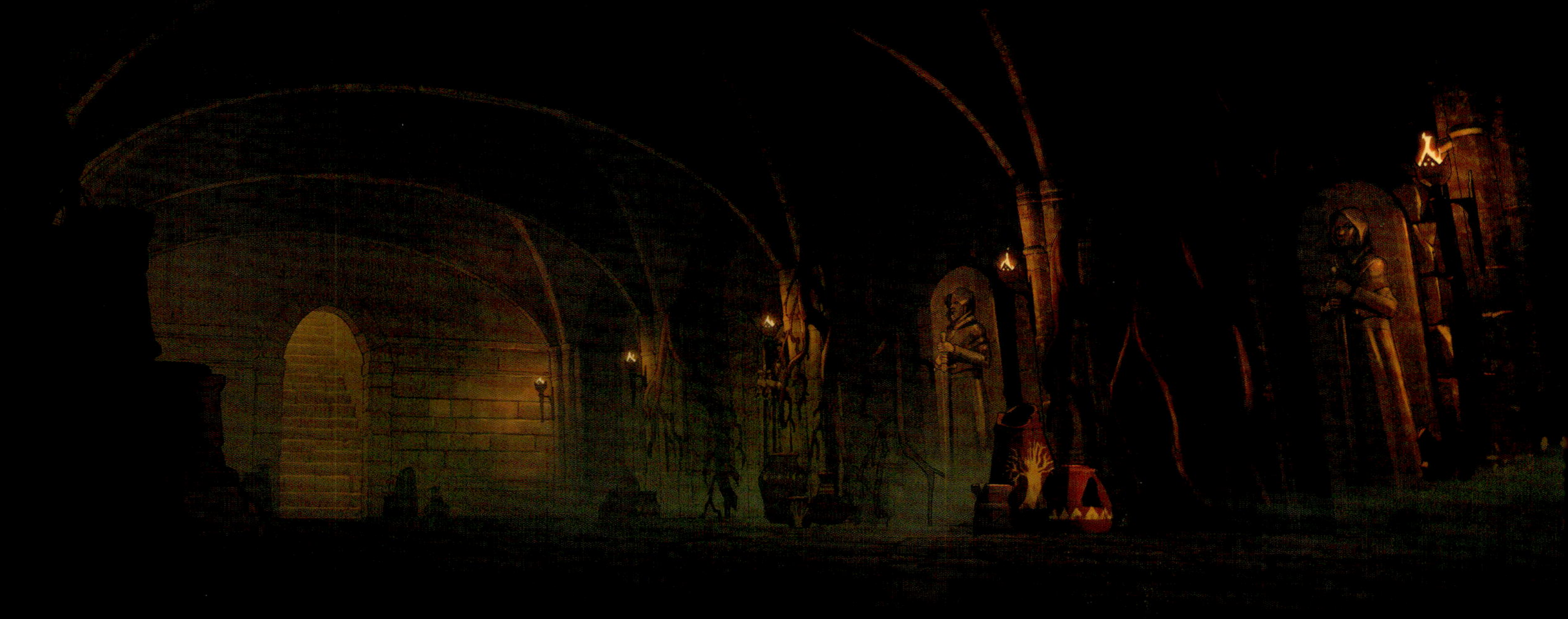

Whitestone Dungeon

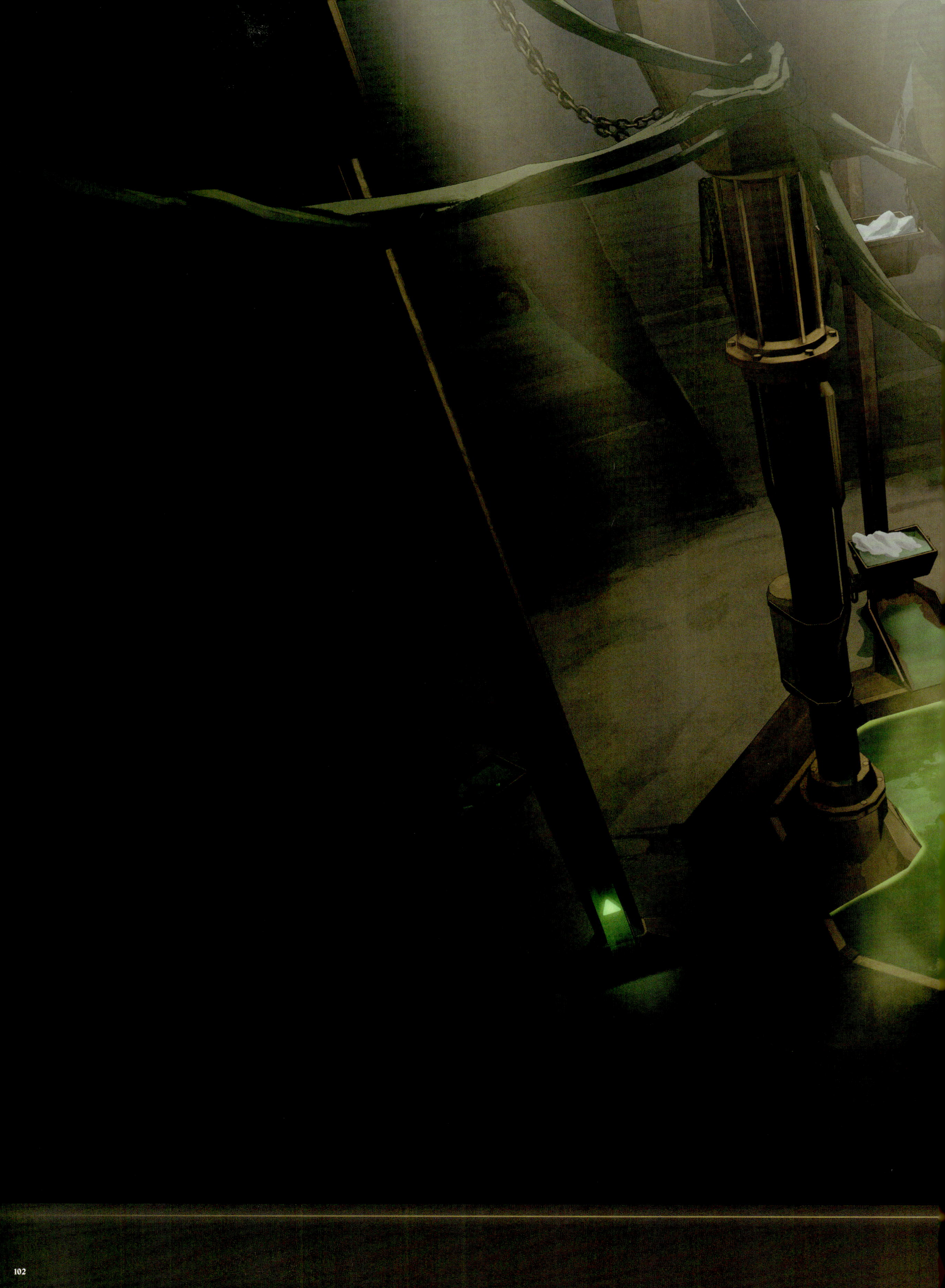

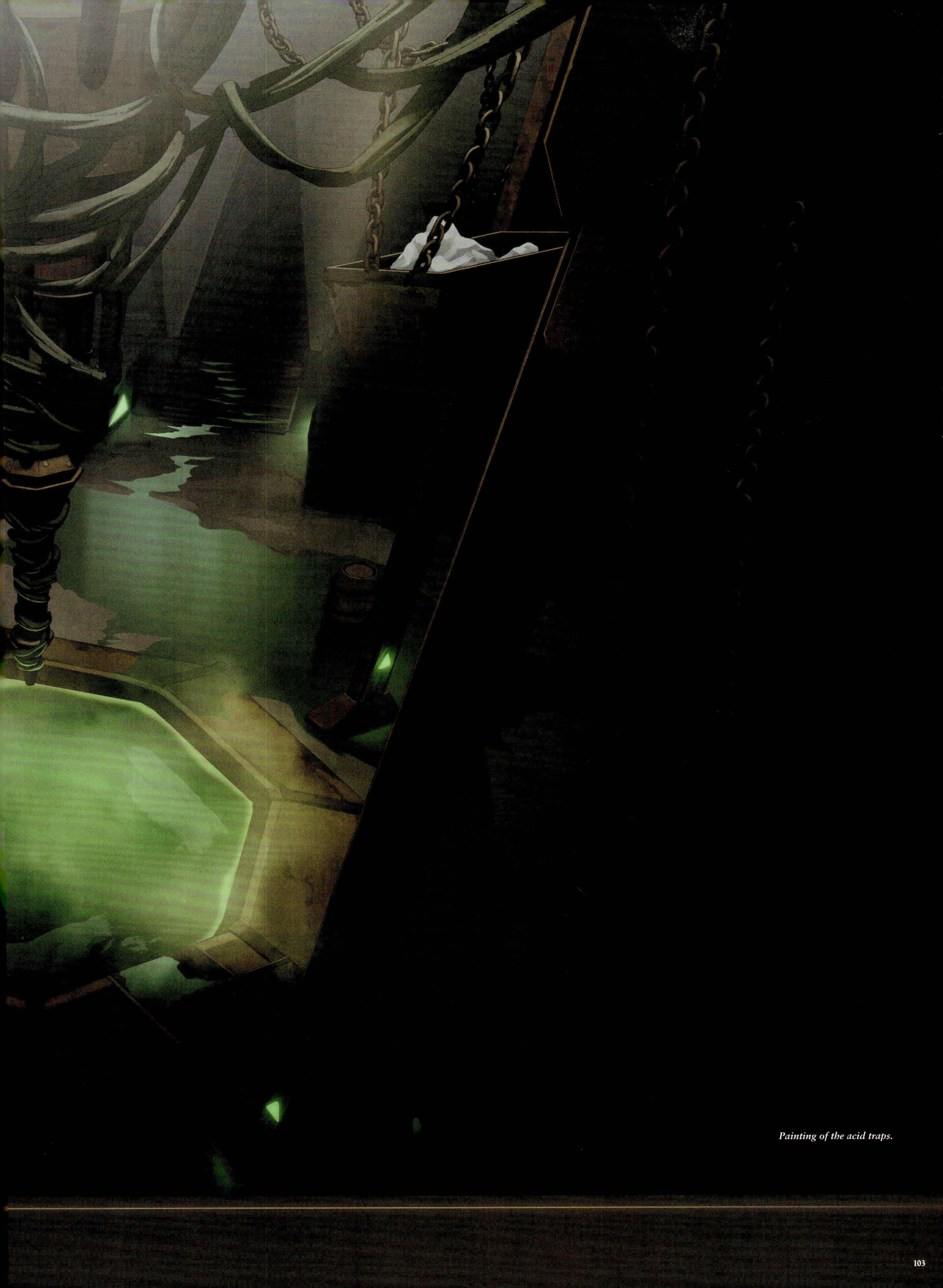

Painting of the acid traps.

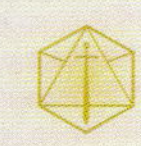

Residuum Distillery

For the purposes of the show, Arthur Loftis wanted everything to make sense in the world without the context of a tabletop RPG around it. The room was designed not as a trap, but as the industrial space employed by The Briarwoods to refine residuum under Ripley's supervision. Designers went through a few different versions of this room, experimenting with different mechanics behind the residuum production pipeline before arriving at the final design.

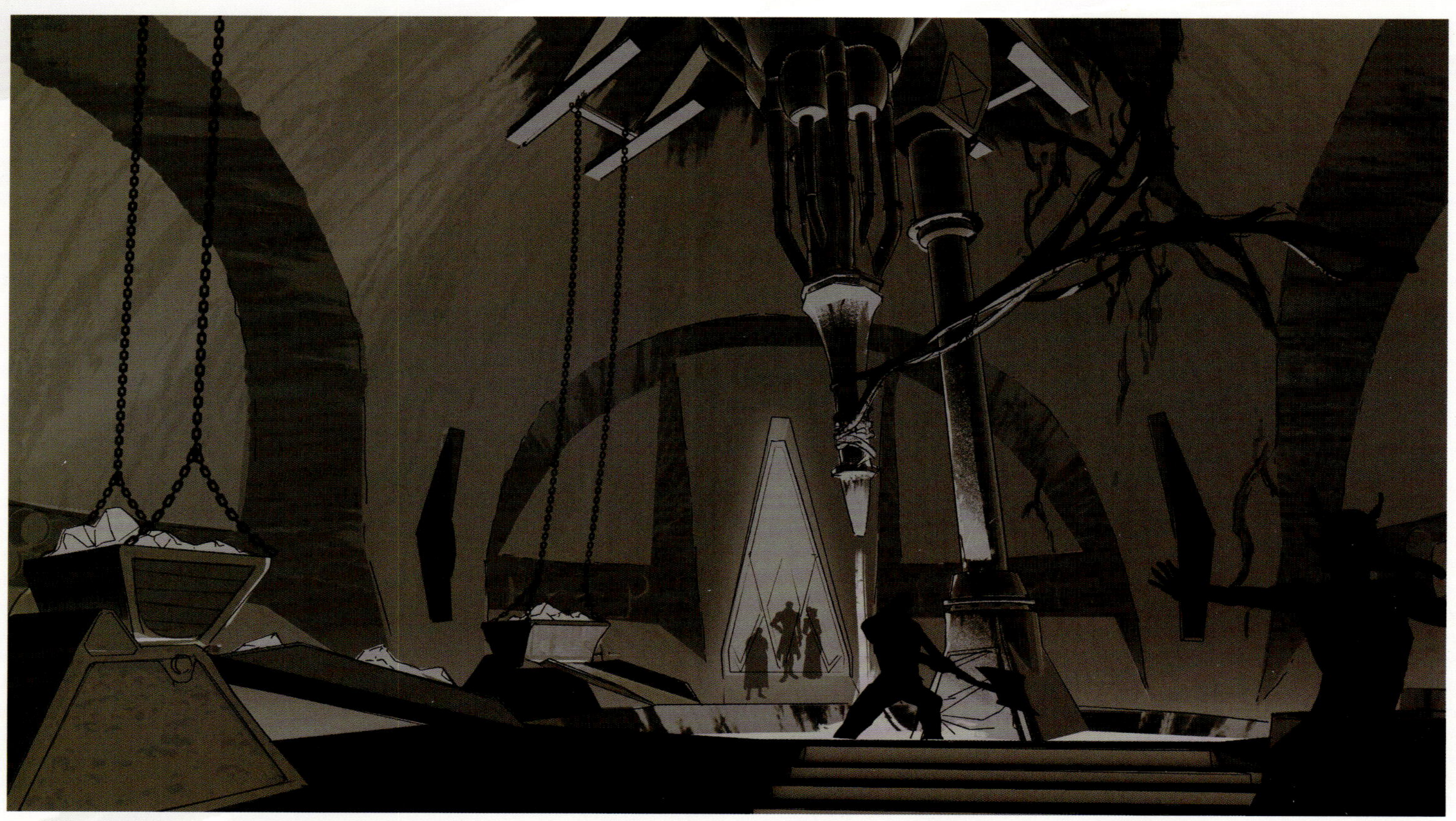

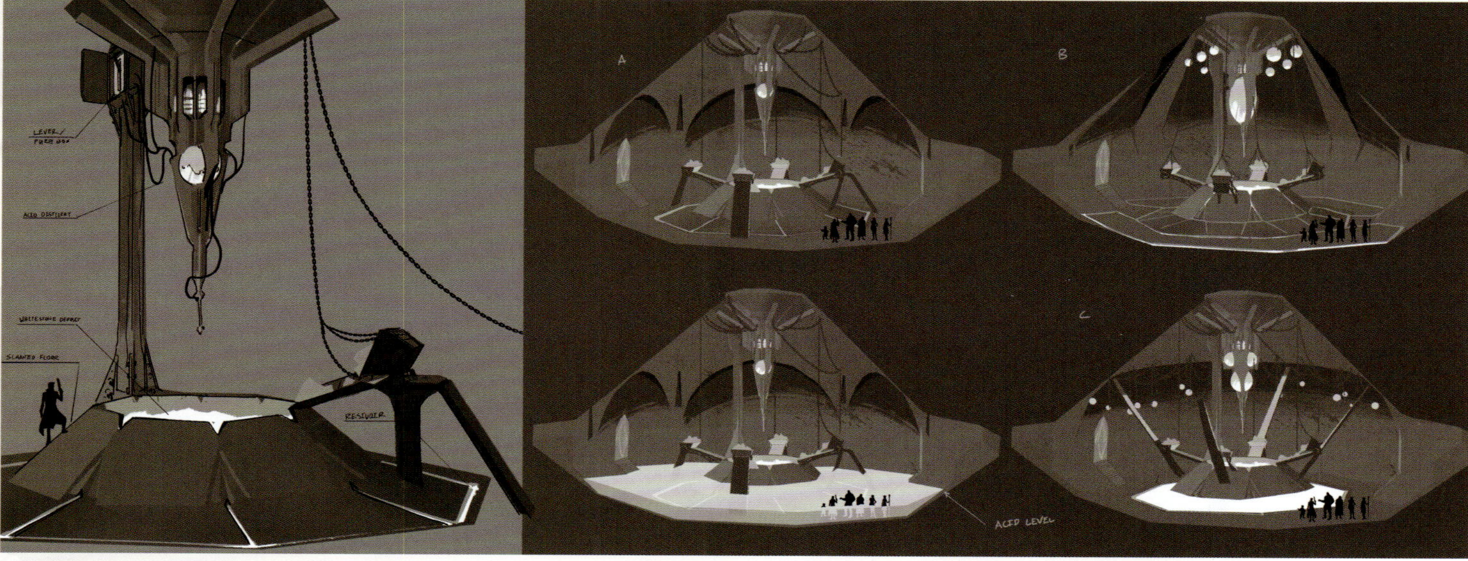

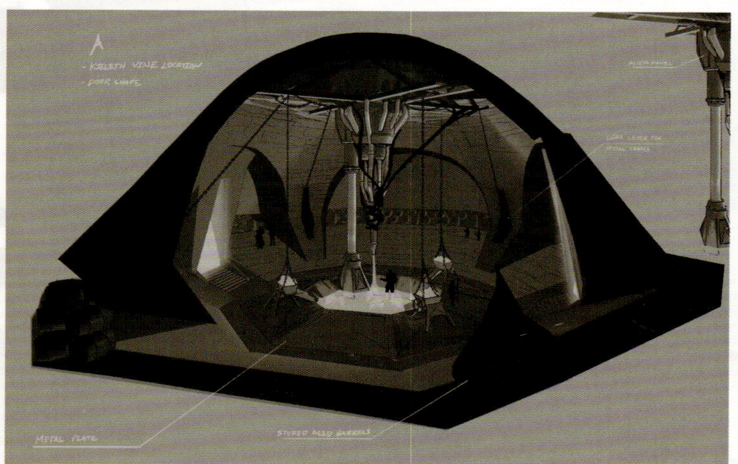

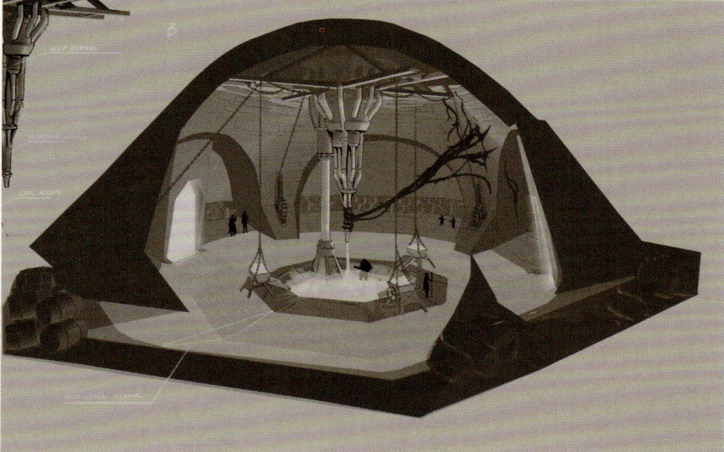

"An acid trap? Oh, real fucking original!" – PIKE, S1E10 "DEPTHS OF DECEIT"

FROM SCRIPT TO SCREEN

TRAPPED IN THE ACID PITS

Scanlan keeps strumming his lute. Giving it all he's got as Ripley checks for the location of the third lever.

174A RIPLEY
There's no visible controls on the outer walls...

Percy mentally calculates – then looks down.

175 PERCY
The drain. The stopper!

Everyone looks down. It's way UNDER THE ACID.

176 KEYLETH
In the acid? You have to be insane to go in–

177 GROG
I'M GOIN' IN!

Grog pulls off his pants and dives naked into the acid!

INSIDE THE ACID, Grog's nude body BURNS. The acid bubbles as it melts his skin, exposing muscle, sinew, and BONE.

Pike leaps down, grabbing onto Percy's foot, dangling over the acid as she reaches for Grog.

178 PIKE
Grog, wait!

Pike, thinking quickly, casts a healing spell through the acid, restoring Grog's flesh as it simultaneously burns.

Grog <GARGLE-SCREAMS> under the acid, but keeps swimming.

He swims down, plants his feet, strains, and POPS the plug open. Under it is a METAL CASING with a HANDLE. Grog GRABS IT.

Ripley leaps, grabbing onto a chain, and swings over to Percy to help pull the other lever.

179 PERCY
Ready...

QUICK CUTS:

Scanlan strumming like a maniac, his tune increasing in intensity as an illusion hand plucks chords along with him.

Pike using her healing powers to protect Grog–

Grog, his body burning in the acid, reaching for the lever–

Percy holding onto the lever–

179A PERCY
NOW!

SPLIT SCREEN - CLOSE ON Percy, Ripley, and Grog's hands as they PULL all three handles at the same time.

The CHAMBER RESETS – stopper opens, acid drains, the glass wall raises.

As the acid drains, it swirls around Grog, causing further damage and burning his body. He <GARGLE-SCREAMS> in pain.

An exhausted Scanlan's hand moves them to a dry spot, but then immediately dissipates – they plop down. Now safely back on solid ground, Percy and Vex share a look.

180 VEX'AHLIA
Good to have you back, Percival.

Percy nods, managing the hint of a smile. Then turns to Ripley.

181 RIPLEY
Since I helped out, don't you think I earned my freedom?

182 PERCY
If you're lucky, you've earned another hour of life.

Ripley looks sour.

Pike casts another healing spell on Grog, who is still nude. His skin sizzles, then reforms, his wounds closing.

183 PIKE
You okay, Grog?

184 GROG
I dunno. Is is... *Captain Winky* still there?

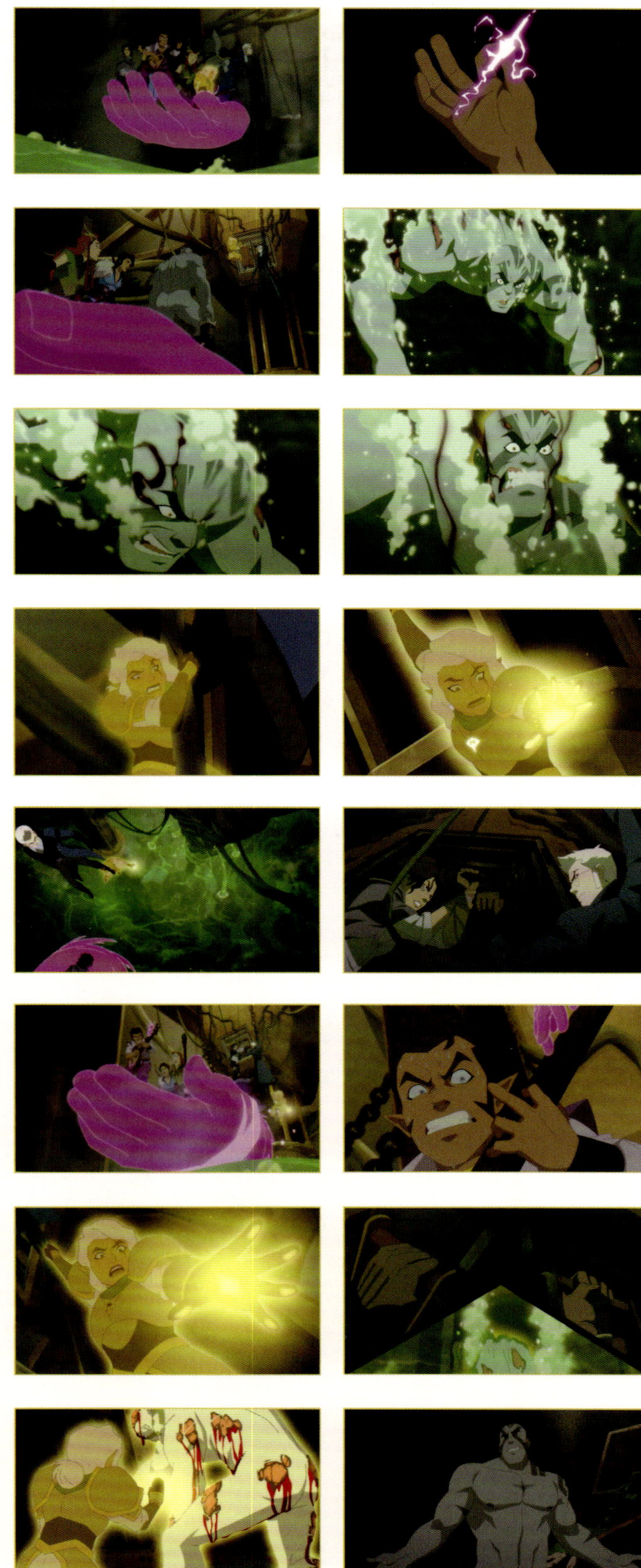

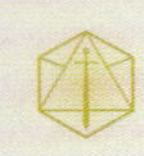

EPISODE 11

WHISPERS AT THE ZIGGURAT

"Question to everyone, can we ever have a ritual that doesn't involve a blood sacrifice? Seems a little over-the-top if you ask me. Things aren't looking great for us as Delilah and Sylas grow closer to starting the ritual that will bring back The Whispered One. But then Vex's love for Vax (and a strategically timed punch) manages to knock him out of his trance. Keyleth and Grog team up for the ultimate one-two punch and take down Sylas (for most certainly the last time). Unfortunately, Delilah just doesn't know when to quit, and Keyleth takes a massive amount of necrotic damage during their fight. Our trusty cleric Pike tries to heal her, but she goes poof! No magic allowed in the creepy ritual death room, apparently. We just love a good cliff-hanger, don't we!" – A RECOUNTING OF "WHISPERS AT THE ZIGGURAT" BY SCANLAN SHORTHALT

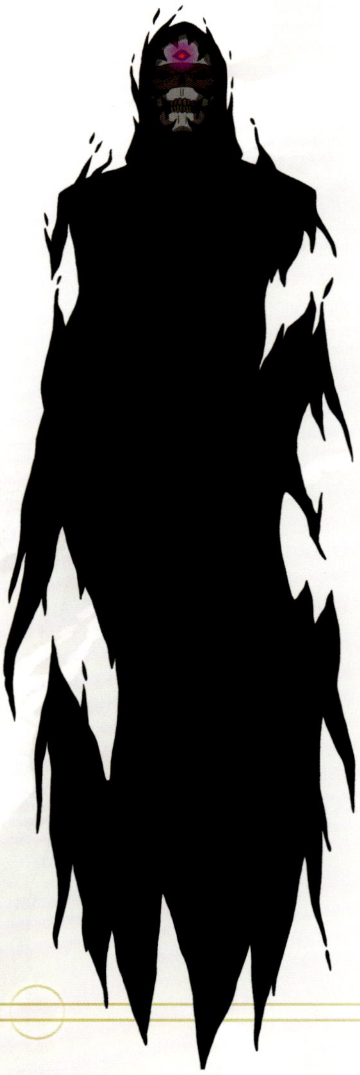

The Whispered One

The "Big Bad" of *The Legend of Vox Machina*.

The Whispered One is a powerful archlich searching for a way to be resurrected and ascend to godhood. His image appears on Delilah's necromancy spellbook.

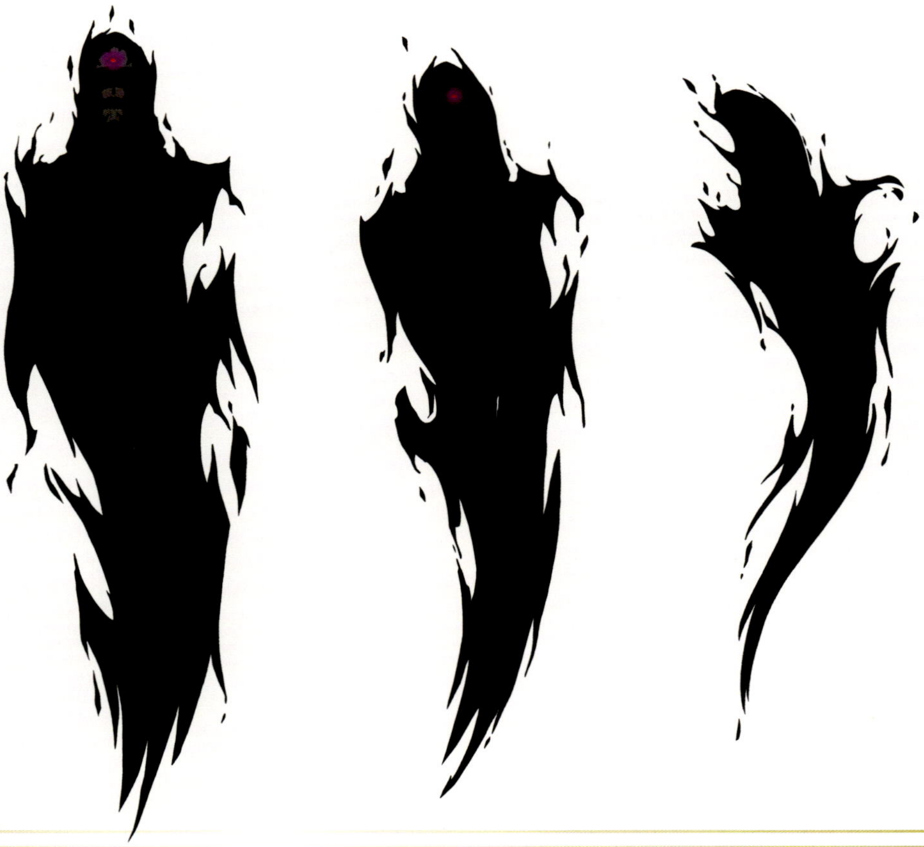

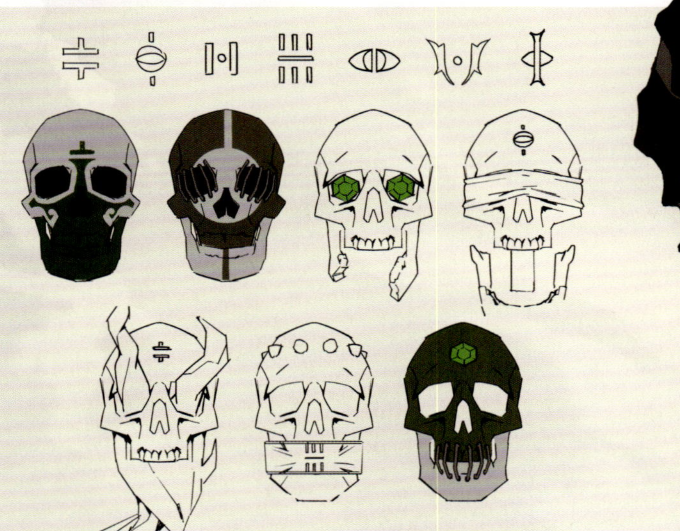

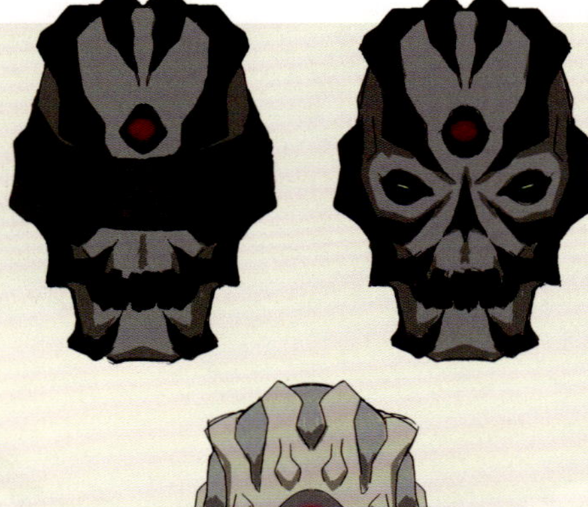

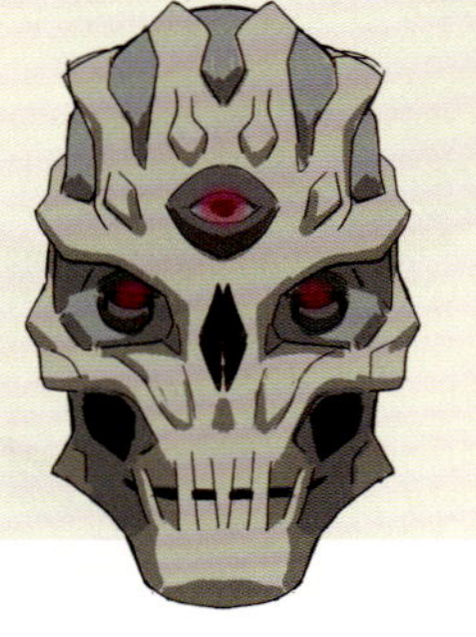

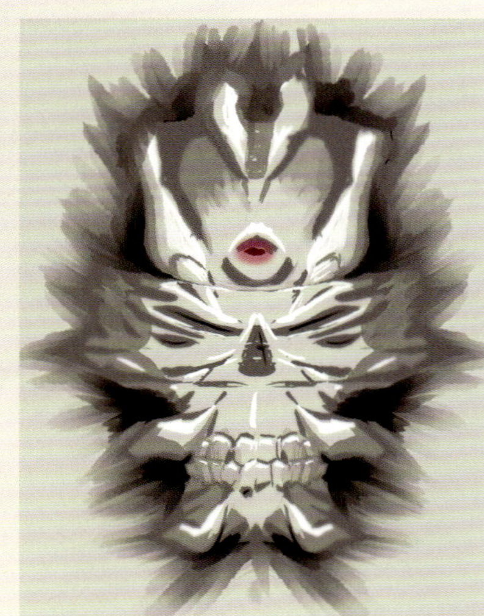

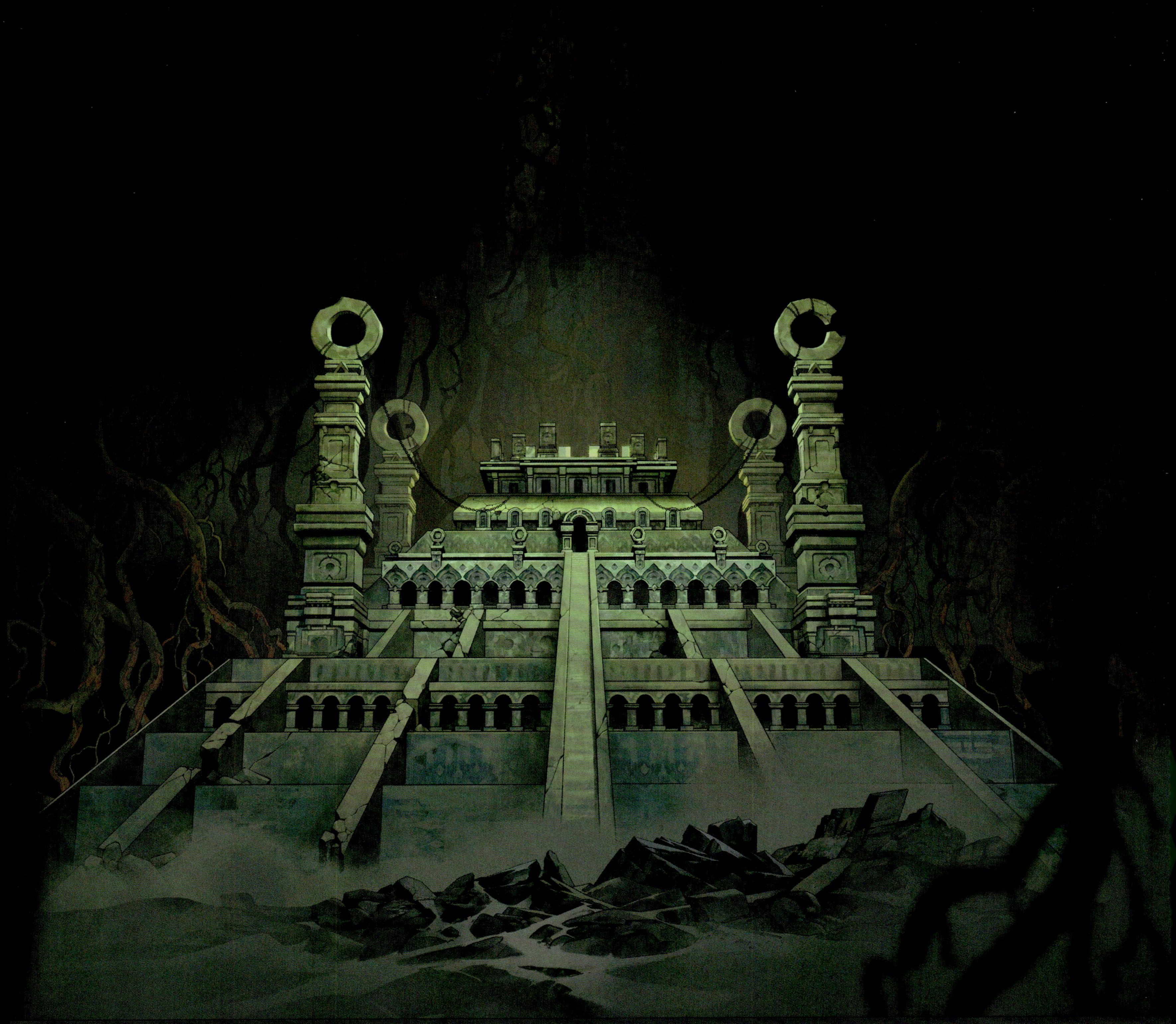

Ziggurat

"Canonically, the Ziggurat is a temple to The Knowing Mistress that's been repurposed by The Briarwoods for their evil plans. We designed it knowing that there would be more Knowing Mistress architecture later in the series (including the floating arena that Kamaljiori tests Vox Machina on in season two.)" – ARTHUR LOFTIS (ART DIRECTOR)

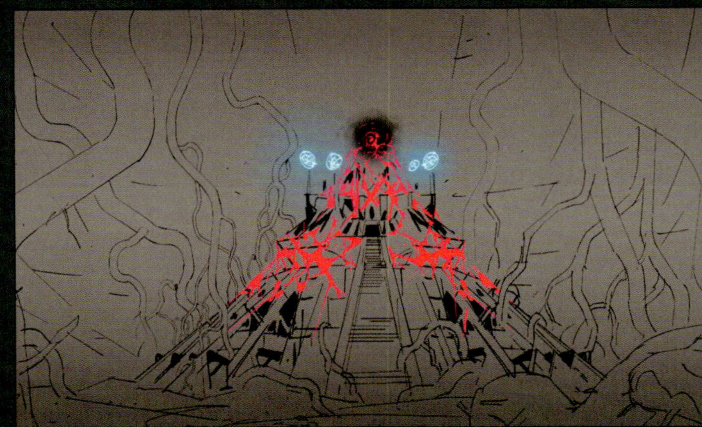

Early drawing of the ziggurat to show magical abilities.

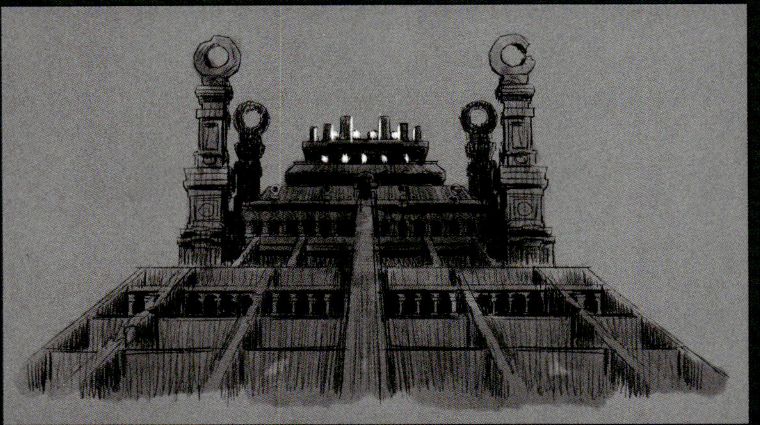

Black and white sketch of the ziggurat.

[top] Painted background of the Sun Tree roots when Keyleth unleashes her sunlight spell on Sylas. [bottom] Shot of the floor of the exterior of the ziggurat, glowing green with power.

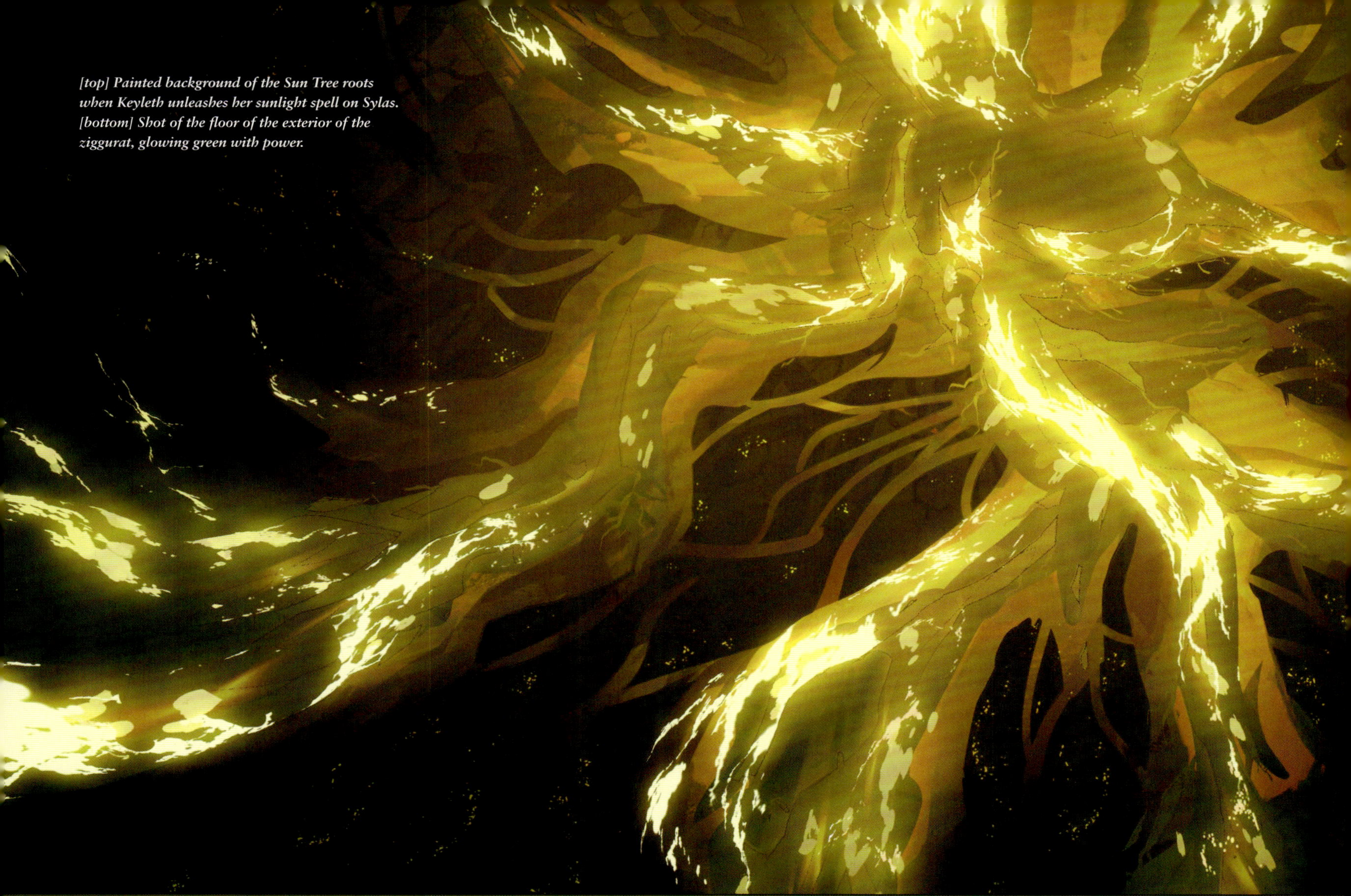

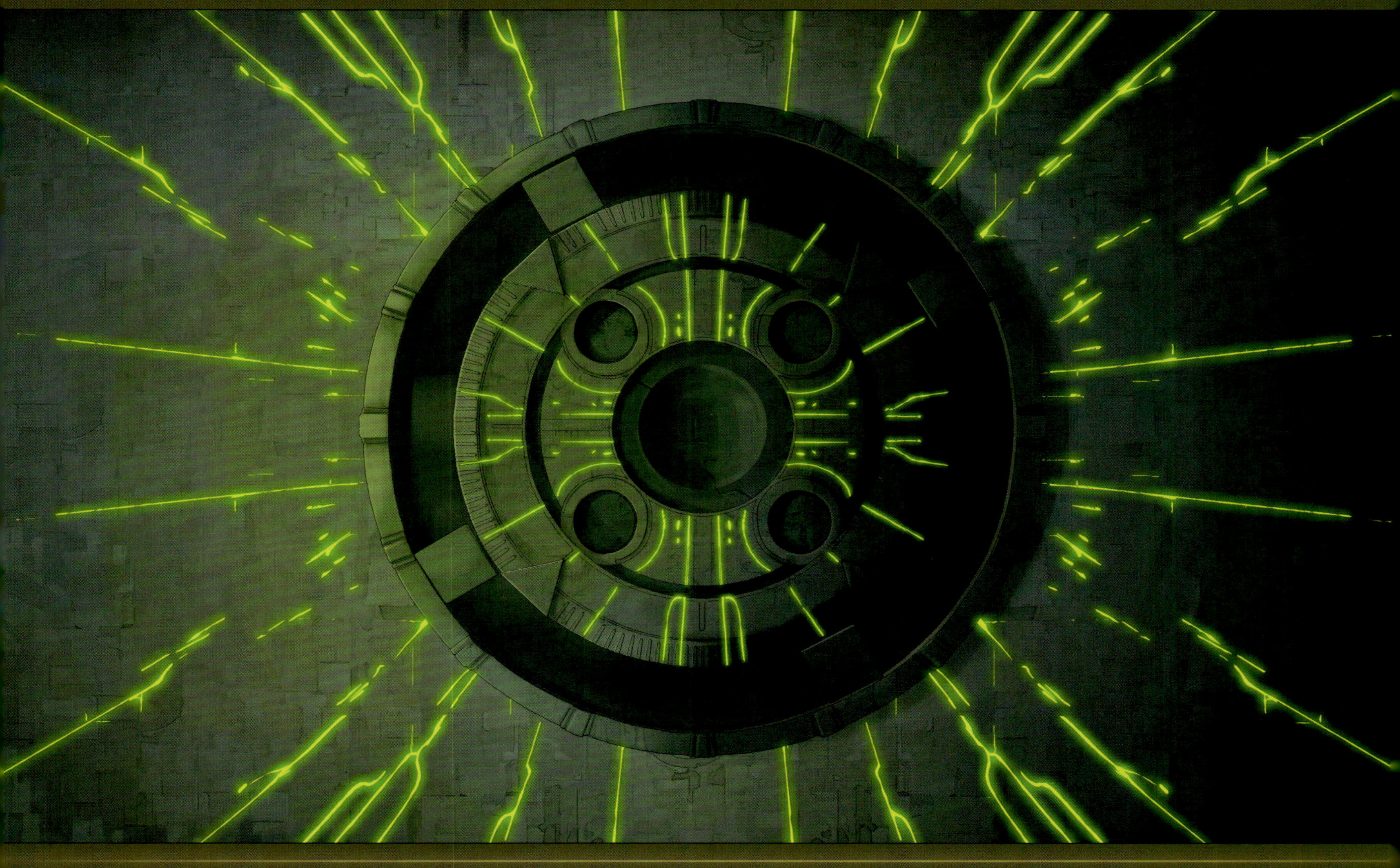

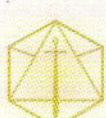

Ritual Chamber

The ritual inside the Ziggurat was one of the more complex setups in the first season. The walls are lined with the writhing bodies of villagers sacrificed by Delilah and Sylas in the name of The Whispered One. The design team built a CG body model to duplicate and help cover the sheer number of bodies in each shot along with layering additional lighting and effects to create the chaos of the ritual.

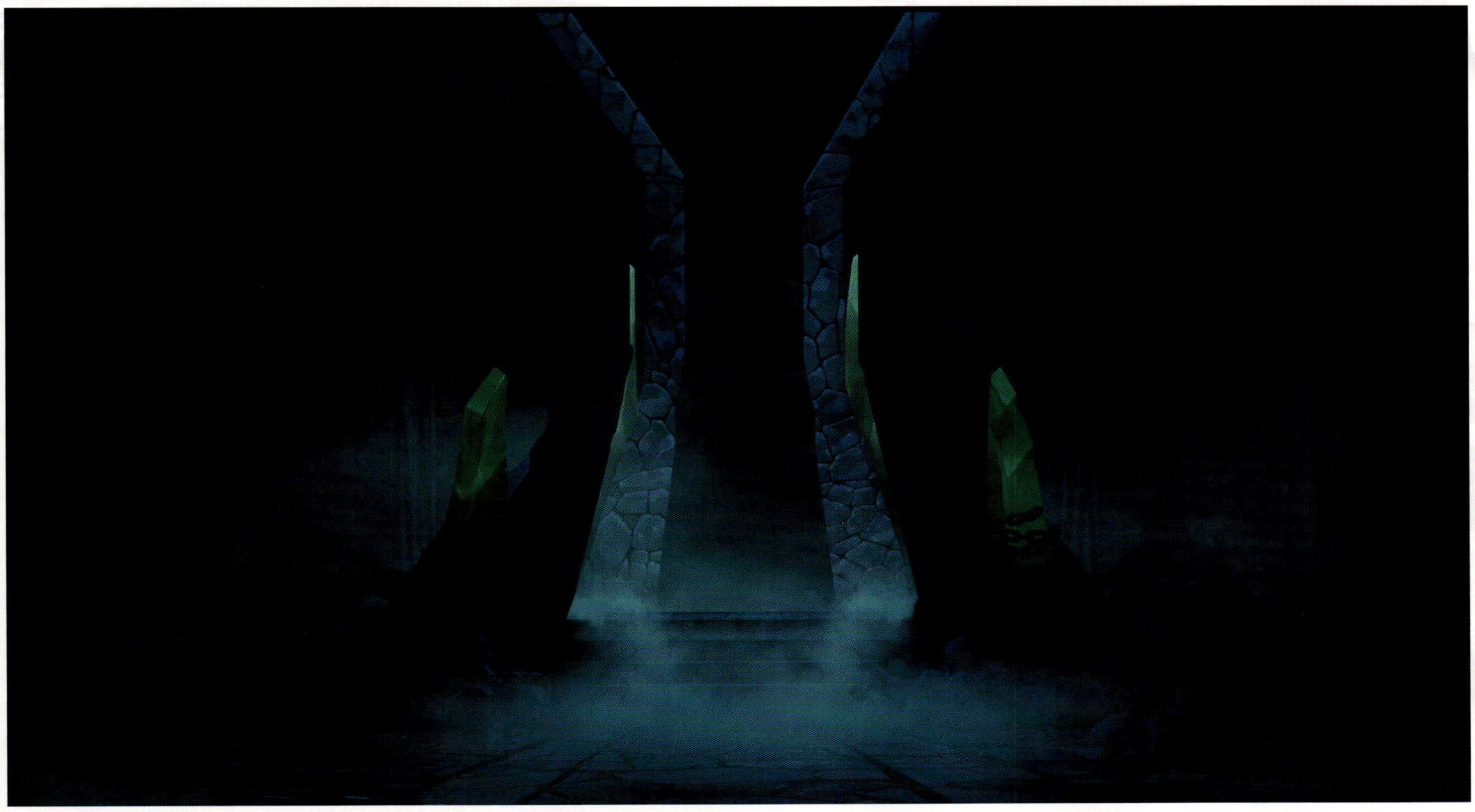

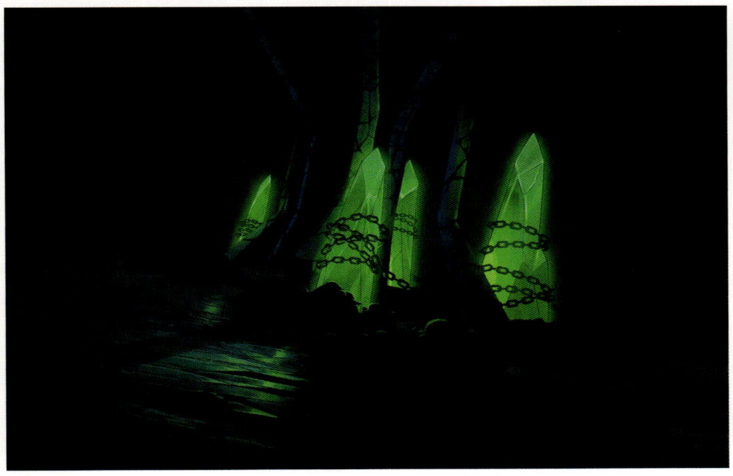

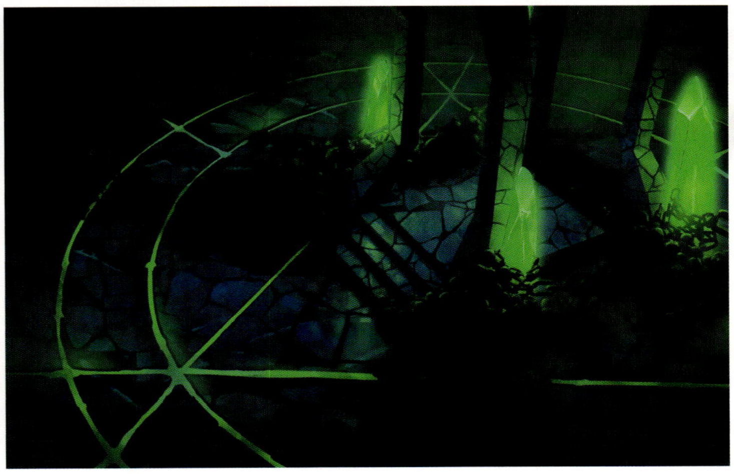

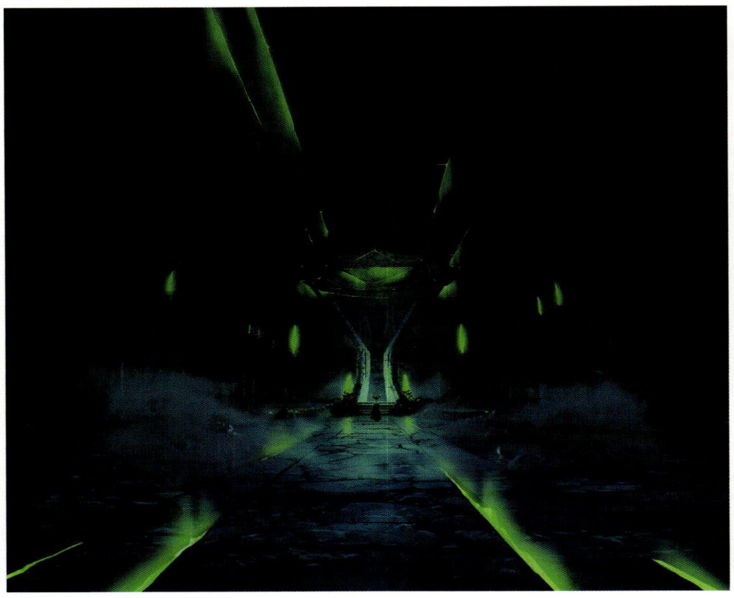

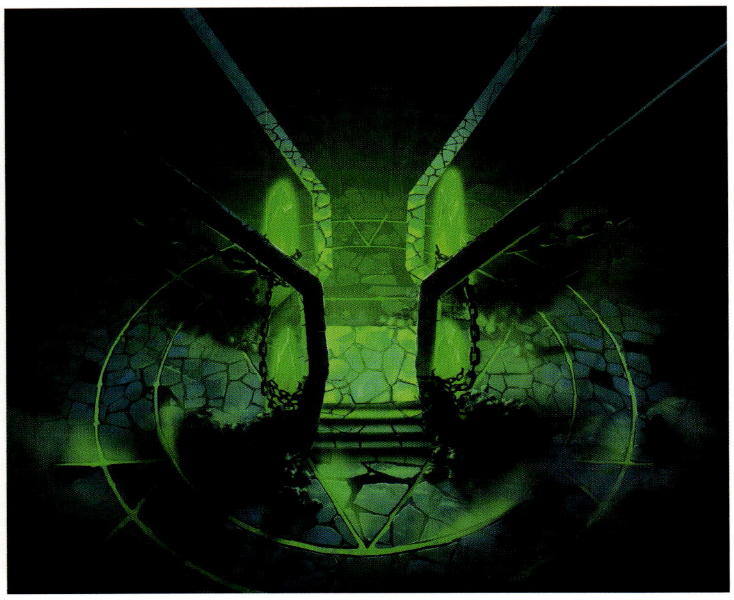

Backgrounds showing the lighting design in The Ritual Chamber.

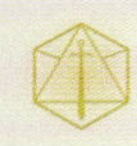

EPISODE 12

THE DARKNESS WITHIN

"Percy forgot to read the user agreement when he struck that deal with Orthax, and now Orthax wants to collect. In typical asshole demon fashion, he takes over Percy's mind and forces him to relive all his toxic family dinners from growing up. Once again, I, Scanlan Shorthalt, SAVE THE MOTHERFUCKING DAY when I destroy Percy's pepperbox, thereby vanquishing the vessel tying Orthax to the mortal plane once and for all. We return as heroes to Emon! Scratch that, heroes to all of Tal'Dorei! Nothing can stop us now. Except for... shit, dragons." – A RECOUNTING OF "THE DARKNESS WITHIN" BY SCANLAN SHORTHALT

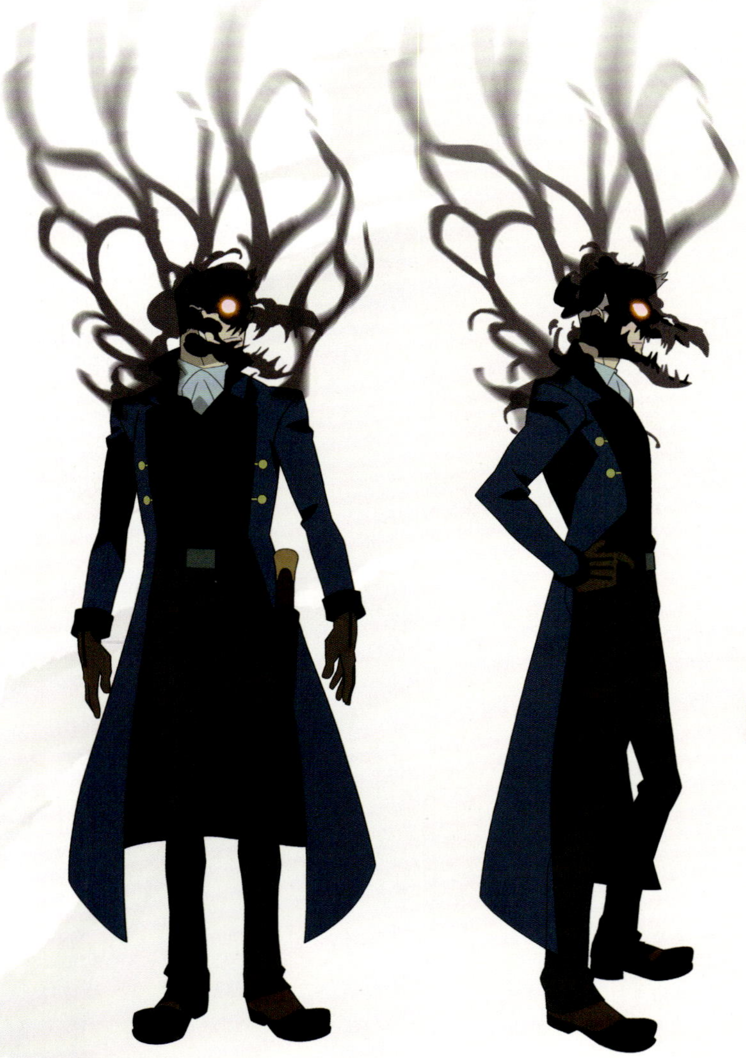

Orthax

In the original campaign and on the page of the script, Orthax is written as a smoke monster. Because this character is essentially built entirely out of effects, figuring out how to animate it was an extremely daunting task. The design team attempted to pitch a version that was mostly corporeal to save animation and post-production some headaches. Ultimately, those options didn't feel faithful enough to the original vision of the character, so those ideas were scrapped, and they went all in with the smoke monster.

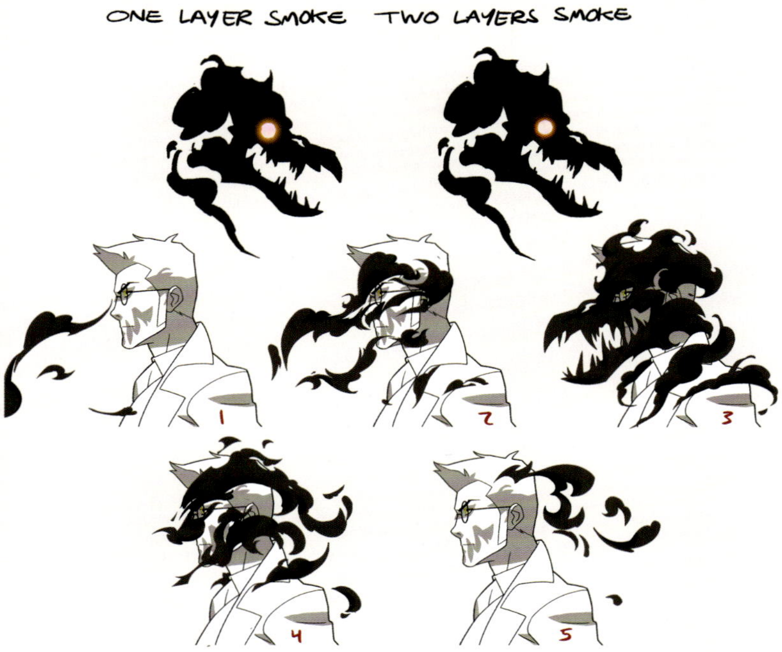

ONE LAYER SMOKE
TWO LAYERS SMOKE
1
2
3
4
5

Concept designs of Orthax taking over Percy during his final stand.

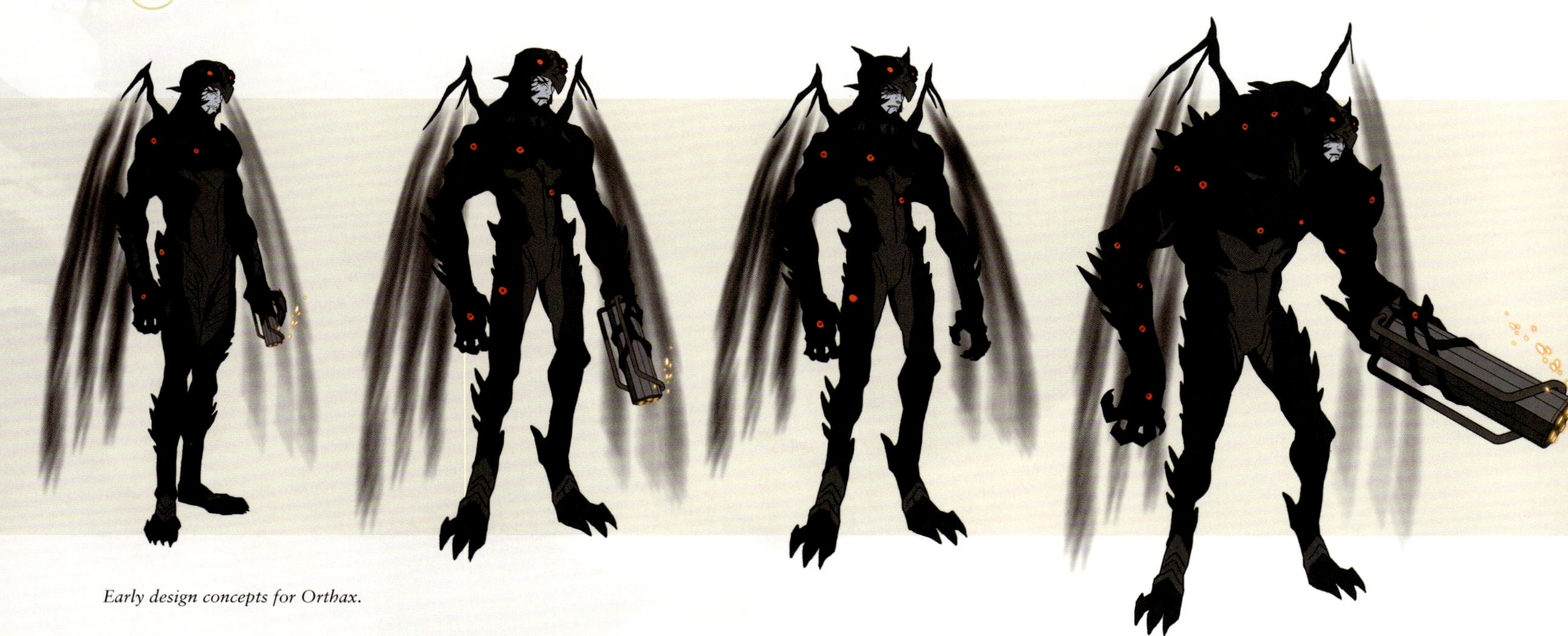

Early design concepts for Orthax.

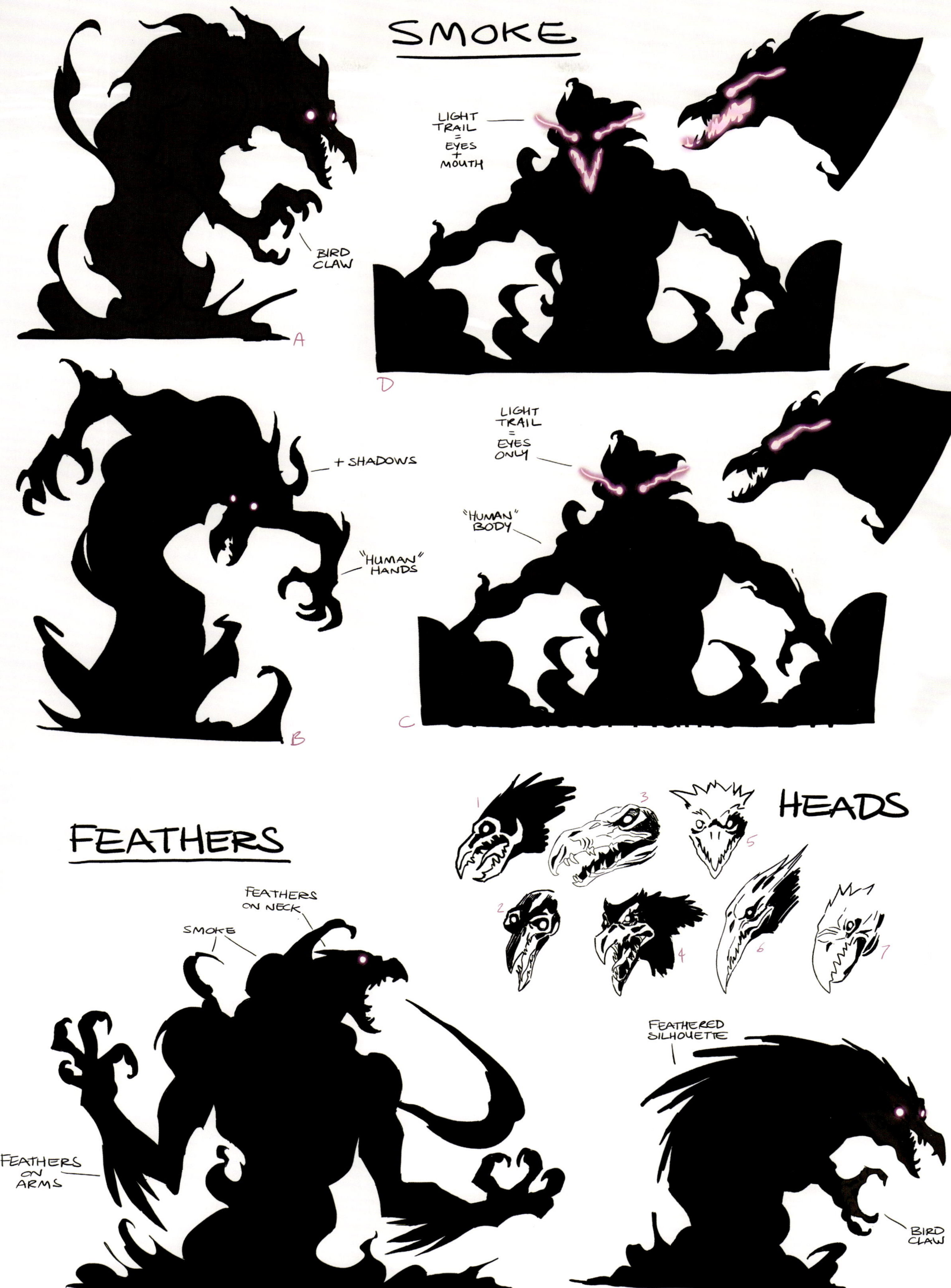
SMOKE
LIGHT TRAIL = EYES + MOUTH
BIRD CLAW
A
D
LIGHT TRAIL = EYES ONLY
+ SHADOWS
"HUMAN" BODY
"HUMAN" HANDS
B
C
FEATHERS
HEADS
1
2
3
4
5
6
7
FEATHERS ON NECK
SMOKE
FEATHERS ON ARMS
FEATHERED SILHOUETTE
BIRD CLAW
E
F

Painted backgrounds of Orthax lording over Percy during their fight in his mindscape.

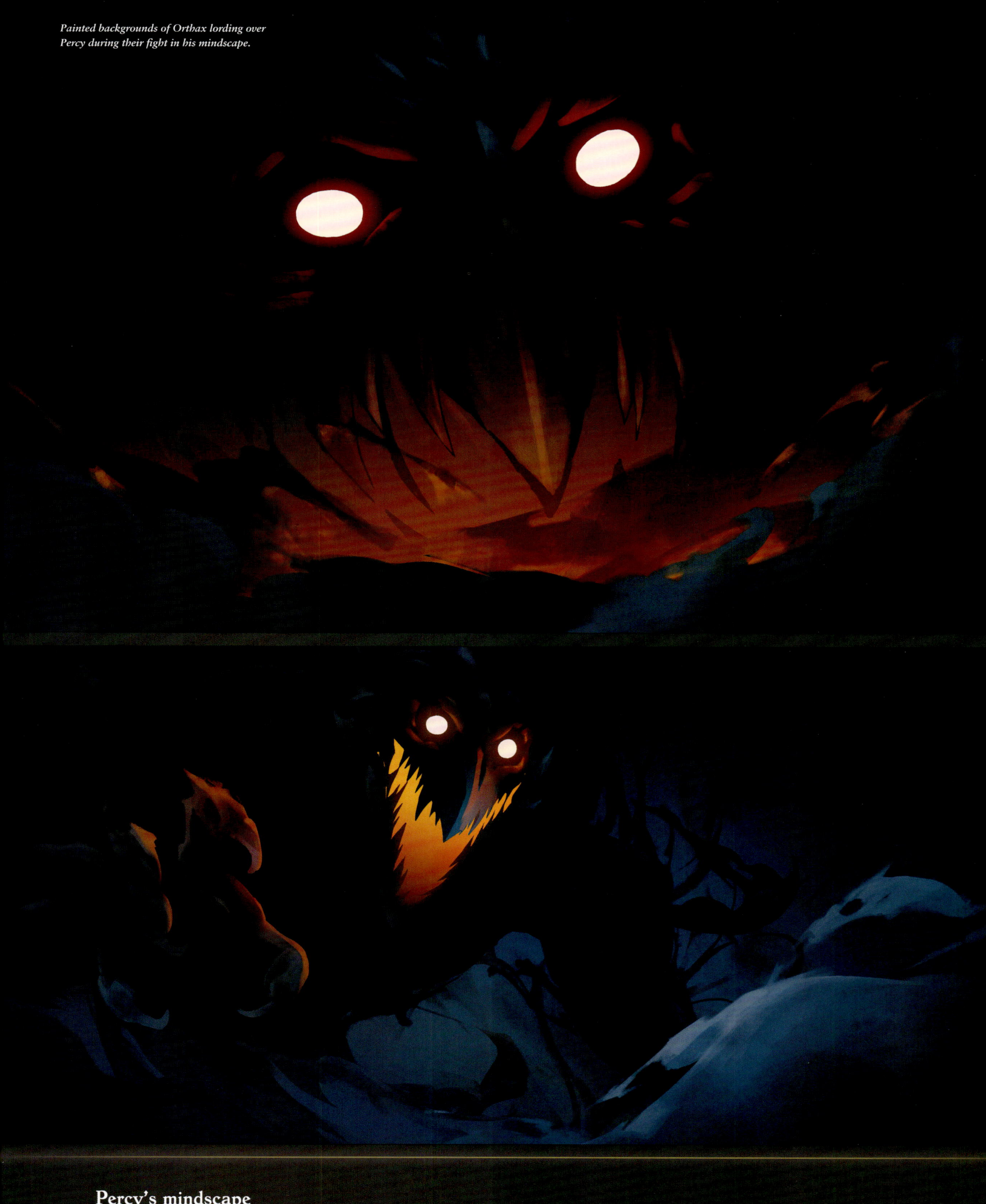

Percy's mindscape

Unsure of who is friend or foe, Percy struggles against his own desires for revenge in a final make-it-or-break-it moment, ultimately hearing the call of his friends to let it all go.

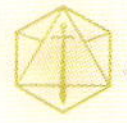

FROM SCRIPT TO SCREEN

PERCY FIGHTING VOX MACHINA IN HIS MINDSCAPE

INT. ACID PITS/DISTILLERY - REALITY - CONTINUOUS

Except he's actually firing at Keyleth, Cassandra, and Vex, who hide behind an overturned workbench for cover.

81 PERCY
I won't let you take them!

Vax leaps out of the way of the flying bullets and joins the group behind the workbench.

82 VAX'ILDAN
So we just wait for him to kill us?

83 VEX'AHLIA
He has to reload eventually...

Another shot explodes through the workbench, right next to Vex's face.

84 VEX'AHLIA
Right?

Through the hole in the workbench they see Orthax billowing above Percy.

INT. PERCY'S MINDSCAPE - CONTINUOUS

Percy finishes firing at his enemies, but when he looks around his parents and family are still - DEAD. They lurch at him, with open eyes and vacant expressions, arrows through their necks. Lady and Lord de Rolo grab Percy by the arm.

85 LADY DE ROLO
You have failed us, son.

86 LORD DE ROLO
A family slaughtered... a legacy lost. You must avenge us.

87 LADY DE ROLO
Avenge us!

87A LORD DE ROLO
Avenge us!

He looks horrified as his dead parents cling onto him-

INT. ACID PITS/DISTILLERY - REALITY - CONTINUOUS

His anguished face mirrors his hallucination.

88 PERCY
I'm sorry Mother...

Grog has Percy in a headlock, in an effort to prevent his destruction. Orthax/Percy blasts them both backwards, slamming Grog into a wall allowing Percy to get free.

Orthax/Percy swivels around, weapon pointed at Grog, and opens fire.

Grog dodges the first few, but is finally hit in the shoulder. Grog dives behind a pillar, grasping his injured arm.

88A GROG
Not cool.

Orthax/Percy turns his attention to the rest of Vox hiding behind the table.

89 VEX'AHLIA
Listen to us! You must fight this!

As he stalks towards them, he sees Scanlan out of the corner of his eye and goes after him.

90 PERCY
Fight... yes.

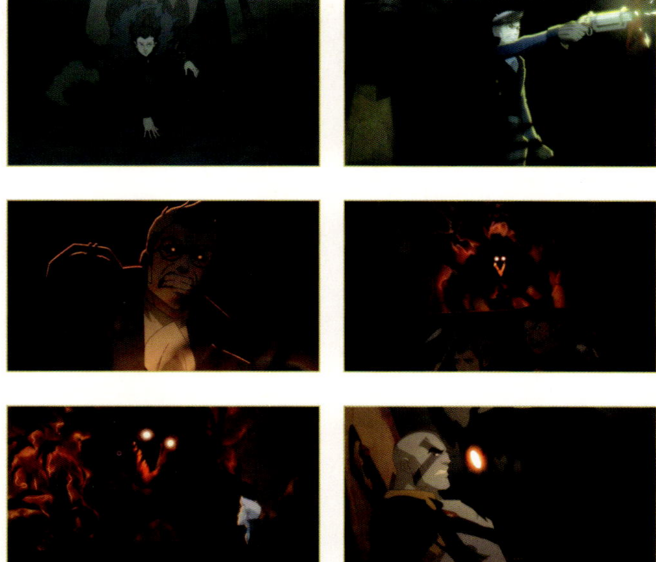

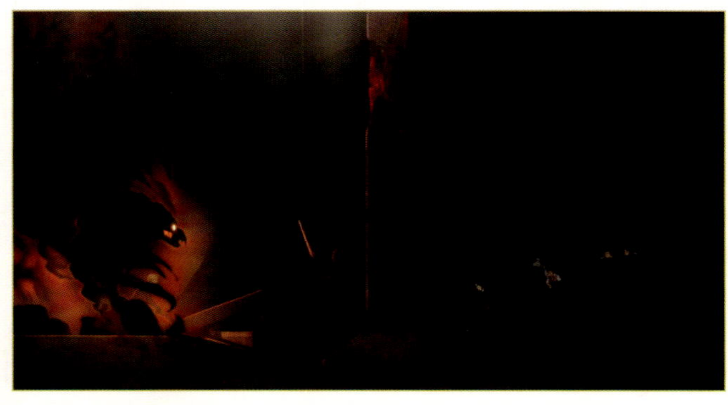

"Your tormented thirst for revenge called me to your side.

An unspoken partnership.

Deep down, you remember welcoming my help.

Welcoming the rage that fueled you to create it… the weapon.

Forged in iron and smoke. We struck a bargain.

I gave you the means for revenge and you give me souls to feast upon." – ORTHAX, S1E12 "THE DARKNESS WITHIN"

"So, that was the most fucked up thing I've ever seen. And I hang out with Scanlan." – VEX, S1E12 "THE DARKNESS WITHIN"

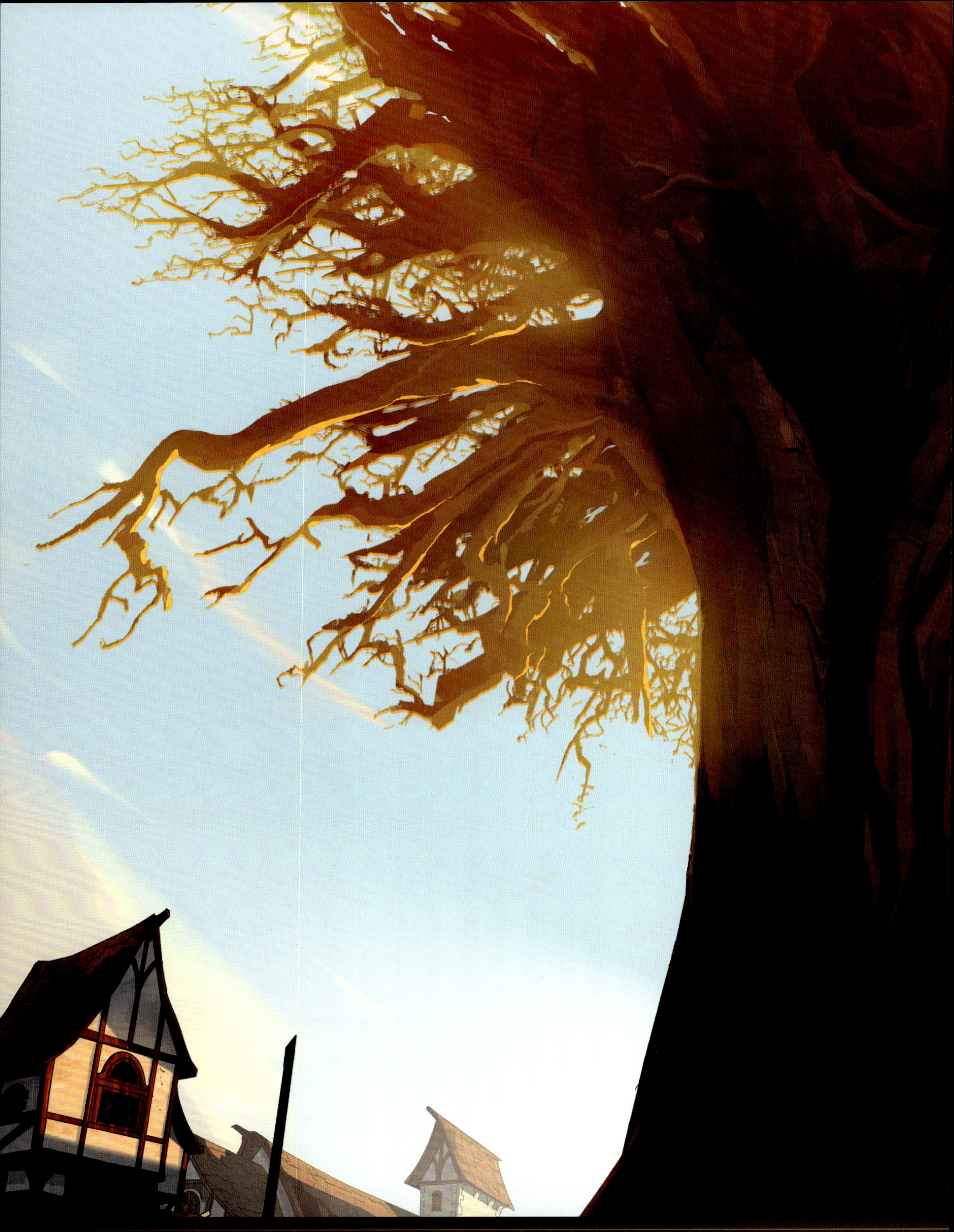

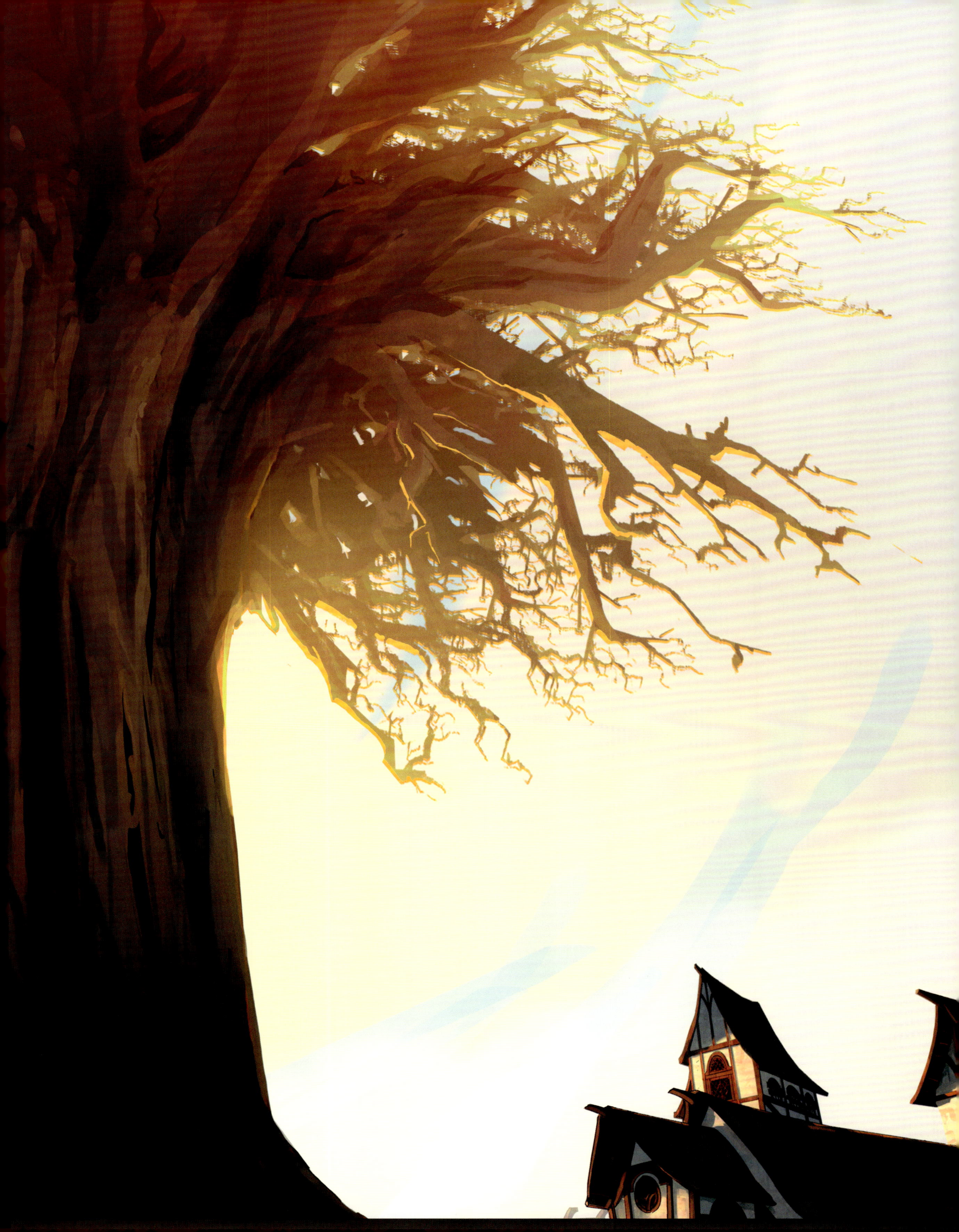

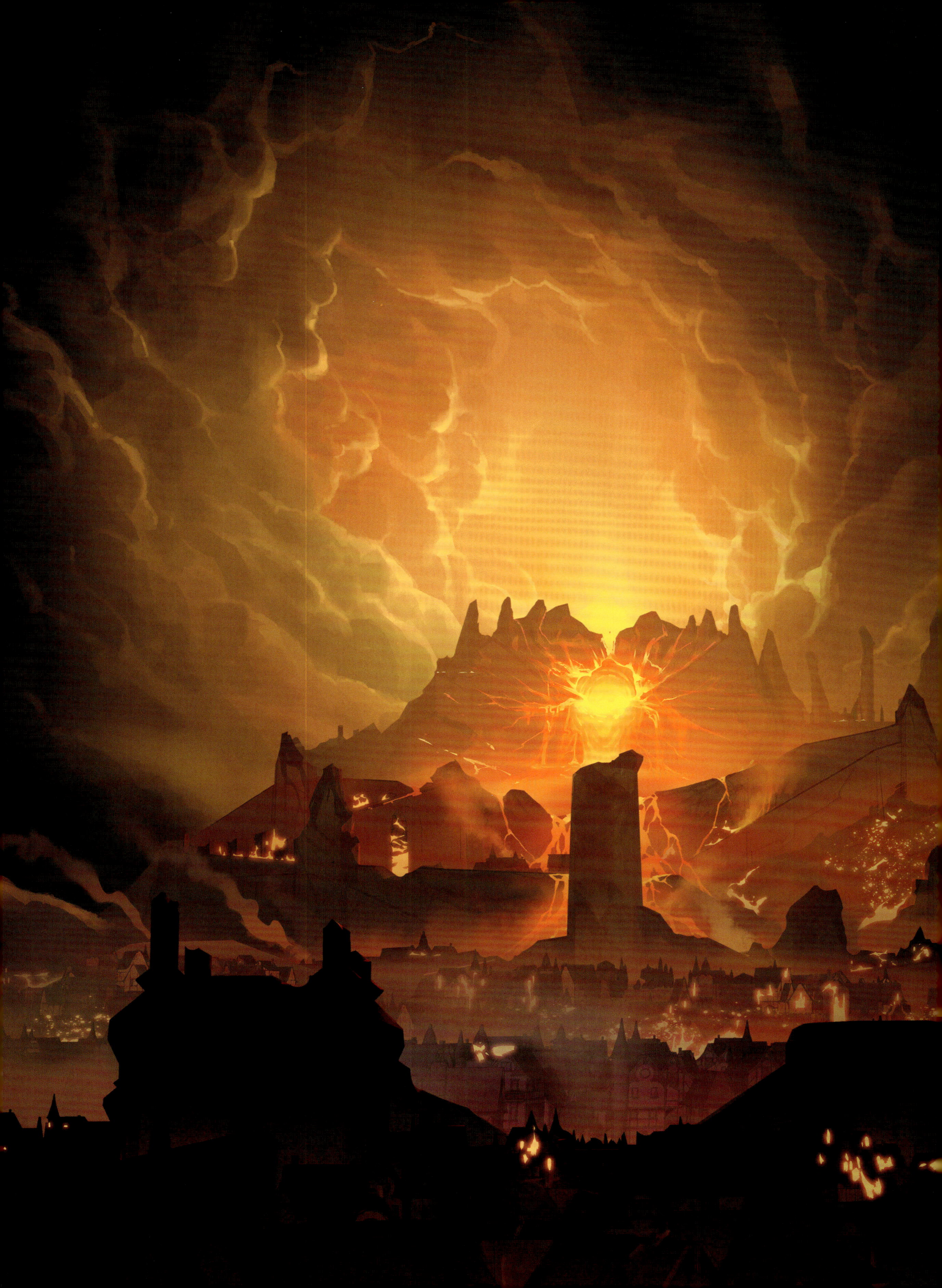

CHAPTER FOUR

SEASON TWO

AND THEY RISE FROM THE FLAMES FOR THE BATTLES AHEAD…

With the heroes of Tal'Dorei returning triumphantly after defeating the Briarwoods, truly nothing could bring Vox Machina down.

Cue the dragon attack…

Having escaped his prison of the Fire Plane, Thordak and his not-so-merry band of dragons are ready to spread destruction through Tal'Dorei and usher in a new age of rule. With everyone looking to Vox Machina (I mean, they defeated one dragon, how hard can four be?), they initially run, then feel bad about it, and the guilt trip drives them to take on the mantle of hero once again. We follow their exploits as they travel to the edges of the continent and beyond to track down the mysterious Vestiges of Divergence–powerful weapons known only in lore to grant their wielders formidable strength.

Despite their lives being on the line, that doesn't stop our heroes from testing the limits of their bond. Apparently, facing death together isn't a cure-all for interpersonal drama. With their group therapy sessions being far from over, we are treated to daddy issues, mommy issues, unrequited love, overly requited love, and a talking sword that may or may not be driving Grog to madness. What's that old saying? Maybe the real Vestiges of Divergence are the friends we made along the way?

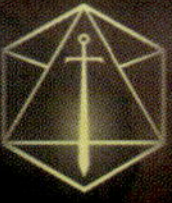

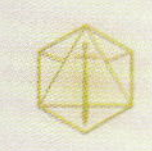

DESIGNING THE SEASON TWO POSTER

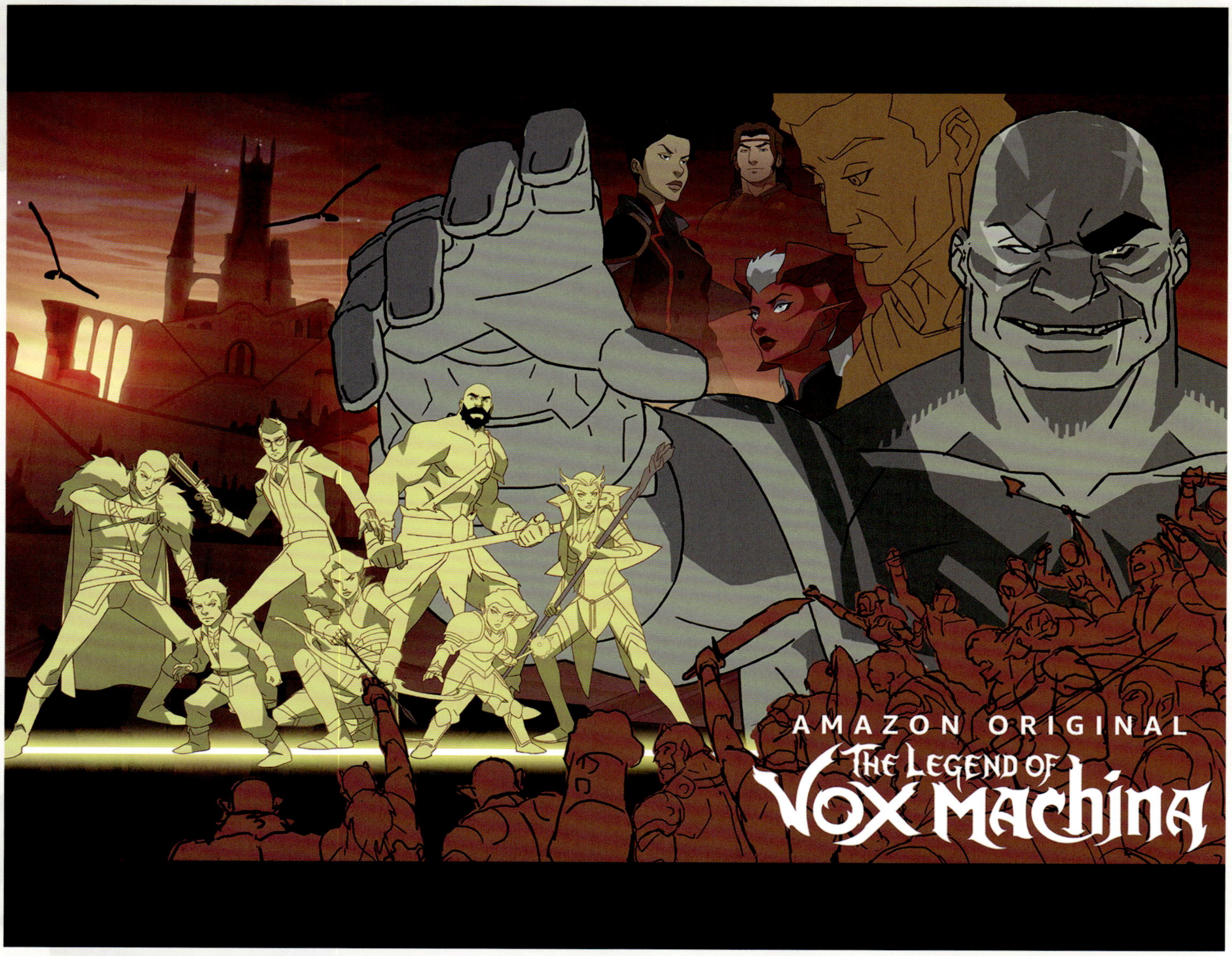

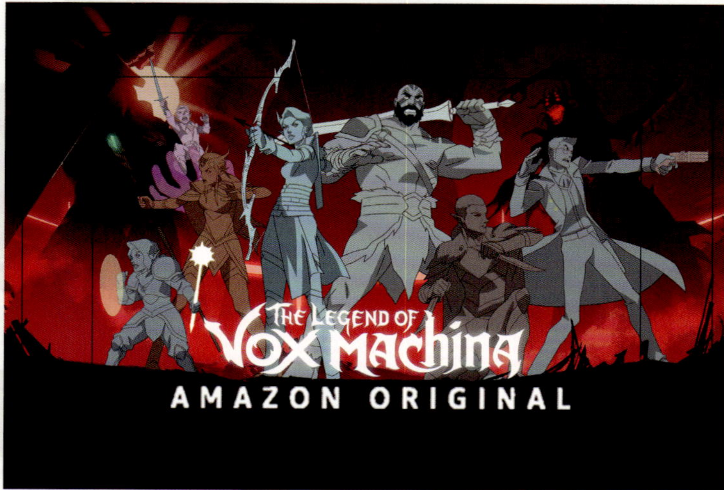

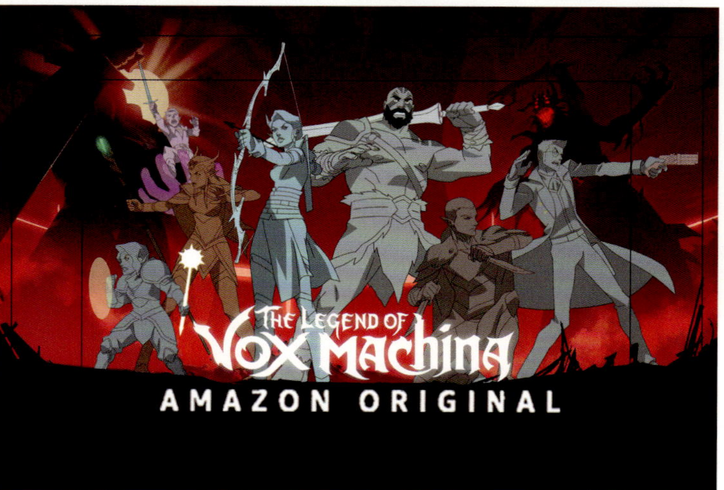

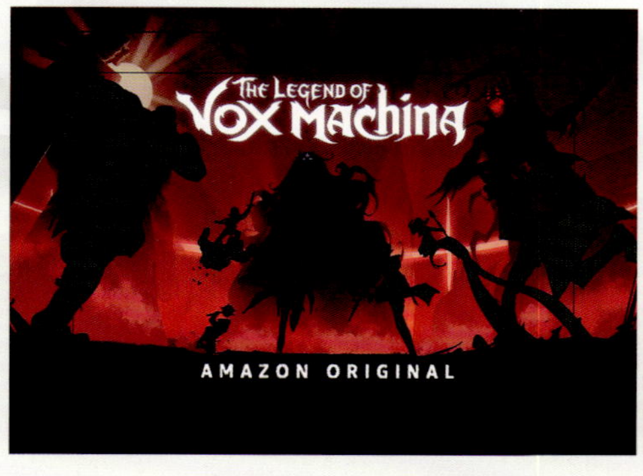

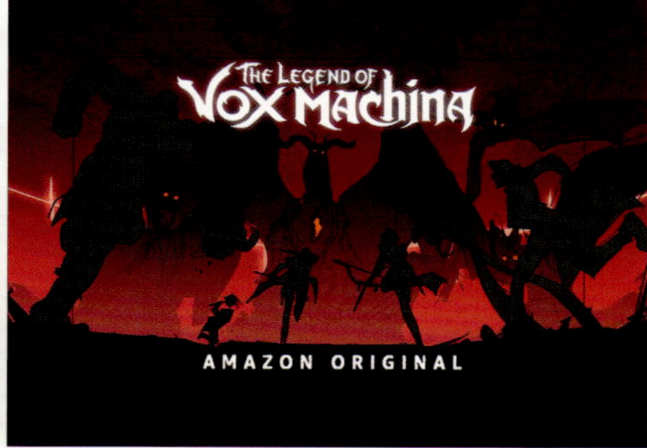

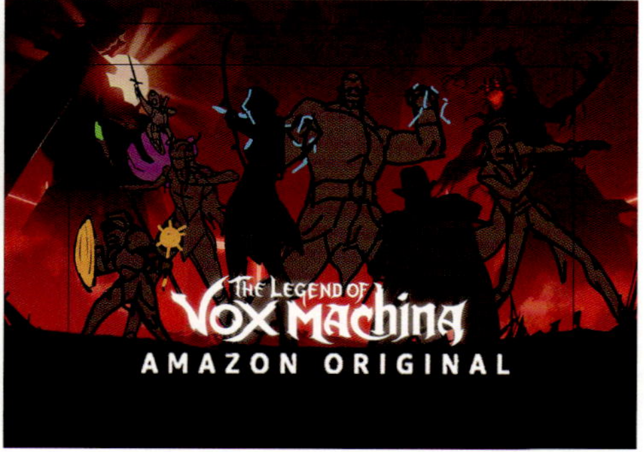

Mock ups for the Season Two launch poster.

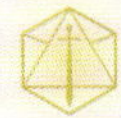

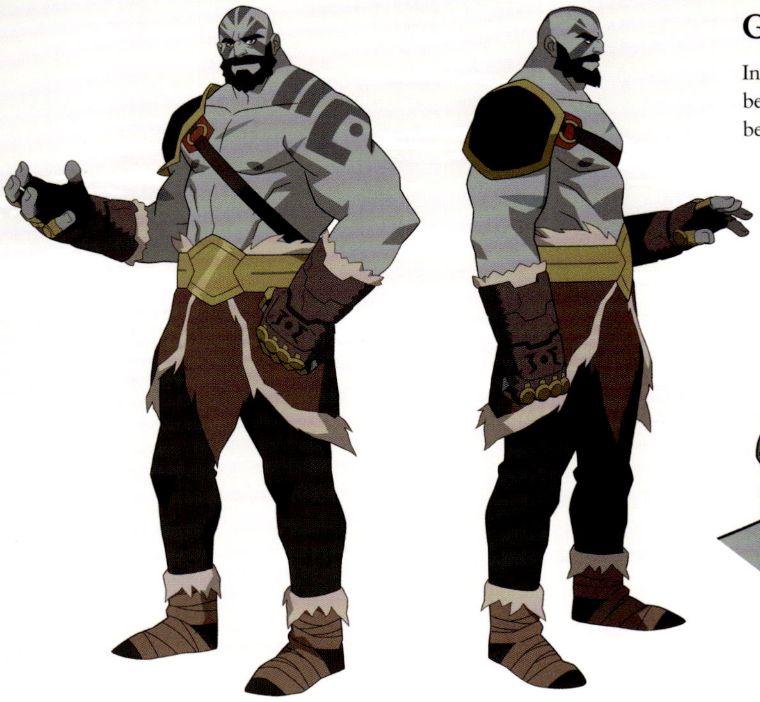

Grog

In season two, Grog gets a new dwarven belt of strength that comes with a surprise beard, to everyone's delight. The new belt was a great opportunity to simplify the original belt design and economize the number of lines in Grog's overall design for animation.

Eventually, Grog also inherits his uncle's Titanstone Knuckles, which Phil Bourassa admits to being challenging to animate. The Knuckles' mechanics required extra attention, as the exact effects of their growth magic needed to be plotted out for the remainder of the season.

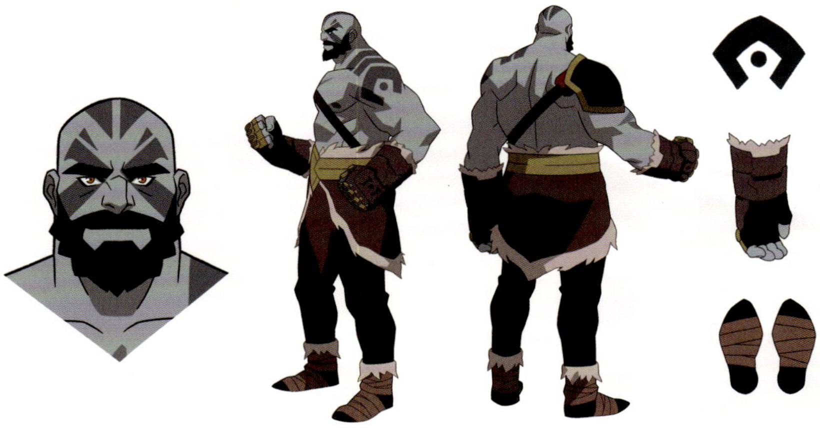

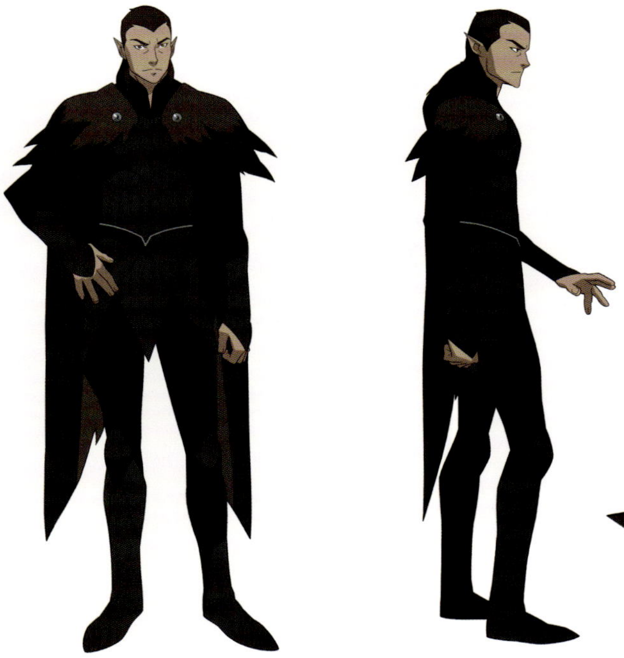

Vax

Vax gets a complete costume redesign to reflect his service to The Matron of Ravens. His design in season one is one of the most detailed of the entire main cast, so his new "uniform" was another chance to simplify the line counts to help out animation. He gets a cape that splits down the middle in the back, which gives him a dynamic winged silhouette when he's dashing around. One thing that was important to Bourassa was for Vax's silhouette to still remain characteristically him. In season one, he had the big fur mantle around his shoulders, so they were sure to keep a similar shape on his upper half to keep him easily recognizable.

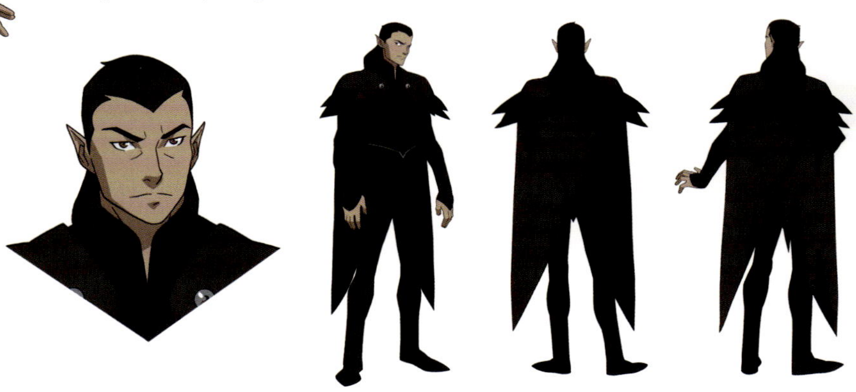

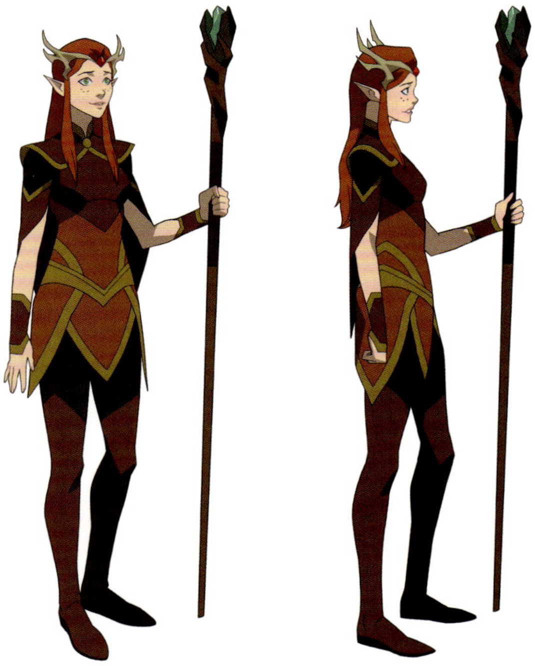

Keyleth

Keyleth's new outfit design reflects her mastery of the element of fire. Bourassa likens it to her "Dark Phoenix" moment in that it's the audience's first glimpse at her truly terrifying potential. The goal was always to keep it simple and elegant and focus on the change through color. When a character's overall silhouette changes drastically, it can be challenging for the audience to have a visual throughline of the character. Keeping her loyal to season one Keyleth was always the goal while still adjusting elements to show her character progression.

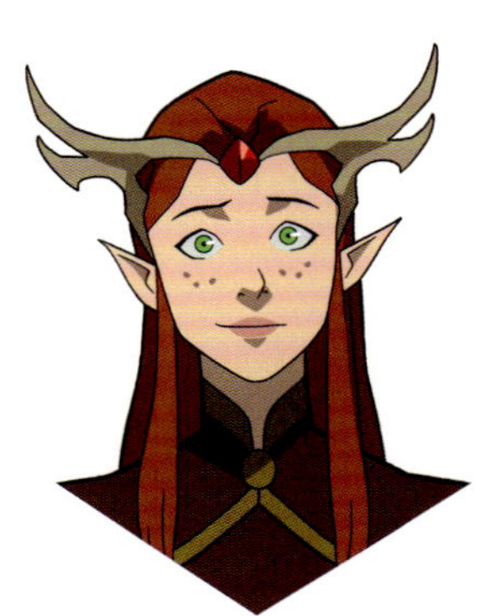

"Keyleth is such an interesting character because she's so humble and unsure of herself, and yet she might be the most powerful person in the group. She masters fire in a crisis. I was excited to do her redesign because a lot of her look from season one was based on her established art, and this was a new angle we got to figure out on our own." – PHIL BOURASSA

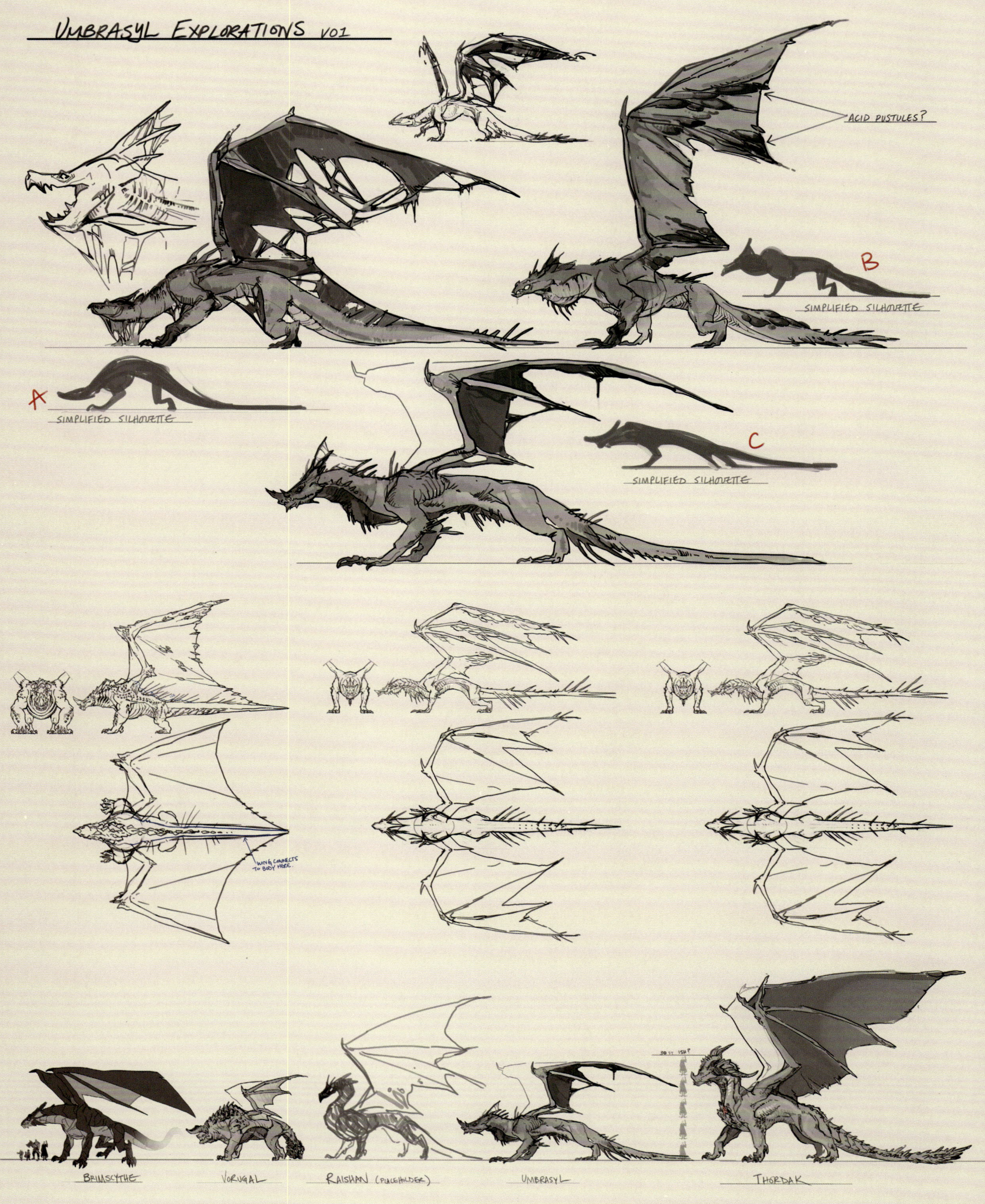

"Our vision of the dragons moving into season two was for them to appear like detailed painted miniatures straight from a tabletop game. Eddie Gonzalez (CG Supervisor) also happens to be a huge dragon nut and was able to give us very specific notes about the physics behind wing movement and how a dragon would need to move to be physically able to fly." — ARTHUR LOFTIS

THE CHROMA CONCLAVE

Due to their increased presence in the storyline, the 3D dragon models for season two had to shift in order to accommodate the amount of screen time. The artists added additional highlights and texture layers to aid in the realism of their movements.

Thordak–The Cinder King

Ancient Red Dragon–Breath Weapon: Fire

Trapped for years in the Elemental Plane of Fire, Thordak struck a deal with Raishan to help him escape by embedding the soul anchor that was imprisoning him directly into his chest. The areas of his neck that light up with flame are inspired by a car engine and are meant to show his breath weapon "revving" up. He comes off as a kingly creature–arrogant and unrelenting in his pursuit of power.

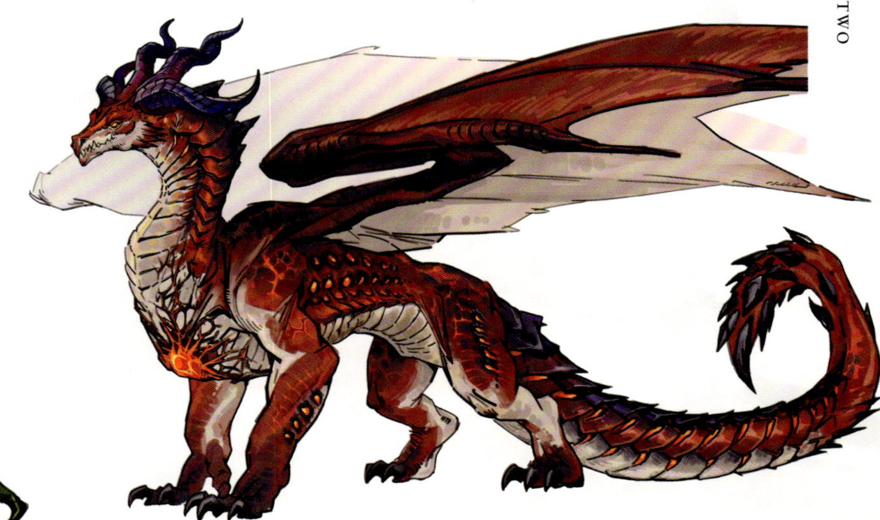

> *"Hear me, insects. You live out of mercy. Fight or flee, and you forfeit that mercy. A new age is upon you, the rule of the Chroma Conclave!"* – THORDAK, S1E1 "RISE OF THE CHROMA CONCLAVE"

Raishan–The Diseased Deceiver

Ancient Green Dragon–Breath Weapon: Poison

Seemingly falling apart at the seams, Raishan takes the "diseased" nickname to heart in her design. Her design is more serpentine-inspired to play off her conniving nature.

Vorugal–The Frigid Doom

Ancient White Dragon–Breath Weapon: Ice

This brutish dragon is the most "beast" in nature out of the other Chroma Conclave members. He is the most eager for the hunt and might spend a little too much time playing with his food.

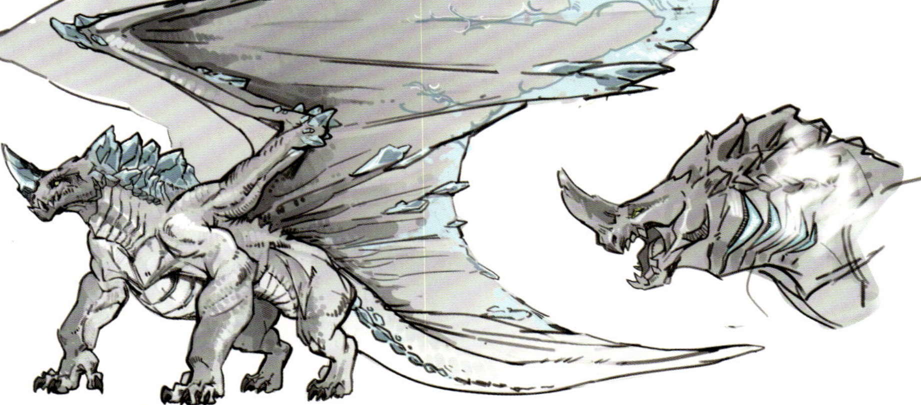

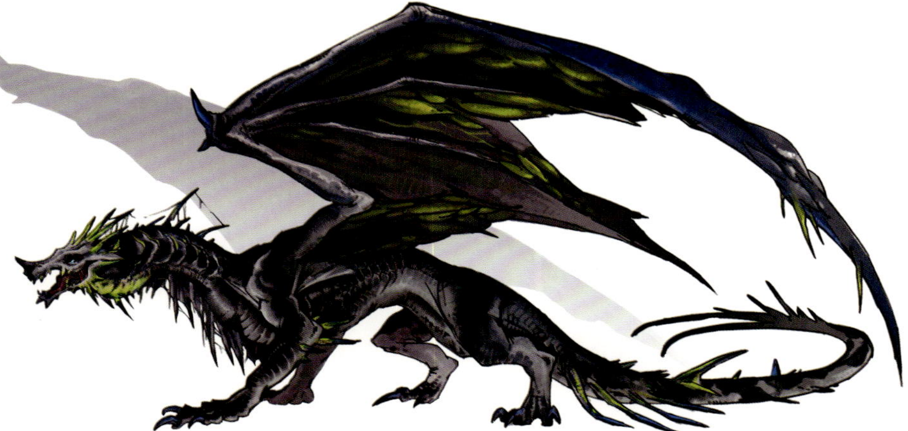

Umbrasyl–The Hope Devourer

Ancient Black Dragon–Breath Weapon: Acid

Umbrasyl's acid breath gives us some of the more terrifying imagery from the Conclave's attack on Emon. He is more of a weasel-inspired swamp creature intended to sludge his way through the battlefield.

Animation Tip: When you're worried about overworking your art team with too many dragon battles, having a dragon that can turn invisible comes in clutch.

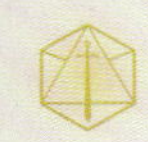

EPISODE 1

THE RISE OF THE CHROMA CONCLAVE

"When the Chroma Conclave attacks, we make like a tree and... get the fuck out of town before we burn to the ground. Led by Thordak, a.k.a. The Cinder King, these dragons threaten to spread their deadly rule across all Tal'Dorei. Man, this continent sure could use a band of heroes stupid enough to take on four dragons right about now, huh? Not us; we're running away to Whitestone. But... someone should definitely help out." – A RECOUNTING OF "RISE OF THE CHROMA CONCLAVE" BY SCANLAN SHORTHALT

Empress Salda Tal'Dorei

Final designs of Sovereign Uriel Tal'Dorei III's wife and children.

Tal'Dorei Kids

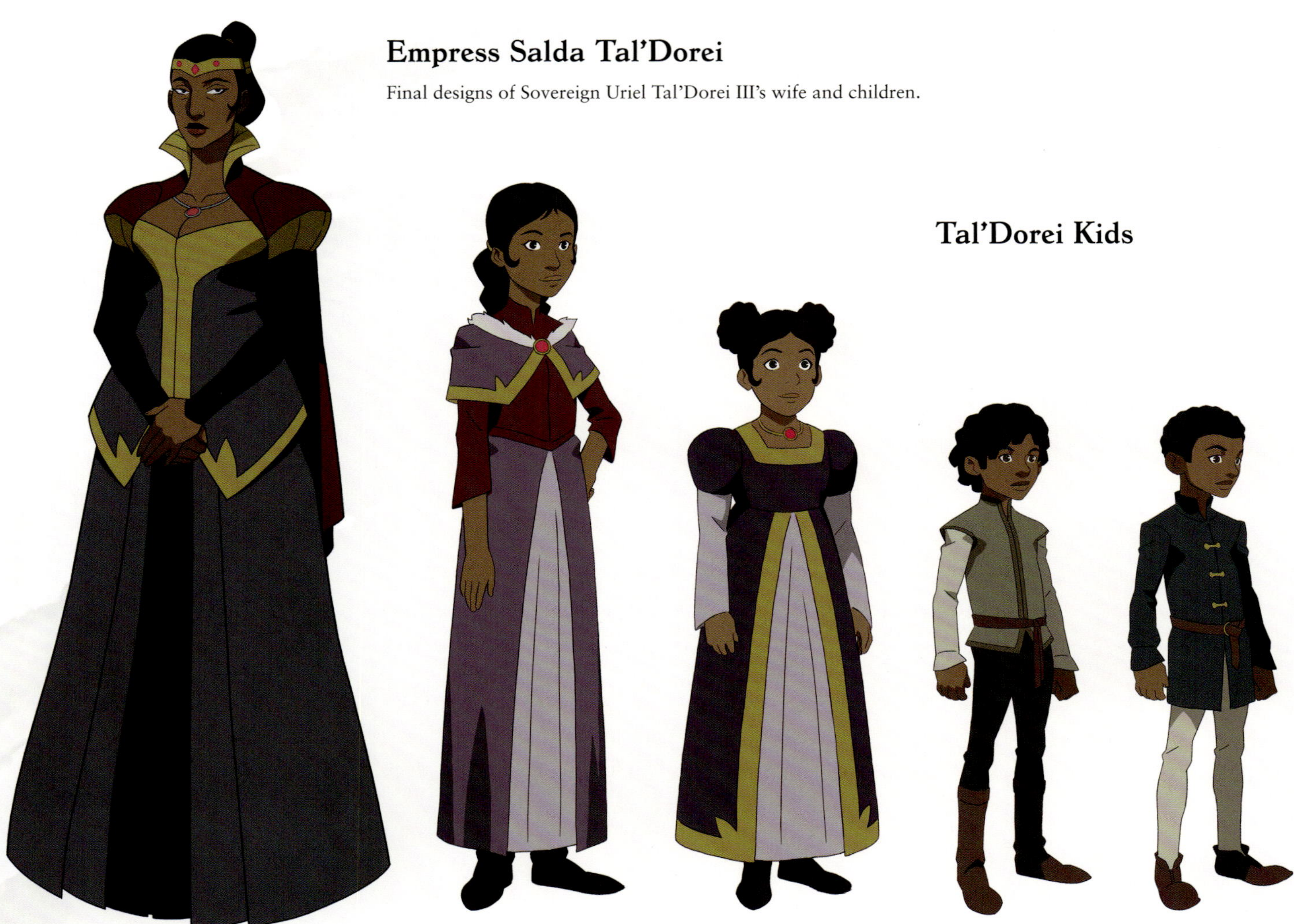

Large Crowd Scenes

The choreography of large crowd scenes, whether it be in battle or a festive party, is a large challenge to surmount. While one may be tempted to copy and paste the same character over and over again, in order to maintain a realistic feel, designers have to go in and create every individual character and give it a different movement cycle so nothing looks too similar. Even a simple shot such as this crowd of refugees escaping Emon can take months to coordinate and get right.

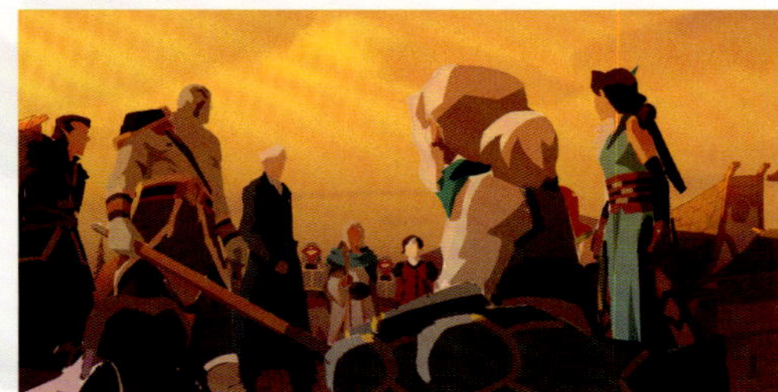

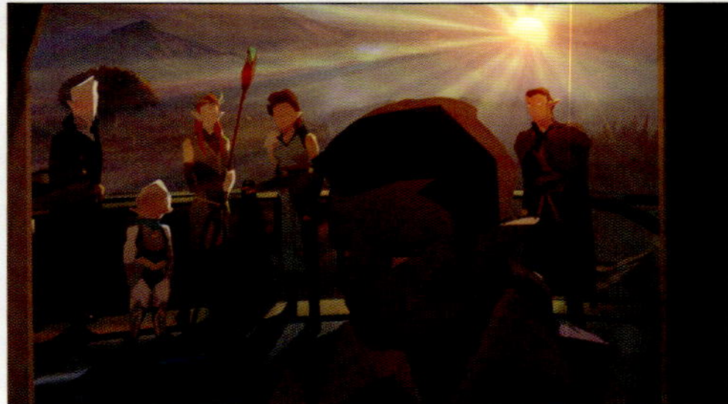

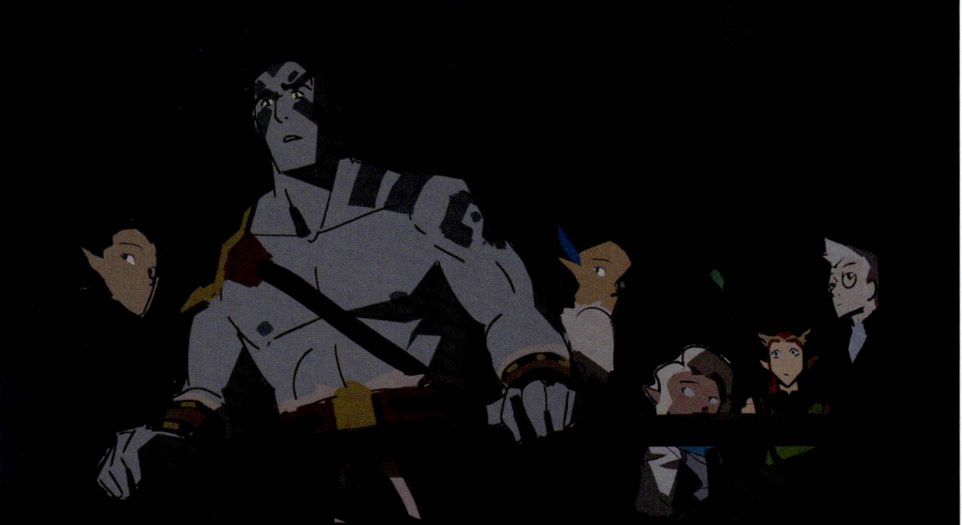

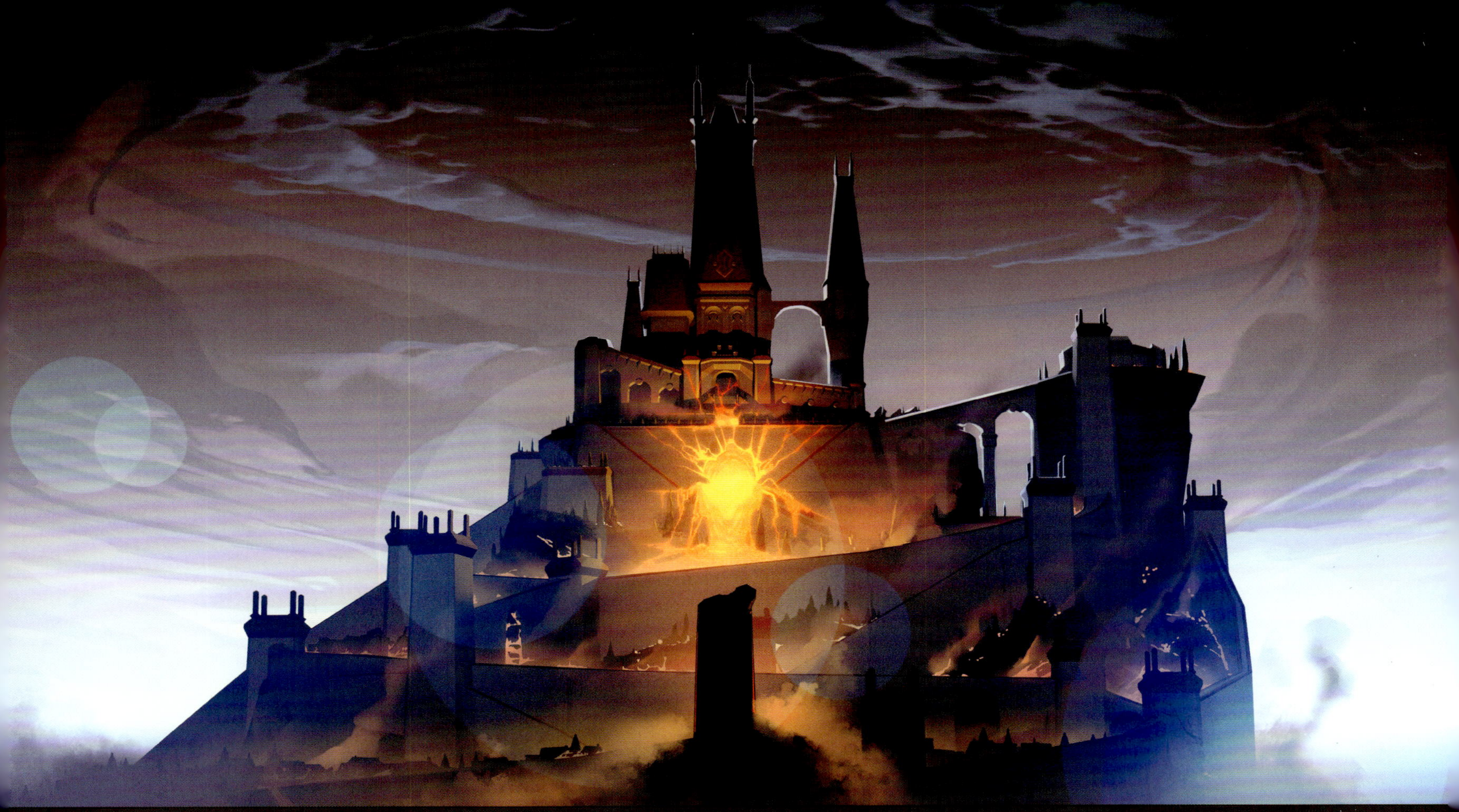

The Destruction of Emon

Following the epic cliffhanger at the end of Season One, the art department was tasked with carefully destroying the entire city of Emon.

A common "cheat code" in animation is reuse. That is when design is able to take existing backgrounds and characters and, as the name implies, reuse them. Unfortunately, the idea of reuse is thrown out the window when you are completely destroying a location and every charred building, flaming rooftop, and frozen street has to be completely redrawn. Designers had to research and develop how specific attacks would cause the buildings of Emon to crumble. As each dragon has a different breath weapon, the final scene is a bloodbath of fire, ice, acid, and poison.

The design team wanted it to be extremely clear which dragon was attacking in each shot, so they developed four distinct looks for the different fighting styles. For example, in a tabletop RPG setting, what is considered acid damage versus poison damage could be easy to overlap. To avoid confusion, the artists pushed Raishan's poison breath into a more gaseous state versus Umbrasyl's liquid acid rivers flowing through the streets.

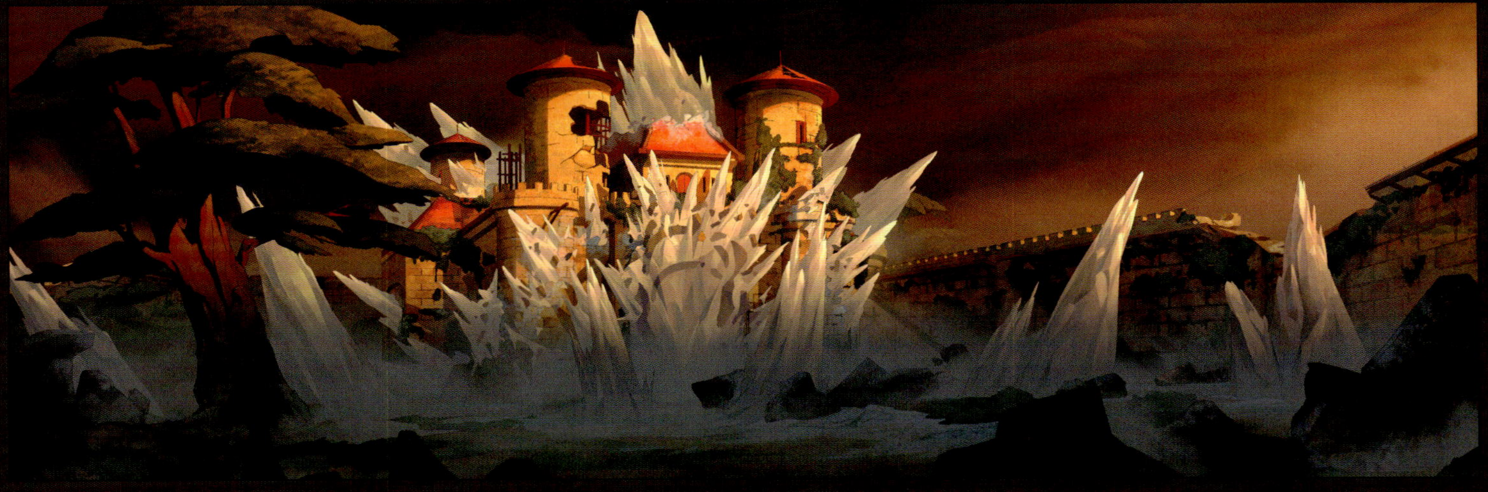

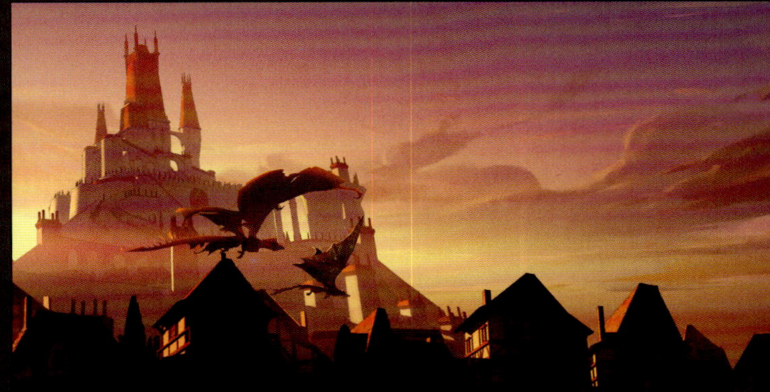

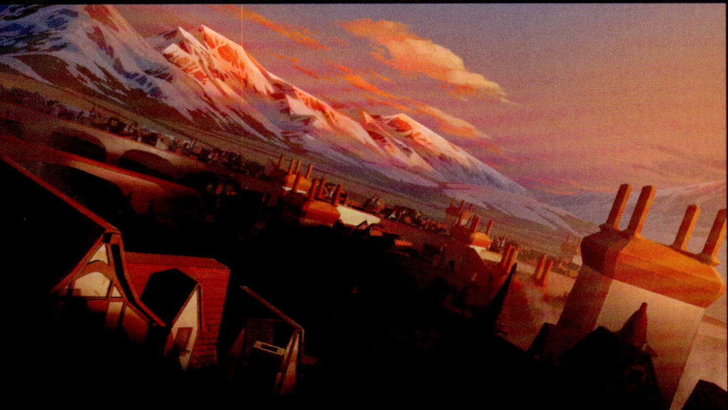

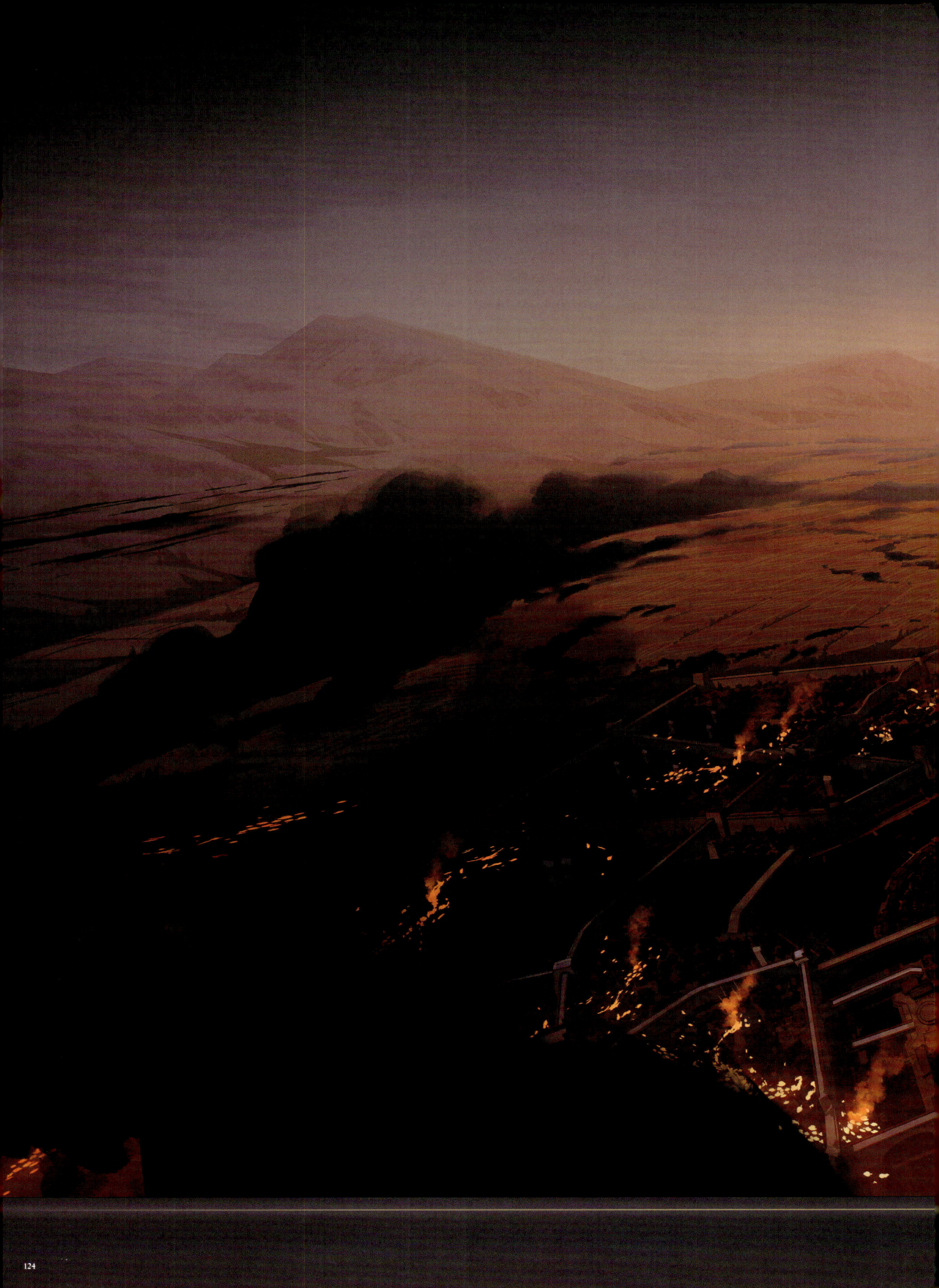

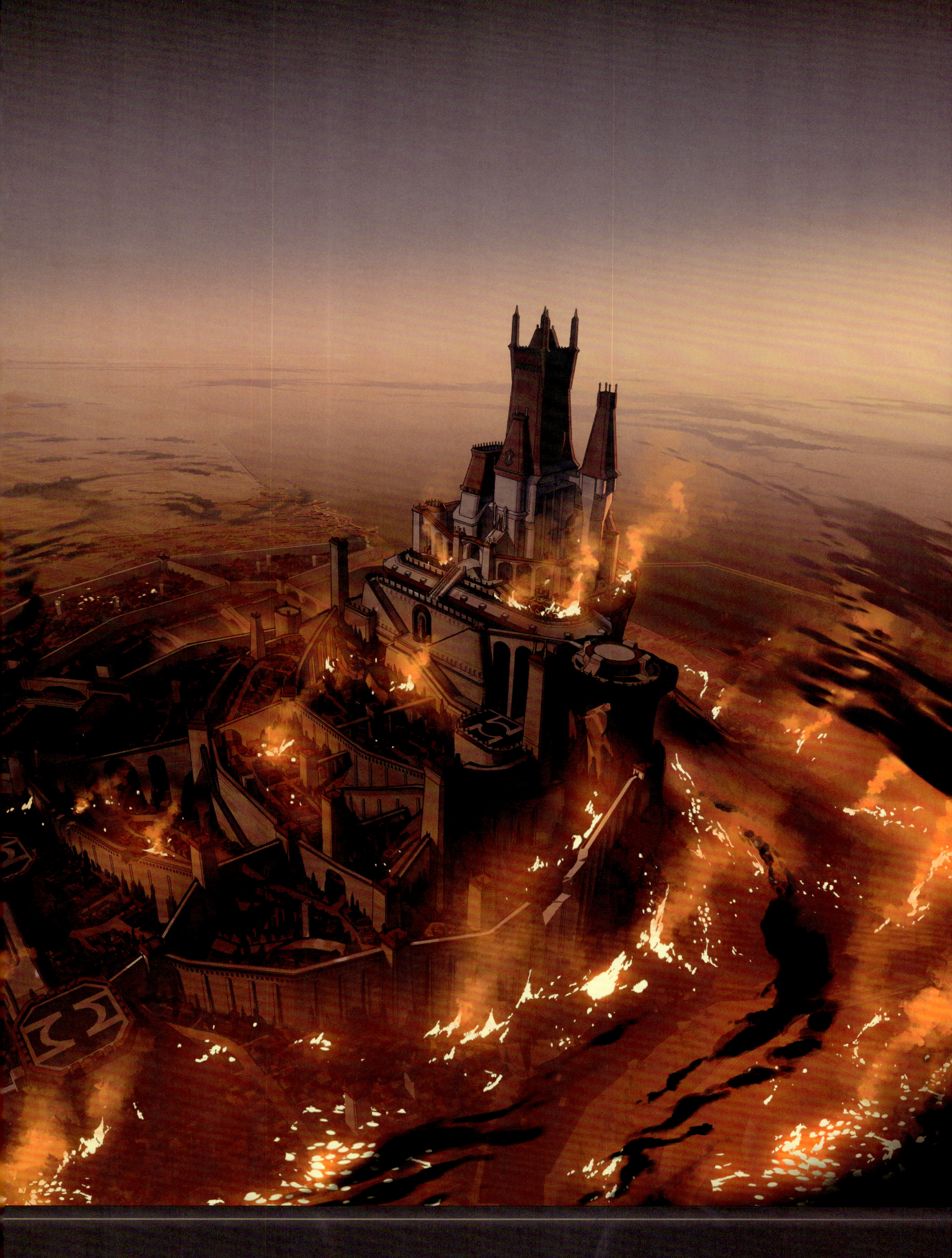

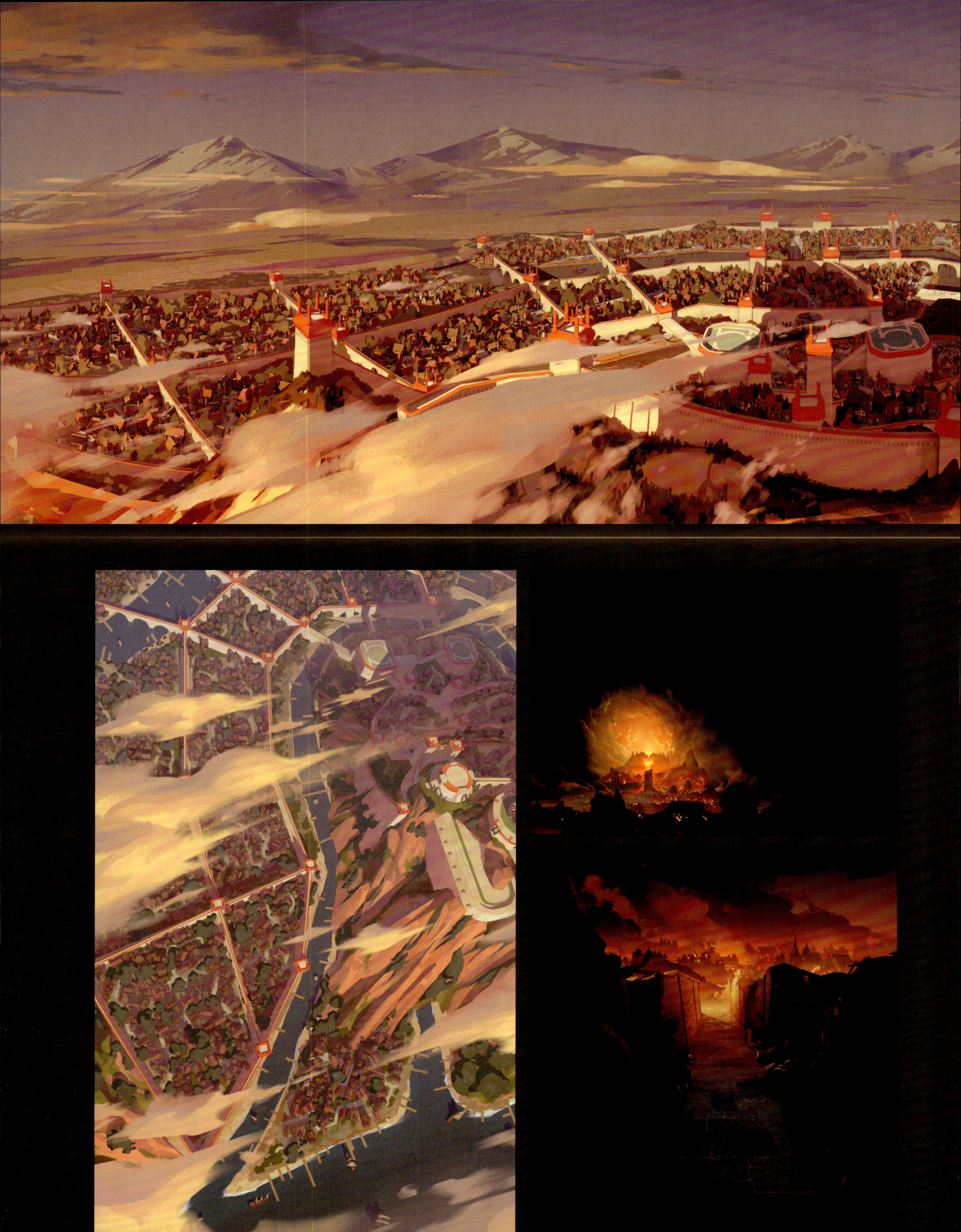

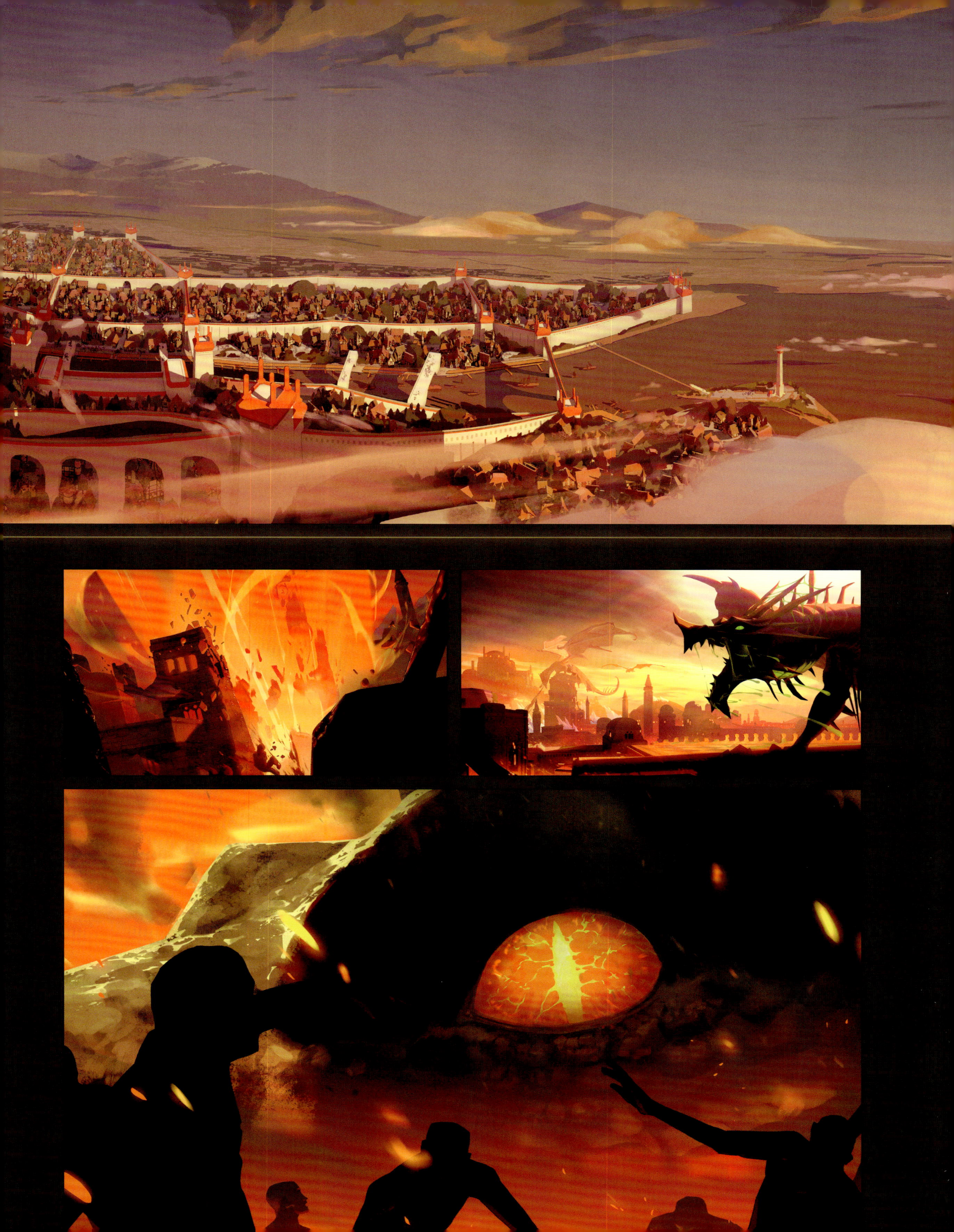

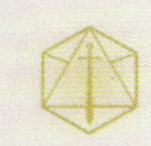

Rebuilding Whitestone

You know that old saying, when a dragon burns down one city, you build another? With the threat of the Briarwoods passed, the citizens of Whitestone get to work on rebuilding their once thriving city. Many backgrounds were repainted to give them a more vibrant color, including The Sun Tree, now flourishing green with the radiance of The Dawnfather.

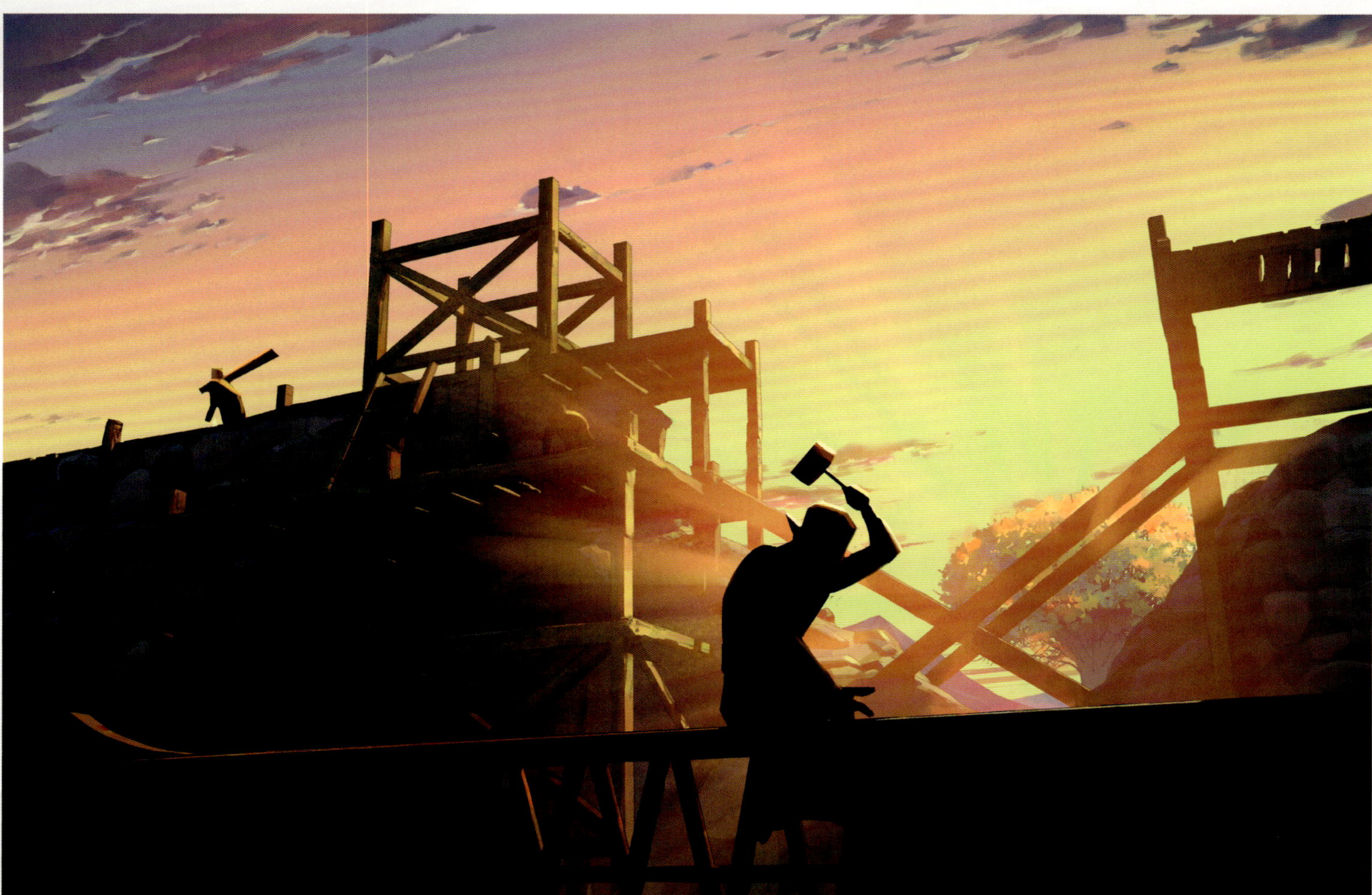

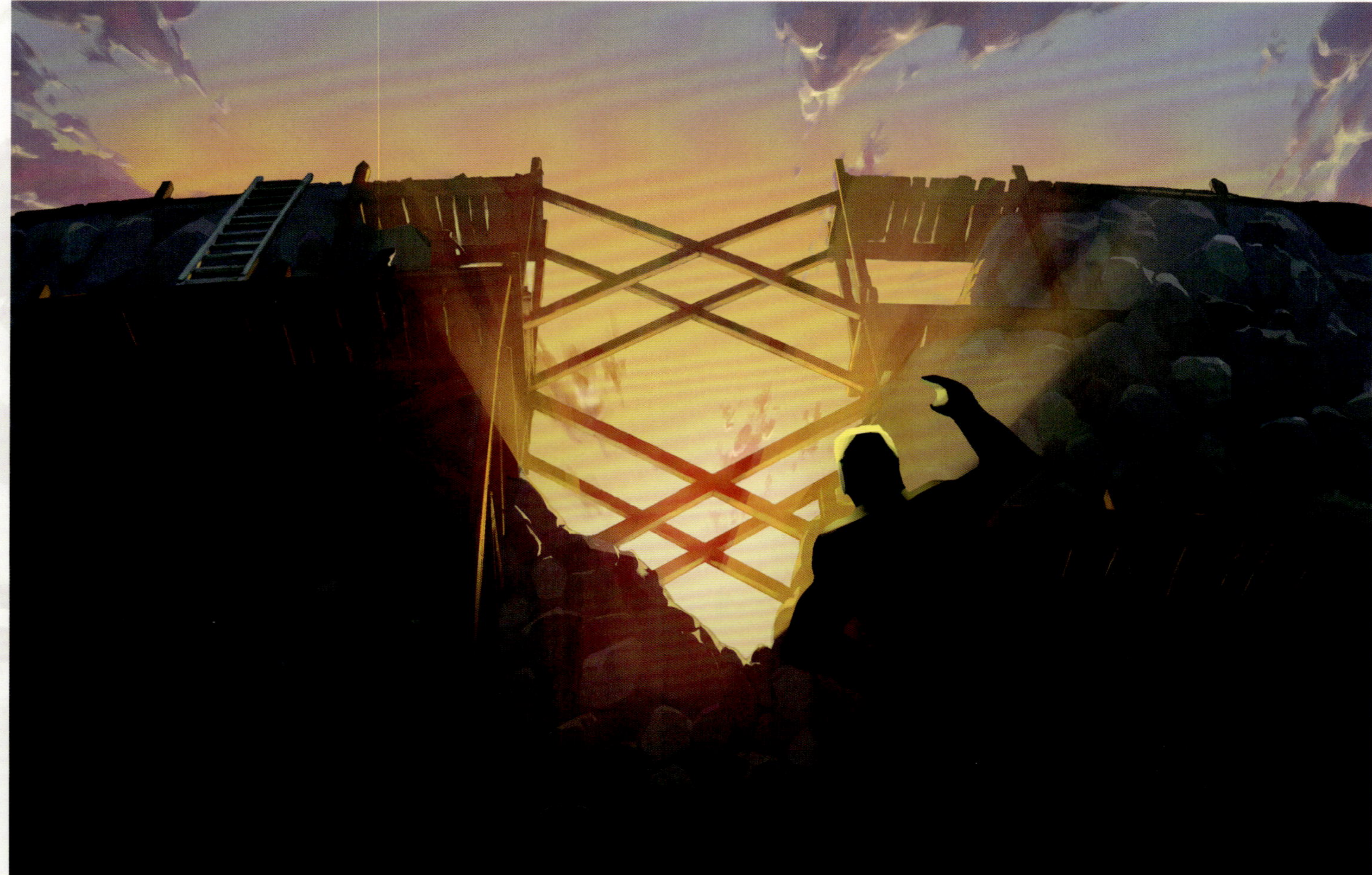

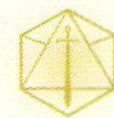

FROM SCRIPT TO SCREEN

GOING THROUGH THE SUN TREE

179 VAX'ILDAN
Not bad for a bunch of assholes who got lucky.

Scanlan has his back to the group as he listens. The rest of VM takes in the view.

180 VEX'AHLIA
We're all frustrated... and scared. But the fight's not over. What do you say, Scanlan? Up for not going quietly into the night?

Scanlan thinks, still conflicted. Suddenly, he hears a hushed voice-

180A LITTLE BOY (O.S.)
It's them! They fought the dragon.

It's the two young refugee kids from earlier, poking their heads around the doorway for a glimpse of VM.

180B LITTLE GIRL
Shh... hide.

The kids run away giggling excitedly. Scanlan is touched.

181 SCANLAN
<sigh> Yeah, alright, let's do it. After all, I can't do my world tour without the rest of the band...

EXT. SUN TREE - LATER

Vox Machina (with Trinket) stands by the tree, along with Cassandra, Keeper Yennen, and Gilmore. Keyleth looks concerned.

182 YENNEN
Legends speak of forces hidden in Vasselheim. Make your appeal for help at the Platinum Sanctuary, but failing that, seek out help where ever you can.

183 KEYLETH
I've never been to Vasselheim. My teleport spell only works if I'm familiar with the tree on the other side.

184 YENNEN
I know the tree. You merely need to visualize it.

185 KEYLETH
Oh. Okayyy, maybe that'll work.
(then)
What's the tree look like?

Keyleth begins swinging her staff to start her spell.

186 YENNEN
Big. But not TOO big. Pink buds... or were they yellow? Her branches swaying in the breeze... a fabulous oak tree... maybe walnut?

187 PIKE
Uhhh, is that enough, Keyleth?

Keyleth closes her eyes, pictures the tree in her head and waves her staff. A glowing PORTAL "opens up" in the Sun Tree.

Vox Machina steps up to the portal.

188 PERCY
Onward. To Vasselheim.

With that, the team leaps through the portal.

188A SCANLAN
Beauty first!

188B PIKE
Last one in is a troll dick!

188C VEX'AHLIA
Here goes nothing.

188D GROG
Hoo-hoo-hoo, yeah!

Before Percy steps through he looks back and nods at Cassandra, then leaps through.

189 CASSANDRA
Let's hope they made it. For all our sakes...

As the portal closes SHUT...

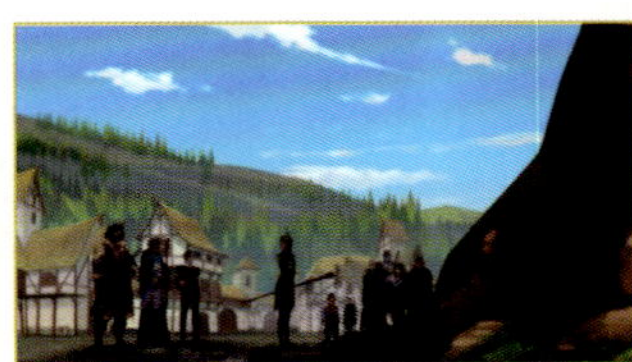
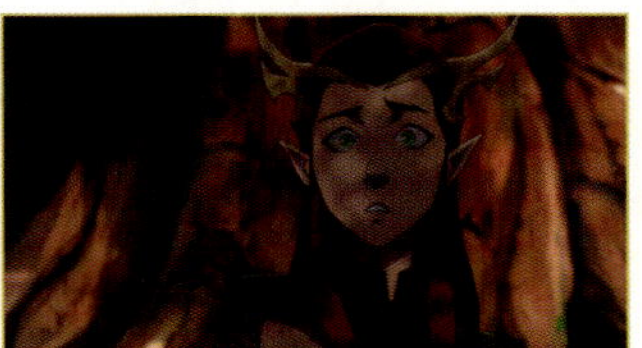
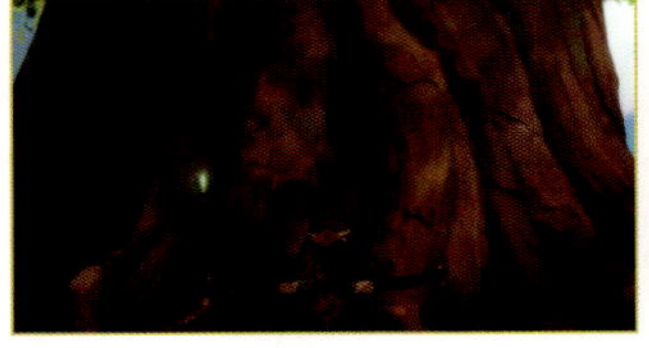
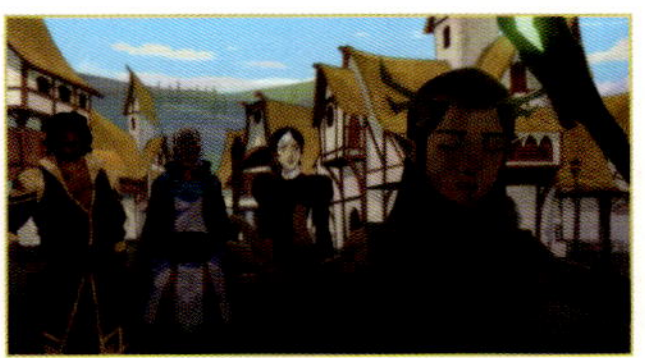
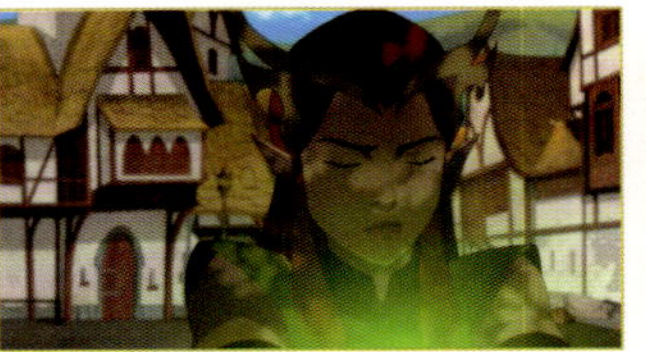
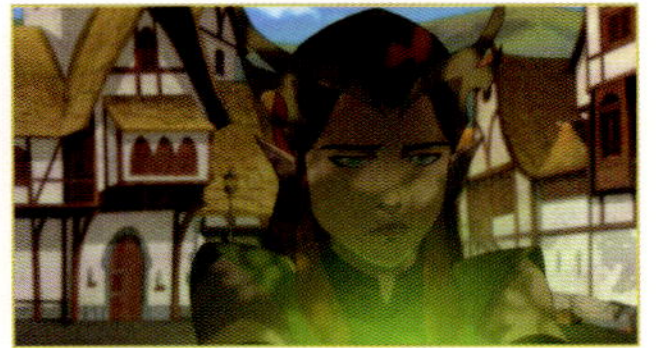
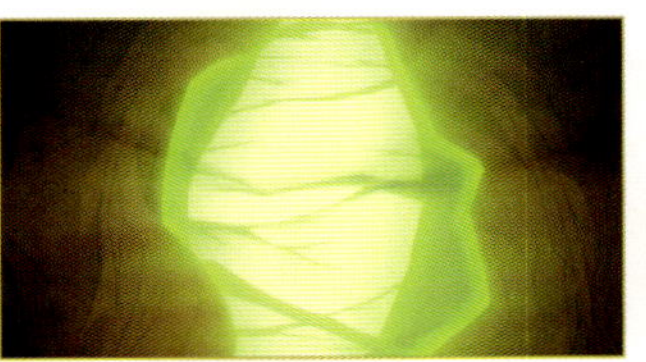
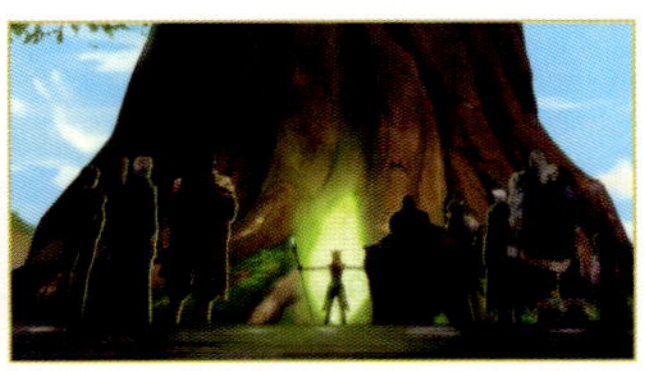
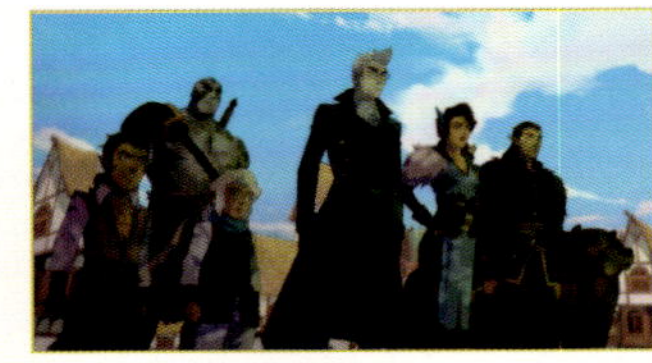
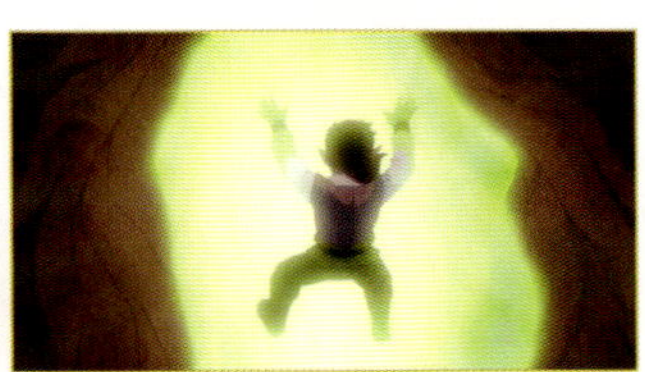
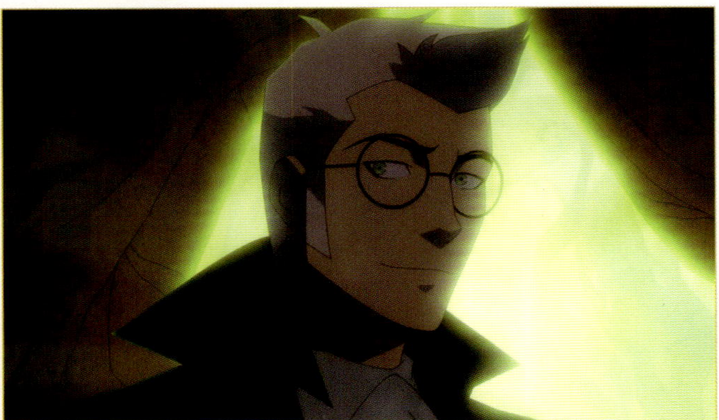

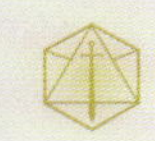

EPISODE 2

THE TRIALS OF VASSELHEIM

"We go to Vasselheim, hoping to recruit an army to take on the Chroma Conclave, and wind up getting tossed out on our asses. Vex has the stupid idea of asking for help from The Slayer's Take, a band of ruthless monster hunters, but we just get bullied by a gynosphinx for NO REASON. Seriously, why did Osysa have to go that hard? Oh, and has anybody seen Grog?"

– A RECOUNTING OF "THE TRIALS OF VASSELHEIM" BY SCANLAN SHORTHALT

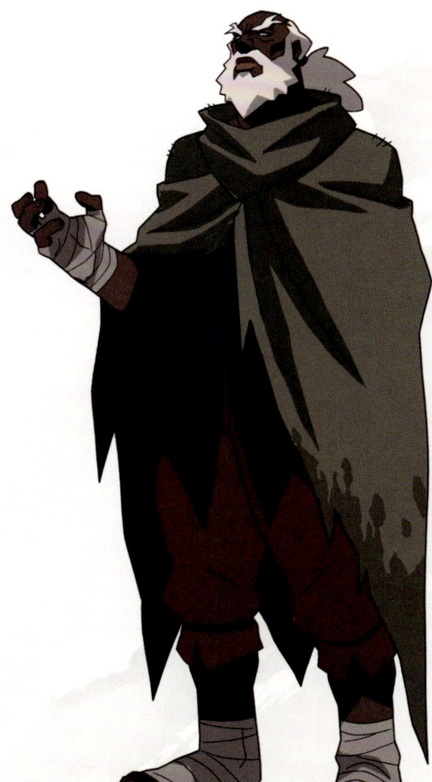

Earthbreaker Groon

Designed with the classic videogame fighter build, Earthbreaker Groon needed to be equally stacked with muscles and stoicism. He presides over the Temple of The Stormlord and gets the honor of being among the few who have ever handed Grog's ass to him.

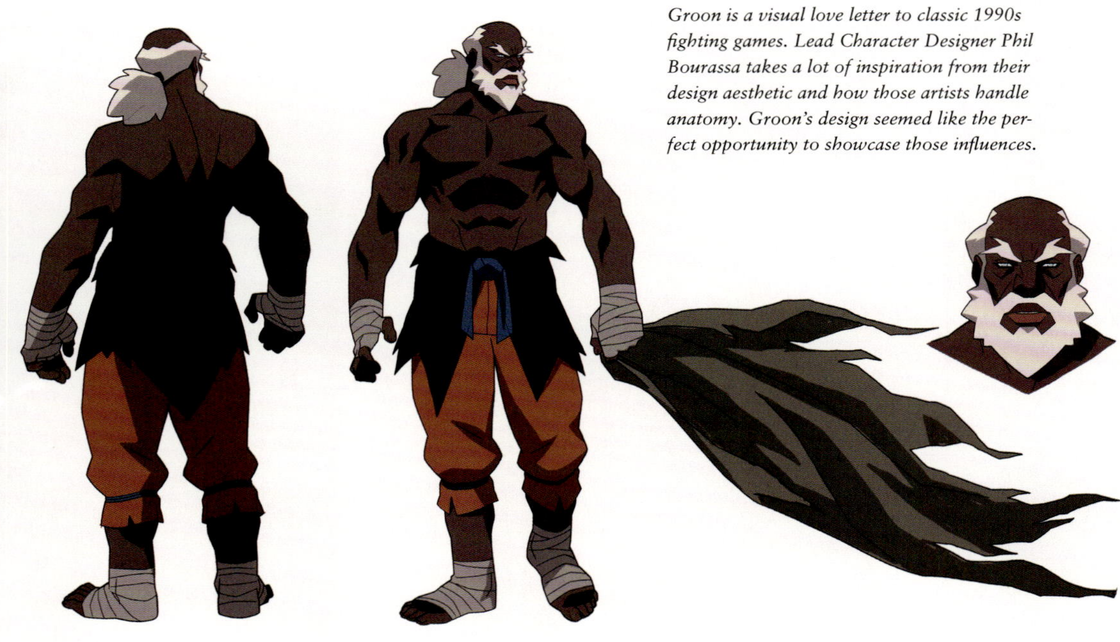

Groon is a visual love letter to classic 1990s fighting games. Lead Character Designer Phil Bourassa takes a lot of inspiration from their design aesthetic and how those artists handle anatomy. Groon's design seemed like the perfect opportunity to showcase those influences.

Kashaw

Zahra

Matt Mercer as Rob, the Vasselheim front gate guard

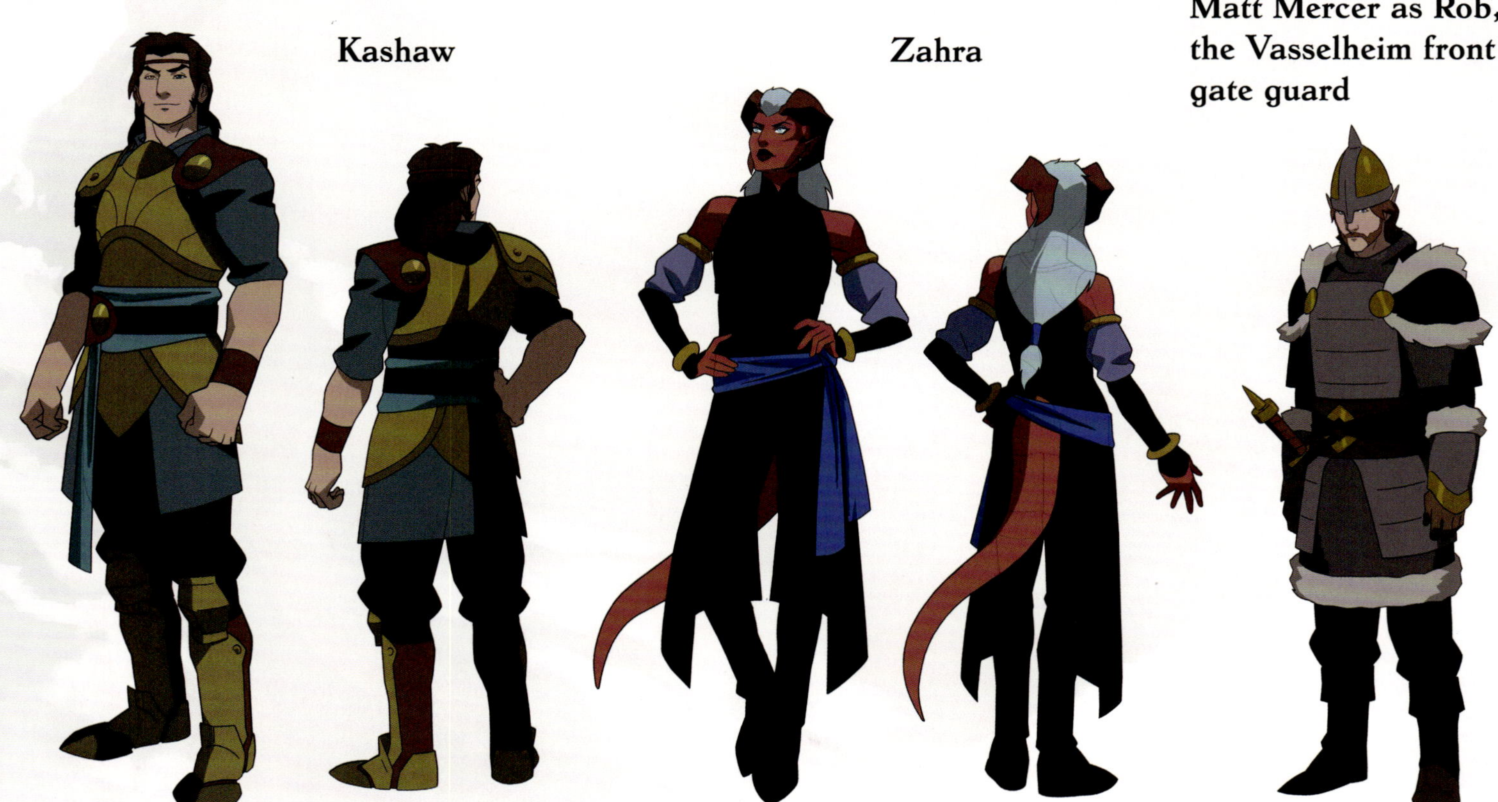

Two members of The Slayer's Take who begrudgingly aid Vox Machina on their quest. Some would call them "friends."

Another hidden Matt Mercer–as always, the bear waits outside.

Victor

Our resident gunpowder expert who definitely still has all his original teeth.

Highbearer Vord

Ruler over The Platinum Sanctuary in Vasselheim.

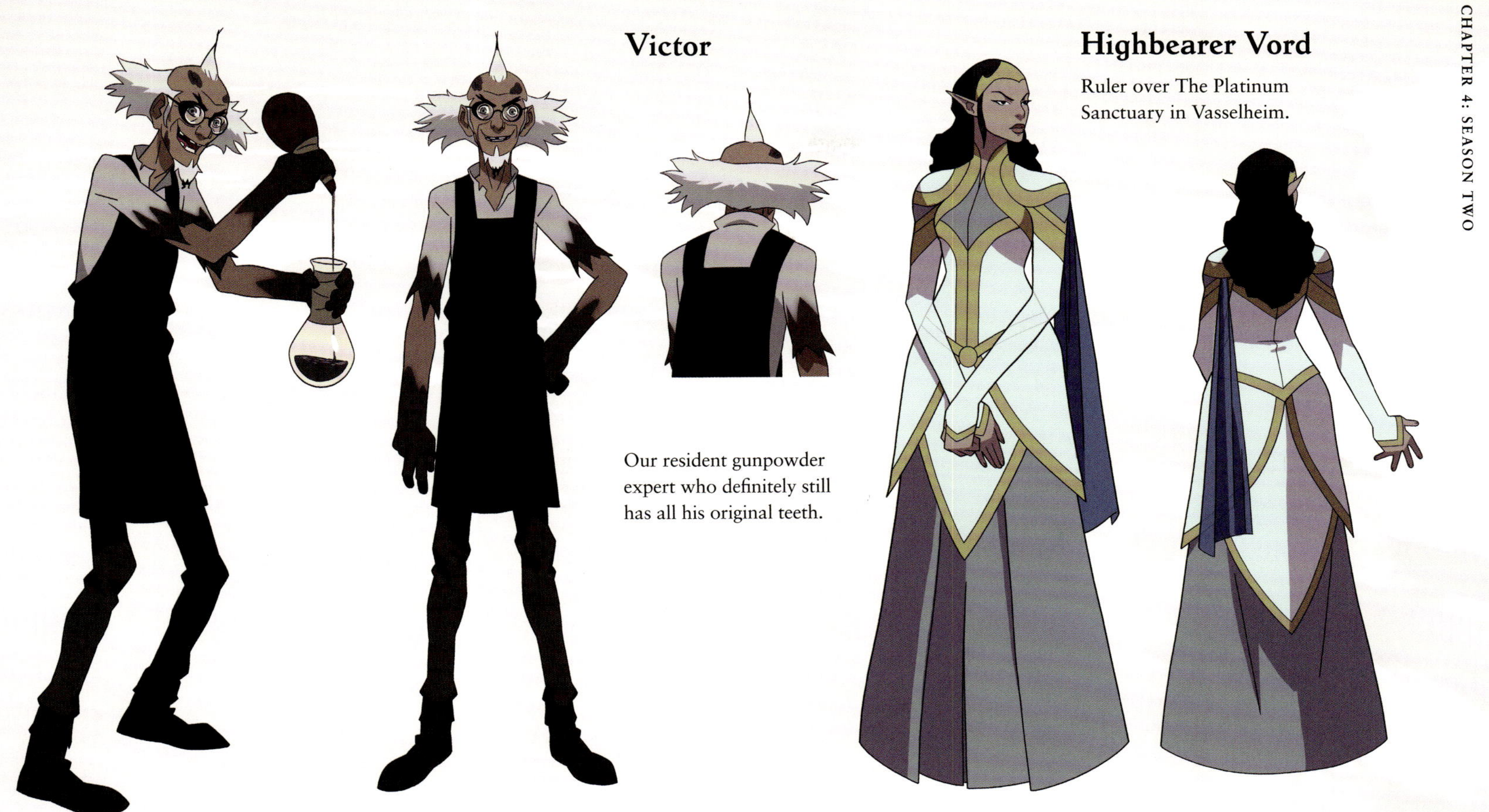

Osysa

Early explorations of the gynosphinx Osysa. Designed in CG, the team opted for a metallic motif to simplify animation.

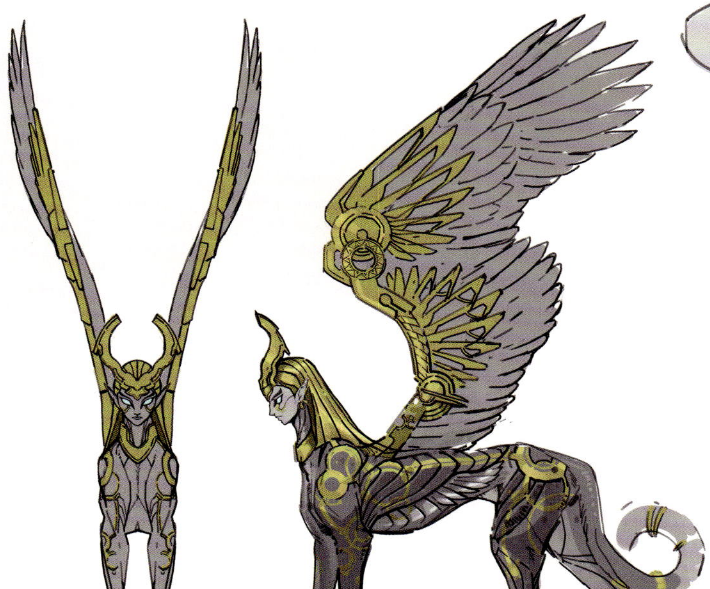

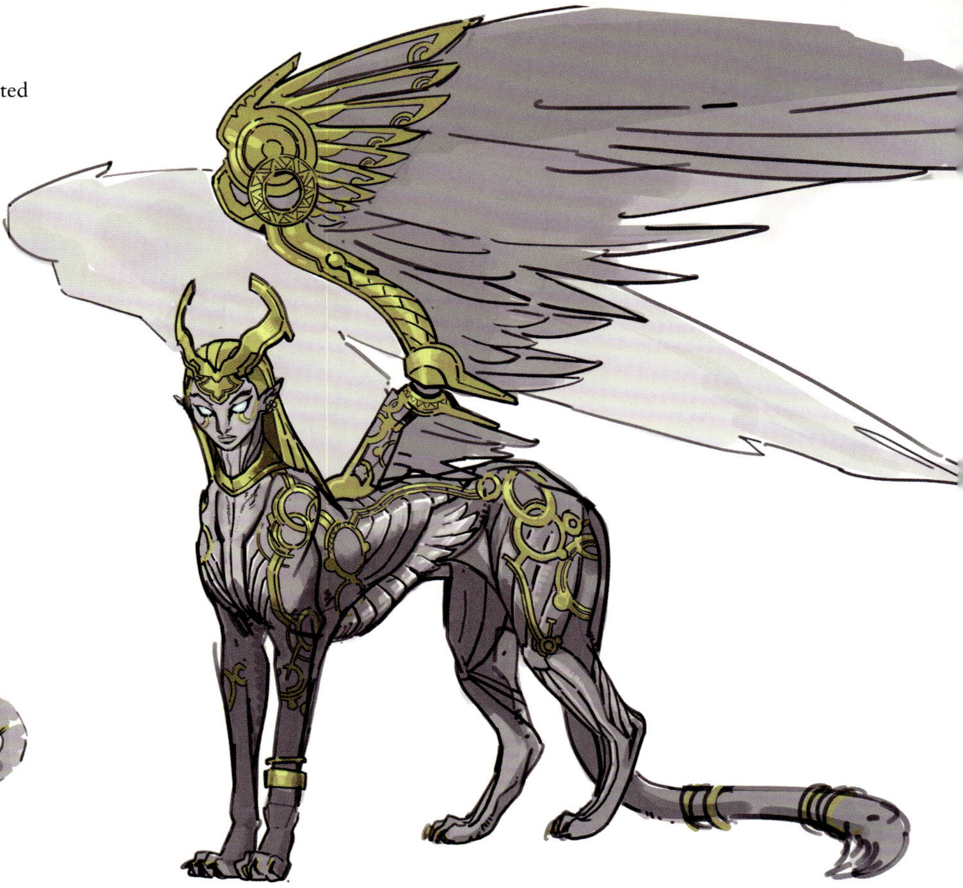

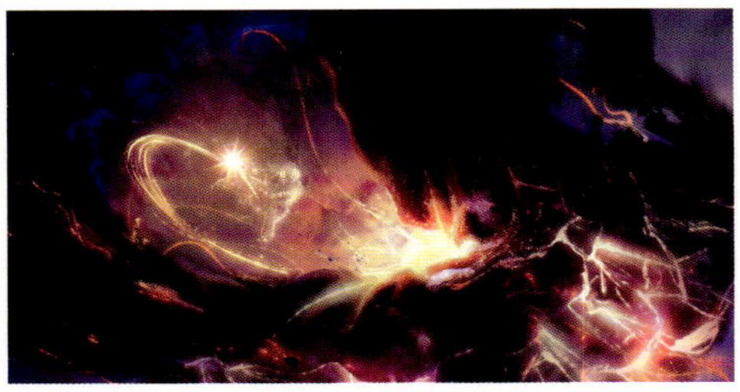

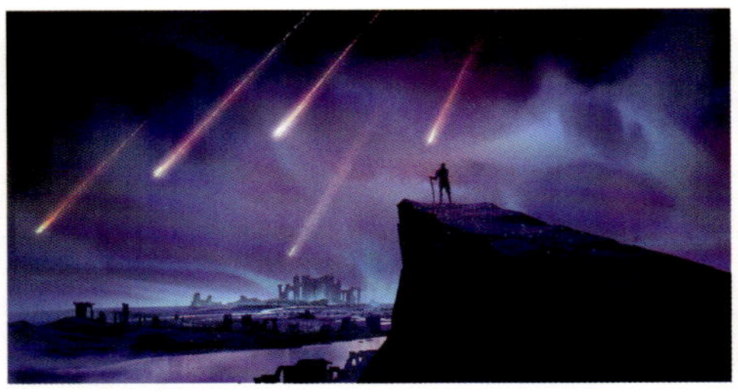

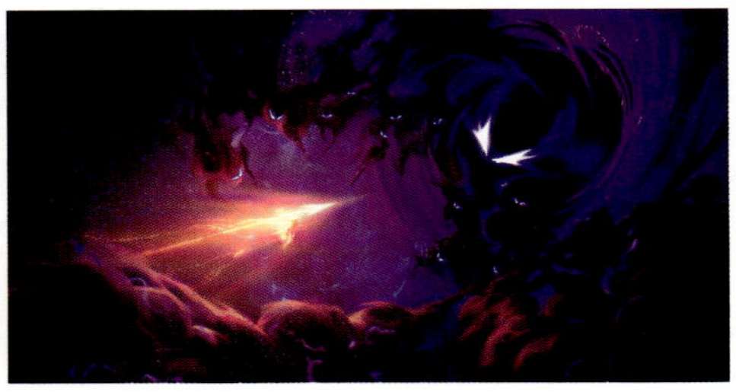

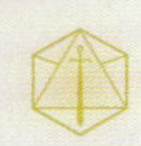

Vasselheim

Vasselheim is an ancient fortress city and home to many of the oldest temples in the world. As a bastion of many religions, the design team sought to include themes of unity and diversity within the architecture to represent different ideologies coexisting peacefully within those massive walls. The primary design element of Vasselheim is the intertwining cobalt pattern seen on the mountain and walls. The knotted shapes represent many people of differing ideologies coming together to form something stronger.

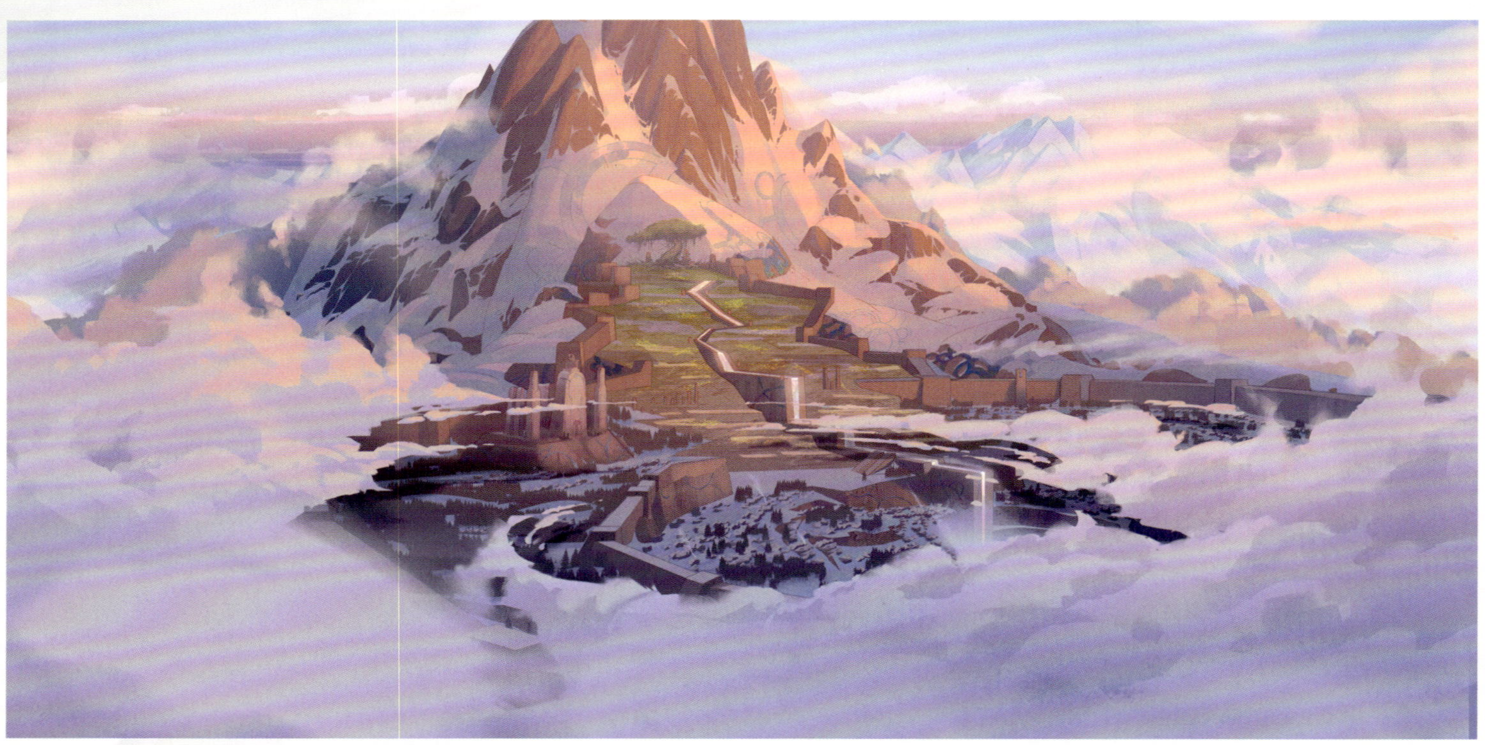

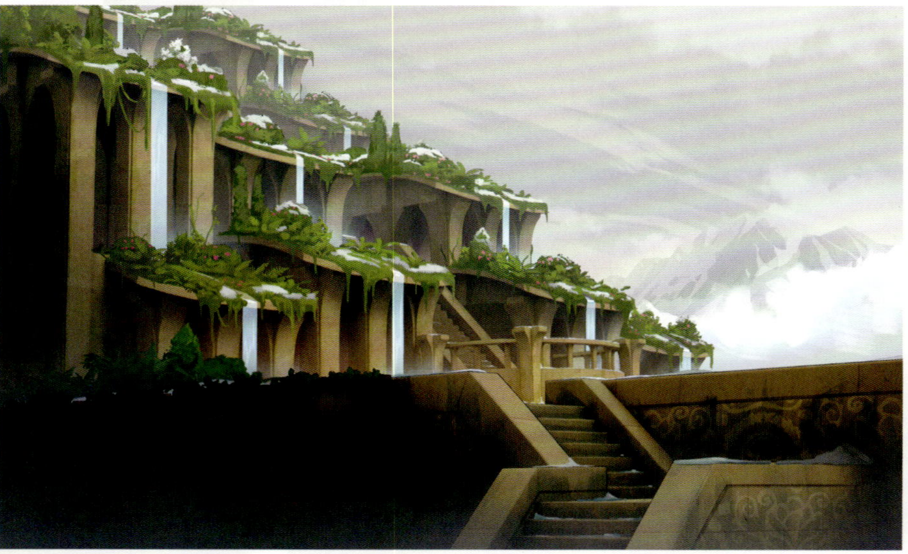

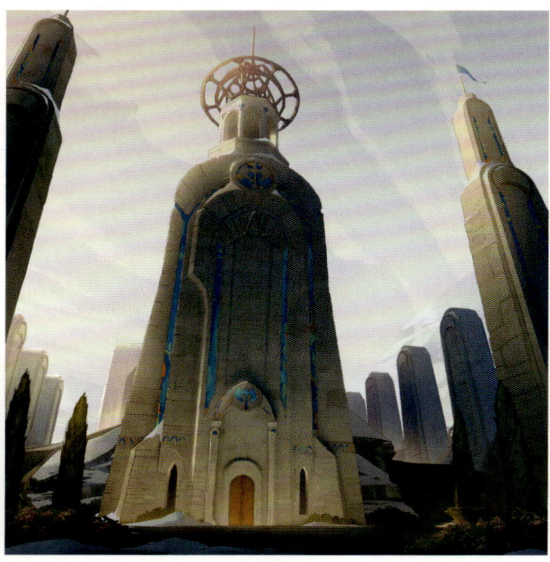

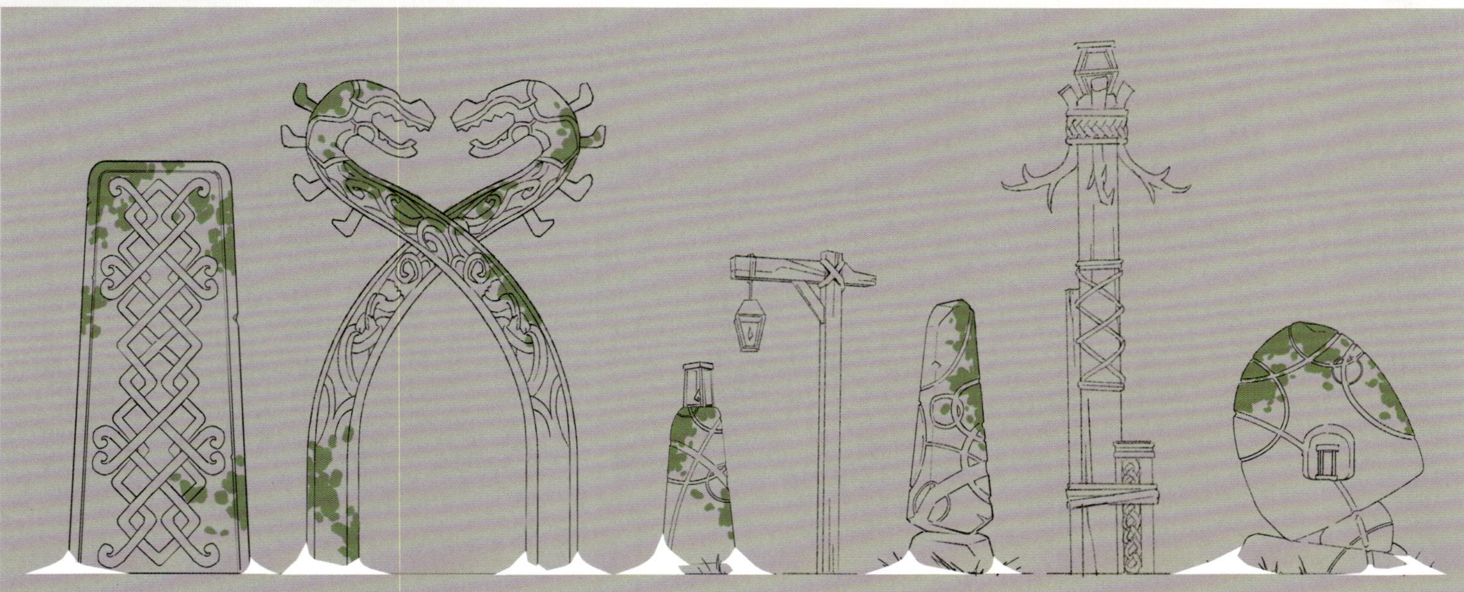

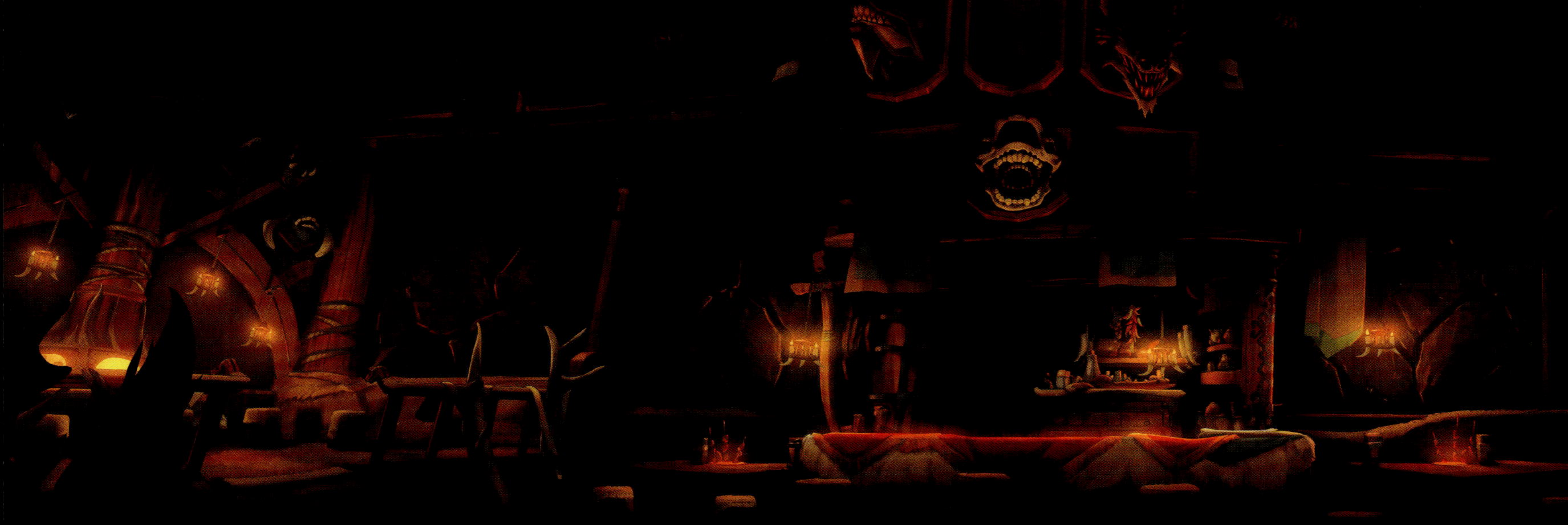

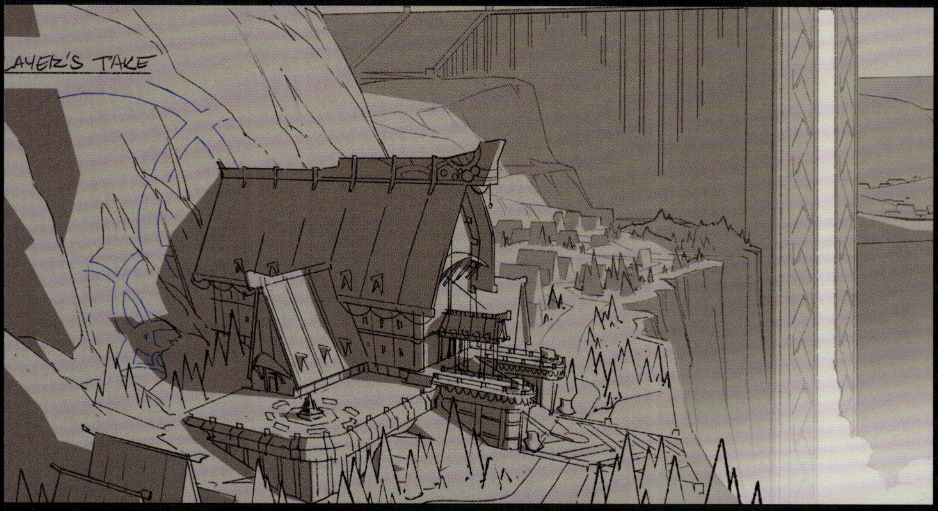

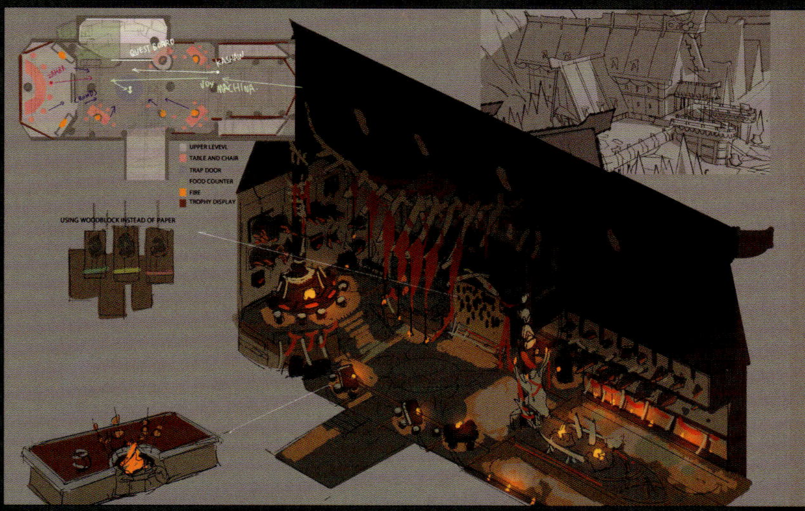

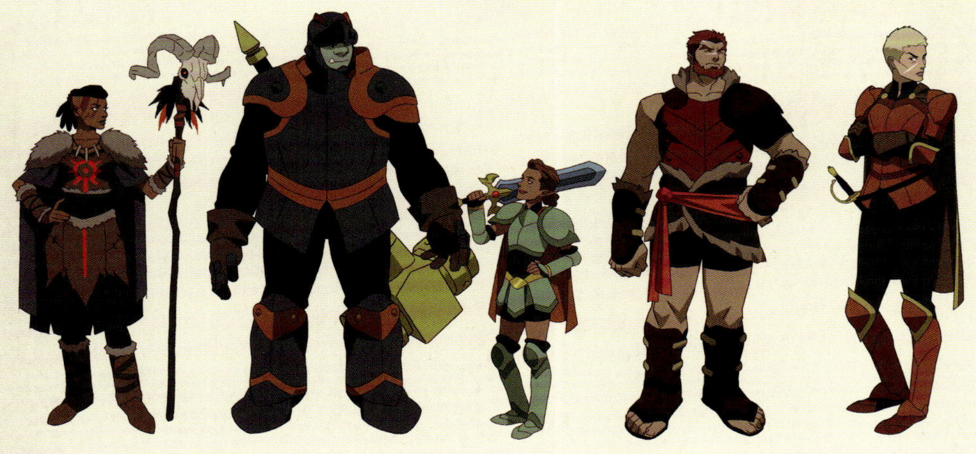

Slayer's Take

A tavern in Vasselheim that is home to a band of skilled monster hunters. The skulls of said monsters can be seen adorning the walls.

For Bourassa, nothing is more fun than populating a guildhall full of mercenaries in a fantasy world. Truly anything goes! For him, it was an opportunity to hint at cultural and factional diversity that exists beyond the borders of the script. Usually, you don't want incidentals to compete with the main characters, but in this context, every adventurer is the main character of their own story.

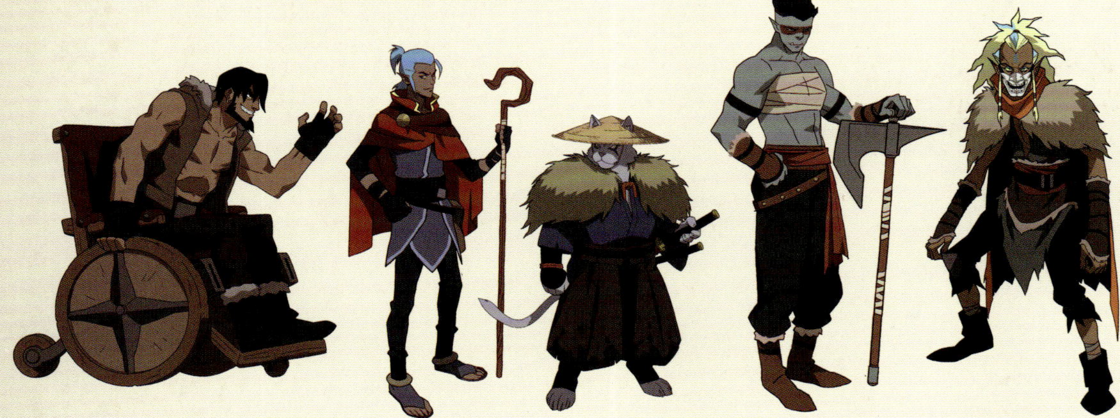

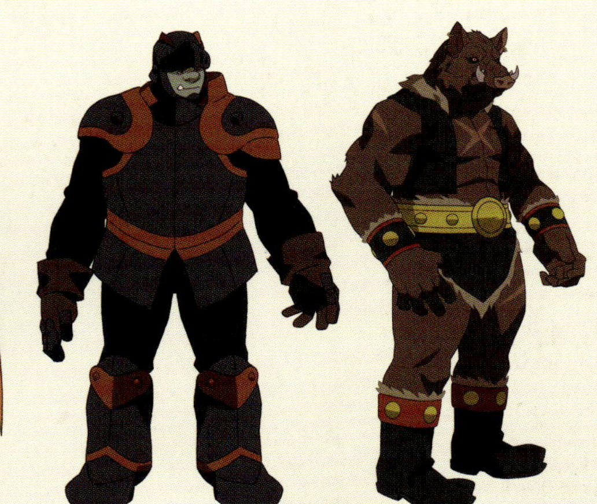

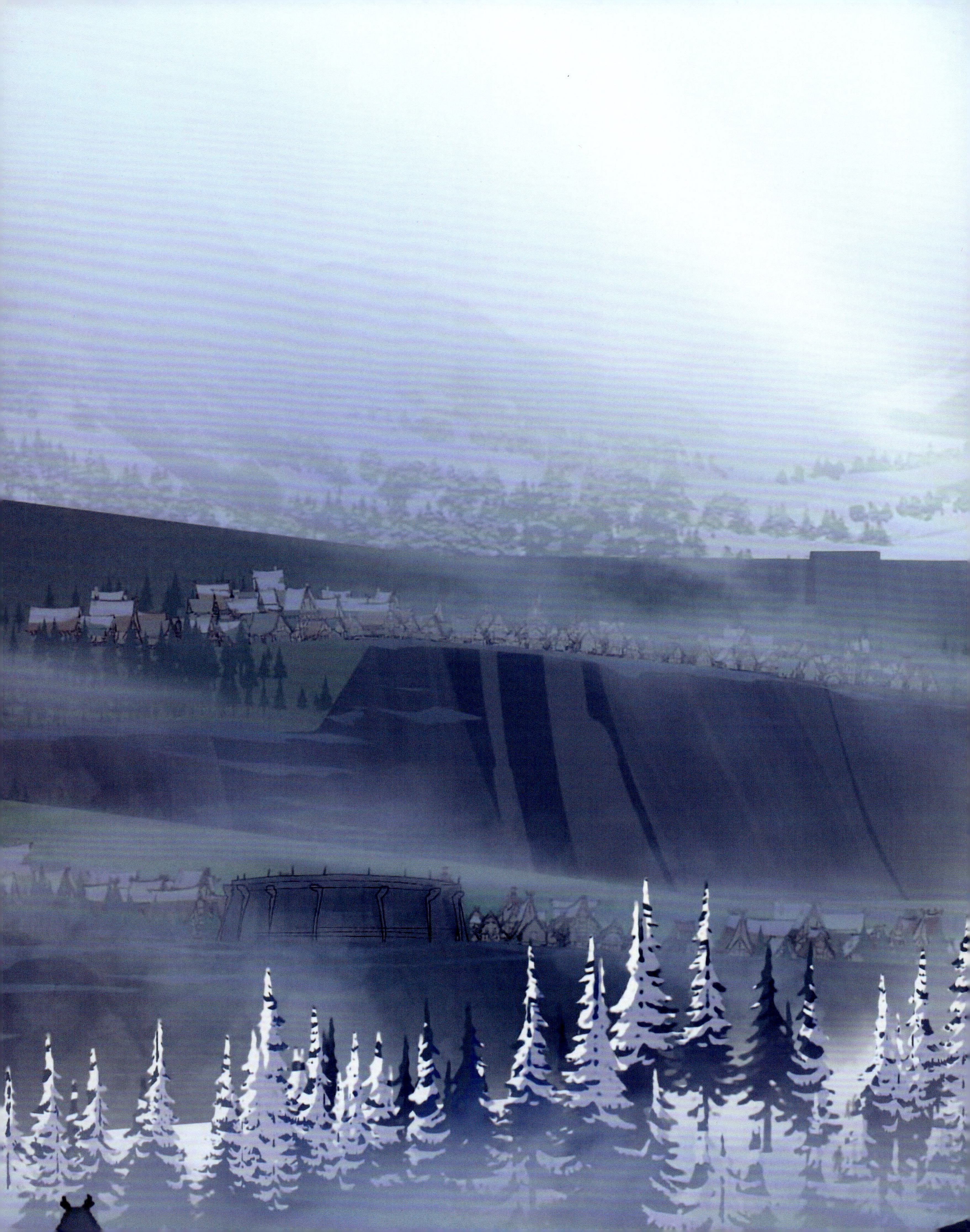

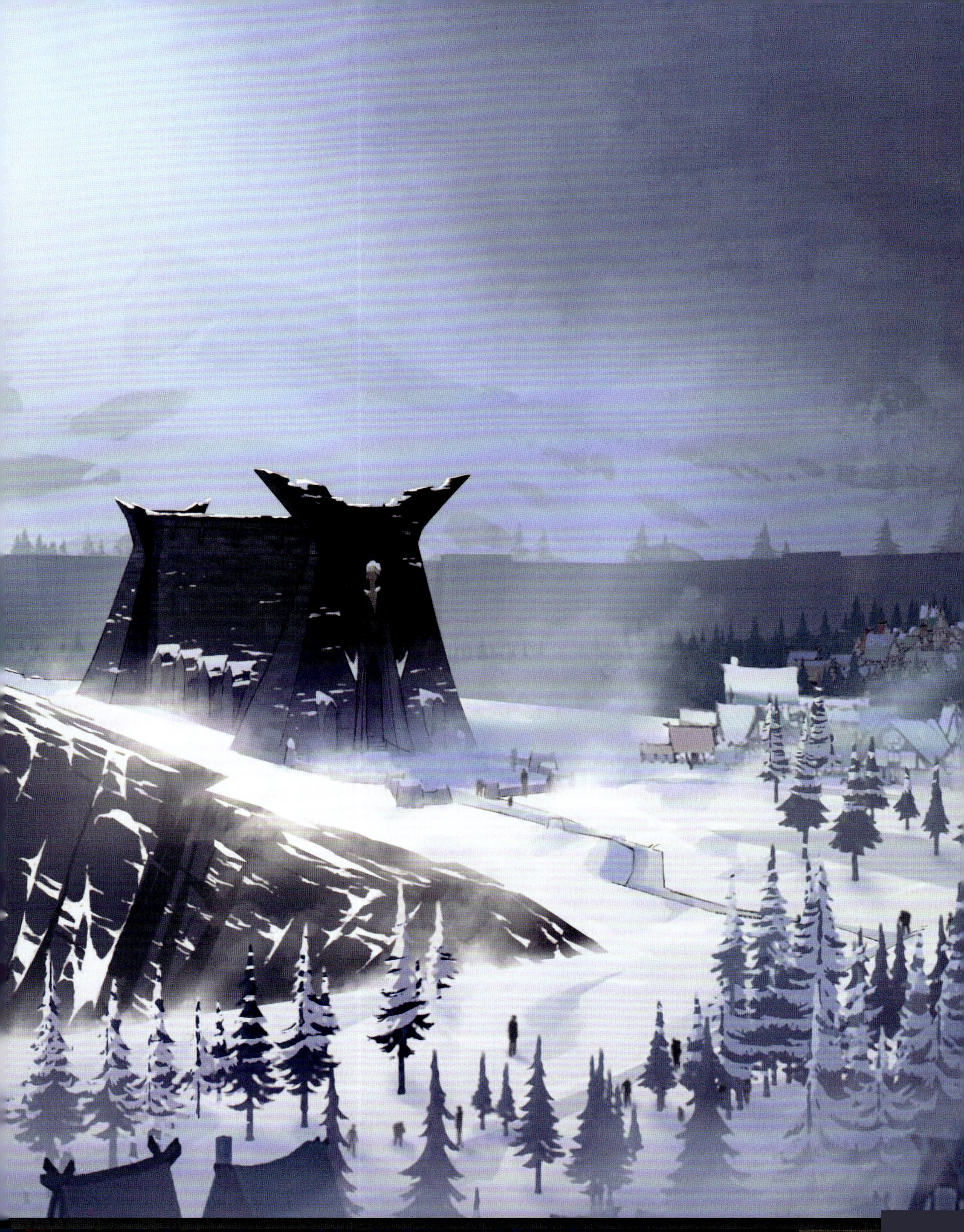

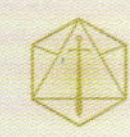

Platinum Sanctuary

The Platinum Sanctuary is a grand stone fortress that is described as looking "older than time itself." While a few iterations were pitched for the structure, the design team ultimately opted for a towering, monolithic building to visually reinforce the power of the religion it embodies.

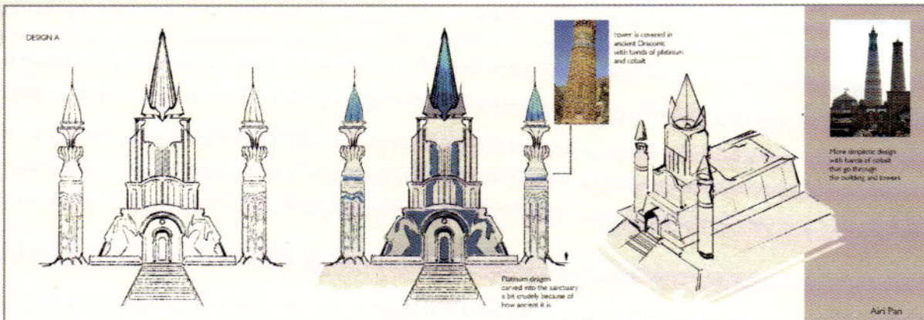

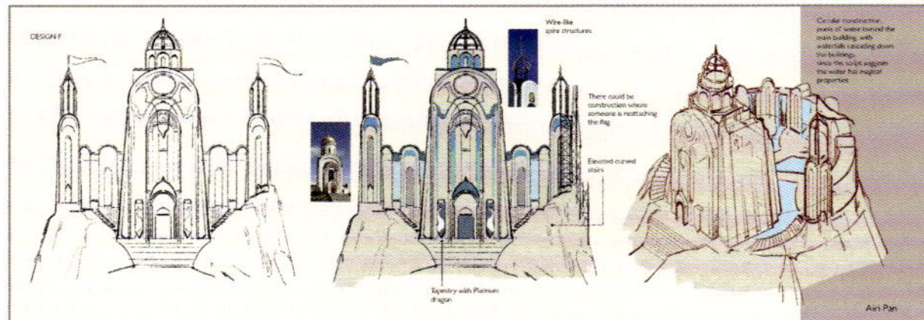

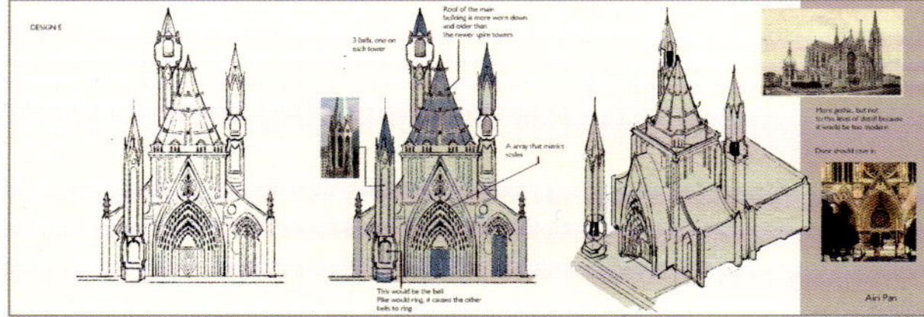

Early concept drawings of The Platinum Sanctuary that played around with the building's silhouette.

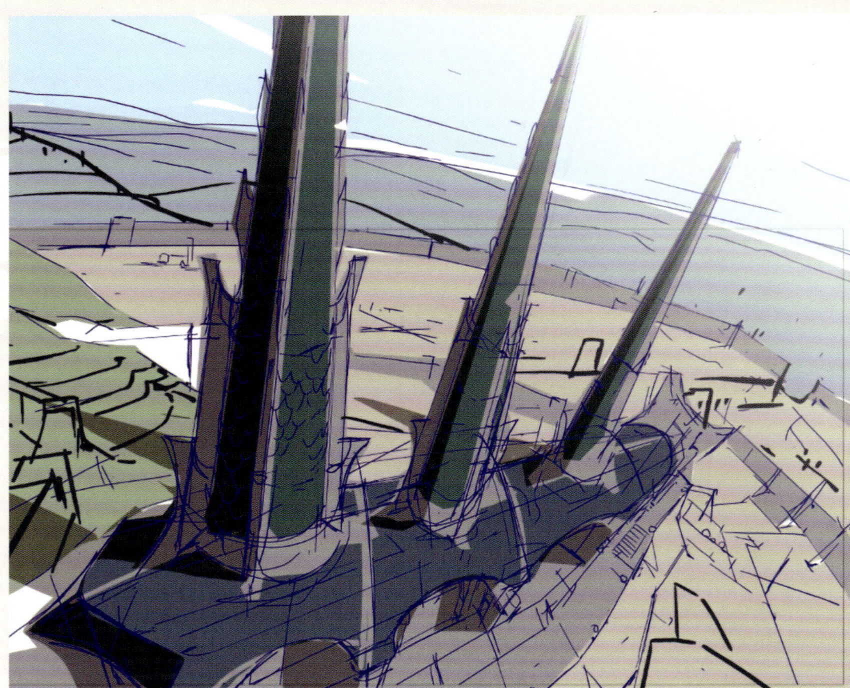

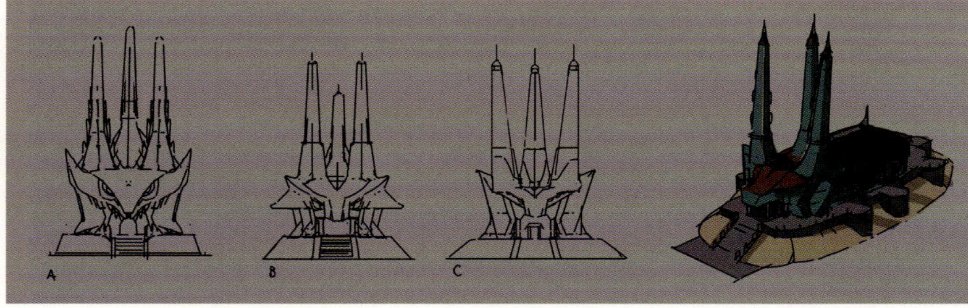

Temple of the Stormlord

The Stormlord Temple is a reference to a god more prominently featured in the second Critical Role campaign, which the animated series only had a few seconds to showcase. In situations like these, the art team usually goes for big impact over subtlety. The lightning bolt shapes that are featured in the Stormlord's symbol are the core design motif for the temple.

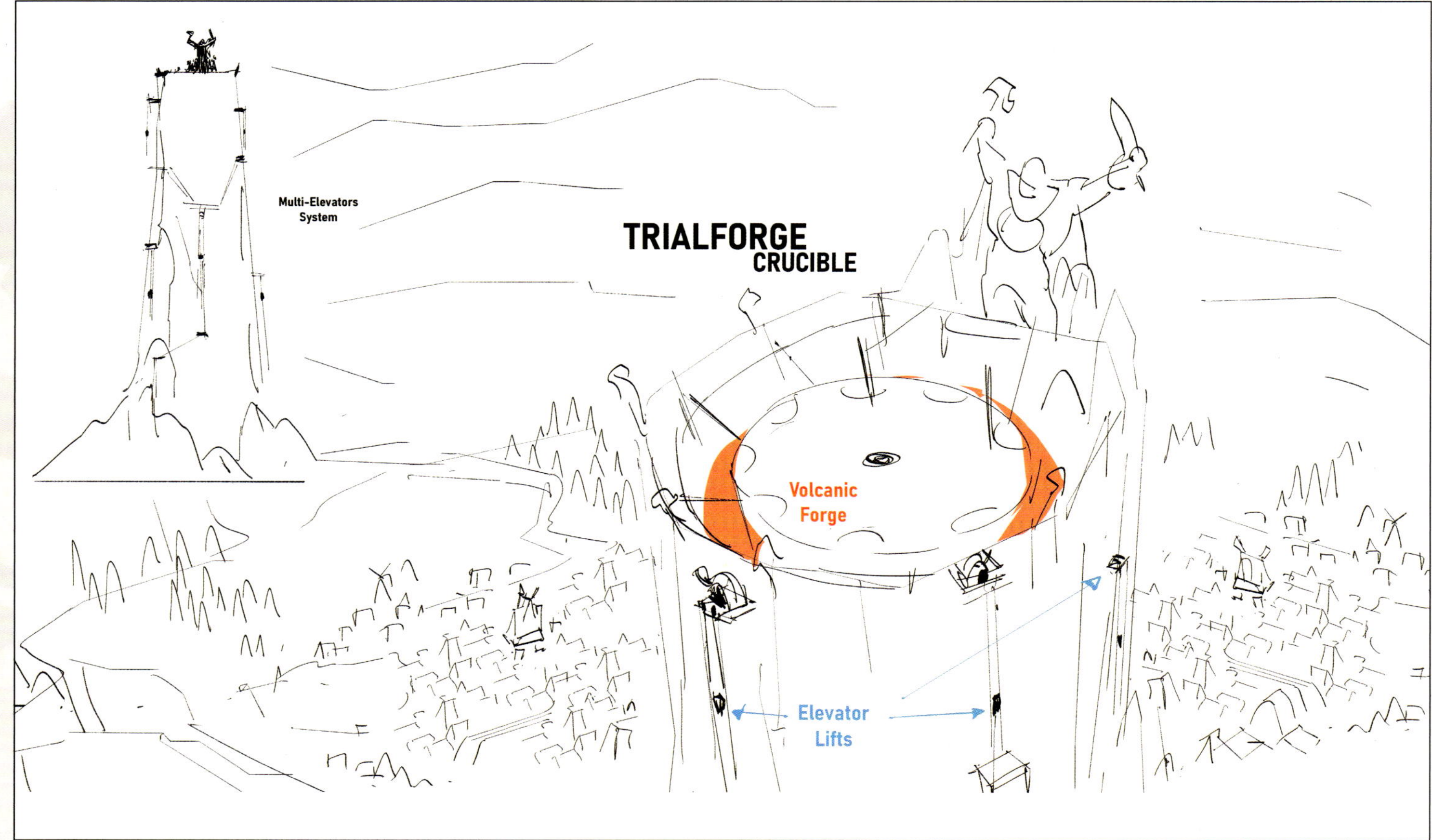

Early concept drawings of the Temple of the Stormlord. Originally pitched to be raised above the city with an elevator system to access.

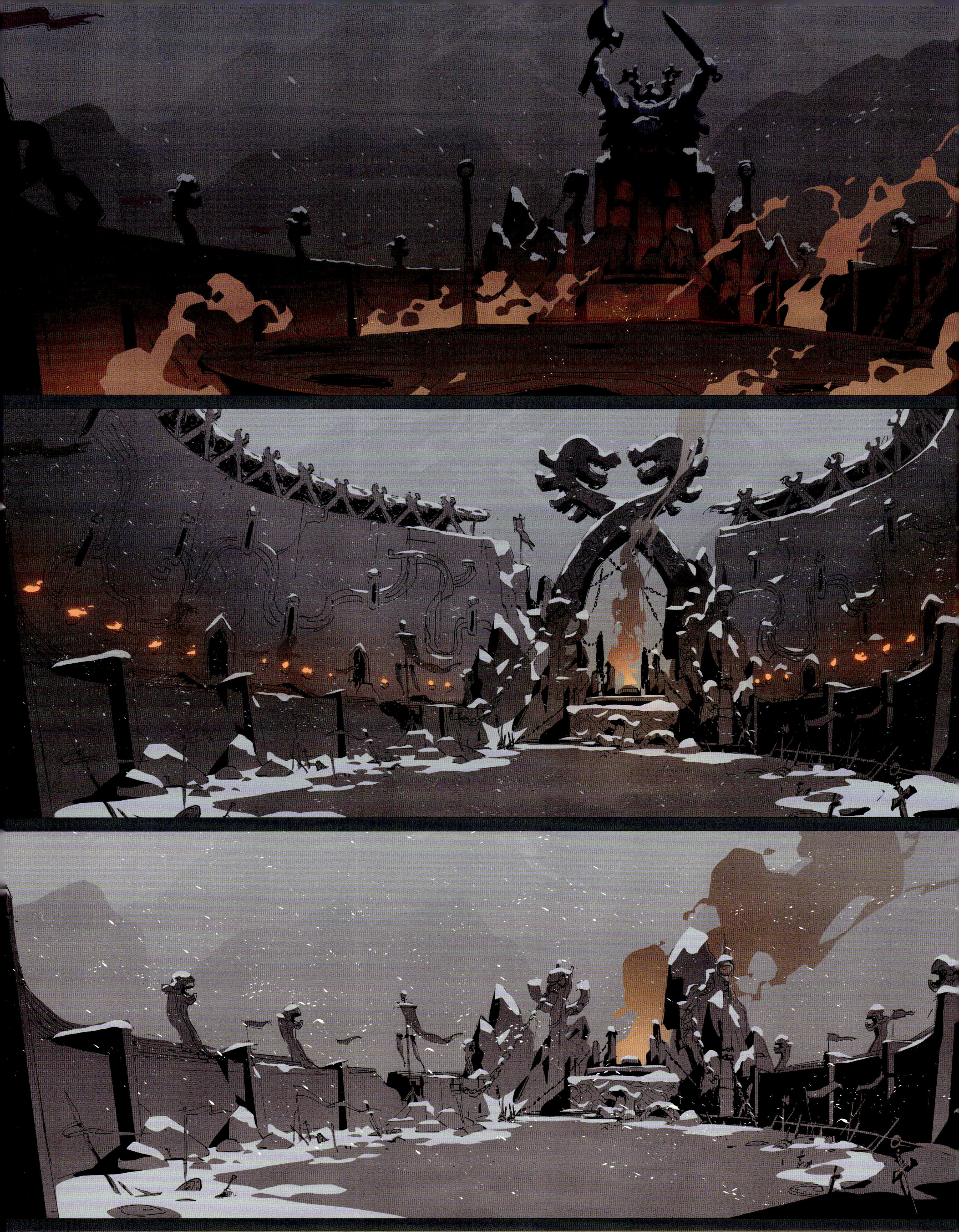

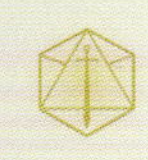

EPISODE 3 & 4

THE SUNKEN TOMB AND THOSE WHO WALK AWAY

"It wouldn't be a real adventure without delving into more tragic backstory, now, would it? Vex and Vax give us a glimpse into their angsty teen years before we try our hand at grave robbing to get one of The Vestiges of Divergence; ancient weapons that will aid in our fight against the Chroma Conclave. Of course, Vex dies, and Vax, having absolutely no chill, strikes a deal with the goddess of death to save his sister in exchange for his service as her champion. Good thing he already has the wardrobe to match!"

– A RECOUNTING OF "THE SUNKEN TOMB" AND "THOSE WHO WALK AWAY" BY SCANLAN SHORTHALT

Teen Vax

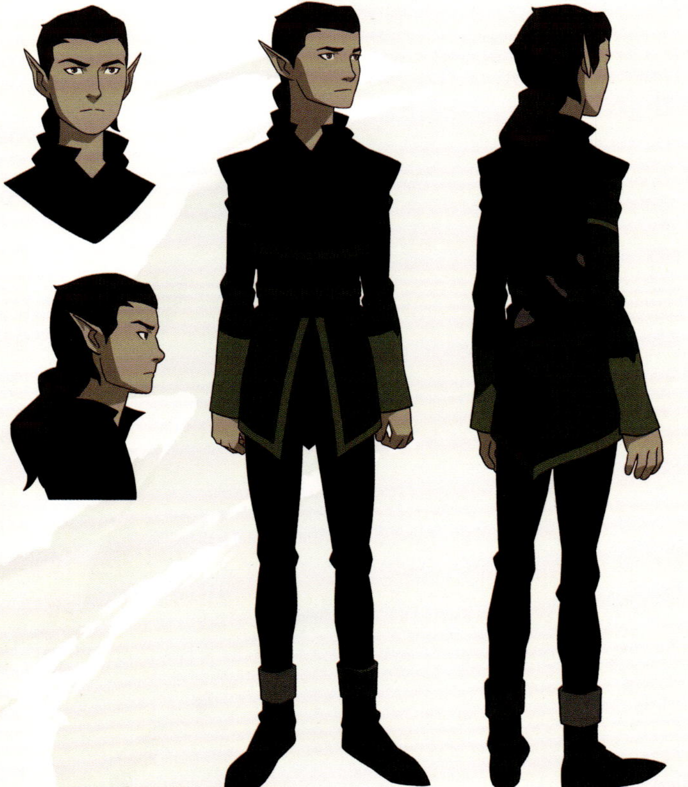

Teen Vex

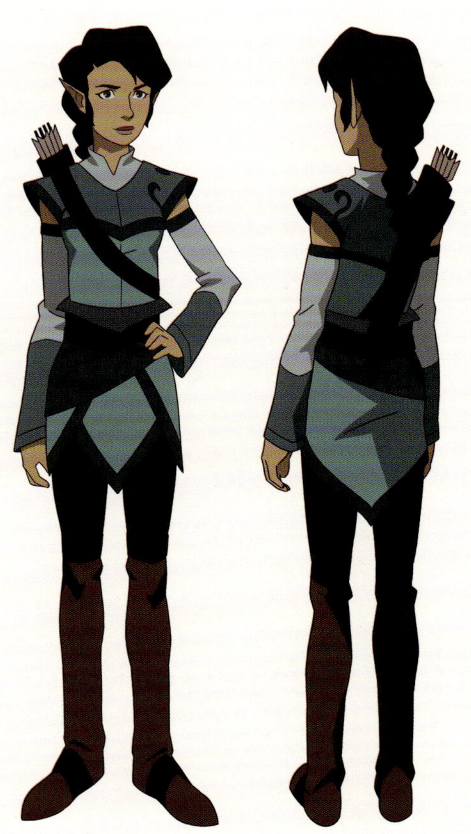

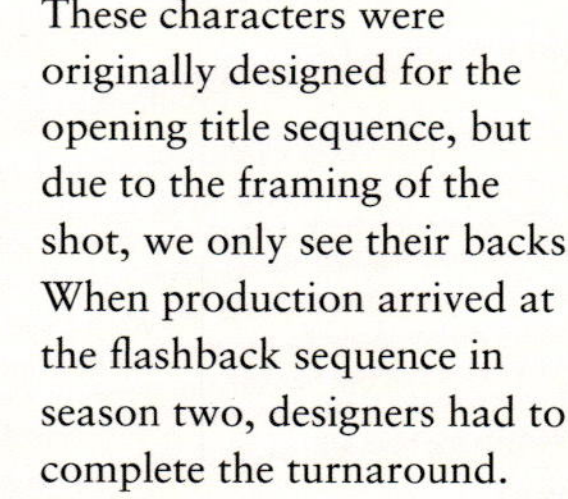

These characters were originally designed for the opening title sequence, but due to the framing of the shot, we only see their backs. When production arrived at the flashback sequence in season two, designers had to complete the turnaround.

Adaro (Fish People)

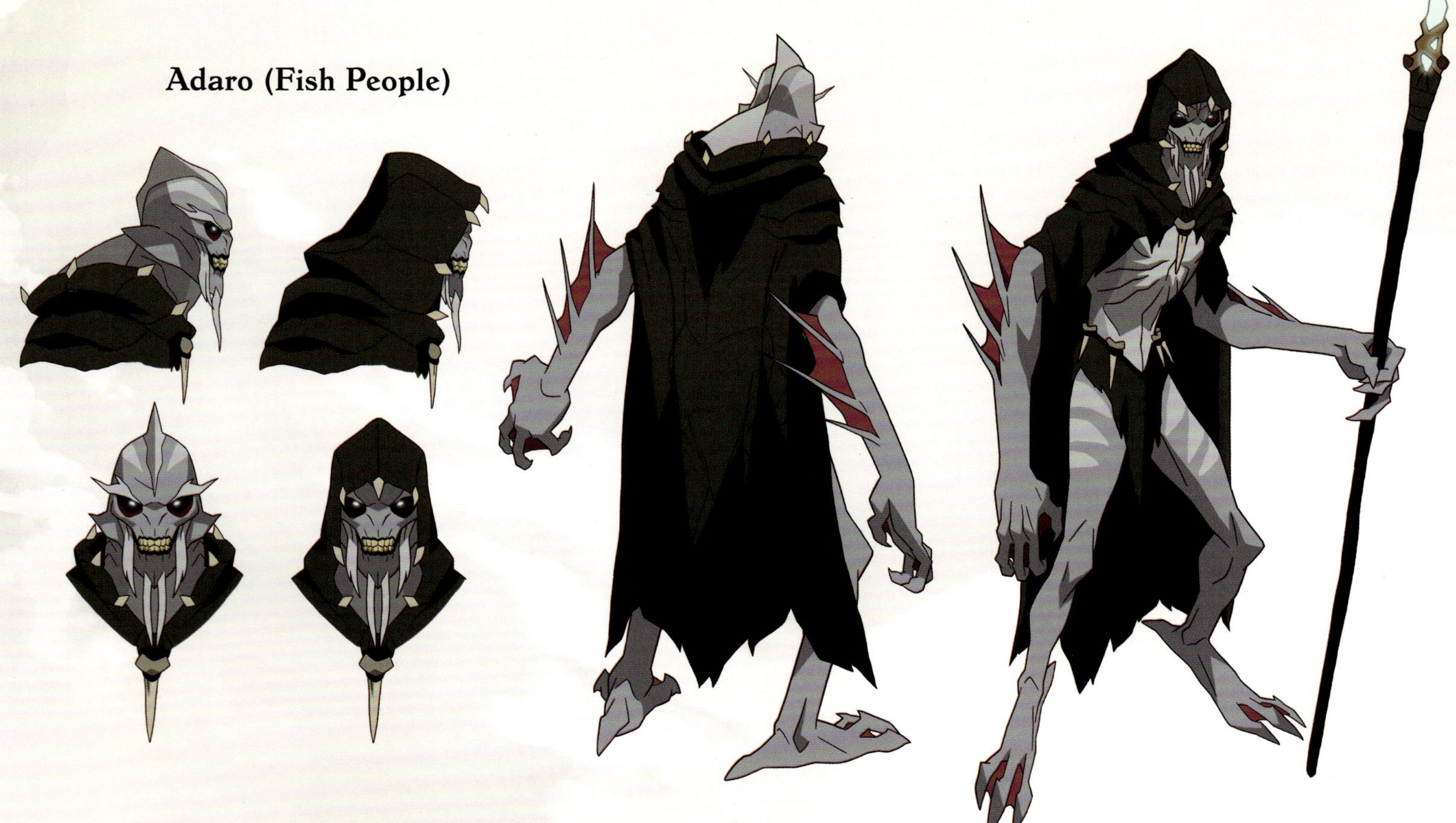

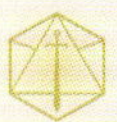

Purvan Suul

The last champion of The Matron of Ravens and current owner of The Deathwalker's Ward.

The Onlooker

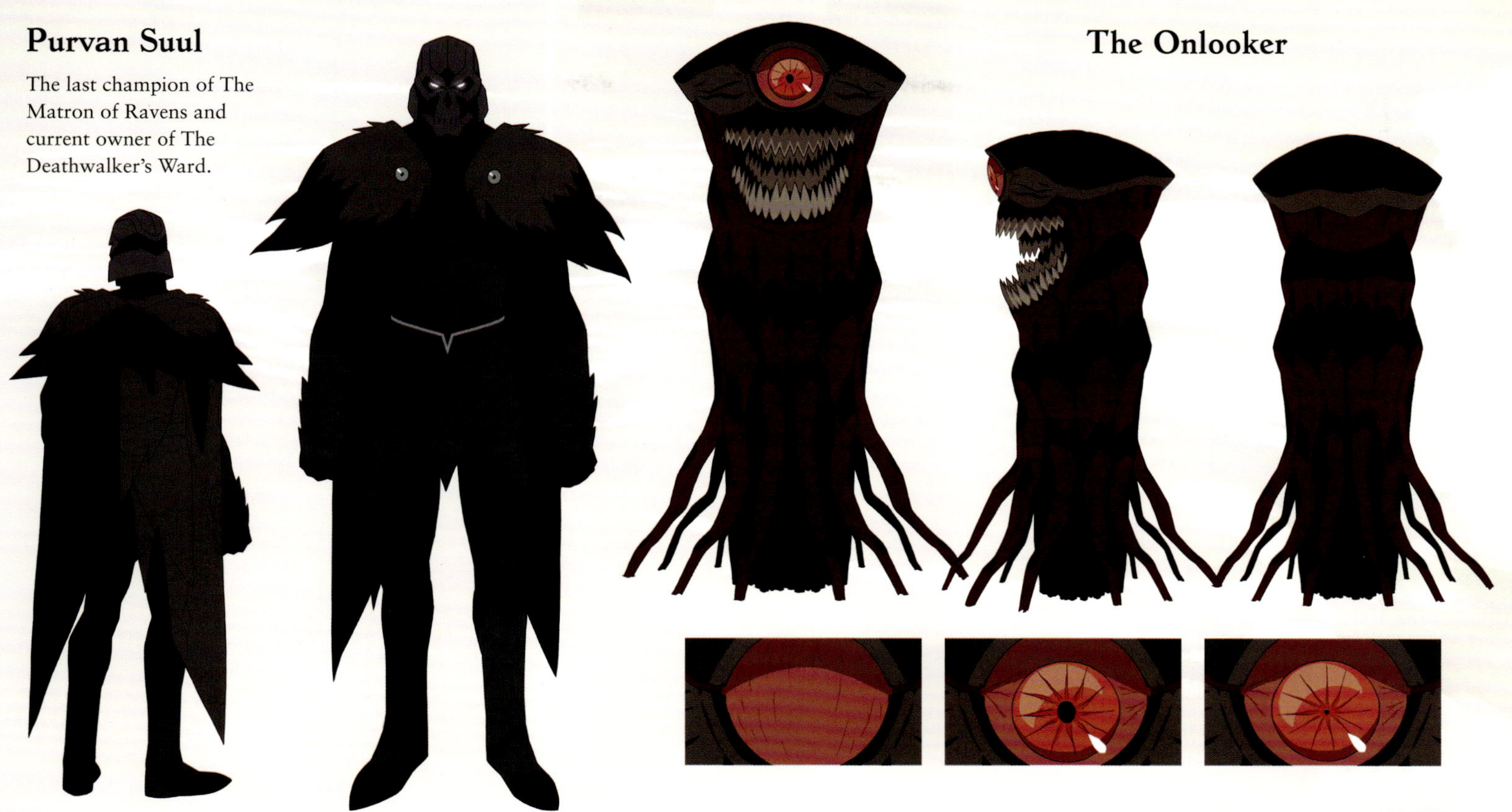

The Matron of Ravens

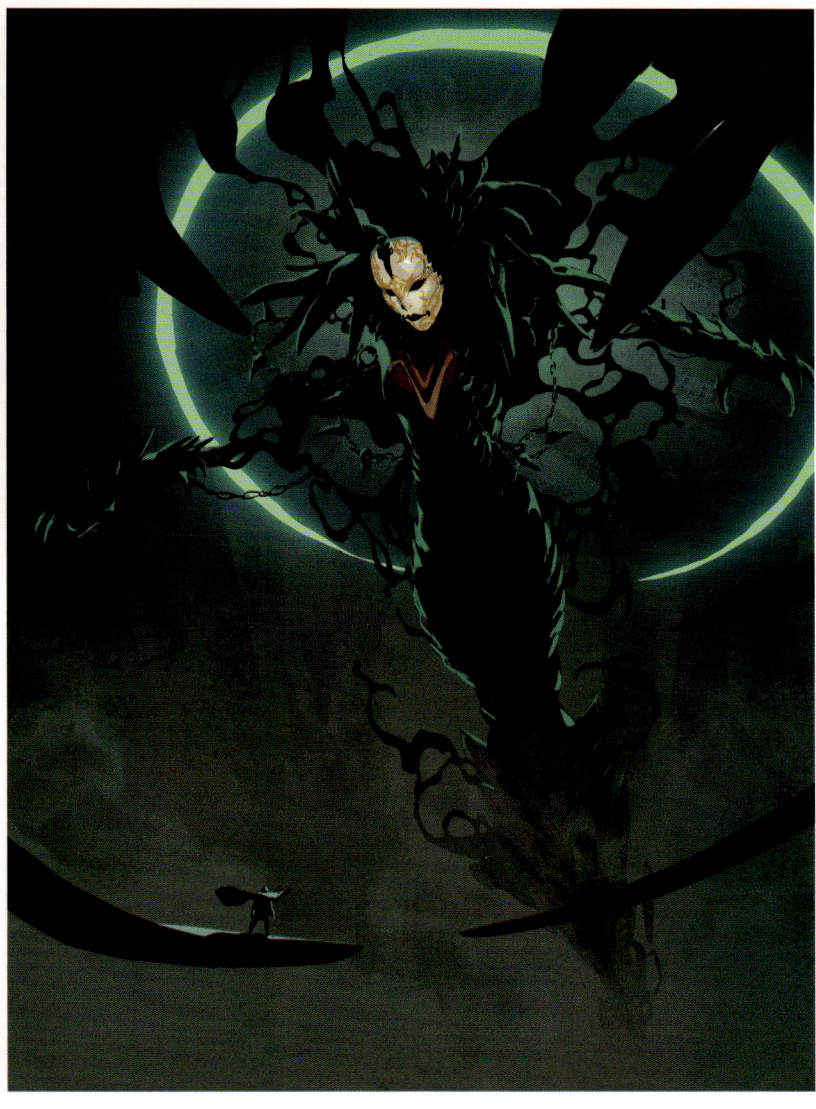

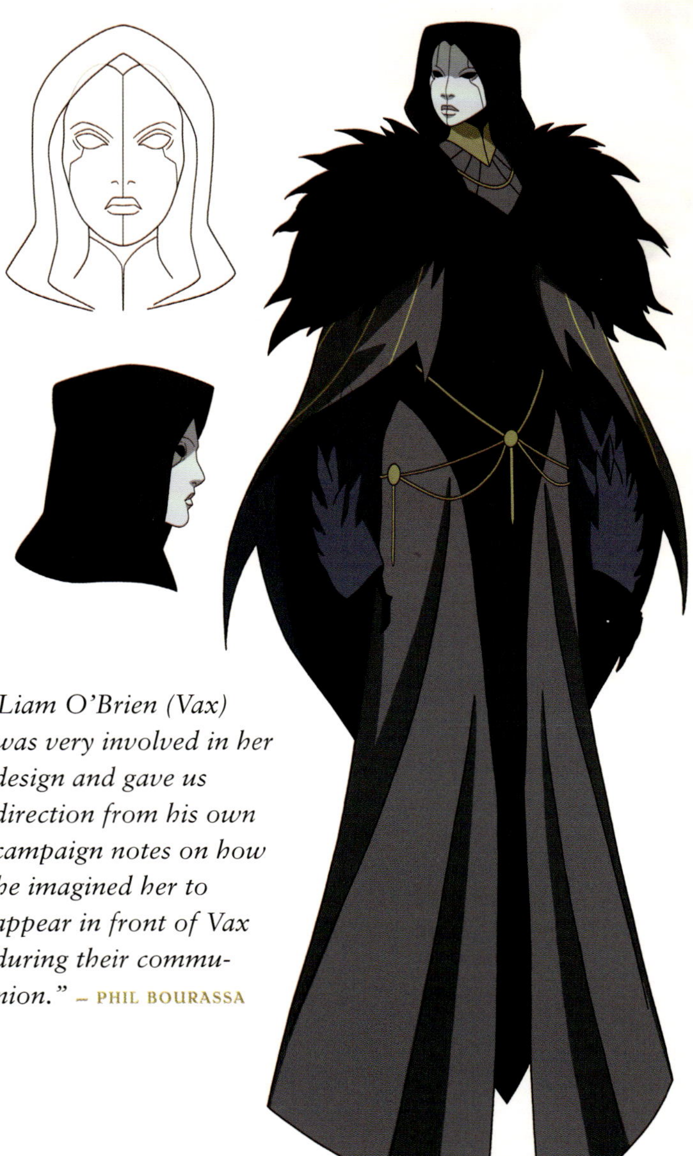

"Liam O'Brien (Vax) was very involved in her design and gave us direction from his own campaign notes on how he imagined her to appear in front of Vax during their communion." – PHIL BOURASSA

Known by many names, The Matron of Ravens ushers the dead to the afterlife. While she takes different forms throughout the series, her white emotionless mask, elongated limbs, and black raven feathers are key to the design.

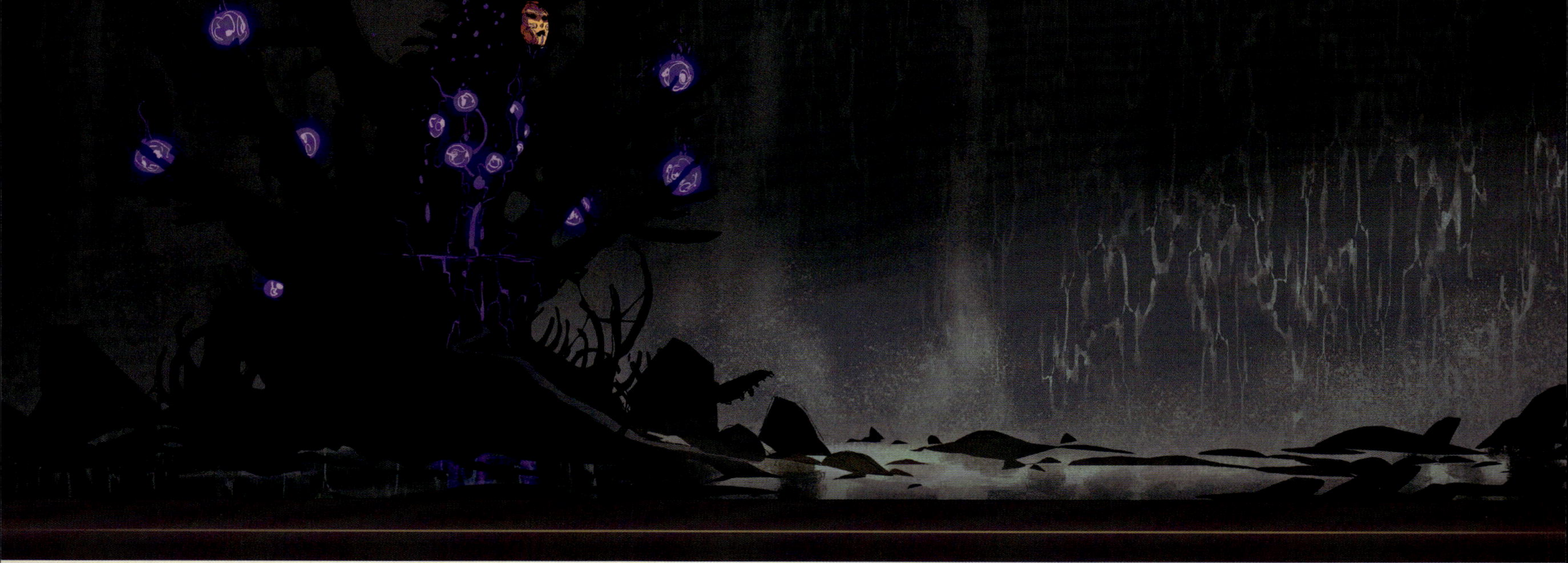

The Sunken Tomb

The temple's imagery revolves around raven skulls and feathers, which are intricately woven into each pillar throughout the structure. Nestled at its core lies the actual tomb, adorned with numerous statues commemorating past champions of The Matron of Ravens.

"The tomb was built for The Matron of Ravens–the goddess of death. It enshrines the body of her ancient champion, the highest of her order. Striking fear into the hearts of her enemies. His name was... Purvon." – KASH, S2E3 "THE SUNKEN TOMB"

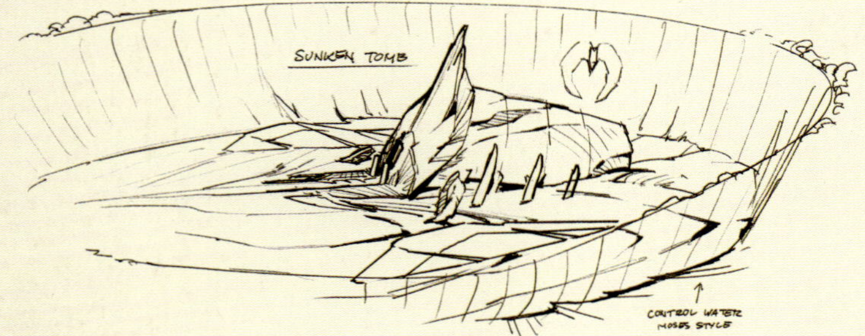

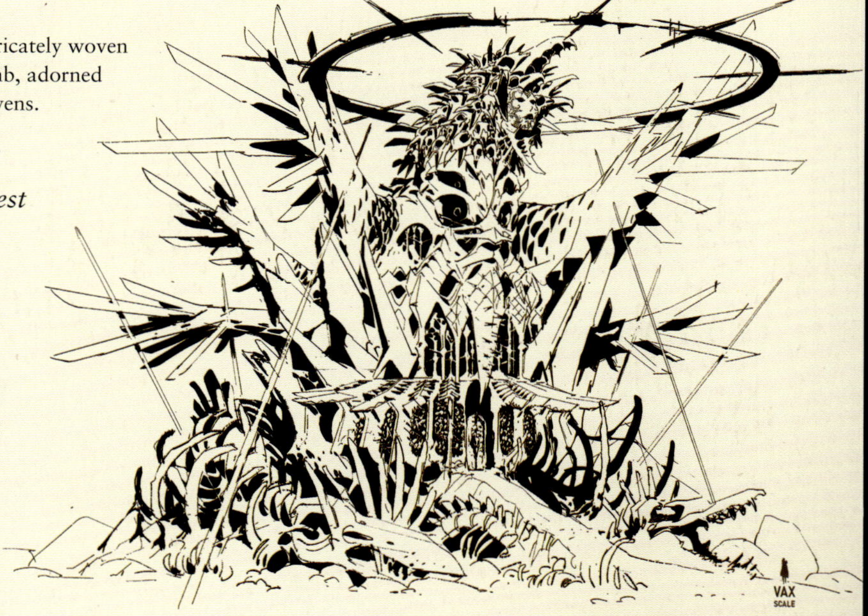

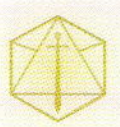

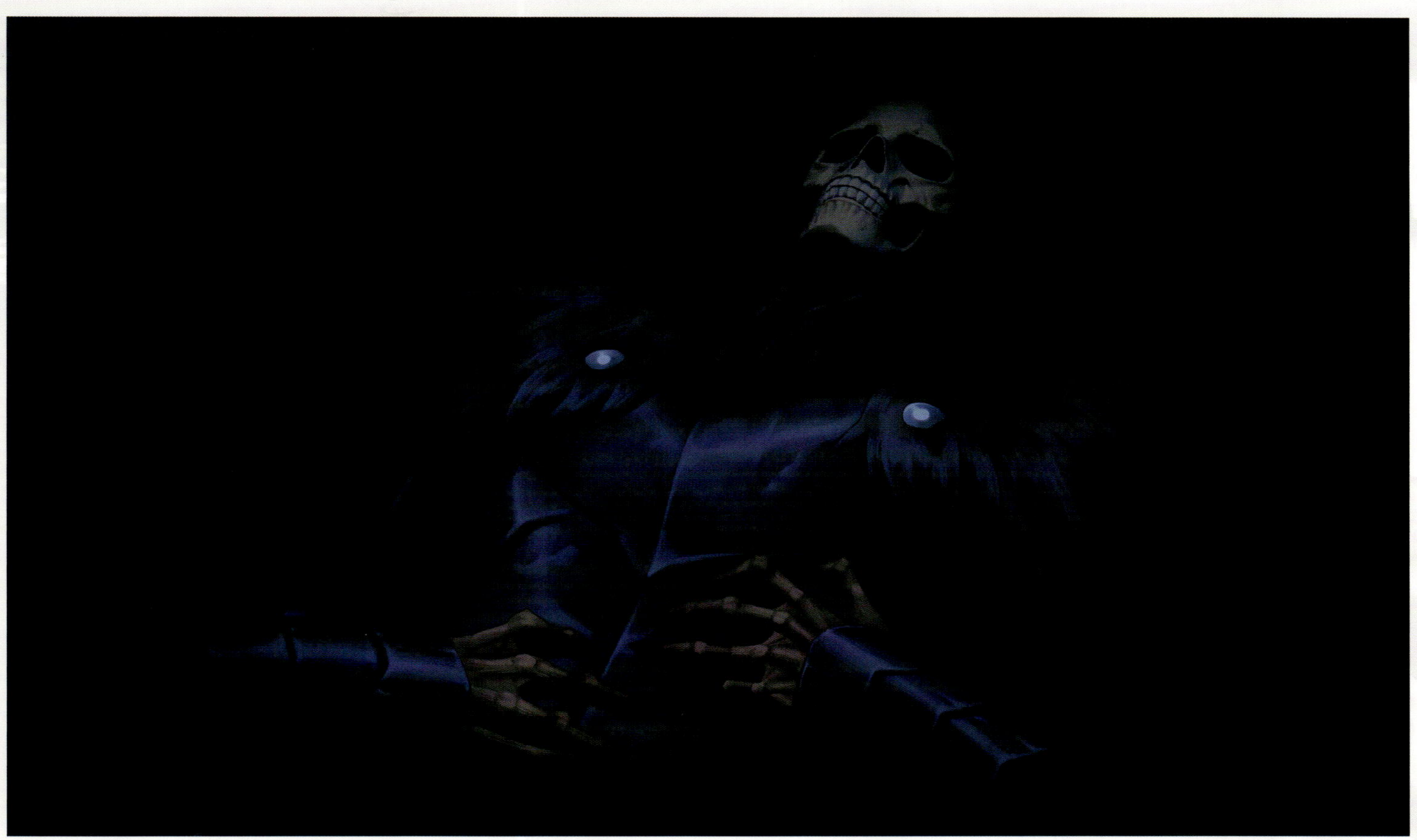

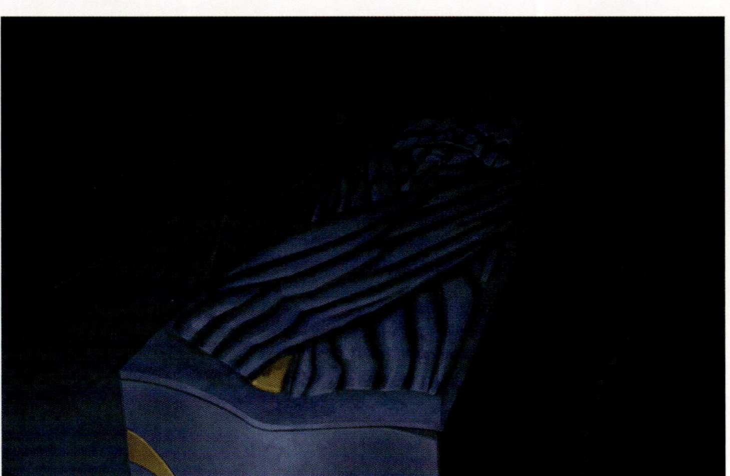

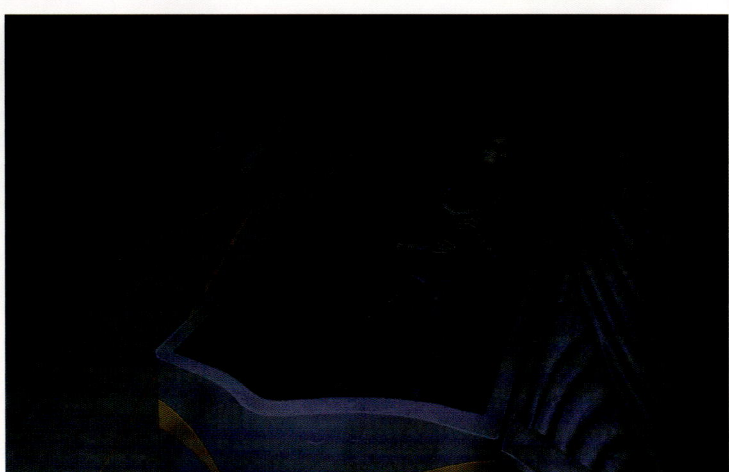

Deathwalker's Ward

Once donned, Vax is unable to remove this armor, which grants him super speed. Later, it reveals additional power–allowing Vax to fly.

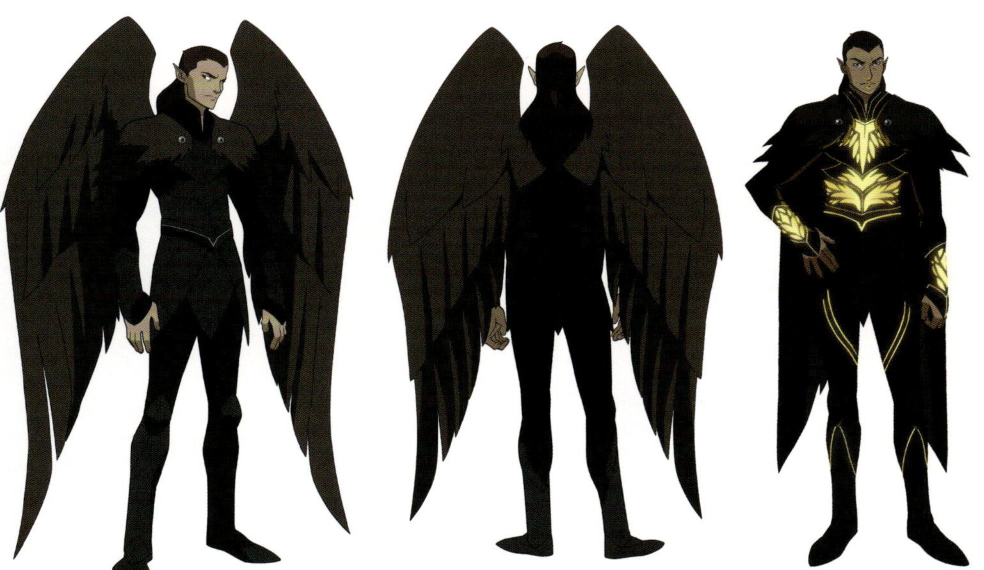

Grog's Belt

Find yourself a man who looks at you the way Grog looks at his beard.

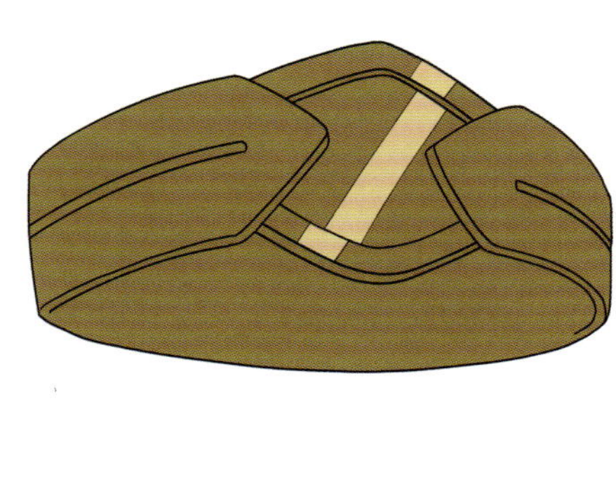

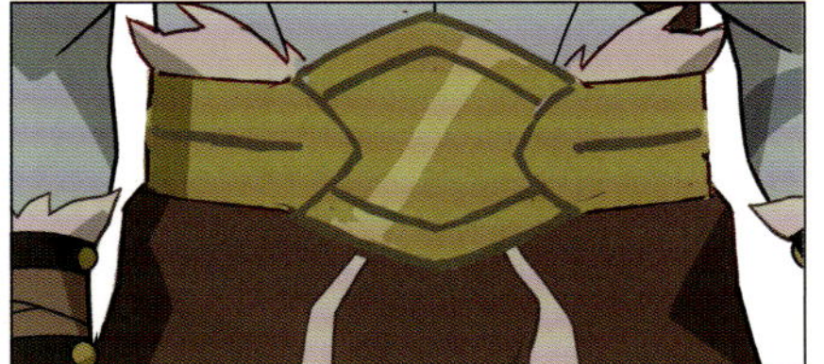

Storyboards from Vex's Death Scene in The Sunken Tomb

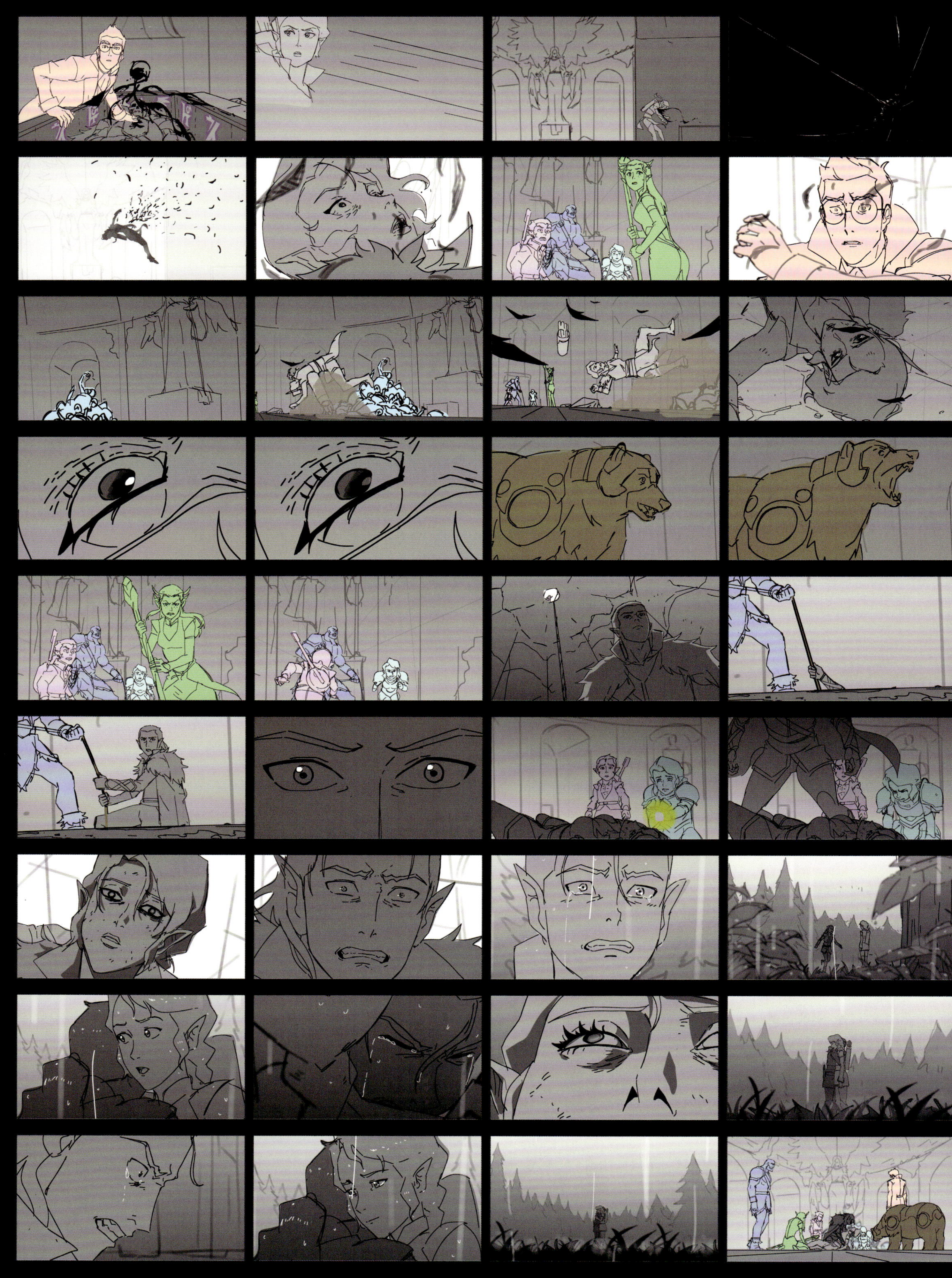

"Take me instead, you raven bitch!" – VAX

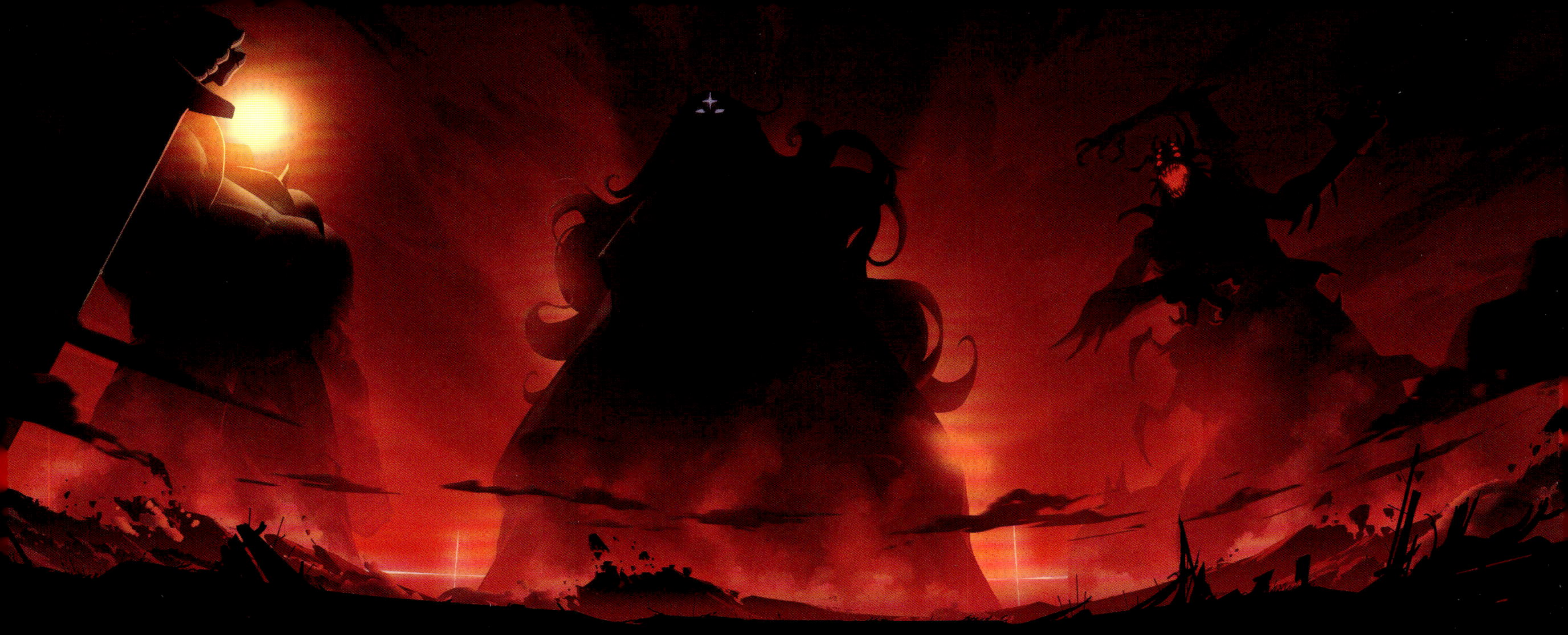

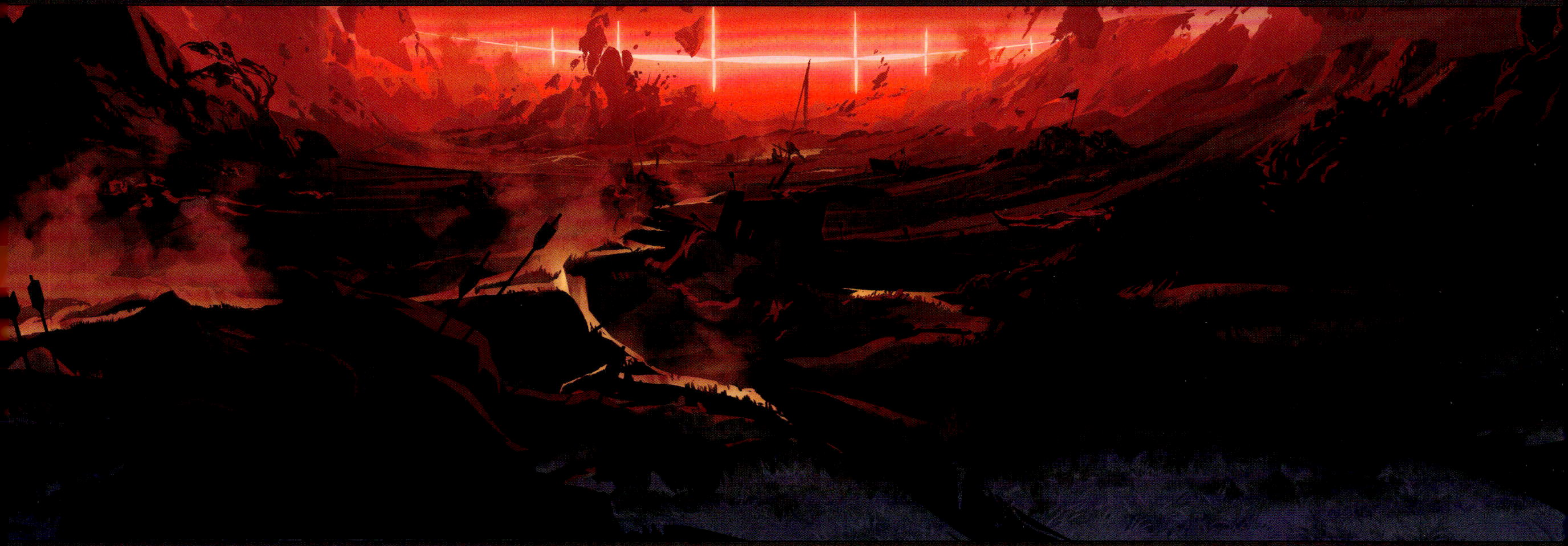

The Calamity

Visions seen by Vax in The Sunken Tomb of an ancient battle fought amongst gods.

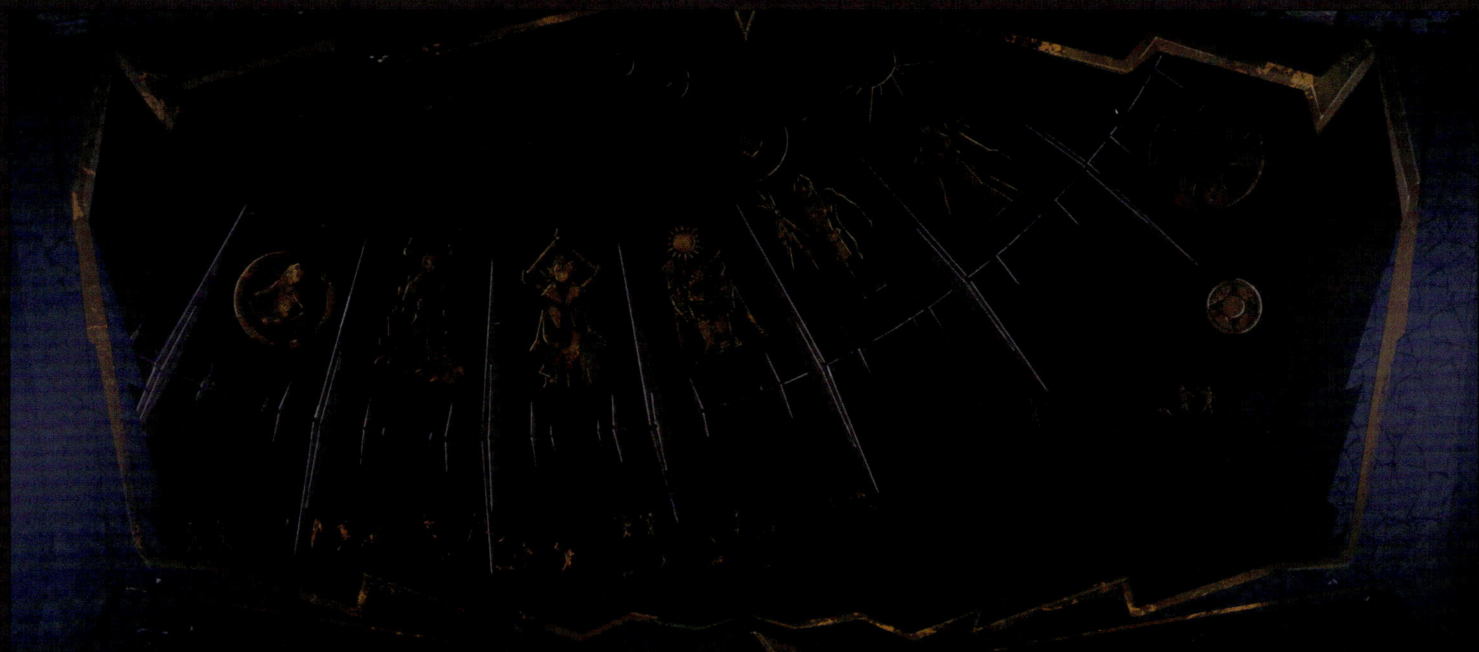

Top: From L to R: The Dawnfather, The Arch Heart, The Crawling King. Middle: Aftermath of The Calamity. Bottom: Engravings on the wall in The Sunken Tomb–They lay out the pantheon of gods in Exandria. Each simplified engraving of a god ties back into the lore spelled out by Matt Mercer, and many of the same gods are seen again in Vax's visions throughout the rest of the episode.

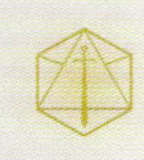

EPISODE 5

PASS THROUGH FIRE

"When our mission takes us near Pyrah, we charge in like a bunch of idiots to help them seal the rift that Thordak blew open during his escape from the Fire Plane. Unfortunately, a brief family reunion with Keyleth's dad brings on a massive guilt trip, and she begins to wonder if she should start focusing on completing her Aramente. Oh, and Grog takes a very uneventful shit."

– A RECOUNTING OF "PASS THROUGH FIRE" BY SCANLAN SHORTHALT

Vilya (Keyleth's Mother)

Young Keyleth

"Little flower, listen to your power." – VILYA, S1E5 "PASS THROUGH FIRE"

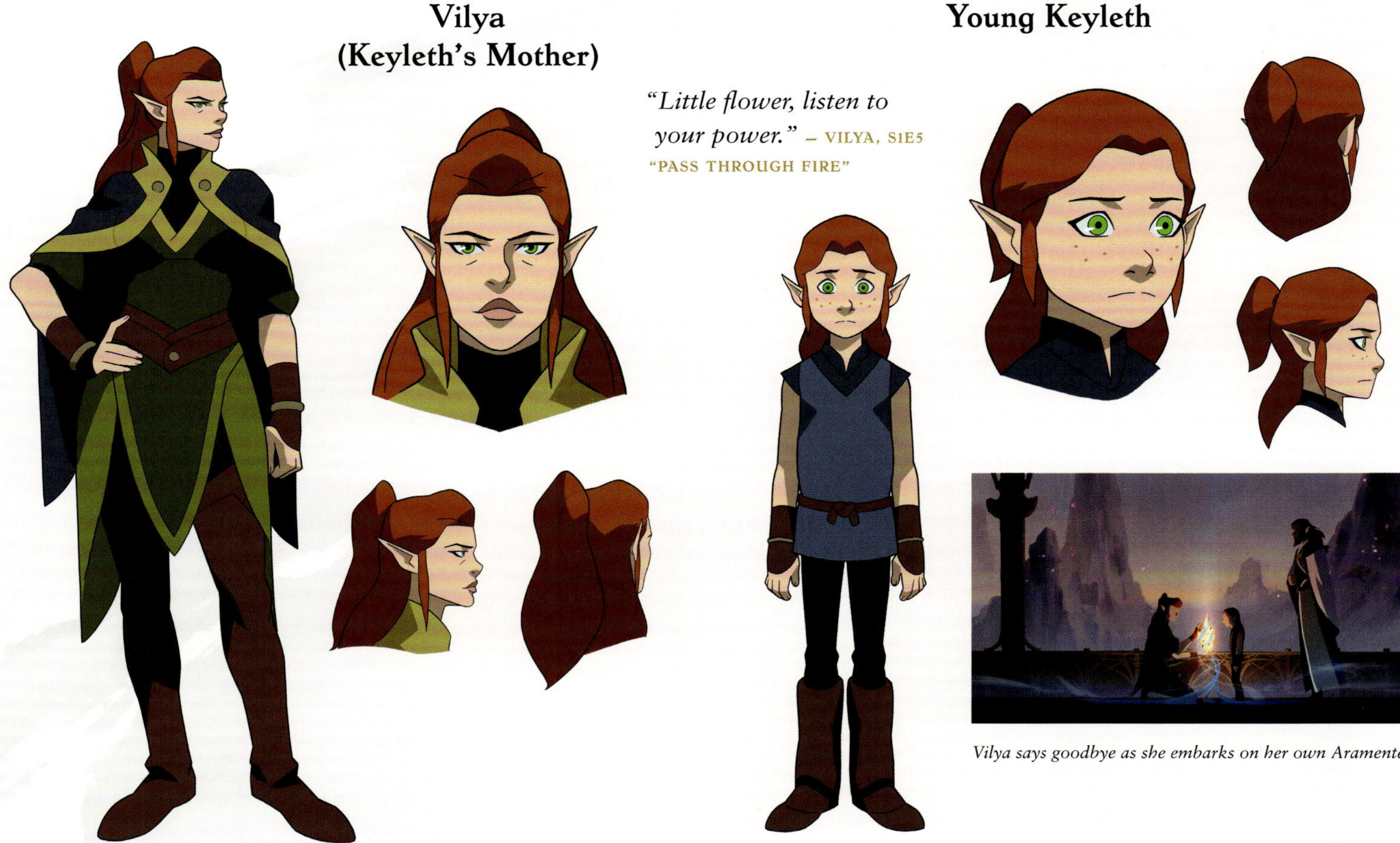

Vilya says goodbye as she embarks on her own Aramente.

Korrin

Keyleth's father and temporary headmaster to the Air Ashari while Keyleth completes her Aramente.

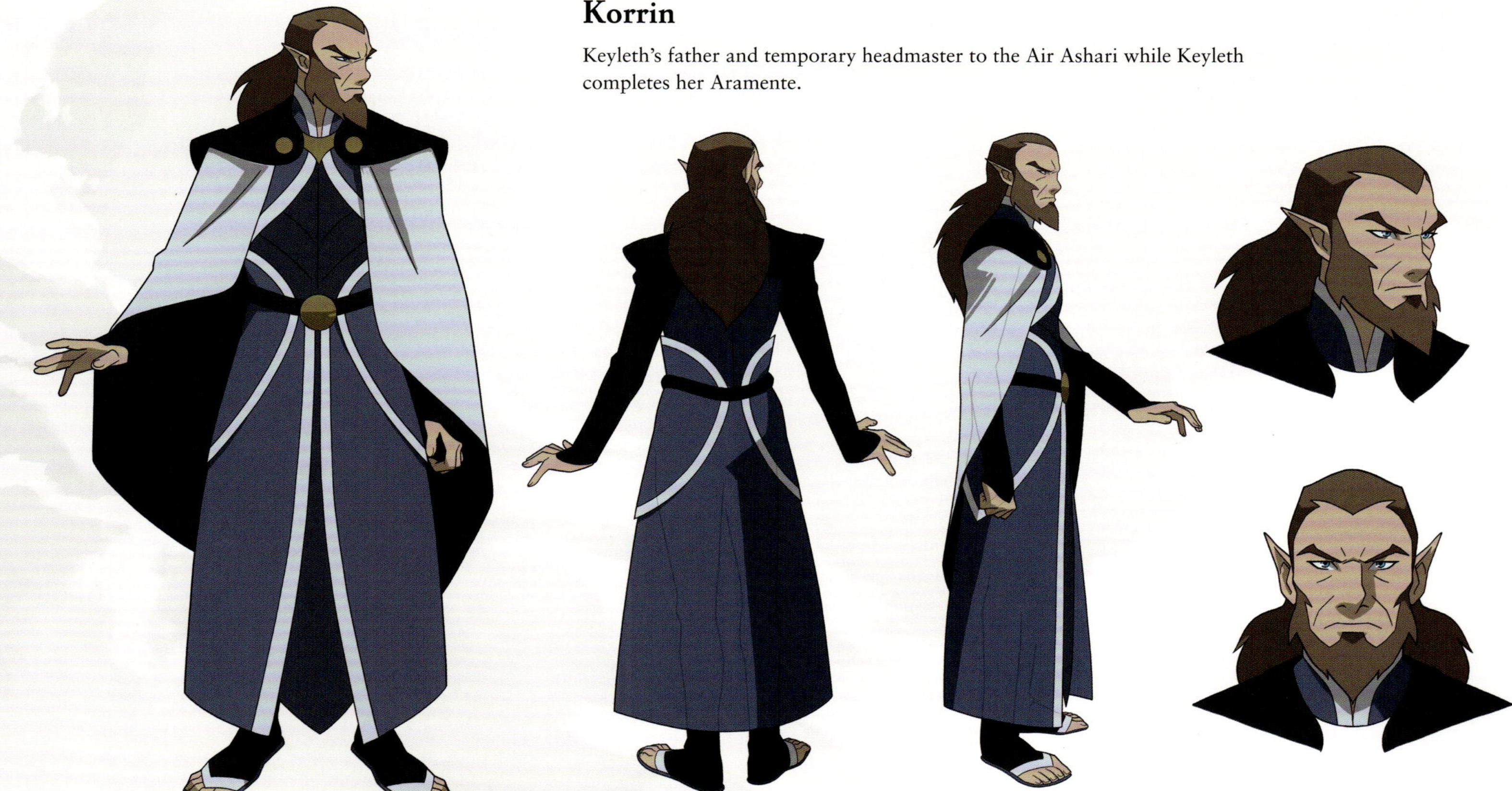

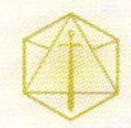

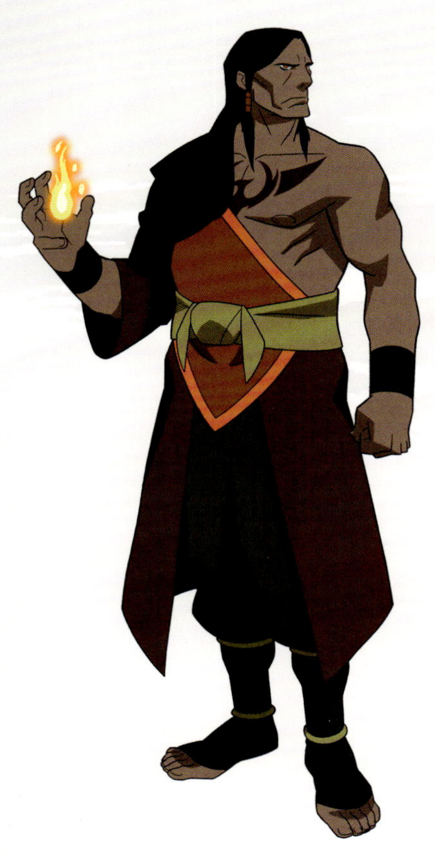

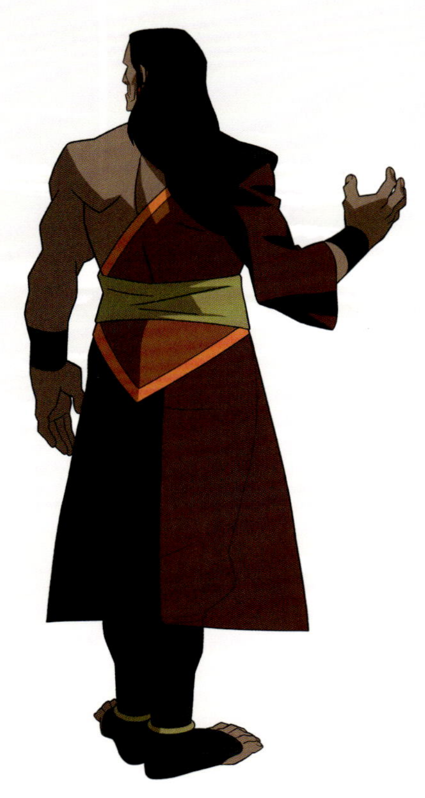

Cerkonos "Flamespeaker"

Leader of the Fire Ashari, he gives Keyleth the blessing of Pyrah after she completes her Fire Trial for her Aramente.

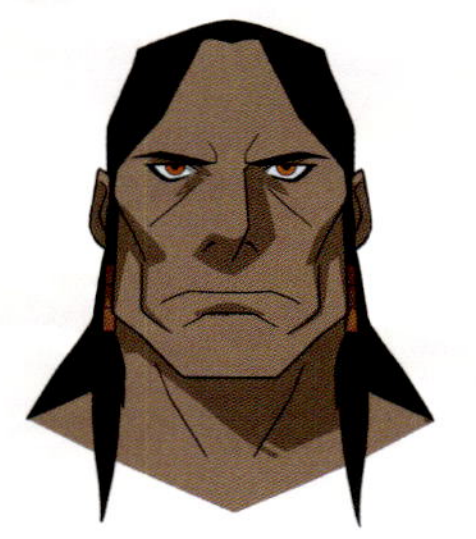

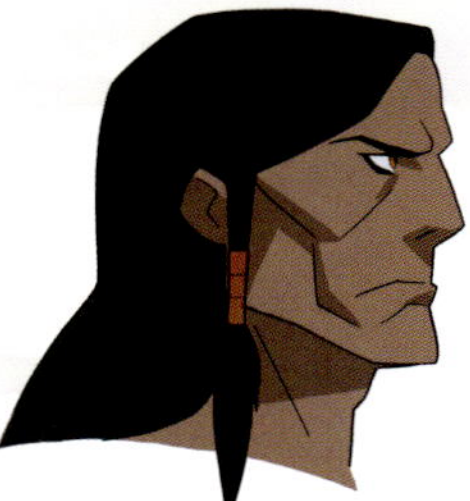

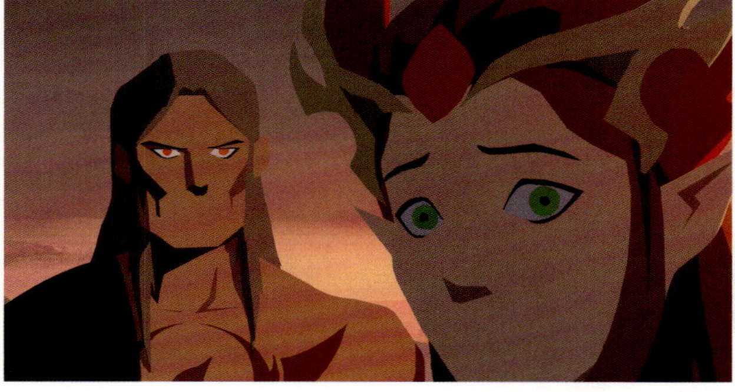

Keyleth in Fire Elemental Form

You can tell it's Keyleth because she still has her antlers!

"I was made to pass through fire." – KEYLETH, S1E5 "PASS THROUGH FIRE"

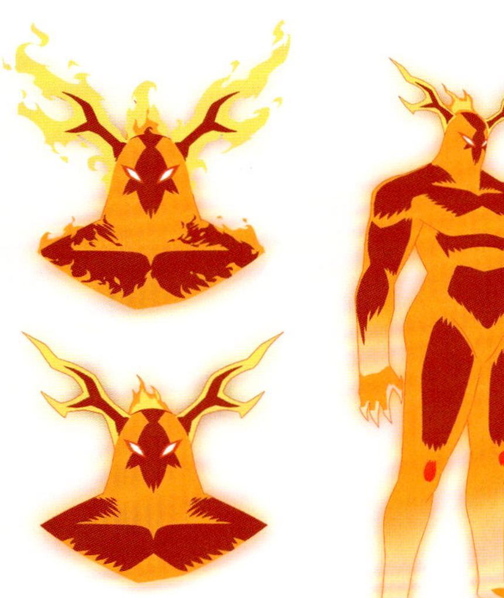

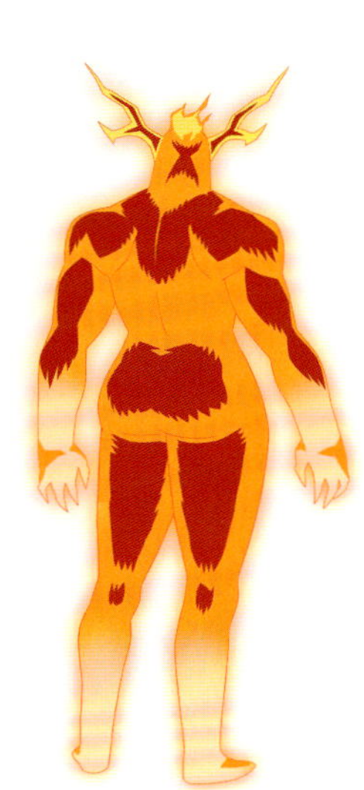

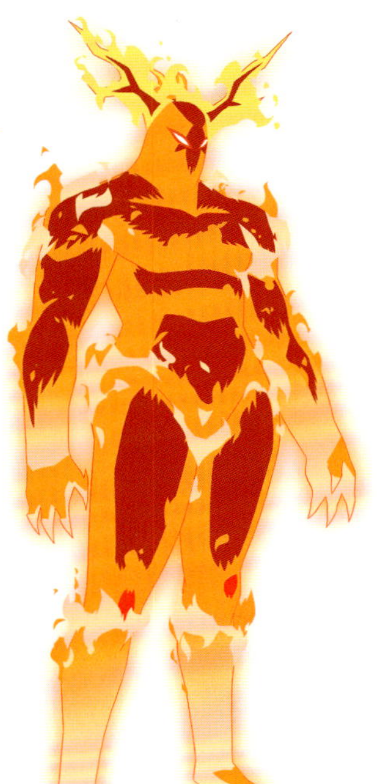

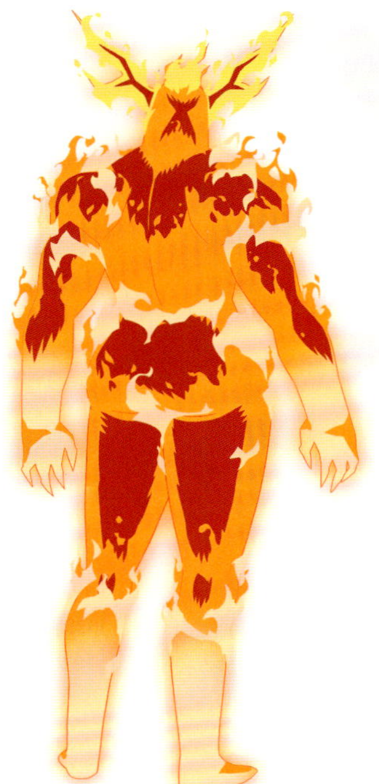

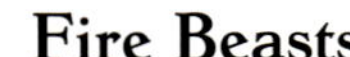

Fire Beasts

Explorations of the different creatures in the Fire Plane. When slain, they bleed ash and lava instead of blood, further starving Craven Edge.

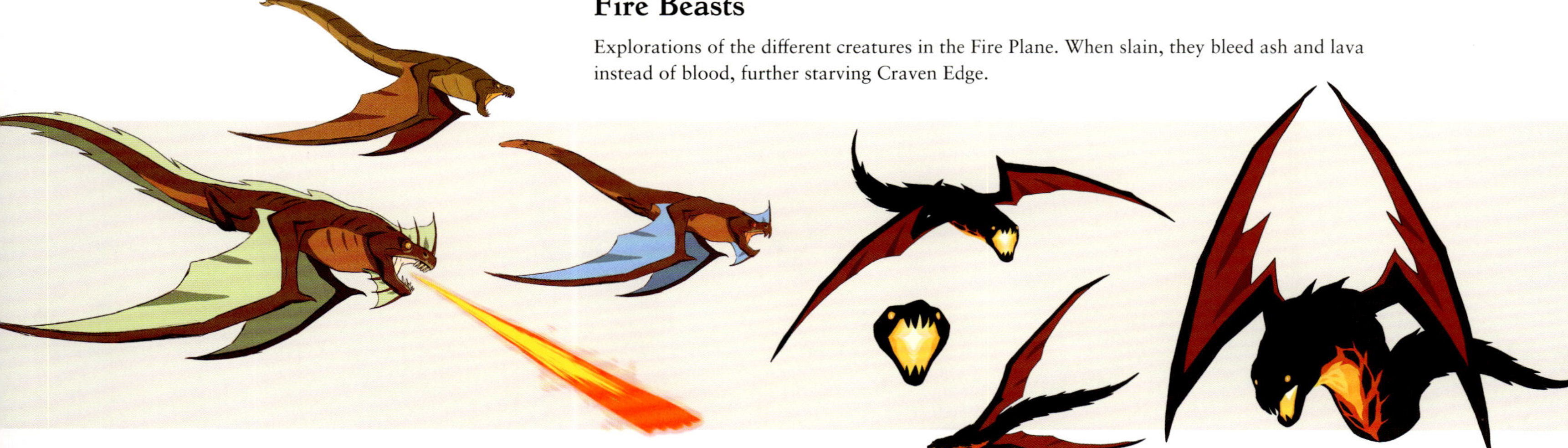

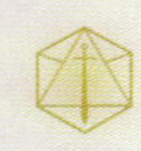

Zephrah

Home to the Air Ashari and where Keyleth grew up before embarking on her Aramente. When developing the look for Zephrah, Matt Mercer noted that he had always imagined cherry blossoms in this environment, and adding them to the backgrounds helped designers give a visual queue to "air." The village itself spans a series of peaks, linked together by long bridges. Arthur Loftis took influence from Chinese watercolor paintings for the shape of the curved mountain-tops and focused on tall, thin, elegant architecture to embody the lightness of air and mirror the mountainous environment.

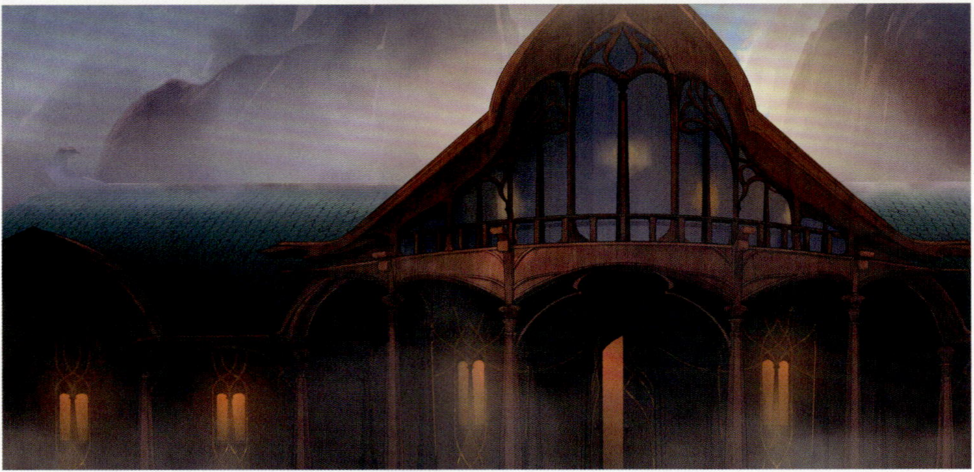

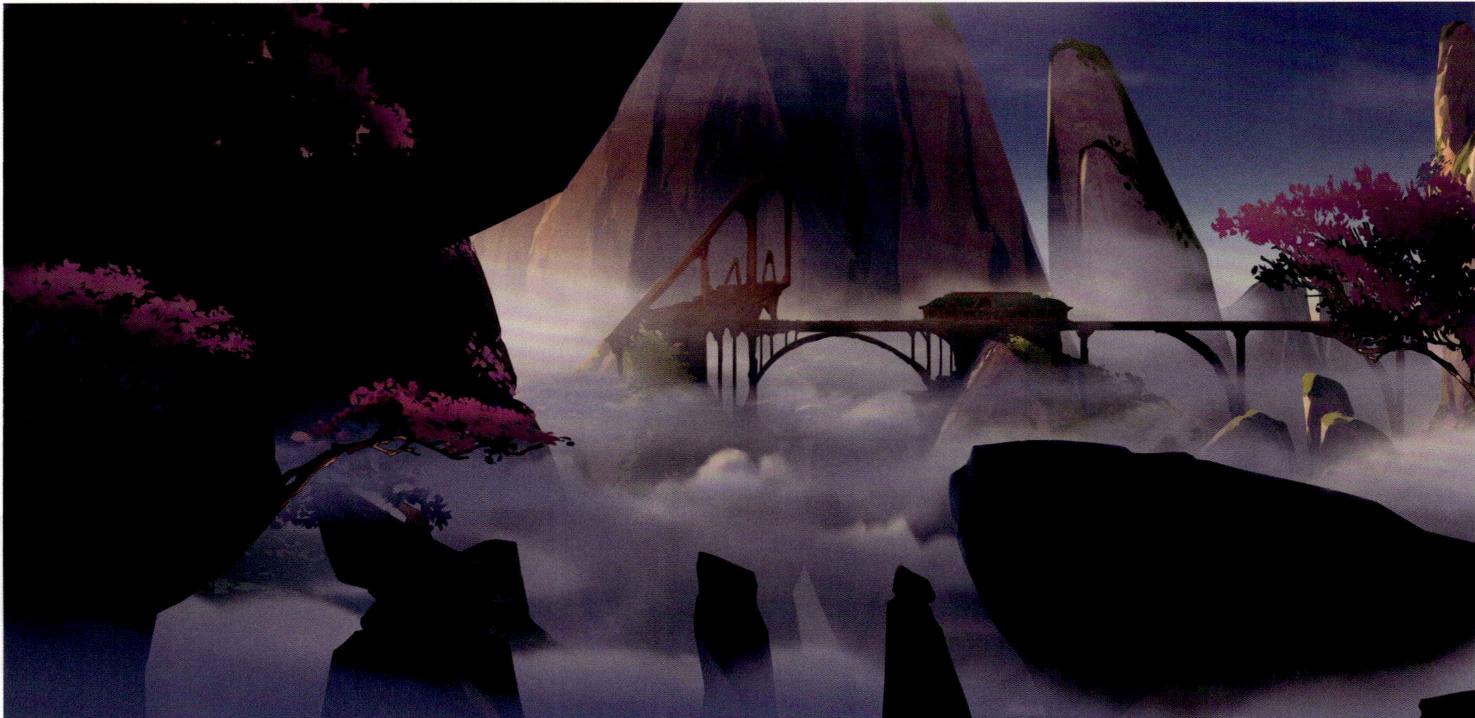

Pyrah

Pyrah is home to the Fire Ashari people, and where they guard a rift to the Fire Plane. The village was built around a volcano, where villagers can access the fertile volcanic soil. Arthur Loftis imagined that the Fire Ashari employed terrace farming as their primary food source and included areas for crop growing at the base of the volcano, while the houses were built directly into the mountainside as if the Ashari magically molded the earth outward to form the walls.

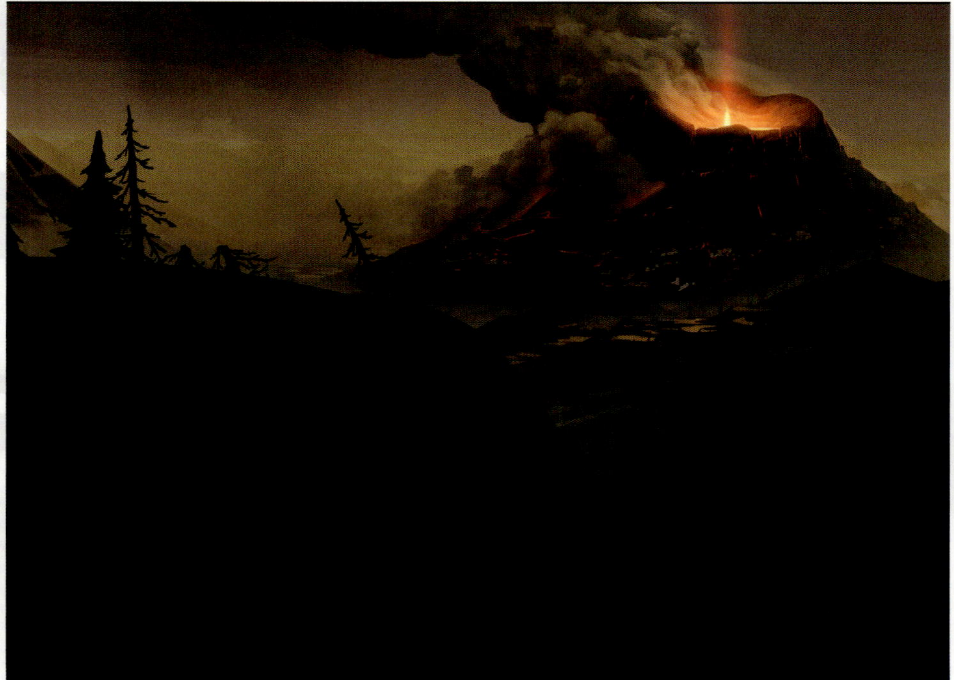

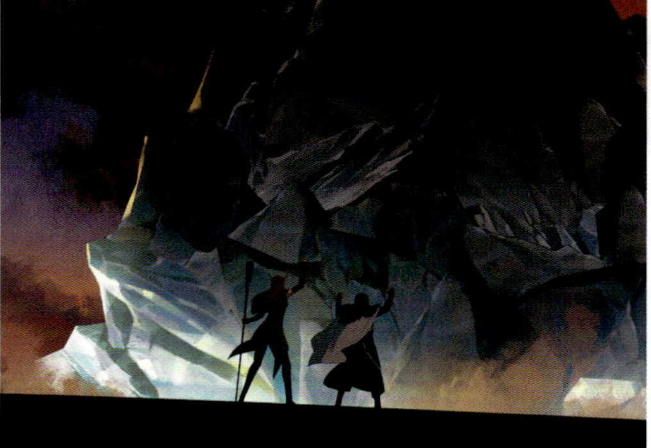

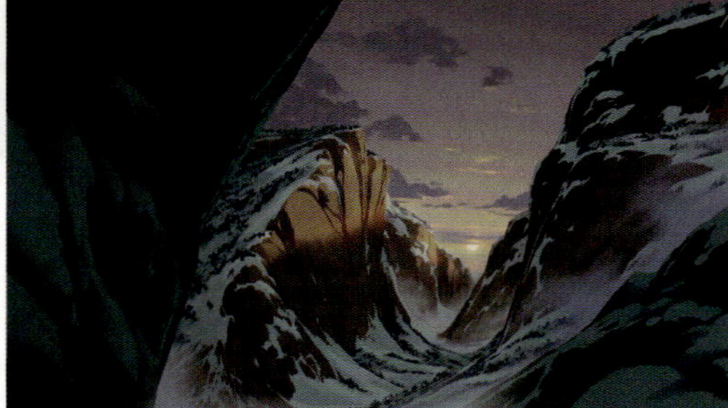

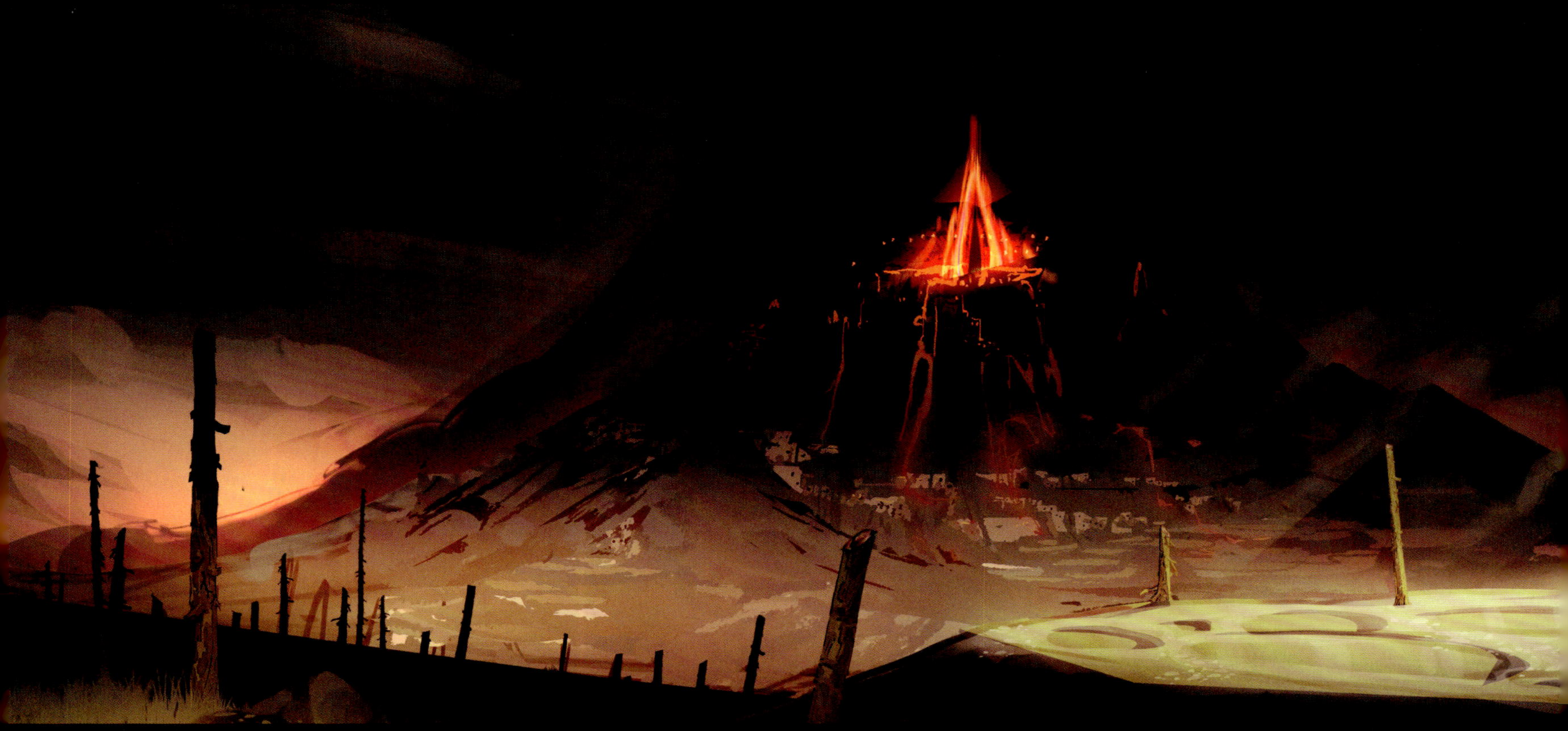

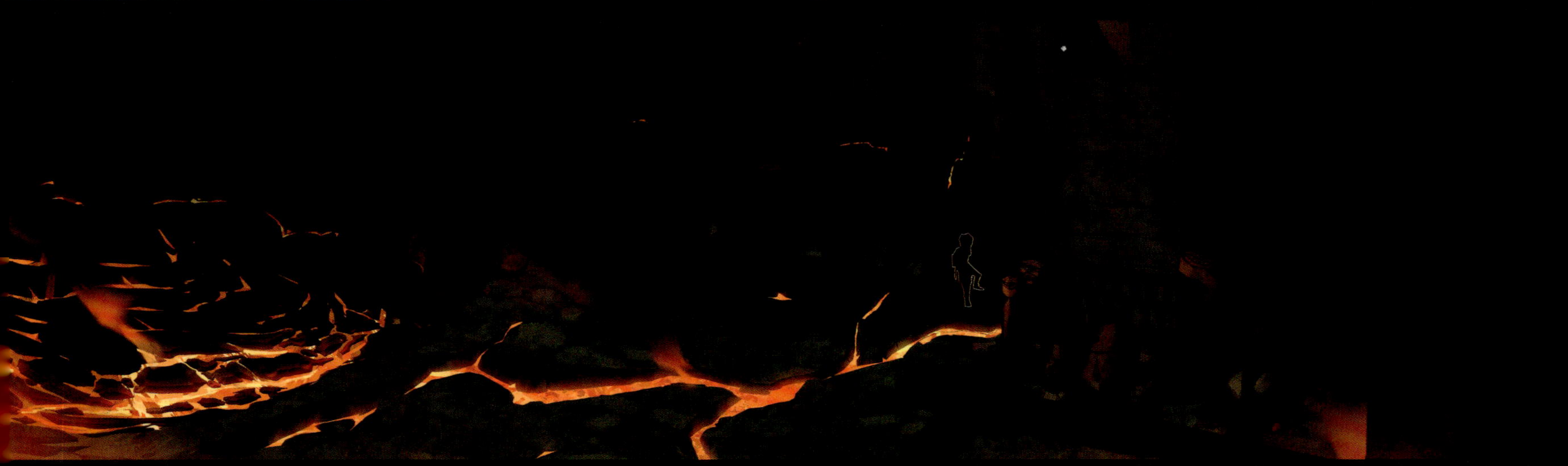

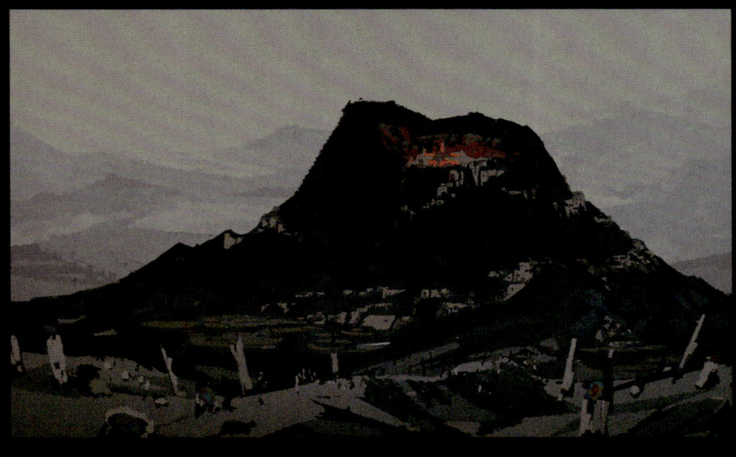

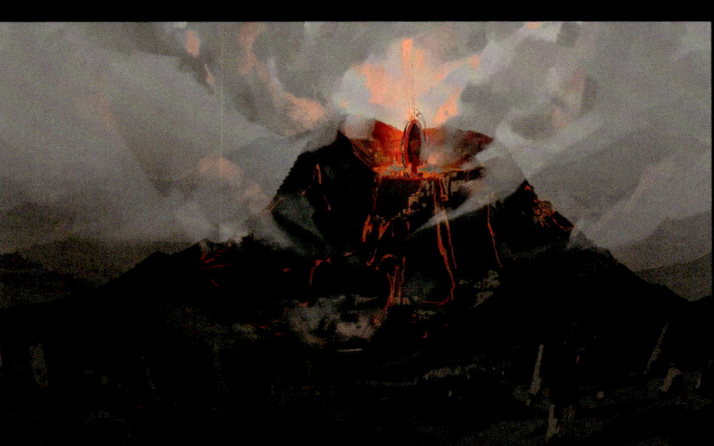

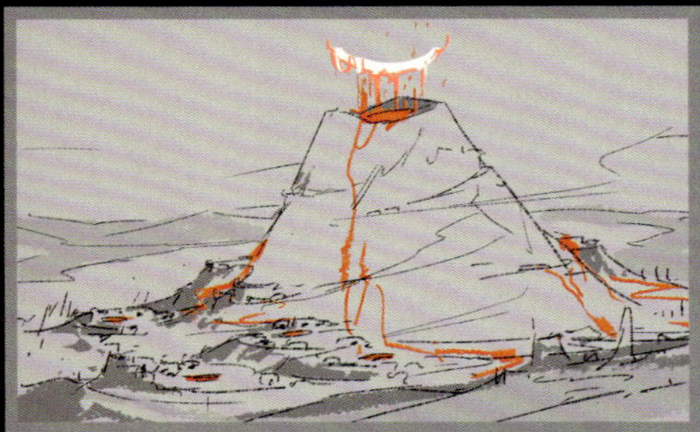

ver. A
ringed settlements around volcano
circle represent symbol of containment of fire

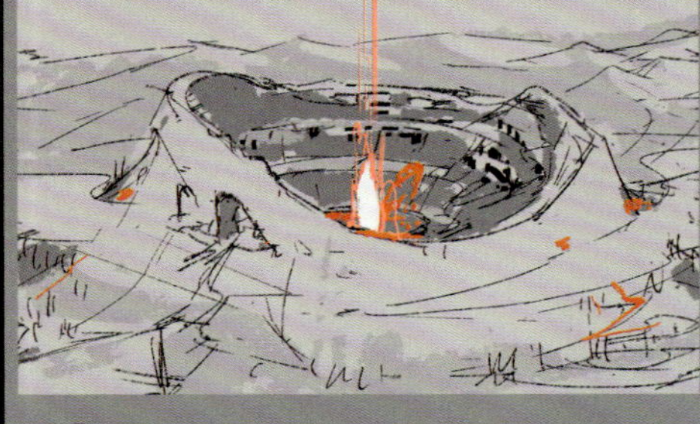

ver. B
settlement built within volcano inner wall
symbiosis with volcano

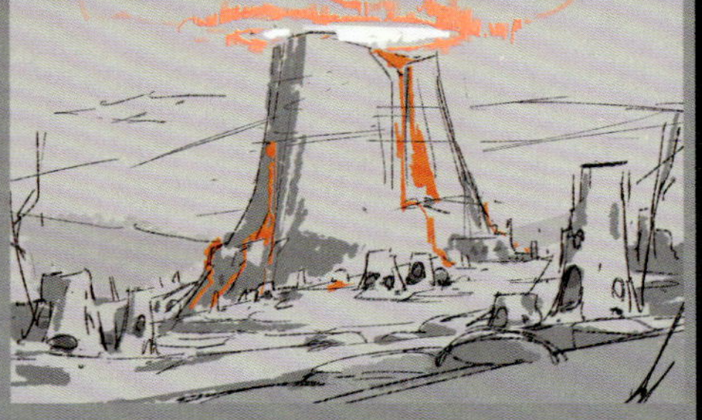

ver. C
calcification landscape & pools
settlement carved out from giant petrified wood forest

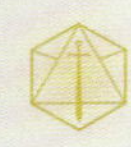

Fire Plane

The Ashari people live across Exandria and guard the regions where the different elemental planes (Fire, Earth, Water, and Air) have openings into the Material Plane. In every generation, a leader from the four tribes is chosen and must complete their Aramente by traveling to the four regions and venturing into the Elemental Planes.

"The fire plane was designed to be as alien as possible–a realm made entirely of molten rock islands amidst seas of flame. We imagined some areas get so hot that the flame would turn from orange to bright blue, like the after-burner of a jet. In the distance, we added huge solar flares that gradually slide across the sky." – ARTHUR LOFTIS

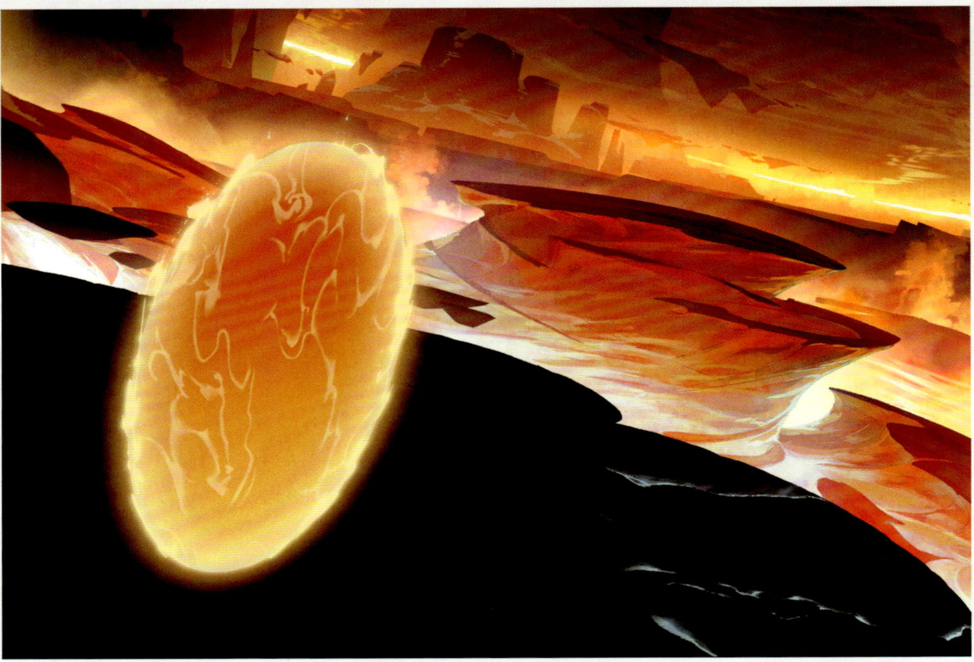

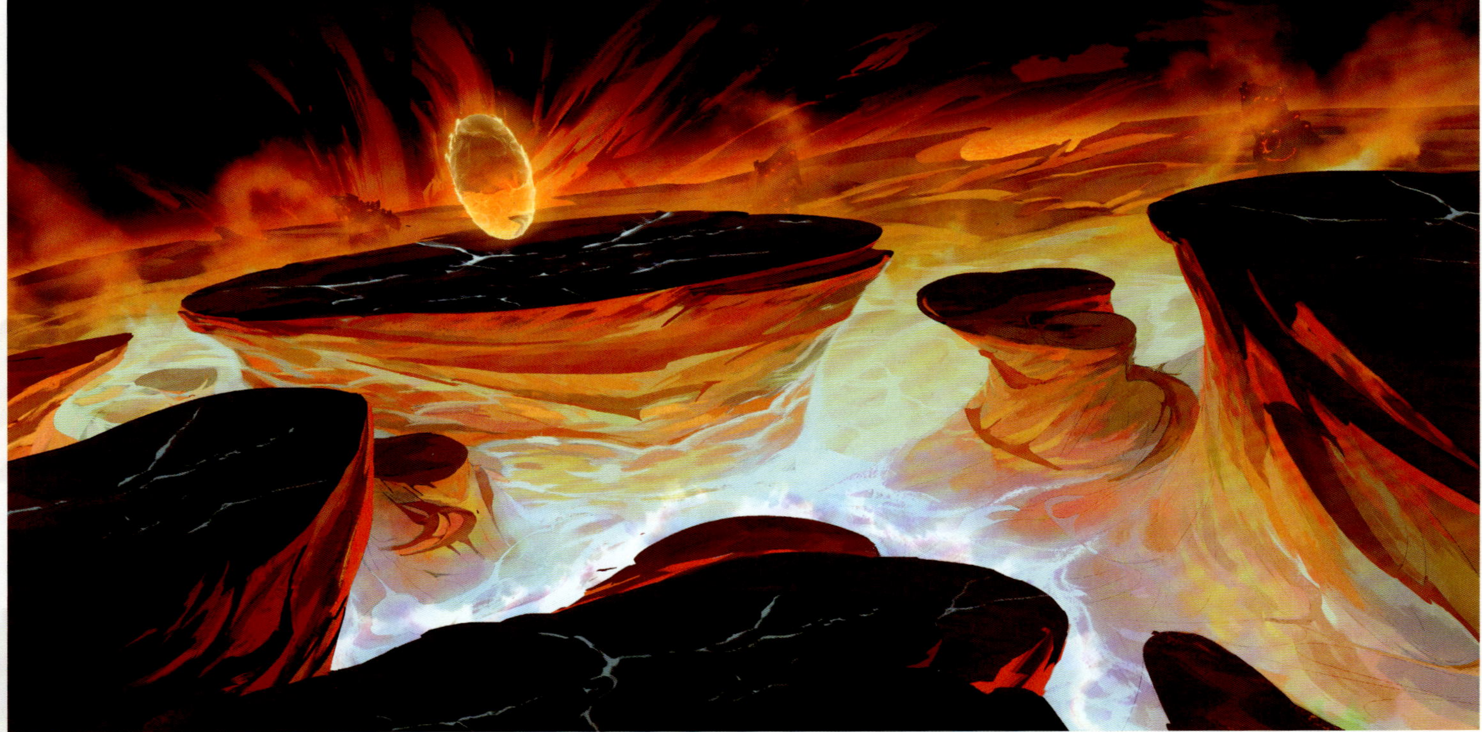

Vex's Broom

Found in Gilmore's shop, just say "volantier," and off you go!

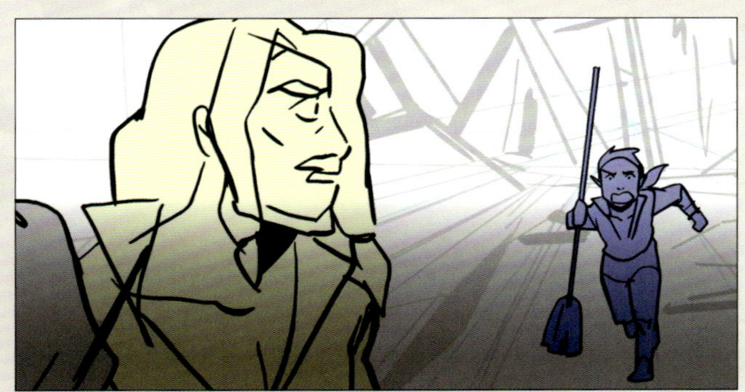

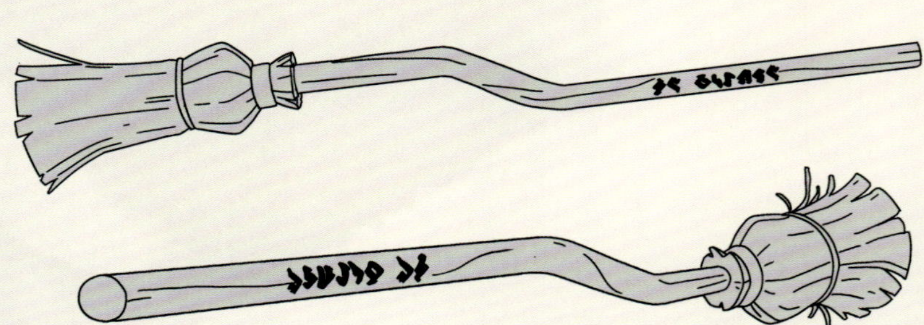

Storyboards from Keyleth Going Fire Elemental

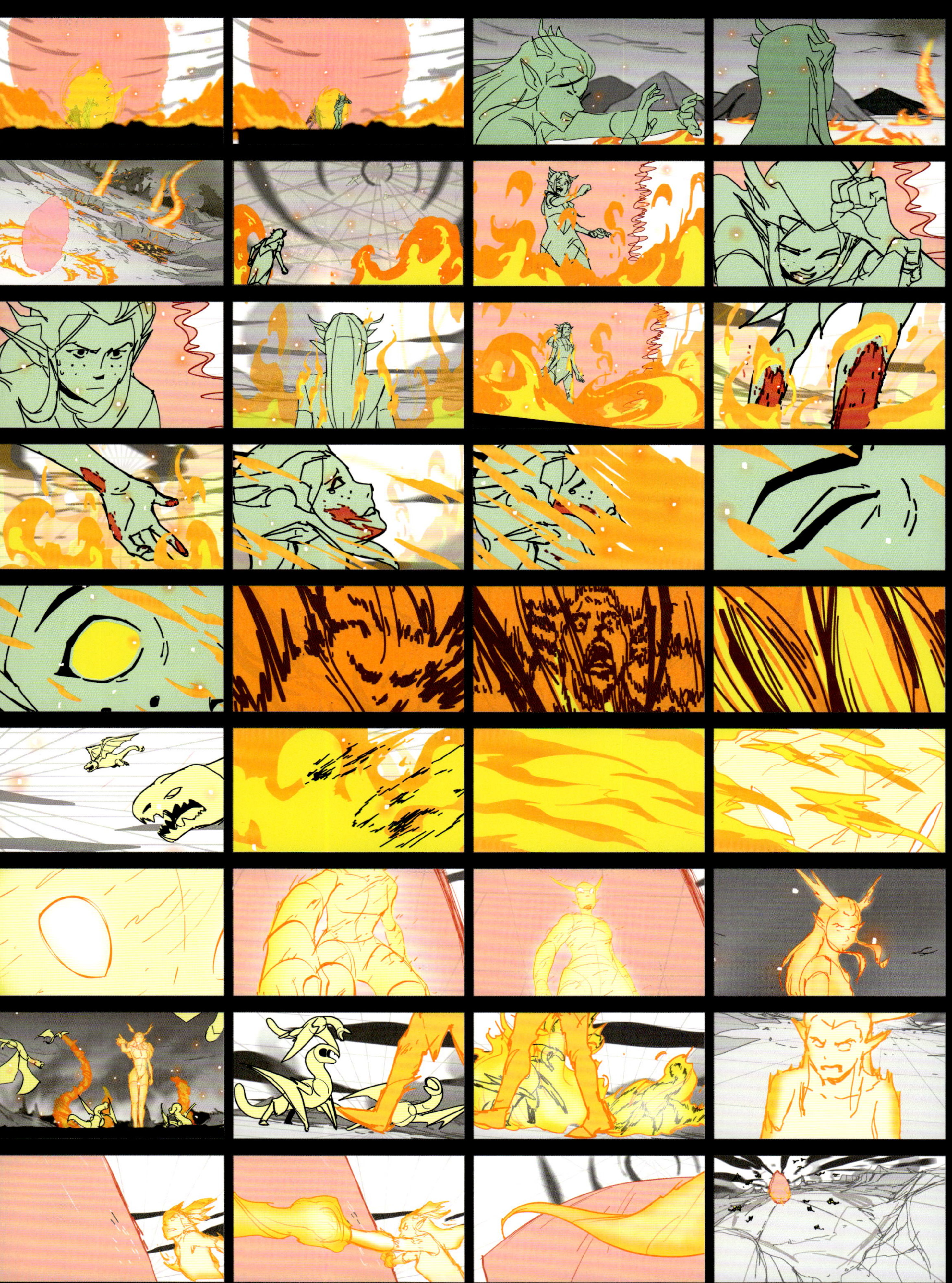

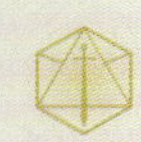

EPISODE 6

INTO RIMECLEFT

"I always say, when you can't beat 'em, join them in a beautiful love song duet sure to make even the coldest of hearts weep with joy. My quick thinking gets us out of a jam when we face off against yet another sphinx by the name of Kamaljiori. Kam and I become fast friends, and he gifts us Mythcarver, a kickass sword that will point us in the direction of all the other vestiges! But just when we think we've added another point to team Vox, that shit-stirring dragon Umbrasyl knocks on our door and steals it. Fortunately, my song was enchanting and the only thing worth remembering anyway." – A RECOUNTING OF "INTO RIMECLEFT" BY SCANLAN SHORTHALT

Kamaljiori

Osysa's mate who offers to help Vox Machina if they are able to "wound him." In his eons of life, he has never felt pain, but Scanlan is able to touch his heart through song.

The character designers did not want Kamaljiori and Osysa to be identical, so they focused on the lithe, cat-like qualities of a sphinx for Osysa, whereas Kamaljiori's build was more stone-like and lion in nature.

The sphinx's forcefield powers come from The Knowing Mistress. Kamaljiori and Osysa are her chosen entities tasked with protecting her knowledge while she is in exile. The circular markings that appear in their magic can be seen throughout the series, most notably on the exterior walls of Vasselheim.

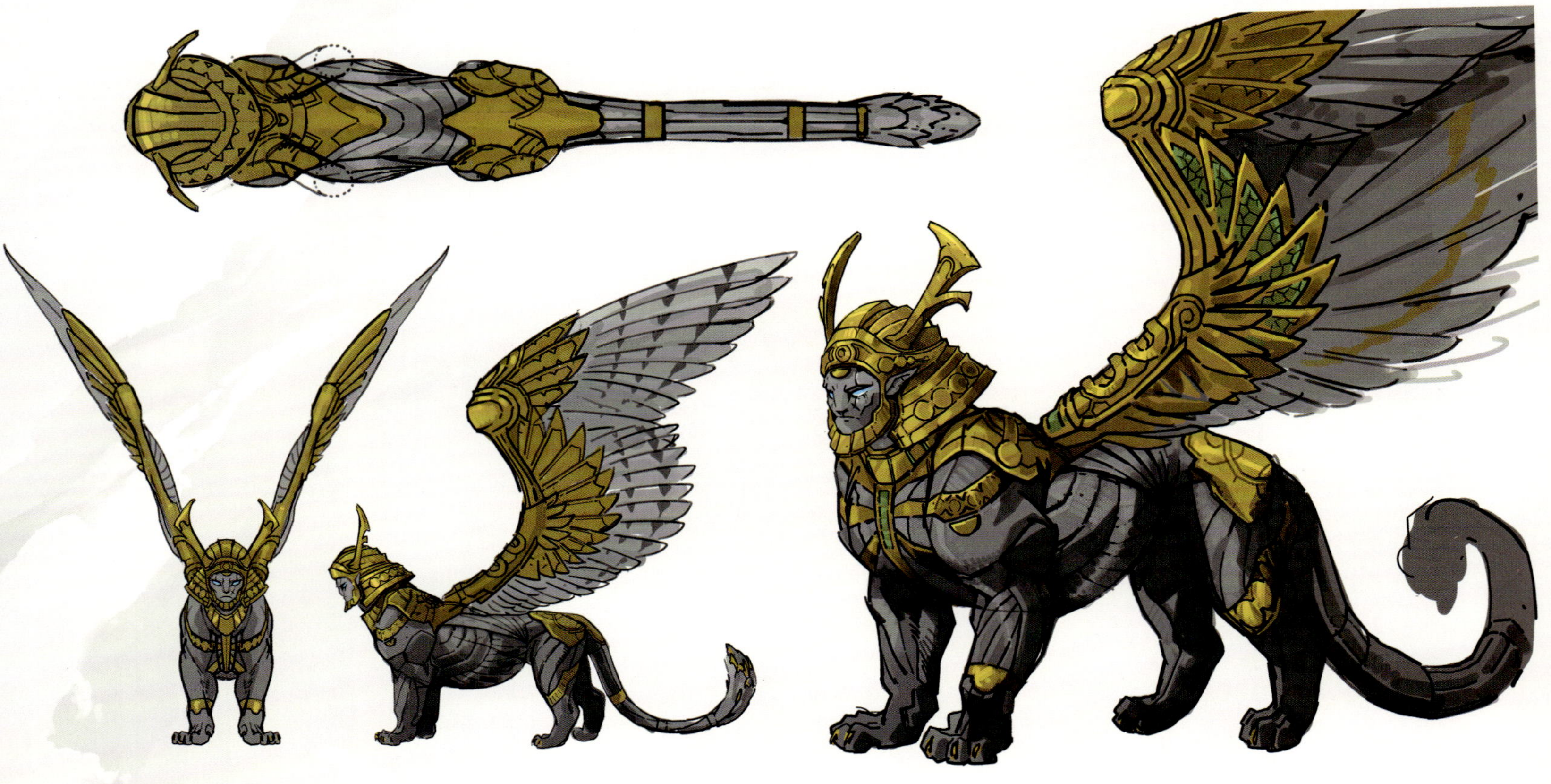

Rimecleft

Rimecleft is a unique location created for the animated series. While plotting the storyline, the directors did not want Vox Machina repeatedly bouncing back and forth between the continent of Tal'Dorei and Issylra, where Kamaljiori's lair was in the original campaign.

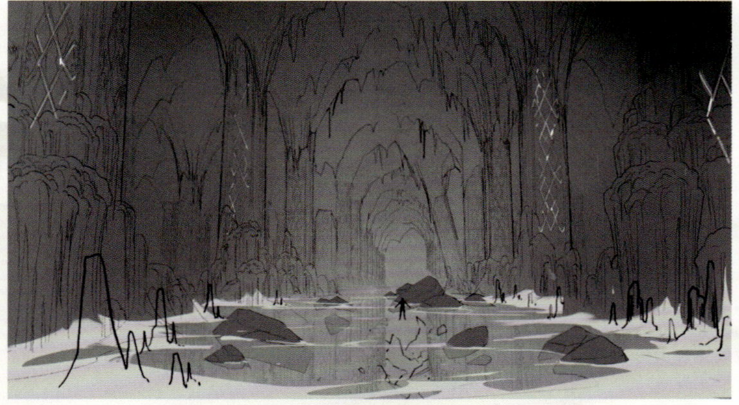

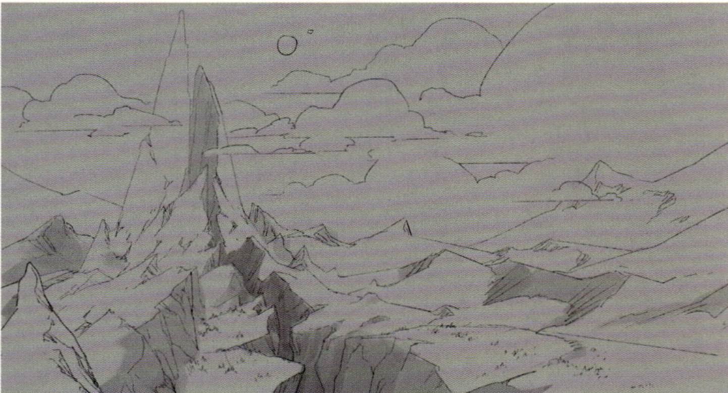

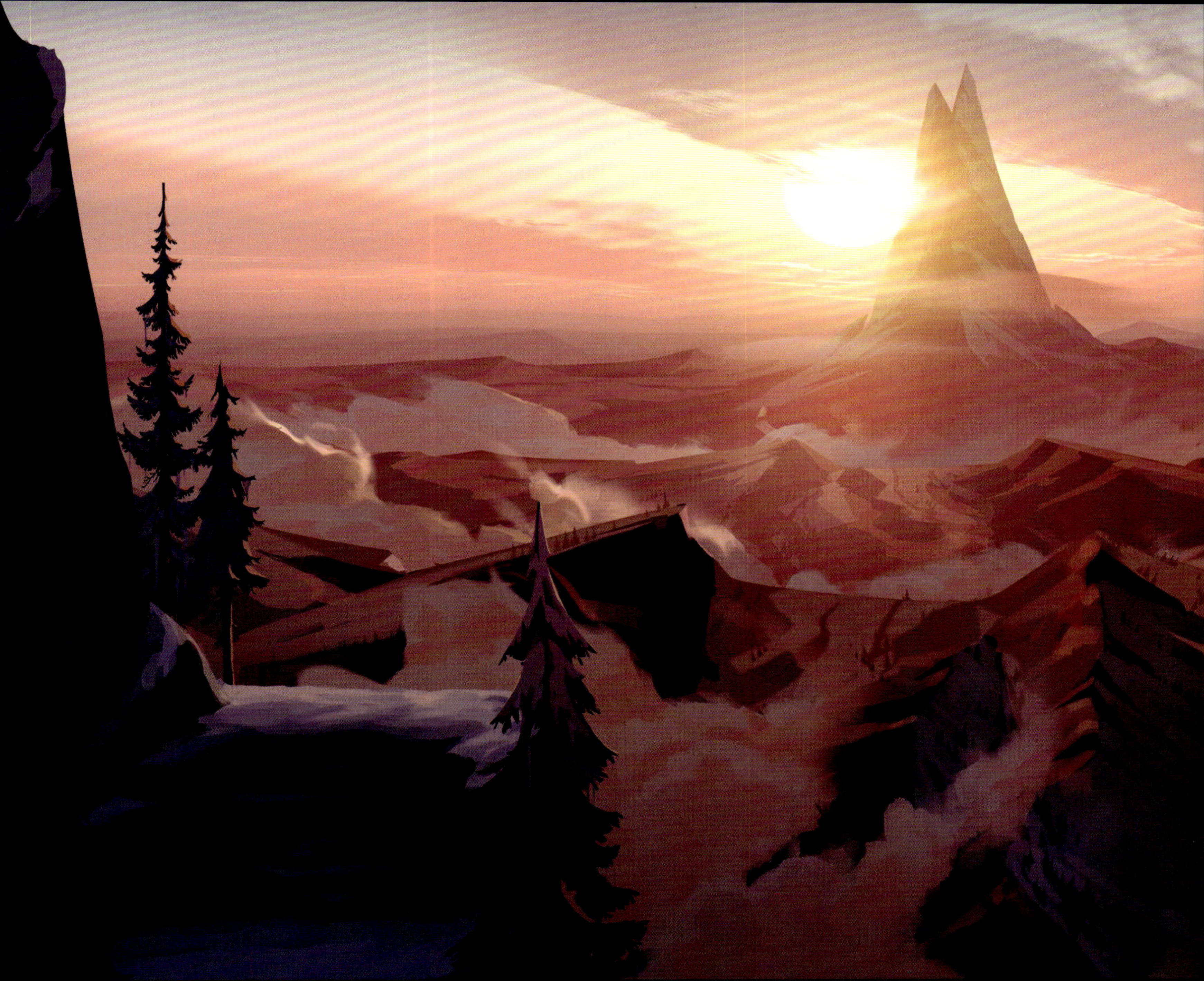

The history behind Rimecleft is that it is a mountain torn in half during an ancient cataclysm, permanently freezing the surrounding area. The design team focused on jagged shapes for these landscapes to show the treacherousness of Vox Machina's journey to Kamaljiori's lair.

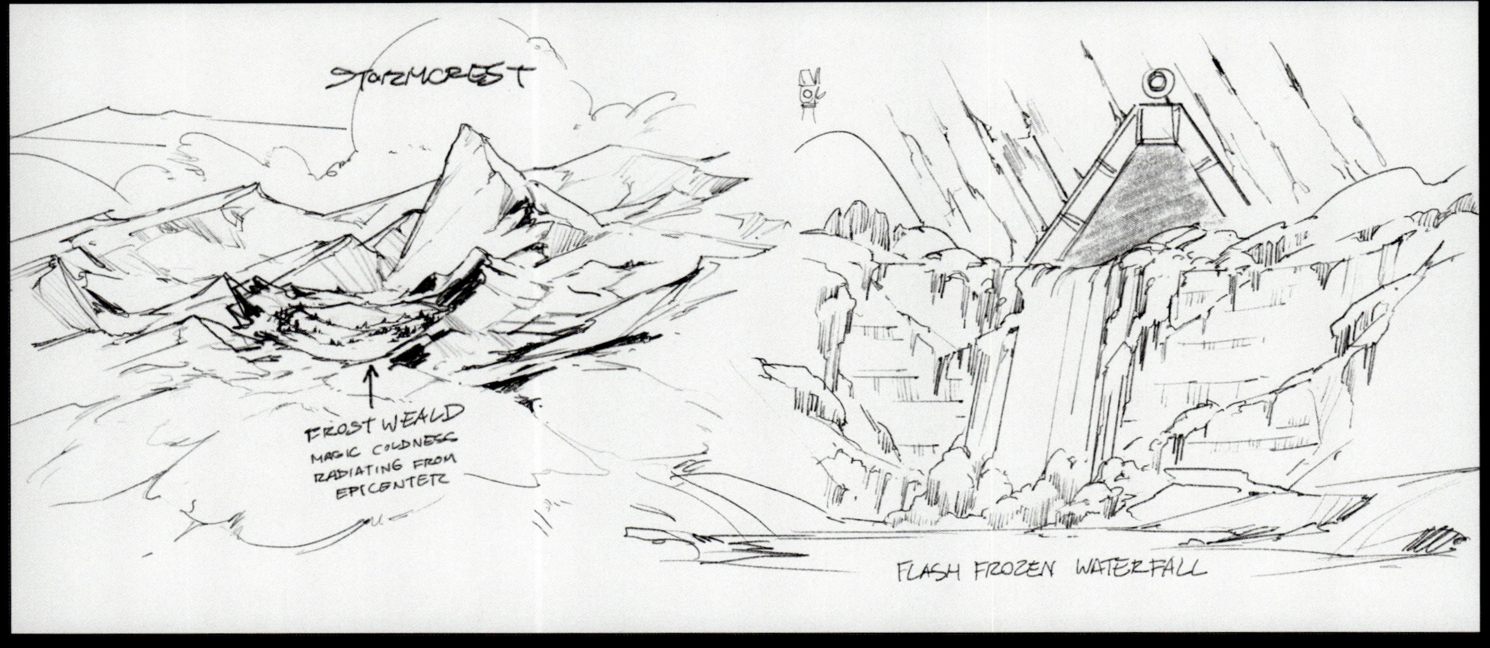

Early sketches of the Frostweald (later reworked as Rimecleft) with the obelisk sitting atop a frozen waterfall.

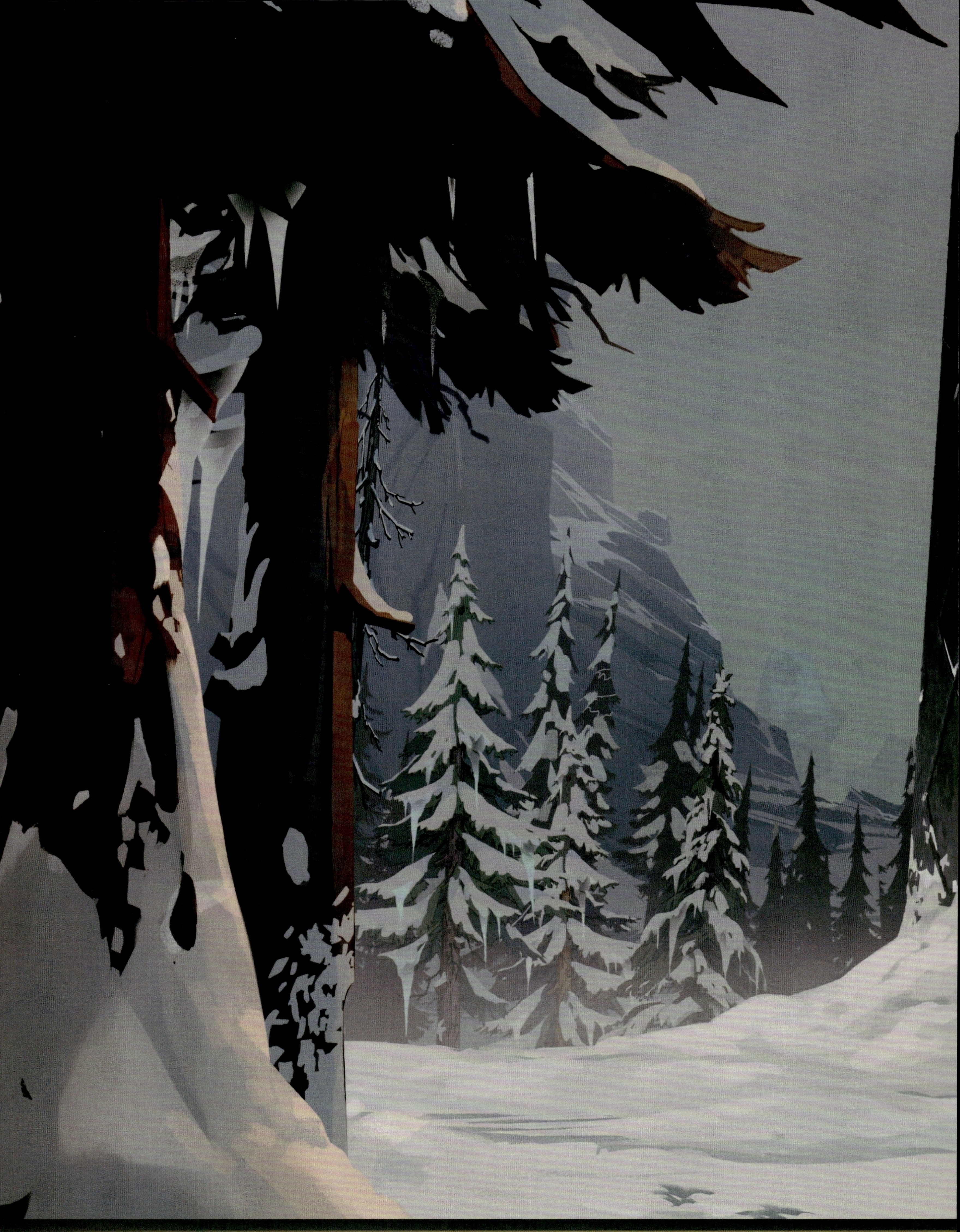

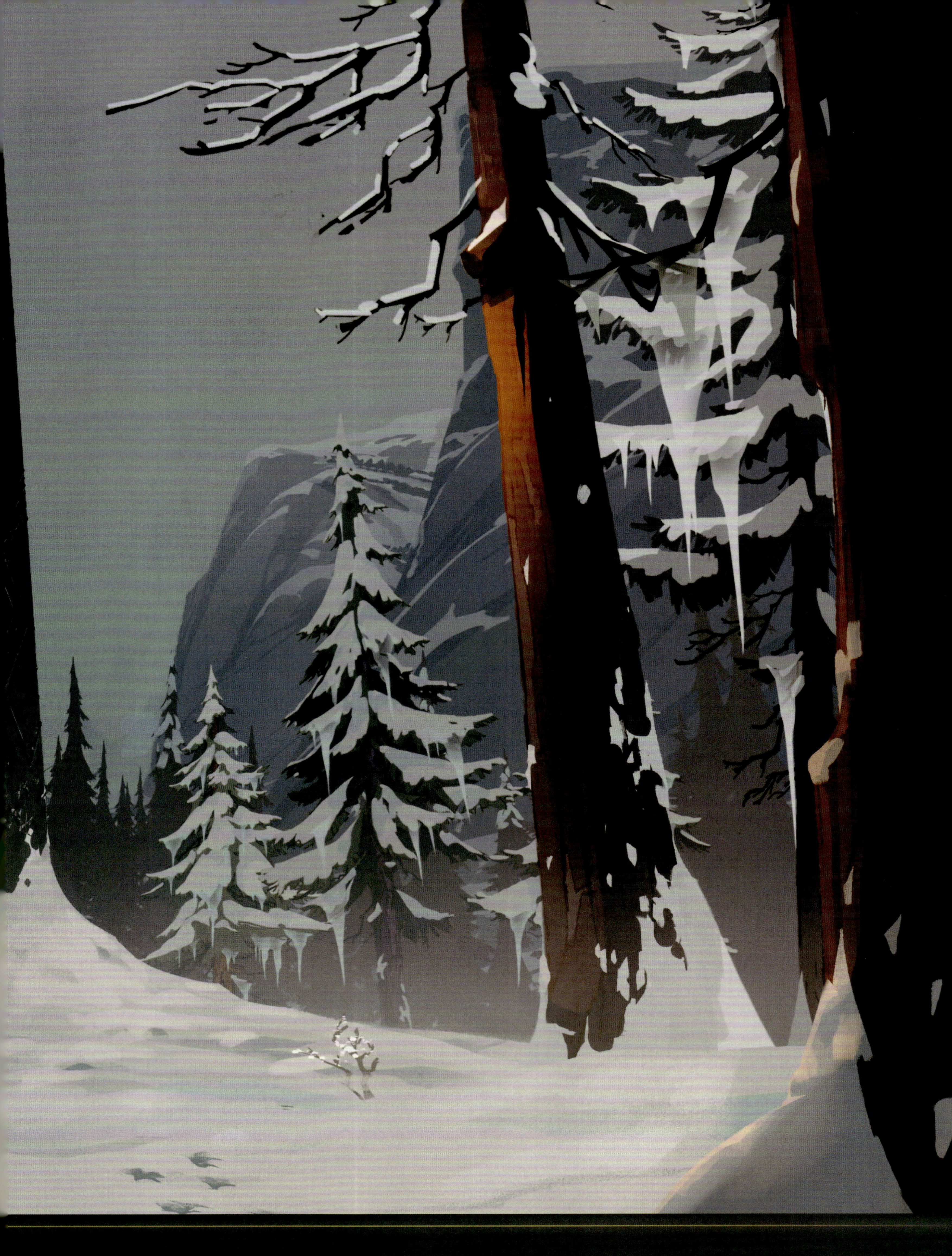

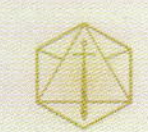

Obelisk

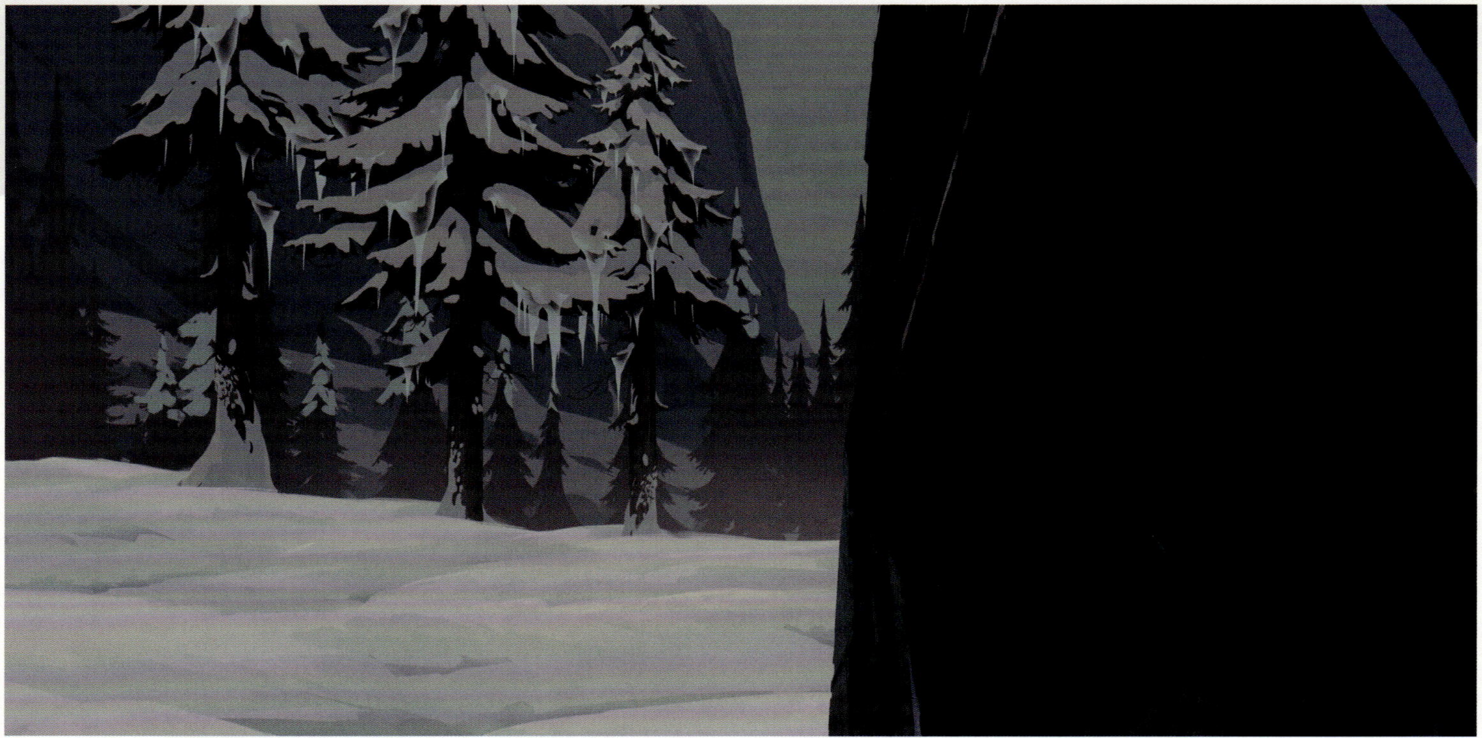

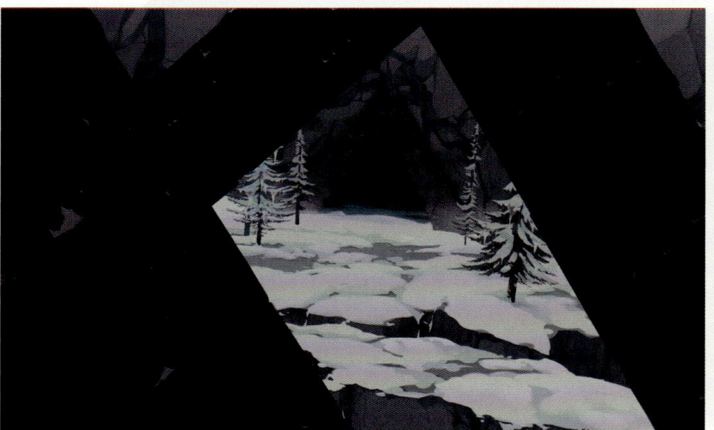

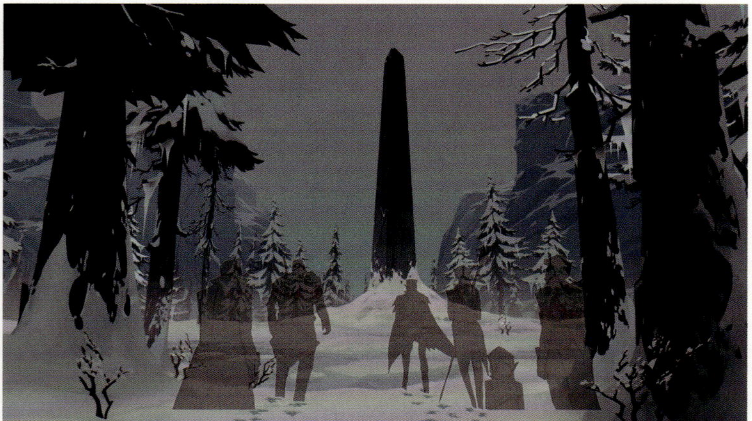

Mythcarver

A Vestige of Divergence given to Scanlan by Kamaljiori. Its original owner forged it with song, making it a natural weapon for Scanlan to wield.

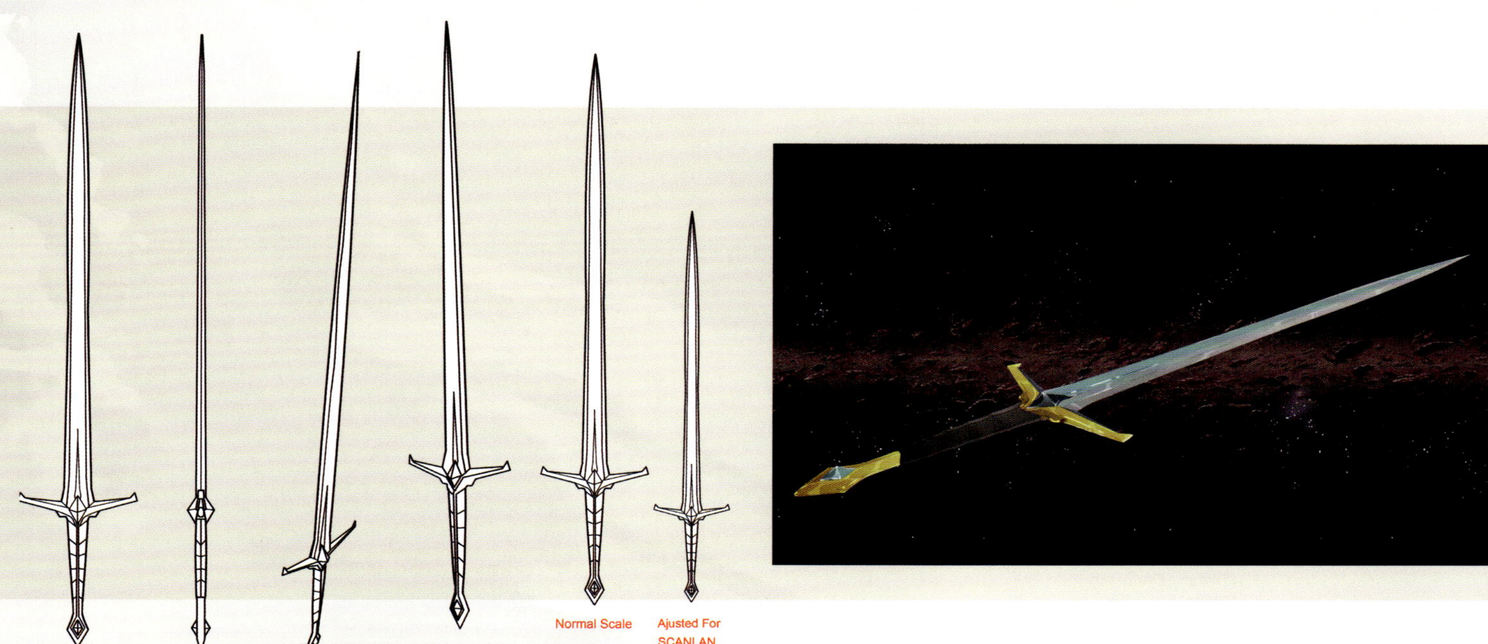

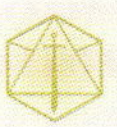

Sphinx's Temple

When deciding on the temple's scale, the design team had to consider the epic fight between Kamaljiori and Umbrasyl. The structure needed to be large enough for two large creatures to enter into battle while allowing the audience to also see Vox Machina below.

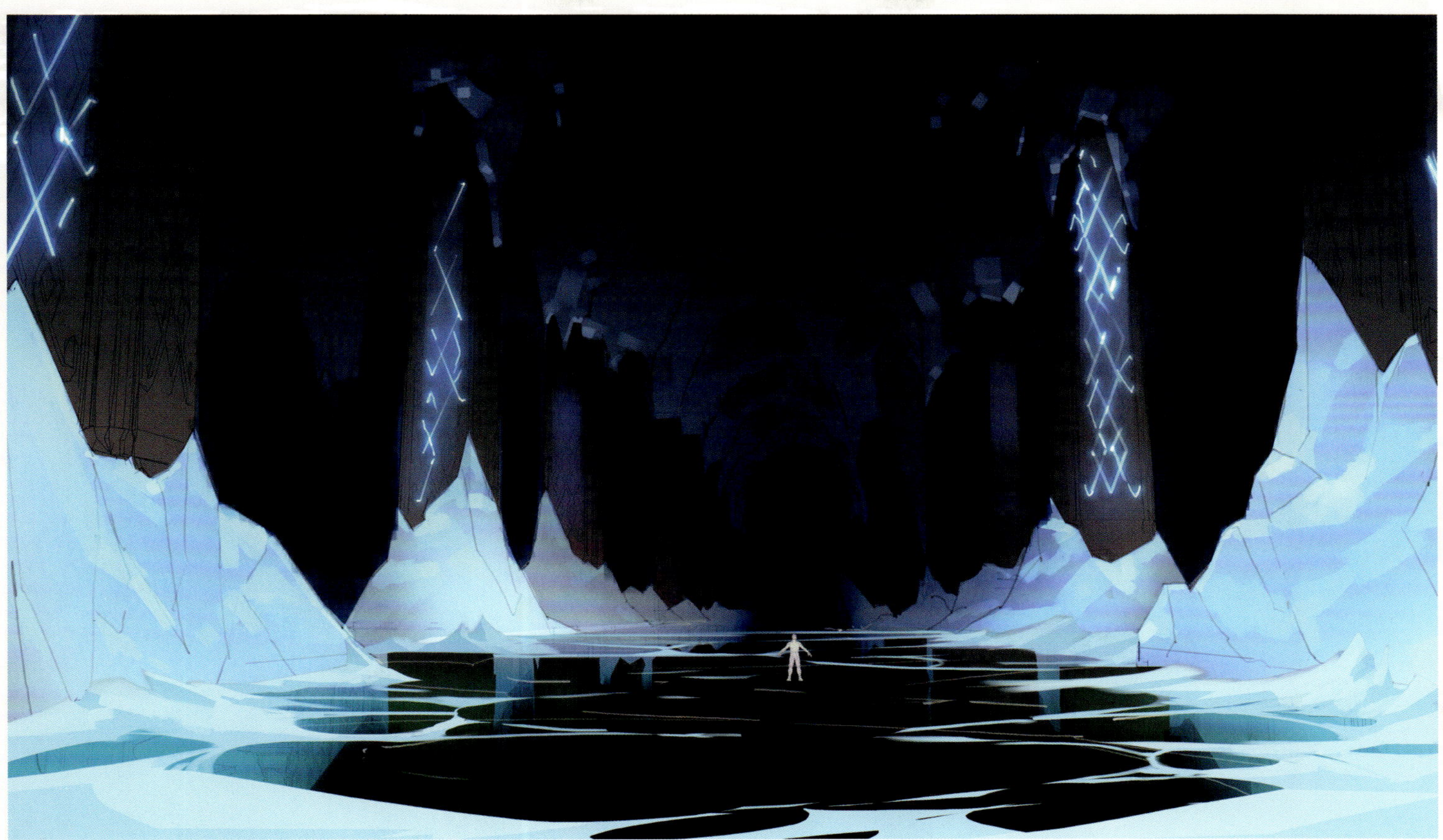

The columns contain the circular markings of The Knowing Mistress and light up when Kamaljiori moves through.

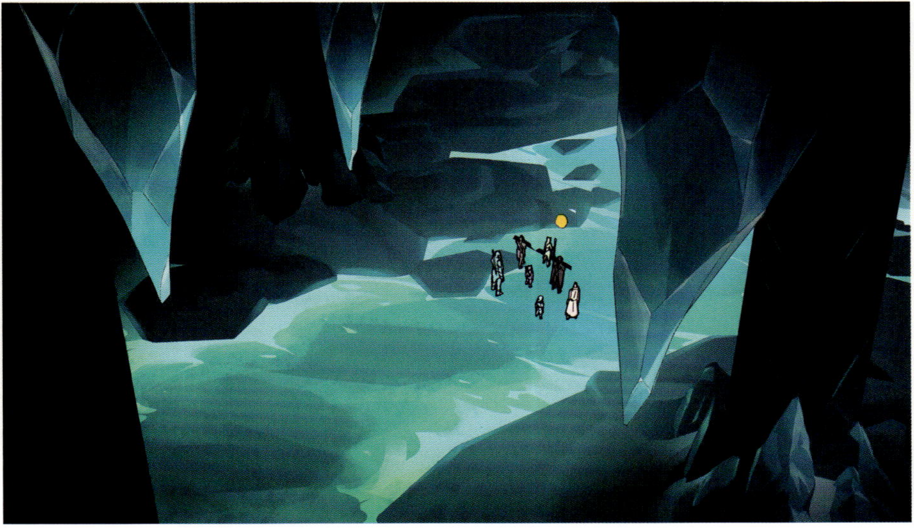

The perfect setting for a power ballad love song if you ask me.

Sketches of Early Temple Traps

While the story eventually took a different route, early explorations of the Sphinx's temple included various puzzles and traps to foil Vox Machina.

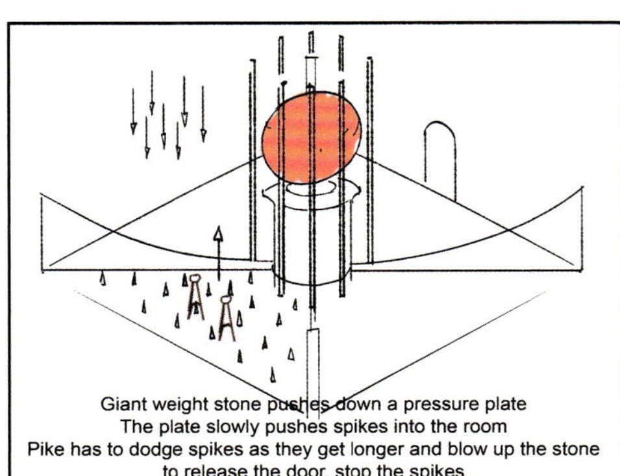

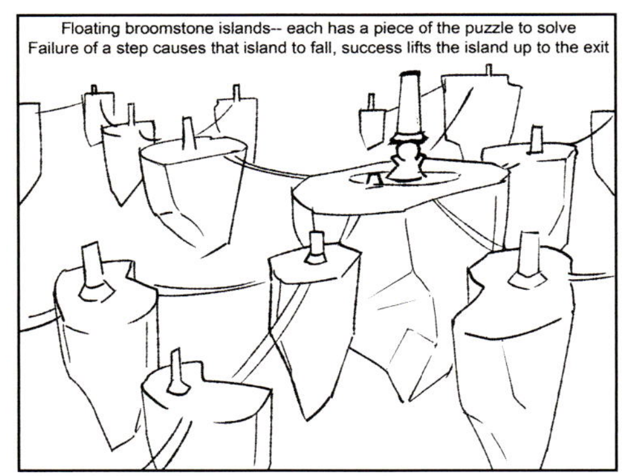

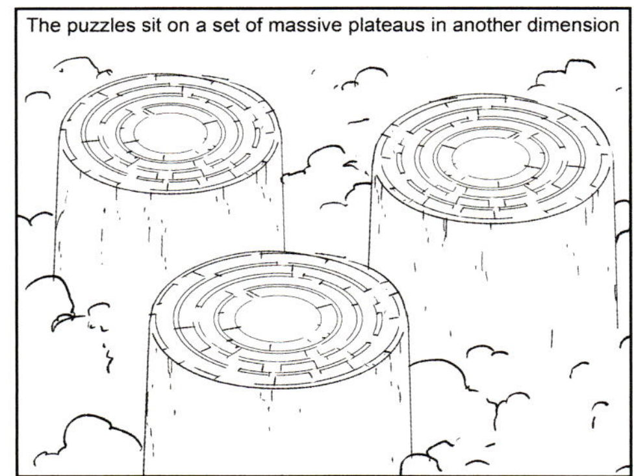

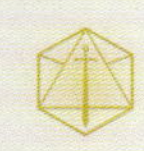

EPISODE 7

THE FEY REALM

"Grog finally sees reason and destroys the bloodsucking sword Craven Edge. Unfortunately, it decides to zap him of his muscles as a last act of revenge, leaving Pike and I to lug his slightly smaller ass across Tal'Dorei for help. Meanwhile, the twins, Keyleth, and Percy go for a jaunt through The Fey Realm and learn a thing or two about 'connecting with nature.'" – A RECOUNTING OF "THE FEY REALM" BY SCANLAN SHORTHALT

Garmelie

A mischievous satyr encountered by Vox Machina in the Fey Realm, he is later revealed to be the archfey Artagan in disguise.

Artagan

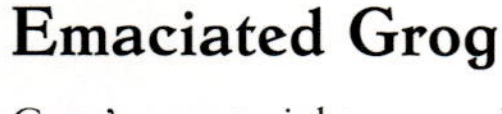

Emaciated Grog

Grog's worst nightmare–a less swole Grog. At least he still has his beard!

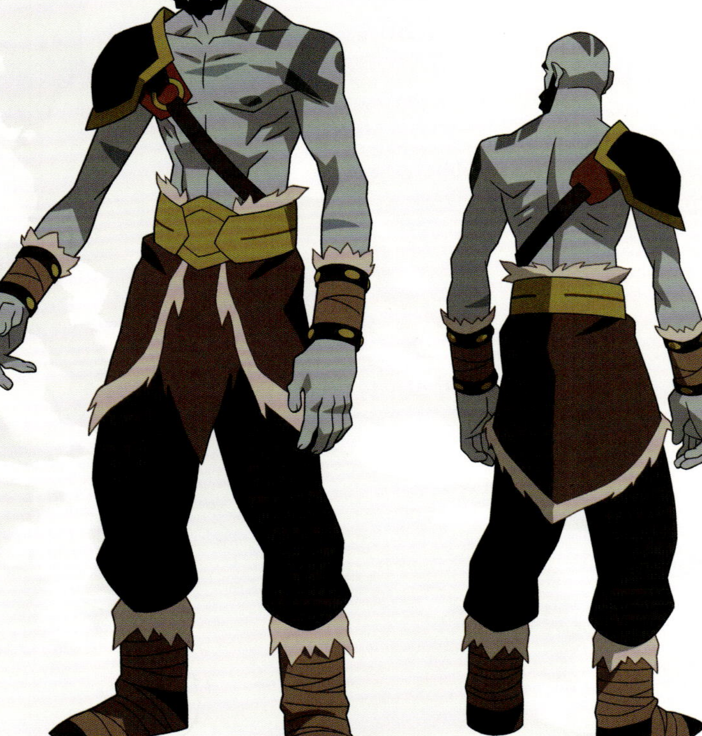

Creatures of the Fey Realm

Various designs of creatures as otherworldly as the land they inhabit.

The middle-top design is inspired by Marisha and Matt's beloved bird, Dagon, who passed away during production.

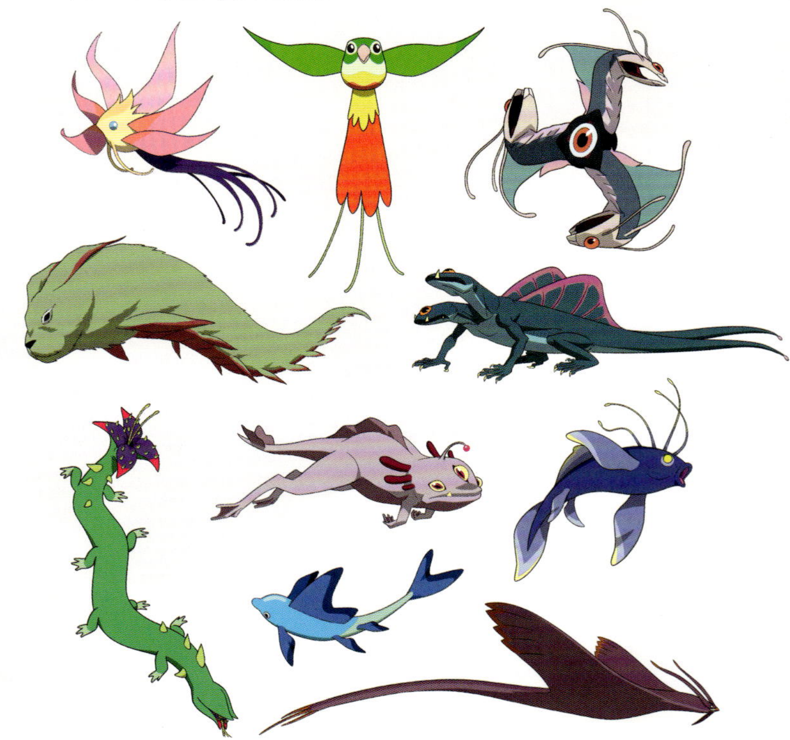

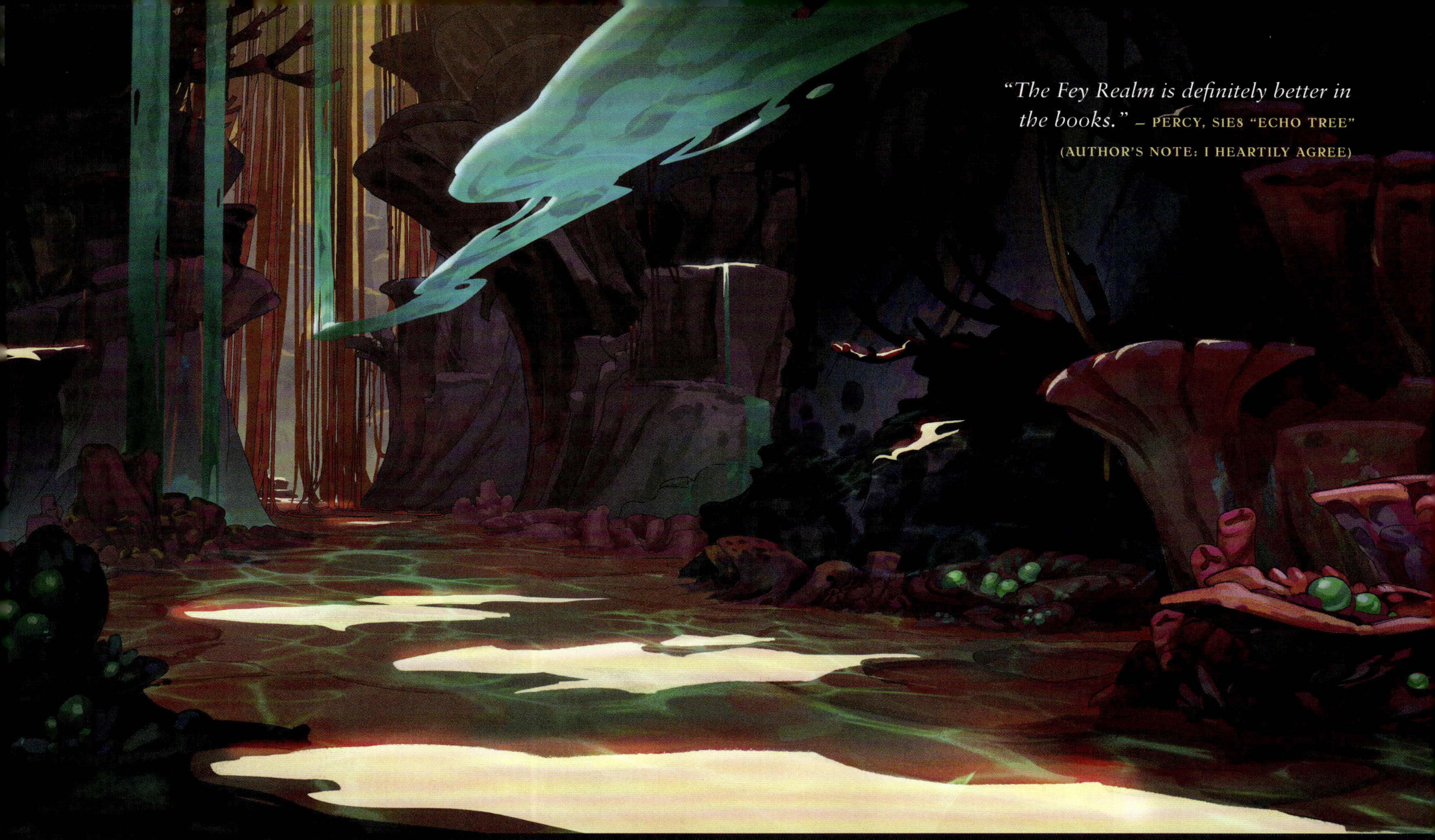

"The Fey Realm is definitely better in the books." – PERCY, S1E8 "ECHO TREE"

(AUTHOR'S NOTE: I HEARTILY AGREE)

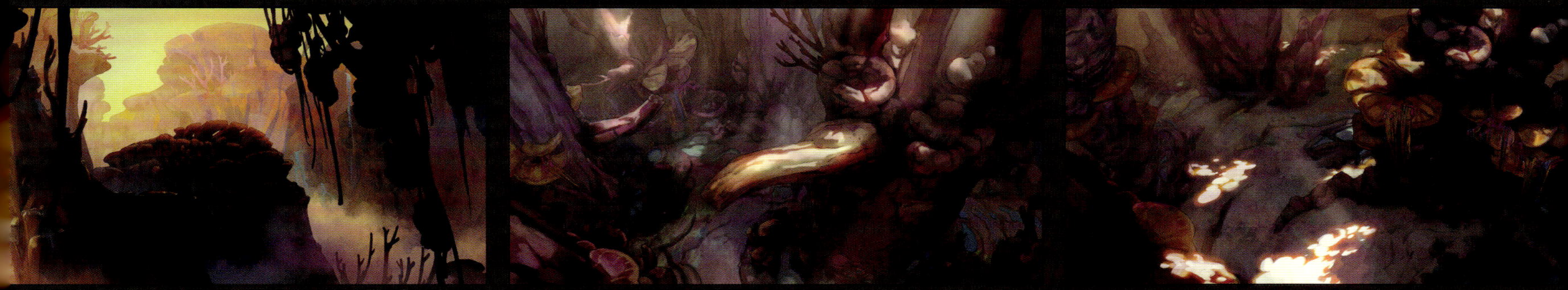

The Fey Realm

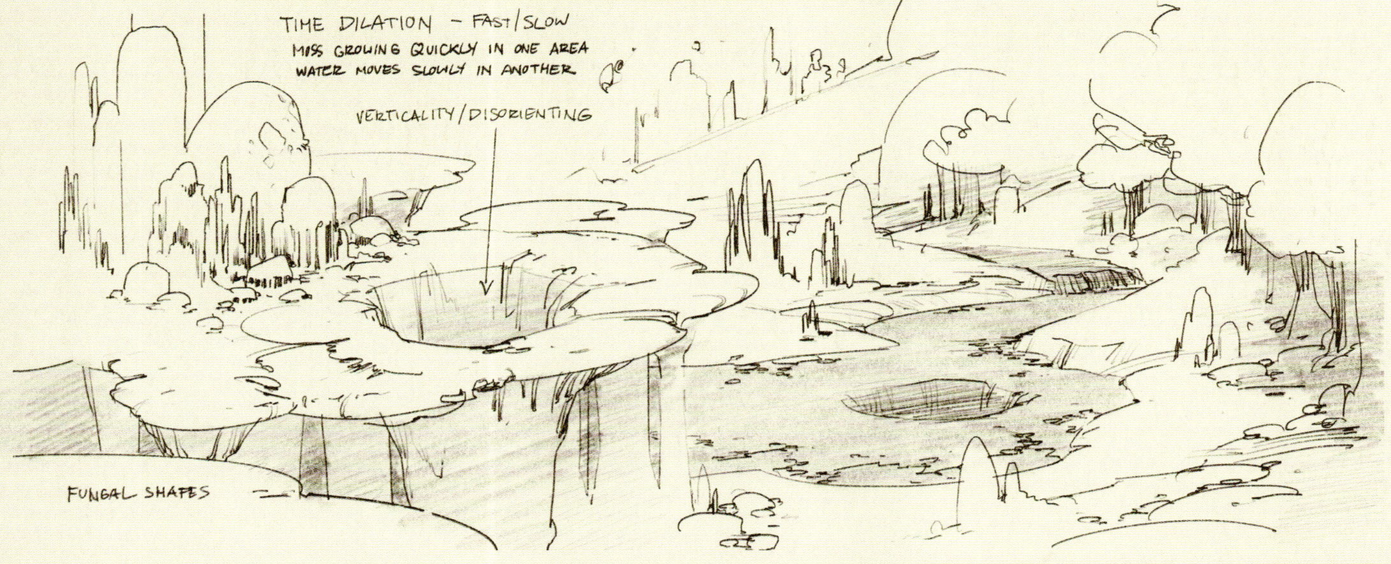

Though Vox Machina's time in this world was short, it didn't prevent the artists from pulling out all the stops. Introducing a distinct color palette gave the space an easily distinguishable look while cutting back and forth between the Fey Realm and Tal'Dorei.

The Fey Realm was intended to be the most alien environment in Vox Machina's journeys. The design team started by looking at coral reefs for unique shapes that felt believable yet unlike anything designed for the series thus far. Each area the characters trek through has a new form of wildlife, such as an upside-down waterfall, the living vine jungle, or the rainbow grass fields that respond to sound.

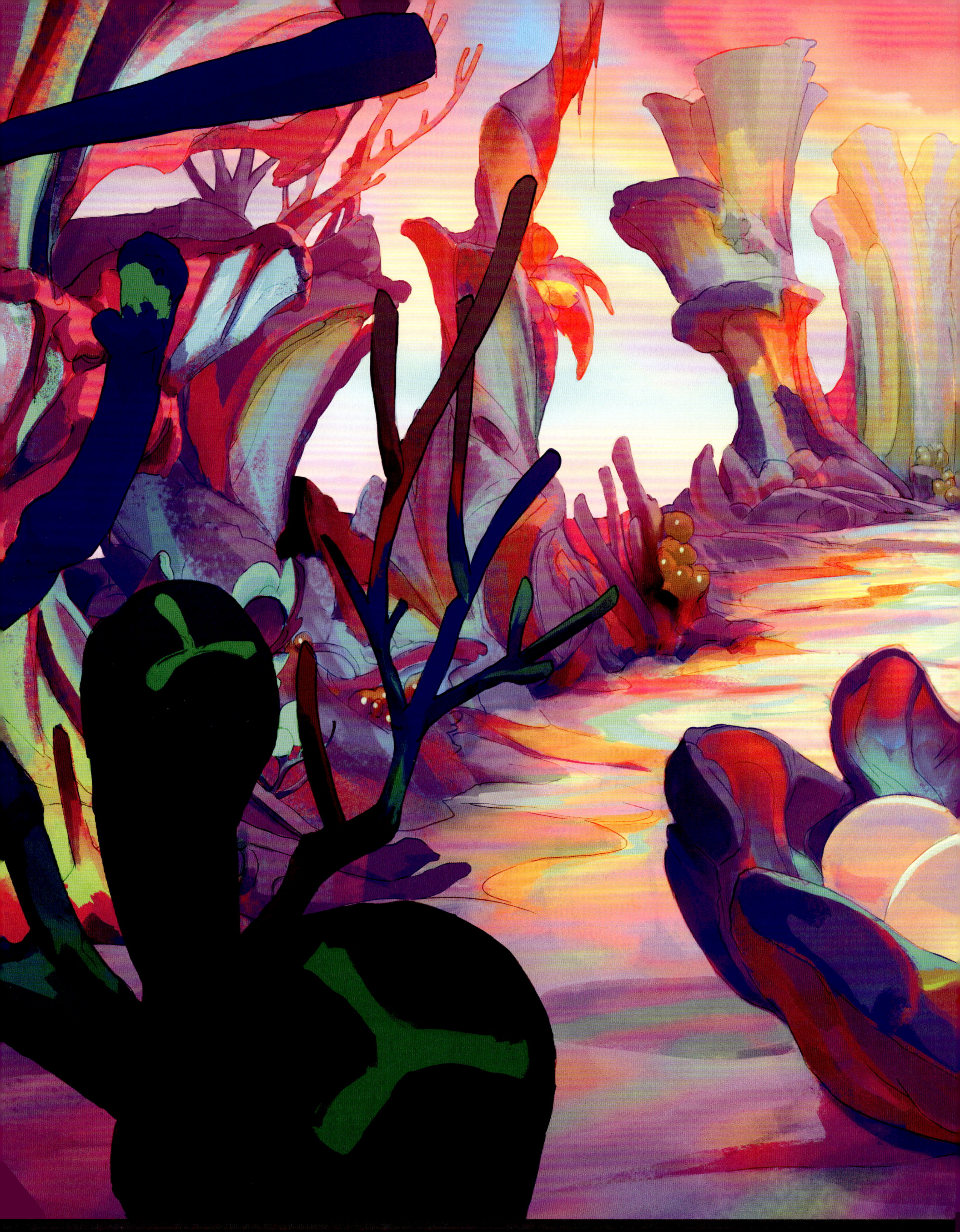

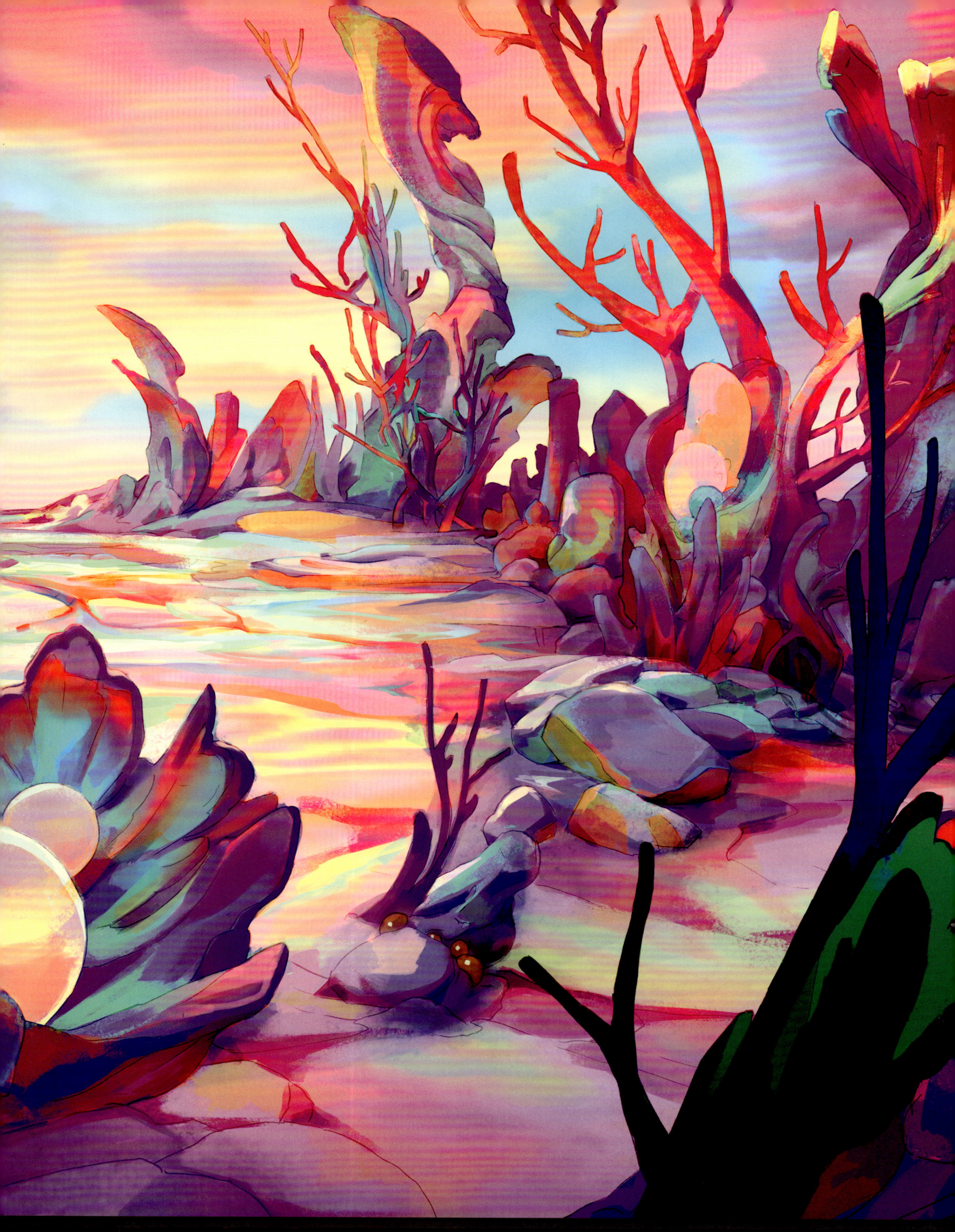

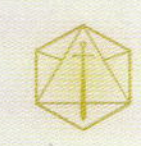

Visions from Vox Machina's Drug Trip in the Fey Realm

While the Fey Realm might be Percy's wet dream, a rogue encounter with mystical spores gives Keyleth and Vex psychedelic visions. Original ideas for this drug scene sequence included superimposing Laura Bailey and Marisha Ray's actual faces onto their characters. The test was deemed too disturbing to include in the final cut.

"It feels like a hangover without any of the fun." – VEX, S1E7 "THE FEY REALM"

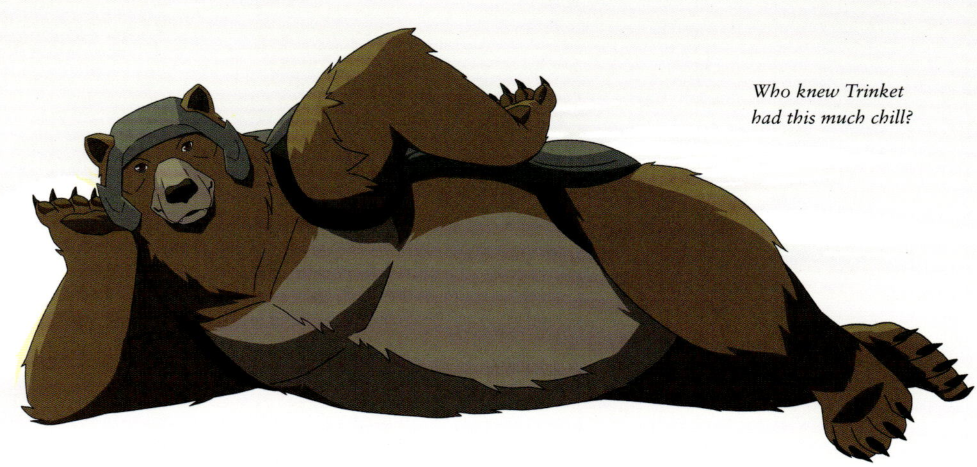

Who knew Trinket had this much chill?

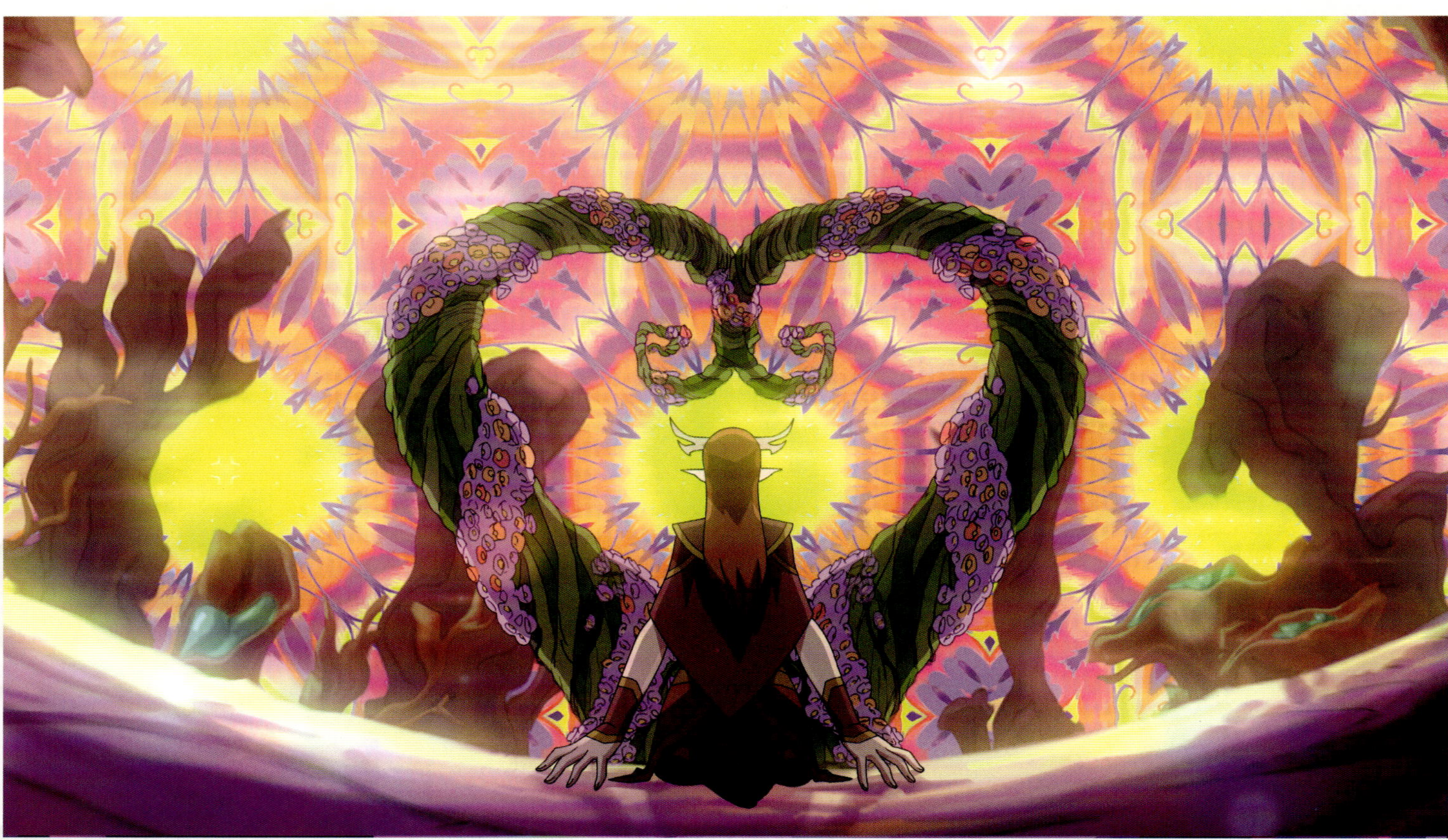

Garmelie's Notebook

Garmelie might be a bit of a dick, but he also draws them!

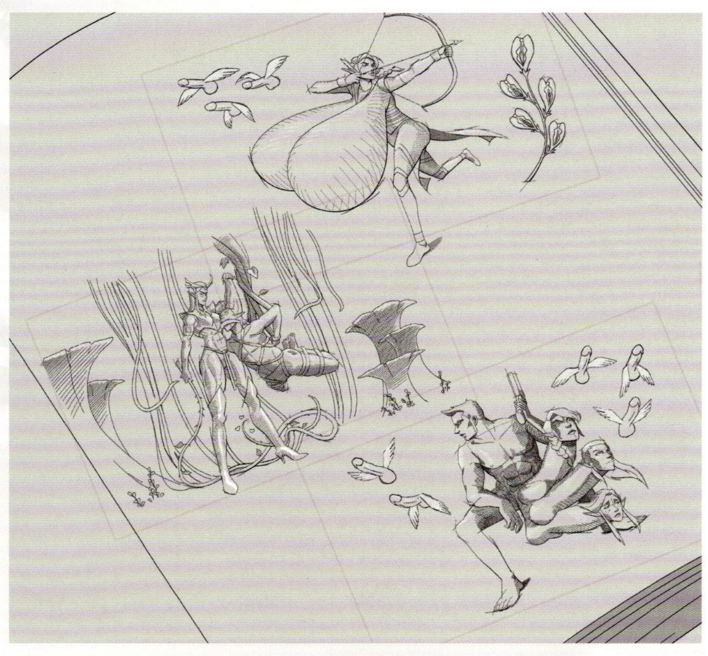

Diplomacy

Another weapon from our resident tinkerer Percy, the glove produces an electric shock when properly charged. Keyword is *properly*.

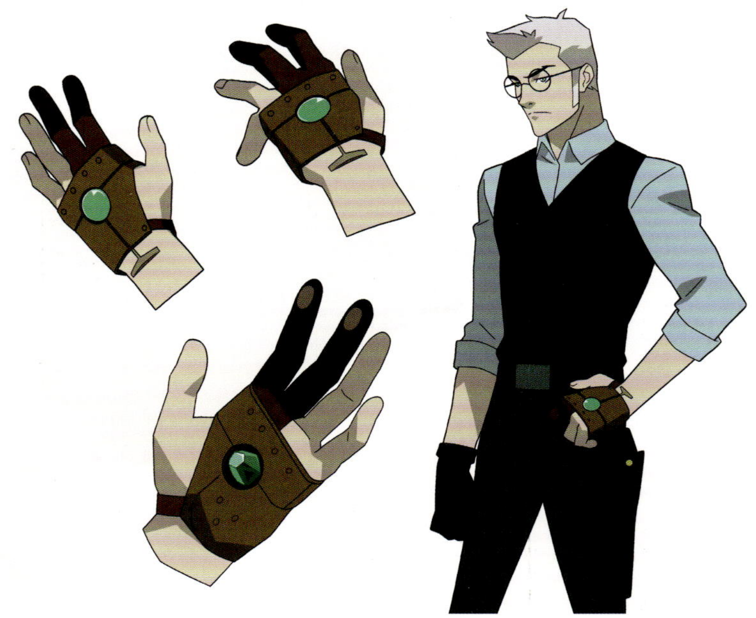

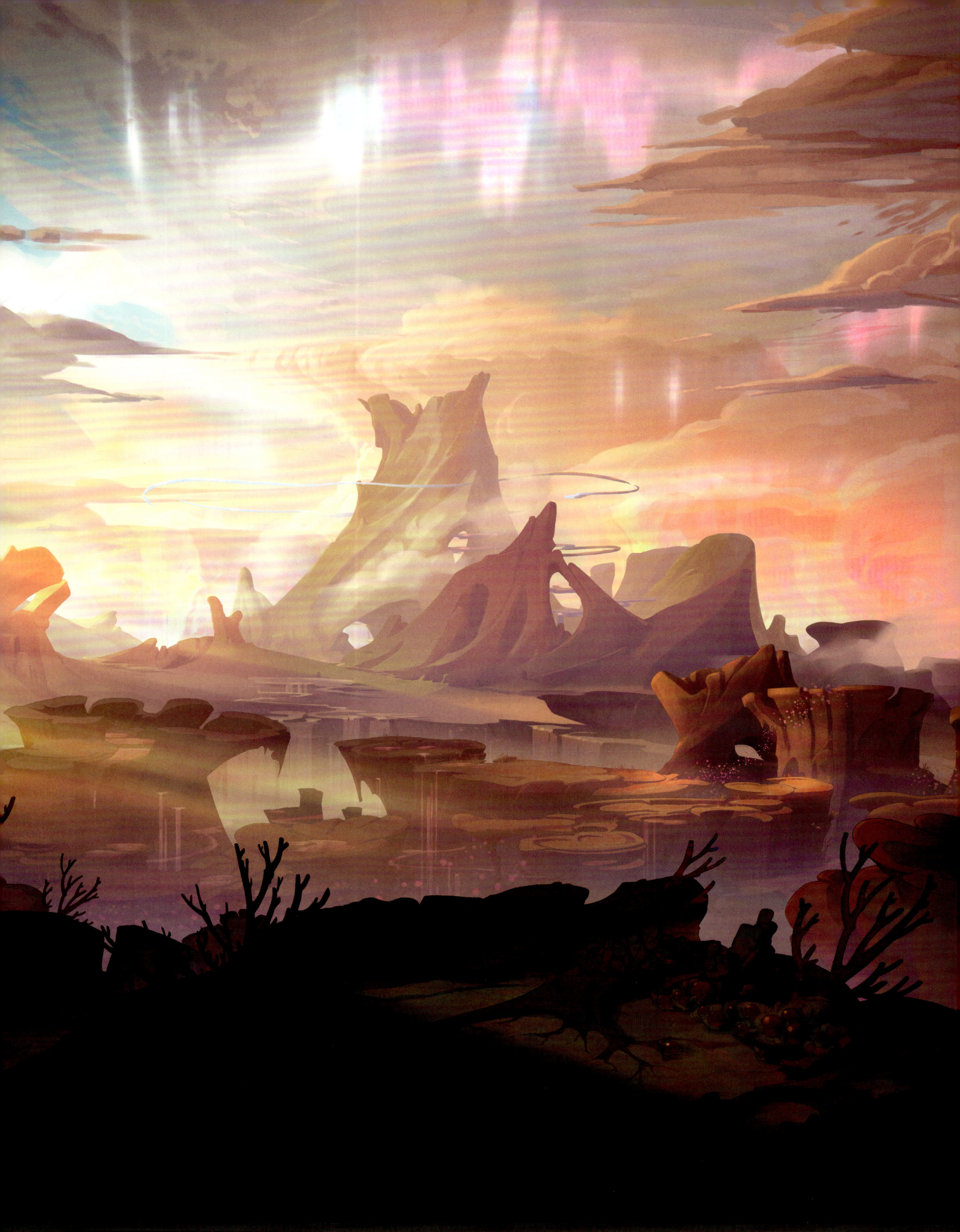

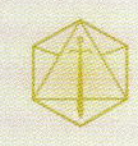

EPISODE 8

THE ECHO TREE

"Vex and Vax meet up with their deadbeat dad and teach everyone the meaning of 'awkward situation.' Then Percy grants Vex a title and begins the age-old tradition of giving meaningless promotions with no change in responsibilities or pay bump. I wasn't there, but I think they spend the rest of the episode cutting down a tree? Back with your boy Scanlan, Pike takes our relationship to the next level and introduces me to her granddad. I think it's getting serious!" – A RECOUNTING OF "ECHO TREE" BY SCANLAN SHORTHALT

Cameo of Brandon Auman (Series Showrunner)

"Nice melons."

Syldor

Scornful of Vax and Vex's human ancestry, Syldor's look needed to portray "elf" right off the bat. He also needed to convey an aristocratic air and an indignant vibe. Essentially, a prick.

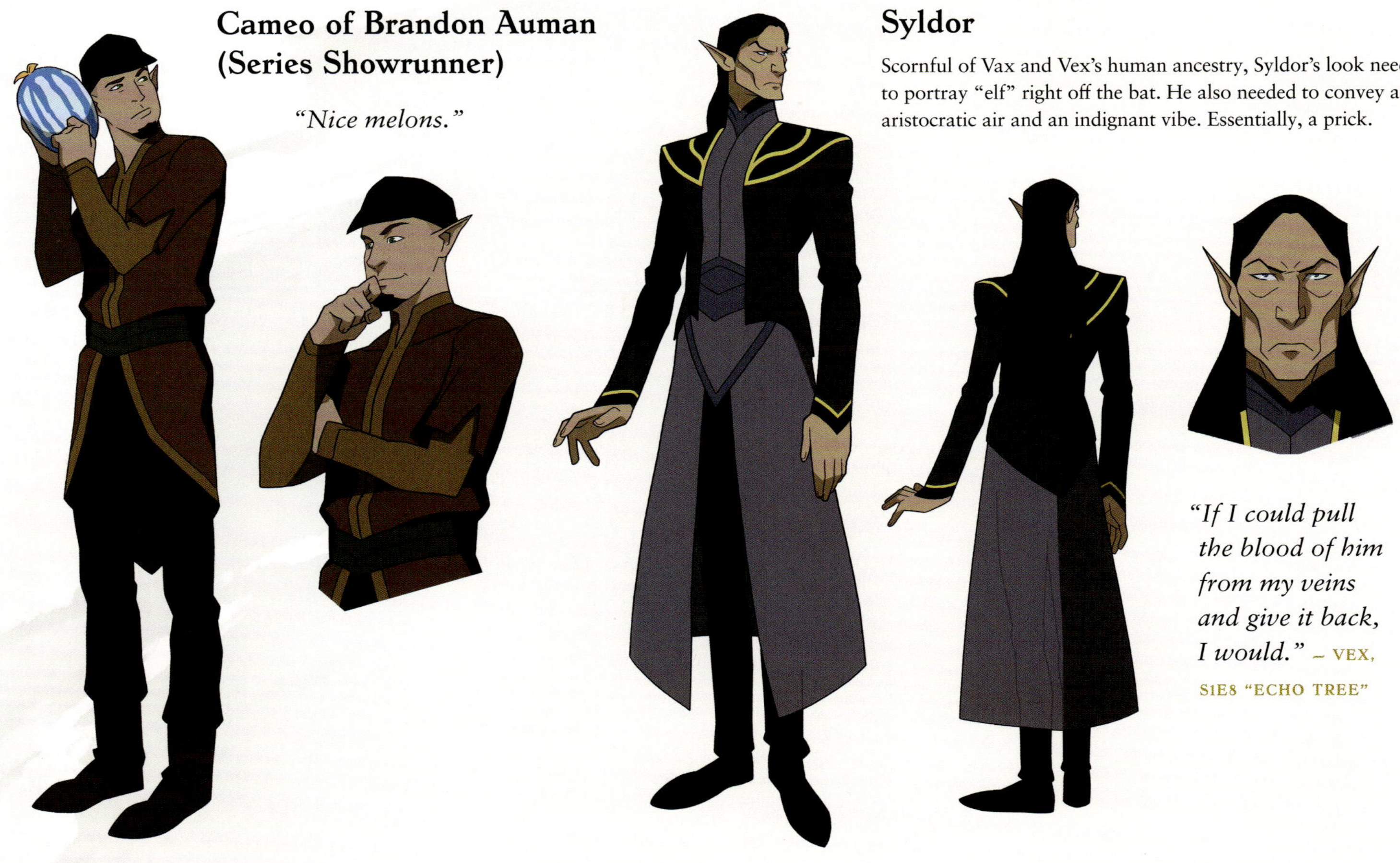

"If I could pull the blood of him from my veins and give it back, I would." – VEX, S1E8 "ECHO TREE"

Devana

Vex and Vax's stepmother.

Velora

Vex and Vax's half-sister.

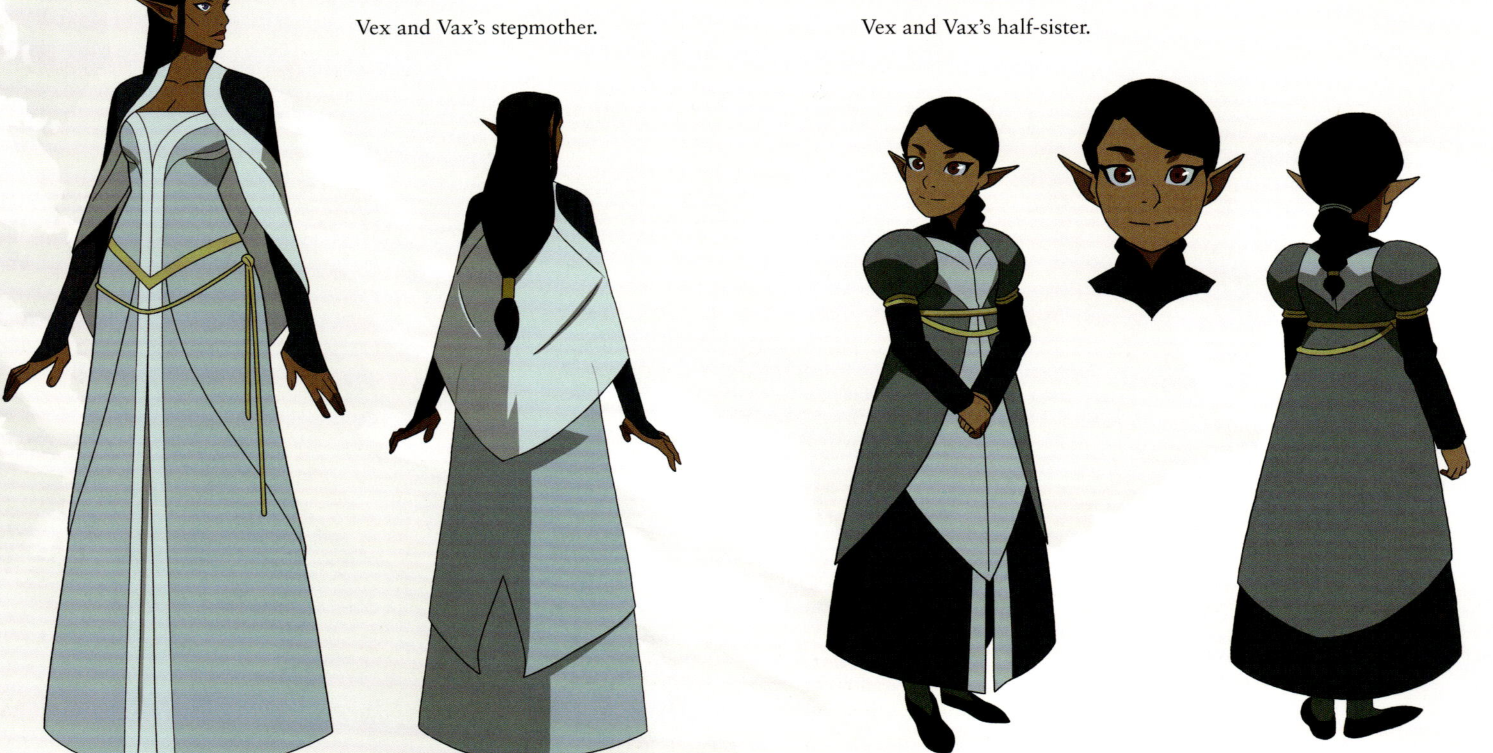

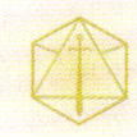

Wilhand Trickfoot

Pike's grandpappy who took in Grog after his exile from the herd. His look invokes the infectious *joie de vivre* that passes on to everyone he meets.

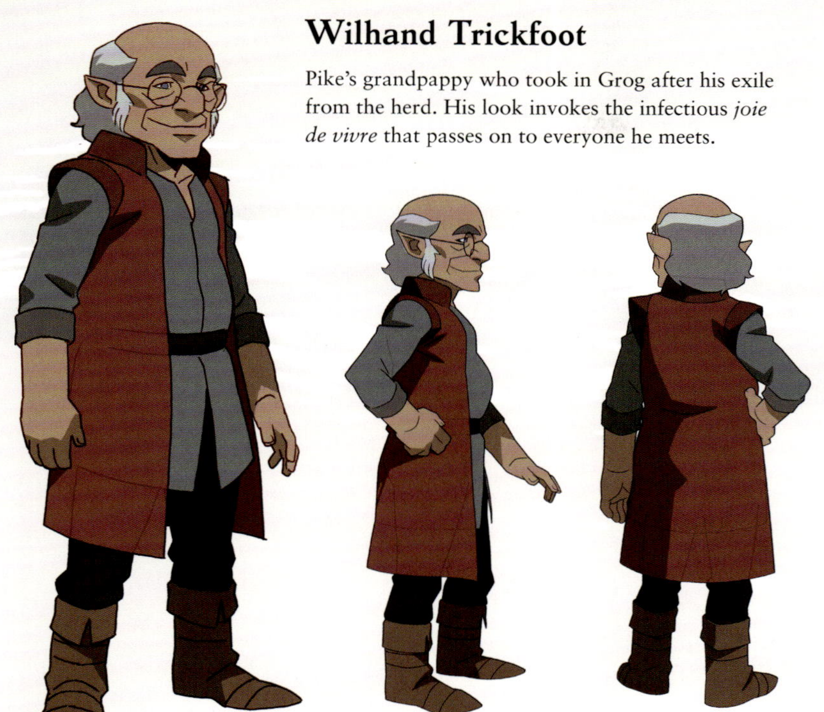

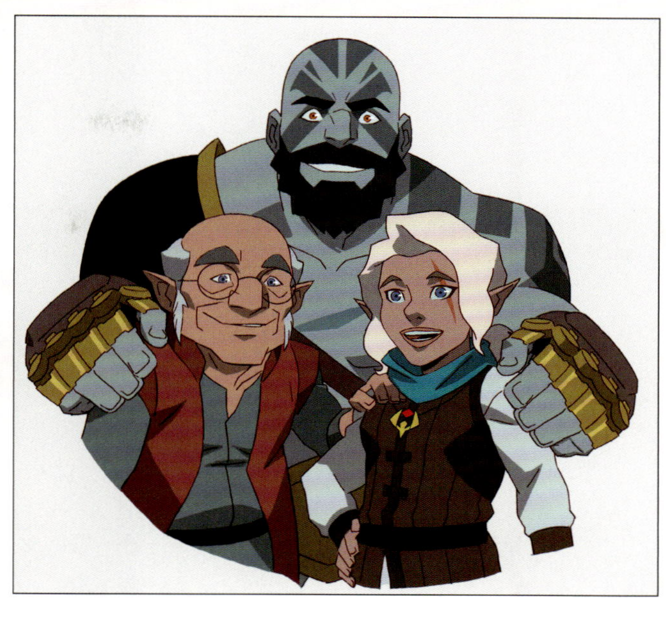

"Violence was all that mattered to us. I took anything I wanted without a second thought. Nothing and no one could stop me. Until the day I met him." – GROG, S1E9 "A TEST OF PRIDE"

Saundor

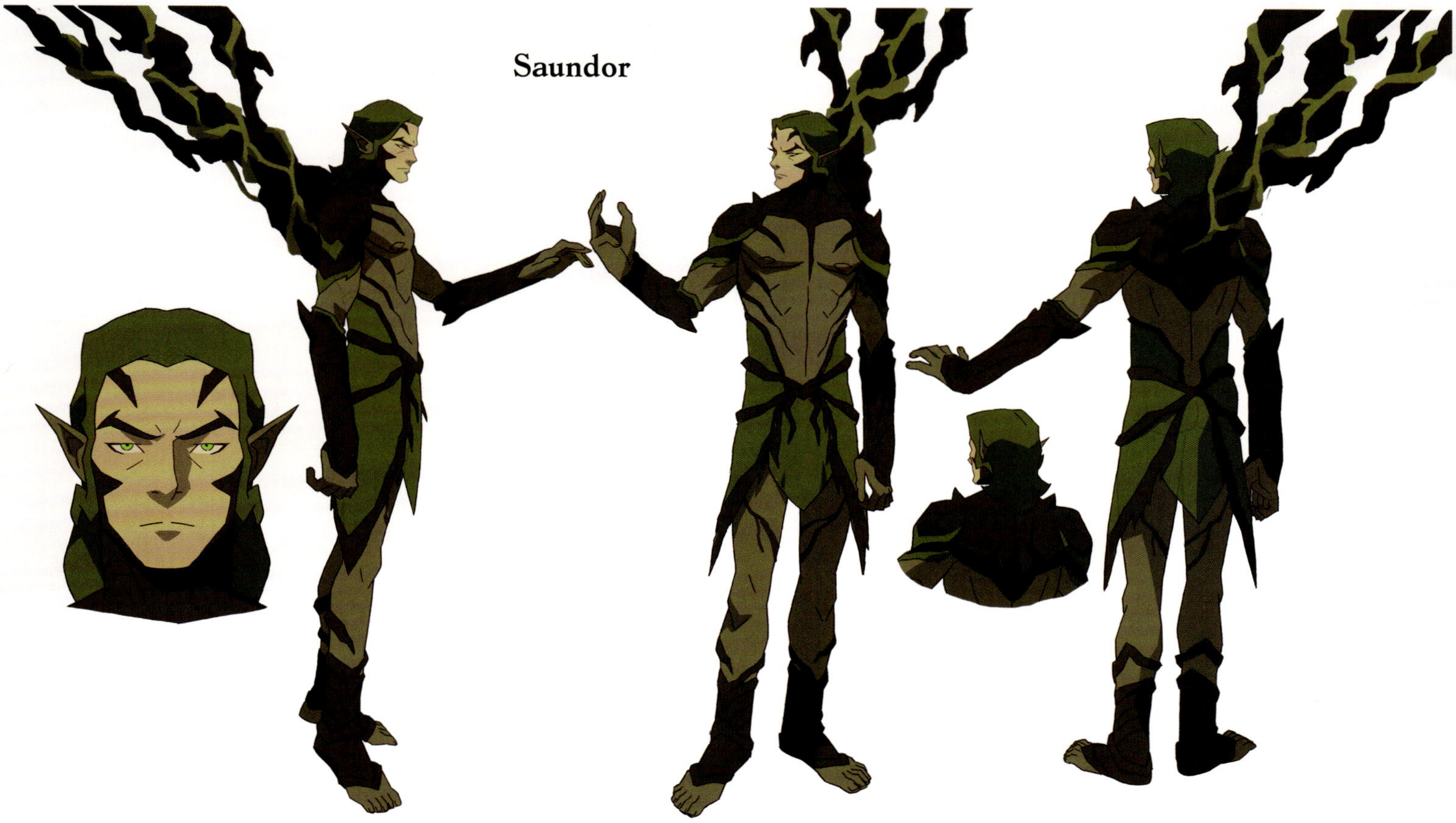

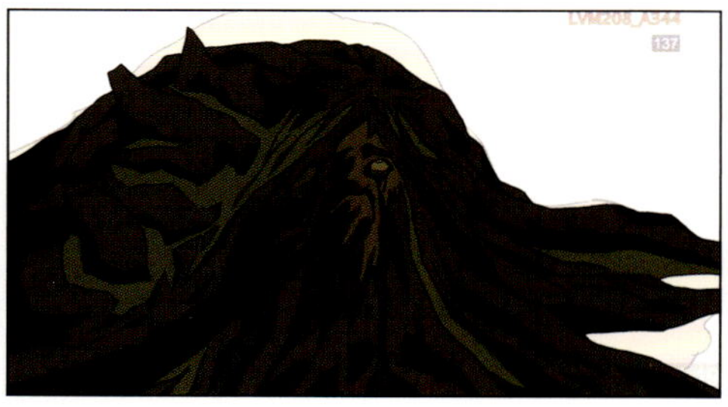

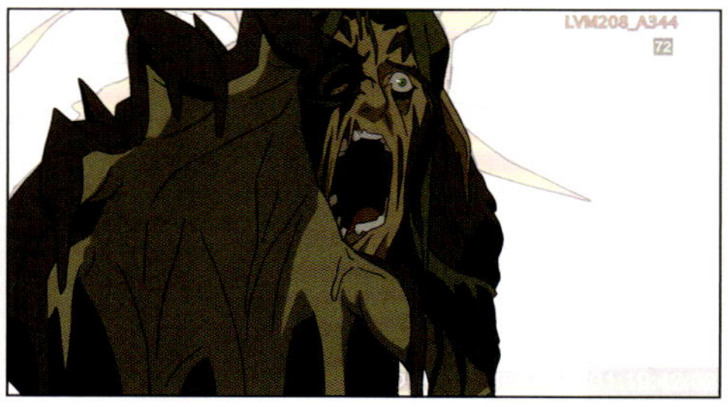

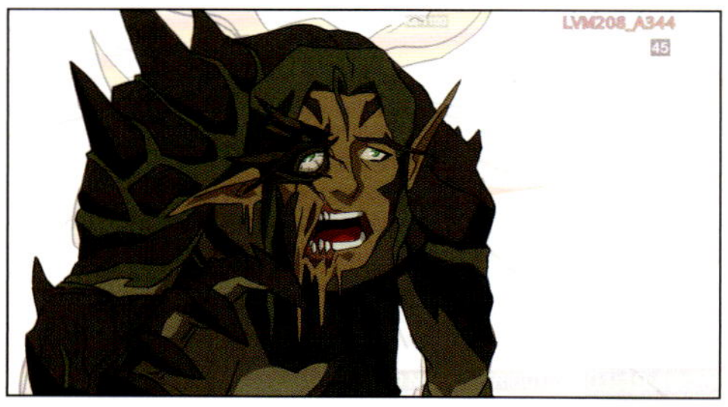

Having been betrayed by the woman he loved, corruption took over Saundor's heart. That corruption spread throughout the land surrounding his arboreal prison. His design needed to be appealing enough to be an enticing option for Vex while still remaining a sinister foe.

The storyboard and design team were challenged by Saundor's mobility during his confrontation with Vex. They opted to give him a vine-like suspension from his back for freer movement while also giving him the appearance of being shackled to the trees.

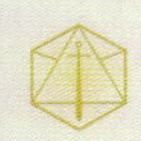

Syngorn

Originally in Tal'Dorei, the city of Syngorn transported itself to the Fey Realm for safety when the Chroma Conclave attacked. The magical walls that enclose the city are dotted with massive threshold crests that enable the teleportation magic. It's a city that celebrates nature, so all of the architecture blends the line between dwelling and tree as if the buildings were magically formed from a forest. Elves are not the dominant species in this world, so Syngorn is a vestige of former elven glory.

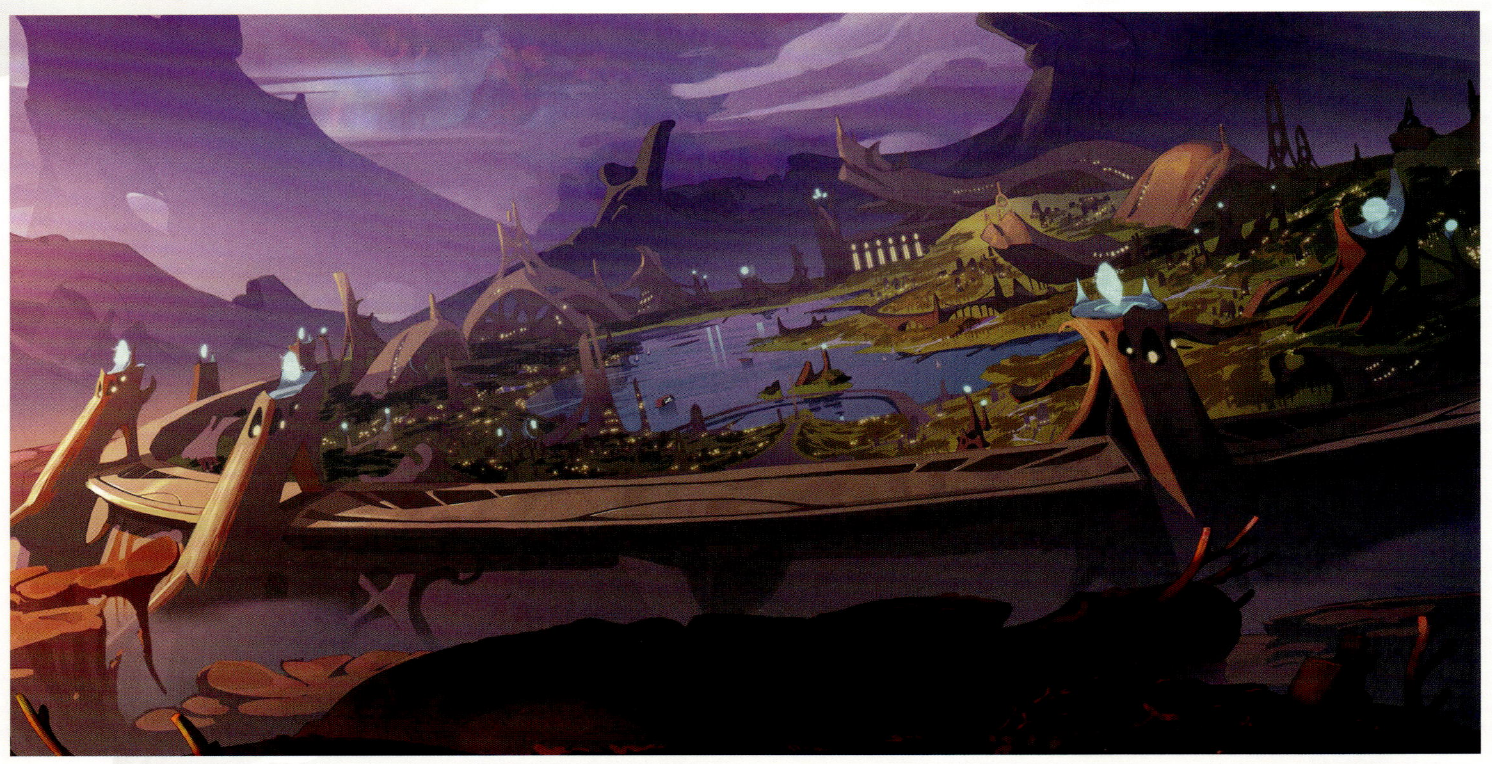

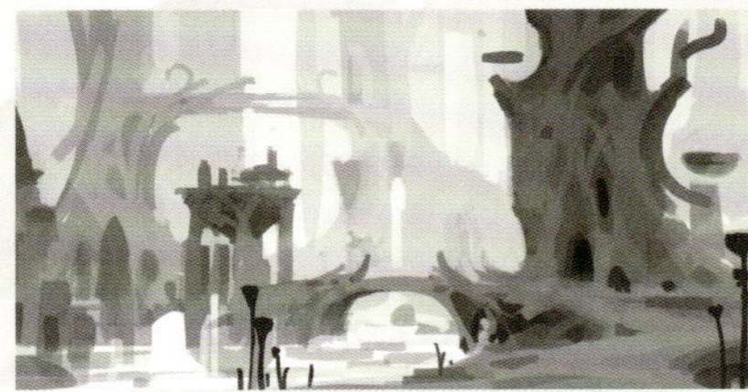

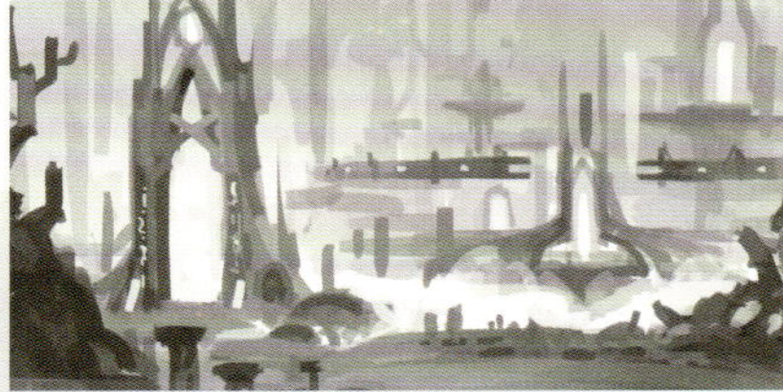

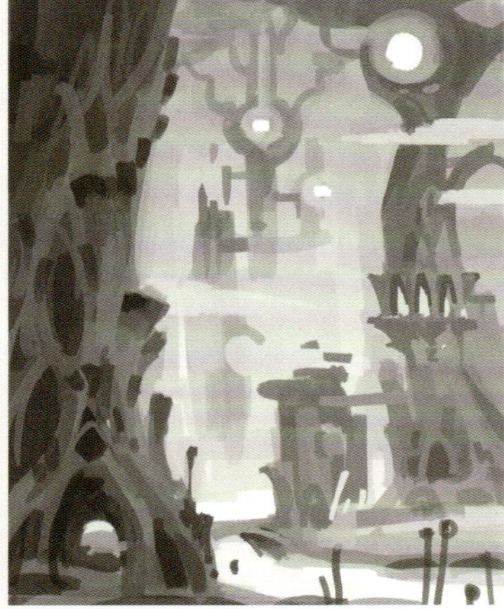

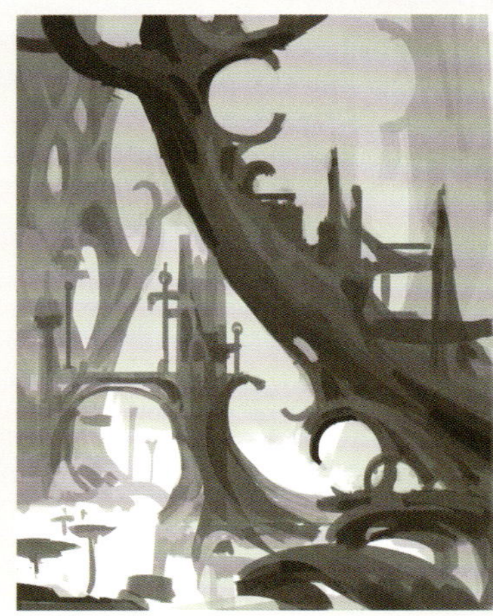

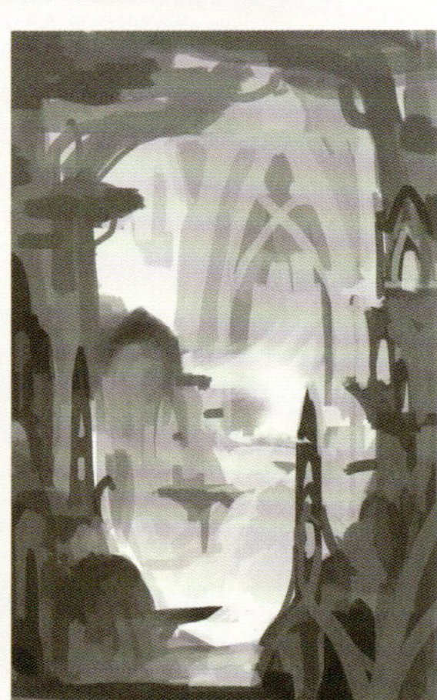

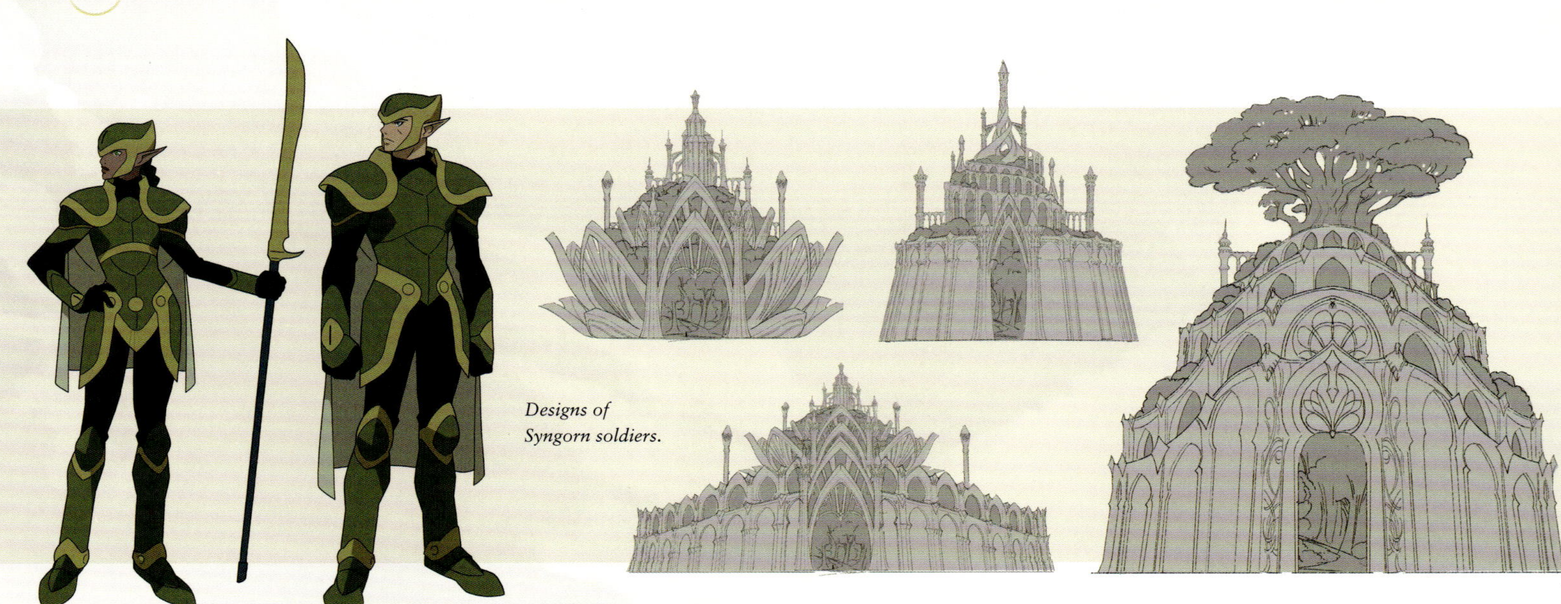

Designs of Syngorn soldiers.

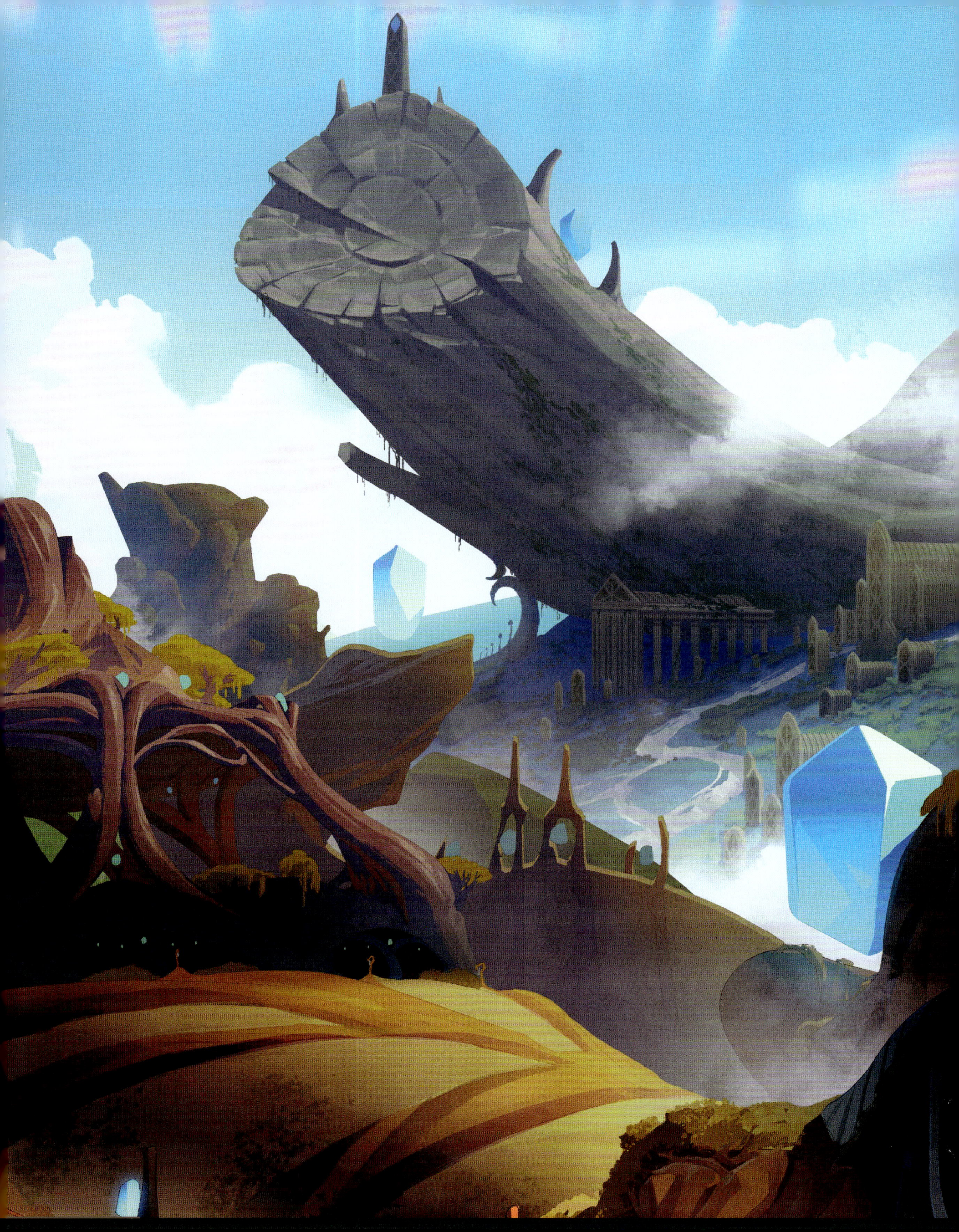

"We created Syldor's house as a testament to his own ego. The foyer puts any visitor below a raised balcony that he can beckon them from. The study is an entire wing of the house, filled to the brim with his books. The window that he smokes by encompasses an entire wall. How anyone puts up with this guy is a mystery."

— ARTHUR LOFTIS

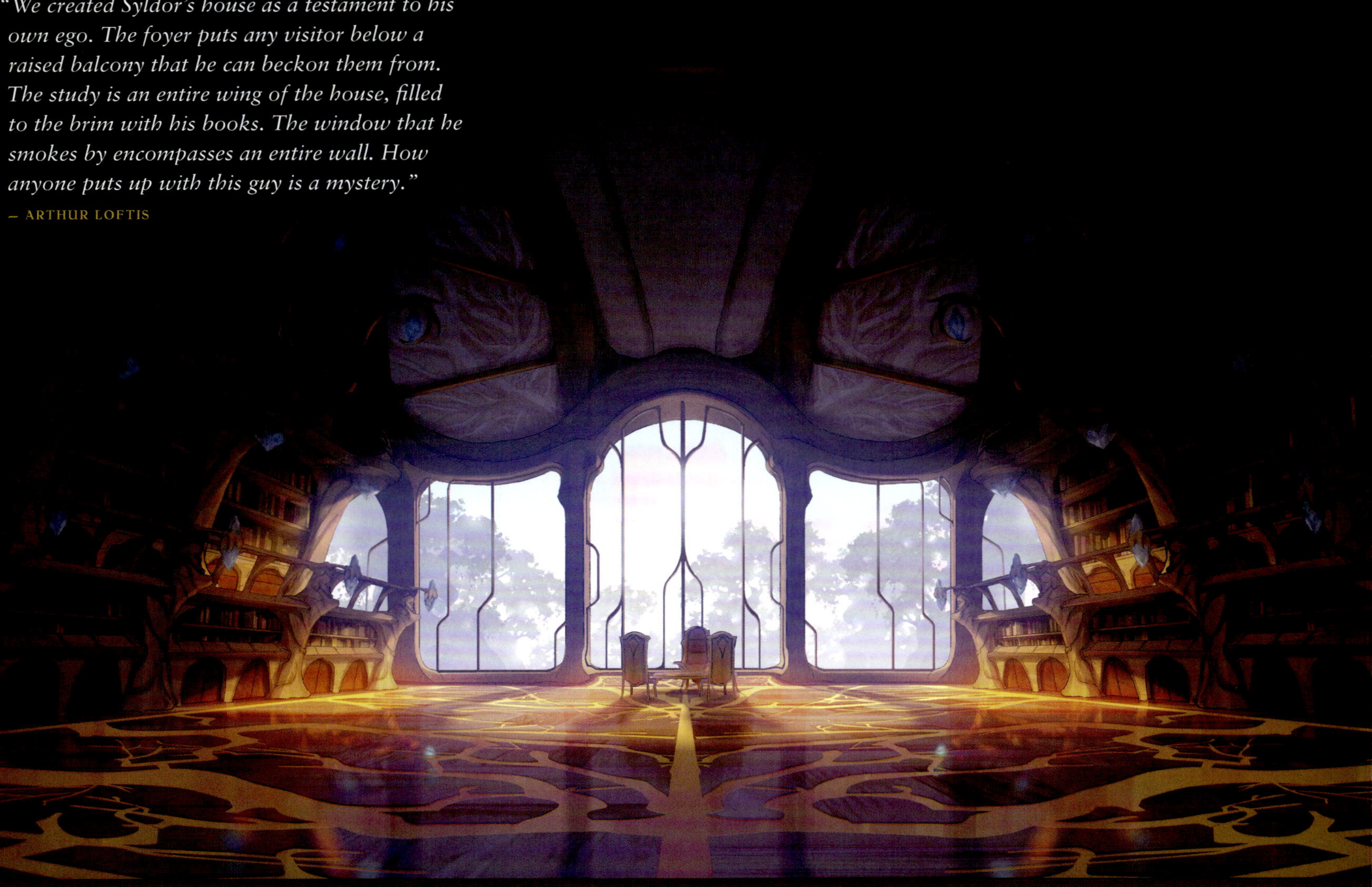

Syldor's Chateau

Syldor's Chateau was inspired by a roman basilica with an Art Nouveau style. Organic line work with tree imagery is present in the carvings seen on the floors and walls.

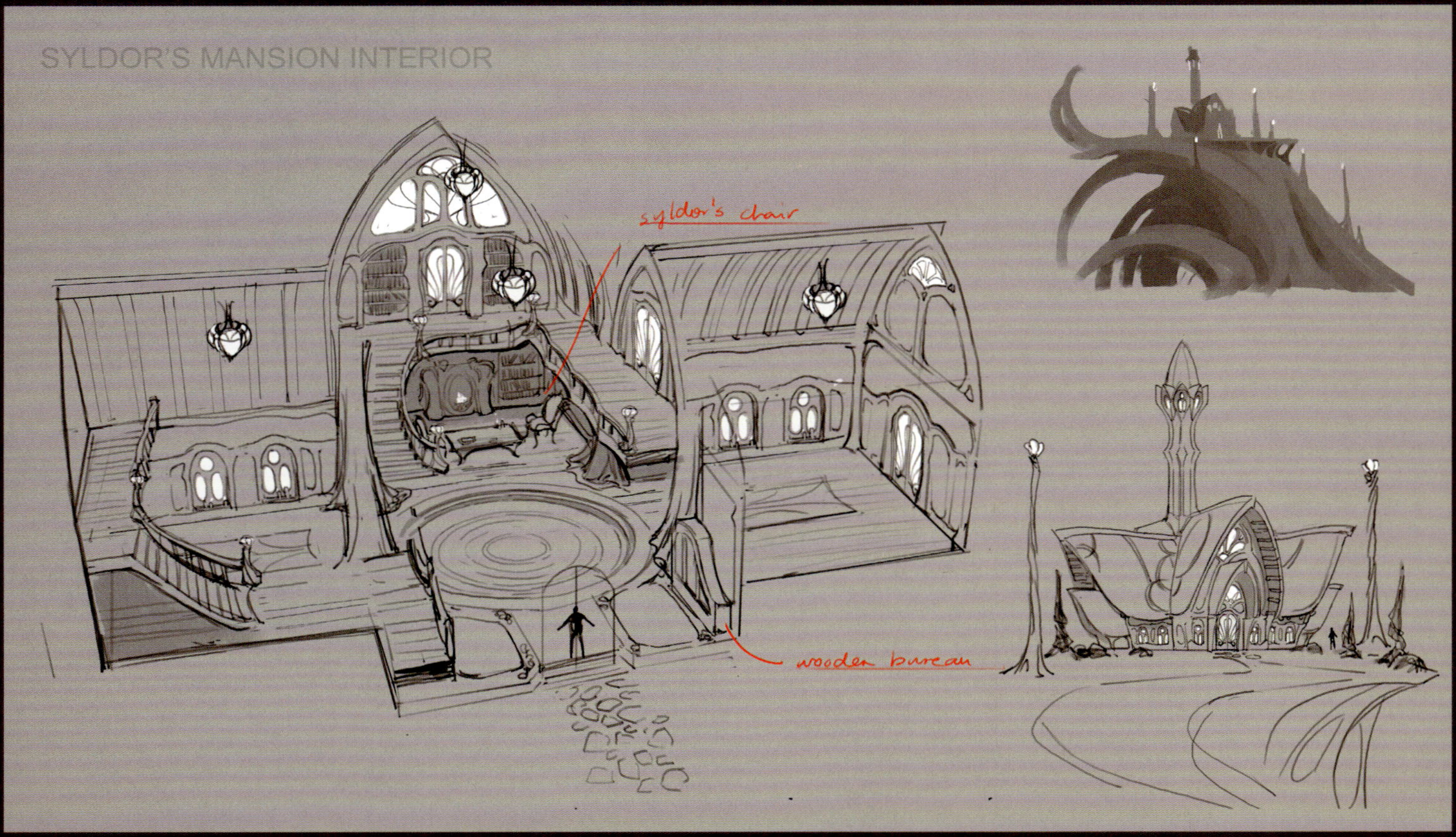

SYLDOR'S MANSION INTERIOR

syldor's chair

wooden bureau

Interior sketches of Syldor's home.

Shademurk Bog

Poisoned by Saundor's corruption, the Shademurk's environment is meant to evoke tar or oil pollution.

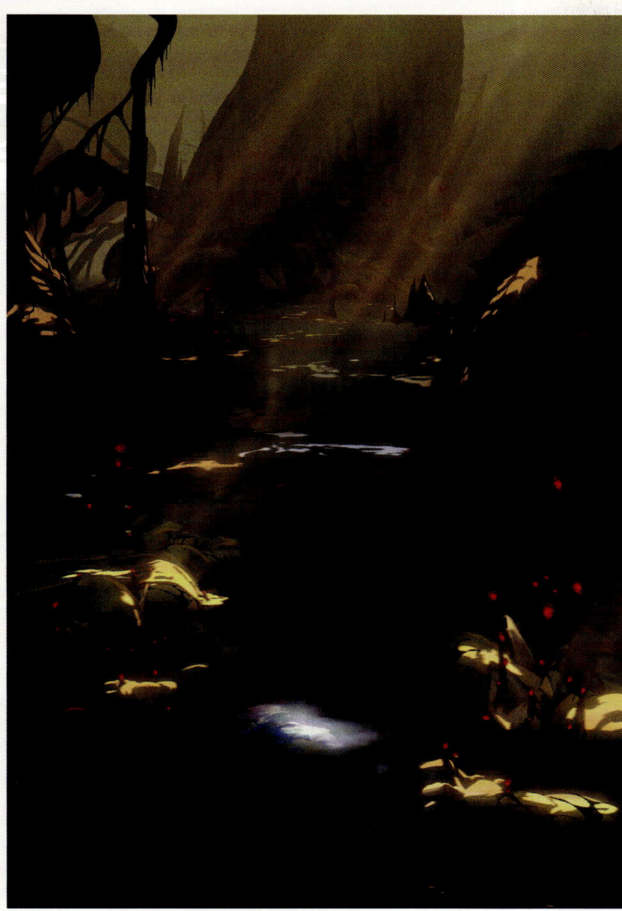

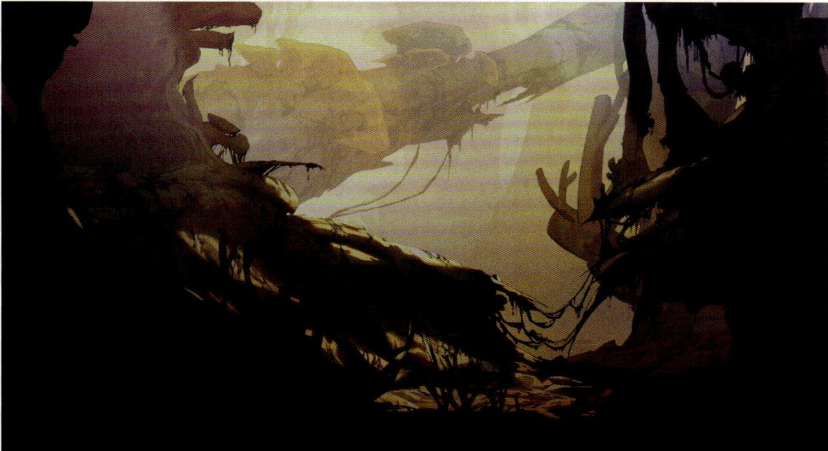

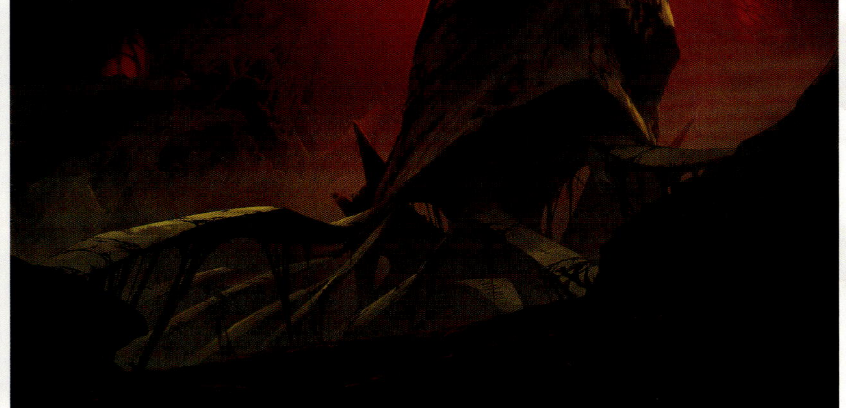

Wilhand Trickfoot's Cottage

Home of Pike's grandpappy, Wilhand Trickfoot. He lives a modest life in his charming woodland cottage.

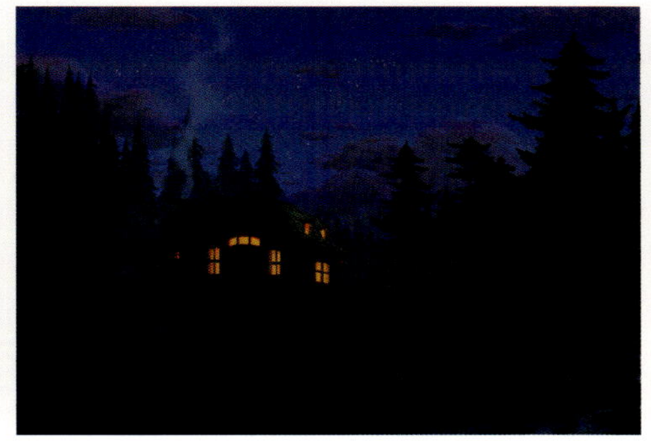

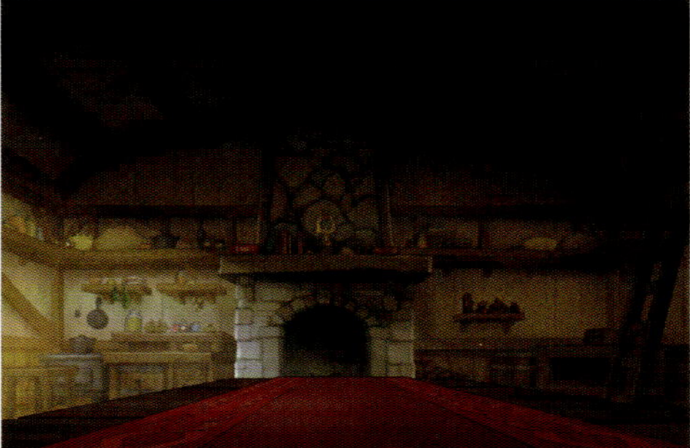

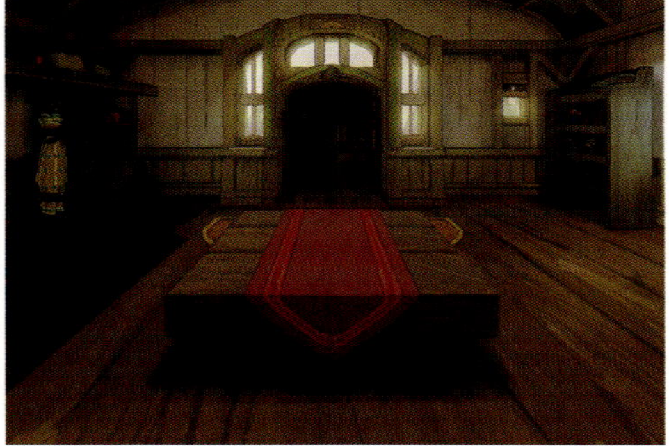

Fenthras Bow

A powerful relic rumored to fire arrows strong enough to wound a Titan. The elven name "Fenthras" has its roots in the ancient Elvish words for "protector" and "growth." It is a living weapon with the ability to shoot a variety of different elemental-based attacks.

Concept art of the Fenthras Bow–Artist Arthur Tang created several options for the bow, all intended to showcase the bow's organic nature.

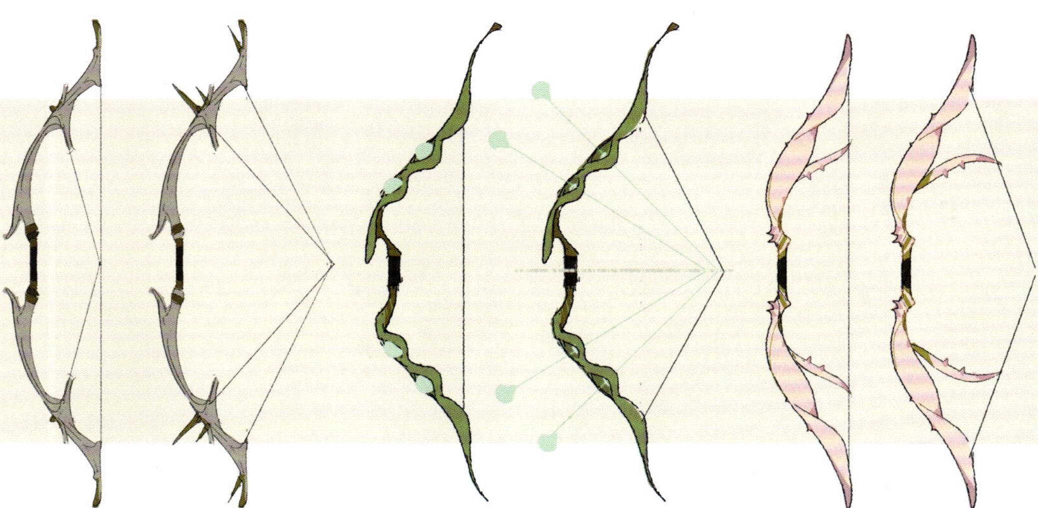

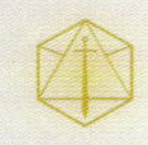

EPISODE 9 & 10

A TEST OF PRIDE AND KILLBOX

"After a fun trauma dump by Grog, he gets a second chance to face off against his childhood abuser, Uncle Kevdak. Just when we think history might be repeating itself, the stage is set for Percy, Keyleth, Vex, and Vax to arrive JUST IN THE NICK OF TIME and kick all y'all's asses. For an encore, we get the plot twist of a lifetime and learn that I, Scanlan Shorthalt, am a daddy (and not in a fun, sexy way!)" – A RECOUNTING OF "A TEST OF PRIDE" AND "KILLBOX" BY SCANLAN SHORTHALT

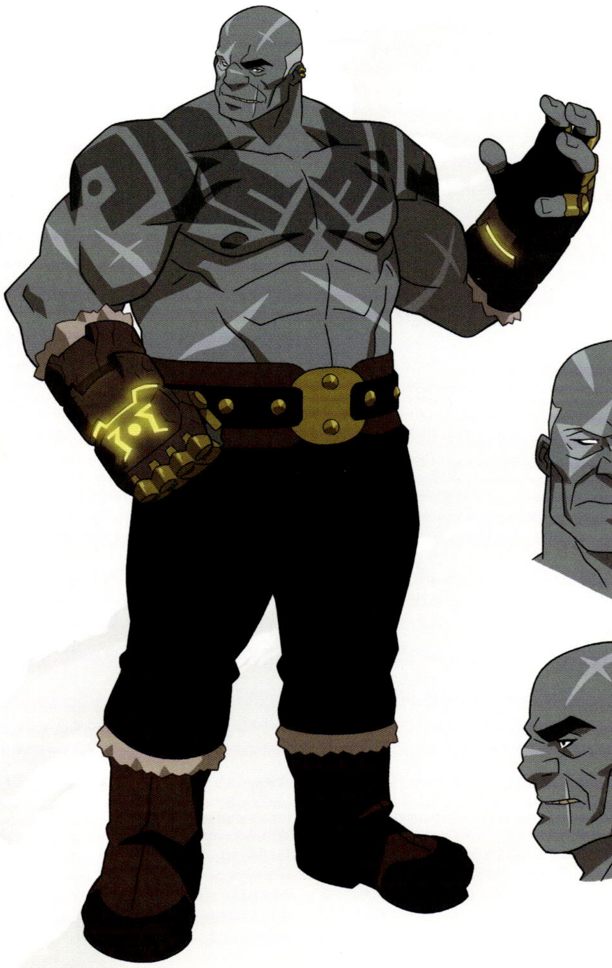

Kevdak

Grog's uncle–leader of The Herd of Storms.

Bourassa didn't want his design to be too evocative of a native hunter or a warrior as that would feel too similar to Grog. Travis Willingham (Grog) and Matt Mercer steered the artists toward a more "apocalyptic warlord gone mad" look for the final design.

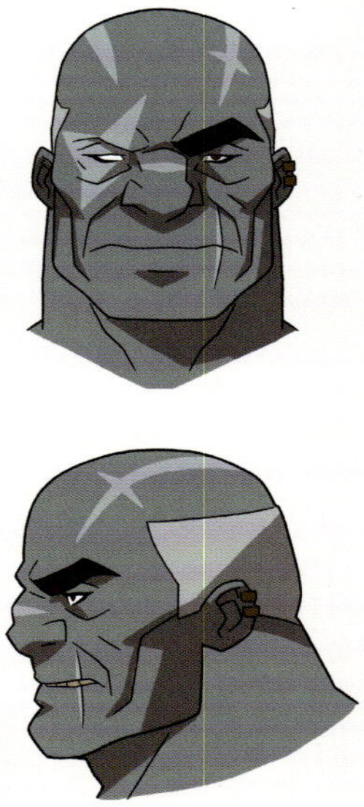

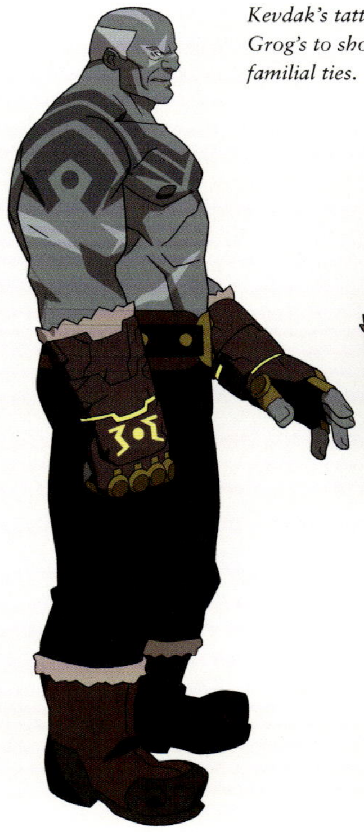

Kevdak's tattoos mirror Grog's to show their familial ties.

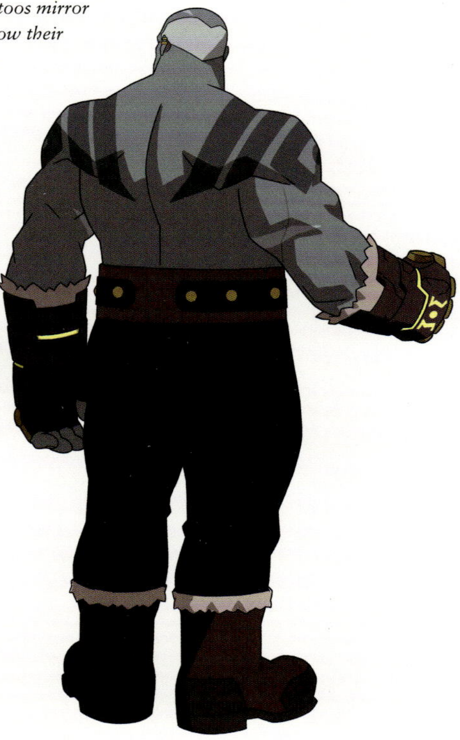

Titanstone Knuckles

A Vestige of Divergence owned by Grog's ruthless Uncle Kevdak. They grant the wearer enormous size and strength during battle.

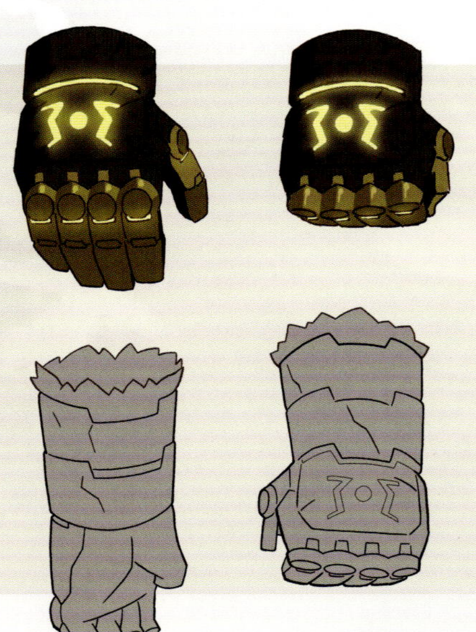

Kevdak's Bloodaxe

Soon to be Grog's bloodaxe. Finders keepers!

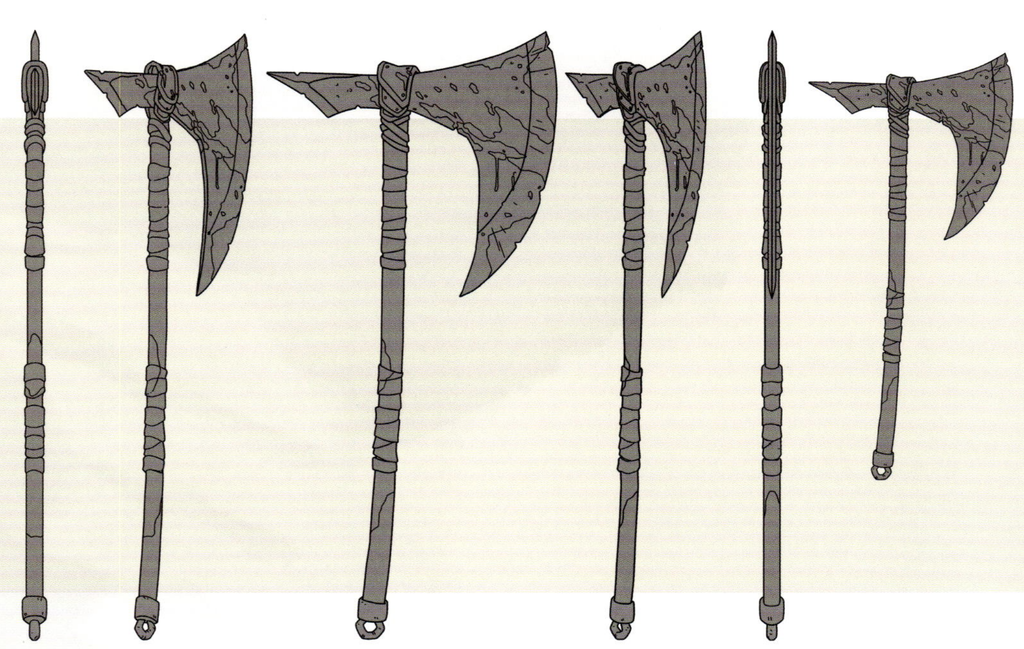

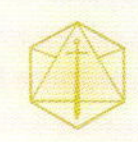

Zanror

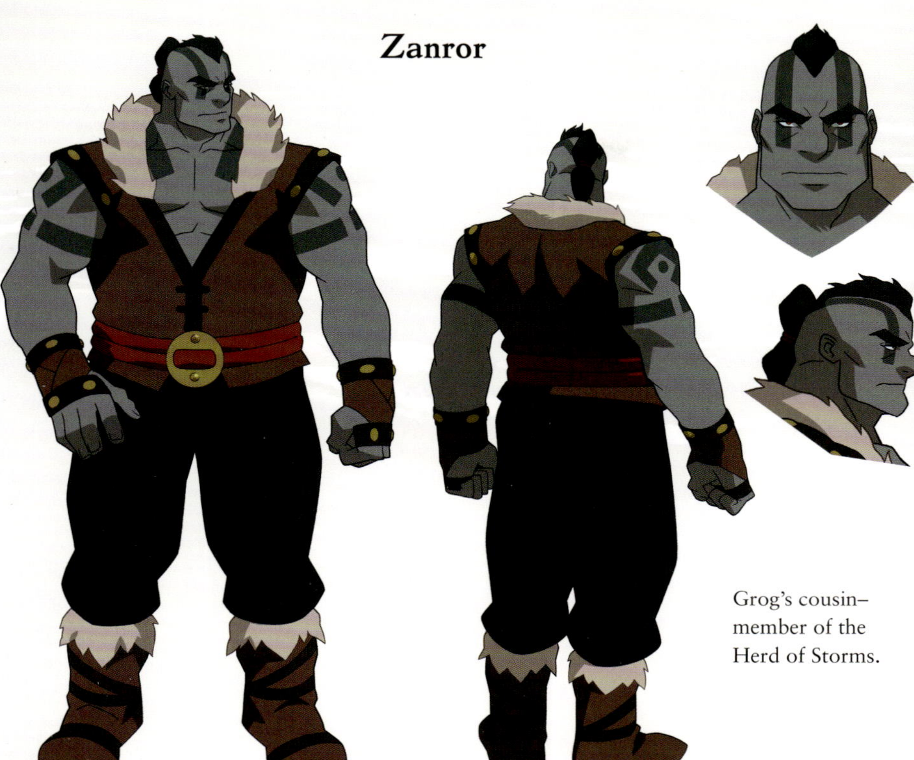

Grog's cousin–member of the Herd of Storms.

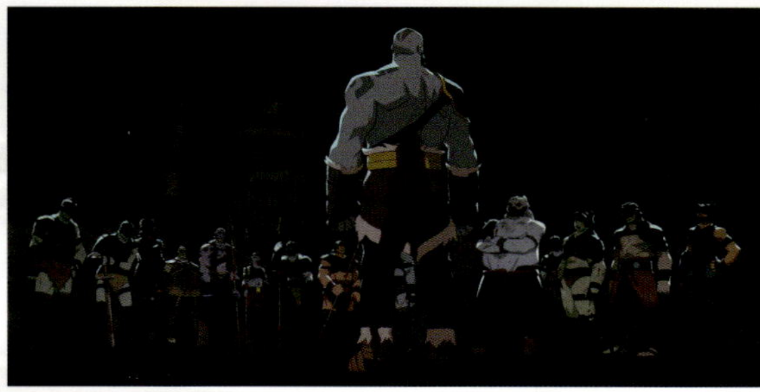

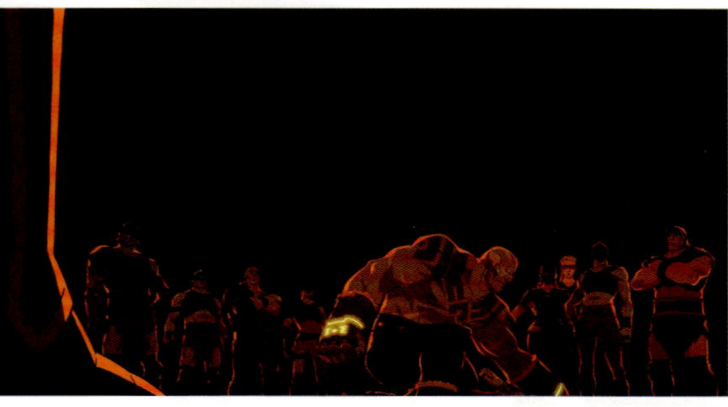

Images laying out the lighting design during Grog and Kevdak's final battle.

Members of the Herd of Storms

The Herd of Storms is a band of nomadic warriors and bandits that wander through Tal'Dorei, raiding villages and leaving a wake of destruction. The challenge with the herd lineup was to include as much variety as possible while still having unifying elements to show they are part of the same tribe. To streamline animation, Phil Bourassa developed a modular design kit with various body sections to mix and match together.

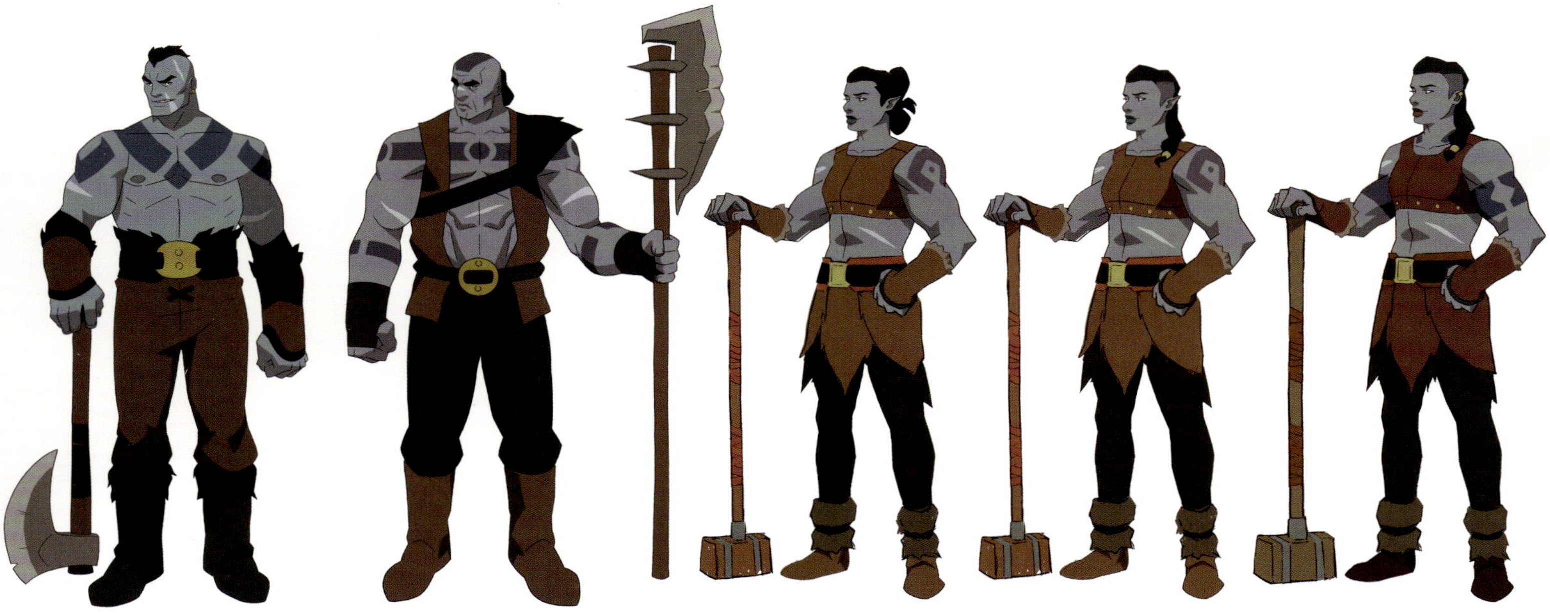

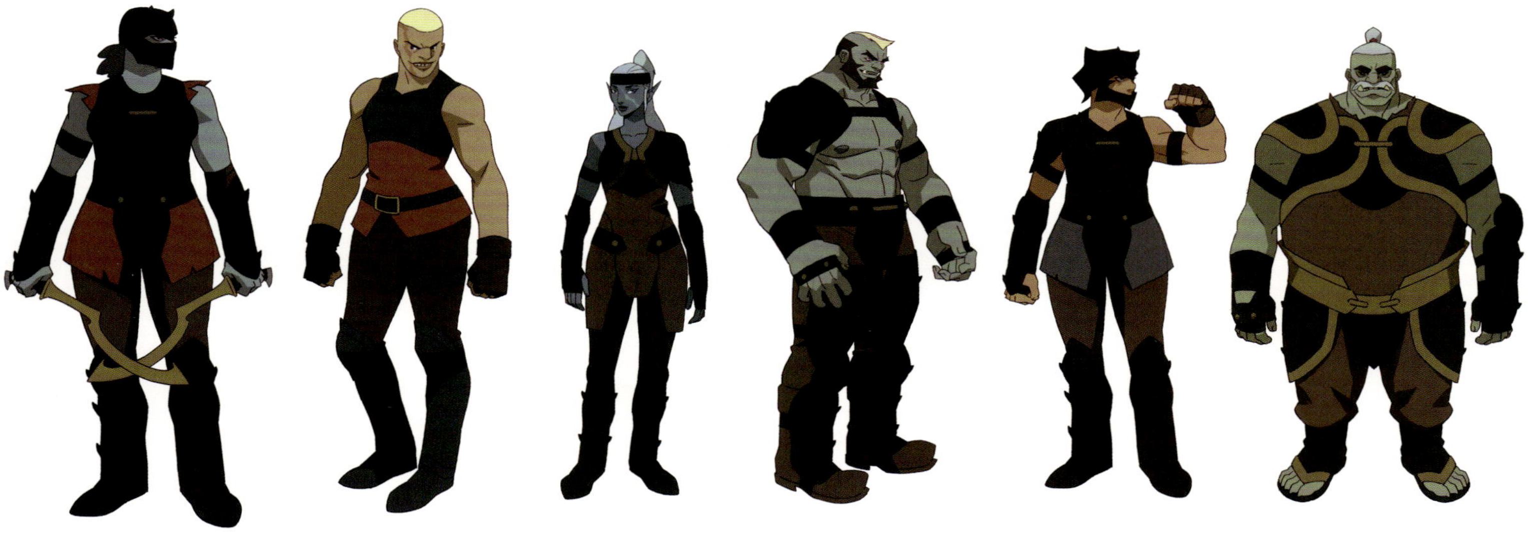

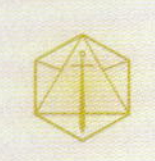
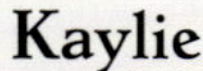

Kaylie

She's got spunk and sass built up over a lifetime of fending for herself.

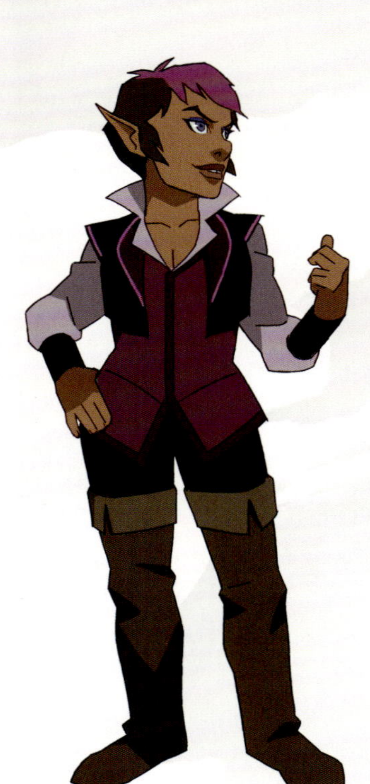
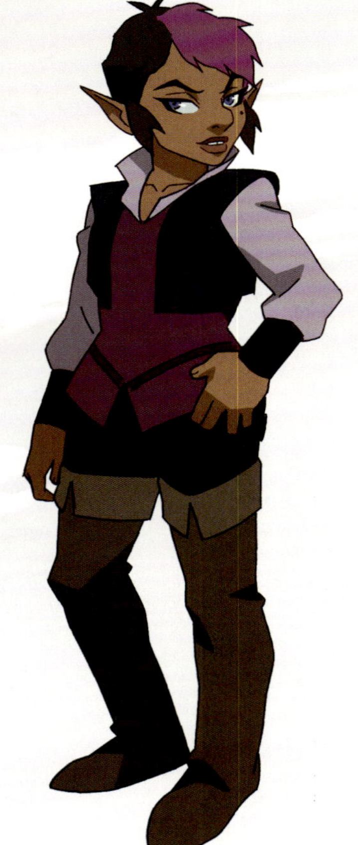

Scanlan a.k.a. "Daddy"

Everyone owns monogrammed underwear, don't they?

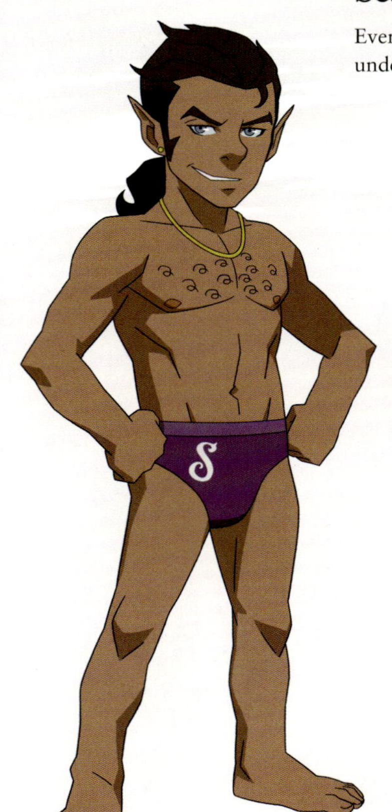
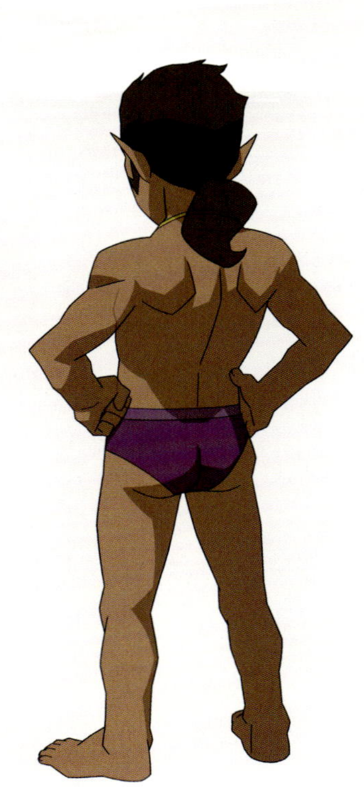

Dr. Dranzel and His Traveling Troupe

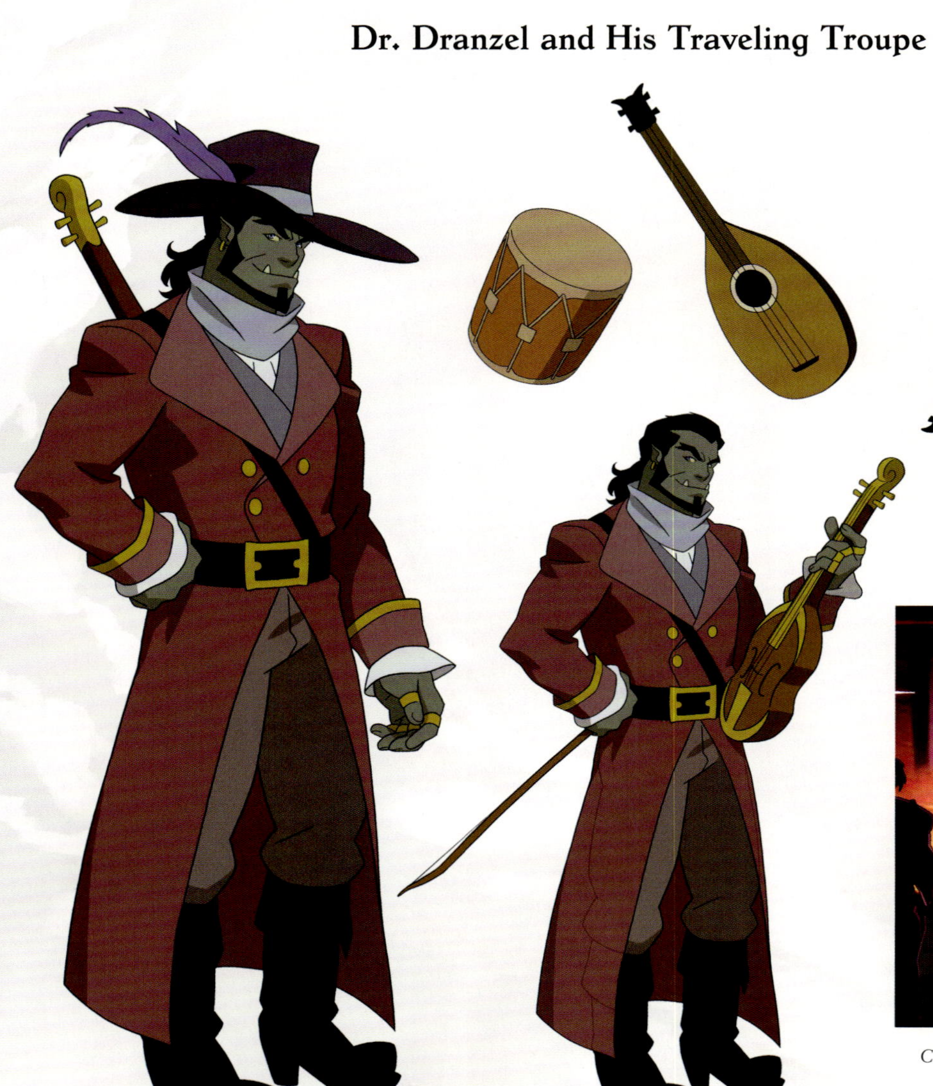
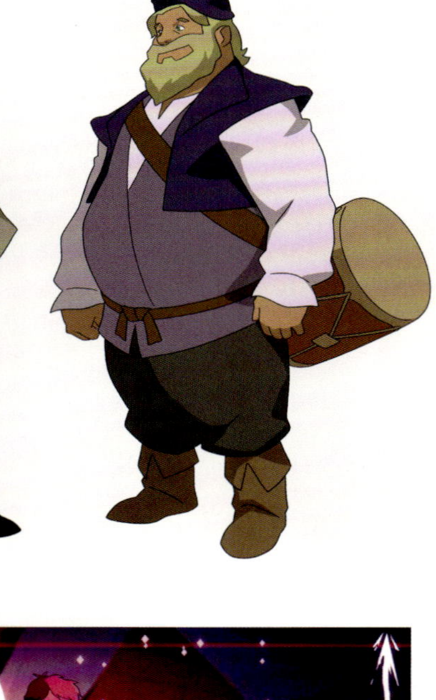
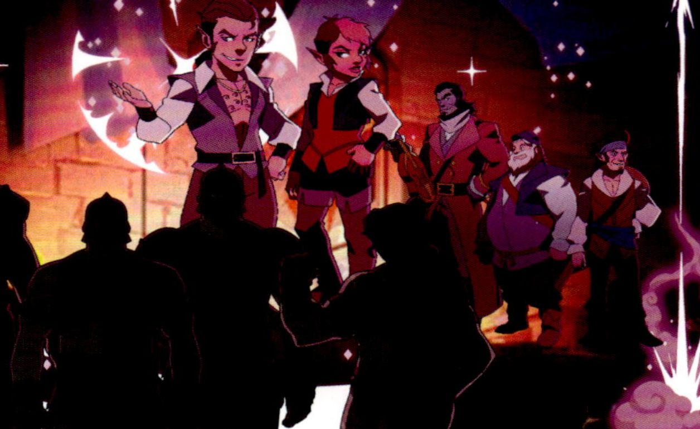

Composition of Scanlan and Kaylie's performance along with magical effects.

Westruun

Whenever a large city appears in the series, chances are a 3D model has been built out as a foundation to guide the board artists and animation teams. This allows shots to be easily choreographed and composed. Modelers used Matt Mercer's notes and maps as reference when planning the city.

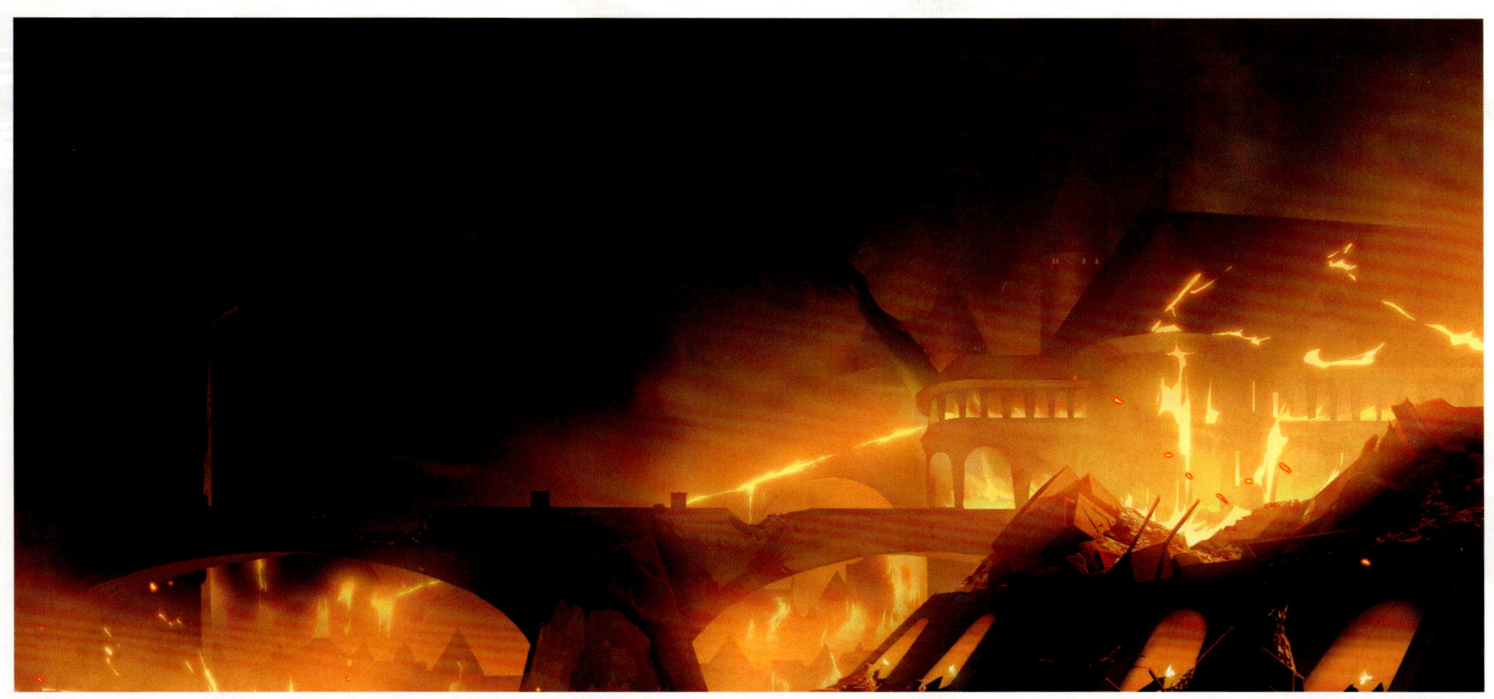

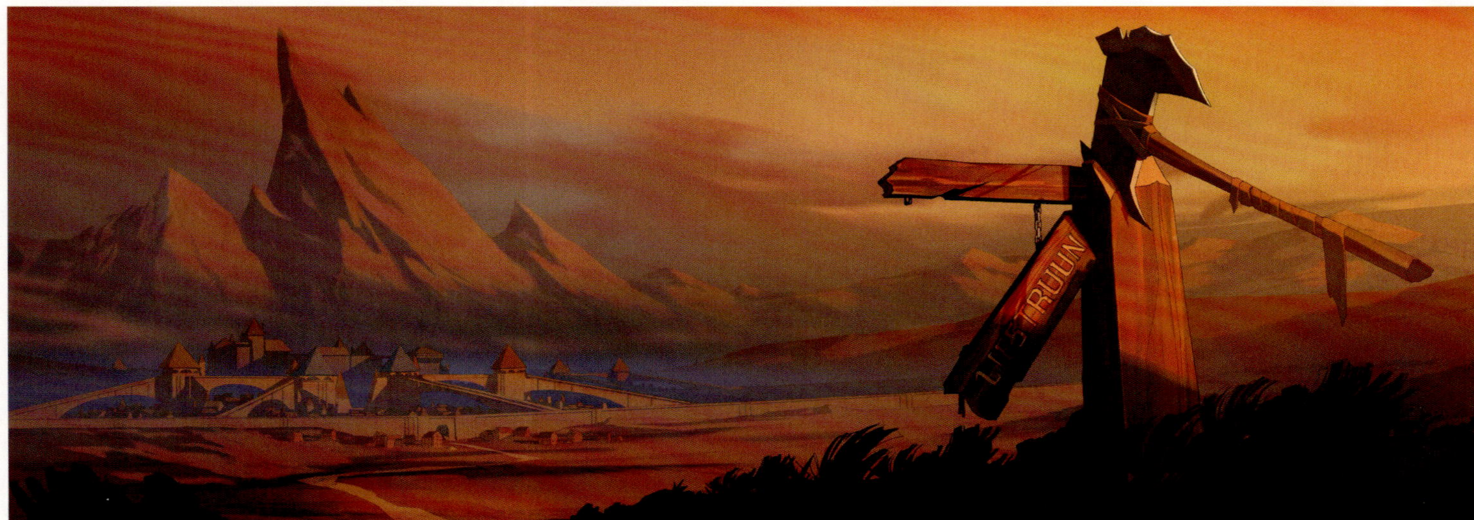

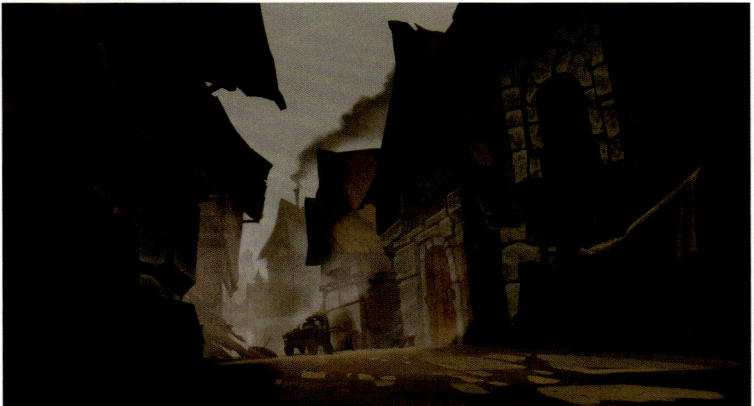

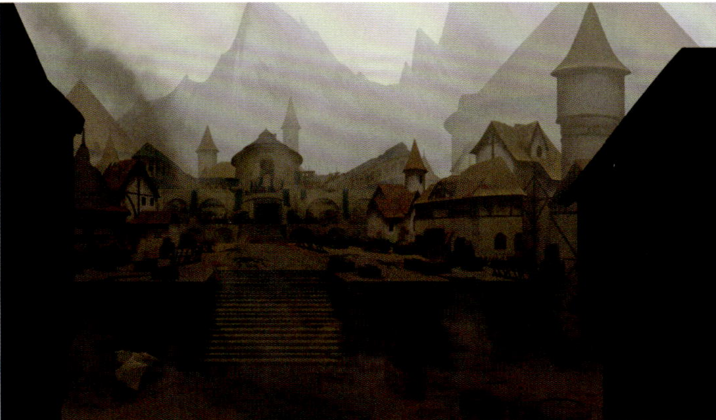

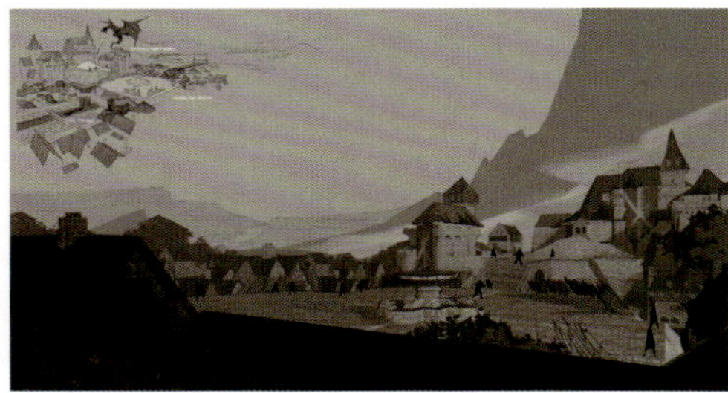

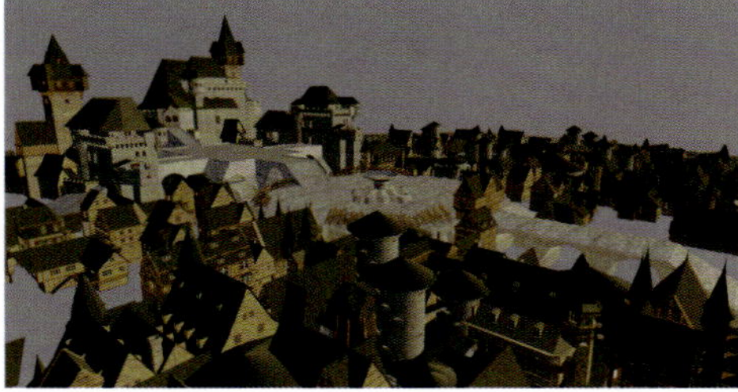

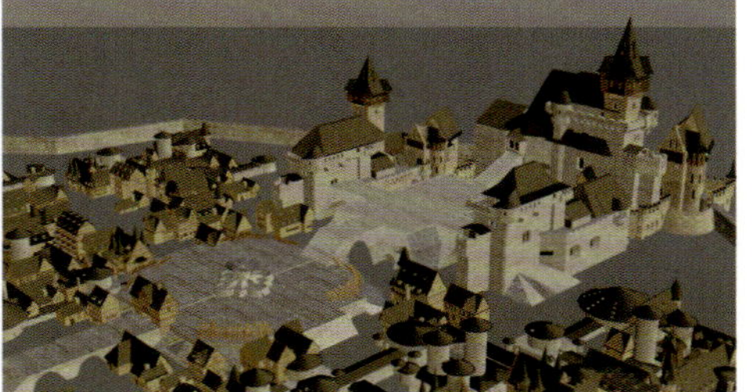

Renders of Westruun's 3D model.

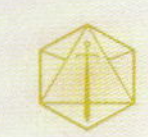

The Margrave's Mansion

The margrave was essentially the mayor of Westruun who was met with the wrong side of a sword when The Herd of Storms came through. Arthur Loftis gave the mansion a massive courtyard where he might have housed caravans from neighboring towns in better days. The inside of the house features a large central hall used as a home base for the Herd during their takeover.

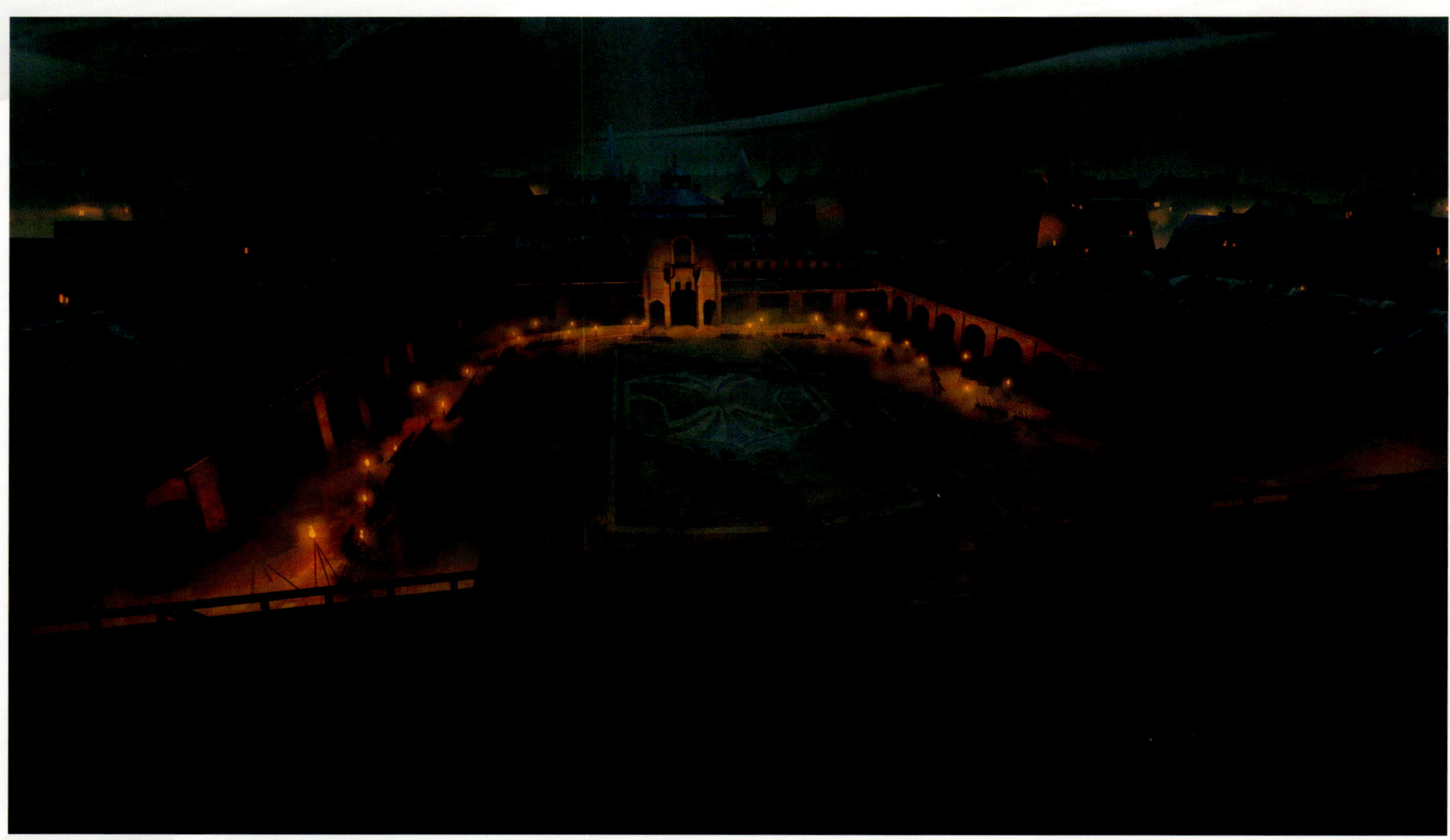

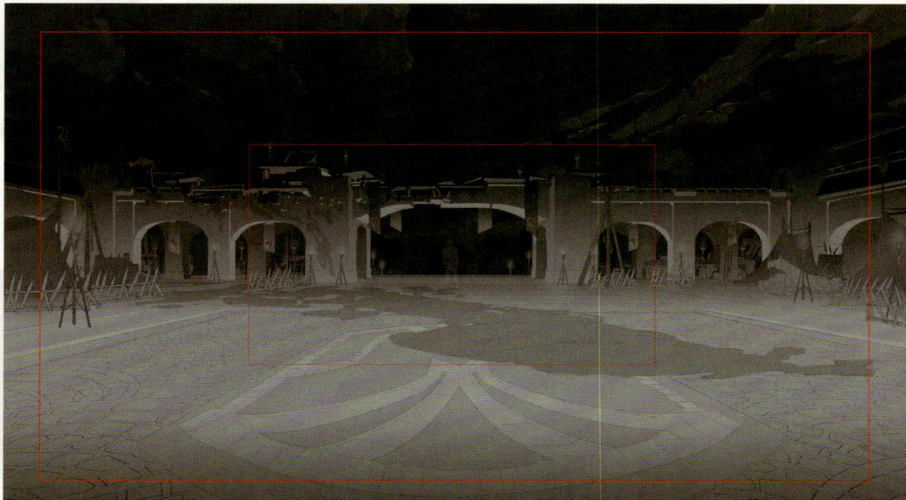

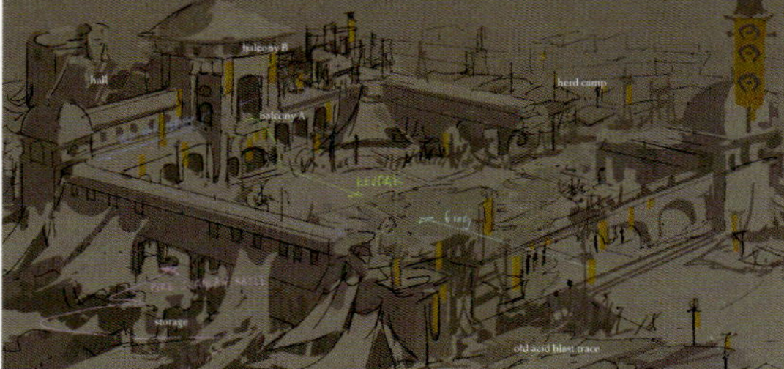

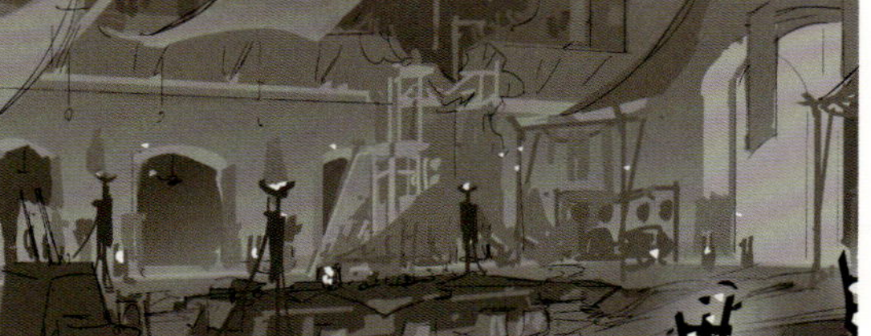

Manor Bedroom

Design imagined that Scanlan used the margrave's personal bedroom for his private discussion with Kaylie, so the space is filled with luxurious furniture, emptied chests, and more recent damage from the new owners.

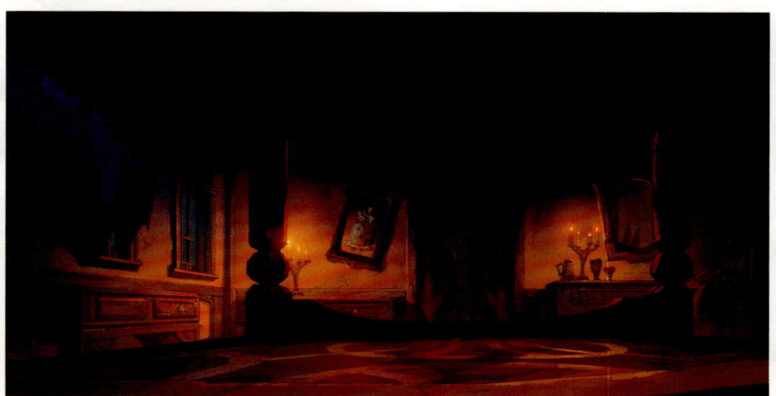

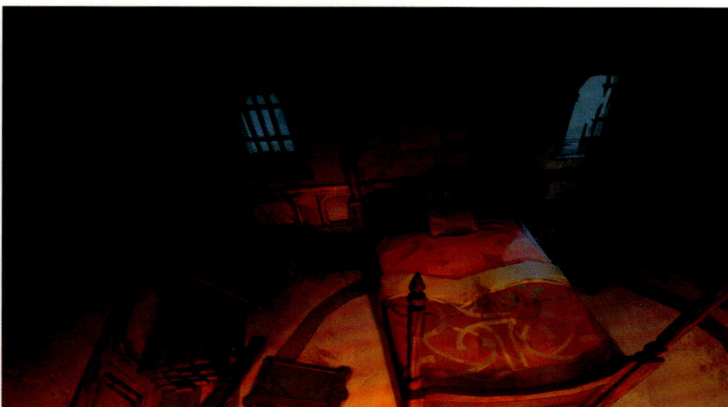

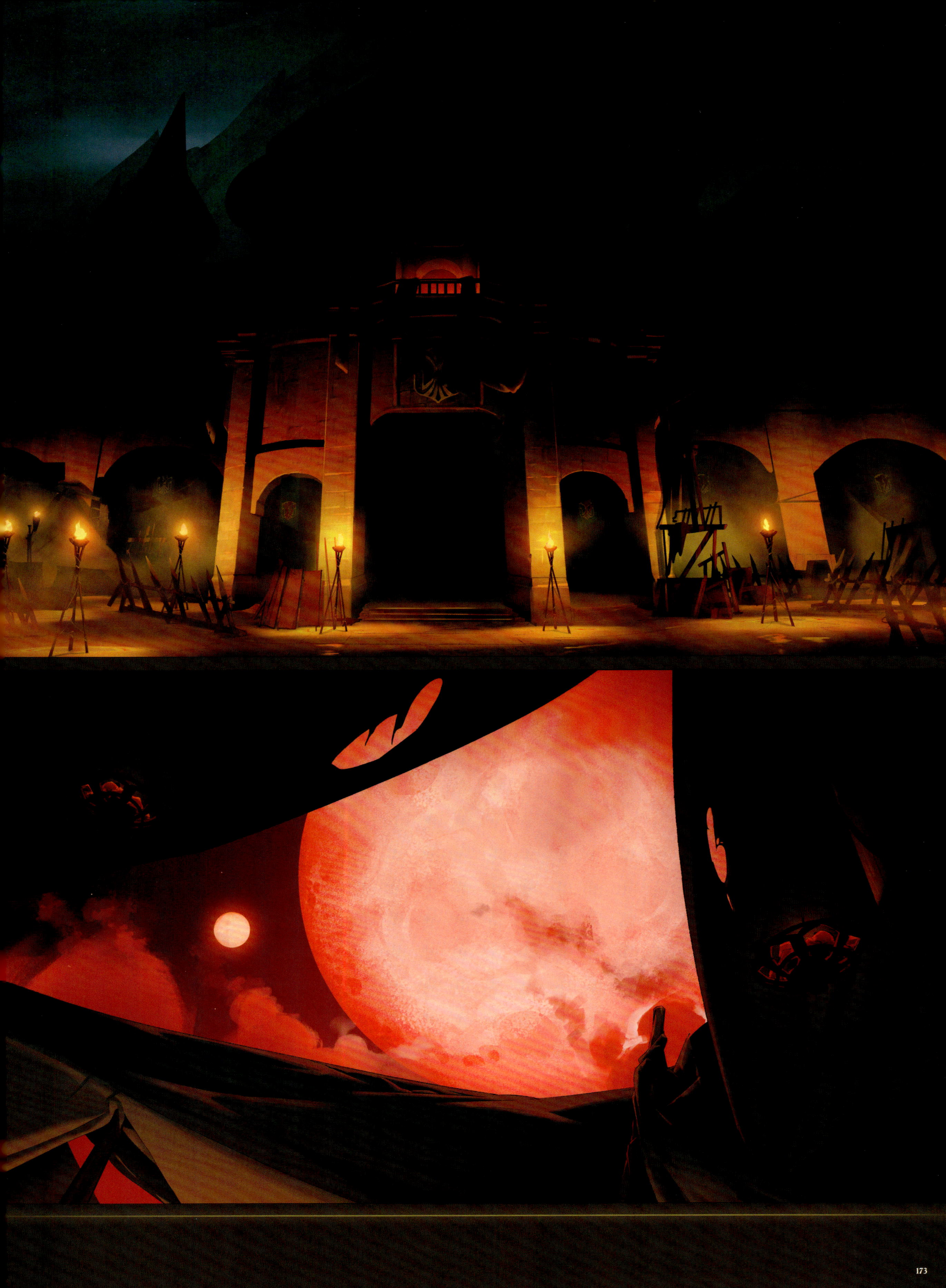

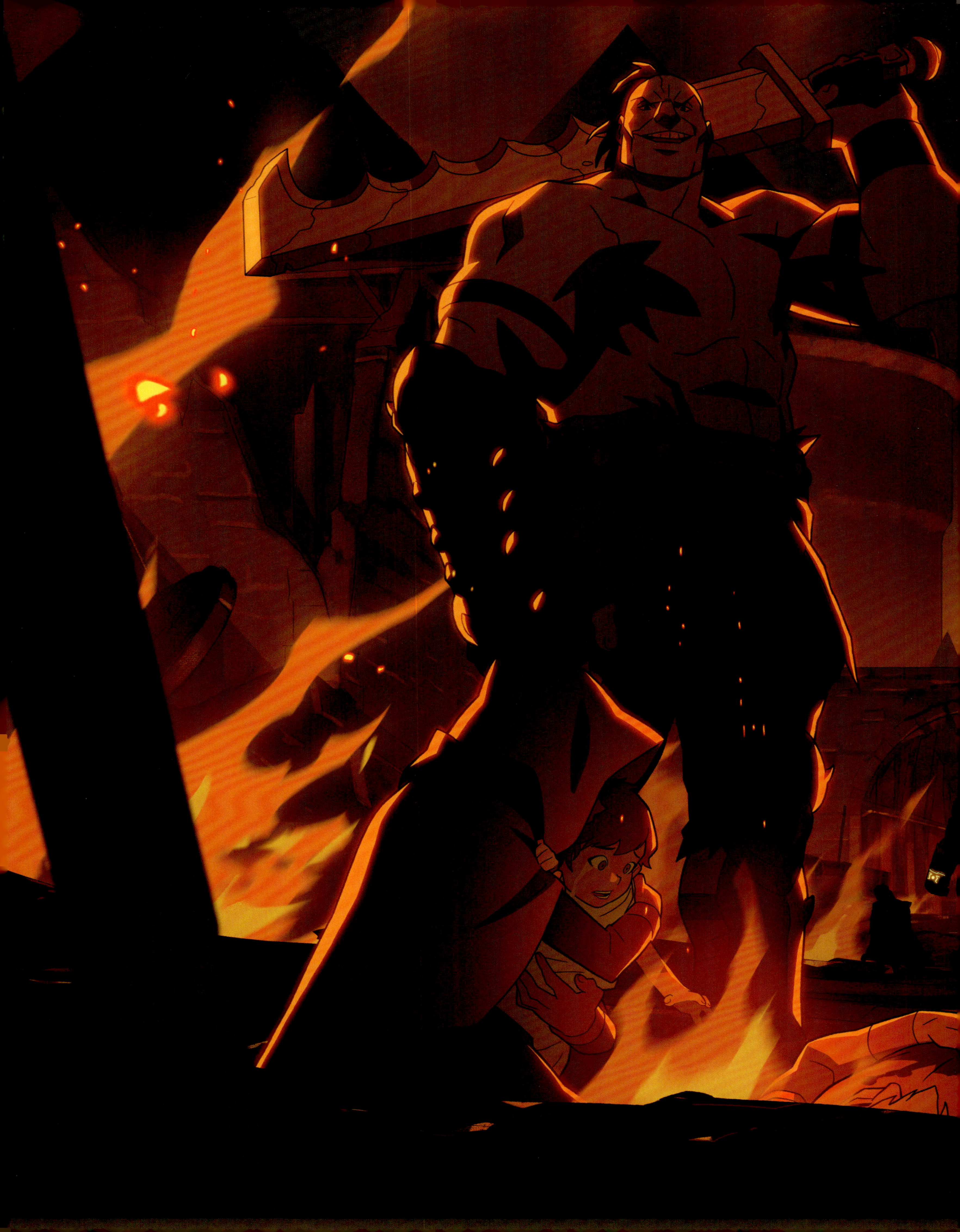

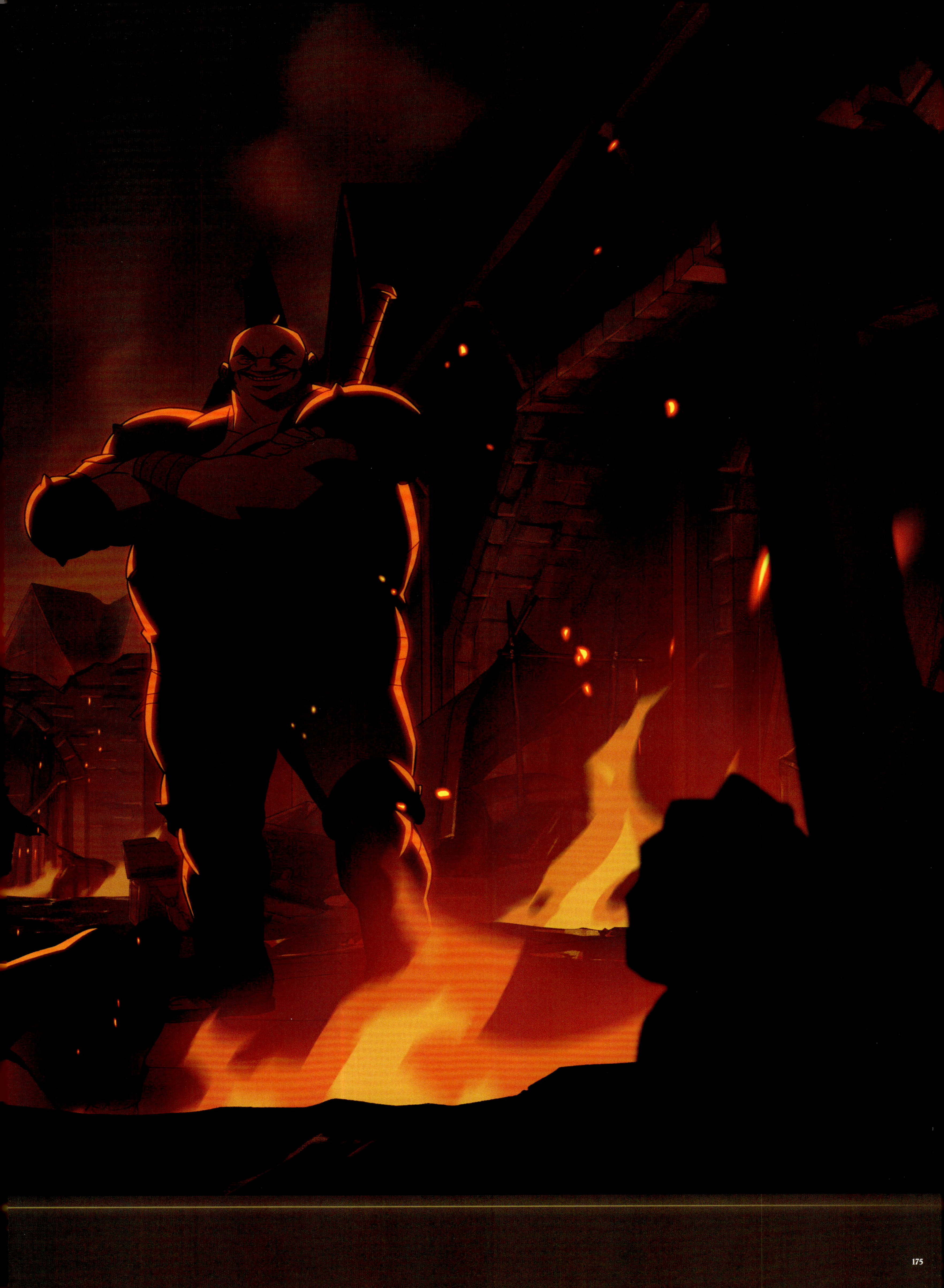

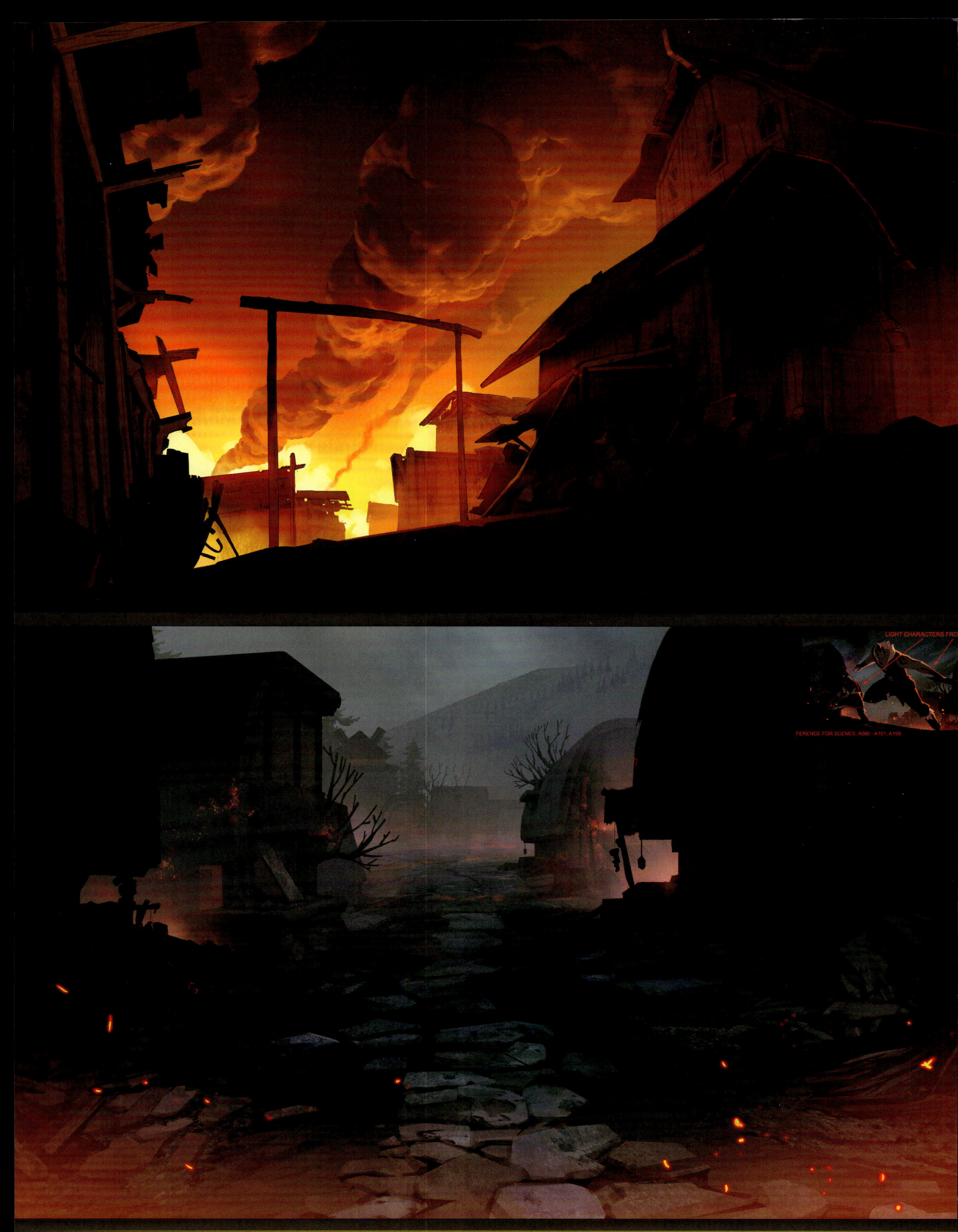
LIGHT CHARACTERS
FOR SCENES: A090 - A101, A159

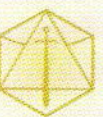

Grog's Past

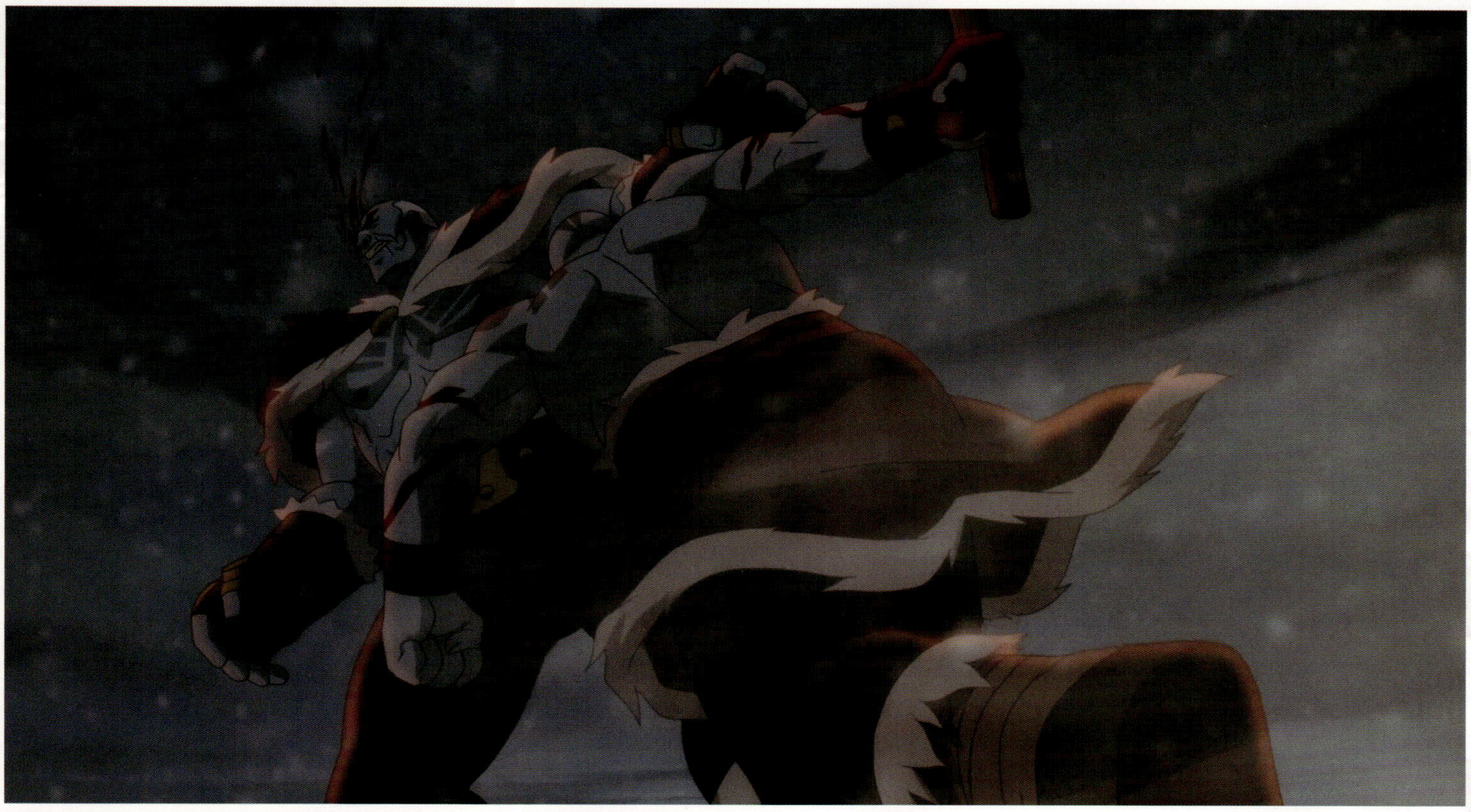

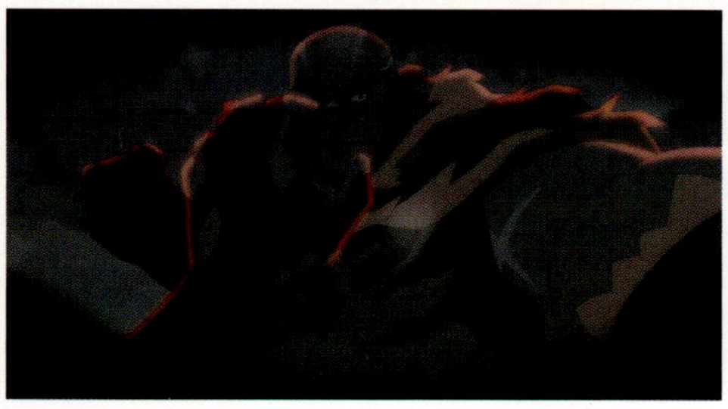

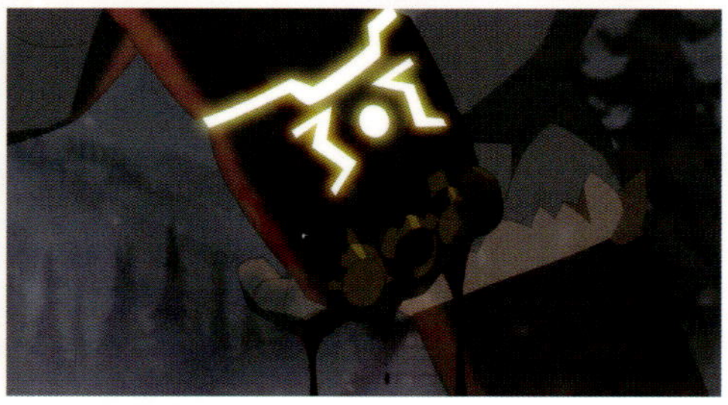

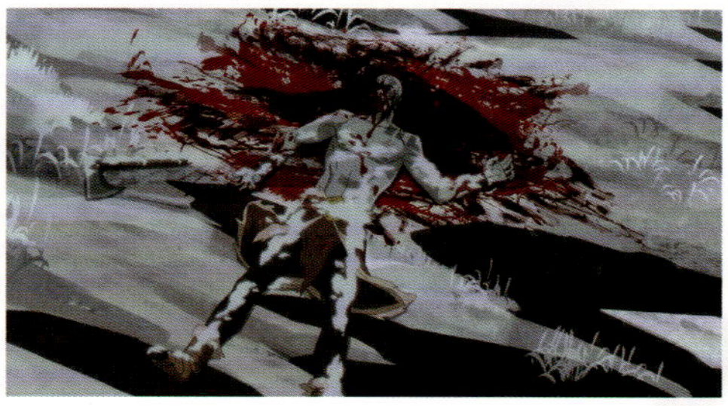

Kevdak leaving Grog to die.

Young Grog, Pike and Wilhand meeting for the first time.

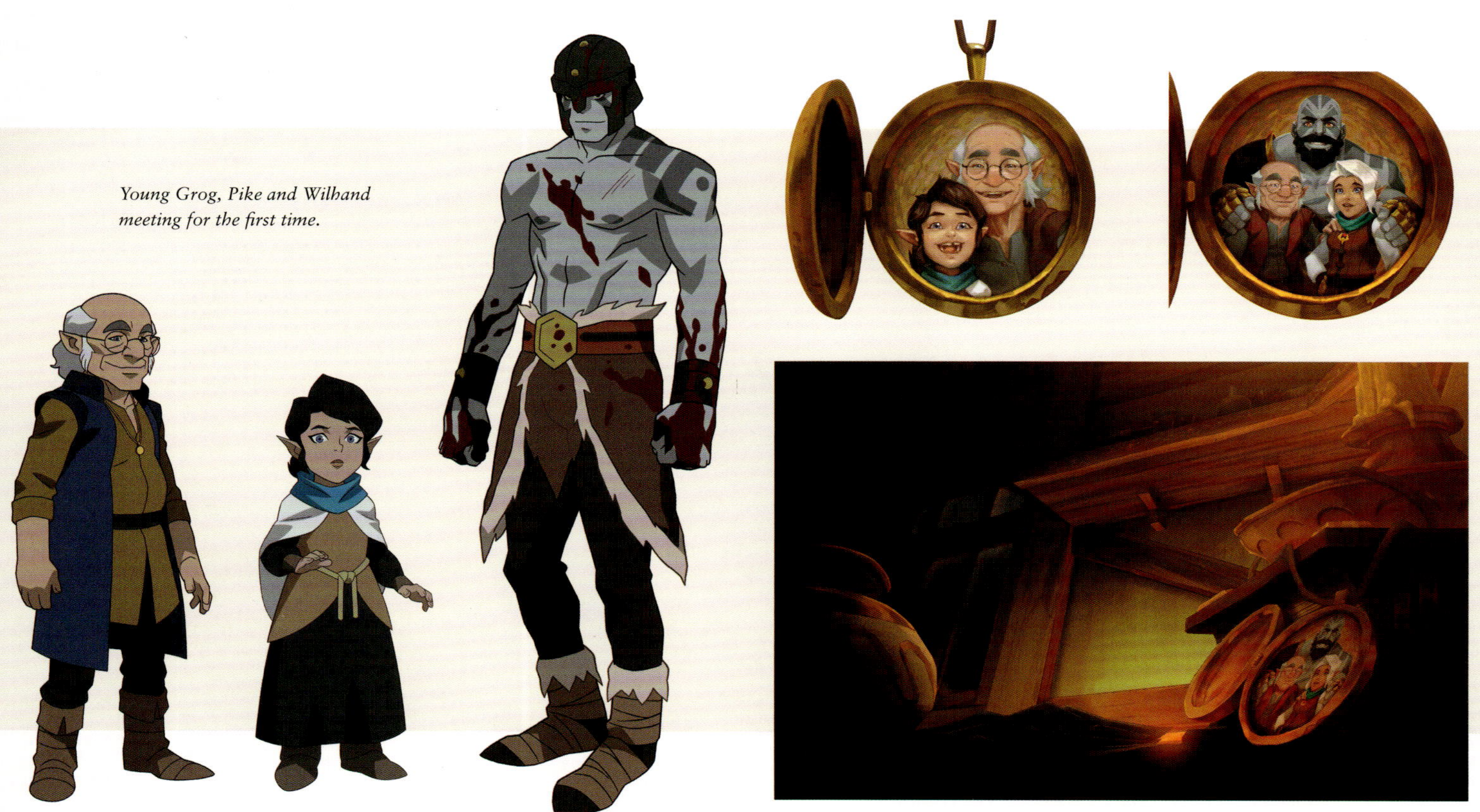

Storyboards from Grog's Battle with Kevdak

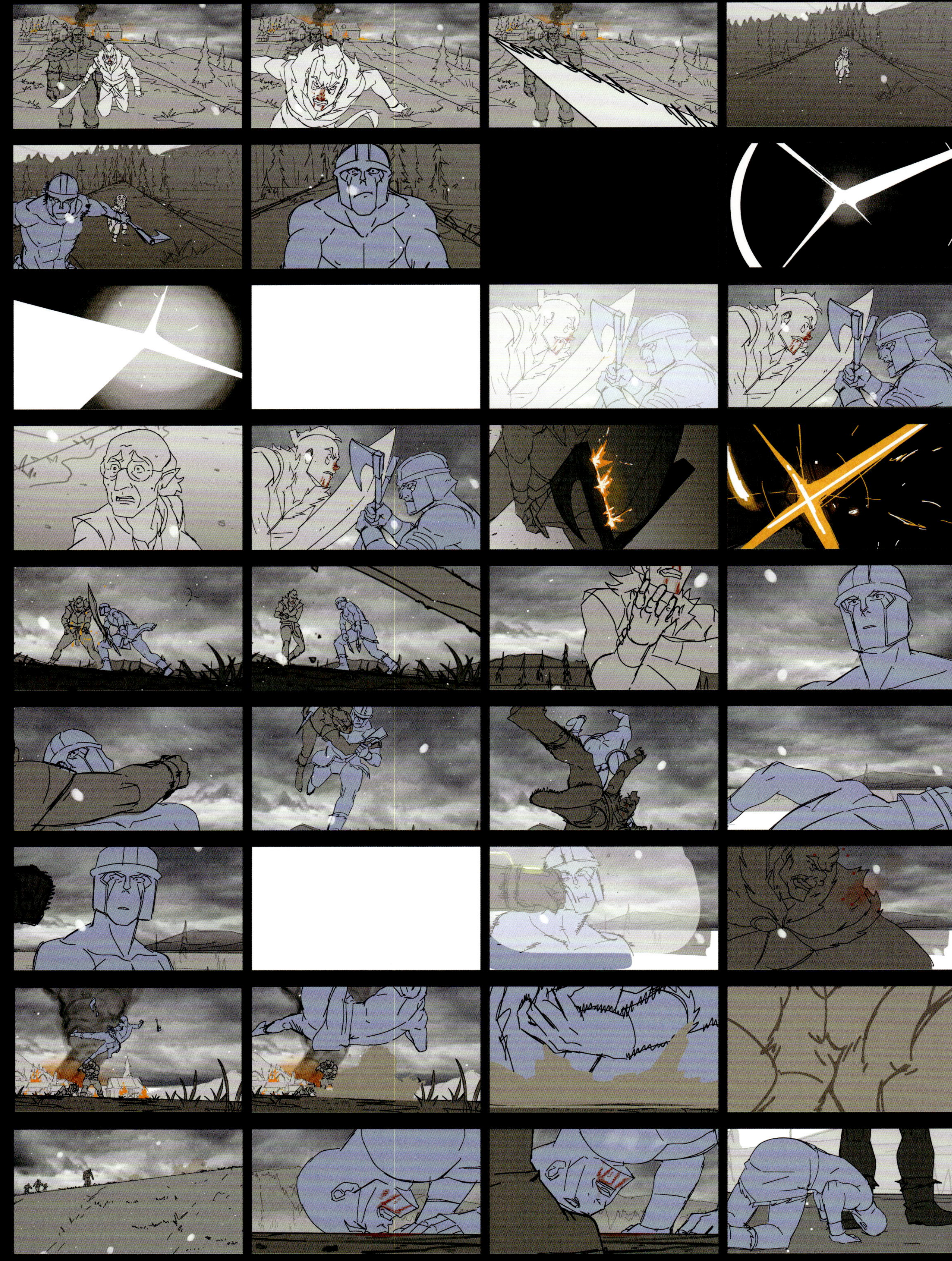

"The rules of herd combat are thus; the fight ends when someone dies." – KEVDAK

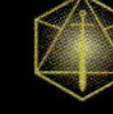

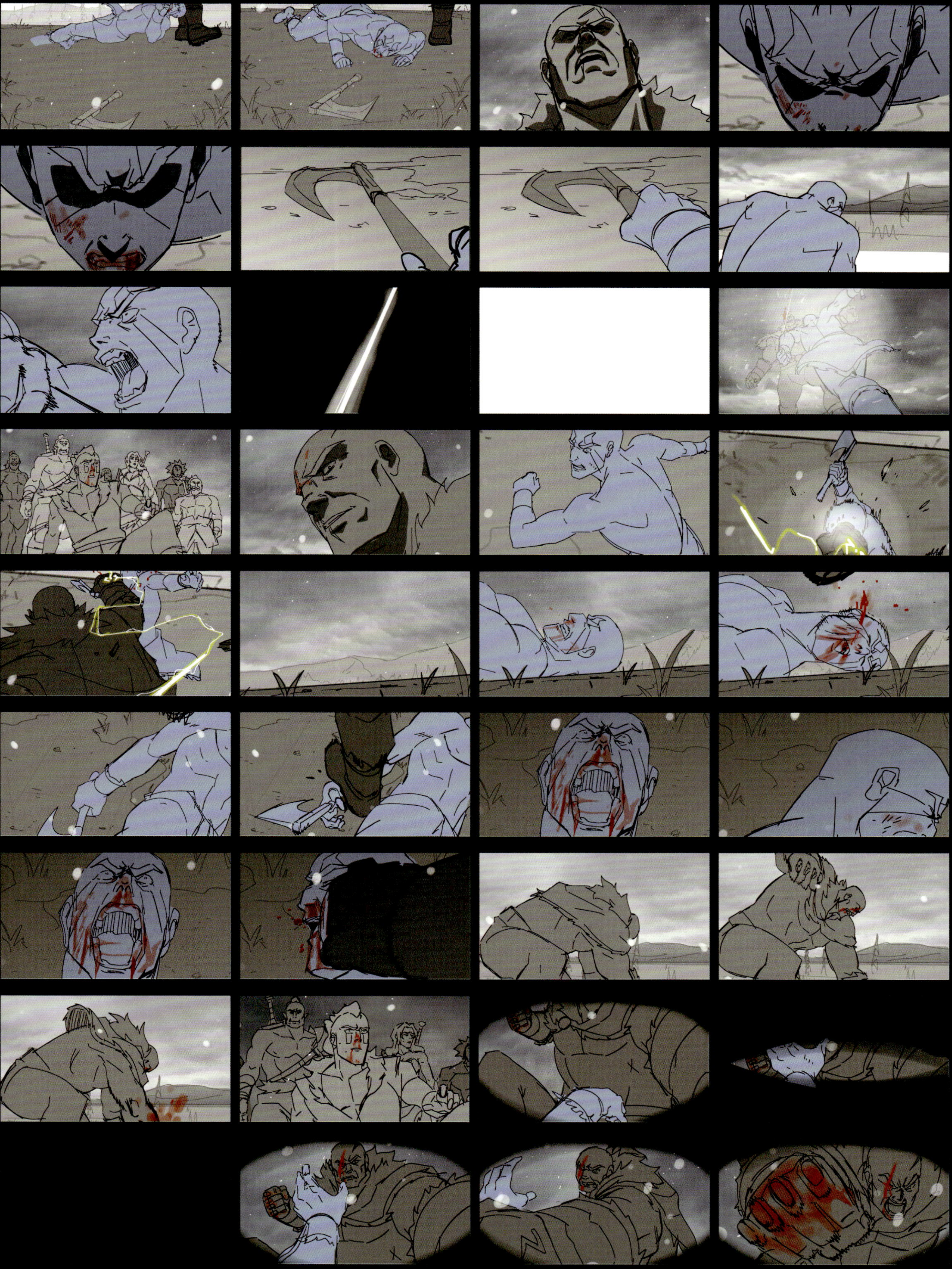

"I would like to rage!" – GROG

EPISODE 11

THE BELLY OF THE BEAST

"Being a father changes you. Being tied to a bed and threatened by your long-lost daughter changes you even more. Not to be outdone in the moody department by me, Vax goes on a lonely boy walk and communes with The Matron of Ravens before fully accepting himself as her champion. Perfect timing because we have a dragon to slay!" – A RECOUNTING OF "THE BELLY OF THE BEAST" BY SCANLAN SHORTHALT

Communion Pool

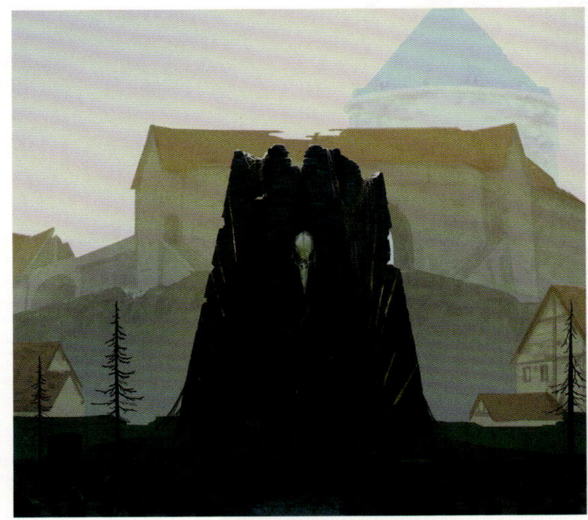

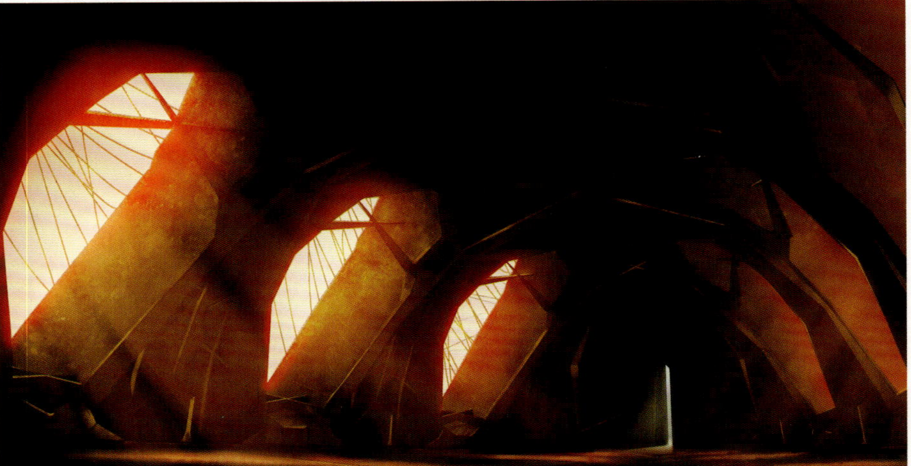

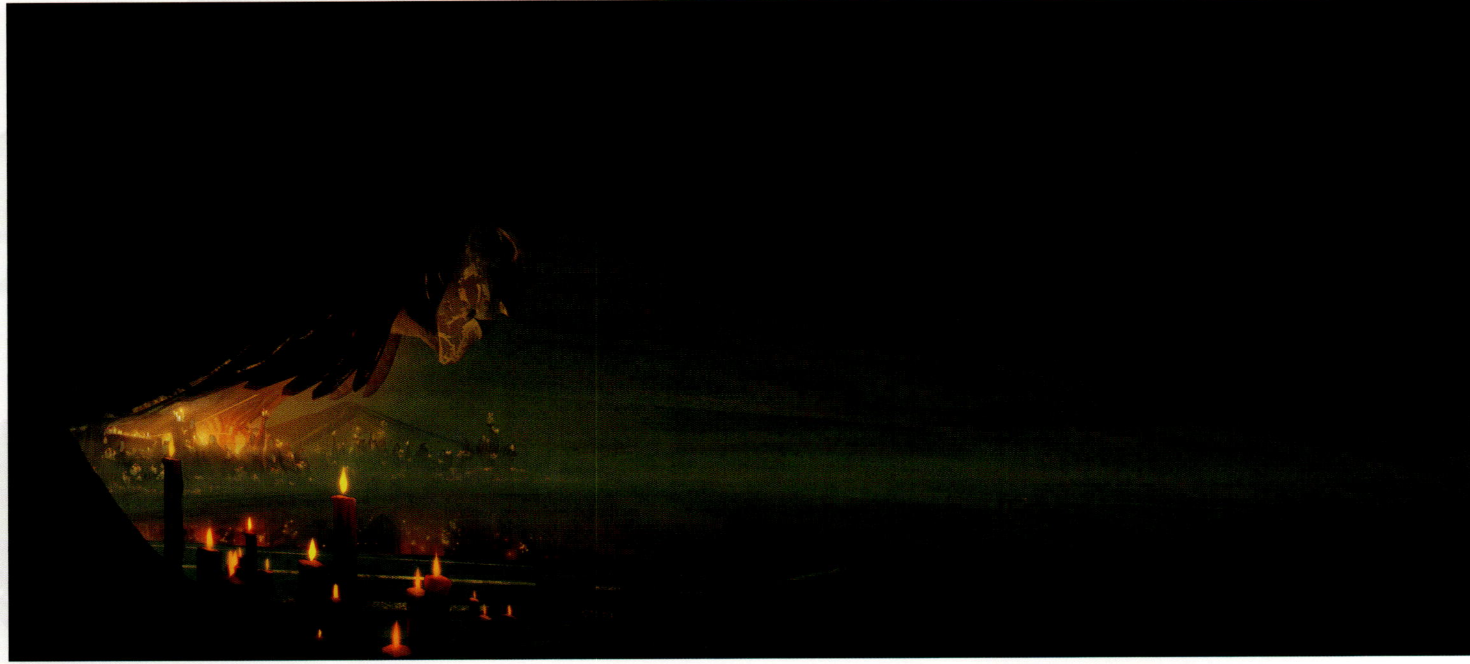

Scanlan's Backpack (Critical Role Logo Easter Egg)

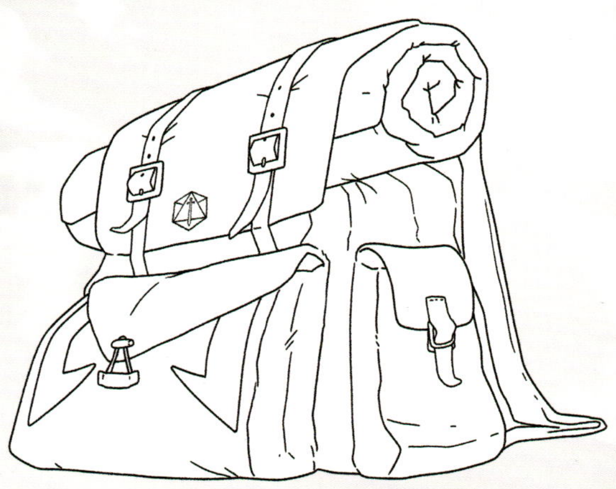

Immoveable Dagger

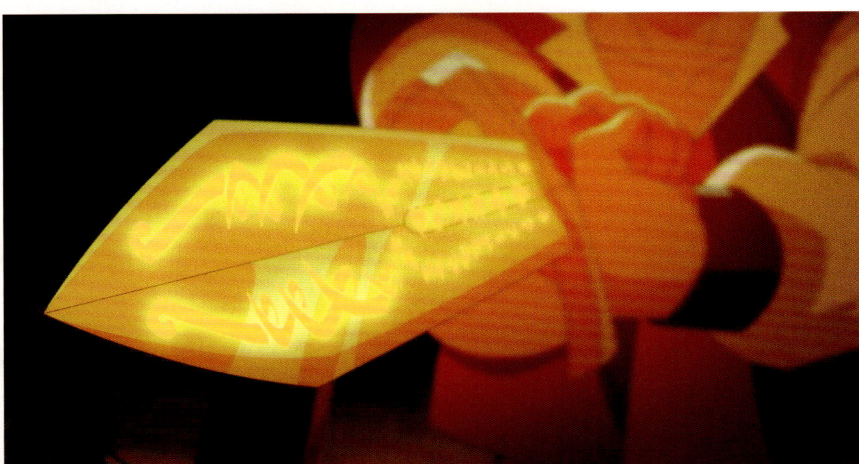

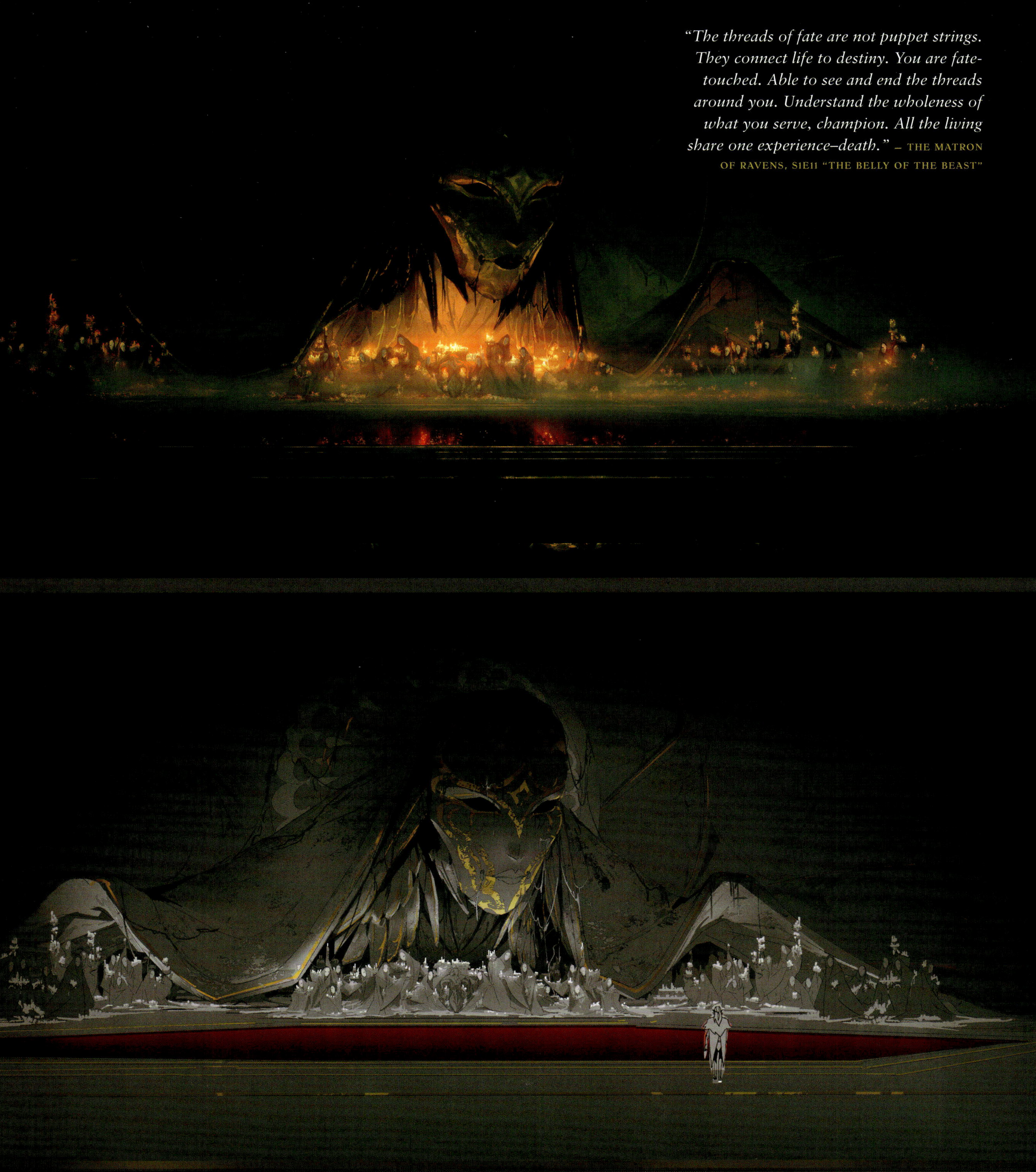

"The threads of fate are not puppet strings. They connect life to destiny. You are fate-touched. Able to see and end the threads around you. Understand the wholeness of what you serve, champion. All the living share one experience–death." – THE MATRON OF RAVENS, S1E11 "THE BELLY OF THE BEAST"

The Matron of Ravens' Temple in Westruun

Uncertain about what his bargain with The Matron of Ravens means, Vax seeks answers within her temple located in Westruun. After entering her communion pool of blood, she informs him that his purpose as her champion is to protect the sanctity between life and death. In classic Vax fashion, this experience seems to cheer him up.

The space is designed to give the Matron scale and importance. Her massive mask presides over smaller statues and mountains of candles. All of this looms over a lake of blood, which is the portal to a deeper connection with the matron herself.

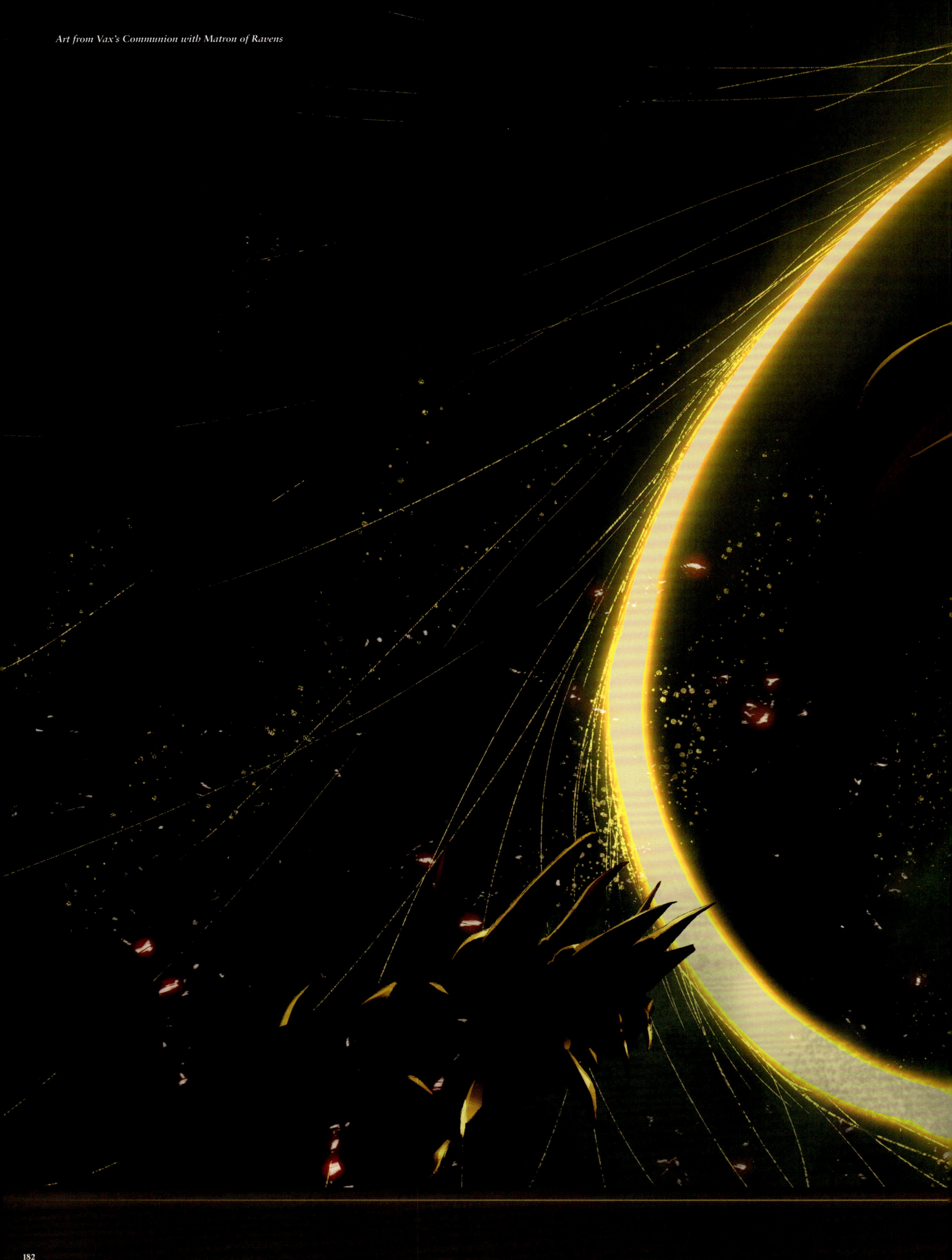

Art from Vax's Communion with Matron of Ravens

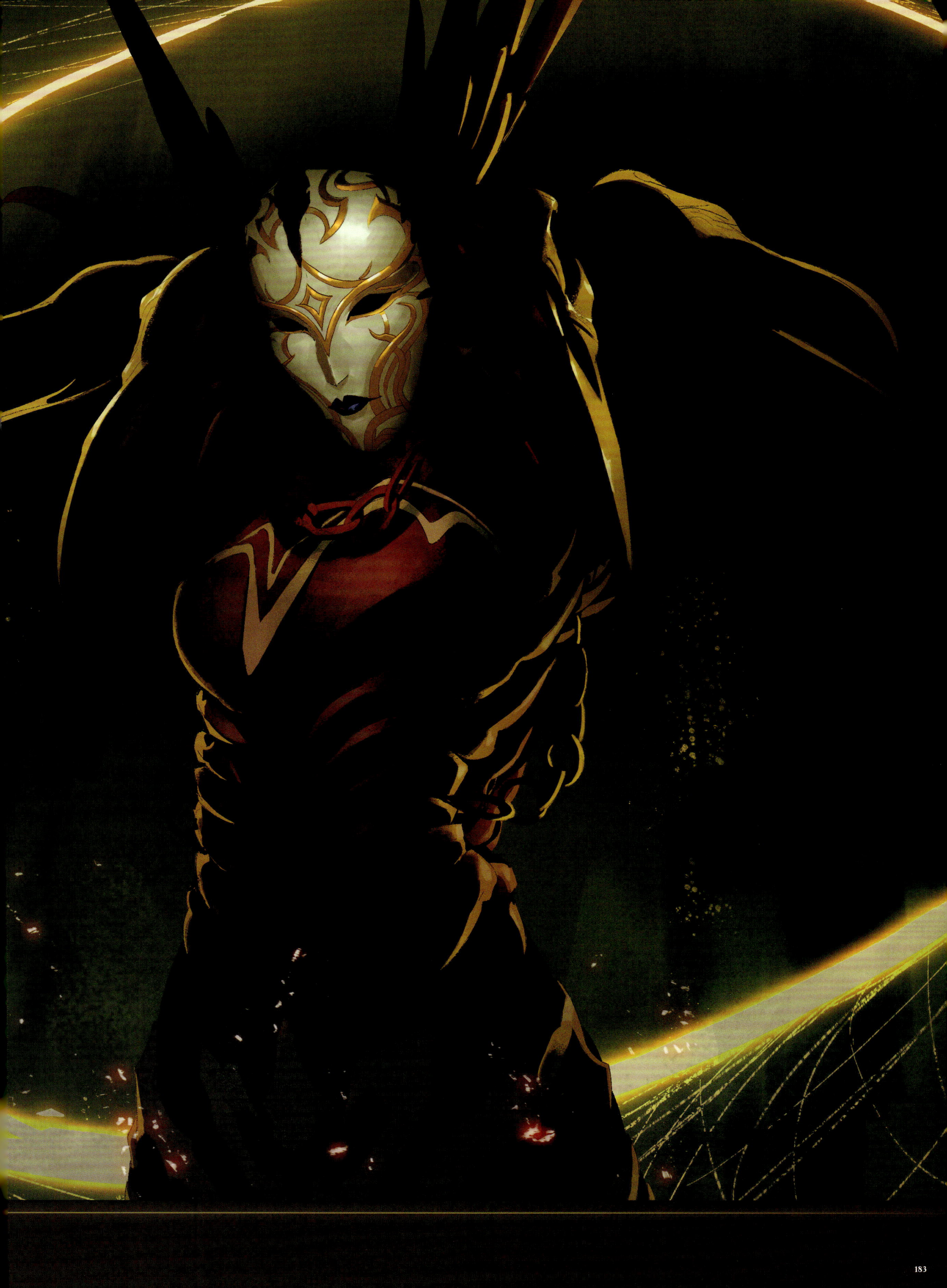

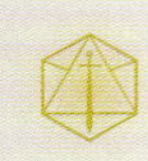

EPISODE 12

THE HOPE DEVOURER

"We're coming at you live from inside Umbrasyl's stomach! I have to be honest; this isn't my favorite acid trip of all time, but it's close. We corner Umbrasyl in Gatshadow Mountain, and after an epic battle worthy of song, we defeat that motherfucker once and for all!" – A RECOUNTING OF "THE HOPE DEVOURER" BY SCANLAN SHORTHALT

Scanlan and Kaylie Grow Old Together

Scanlan's visions of a future with Kaylie and their growing family.

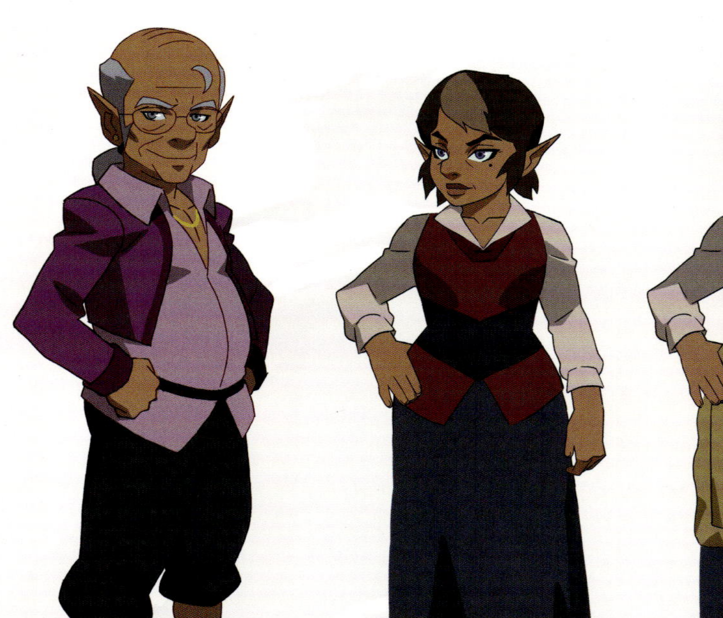

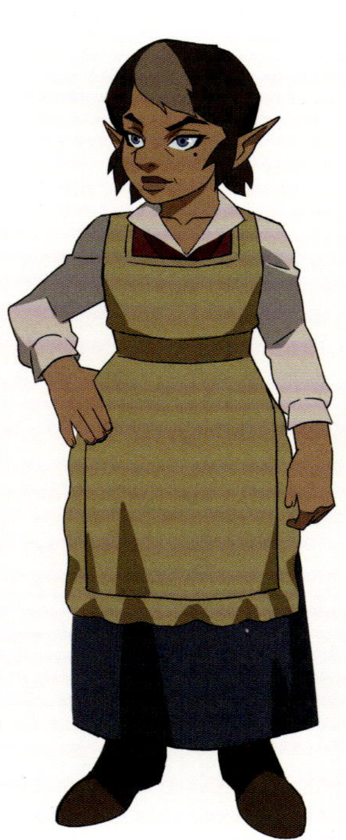

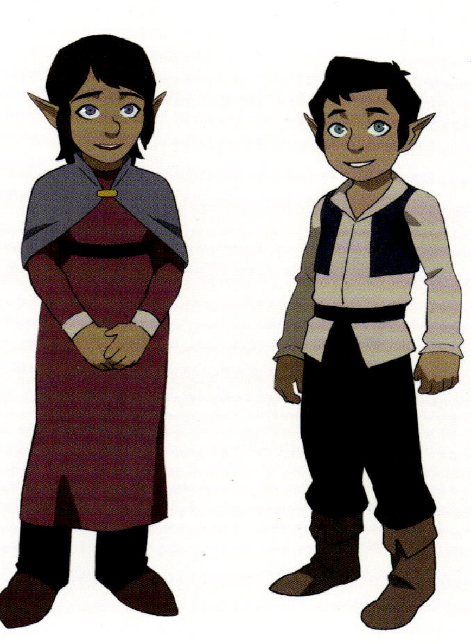

A Portrait of Vox Machina

During Scanlan's imaginings of a life growing old as a father to Kaylie, he dreams of how his continued friendship with Vox Machina would look and envisions a portrait of their big, happy family.

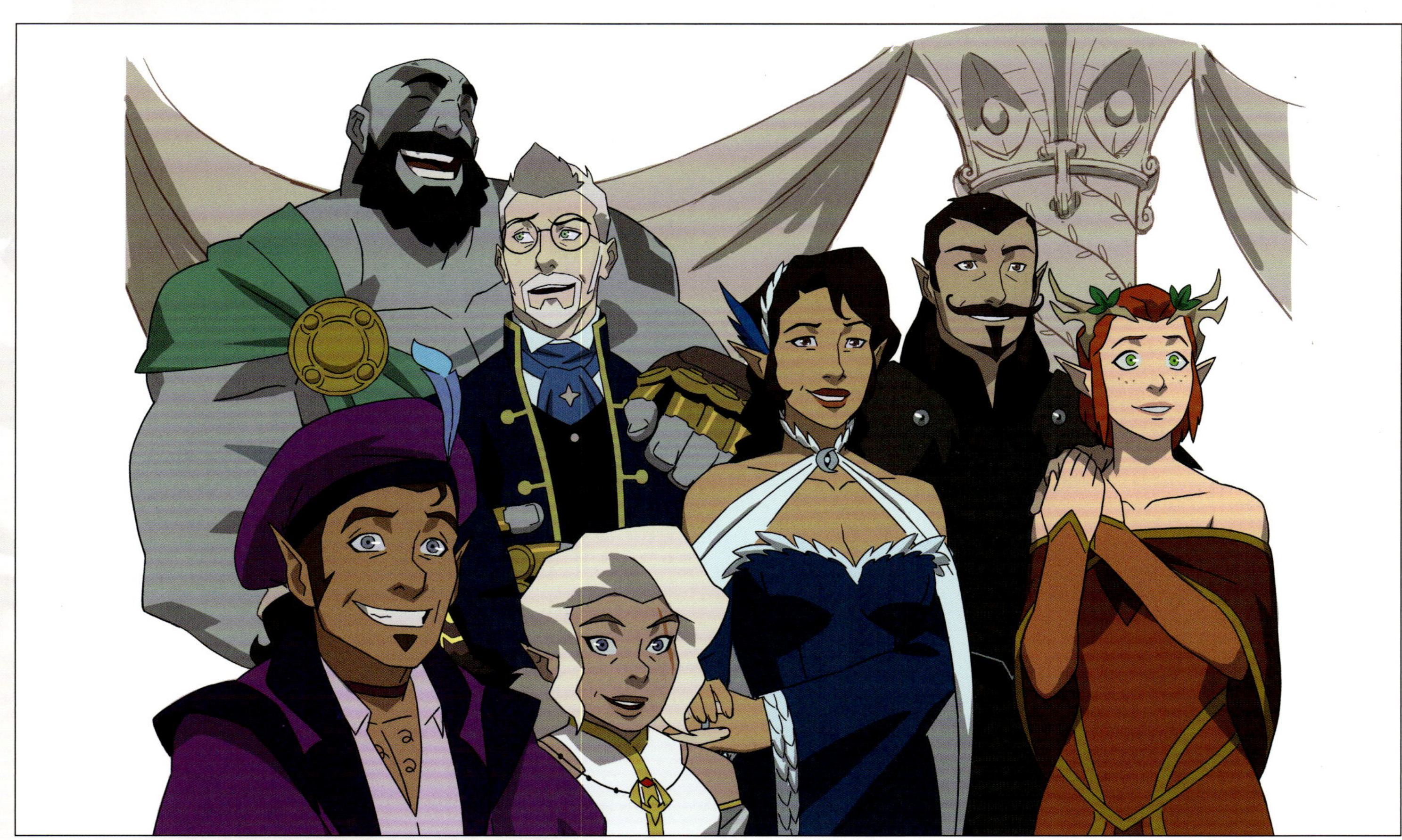

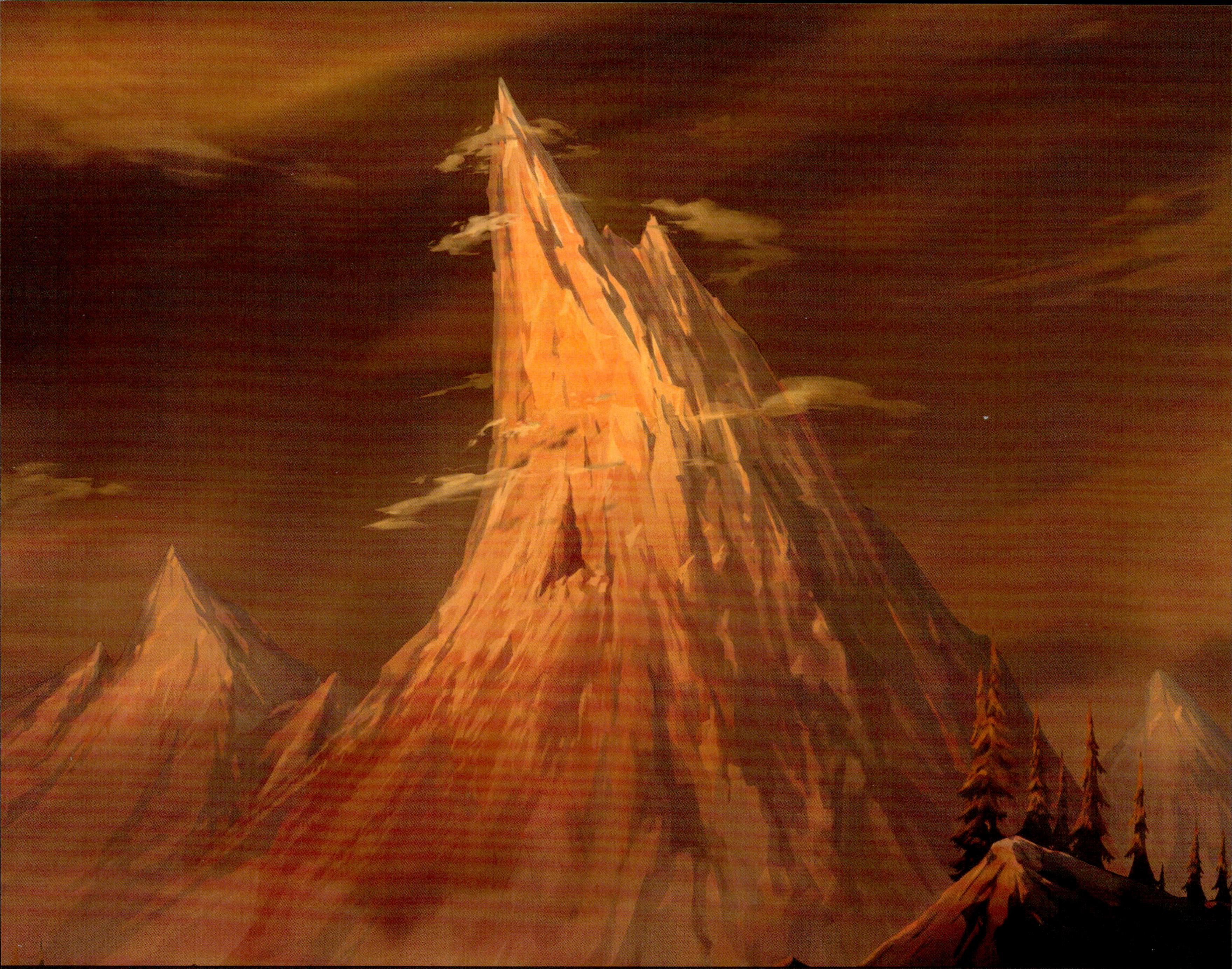

Gatshadow

Gatshadow Mountain stands foreboding amongst the neighboring peaks of The Cliffkeep Mountain Range.

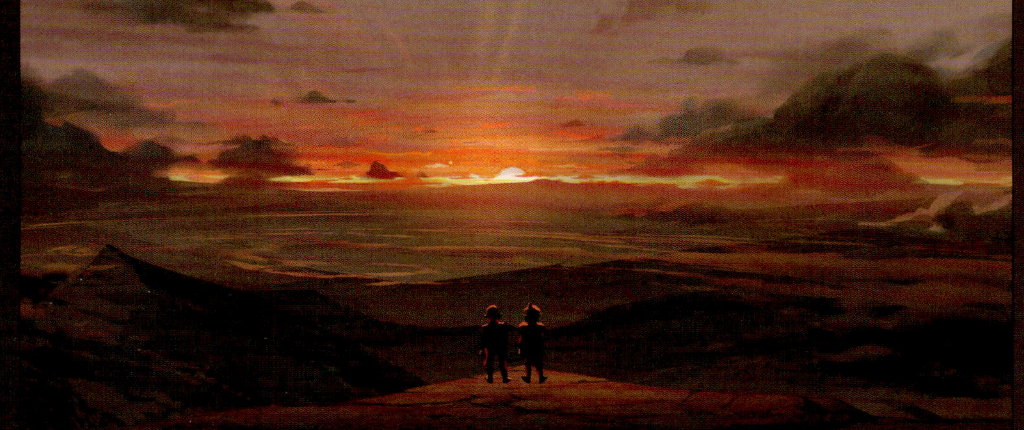

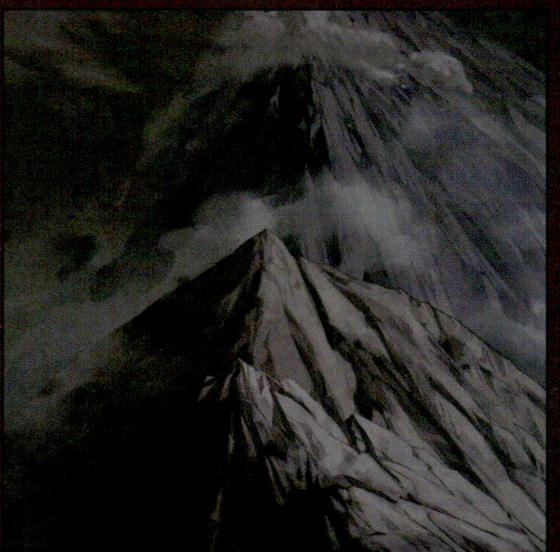

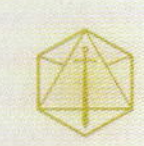

Umbrasyl's Lair

Similar to staging the sphinx sequences, artists had to take into account Umbrasyl's size in comparison to Vox Machina when designing Umbrasyl's lair.

Like Anders, Umbrasyl is also a collector. His lair is a much grittier museum of trophies containing primarily the skulls of his victims. Design chose to dot the caves with crystals, which are endemic to the Gatshadow, to help break up the darkness of the surrounding rocks. Green pools of acid flow throughout to show this as a regular resting place for The Hope Devourer.

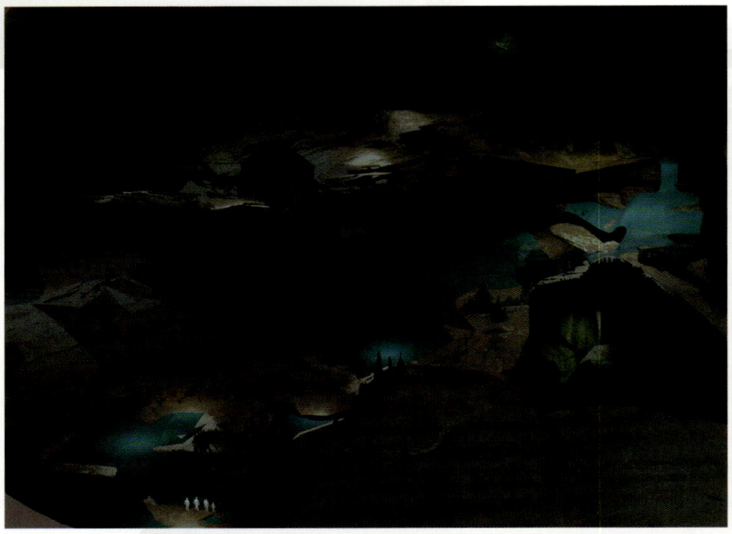

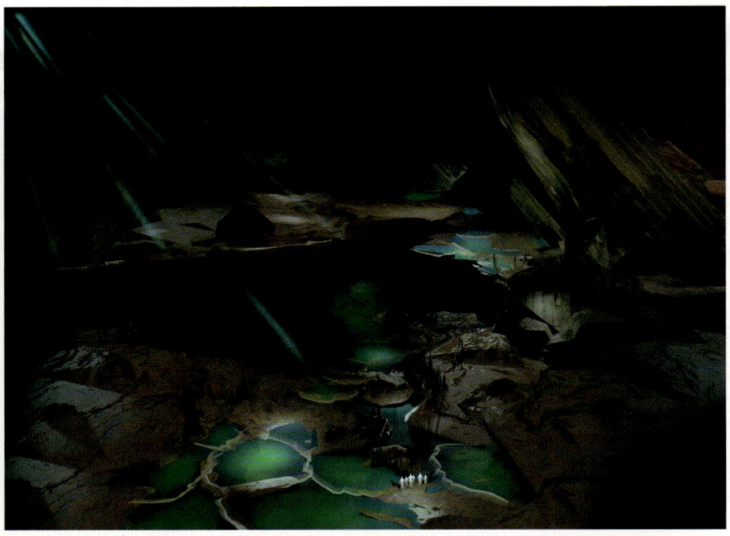

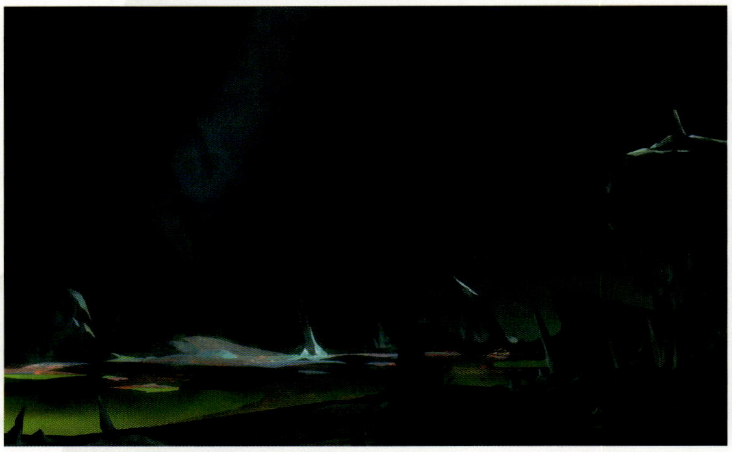

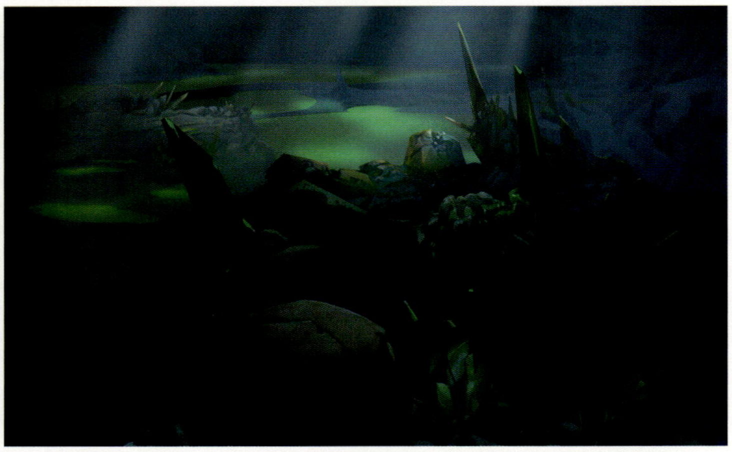

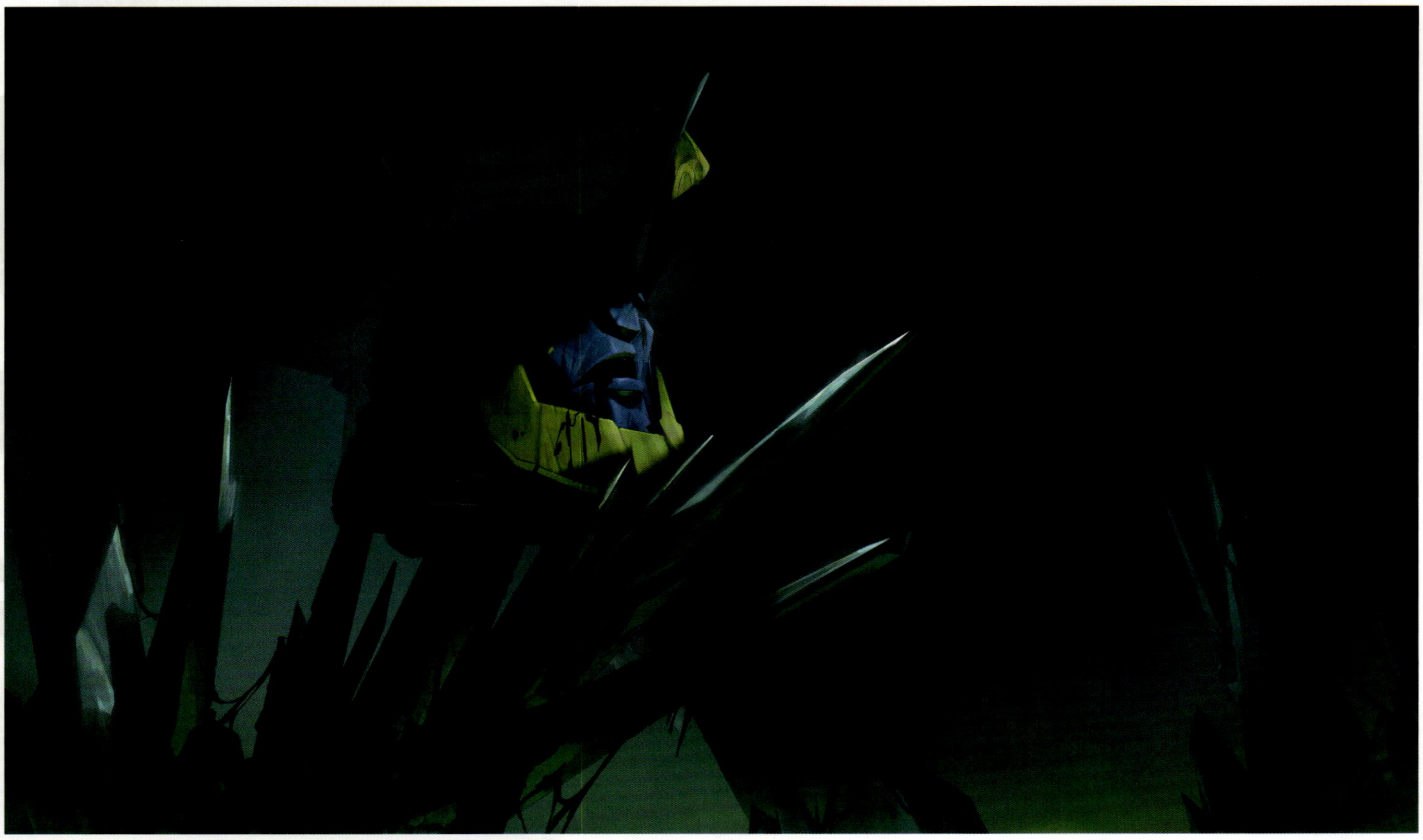

One of Umbrasyl's many trophies, the head of Kamaljiori sits as a warning to those who wish to challenge Umbrasyl.

Storyboards from *that* Vax and Scanlan Butthole Moment

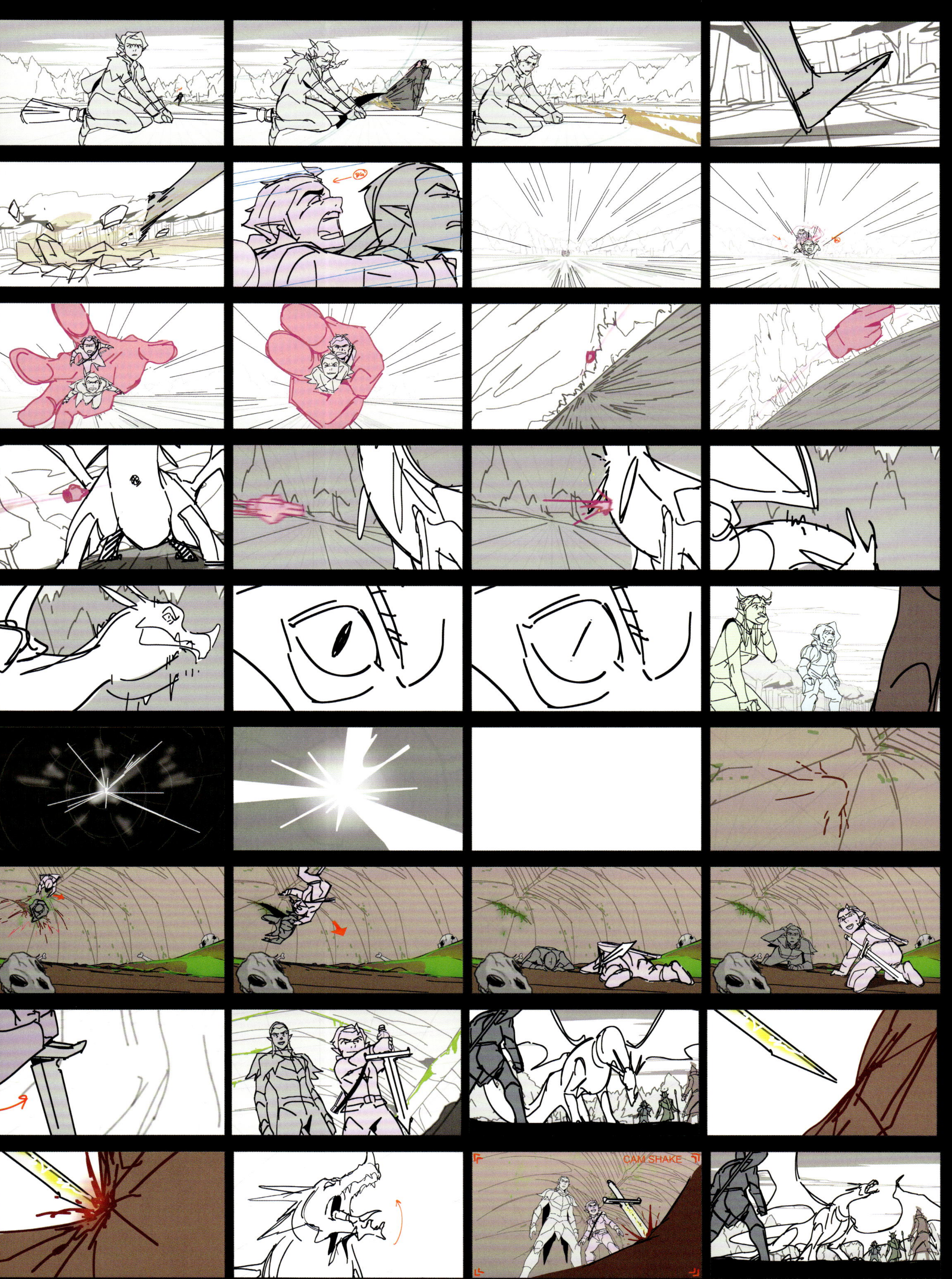

When you can't cut through Dragonscale, maybe find another opening?

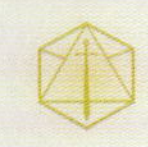

Inside Umbrasyl's Stomach

Painted backgrounds from inside Umbrasyl's stomach.

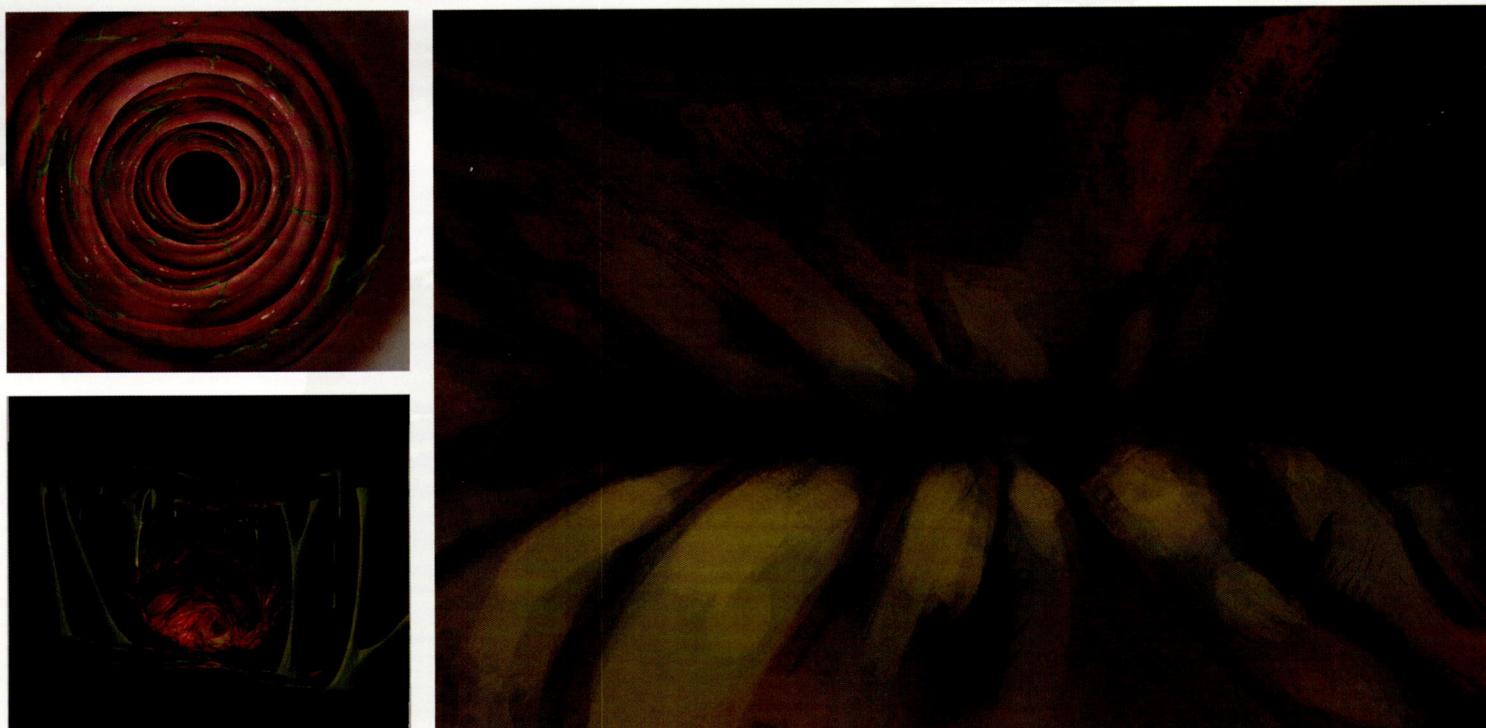

Keeper Yennen Reveals Herself to Vox Machina as Raishan in Disguise

After defeating Umbrasyl, Vox Machina returns triumphant to Whitestone to plan their next move on the Chroma Conclave. Off the high of victory, "Keeper Yennen" shocks everyone by revealing herself to be Raishan in disguise. In a wild cliffhanger ending, she leaves the audience wondering, is she here as friend or foe?

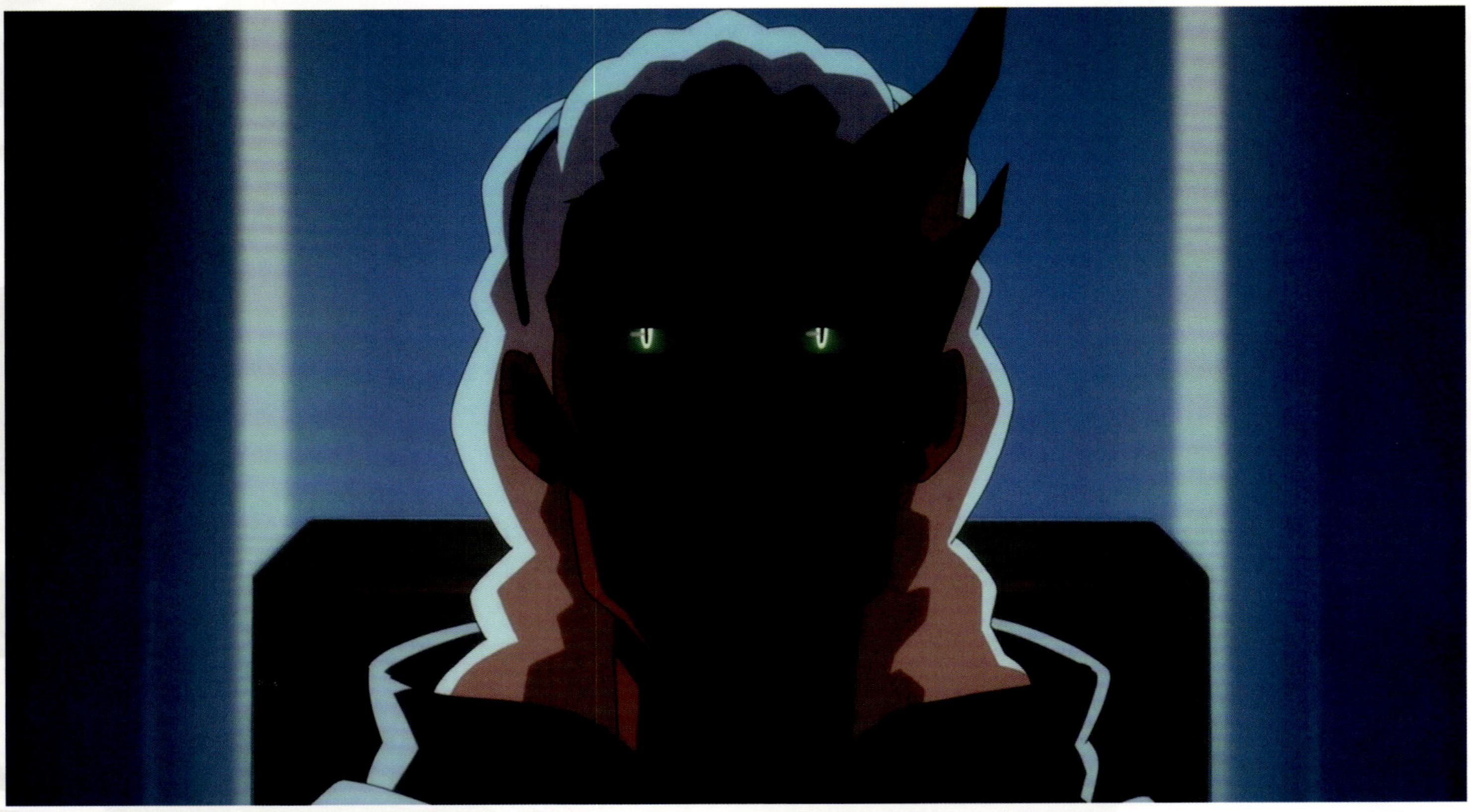

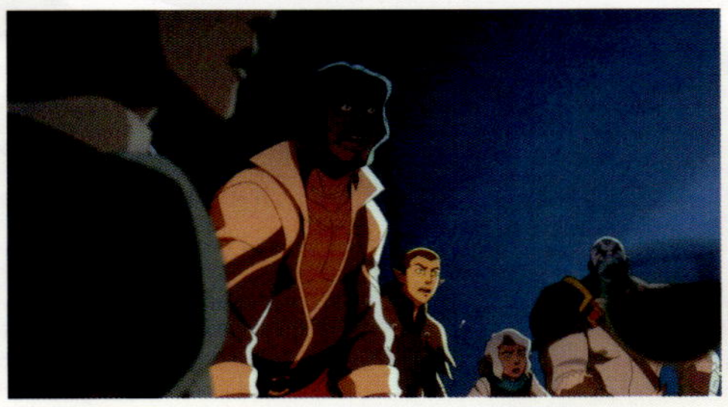

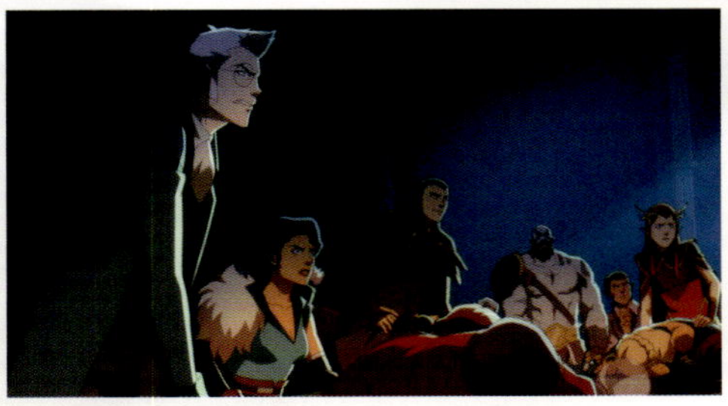

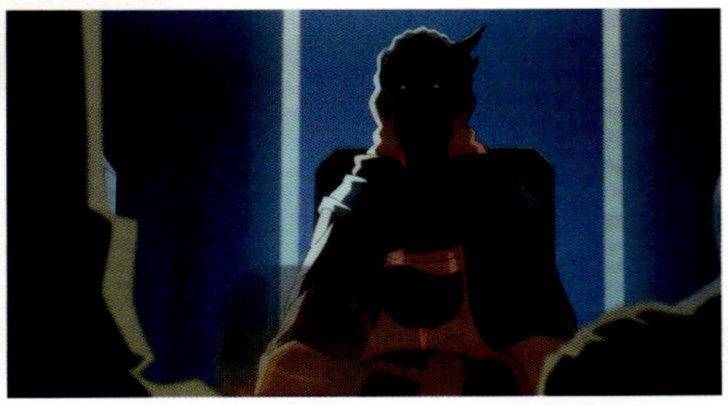

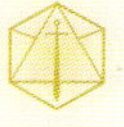

FROM SCRIPT TO SCREEN

PIKE AND SCANLAN KISS

As the dragon trembles, Scanlan won't let go - pushing the sword in FURTHER. He <sings> a triumphant note, and Mythcarver rings out in harmony. The blade GLOWS as a bolt of energy BURSTS OUT, BLASTING through the opposite side of the dragon's head.

The dragon's <ROAR> turns into a shrieking DEATH RATTLE.

Umbrasyl plummets to the ground, landing hard.

In a remote corner of the cavern, Ripley - shrouded in shadow - watches Umbrasyl fall. She pulls her cloak up, and steals away without anyone seeing.

The team watches, awe-struck, as the life goes out of the dragon's snarling features. The monster is finally dead.

Then Pike realizes -

162 PIKE
Wait. Where's *Scanlan?!*

They follow Pike's worried eye-line to Scanlan's unconscious body sticking out from under the dead dragon's neck.

163 PIKE
Oh no.

Grog picks up the Titanstone Knuckles.

163A GROG
Vax, give me a hand!

With Vax's help, Grog uses the knuckles to <SHOVE> the dragon's head aside revealing Scanlan underneath. He lies there, battered, seemingly dead.

Pike tries to heal Scanlan, but it doesn't seem to work.

163B PIKE
Come on. Come on! Oh God... no.

165 VEX'AHLIA
Pike, can't you...?

Pike shakes her head. She has no magic left. No way to heal.

She kneels, taking Scanlan's lifeless hand in hers.

166 PIKE
(whispers, teary)
Scanlan. You did it. You might not have known what you could do. But I always did.

She strokes his hair. And gives a soft <u>kiss</u> on his lips.

166A PIKE
Your daughter would have been proud.

A long beat. Some tears.

Then, from the corner of his mouth...

166B SCANLAN
(doing Pike's voice)
"And I'm in love with you, too, Scanlan."

Pike's eyes go wide.

Scanlan's eyes open. He's all smiles.

166C PIKE
Wait. You're alive, motherfucker?

166D SCANLAN
Oops.

Pike THROWS HER ARMS AROUND HIM. Everyone breathes a big <sigh of relief>.

166DA VEX'AHLIA
You idiot.

166DB KEYLETH
Scanlan! Don't do that again.

166DC PERCY
Well done!

Pike gives him a playful punch on the shoulder. As the team finally relaxes, Scanlan notices a GOLDEN GLIMMER coming from deep inside the lair.

166E SCANLAN
Uh, what's that glow?

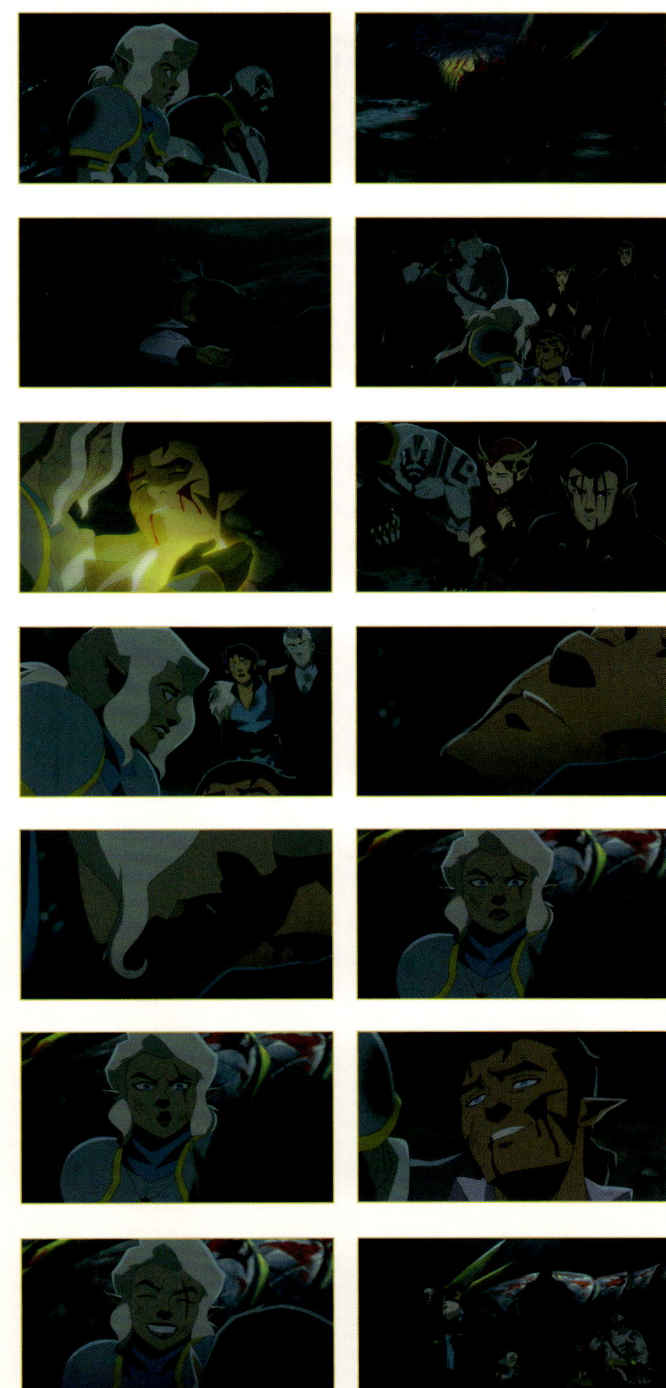

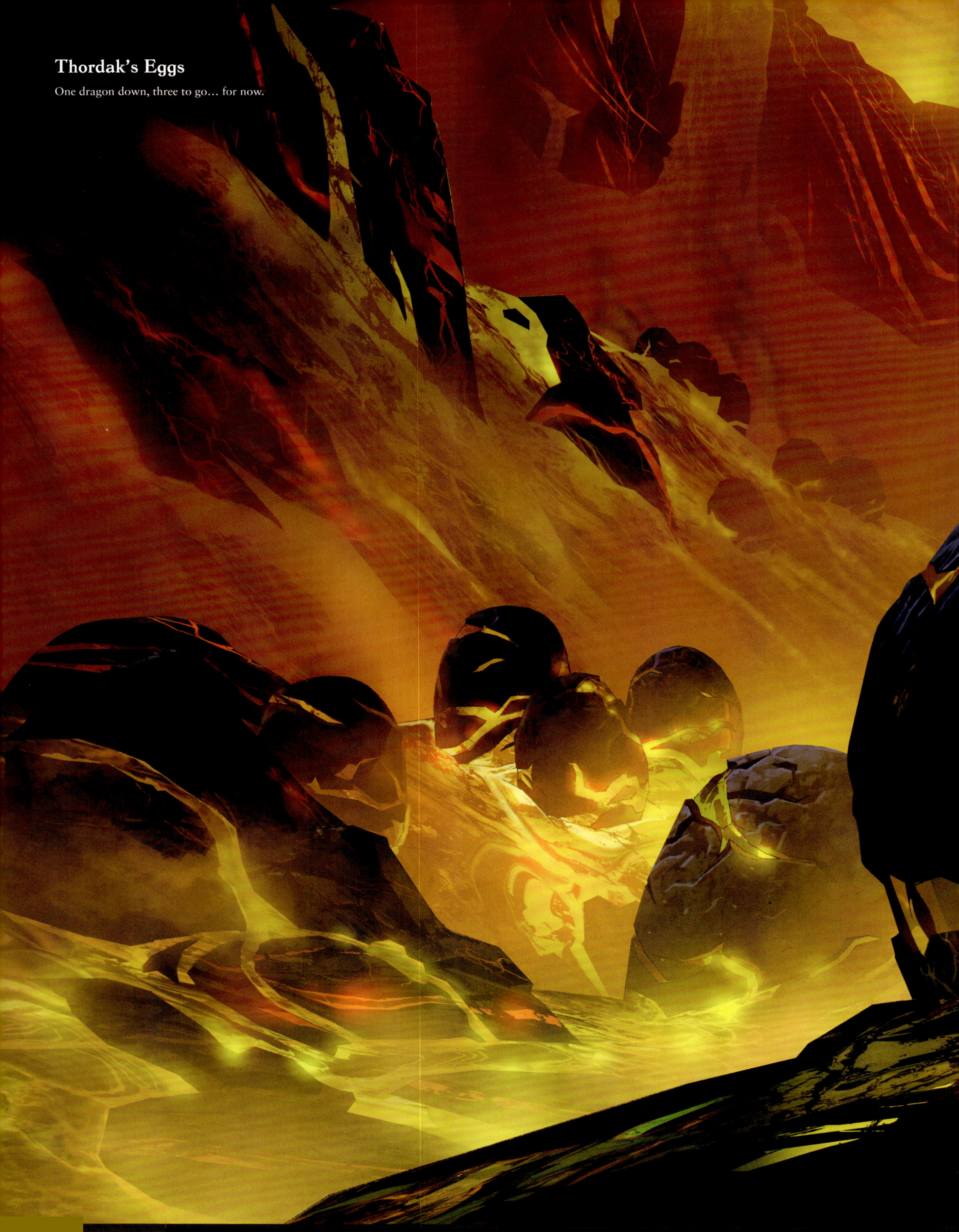

Thordak's Eggs

One dragon down, three to go… for now.

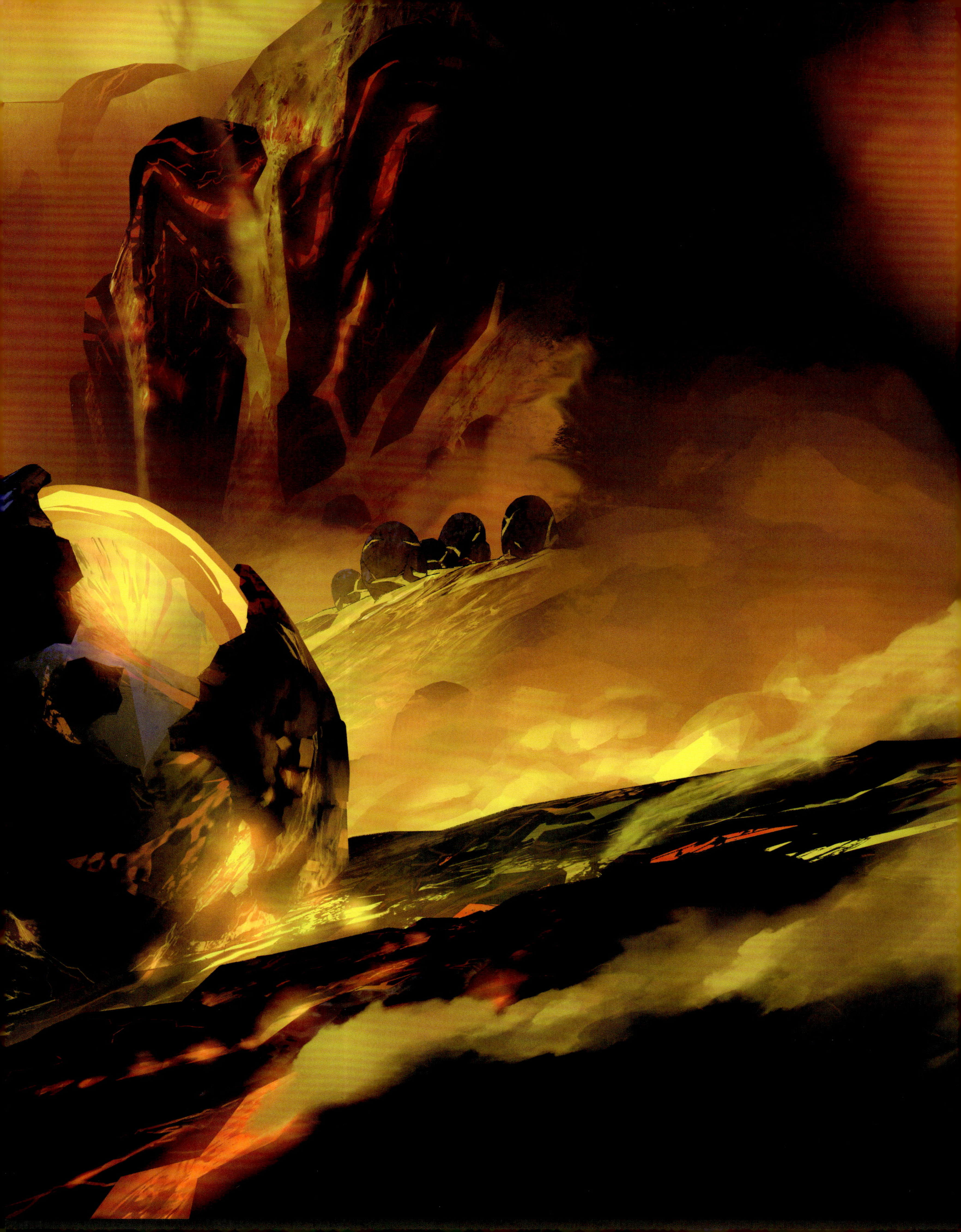

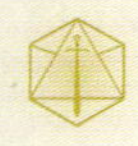

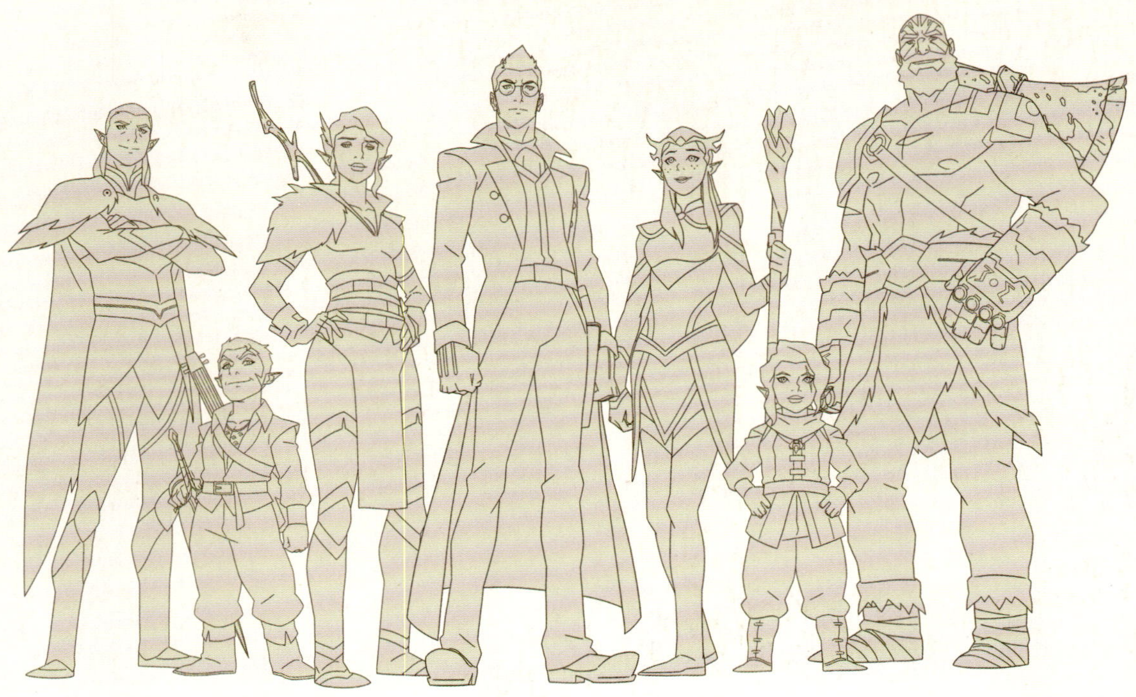

ARTIST CREDITS

CHARACTER TEAM

Phil Bourassa
Dusty Abell
Luke Ashworth
Christine Bian
Dan Holland
Dou Hong
Nick Lombardo
Jessica Mahon
Will Nichols
Shaun O'Neil
Bertrand Todesco
Xiyin Wang

PROP & FX TEAM

Simon Baek
Kyle Bowman
Eric Brown
April Erikkson
Jermz Gallardo
Juan Gutierrez
Damon Moran
Celina Sarmiento
Alastair Sew Hoy
Brian Uchida

COLOR TEAM

James Batrez
Ashley Fisher
Lane Garrison
Camille Stancin
Ashley Stoddard
Victoria Thornberry
Roger Webb
Kasey Williams

BACKGROUND DESIGN TEAM

Ridell Apellanes
Gael Bertrand
Antonio Caggiano
Cullen Cole
Grace Kum
Khang Le
Joseph Martinez
William Niu
Roger Oda
Airi Pan
Arthur Tang
Jessica Woulfe
Ryo Yambe

BACKGROUND PAINT TEAM

Sherwin Abesamis
Addison Bell
Richard Chang
Mikell Chung
Tiffany Deng
Leah Douw
Pavel Elagin
Amber Blade Jones
Toly Kivshar
Garrett Lee
Wing Luk
Ryan Magno
Mike McCain
Diego Penuela
Pablo Rivera
Kirk Shinmoto
Wayne Tsay
Ed Vargas
Bobby Walker
Randolph Williams
Daniel Willardson
Salvatore Yazzie
Ellen Zhang

COLOR SCRIPT ARTIST

Howard Chen

CG TEAM

Eddie Gonzalez
Joshua Brock
Meg Higginbotham
Laura Hohman
Oganes Kharikian
Sergio Lorenzo
Emmanuel Marenco
Allan Parker
Katherina Schuhmacher
Rex Sheen

ANIMATION SERVICES BY

Production Reve

STORYBOARD TEAM

Sung Jin Ahn
Vince Aparo
Mavin Britt
Servan Castillo
Alicia Chan
Sean Christopher
Li Cree
Karen Guo
Young Heller
Morgan Hillebrand
Sinae Jung
Cassey Kuo
Eugene Lee
Jessica Lin
Grace Mi
Brian Pak
William Rowe
Richard Suh
Sheldon Vella
Stanley Von Medvey
Erin Won
Aeri Yoon

PRODUCTION TEAM

Steven Carson
Jasmine Don
Jake Humphrey
Joo-Young Kim
Alex Klein
Elizabeth Schantz
Kay Tinder
Rebecca Ung

TAL'DOREI MAP ILLUSTRATION

Deven Rue

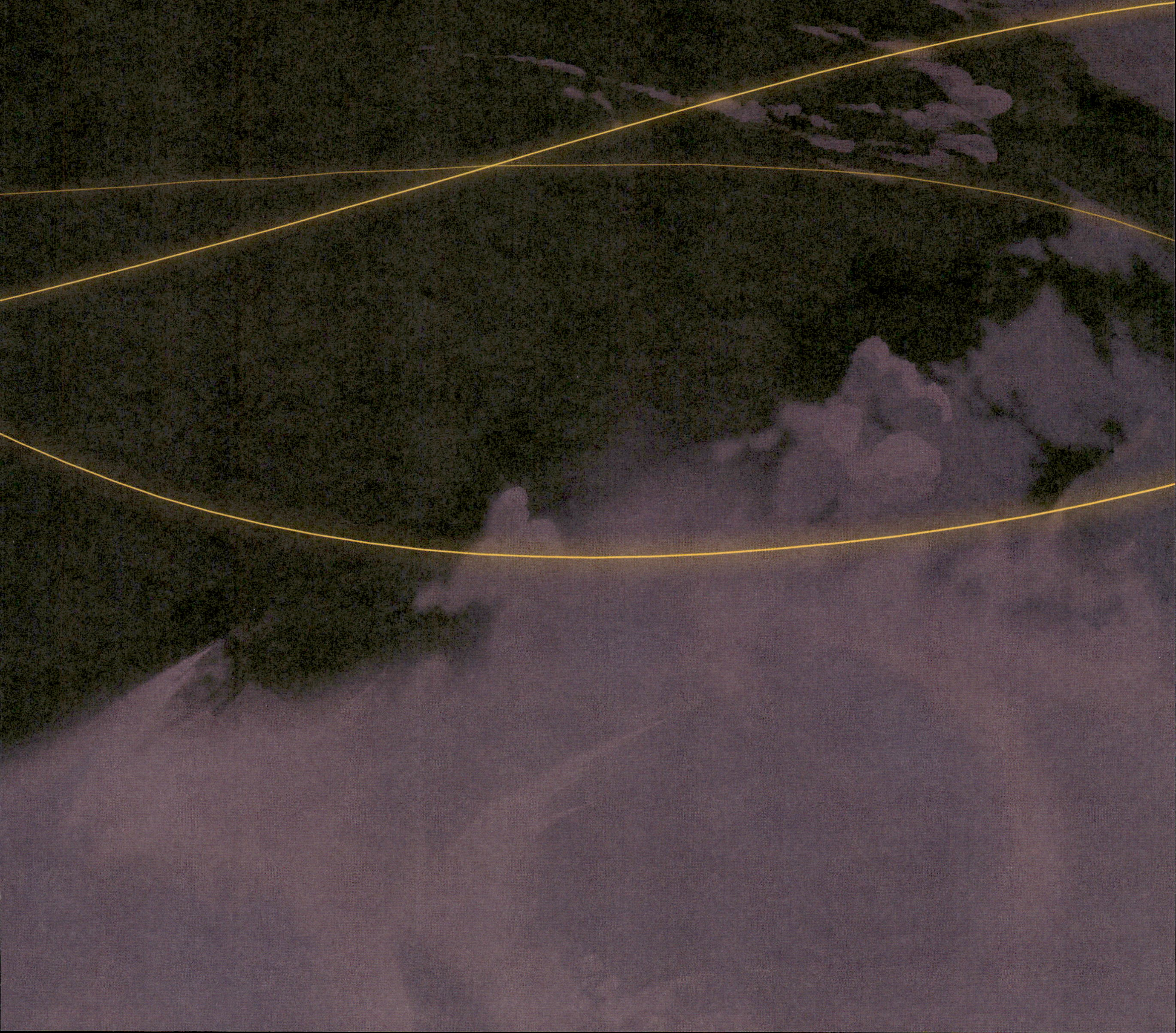

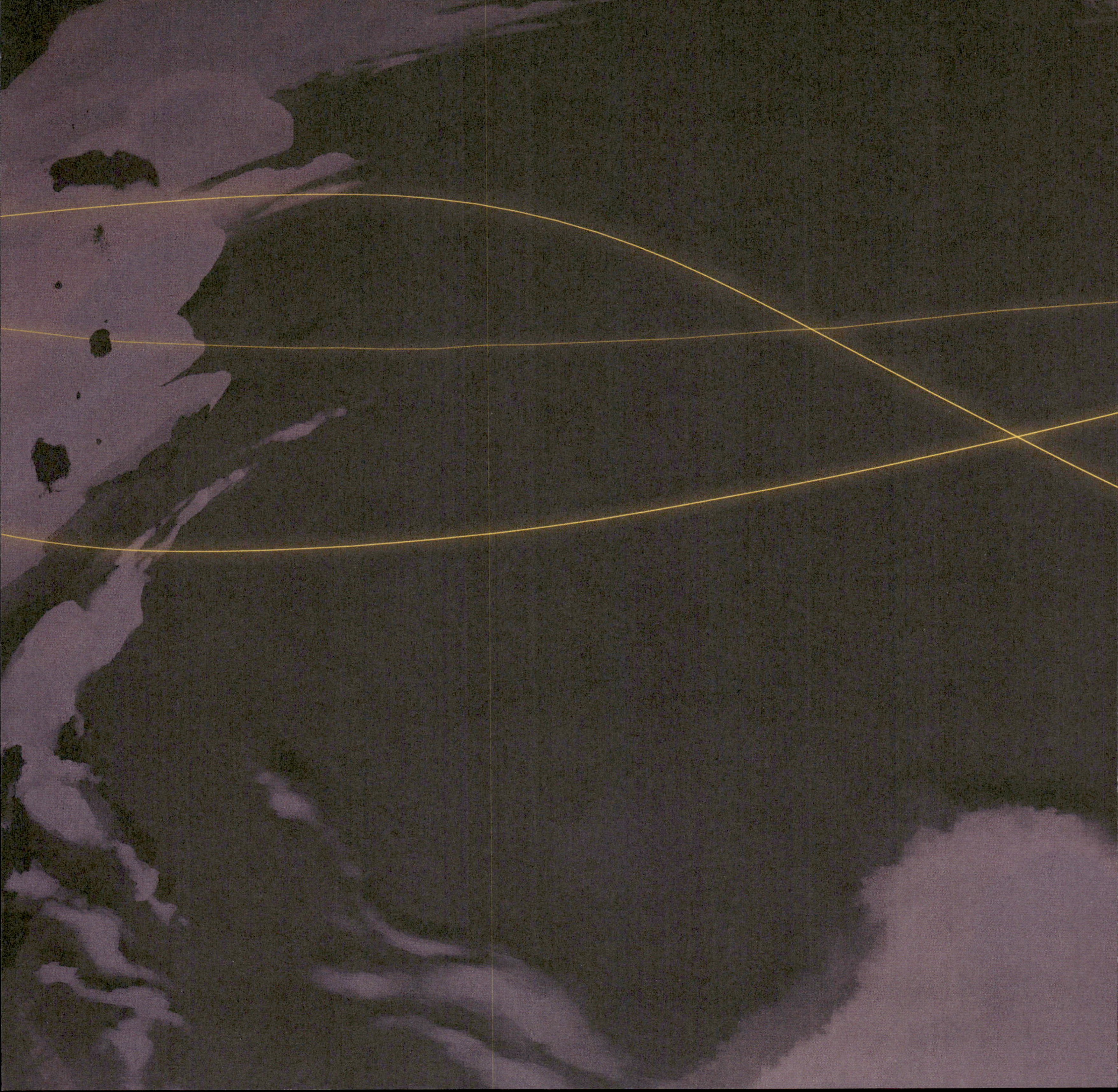